HENRY JAMES

The Ambassadors

Edited with an Introduction and Notes by
ADRIAN POOLE

PENGUIN BOOKS

PENGUIN CLASSICS

Published by the Penguin Group
Penguin Books Ltd, 80 Strand, London WC2R ORL, England
Penguin Group (USA) Inc., 375 Hudson Street, New York, New York 10014, USA
Penguin Group (Canada), 90 Eglinton Avenue East, Suite 700, Toronto, Ontario, Canada M4P 2Y3
(a division of Pearson Penguin Canada Inc.)
Penguin Ireland, 25 St Stephen's Green, Dublin 2, Ireland
(a division of Penguin Books Ltd)
Penguin Group (Australia), 250 Camberwell Road, Camberwell, Victoria 3124, Australia
(a division of Pearson Australia Group Pty Ltd)
Penguin Books India Pvt Ltd, 11 Community Centre, Panchsheel Park, New Delhi – 110 017, India
Penguin Group (NZ), 67 Apollo Drive, Rosedale, North Shore 0632, New Zealand
(a division of Pearson New Zealand Ltd)
Penguin Books (South Africa) (Pty) Ltd, 24 Sturdee Avenue, Rosebank, Johannesburg 2196, South Africa

Penguin Books Ltd, Registered Offices: 80 Strand, London WC2R ORL, England

www.penguin.com

First published 1903
New York Edition published 1909
Published in Penguin Classics 2008

1

Introduction and editorial material copyright © Adrian Poole, 2008
Chronology copyright © Philip Horne, 2008
All rights reserved

The moral right of the editors has been asserted

Set in 10.25/12.25 pt PostScript Adobe Sabon
Typeset by Rowland Phototypesetting Ltd, Bury St Edmunds, Suffolk
Printed in Great Britain by Clays Ltd, St Ives plc

ISBN: 978-0-141-44132-0

1005800161

Contents

List of Abbreviations

This list applies to works frequently cited in the Introduction and the Notes.

Autobiography	*Henry James: Autobiography*, ed. Frederick V. Dupee (Princeton, NJ: Princeton University Press, 1983).
CN	*The Complete Notebooks of Henry James*, ed. Leon Edel and Lyall H. Powers (New York and Oxford: Oxford University Press, 1987).
EH	Henry James, *English Hours* (1905), ed. Leon Edel (New York and Oxford: Oxford University Press, 1981).
Horne	*Henry James: A Life in Letters*, ed. Philip Horne (London: Penguin, 1999).
LC	*Henry James: Literary Criticism*, ed. Leon Edel with the assistance of Mark Wilson, 2 vols. (New York and Cambridge: Library of America, 1984).
Letters	*Henry James: Letters*, ed. Leon Edel, 4 vols. (Cambridge, MA: Belknap Press, 1974–84).
PE	Henry James, *The Painter's Eye: Notes and Essays on the Pictorial Arts*, ed. John L. Sweeney (Cambridge, MA: Harvard University Press, 1956).
PS	Henry James, *Parisian Sketches: Letters to the New York Tribune 1875–76*, ed. Leon Edel and Ilse Dusoir Lind (New York: New York University Press, 1957).

SA   Henry James, *The Scenic Art: Notes on Acting
               and Drama 1872–1901*, ed. Allan Wade
               (London: Rupert Hart-Davis, 1949).

Chronology

1843 *15 April*: HJ born at 21 Washington Place in New York City, second of five children of Henry James (1811–82), speculative theologian and social thinker, whose strict entrepreneur father had amassed wealth estimated at $3 million, one of the top ten American fortunes of his time, and his wife Mary (1810–82), daughter of James Walsh, a New York cotton merchant of Scottish origin.

1843–5 Accompanies parents to Paris and London.

1845–7 James family returns to USA and settles in Albany, New York.

1847–55 Family settles in New York City; HJ taught by tutors and in private schools.

1855–8 Family travels in Europe: Geneva, London, Paris, Boulogne-sur-Mer. Returns to USA and settles in Newport, Rhode Island.

1859–60 Family in Europe again: HJ attends scientific school, then the Academy (later the University) in Geneva. Learns German in Bonn.

> *September 1860*: Family returns to Newport. HJ makes friends with future critic T. S. Perry (who records that HJ 'was continually writing stories, mainly of a romantic kind') and artist John La Farge.

1861–3 Injures his back helping to extinguish a fire in Newport and is exempted from military service in American Civil War (1861–5).

> *Autumn 1862*: Enters Harvard Law School for a term. Begins to send stories to magazines.

1864 *February*: First short story, 'A Tragedy of Error', published anonymously in *Continental Monthly*.

May: Family moves to 13 Ashburton Place, Boston, Massachusetts.

October: Unsigned review published in *North American Review*.

1865 *March*: First signed tale, 'The Story of a Year', appears in *Atlantic Monthly*. HJ's criticism published in first number of the *Nation* (New York).

1866–8 Continues reviewing and writing stories.

Summer 1866: W. D. Howells, novelist, critic and influential editor, becomes a friend.

November 1866: Family moves to 20 Quincy Street, beside Harvard Yard, in Cambridge, Massachusetts.

1869 Travels for his health to England, where he meets John Ruskin, William Morris, Charles Darwin and George Eliot; also visits Switzerland and Italy.

1870 *March*: Death in USA of his much-loved cousin Minny Temple.

May: HJ, still unwell, is reluctantly back in Cambridge.

1871 *August–December*: First short novel, *Watch and Ward*, serialized in *Atlantic Monthly*.

1872–4 Accompanies invalid sister Alice and aunt Catherine Walsh ('Aunt Kate') to Europe in May 1872. Writes travel pieces for the *Nation*. Between October 1872 and September 1874 spends periods of time in Paris, Rome, Switzerland, Homburg and Italy without his family.

Spring 1874: Begins first long novel, *Roderick Hudson*, in Florence.

September 1874: Returns to USA.

1875 *January*: Publishes *A Passionate Pilgrim, and Other Tales*, his first work to appear in book form. It is followed by *Transatlantic Sketches* (travel pieces) and then by *Roderick Hudson* in November. Spends six months in New York City (111 East 25th Street), then three in Cambridge.

11 November: Arrives at 29 rue de Luxembourg, Paris as correspondent for the *New York Tribune* on return to Europe.

December: Begins new novel *The American*.

1876 Meets Gustave Flaubert, Ivan Turgenev, Edmond de Goncourt, Alphonse Daudet, Guy de Maupassant and Émile Zola.

December: Moves to London and settles at 3 Bolton Street, just off Piccadilly.

1877 Visits Paris, Florence and Rome.

May: *The American* is published.

1878 Meets William Gladstone, Alfred Tennyson, and Robert Browning.

February: Collection of essays, *French Poets and Novelists*, is the first book HJ publishes in London.

July: Novella 'Daisy Miller' serialized in *The Cornhill Magazine*; in November Harper's publishes it in the USA, establishing HJ's reputation on both sides of the Atlantic.

September: Publishes novel *The Europeans*.

1879 *December*: Publishes novel *Confidence* and *Hawthorne* (critical study).

1880 *December*: Publishes novel *Washington Square*.

1881 *October*: Returns to USA; visits Cambridge.

November: Publishes novel *The Portrait of a Lady*.

1882 *January*: Death of mother. Visits New York and Washington D.C.

May: Travels back to England but returns to USA on death of father in December.

1883 *Summer*: Returns to London.

November: Fourteen-volume collected edition of fiction published by Macmillan.

December: Publishes *Portraits of Places* (travel writings).

1884 Sister Alice moves to London and settles near HJ.

September: Publishes *A Little Tour in France* (travel writings) and *Tales of Three Cities*; his important artistic statement 'The Art of Fiction' appears in *Longman's Magazine*.

Becomes a friend of R. L. Stevenson and Edmund Gosse. Writes to his American friend Grace Norton: 'I shall never marry . . . I am both happy enough and miserable enough, as it is.'

1885-6 Publishes two serial novels, *The Bostonians* and *The Princess Casamassima*.

6 March 1886: Moves into flat at 34 de Vere Gardens.

1887 *Spring and summer*: Visits Florence and Venice. Continues friendship (begun in 1880) with American novelist Constance Fenimore Woolson.

1888 Publishes novel *The Reverberator*, novella 'The Aspern Papers' and *Partial Portraits* (criticism).

1889 Collection of tales *A London Life* published.

1890 Novel *The Tragic Muse* published.

1891 Play version of *The American* has a short run in the provinces and London.

1892 *February*: Publishes *The Lesson of the Master* (story collection).

March: Death of Alice James in London.

1893 Three volumes of tales published: *The Real Thing* (March), *The Private Life* (June), *The Wheel of Time* (September).

1894 Deaths of Constance Fenimore Woolson and R. L. Stevenson.

1895 *5 January*: Play *Guy Domville* is greeted by boos and applause on its premiere at St James's Theatre; HJ abandons playwriting for many years.

Visits Ireland. Takes up cycling. Publishes two volumes of tales, *Terminations* (May) and *Embarrassments* (June).

1896 Publishes novel *The Other House*.

1897 Two novels, *The Spoils of Poynton* and *What Maisie Knew*, published.

February: Starts dictating, due to wrist problems.

September: Takes lease on Lamb House, Rye, Sussex.

1898 *June*: Moves into Lamb House. Sussex neighbours include the writers Joseph Conrad, H. G. Wells and Ford Madox Hueffer (Ford).

August: Publishes *In the Cage* (short novel).

October: 'The Turn of the Screw', ghost story included in *The Two Magics*, proves his most popular work since 'Daisy Miller'.

1899 *April*: Novel *The Awkward Age* published.

    August: Buys the freehold of Lamb House.

1900 Shaves off his beard.

    August: Publishes collection of tales *The Soft Side*.

    Friendship with American novelist Edith Wharton develops.

1901 *February*: Publishes novel *The Sacred Fount*.

1902 *August*: Publishes novel *The Wings of the Dove*.

1903 *February*: Publishes collection of tales *The Better Sort*.

    September: Publishes novel *The Ambassadors*.

    October: Publishes memoir *William Wetmore Story and his Friends*.

1904 *August*: Sails to USA, his first visit for twenty-one years. Travels to New England, New York, Philadelphia, Washington, the South, St Louis, Chicago, Los Angeles and San Francisco.

    November: Publishes novel *The Golden Bowl*.

1905 *January*: Is President Theodore Roosevelt's guest at the White House. Elected to the American Academy of Arts and Letters.

    July: Back in Lamb House, begins revising works for the New York Edition of *The Novels and Tales of Henry James*.

    October: Publishes *English Hours* (travel essays).

1906–8 Selects, arranges, writes prefaces and has illustrations made for New York Edition (published 1907–9, twenty-four volumes).

1907 *January*: Publishes *The American Scene* (travel essays).

1908 *March*: Play *The High Bid* produced at Edinburgh.

1909 *October*: Publishes *Italian Hours* (travel essays). Health problems.

1910 *August*: Travels to USA with brother William, who dies a week after their return.

    October: Publishes *The Finer Grain* (tales).

1911 *August*: Returns to England.

    October: Publishes *The Outcry* (novel adapted from play). Begins work on autobiography.

1912 *June*: Receives honorary doctorate from Oxford University.

October: Takes flat at 21 Carlyle Mansions, Cheyne Walk, Chelsea; suffers from shingles.

1913 *March*: Publishes *A Small Boy and Others* (first volume of autobiography). Portrait painted by John Singer Sargent for seventieth birthday.

1914 *March*: Publishes *Notes of a Son and Brother* (second volume of autobiography).

August: Outbreak of World War One; HJ becomes passionately engaged with the British cause and helps Belgian refugees and wounded soldiers.

October: Publishes *Notes on Novelists*.

1915 Is made honorary president of the American Volunteer Motor Ambulance Corps.

July: Becomes a British citizen.

Writes essays about the war (collected in *Within the Rim* (1919)) and the Preface to *Letters from America* (1916) by the poet Rupert Brooke, who had died the previous year.

2 December: Suffers a stroke.

1916 Awarded the Order of Merit in New Year Honours.

28 February: Dies. After his funeral in Chelsea Old Church, his ashes are smuggled back to USA by sister-in-law and buried in the family plot in Cambridge.

Philip Horne

Introduction

First-time readers should be aware that details of the plot are revealed in this introduction.

In May 1900, a few weeks after he turned fifty-seven, Henry James shaved off his beard: 'Now, I feel *forty* and clean and light' (*Letters*, IV, p. 139). He was steeled for the new century, he had escaped from London to Lamb House in Rye and he was about to embark on the three great novels in which his career would climax: *The Ambassadors* (1903), *The Wings of the Dove* (1902) and *The Golden Bowl* (1904). (*The Wings of the Dove* was published first, though second in order of writing.) As the previous century drew to a close James told Henrietta Reubell, an American expatriate friend living in Paris who would model for Miss Barrace in *The Ambassadors*, that he liked being the age he was, 'the compensations, simplifications, freedoms, independences, memories, advantages of it' (Horne, p. 330). Once your mid-point is certainly past there is much you will never recover, but there is everything from which – and for which – you are now free. James sat down to a novel that would explore this double sense of loss and gain.

He was ready to return to old stories about wide-eyed Americans in scheming old Europe, their dreams and their fears of freedom. They had helped make his name twenty-five years earlier, with *Roderick Hudson* (1875), *The American* (1877), 'Daisy Miller' (1878) and *The Portrait of a Lady* (1881). In the heroine of this last James had rewritten Christopher Newman's story in *The American*; he thought of Isabel Archer as an 'Americana'. Now he wanted to rewrite it again with the same Parisian setting but an older, more sensitive male protagonist. Newman had been so many things that his author was not and never much hoped to be – ruthless in business, devoid of

imagination, unresponsive to art, sexually confident, certain of always getting his way. (This is slightly unfair to Newman.) Such a conventional image of male 'success', a young or still young enough man on the make, does feature at the centre of *The Ambassadors*, but we do not see things from his point of view. For this James chose a male figure closer to himself, or ideas he had about himself. He urged his young friend Jocelyn Persse to 'try to like the poor old hero, in whom you will perhaps find a vague resemblance (though not facial!) to yours always' (*Letters*, IV, p. 286). Many details are left unspecified in this novel, but the age of the poor old hero, Lambert Strether, is precisely given as fifty-five, just younger than the author himself at the time of writing.

James was also harking back to *Roderick Hudson*, where the relationship between Rowland Mallett – patron, mentor, minder – and the eponymous young artist, his glamorous protégé, would be partially repeated in the responsibility Strether is given for the handsome, debonair, self-assured Chad Newsome. Roderick and Chad both fall for dazzling dangerous women, but whereas Roderick is doomed by Christina Light, Chad escapes from his affair with Madame de Vionnet unscathed, and indeed enriched by it. In the earlier novel the man is the sacrificial victim, in the later the woman. *Roderick Hudson* is unusual, for James, in harbouring two leading characters who reappear in subsequent novels: Christina Light in the title-role of *The Princess Casamassima* (1886) and the artist Gloriani in *The Ambassadors*. Strether first meets Christina's successor Madame de Vionnet in Gloriani's garden, where they appear to him the epitome of male and female worldly success.

James's sensitive young men fear they may never get a real chance in life or be able to take it. Strether feels he has had his moment and missed it: 'it's as if,' he declares, 'the train had fairly waited at the station for me without my having had the gumption to know it was there. Now I hear its faint receding whistle miles and miles down the line' (p. 176). His youthful ambitions are interred in the memory of a honeymoon trip to Paris thirty years before, just after the American Civil War (1861–5). His young wife died (presumably in childbirth), and

so did their son ten years later. Since then his life has been, he thinks to himself, 'a dreadful cheerful sociable solitude' (79), conscientious and strenuous and arid. He has not made money, felt passion or done much to be proud of, save to edit a high-minded New England journal. His very name seems to connote stress and strain and the end of a tether: 'poor fine melancholy, missing, striving Strether', James described him to his New York publishers (*CN*, p. 550). 'Had ever a man,' he makes Strether conclude in remorse and self-pity, 'lost so much and even done so much for so little?' (80).

Strether's personal tether is to a wealthy widow in Woollett, Massachusetts called Mrs Newsome, whose unscrupulous husband has enjoyed the same sort of business success as his near namesake Christopher Newman. The family money has been made from manufacturing 'a small, trivial, rather ridiculous object of the commonest domestic use' (63). James teases his readers by never naming it, though this has not stopped their speculating about alarm-clocks, button-hooks and chamber-pots. Strether's friend Maria Gostrey has some guesses too, but she is not even close, he tells her. We never get to know the source of the fortune and we never get to see the Queen of Woollett, whom James rightly thought one of the novel's triumphs. The invisible monarch is present in and represented by her ambassadors, first Strether and then her daughter, the imposing, imperturbable Sarah Pocock. Strether is haunted by her mother and scared of them both, with good reason.

He is bound to Mrs Newsome by the temperate prospect of marriage and comfort to the end of his days. He has been content to settle for this until Mrs Newsome deputes him to rescue the errant son who has, as it were, gone native in Paris. Strether's mission is to save Prince Chad from the wicked French witch, Madame de Vionnet, who holds him in thrall. This is the romance version embraced and promulgated by the Newsome–Pococks, who conceive the world in terms of good and evil. The novel is amongst other things an allegory about America and its future. Chad has been up to no good in the modern Babylon for five-and-a-half years, and for reasons at once vague and imperative the son and heir must now return

home to take up his post in the family business. Otherwise – and this novel, as all of James's, is much concerned with financial realities – Chad will stand to lose a great deal of money. So too will Strether, for he must pass this test to win the queen's hand: the two men's futures are bound up together. At the outset Strether believes that Chad needs 'the general safety of being anchored by a strong chain'. The young man wants, Strether thinks, 'to be protected. Protected I mean from life' (70). But he is talking about himself, his own fears and desires.

What neither Mrs Newsome nor Strether has reckoned with is the effect on her ambassador of his journey to the old world he once touched, glimpsed and tasted as a young man. For like Isabel Archer in *The Portrait of a Lady*, Hyacinth Robinson in *The Princess Casamassima*, Maisie Farange in *What Maisie Knew*, Fleda Vetch in *The Spoils of Poynton*, the governess in *The Turn of the Screw*, Strether is highly impressionable, vulnerable or (a favourite word) penetrable. (From the Hôtel des Trois Empereurs, Rue de Rivoli, the seventeen-year-old James told a friend that he was 'more than ever "penetrated" with Paris' (*Letters*, I, p. 35).) If ambassadors should have no views or ideas that are not identical to those of the powers they serve, then Strether is as hopelessly miscast as his successor Sarah Pocock is ideal. From the moment he lands in Liverpool and strays to Chester, he is a prey to distraction, digression, memory, fantasy. He walks around in a state of childlike wonder. Everything in Europe surprises him. There is a delightful scene at the Comédie Française when a charming suave stranger slips into Strether's box before he realizes that it is Chad, changed not for the worse as Woollett had feared but, magically, all for the better. If this is what the wicked witch has to offer, then perhaps Strether could have a dose of it too? Sure enough, when he eventually meets her, the ghastly slut he has been led to expect seems more like an angel, a vision of grace, loveliness, elegance. Why, he might even fall for her himself.

But then everything is different from what Woollett predicted. Madame de Vionnet personifies something Strether might once have wished for and could never hope to find in America. He is almost angered by his inability wholly to shed

the habits of Woollett, as for instance 'his odious ascetic suspicion of any form of beauty' (159). He is disturbed by the risk
he now runs of betraying his mission and going over to 'the
enemy'. He solves this dilemma, or keeps it at bay, with the
help of one of Chad's friends, John Little Bilham (inevitably
known as 'little Bilham'), who tells Strether that Chad and
Madame de Vionnet enjoy a 'virtuous attachment' (149).
Strether permits himself to believe this comforting formula. He
can remain loyal to Mrs Newsome, or not wholly disloyal, by
trying to persuade her that Woollett's story is wrong. 'You
don't want to get back to Mother?' Chad asks him. 'Not just
yet,' he replies. 'I'm not ready' (253).

But Woollett cannot wait. A second embassy is dispatched to
relieve Strether of his duties, the formidable Sarah Pocock, her
less reliable but effectively cowed husband Jim, and his young
sister Mamie, the American princess designed to help Chad
realize what he has been missing back home. What *has* Strether
been playing at? He cannot believe the Pococks will not see for
themselves that Chad has not gone to the bad but the good.
And when they see Madame de Vionnet, surely . . . ? There is a
fine scene in which Strether surprises young Mamie on her own,
and realizes that she at least can appreciate what has happened
to Chad. But her sister-in-law is impervious. Sarah will not
relax, let alone relinquish, the black-and-white fable with which
she has been charged. She rebuffs Madame de Vionnet's over-
tures in a brilliant diplomatic encounter simmering with animus
beneath the courtesies. Finally Sarah unleashes on Strether her
pent-up opprobrium. Does he consider Madame de Vionnet
'even an apology for a decent woman?' (376). As for what
Strether is pleased to call Chad's 'fortunate development', she
pronounces it 'hideous' (378). Though it is hard to imagine,
Strether has been Sarah's stepfather elect. Now at least he is
free of *that* grim future.

Strether's own fortunate development has another big twist
still to come. He makes an excursion into the countryside. This
brings back delicious memories of a small French painting he
once nearly bought, and as he sinks blissfully into the enveloping medium, at once nature and art, both real and sublime,

a treat for all the senses not excluding the foretaste of 'something fried and felicitous' (412) awaiting him at the local inn, the idyll turns cold. A boat floats into the picture frame; it contains Chad and Madame de Vionnet. Even Strether must now realize that their attachment is not after all 'virtuous' in the sense that Woollett understands it. His revels now are ended. Strether's terms and categories and frames for making sense of the world have been sorely tested, but until this point he has not abandoned the sense in which 'virtuous' is a judgement on sexual conduct. Now he realizes that he has been fooled, and fooled himself, for Chad and Madame de Vionnet have of course been lovers all along. 'I had flights,' he admits to Maria Gostrey. 'Yes, but things must have a basis,' she responds (451).

It would take a depressingly moralistic reader to condemn Strether for emancipating himself from the ethos of Woollett. But unlikely as they have ever been to persevere with the novel or even pick it up in the first place, such readers were more readily imaginable at the time James wrote it than they are now. The novel tries to mark the passing of a specific era. Strether begins life in the Victorian age and steps out into the Edwardian. In the future that lies ahead of him, he is unlikely too blatantly to indulge in the increased licence sponsored by Edward VII, the monarch vulgarly known as Edward the Caresser – especially if he returns to Woollett, as he seems bound to. But Strether will breathe more easily for accepting that he has been able to admire and even envy the 'attachment' between Chad and Madame de Vionnet, whatever it is called.

O brave new world. If only the two lovers could live up to the ideal Strether imagines for them. Perhaps Madame de Vionnet could, but Chad cannot. Strether protests that he will never forgive the young man if he now abandons her, but that is exactly what Chad is going to do, lured back to run the advertising for the family company. Chad may well have been changed but he has not been entirely transformed, and Woollett will – no thanks to Strether – welcome back the prodigal son. At the close Strether and Chad have exchanged the positions from which they began, thus giving the novel, as E. M. Forster described it in *Aspects of the Novel* (1927), the shape of an hourglass.

If the four main players are Strether and Chad, Mrs Newsome and Madame de Vionnet, there is a further symmetry to the way each is supported by ancillary figures, one male and one female. Mrs Newsome is so effectively represented by her daughter Sarah that they amount in this scheme to the single figure of Woollett Woman. Sarah is flanked by husband Jim and his sister Mamie. Chad is similarly partnered by little Bilham and Miss Barrace, the two friends deployed to deal with Strether; he enjoys with them some confidential exchanges that bewilder and enlighten him in about equal measure. The male figure with whom Marie de Vionnet is associated appears only once but to enormous effect, on Strether at least – the artist Gloriani, in whose garden Strether first encounters her. On the other side is her daughter Jeanne, sufficiently eligible for Strether to be confused by the possibility that it is she with whom Chad is in love. This would simplify matters, by reducing the conflict between Woollett and Paris to a duel between Jeanne de Vionnet and Mamie Pocock.

Strether is himself associated with his old friend Waymarsh, a lawyer from Milrose, Connecticut, and his new friend Maria Gostrey, a modern independent woman who shepherds Americans round Europe. They both think that Strether needs looking after, and there is something of a duel between them over who will play his good angel. Strether spends more time than he should wondering what Waymarsh thinks of him and his relations with Maria. In one of his more fanciful excursions, Strether imagines Waymarsh imagining Miss Gostrey as 'a Jesuit in petticoats, a representative of the recruiting interests of the Catholic Church ... the monster of bulging eyes and far-reaching quivering groping tentacles' (47). Strether is constantly getting carried away and sternly trying to rein himself in. Waymarsh is a richly comic character whose loyalties lie so entirely with the values of Woollett that he makes a natural partner for Sarah Pocock, with whom he forms an impeccably virtuous attachment.

Maria Gostrey is a more complex 'case' (a word to which James and his characters have frequent recourse). We are told early on that Strether and she 'might have been brother and

sister' (26). This would be more than enough for Strether, who enjoys the benefits of Maria's friendship, worldly wisdom and general solicitude with diminishing qualms for what Woollett may think. But her feelings for him evidently go beyond this, and to this extent she represents the possibility of a real alternative to Mrs Newsome. Why doesn't he settle for – settle *with* – Maria, in her comfortable Paris apartment? Readers have been known to feel indignation on her behalf, and regret on his, that he turns her offer down at the end of the novel (especially readers who see here a tendentious version of James's real relations with Constance Fenimore Woolson, the close friend whose death in Venice in 1894 shook him deeply). It is notable that in comments external to the novel James speaks of Maria in distinctly distancing terms – 'clever, independent, humorous, shrewd, a little battered, a little hard', 'mere lone, lean, migratory spinster as she is', 'poor convenient, amusing, unforgettable, impossible Gostrey' (*CN*, pp. 546, 575). Her first name brings her temptingly close to Marie de Vionnet and prompts speculation about different 'types' of Mary (the Virgin Mary, Mary Magdalene, Mary Queen of Scots). But the sound of her surname ('gawky', 'ostrich') has a mildly disenchanting effect that assists Strether and James in their joint need, as it seems, to keep her at bay.

Virtually all the novel's characters are clearly American, the exceptions being Madame de Vionnet (half-French and half-English), her daughter Jeanne and Gloriani (unfathomably cosmopolitan, wholly Europeanized, though credited with American origins in the revised version of *Roderick Hudson* that James prepared for the New York Edition of *The Novels and Tales of Henry James* (1907–9)). As in James's earlier fiction, Europe is a kind of theatre in which Americans find themselves exposed to each others' views. In the Preface to 'Daisy Miller' for the New York Edition he described Europe as 'the more salient American stage'. Everything stands out, even the most mundane decisions. Should Strether agree to visit Madame de Vionnet on Tuesday at half-past five or at six? Sarah Pocock and Waymarsh are hanging on his answer: 'It was indeed as if they were arranged, gathered for a performance, the

performance of "Europe" by his confederate and himself. Well, the performance could only go on. "Say five forty-five"' (304). What a smooth practised confederate Strether has become. All Woollett's worst fears are confirmed.

The novel conducts a kind of debate about what it might mean to be American. In 1900 the possible answers were different from what they had been twenty years earlier when James wrote *The Portrait of a Lady*, or even fifteen, when he wrote *The Bostonians*. Of course James had continued his communications and his contacts, but through the 1890s Americans did not feature in his work and he did not see his native land. When he finally revisited America in 1904 it was over twenty years since he had last been there. But from around 1895 he began actively to think about America and Americans again, and to imagine the possible future. All too luridly, if a famous entry in his notebook for 15 July 1895 is to be credited: 'The Americans looming up – dim, vast, portentous – in their millions – like gathering waves – the barbarians of the Roman Empire' (*CN*, p. 126). Well, maybe: but this is not the scale on which James's novels work, nor is it their temper. (He could admire the novels of Zola, his near contemporary, on this score, and did so, with reservations, in an essay published the same year as *The Ambassadors*.) He had used just this image of the looming barbarians in *The Princess Casamassima*, but there they were supposed, too optimistically by the Princess herself, to be the oppressed proletariat. James could never deal successfully with masses of characters nor with 'mass' effects, as could Dickens, Hugo, Tolstoy or Zola, but he could focus to fine effect on particular exemplary 'barbarians' (such as the Princess and her henchman Paul Muniment). It would be absurd to describe all the Americans who repopulate his novels in the early years of the twentieth century as 'barbarians'. Nevertheless there is a sense, much more subtle than the notebook entry suggests, in which from the perspective of old Europe the Newsomes and Pococks and their henchman Waymarsh are indeed barbaric, and deserve all the high scornful mirth they engender. Need we try to be as fair to Mrs Newsome as Strether himself is? It

is hard to resist Maria Gostrey's judgement: 'intensity with ignorance – what do you want worse?' (407). If Strether is haunted by the spectre of Mrs Newsome, then so too are we a century later, for she is still thriving, albeit in different political circumstances. As for her son Chad, he is heading a global conglomerate and running for high political office. But so too might she be, herself.

Strether represents a sweeter improbable dream. This is fostered by Paris though it does not reside there. James got the 'germ' of the novel in October 1895 from a young friend called Jonathan Sturges. They had been chatting about James's old friend and fellow-writer W. D. Howells, and Sturges recalled the advice Howells had given him on a recent brief stay in Paris: 'Oh, you are young, you are young – be glad of it: be glad of it and *live*. Live all you can: it's a mistake not to' (*CN*, p. 141). This is the basis for Strether's famous declaration to little Bilham in Gloriani's garden just after he has met Madame de Vionnet for the first time (Book Fifth, II). As so often James saw 'a little situation' that grew well beyond his initial calculations. He could draw on the experience of other ageing Americans such as his old friend Henry Adams, eminent man of letters, and himself, and speak to the idea of *anyone* struck with the sense, as Strether simply says, 'It's too late' (176). The long entry in his notebook conveys the excitement with which he began to develop this idea:

> the figure of an elderly man who hasn't 'lived', hasn't at all, in the sense of sensations, passions, impulses, pleasures – and to whom, in the presence of some great human spectacle, some great organization for the Immediate, the Agreeable, for curiosity, and experiment and perception, for Enjoyment, in a word, becomes, *sur la fin*, or toward it, sorrowfully aware. (*CN*, p. 141)

Was Paris too obvious? He would risk it.

So far from being the place where good Americans at the end (*sur la fin*) go to die, Paris would be the place where James's hero is brought back to life if not wholly reborn. For plangent

as Strether's words are, he is wrong to suppose that the injunction to 'Live all you can' does not still apply to himself. James
would certainly have agreed with Strether and approved of his
sentiments, but this is not James speaking. Strether is feeling
sorry for himself and trying to take comfort in the thought that
he is now entirely out of it. There was only ever one chance –
one train! – and he missed it. But this is no more than a
metaphor, like the frankly absurd one he goes on to develop
about life being 'a helpless jelly' poured into a tin mould chosen
by 'the great cook' (176). The speech is at once a high point
and low point for Strether. It is a moment of true recognition,
that what's done is done, but it is also a false because premature
conclusion: the novel is not yet half over. Strether has a second
chance such as not everyone gets (his dead wife and son, for
example), and such as will never permit him, it's true, to be a
Gloriani or to have a Madame de Vionnet. There are other
options, such as being himself and having a life of his own,
instead of always living 'for others'. In Woollett he lived, if that
is not too strong a word, 'for' Mrs Newsome, while in Paris he
starts living 'for' Chad and Madame de Vionnet. This is an
improvement but it is still not as good as where he ends up,
declining Maria Gostrey's kind but still tethering terms, fully
freed at last. Freed above all from 'the terror' he described near
the start when he told her: 'I'm always considering something
else . . . than the thing of the moment. The obsession of the
other thing is the terror' (32).

   Paris is everything that Woollett is not. 'Woollett isn't sure it
ought to enjoy. If it were it would', reflects Strether (30). In Paris
there is so much to talk about; he has never heard so many
opinions on so many subjects: 'There were opinions at Woollett,
but only on three or four' (144). As Egypt is to Rome in *Antony
and Cleopatra* – and Madame de Vionnet makes Strether think
of Shakespeare's heroine and her 'infinite variety' – so is Paris,
the city of art and artifice, imagination and illusion, delight and
delirium, to plain, literal, powerful, moneyed Woollett (rhymes
with 'bullet'). In a passage that everyone likes to quote, Paris
dazzles Strether with its suspension of the 'differences' we
normally depend on to know what we are dealing with:

It hung before him this morning, the vast bright Babylon, like
some huge iridescent object, a jewel brilliant and hard, in which
parts were not to be discriminated nor differences comfortably
marked. It twinkled and trembled and melted together, and what
seemed all surface one moment seemed all depth the next. (83)

Hard and soft, solid and liquid, surface and depth, this place is
an all-round enveloping treat to the senses, appealing not to
one but to all, touch, taste, smell, ear, eye. The whole process
of reanimation begins for Strether with Maria Gostrey in
Chester and London: 'the moment filled to the brim' (55). By
the time he pulls up a penny chair in the Luxembourg Gardens
in Paris 'the cup of his impressions seemed truly to overflow'
(77). He is happily invaded by hums and clicks and vibrations,
by a 'roundabout echo' (103). He seizes eagerly on the wonderful supply of cigarettes Chad has thoughtfully left behind.
It is a world, as it seems for these leisured Americans, of
endless consumption, the fabled land of Cockaigne. Only Maria
Gostrey seems to have some work to do. Little Bilham has an
occupation, we are told, 'but it was only an occupation
declined' (110). Like Chad they are all on a long if not perma-
nent break, and their Paris – Gloriani apart – is a world away
from one in which anything gets made, let alone trivial objects
of common domestic use. It is intoxicating and delicious, of
course, as anyone knows who has ever been remotely as fam-
ished and wearied as Strether. Paris is supremely refreshing: it
is the *omelette aux tomates* and the bottle of straw-coloured
Chablis and the intensely white tablecloth and the bliss of being
with Madame de Vionnet, who speaks 'as if her art were all an
innocence, and then again as if her innocence were all an art'
(312). Strether has forgotten how to live in the moment, if he
has ever really known, and Madame de Vionnet, the spirit of
Paris incarnate, helps to save and revive him. At such moments
of ecstasy Strether might well murmur, with another Shakespearean lover, 'If it were now to die, / 'Twere now to be most
happy' (*Othello*, II. i.188–9).

*

Like many great artists before the twentieth century diminished the imaginative supremacy of the sea, James was drawn to metaphors of voyage and flood, of embarking and being launched and shipwrecked and cast ashore on a desert island, of floating and sinking and drowning, of being immersed and saturated. Such images of risk, of potential self-loss and self-surrender have deep literary associations, not least promoted by Shakespeare, in *The Winter's Tale* and above all *The Tempest*, to which James was particularly drawn. (He wrote an astonishing essay, if not exactly 'on' then certainly inspired by *The Tempest*, for volume 16 of the Renaissance Edition of the plays (New York, 1907).) James freely employs such images for his own adventures as creative artist, as well as for those of his fictional characters.

Paris stimulates and gratifies the senses. It also excites the imagination, especially when you linger: 'wherever one paused in Paris the imagination reacted before one could stop it' (88). Can it always be trusted? Here Strether's tale turns out to be no less cautionary than inspiring. It does not vindicate the view of Woollett and Waymarsh that the imagination is all a snare and a delusion, but nor does it vindicate Strether's burgeoning belief in miracles and magic. If Strether identifies with Chad, that is because he projects on to him his need to see a resurrected image of his lost youth (which includes the dead son as well as his own younger self). If Madame de Vionnet seems a dream come true, that is because she gives flesh and blood to ideas, images and appetites he never realized he possessed and that now threaten to smother and drown him. She seems endlessly to inspire metaphors in him, as if she were a figure for the act of imagination itself (like Shakespeare's Cleopatra).

Et in Arcadia ego: time does not stop even in the land of Cockaigne or in Arcadia, and death awaits every reveller. For a time, the best of times, Strether bathes in 'a vast warm fragrant medium . . . in which rewards were immediate and reckonings postponed' (270). But the clock is silently ticking. James was particularly concerned with rendering the passage of time. He urged one of his readers to take this novel 'very easily and

gently: read five pages a day – be even as deliberate as that – but *don't break the thread*.' By this stage in his career he thought that 'the very most difficult thing in the art of the novelist is to give the impression and illusion of the real *lapse of time, the quantity* of time, represented by our poor few phrases and pages' (*Letters*, IV, pp. 302–3). One of the ways he found to assist this 'impression and illusion' was the alternation and blending of tenses. Within the retrospective past tense of third-person narration, there is the present of direct speech, the sense of 'now' promoted by such phrases as 'at the present sharp hour' and 'on the spot' (a particular favourite). There is the pluperfect for events, actions, thoughts and feelings completed before the notional 'now': 'It wasn't the first time Strether had sat alone in the great dim church' (231). ('Had' is a particularly reverberant little word, suggestively rhyming with 'Chad', such that at one point we are treated to the triple beat of 'Chad had had' (120).) There is the double sense of prospect and retrospect in the formula especially adapted to Strether's ability to look before and after: 'He *was to* feel many things on this occasion' (238), or 'He *was to* reflect later on' (420 – emphases added). This reaches a climax in the elaborate sentence with which Strether approaches Madame de Vionnet for their final encounter: 'He knew in advance he should look back on the perception actually sharpest with him . . .' (434).

Strether's apprehension of mortality is located in what James calls his 'historic sense'. Strether sees or imagines he sees in Madame de Vionnet not just a beautiful desirable woman but a living embodiment of history and, specifically, the violent dramatic history of modern France. Paris is not only the city of Art but also of bloody political violence. Strether's sense of this draws on his predecessor Hyacinth Robinson's recognition 'that the most brilliant city in the world was also the most blood-stained' (*The Princess Casamassima*, Book Fourth, XXIX). The blood was not a remote myth but a living memory of revolutionary violence, not only in the 1790s but also in 1830 and 1848 and, above all, within James's own adulthood, during the Commune of 1871. Traces of this living history help to divide Strether from his own younger self. Strolling across

Paris toward the Quartier Latin (in Chad's footsteps), he passes through the Tuileries gardens, where the palace was burnt down in 1871: 'when he gazed into the irremediable void of its site the historic sense in him might have been freely at play – the play under which in Paris indeed it so often winces like a touched nerve' (76). What does this mean to Strether, this void? 'Might have been' is curiously non-committal, as if he is unsure how freely he can afford to let the historic sense play in him, how deeply he wants to be touched.

Paris abounds with pleasures but Strether has also to reckon with pain. This leads him to Marie de Vionnet's dwelling in the rue de Bellechasse, which excites his historic sense as if with the promise of initiation into innermost mystery. On his first visit the place makes him think of 'some glory, some prosperity of the First Empire, some Napoleonic glamour, some dim lustre of the great legend'; it is full of 'relics . . . of a private order', 'old accumulations' inherited from her French father, he decides (unlike Maria Gostrey's or Chad's); it exhales 'the air of supreme respectability'. He admires it all, especially 'the mistress of the scene before him' (196, 197). He is curious, intrigued, slightly troubled. On his next visit, in the high square antechamber, 'a little cold and slippery even in summer' (320), Madame de Vionnet tells him, as he is leaving, that her daughter Jeanne's marriage has been arranged in the traditional high Continental fashion. For Strether it marks a new depth to the differences of manners and morals: 'It was – through something ancient and cold in it – what he would have called the real thing' (322). At some level beneath the codes of conduct for everyday life, Strether is shocked. 'He was prepared to suffer – before his own inner tribunal – for Chad; he was prepared to suffer even for Madame de Vionnet. But he wasn't prepared to suffer for the little girl.' Though he is too polite to say anything, he registers the injustice and begins to pass judgement on Madame de Vionnet for her complicity in it. At his final encounter with her in these rooms the 'historic sense' plays very freely indeed. He fantasizes that it is like the eve of some great violent public event. The sounds, the smells, the omens – 'They were the smell of revolution, the smell of the public temper – or

perhaps simply the smell of blood' (433). And Madame de Vionnet is the sacrificial victim, another Madame Roland going to the scaffold at the height of the revolutionary Terror.

How far does Strether's vision of her derive from his own needs and desires? It seems clear that Madame de Vionnet is indeed a victim; what is more open to doubt and interpretation is the nature of Strether's feelings about her. A sympathetic reading would credit him with grasping the rules of the game as it is played in the world to which Marie de Vionnet and her daughter are bound. Because he is not a glossy male tiger like Gloriani or Chad but a milder creature whose own sexual preferences are undetermined, Strether can see truly what these women have to endure. When he imagines Marie de Vionnet as Madame Roland, he is perceiving a terrible truth about the perpetuation through history of the baneful models that victimize women. But a darker reading would go further than this. Strether may be less rampant and more scrupulous than other men, but he still enjoys the privileges of the gender he shares with them. He is at least complicit with the system that dooms Madame de Vionnet, and he could at worst be accused of deriving satisfaction from it. Perhaps at some level he wants to see a woman suffer and at last he has found just the one for the role. Is he taking a kind of displaced revenge for what he has suffered from Mrs Newsome? We cannot tell. Such thoughts may be grossly unjust. Strether's story is dramatized in such a way as to tempt our imagination and judgement – just as Strether himself and the other ambassadors have been tempted by Madame de Vionnet. Perhaps we should refrain and turn softly away.

James took pains to embroil the reader in Strether's experience. Quite how far he goes in this respect can be judged by comparing the finished novel with the summary he provided for his New York publishers in the autumn of 1900 as the writing was well under way. James's 'Project of Novel' is remarkable for its length and detail, no less than 20,000 words (see CN, pp. 541–76). Unusually for James, the novel did not yet have a name. It probably acquired its title from the famous painting

by Hans Holbein (1497–1543) in the National Gallery, London. Now known as *The Ambassadors* (1533), it only acquired this name after Mary F. S. Hervey proved – in a book published in 1900 – that the two men portrayed were French ambassadors to the court of Henry VIII and not, as had been previously thought, the 'King's antiquary' John Leland and the courtier-poet Thomas Wyatt.

The Project reveals that James changed some details in the course of writing: Waymarsh was originally Waymark, John Little Bilham was Glenn Burbage, Strether's son was going to be a difficult adolescent and die in a swimming accident about the age of sixteen, Strether once thought of taking Chad off 'for some small sanitary and, as it were disinfecting jaunt through some one of those regions vaguely figuring to Strether as the more marked homes and haunts of earnestness' like Norway or Sweden (*CN*, p. 561). Many of the Project's expressions, however, seem perfectly apt to the novel. In the portrayal of Mrs Newsome, for instance, James says that he aims at 'an especially refined hardness and dryness of grain and strain'. Of the effect on Strether of Chad's story of his relations with Madame de Vionnet and her daughter, James describes it as 'moving him without really quite convincing him'; Strether 'assents, in a word, without quite believing' (*CN*, p. 562). As for the whole impact of the Parisian world on Strether, James memorably affirms: 'Well, he finds himself sinking, as I say, up to his middle in the Difference – difference from what he expected, difference in Chad, difference in everything; and the Difference, I also again say, is what I give' (*CN*, p. 562).

There is a certain comedy, familiar to readers of James's Notebooks and Prefaces, in the struggle the author depicts between himself and his material, or if one prefers, between two aspects of his artistry, the spender and saver. The recklessly prolific inventor of characters, incidents, scenes is constantly being called to order by the stern hand of bursarial restraint. Hence in the Project that grew and grew we get the sense of endlessly proliferating potential that would have to be curtailed when it came to the novel itself: the Pococks, for instance, and the endless fun that *could* be had with Jim, in particular, at

large in Paris. So too with the details of Strether's past – the back-story, as we would now say. One can see for example why James decided to kill off the son at the age of ten to avoid the complications of Oedipal struggle between father and son; better to bury the boy more deeply in the past. The novel thins the thicket of detail that could have run riot, turning the garden into a jungle. It also eschews some of the violence promised in the Project, as for example a scene in which Chad 'really lets fly' at his sister Sarah 'for the folly of her supposing him amenable to her ridiculous view of the little Pocock', that is, that Mamie would be a good match for him (*CN*, p. 566). There are meannesses and lies and rudeness imagined in the Project that are masked or displaced in the finished novel, though they lurk all the more effectively just behind the scenes we get to see, in the 'glitter' of Sarah Pocock's hard eyes, for example.

The main obvious difference between Project and novel is that the former boasts a voice that almost completely disappears from the latter. Instead of the author telling us what's what from a controlling external perspective, we get to experience the world of the novel from an unprivileged position inside it, Strether's own 'point of view'. Weak-minded readers may well yearn for the clarity and certitudes of the Project. Not just for the knowledge that James had in mind for Woollett 'an American city of the second order . . . like Providence, R. I., or like Worcester, Mass., or like Hartford, Conn.' (*CN*, p. 547), but for sheer assistance in grasping what is going on. Instead readers are made to share Strether's state of being 'so often at sea' (102), of 'moving verily in a strange air and on ground not of the firmest' (212), of 'moving in a maze of mystic closed allusions' (222). Not that there is much that James says in the Project we should not eventually work out for ourselves. Amid all the ambiguities surrounding Madame de Vionnet's relations with Chad, James describes in the Project his plans for Strether, whereby 'one or two convictions and impressions thicken for him, stiffen, harden – and one of these is the estimate of the value of such a relation, for any young man, as such a woman as Mme de Vionnet represents' (*CN*, p. 560). In the novel itself

we are invited to share all the sensuous stiffening and hardening and softening and melting, the pleasure of the text.

This points to further related differences. Woollett is all for literal meanings, for simplification, for telegrams and headlines. The Project is relatively sparing with metaphors, though when they do occur they are telling, as in Strether's 'sense of what he has lost, or only caught the last whisk of the tip of the tail of' (CN, p. 545). The novel itself gives free rein to the figurative. Strether and his author revel – and the reader is invited to join them – in exuberant, elastic, buoyant excess. There is also an important contrast between metaphor and platitude. Much of the novel's comedy depends on the scope for misunderstanding over apparently simple words of approbation such as 'good', 'free', 'honest', 'virtuous', 'straight', 'grand', 'fine', 'wonderful', 'magnificent', 'sublime'. People hear in these words, very much as they see, just what they want or expect to. The rarity is the person, like Strether, who can revise those expectations when they are not confirmed or positively contradicted. Woollett will not change its mind. This is where Strether's openness to the language of metaphor helps him get in touch with what he really thinks and feels and believes. Thus for example he thinks of Mrs Newsome as 'pure and by the vulgar estimate "cold", but deep devoted delicate sensitive noble' (262). Later on we get closer to what he truly feels about her cold massive impenetrability when he imagines her as a giant iceberg (406). He is similarly wary of letting Chad inspire him to metaphor. He admires him of course, as he admires Chad's mother, and yet 'strong and sleek and gay, easy and fragrant and fathomless' (249) – these words do not really tell us much. They are polished platitudes, and it is exactly the 'polish' of Chad's appearance (especially his teeth) that impresses – and rebuffs – Strether. We may conclude that it is exactly the polish Chad learns from Europe that he will apply to the art of advertising. It is a different matter when it comes to Gloriani and Madame de Vionnet. They do inspire Strether to metaphor; indeed at times, especially with Madame de Vionnet, he seems barely able to restrain the flood.

But then right from the start Strether has shown his capacity for poetry. Here he is leaning on the ramparts at Chester looking up at the cathedral.

> He leaned back on this support with his face to the tower of the cathedral, now admirably commanded by their station, the high red-brown mass, square and subordinately spired and crocketed, retouched and restored, but charming to his long-sealed eyes and with the first swallows of the year weaving their flight all round it. (30–31)

The sentence could easily have stopped at 'long-sealed eyes'; the extra 'flight' is gratuitous, a lingering verbal caress. Strether, we realize, is not like this in Woollett. Here is a further example. Strether is generously reflecting that Mrs Newsome cannot after all be expected to appreciate the change in Chad. She is not 'on the spot'. No wonder she is out of touch. 'Her tact had to reckon with the Atlantic Ocean, the General Post-Office and the extravagant curve of the globe' (145). He is trying to be fair to the Woollett way of seeing and thinking. This is after all the literal route by which Mrs Newsome's missives have to travel. And yet in its carelessly sensuous rhythm 'the extravagant curve of the globe' connotes everything to which she will never do justice.

The Ambassadors can be understood as a long unfinished farewell, but it is also a wonderful harvest, both for Strether and the reader. He tells Maria Gostrey at the end that his only 'logic' is this: 'Not, out of the whole affair, to have got anything for myself' (470). She rightly protests that with his 'wonderful impressions' he has got a great deal. In Gloriani's garden he felt the waters rise within him and overflow, not into tears but into the elegy for his own lost youth and his declaration to little Bilham, a potential son and heir, to 'Live all you can!' This is memorable and moving, but it leaves open all sorts of question about how much 'you can'. Strether's final scene with Madame de Vionnet sees the waters rise and overflow – around *her*. This, too, is a scene of mourning, but now she shows Strether what it might mean to 'live all you can'. It might mean giving yourself

up in a more personal sense than Strether has done; it might mean running the risk of being abandoned as she now knows she will be. Has Marie de Vionnet lived all she could? How can we know? Now Strether sees – so much more deeply than his risible metaphor of jelly and mould had suggested – the real limits to what anyone 'can', circumscribed as we are sure to be by sex, age, education, class, money, history, all the 'old accumulations'.

Where does this all leave us, the readers? We are told early on that Strether is burdened with 'the oddity of a double consciousness. There was detachment in his zeal and curiosity in his indifference' (22). The very act of reading requires some such doubleness, but the novel asks us to reflect on the value of such a capacity. Strether's odd consciousness never works harder than in this last great scene, where he attends to the misery at the heart of beauty, elegance, wealth and privilege, 'consenting to it as he had consented to the rest, and even conscious of some vague inward irony in the presence of such a fine free range of bliss and bale' (441). It is at once disconcerting and heartening to discover that we have shared, both with Strether and James, 'such a fine free range of bliss and bale'. And to find ourselves left with the endless puzzle of living all we can.

Further Reading

See also works cited in the List of Abbreviations on p. vii.

BY HENRY JAMES

The Complete Letters of Henry James, ed. Pierre A. Walker and Greg Zacharias (Lincoln, NE: University of Nebraska Press, 2006–).

The Complete Plays of Henry James, ed. Leon Edel (London: Rupert Hart-Davis, 1949).

Complete Stories, 5 vols. (New York and Cambridge: Library of America, 1996–9).

The Letters of Henry James, ed. Percy Lubbock, 2 vols. (London: Macmillan, 1920).

BIOGRAPHY, CRITICISM AND REFERENCE

Edel, Leon, *Henry James: A Life* (New York: Harper & Row, 1985).

—— and Dan H. Laurence, *A Bibliography of Henry James*, third edn. revised with the assistance of James Rambeau (Oxford: Oxford University Press, 1982).

Gard, Roger (ed.), *Henry James: The Critical Heritage* (London: Routledge & Kegan Paul, 1968). Contains a very full selection of contemporary reviews and comments.

Graham, Kenneth, *Henry James: A Literary Life* (Basingstoke: Macmillan, 1995).

Kaplan, Fred, *Henry James: The Imagination of Genius* (London: Hodder & Stoughton, 1992).

Nowell-Smith, Simon (compiler), *The Legend of the Master* (London: Constable, 1947).

P.H.

CRITICAL WORKS RELATING TO *THE AMBASSADORS*

Armstrong, Paul B., *The Phenomenology of Henry James* (Chapel Hill: University of North Carolina Press, 1983).

Bell, Millicent, *Meaning in Henry James* (Cambridge, MA: Harvard University Press, 1991).

Bersani, Leo, *A Future for Astyanax: Character and Desire in Literature* (London: M. Boyars, 1978).

Bradbury, Nicola, *Henry James: The Later Novels* (Oxford: Clarendon Press, 1979).

Brooks, Peter, *The Melodramatic Imagination* (New Haven, CN: Yale University Press, 1976).

Buelens, Gert (ed.), *Enacting History in Henry James: Narrative, Power, and Ethics* (Cambridge: Cambridge University Press, 1997).

Chatman, Seymour, *The Later Style of Henry James* (Oxford: Blackwell, 1972).

Ellmann, Maud, ' "The Intimate Difference": Power and Representation in *The Ambassadors*', in *Henry James: Fiction as History*, ed. Ian F. A. Bell (London: Vision Press, 1984); revised in Norton Critical Edition of *The Ambassadors*, ed. S. P. Rosenbaum (New York: W. W. Norton, 1994), pp. 501–14.

Fogel, Daniel Mark, *Henry James and the Structure of the Romantic Imagination* (Baton Rouge: Louisiana State University Press, 1981).

Freedman, Jonathan, *Professions of Taste: Henry James, British Aestheticism, and Commodity Culture* (Stanford, CA: Stanford University Press, 1990).

—— (ed.), *The Cambridge Companion to Henry James* (Cambridge: Cambridge University Press, 1998).

Fussell, Edwin Sill, *The French Side of Henry James* (New York: Columbia University Press, 1990).

——, *The Catholic Side of Henry James* (Cambridge: Cambridge University Press, 1993).

Goode, John (ed.), *The Air of Reality: New Essays on Henry James* (London: Methuen, 1972).

Greenslade, William, 'The Power of Advertising: Chad Newsome and the Meaning of Paris in *The Ambassadors*', *English Literary History*, 49 (1982), 99–122.

Griffin, Susan M., *The Historical Eye: The Texture of the Visual in Late James* (Boston: Northeastern University Press, 1991).

Hadley, Tessa, *Henry James and the Imagination of Pleasure* (Cambridge: Cambridge University Press, 2002).

Haralson, Eric, 'Lambert Strether's Excellent Adventure', in *The Cambridge Companion to Henry James*, ed. Jonathan Freedman (Cambridge: Cambridge University Press, 1998), pp. 169–86.

Hocks, Richard A., *Henry James and Pragmatistic Thought: A Study in the Relationship between the Philosophy of William James and the Literary Art of Henry James* (Chapel Hill: University of North Carolina Press, 1974).

Hutchinson, Stuart, *Henry James: An American as Modernist* (London: Vision Press, 1982).

Hutchison, Hazel, 'The Other Lambert Strether: Henry James's *The Ambassadors*, Balzac's *Louis Lambert* and J. H. Lambert', *Nineteenth Century Literature*, 58 (2003), 230–58.

——, 'James's Spectacles: Distorted Vision in *The Ambassadors*', *Henry James Review*, 26.1 (Winter 2005), 39–51.

McWhirter, David, *Desire and Love in Henry James: A Study of the Late Novels* (Cambridge: Cambridge University Press, 1989).

Meissner, Collin, *Henry James and the Language of Experience* (Cambridge: Cambridge University Press, 1999).

Nussbaum, Martha C., 'Perceptive Equilibrium: Literary Theory and Ethical Theory', in *Love's Knowledge: Essays on Philosophy and Literature* (New York and Oxford: Oxford University Press, 1990), pp. 168–94.

Perosa, Sergio, *Henry James and the Experimental Novel* (Charlottesville: University of Virginia Press, 1978).

Pippin, Robert B., *Henry James and Modern Moral Life* (Cambridge: Cambridge University Press, 2000).

Posnock, Ross, *The Trial of Curiosity: Henry James, William James, and the Challenge of Modernity* (New York and Oxford: Oxford University Press, 1991).

Rivkin, Julie, *False Positions: The Representational Logics of Henry James's Fiction* (Stanford, CA: Stanford University Press, 1996).

Rowe, John Carlos, *The Theoretical Dimensions of Henry James* (London: Methuen, 1985).

Salmon, Richard, *Henry James and the Culture of Publicity* (Cambridge: Cambridge University Press, 1997).

Stevens, Hugh, *Henry James and Sexuality* (Cambridge: Cambridge University Press, 1998).

Stone, Albert E., Jr. (ed.), *Twentieth-Century Interpretations of 'The Ambassadors': A Collection of Critical Essays* (Englewood Cliffs, NJ: Prentice-Hall, 1969).

Tintner, Adeline R., *The Book World of Henry James: Appropriating the Classics* (Ann Arbor, MI: UMI Research Press, 1987).

——, *Henry James and the Lust of the Eyes* (Baton Rouge: Louisiana State University Press, 1993).

Walker, Pierre A., *Reading Henry James in French Cultural Contexts* (DeKalb: Northern Illinois University Press, 1995).

Watt, Ian, 'The First Paragraph of *The Ambassadors*: An Explication', *Essays in Criticism*, 10 (July 1960), 250–74; reprinted in *Twentieth-Century Literary Criticism: Reader*, ed. David Lodge (London: Longman, 1972), pp. 528–45.

Williams, Merle A., *Henry James and the Philosophical Novel: Being and Seeing* (Cambridge: Cambridge University Press, 1993).

Winner, Viola Hopkins, *Henry James and the Visual Arts* (Charlottesville: University of Virginia Press, 1970).

Yeazell, Ruth Bernard, *Language and Knowledge in the Late Novels of Henry James* (Chicago: University of Chicago Press, 1976).

A.P.

A Note on the Text

Four versions of *The Ambassadors* were published in the author's lifetime, the first three all in 1903: a twelve-part serial in an American journal and the first English and American editions in volume form. The final version was issued in 1909 as part of the New York Edition of *The Novels and Tales of Henry James*, of which it comprised Volumes XXI and XXII.

In the summer of 1901, about a year after he started writing the novel, James signed an agreement with the New York publishers Harper and Brothers (to whom he had sent his 'Project of Novel' the previous September). Harper however delayed so long that *The Wings of the Dove* had been written and published (in August 1902) before *The Ambassadors* began to appear as a serial in January 1903, not in *Harper's Monthly* as James had expected, but in another Harper's journal, the prestigious *North American Review*. James had planned the novel with serialization in mind but was forced to withhold three and a quarter chapters because he was overrunning the 10,000-word limit for each instalment. These were part of chapter V (now Book Second, I), and in their entirety chapters XIX (Book Eighth, I), XXVIII (Book Eleventh, I), and XXXV (Book Twelfth, IV). All these concern Chad, or to be more exact, Strether's relations with Chad.

For volume publication James restored these passages. He revised the serial version twice as it was appearing in the *North American Review*, first for Harper in America, then for Methuen in Britain. Harper was again so slow that the first English edition appeared on 24 September 1903, six weeks before the American edition. There are some interesting minor

differences between the two, but the most spectacular, indeed notorious, is the order in which chapters XXVIII and XXIX appeared (now Book Eleventh, I and II). The former had been omitted from the serial version, and when it was reinstated in the first American edition it was inserted after chapter XXIX, out of chronological sequence. In the first English edition, however, the 'correct' sequence was restored. The real oddity is that when it came to the New York Edition of 1909 James repeated what seems to be the error in the Harper edition rather than following the corrected Methuen sequence. This is odd, but it is a consequence of James's choice of the American edition as the text on which the New York Edition is based. It is no less odd that nobody noticed for another forty years. There is an ingenious argument that James deliberately retained the 'error' but this seems unlikely. This aside, James revised the American text for the New York edition in his usual scrupulous manner, though the revisions are unsurprisingly less substantial than for earlier novels such as *The American* and *The Portrait of a Lady*. A sample of the more interesting textual variations is provided at the end of the volume.

The text reprinted here is that of the New York Edition, save that Book Eleventh, I and II follow the order of the first English edition. Some minor adjustments have been made to punctuation, including the substitution of n-rule dashes for m-rule and the closing up of the spaced contractions ('is n't', 'was n't' and so on) favoured by James, but which now seem distracting. Single quotation marks replace double ones and 'ize' spellings have been standardized throughout, in accordance with Penguin Classics style. There has been no attempt to regularize James's inconsistent use of italics for French words and expressions.

A.P.

The Ambassadors

PREFACE

Nothing is more easy than to state the subject of 'The Ambassadors', which first appeared in twelve numbers of the *North American Review* (1903) and was published as a whole the same year. The situation involved is gathered up betimes, that is in the second chapter of Book Fifth, for the reader's benefit, into as few words as possible – planted or 'sunk', stiffly and saliently, in the centre of the current, almost perhaps to the obstruction of traffic. Never can a composition of this sort have sprung straighter from a dropped grain of suggestion, and never can that grain, developed, overgrown and smothered, have yet lurked more in the mass as an independent particle. The whole case, in fine, is in Lambert Strether's irrepressible outbreak to little Bilham on the Sunday afternoon in Gloriani's garden, the candour with which he yields, for his young friend's enlightenment, to the charming admonition of that crisis. The idea of the tale resides indeed in the very fact that an hour of such unprecedented ease should have been felt by him *as* a crisis, and he is at pains to express it for us as neatly as we could desire. The remarks to which he thus gives utterance contain the essence of 'The Ambassadors', his fingers close, before he has done, round the stem of the full-blown flower; which, after that fashion, he continues officiously to present to us. 'Live all you can; it's a mistake not to. It doesn't so much matter what you do in particular so long as you have your life. If you haven't had that what *have* you had? I'm too old – too old at any rate for what I see. What one loses one loses; make no mistake about that. Still, we have the illusion of freedom; therefore don't, like me to-day, be without the memory of that illusion.

I was either, at the right time, too stupid or too intelligent to
have it, and now I'm a case of reaction against the mistake. Do
what you like so long as you don't make it. For it *was* a mistake.
Live, live!' Such is the gist of Strether's appeal to the impressed
youth, whom he likes and whom he desires to befriend; the
word 'mistake' occurs several times, it will be seen, in the course
of his remarks – which gives the measure of the signal warning
he feels attached to his case. He has accordingly missed too
much, though perhaps after all constitutionally qualified for a
better part, and he wakes up to it in conditions that press the
spring of a terrible question. *Would* there yet perhaps be time
for reparation? – reparation, that is, for the injury done his
character; for the affront, he is quite ready to say, so stupidly
put upon it and in which he has even himself had so clumsy a
hand? The answer to which is that he now at all events *sees*; so
that the business of my tale and the march of my action, not to
say the precious moral of everything, is just my demonstration
of this process of vision.

Nothing can exceed the closeness with which the whole fits
again into its germ.[1] That had been given me bodily, as usual,
by the spoken word, for I was to take the image over exactly
as I happened to have met it. A friend had repeated to me, with
great appreciation, a thing or two said to him by a man of
distinction, much his senior, and to which a sense akin to that
of Strether's melancholy eloquence might be imputed – said
as chance would have, and so easily might, in Paris, and in a
charming old garden attached to a house of art, and on a
Sunday afternoon of summer, many persons of great interest
being present. The observation there listened to and gathered
up had contained part of the 'note' that I was to recognize on
the spot as to my purpose – had contained in fact the greater
part; the rest was in the place and the time and the scene they
sketched: these constituents clustered and combined to give me
further support, to give me what I may call the note absolute.
There it stands, accordingly, full in the tideway; driven in with
hard taps, like some strong stake for the noose of a cable, the
swirl of the current roundabout it. What amplified the hint to
more than the bulk of hints in general was the gift with it of

the old Paris garden, for in that token were sealed up values infinitely precious. There was of course the seal to break and each item of the packet to count over and handle and estimate; but somehow, in the light of the hint, all the elements of a situation of the sort most to my taste were there. I could even remember no occasion on which, so confronted, I had found it of a livelier interest to take stock, in this fashion, of suggested wealth. For I think, verily, that there are degrees of merit in subjects – in spite of the fact that to treat even one of the most ambiguous with due decency we must for the time, for the feverish and prejudiced hour, at least figure its merit and its dignity as *possibly* absolute. What it comes to, doubtless, is that even among the supremely good – since with such alone is it one's theory of one's honour to be concerned – there is an ideal *beauty* of goodness the invoked action of which is to raise the artistic faith to its maximum. Then truly, I hold, one's theme may be said to shine, and that of 'The Ambassadors', I confess, wore this glow for me from beginning to end. Fortunately thus I am able to estimate this as, frankly, quite the best, 'all round', of all my productions; any failure of that justification would have made such an extreme of complacency publicly fatuous.

I recall then in this connexion no moment of subjective intermittence, never one of those alarms as for a suspected hollow beneath one's feet, a felt ingratitude in the scheme adopted, under which confidence fails and opportunity seems but to mock. If the motive of 'The Wings of the Dove', as I have noted, was to worry me at moments by a sealing-up of its face – though without prejudice to its again, of a sudden, fairly grimacing with expression – so in this other business I had absolute conviction and constant clearness to deal with; it had been a frank proposition, the whole bunch of data, installed on my premises like a monotony of fine weather. (The order of composition, in these things, I may mention, was reversed by the order of publication; the earlier written of the two books having appeared as the later.) Even under the weight of my hero's years I could feel my postulate firm; even under the strain of the difference between those of Madame de Vionnet and those of Chad Newsome, a difference liable to be denounced as

shocking, I could still feel it serene. Nothing resisted, nothing
betrayed, I seem to make out, in this full and sound sense of
the matter; it shed from any side I could turn it to the same
golden glow. I rejoiced in the promise of a hero so mature, who
would give me thereby the more to bite into – since it's only
into thickened motive and accumulated character, I think, that
the painter of life bites more than a little. My poor friend should
have accumulated character, certainly; or rather would be quite
naturally and handsomely possessed of it, in the sense that he
would have, and would always have felt he had, imagination
galore, and that this yet wouldn't have wrecked him. It was
immeasurable, the opportunity to 'do' a man of imagination,
for if *there* mightn't be a chance to 'bite', where in the world
might it be? This personage of course, so enriched, wouldn't
give me, for his type, imagination in *predominance* or as his
prime faculty, nor should I, in view of other matters, have
found that convenient. So particular a luxury – some occasion,
that is, for study of the high gift in *supreme* command of a case
or of a career – would still doubtless come on the day I should
be ready to pay for it; and till then might, as from far back,
remain hung up well in view and just out of reach. The comparative case meanwhile would serve – it was only on the minor
scale that I had treated myself even to comparative cases.

I was to hasten to add however that, happy stopgaps as the
minor scale had thus yielded, the instance in hand should enjoy
the advantage of the full range of the major; since most immediately to the point was the question of that *supplement* of situation logically involved in our gentleman's impulse to deliver
himself in the Paris garden on the Sunday afternoon – or if not
involved by strict logic then all ideally and enchantingly implied
in it. (I say 'ideally', because I need scarce mention that for
development, for expression of its maximum, my glimmering
story was, at the earliest stage, to have nipped the thread of
connexion with the possibilities of the actual reported speaker.
He remains but the happiest of accidents; his actualities, all too
definite, precluded any range of possibilities; it had only been
his charming office to project upon that wide field of the artist's
vision – which hangs there ever in place like the white sheet

suspended for the figures of a child's magic-lantern – a more fantastic and more moveable shadow.) No privilege of the teller of tales and the handler of puppets is more delightful, or has more of the suspense and the thrill of a game of difficulty breathlessly played, than just this business of looking for the unseen and the occult, in a scheme half-grasped, by the light or, so to speak, by the clinging scent, of the gage already in hand. No dreadful old pursuit of the hidden slave with bloodhounds and the rag of association can ever, for 'excitement', I judge, have bettered it at its best. For the dramatist always, by the very law of his genius, believes not only in a possible right issue from the rightly-conceived tight place; he does much more than this – he believes, irresistibly, in the necessary, the precious 'tightness' of the place (whatever the issue) on the strength of any respectable hint. It being thus the respectable hint that I had with such avidity picked up, what would be the story to which it would most inevitably form the centre? It is part of the charm attendant on such questions that the 'story', with the omens true, as I say, puts on from this stage the authenticity of concrete existence. It then *is*, essentially – it begins to be, though it may more or less obscurely lurk; so that the point is not in the least what to make of it, but only, very delightfully and very damnably, where to put one's hand on it.

In which truth resides surely much of the interest of that admirable mixture for salutary application which we know as art. Art deals with what we see, it must first contribute full-handed that ingredient; it plucks its material, otherwise expressed, in the garden of life – which material elsewhere grown is stale and uneatable. But it has no sooner done this than it has to take account of a *process* – from which only when it's the basest of the servants of man, incurring ignominious dismissal with no 'character', does it, and whether under some muddled pretext of morality or on any other, pusillanimously edge away. The process, that of the expression, the literal squeezing-out, of value is another affair – with which the happy luck of mere finding has little to do. The joys of finding, at this stage, are pretty well over; that quest of the subject as a whole

by 'matching', as the ladies say at the shops, the big piece with
the snippet, having ended, we assume, with a capture. The
subject is found, and if the problem is then transferred to the
ground of what to do with it the field opens out for any amount
of doing. This is precisely the infusion that, as I submit, com-
pletes the strong mixture. It is on the other hand the part of the
business that can least be likened to the chase with horn and
hound. It's all a sedentary part – involves as much ciphering,
of sorts, as would merit the highest salary paid to a chief
accountant. Not, however, that the chief accountant hasn't *his*
gleams of bliss; for the felicity, or at least the equilibrium, of
the artist's state dwells less, surely, in the further delightful
complications he can smuggle in than in those he succeeds in
keeping out. He sows his seed at the risk of too thick a crop;
wherefore yet again, like the gentlemen who audit ledgers, he
must keep his head at any price. In consequence of all which,
for the interest of the matter, I might seem here to have my
choice of narrating my 'hunt' for Lambert Strether, of describing the capture of the shadow projected by my friend's anecdote, or of reporting on the occurrences subsequent to that
triumph. But I had probably best attempt a little to glance in
each direction; since it comes to me again and again, over this
licentious record, that one's bag of adventures, conceived or
conceivable, has been only half-emptied by the mere telling of
one's story. It depends so on what one means by that equivocal
quantity. There is the story of one's hero, and then, thanks to
the intimate connexion of things, the story of one's story itself.
I blush to confess it, but if one's a dramatist one's a dramatist,
and the latter imbroglio is liable on occasion to strike me as
really the more objective of the two.

The philosophy imputed to him in that beautiful outbreak,
the hour there, amid such happy provision, striking for him,
would have been then, on behalf of my man of imagination, to
be logically and, as the artless craft of comedy has it, 'led up'
to; the probable course to such a goal, the goal of so conscious
a predicament, would have in short to be finely calculated.
Where has he come from and why has he come, what is he
doing (as we Anglo-Saxons, and we only, say, in our fore-

doomed clutch of exotic aids to expression) in that *galère*?[2] To answer these questions plausibly, to answer them as under cross-examination in the witness-box by counsel for the prosecution, in other words satisfactorily to account for Strether and for his 'peculiar tone', was to possess myself of the entire fabric. At the same time the clue to its whereabouts would lie in a certain *principle* of probability: he wouldn't have indulged in his peculiar tone without a reason; it would take a felt predicament or a false position to give him so ironic an accent. One hadn't been noting 'tones' all one's life without recognizing when one heard it the voice of the false position. The dear man in the Paris garden was then admirably and unmistakeably *in* one – which was no small point gained; what next accordingly concerned us was the determination of *this* identity. One could only go by probabilities, but there was the advantage that the most general of the probabilities were virtual certainties. Possessed of our friend's nationality, to start with, there was a general probability in his narrower localism; which, for that matter, one had really but to keep under the lens for an hour to see it give up its secrets. He would have issued, our rueful worthy, from the very heart of New England – at the heels of which matter of course a perfect train of secrets tumbled for me into the light. They had to be sifted and sorted, and I shall not reproduce the detail of that process; but unmistakeably they were all there, and it was but a question, auspiciously, of picking among them. What the 'position' would infallibly be, and why, on his hands, it had turned 'false' – these inductive steps could only be as rapid as they were distinct. I accounted for everything – and 'everything' had by this time become the most promising quantity – by the view that he had come to Paris in some state of mind which was literally undergoing, as a result of new and unexpected assaults and infusions, a change almost from hour to hour. He had come with a view that might have been figured by a clear green liquid, say, in a neat glass phial; and the liquid, once poured into the open cup of *application*, once exposed to the action of another air, had begun to turn from green to red, or whatever, and might, for all he knew, be on its way to purple, to black, to yellow. At the still wilder

extremes represented perhaps, for all he could say to the contrary, by a variability so violent, he would at first, naturally,
but have gazed in surprise and alarm; whereby the *situation*
clearly would spring from the play of wildness and the development of extremes. I saw in a moment that, should this development proceed both with force and logic, my 'story' would
leave nothing to be desired. There is always, of course, for the
story-teller, the irresistible determinant and the incalculable
advantage of his interest in the story *as such*; it is ever, obviously, overwhelmingly, the prime and precious thing (as other
than this I have never been able to see it); as to which what
makes for it, with whatever headlong energy, may be said to
pale before the energy with which it simply makes for itself. It
rejoices, none the less, at its best, to seem to offer itself in a
light, to seem to know, and with the very last knowledge, what
it's about – liable as it yet is at moments to be caught by us
with its tongue in its cheek and absolutely no warrant but its
splendid impudence. Let us grant then that the impudence is
always there – there, so to speak, for grace and effect and *allure*;
there, above all, because the Story is just the spoiled child
of art, and because, as we are always disappointed when the
pampered don't 'play up', we like it, to that extent, to look all
its character. It probably does so, in truth, even when we most
flatter ourselves that we negotiate with it by treaty.

All of which, again, is but to say that the *steps*, for my fable,
placed themselves with a prompt and, as it were, functional
assurance – an air quite as of readiness to have dispensed with
logic had I been in fact too stupid for my clue. Never, positively,
none the less, as the links multiplied, had I felt less stupid than
for the determination of poor Strether's errand and for the
apprehension of his issue. These things continued to fall
together, as by the neat action of their own weight and form,
even while their commentator scratched his head about them;
he easily sees now that they were always well in advance of
him. As the case completed itself he had in fact, from a good
way behind, to catch up with them, breathless and a little
flurried, as he best could. *The* false position, for our belated
man of the world – belated because he had endeavoured so

long to escape being one, and now at last had really to face his doom – the false position for him, I say, was obviously to have presented himself at the gate of that boundless menagerie primed with a moral scheme of the most approved pattern which was yet framed to break down on any approach to vivid facts; that is to any at all liberal appreciation of them. There would have been of course the case of the Strether prepared, wherever presenting himself, only to judge and to feel meanly; but *he* would have moved for me, I confess, enveloped in no legend whatever. The actual man's note, from the first of our seeing it struck, is the note of discrimination, just as his drama is to become, under stress, the drama of discrimination. It would have been his blest imagination, we have seen, that had already helped him to discriminate; the element that was for so much of the pleasure of my cutting thick, as I have intimated, into his intellectual, into his moral substance. Yet here it was, at the same time, just here, that a shade for a moment fell across the scene.

There was the dreadful little old tradition, one of the platitudes of the human comedy, that people's moral scheme *does* break down in Paris; that nothing is more frequently observed; that hundreds of thousands of more or less hypocritical or more or less cynical persons annually visit the place for the sake of the probable catastrophe, and that I came late in the day to work myself up about it. There was in fine the *trivial* association, one of the vulgarest in the world; but which gave me pause no longer, I think, simply because its vulgarity is so advertised. The revolution performed by Strether under the influence of the most interesting of great cities was to have nothing to do with any *bêtise* of the imputably 'tempted' state; he was to be thrown forward, rather, thrown quite with violence, upon his lifelong trick of intense reflexion: which friendly test indeed was to bring him out, through winding passages, through alternations of darkness and light, very much *in* Paris, but with the surrounding scene itself a minor matter, a mere symbol for more things than had been dreamt of in the philosophy of Woollett.[3] Another surrounding scene would have done as well for our show could it have represented a place in which

Strether's errand was likely to lie and his crisis to await him. The *likely* place had the great merit of sparing me preparations; there would have been too many involved – not at all impossibilities, only rather worrying and delaying difficulties – in positing elsewhere Chad Newsome's interesting relation, his so interesting complexity of relations. Strether's appointed stage, in fine, could be but Chad's most luckily selected one. The young man had gone in, as they say, for circumjacent charm; and where he would have found it, by the turn of his mind, most 'authentic', was where his earnest friend's analysis would most find *him*; as well as where, for that matter, the former's whole analytic faculty would be led such a wonderful dance.

'The Ambassadors' had been, all conveniently, 'arranged for'; its first appearance was from month to month, in the *North American Review* during 1903, and I had been open from far back to any pleasant provocation for ingenuity that might reside in one's actively adopting – so as to make it, in its way, a small compositional law – recurrent breaks and resumptions. I had made up my mind here regularly to exploit and enjoy these often rather rude jolts – having found, as I believed, an admirable way to it; yet every question of form and pressure, I easily remember, paled in the light of the major propriety, recognized as soon as really weighed; that of employing but one centre and keeping it all within my hero's compass. The thing was to be so much this worthy's intimate adventure that even the projection of his consciousness upon it from beginning to end without intermission or deviation would probably still leave a part of its value for him, and *a fortiori* for ourselves, unexpressed. I might, however, express every grain of it that there would be room for – on condition of contriving a splendid particular economy. Other persons in no small number were to people the scene, and each with his or her axe to grind, his or her situation to treat, his or her coherency not to fail of, his or her relation to my leading motive, in a word, to establish and carry on. But Strether's sense of these things, and Strether's only, should avail me for showing them; I should know them but through his more or less groping knowledge of them, since his very gropings would figure among his most interesting motions, and a full

observance of the rich rigour I speak of would give me more of the effect I should be most 'after' than all other possible observances together. It would give me a large unity, and that in turn would crown me with the grace to which the enlightened story-teller will at any time, for his interest, sacrifice if need be all other graces whatever. I refer of course to the grace of intensity, which there are ways of signally achieving and ways of signally missing – as we see it, all round us, helplessly and woefully missed. Not that it isn't, on the other hand, a virtue eminently subject to appreciation – there being no strict, no absolute measure of it; so that one may hear it acclaimed where it has quite escaped one's perception, and see it unnoticed where one has gratefully hailed it. After all of which I am not sure, either, that the immense amusement of the whole cluster of difficulties so arrayed may not operate, for the fond fabulist, when judicious not less than fond, as his best of determinants. That charming principle is always there, at all events, to keep interest fresh: it is a principle, we remember, essentially ravenous, without scruple and without mercy, appeased with no cheap nor easy nourishment. It enjoys the costly sacrifice and rejoices thereby in the very odour of difficulty – even as ogres, with their 'Fee-faw-fum!' rejoice in the smell of the blood of Englishmen.

Thus it was, at all events, that the ultimate, though after all so speedy, definition of my gentleman's job – his coming out, all solemnly appointed and deputed, to 'save' Chad, and his then finding the young man so disobligingly and, at first, so bewilderingly not lost that a new issue altogether, in the connexion, prodigiously faces them, which has to be dealt with in a new light – promised as many calls on ingenuity and on the higher branches of the compositional art as one could possibly desire. Again and yet again, as, from book to book, I proceed with my survey, I find no source of interest equal to this verification after the fact, as I may call it, and the more in detail the better, of the scheme of consistency 'gone in' for. As always – since the charm never fails – the retracing of the process from point to point brings back the old illusion. The old intentions bloom again and flower – in spite of all the blossoms they were

to have dropped by the way. This is the charm, as I say, of adventure *transposed* – the thrilling ups and downs, the intricate ins and outs of the compositional problem, made after such a fashion admirably objective, becoming the question at issue and keeping the author's heart in his mouth. Such an element, for instance, as his intention that Mrs. Newsome, away off with her finger on the pulse of Massachusetts, should yet be no less intensely than circuitously present through the whole thing, should be no less felt as to be reckoned with than the most direct exhibition, the finest portrayal at first hand could make her, such a sign of artistic good faith, I say, once it's unmistakeably there, takes on again an actuality not too much impaired by the comparative dimness of the particular success. Cherished intention too inevitably acts and operates, in the book, about fifty times as little as I had fondly dreamt it might; but that scarce spoils for me the pleasure of recognizing the fifty ways in which I had sought to provide for it. The mere charm of seeing such an idea constituent, in its degree; the fineness of the measures taken – a real extension, if successful, of the very terms and possibilities of representation and figuration – such things alone were, after this fashion, inspiring, such things alone were a gage of the probable success of that dissimulated calculation with which the whole effort was to square. But oh the cares begotten, none the less, of that same 'judicious' sacrifice to a particular form of interest! One's work should have composition, because composition alone is positive beauty; but all the while – apart from one's inevitable consciousness too of the dire paucity of readers ever recognizing or ever missing positive beauty – how, as to the cheap and easy, at every turn, how, as to immediacy and facility, and even as to the commoner vivacity, positive beauty might have to be sweated for and paid for! Once achieved and installed it may always be trusted to make the poor seeker feel he would have blushed to the roots of his hair for failing of it; yet, how, as its virtue can be essentially but the virtue of the whole, the wayside traps set in the interest of muddlement and pleading but the cause of the moment, of the particular bit in itself, have to be kicked out of the path! All the sophistications in life, for

example, might have appeared to muster on behalf of the menace – the menace to a bright variety – involved in Strether's having all the subjective 'say', as it were, to himself.

Had I, meanwhile, made him at once hero and historian, endowed him with the romantic privilege of the 'first person' – the darkest abyss of romance this, inveterately, when enjoyed on the grand scale – variety, and many other queer matters as well, might have been smuggled in by a back door. Suffice it, to be brief, that the first person, in the long piece, is a form foredoomed to looseness, and that looseness, never much my affair, had never been so little so as on this particular occasion. All of which reflexions flocked to the standard from the moment – a very early one – the question of how to keep my form amusing while sticking so close to my central figure and constantly taking its pattern from him had to be faced. He arrives (arrives at Chester) as for the dreadful purpose of giving his creator 'no end' to tell about him – before which rigorous mission the serenest of creators might well have quailed. I was far from the serenest; I was more than agitated enough to reflect that, grimly deprived of one alternative or one substitute for 'telling', I must address myself tooth and nail to another. I couldn't, save by implication, make other persons tell *each other* about him – blest resource, blest necessity, of the drama, which reaches its effects of unity, all remarkably, by paths absolutely opposite to the paths of the novel: with other persons, save as they were primarily *his* persons (not he primarily but one of theirs), I had simply nothing to do. I had relations for him none the less, by the mercy of Providence, quite as much as if my exhibition *was* to be a muddle; if I could only by implication and a show of consequence make other persons tell each other about him, I could at least make him tell *them* whatever in the world he must; and could so, by the same token – which was a further luxury thrown in – see straight into the deep differences between what that could do for me, or at all events for *him*, and the large ease of 'autobiography'. It may be asked why, if one so keeps to one's hero, one shouldn't make a single mouthful of 'method', shouldn't throw the reins on his neck and, letting them flap there as free as in 'Gil Blas' or in

'David Copperfield',[4] equip him with the double privilege of subject and object – a course that has at least the merit of brushing away questions at a sweep. The answer to which is, I think, that one makes that surrender only if one is prepared *not* to make certain precious discriminations.

The 'first person' then, so employed, is addressed by the author directly to ourselves, his possible readers, whom he has to reckon with, at the best, by our English tradition, so loosely and vaguely after all, so little respectfully, on so scant a presumption of exposure to criticism. Strether, on the other hand, encaged and provided for as 'The Ambassadors' encages and provides, has to keep in view proprieties much stiffer and more salutary than any our straight and credulous gape are likely to bring home to him, has exhibitional conditions to meet, in a word, that forbid the terrible *fluidity* of self-revelation. I may seem not to better the case for my discrimination if I say that, for my first care, I had thus inevitably to set him up a confidant or two, to wave away with energy the custom of the seated mass of explanation after the fact, the inserted block of merely referential narrative, which flourishes so, to the shame of the modern impatience, on the serried page of Balzac, but which seems simply to appal our actual, our general weaker, digestion. 'Harking back to make up' took at any rate more doing, as the phrase is, not only than the reader of to-day demands, but than he will tolerate at any price any call upon him either to understand or remotely to measure; and for the beauty of the thing when done the current editorial mind in particular appears wholly without sense. It is not, however, primarily for either of these reasons, whatever their weight, that Strether's friend Waymarsh is so keenly clutched at, on the threshold of the book, or that no less a pounce is made on Maria Gostrey – without even the pretext, either, of *her* being, in essence, Strether's friend. She is the reader's friend much rather – in consequence of dispositions that make him so eminently require one; and she acts in that capacity, and *really* in that capacity alone, with exemplary devotion, from beginning to end of the book. She is an enrolled, a direct, aid to lucidity; she is in fine, to tear off her mask, the most unmitigated and abandoned of

ficelles. Half the dramatist's art, as we well know – since if we don't it's not the fault of the proofs that lie scattered about us – is in the use of *ficelles*; by which I mean in a deep dissimulation of his dependence on them. Waymarsh only to a slighter degree belongs, in the whole business, less to my subject than to my treatment of it; the interesting proof, in these connexions, being that one has but to take one's subject for the stuff of drama to interweave with enthusiasm as many Gostreys as need be.

The material of 'The Ambassadors', conforming in this respect exactly to that of 'The Wings of the Dove', published just before it, is taken absolutely for the stuff of drama; so that, availing myself of the opportunity given me by this edition for some prefatory remarks on the latter work, I had mainly to make on its behalf the point of its scenic consistency. It disguises that virtue, in the oddest way in the world, by just *looking*, as we turn its pages, as little scenic as possible; but it sharply divides itself, just as the composition before us does, into the parts that prepare, that tend in fact to over-prepare, for scenes, and the parts, or otherwise into the scenes, that justify and crown the preparation. It may definitely be said, I think, that everything in it that is not scene (not, I of course mean, complete and functional scene, treating *all* the submitted matter, as by logical start, logical turn, and logical finish) is discriminated preparation, is the fusion and synthesis of picture. These alternations propose themselves all recognizeably, I think, from an early stage, as the very form and figure of 'The Ambassadors'; so that, to repeat, such an agent as Miss Gostrey, pre-engaged at a high salary, but waits in the draughty wing with her shawl and her smelling-salts. Her function speaks at once for itself, and by the time she has dined with Strether in London and gone to a play with him her intervention as a *ficelle* is, I hold, expertly justified. Thanks to it we have treated scenically, and scenically alone, the whole lumpish question of Strether's 'past', which has seen us more happily on the way than anything else could have done; we have strained to a high lucidity and vivacity (or at least we hope we have) certain indispensable facts; we have seen our two or three immediate friends all conveniently and profitably in 'action'; to say nothing of our beginning to

descry others, of a remoter intensity, getting into motion, even if a bit vaguely as yet, for our further enrichment. Let my first point be here that the scene in question, that in which the whole situation at Woollett and the complex forces that have propelled my hero to where this lively extractor of his value and distiller of his essence awaits him, is normal and entire, is really an excellent *standard* scene; copious, comprehensive, and accordingly never short, but with its office as definite as that of the hammer on the gong of the clock, the office of expressing *all that is in* the hour.

The '*ficelle*' character of the subordinate party is as artfully dissimulated, throughout, as may be, and to that extent that, with the seams or joints of Maria Gostrey's ostensible connectedness taken particular care of, duly smoothed over, that is, and anxiously kept from showing as 'pieced on', this figure doubtless achieves, after a fashion, something of the dignity of a prime idea: which circumstance but shows us afresh how many quite incalculable but none the less clear sources of enjoyment for the infatuated artist, how many copious springs of our never-to-be-slighted 'fun' for the reader and critic susceptible of contagion, may sound their incidental plash as soon as an artistic process begins to enjoy free development. Exquisite – in illustration of this – the mere interest and amusement of such at once 'creative' and critical questions as how and where and why to make Miss Gostrey's false connexion carry itself, under a due high polish, as a real one. Nowhere is it more of an artful expedient for mere consistency of form, to mention a case, than in the last 'scene' of the book, where its function is to give or to add nothing whatever, but only to express as vividly as possible certain things quite other than itself and that are of the already fixed and appointed measure. Since, however, all art is *expression*, and is thereby vividness, one was to find the door open here to any amount of delightful dissimulation. These verily are the refinements and ecstasies of method – amid which, or certainly under the influence of any exhilarated demonstration of which, one must keep one's head and not lose one's way. To cultivate an adequate intelligence for them and to make that sense operative is positively to find a charm in any

produced ambiguity of appearance that is not by the same stroke, and all helplessly, an ambiguity of sense. To project imaginatively, for my hero, a relation that has nothing to do with the matter (the matter of my subject) but has everything to do with the manner (the manner of my presentation of the same) and yet to treat it, at close quarters and for fully economic expression's possible sake, as if it were important and essential – to do that sort of thing and yet muddle nothing may easily become, as one goes, a signally attaching proposition; even though it all remains but part and parcel, I hasten to recognize, of the merely general and related question of expressional curiosity and expressional decency.

I am moved to add after so much insistence on the scenic side of my labour that I have found the steps of re-perusal almost as much waylaid here by quite another style of effort in the same signal interest – or have in other words not failed to note how, even so associated and so discriminated, the finest proprieties and charms of the non-scenic may, under the right hand for them, still keep their intelligibility and assert their office. Infinitely suggestive such an observation as this last on the whole delightful head, where representation is concerned, of possible variety, of effective expressional change and contrast. One would like, at such an hour as this, for critical licence, to go into the matter of the noted inevitable deviation (from too fond an original vision) that the exquisite treachery even of the straightest execution may ever be trusted to inflict even on the most mature plan – the case being that, though one's last reconsidered production always seems to bristle with that particular evidence, 'The Ambassadors' would place a flood of such light at my service. I must attach to my final remark here a different import; nothing in the other connexion I just glanced at that such passages as that of my hero's first encounter with Chad Newsome, absolute attestations of the non-scenic form though they be, yet lay the firmest hand too – so far at least as intention goes – on representational effect. To report at all closely and completely of what 'passes' on a given occasion is inevitably to become more or less scenic; and yet in the instance I allude to, *with* the conveyance, expressional curiosity and

expressional decency are sought and arrived at under quite another law. The true inwardness of this may be at bottom but that one of the suffered treacheries has consisted precisely, for Chad's whole figure and presence, of a direct presentability diminished and compromised – despoiled, that is, of its *proportional* advantage; so that, in a word, the whole economy of his author's relation to him has at important points to be redetermined. The book, however, critically viewed, is touchingly full of these disguised and repaired losses, these insidious recoveries, these intensely redemptive consistencies. The pages in which Mamie Pocock gives her appointed and, I can't but think, duly felt lift to the whole action by the so inscrutably-applied side-stroke or short-cut of our just watching, and as quite at an angle of vision as yet untried, her single hour of suspense in the hotel salon, in our partaking of her concentrated study of the sense of matters bearing on her own case, all the bright warm Paris afternoon, from the balcony that overlooks the Tuileries garden – these are as marked an example of the representational virtue that insists here and there on being, for the charm of opposition and renewal, other than the scenic. It wouldn't take much to make me further argue that from an equal play of such oppositions the book gathers an intensity that fairly adds to the dramatic – though the latter is supposed to be the sum of all intensities; or that has at any rate nothing to fear from juxtaposition with it. I consciously fail to shrink in fact from that extravagance – I risk it, rather, for the sake of the moral involved; which is not that the particular production before us exhausts the interesting questions it raises, but that the Novel remains still, under the right persuasion, the most independent, most elastic, most prodigious of literary forms.

HENRY JAMES

BOOK FIRST

I

Strether's first question, when he reached the hotel, was about his friend; yet on his learning that Waymarsh was apparently not to arrive till evening he was not wholly disconcerted. A telegram from him bespeaking a room 'only if not noisy', reply paid, was produced for the enquirer at the office, so that the understanding they should meet at Chester rather than at Liverpool[1] remained to that extent sound. The same secret principle, however, that had prompted Strether not absolutely to desire Waymarsh's presence at the dock, that had led him thus to postpone for a few hours his enjoyment of it, now operated to make him feel he could still wait without disappointment. They would dine together at the worst, and, with all respect to dear old Waymarsh – if not even, for that matter, to himself – there was little fear that in the sequel they shouldn't see enough of each other. The principle I have just mentioned as operating had been, with the most newly disembarked of the two men, wholly instinctive – the fruit of a sharp sense that, delightful as it would be to find himself looking, after so much separation, into his comrade's face, his business would be a trifle bungled should he simply arrange for this countenance to present itself to the nearing steamer as the first 'note', of Europe. Mixed with everything was the apprehension, already, on Strether's part, that it would, at best, throughout, prove the note of Europe in quite a sufficient degree.

That note had been meanwhile – since the previous afternoon, thanks to this happier device – such a consciousness of personal freedom as he hadn't known for years; such a deep taste of change and of having above all for the moment nobody

and nothing to consider, as promised already, if headlong hope were not too foolish, to colour his adventure with cool success. There were people on the ship with whom he had easily consorted – so far as ease could up to now be imputed to him – and who for the most part plunged straight into the current that set from the landing-stage to London; there were others who had invited him to a tryst at the inn and had even invoked his aid for a 'look round' at the beauties of Liverpool; but he had stolen away from every one alike, had kept no appointment and renewed no acquaintance, had been indifferently aware of the number of persons who esteemed themselves fortunate in being, unlike himself, 'met', and had even independently, unsociably, alone, without encounter or relapse and by mere quiet evasion, given his afternoon and evening to the immediate and the sensible. They formed a qualified draught of Europe, an afternoon and an evening on the banks of the Mersey, but such as it was he took his potion at least undiluted. He winced a little, truly, at the thought that Waymarsh might be already at Chester; he reflected that, should he have to describe himself there as having 'got in' so early, it would be difficult to make the interval look particularly eager; but he was like a man who, elatedly finding in his pocket more money than usual, handles it a while and idly and pleasantly chinks it before addressing himself to the business of spending. That he was prepared to be vague to Waymarsh about the hour of the ship's touching, and that he both wanted extremely to see him and enjoyed extremely the duration of delay – these things, it is to be conceived, were early signs in him that his relation to his actual errand might prove none of the simplest. He was burdened, poor Strether – it had better be confessed at the outset – with the oddity of a double consciousness. There was detachment in his zeal and curiosity in his indifference.

After the young woman in the glass cage had held up to him across her counter the pale-pink leaflet bearing his friend's name, which she neatly pronounced, he turned away to find himself, in the hall, facing a lady who met his eyes as with an intention suddenly determined, and whose features – not freshly young, not markedly fine, but on happy terms with each other –

came back to him as from a recent vision. For a moment they stood confronted; then the moment placed her: he had noticed her the day before, noticed her at his previous inn, where – again in the hall – she had been briefly engaged with some people of his own ship's company. Nothing had actually passed between them, and he would as little have been able to say what had been the sign of her face for him on the first occasion as to name the ground of his present recognition. Recognition at any rate appeared to prevail on her own side as well – which would only have added to the mystery. All she now began by saying to him nevertheless was that, having chanced to catch his enquiry, she was moved to ask, by his leave, if it were possibly a question of Mr. Waymarsh of Milrose Connecticut – Mr. Waymarsh the American lawyer.

'Oh yes,' he replied, 'my very well-known friend. He's to meet me here, coming up from Malvern, and I supposed he'd already have arrived. But he doesn't come till later, and I'm relieved not to have kept him. Do you know him?' Strether wound up.

It wasn't till after he had spoken that he became aware of how much there had been in him of response; when the tone of her own rejoinder, as well as the play of something more in her face – something more, that is, than its apparently usual restless light – seemed to notify him. 'I've met him at Milrose – where I used sometimes, a good while ago, to stay; I had friends there who were friends of his, and I've been at his house. I won't answer for it that he would know me,' Strether's new acquaintance pursued; 'but I should be delighted to see him. Perhaps,' she added, 'I shall – for I'm staying over.' She paused while our friend took in these things, and it was as if a good deal of talk had already passed. They even vaguely smiled at it, and Strether presently observed that Mr. Waymarsh would, no doubt, be easily to be seen. This, however, appeared to affect the lady as if she might have advanced too far. She appeared to have no reserves about anything. 'Oh,' she said, 'he won't care!' – and she immediately thereupon remarked that she believed Strether knew the Munsters; the Munsters being the people he had seen her with at Liverpool.

But he didn't, it happened, know the Munsters well enough to give the case much of a lift; so that they were left together as if over the mere laid table of conversation. Her qualification of the mentioned connexion had rather removed than placed a dish, and there seemed nothing else to serve. Their attitude remained, none the less, that of not forsaking the board; and the effect of this in turn was to give them the appearance of having accepted each other with an absence of preliminaries practically complete. They moved along the hall together, and Strether's companion threw off that the hotel had the advantage of a garden. He was aware by this time of his strange inconsequence: he had shirked the intimacies of the steamer and had muffled the shock of Waymarsh only to find himself forsaken, in this sudden case, both of avoidance and of caution. He passed, under this unsought protection and before he had so much as gone up to his room, into the garden of the hotel, and at the end of ten minutes had agreed to meet there again, as soon as he should have made himself tidy, the dispenser of such good assurances. He wanted to look at the town, and they would forthwith look together. It was almost as if she had been in possession and received him as a guest. Her acquaintance with the place presented her in a manner as a hostess, and Strether had a rueful glance for the lady in the glass cage. It was as if this personage had seen herself instantly superseded.

When in a quarter of an hour he came down, what his hostess saw, what she might have taken in with a vision kindly adjusted, was the lean, the slightly loose figure of a man of the middle height and something more perhaps than the middle age – a man of five-and-fifty, whose most immediate signs were a marked bloodless brownness of face, a thick dark moustache, of characteristically American cut, growing strong and falling low, a head of hair still abundant but irregularly streaked with grey, and a nose of bold free prominence, the even line, the high finish, as it might have been called, of which, had a certain effect of mitigation. A perpetual pair of glasses astride of this fine ridge, and a line, unusually deep and drawn, the prolonged pen-stroke of time, accompanying the curve of the moustache from nostril to chin, did something to complete the facial furni-

ture that an attentive observer would have seen catalogued, on
the spot, in the vision of the other party to Strether's appointment. She waited for him in the garden, the other party, drawing
on a pair of singularly fresh soft and elastic light gloves and
presenting herself with a superficial readiness which, as he
approached her over the small smooth lawn and in the watery
English sunshine, he might, with his rougher preparation, have
marked as the model for such an occasion. She had, this lady,
a perfect plain propriety, an expensive subdued suitability, that
her companion was not free to analyse, but that struck him, so
that his consciousness of it was instantly acute, as a quality
quite new to him. Before reaching her he stopped on the grass
and went through the form of feeling for something, possibly
forgotten, in the light overcoat he carried on his arm; yet the
essence of the act was no more than the impulse to gain time.
Nothing could have been odder than Strether's sense of himself
as at that moment launched in something of which the sense
would be quite disconnected from the sense of his past and
which was literally beginning there and then. It had begun in
fact already upstairs and before the dressing-glass that struck
him as blocking further, so strangely, the dimness of the
window of his dull bedroom; begun with a sharper survey of
the elements of Appearance than he had for a long time been
moved to make. He had during those moments felt these
elements to be not so much to his hand as he should have liked,
and then had fallen back on the thought that they were precisely
a matter as to which help was supposed to come from what he
was about to do. He was about to go up to London, so that hat
and necktie might wait. What had come as straight to him as
a ball in a well-played game – and caught moreover not less
neatly – was just the air, in the person of his friend, of having
seen and chosen, the air of achieved possession of those vague
qualities and quantities that collectively figured to him as the
advantage snatched from lucky chances. Without pomp or circumstance, certainly, as her original address to him, equally
with his own response, had been, he would have sketched to
himself his impression of her as: 'Well, she's more thoroughly
civilized –!' If 'More thoroughly than *whom*?' would not have

been for him a sequel to this remark, that was just by reason of his deep consciousness of the bearing of his comparison.

The amusement, at all events, of a civilization intenser was what – familiar compatriot as she was, with the full tone of the compatriot and the rattling link not with mystery but only with dear dyspeptic Waymarsh – she appeared distinctly to promise. His pause while he felt in his overcoat was positively the pause of confidence, and it enabled his eyes to make out as much of a case for her, in proportion, as her own made out for himself. She affected him as almost insolently young; but an easily carried five-and-thirty could still do that. She was, however, like himself, marked and wan; only it naturally couldn't have been known to him how much a spectator looking from one to the other might have discerned that they had in common. It wouldn't for such a spectator have been altogether insupposable that, each so finely brown and so sharply spare, each confessing so to dents of surface and aids to sight, to a disproportionate nose and a head delicately or grossly grizzled, they might have been brother and sister. On this ground indeed there would have been a residuum of difference; such a sister having surely known in respect to such a brother the extremity of separation, and such a brother now feeling in respect to such a sister the extremity of surprise. Surprise, it was true, was not on the other hand what the eyes of Strether's friend most showed him while she gave him, stroking her gloves smoother, the time he appreciated. They had taken hold of him straightway, measuring him up and down as if they knew how; as if he were human material they had already in some sort handled. Their possessor was in truth, it may be communicated, the mistress of a hundred cases or categories, receptacles of the mind, subdivisions for convenience, in which, from a full experience, she pigeon-holed her fellow mortals with a hand as free as that of a compositor scattering type. She was as equipped in this particular as Strether was the reverse, and it made an opposition between them which he might well have shrunk from submitting to if he had fully suspected it. So far as he did suspect it he was on the contrary, after a short shake of his consciousness, as pleasantly passive as might be. He really had

a sort of sense of what she knew. He had quite the sense that she knew things he didn't, and though this was a concession that in general he found not easy to make to women, he made it now as good-humouredly as if it lifted a burden. His eyes were so quiet behind his eternal nippers[2] that they might almost have been absent without changing his face, which took its expression mainly, and not least its stamp of sensibility, from other sources, surface and grain and form. He joined his guide in an instant, and then felt she had profited still better than he by his having been, for the moments just mentioned, so at the disposal of her intelligence. She knew even intimate things about him that he hadn't yet told her and perhaps never would. He wasn't unaware that he had told her rather remarkably many for the time, but these were not the real ones. Some of the real ones, however, precisely, were what she knew.

They were to pass again through the hall of the inn to get into the street, and it was here she presently checked him with a question. 'Have you looked up my name?'

He could only stop with a laugh. 'Have you looked up mine?'

'Oh dear, yes – as soon as you left me. I went to the office and asked. Hadn't *you* better do the same?'

He wondered. 'Find out who you are? – after the uplifted young woman there has seen us thus scrape acquaintance!'

She laughed on her side now at the shade of alarm in his amusement. 'Isn't it a reason the more? If what you're afraid of is the injury for me – my being seen to walk off with a gentleman who has to ask who I am – I assure you I don't in the least mind. Here, however,' she continued, 'is my card, and as I find there's something else again I have to say at the office, you can just study it during the moment I leave you.'

She left him after he had taken from her the small pasteboard she had extracted from her pocket-book, and he had extracted another from his own, to exchange with it, before she came back. He read thus the simple designation 'Maria Gostrey', to which was attached, in a corner of the card, with a number, the name of a street, presumably in Paris, without other appreciable identity than its foreignness. He put the card into his waistcoat pocket, keeping his own meanwhile in evidence; and as he

leaned against the door-post he met with the smile of a straying thought what the expanse before the hotel offered to his view. It was positively droll to him that he should already have Maria Gostrey, whoever she was – of which he hadn't really the least idea – in a place of safe keeping. He had somehow an assurance that he should carefully preserve the little token he had just tucked in. He gazed with unseeing lingering eyes as he followed some of the implications of his act, asking himself if he really felt admonished to qualify it as disloyal. It was prompt, it was possibly even premature, and there was little doubt of the expression of face the sight of it would have produced in a certain person. But if it was 'wrong' – why then he had better not have come out at all. At this, poor man, had he already – and even before meeting Waymarsh – arrived. He had believed he had a limit, but the limit had been transcended within thirty-six hours. By how long a space on the plane of manners, or even of morals, moreover, he felt still more sharply after Maria Gostrey had come back to him and with a gay decisive 'So now –!' led him forth into the world. This counted, it struck him as he walked beside her with his overcoat on an arm, his umbrella under another and his personal pasteboard a little stiffly retained between forefinger and thumb, this struck him as really, in comparison, his introduction to things. It hadn't been 'Europe' at Liverpool, no – not even in the dreadful delightful impressive streets the night before – to the extent his present companion made it so. She hadn't yet done that so much as when, after their walk had lasted a few minutes and he had had time to wonder if a couple of sidelong glances from her meant that he had best have put on gloves, she almost pulled him up with an amused challenge. 'But why – fondly as it's so easy to imagine your clinging to it – don't you put it away? Or if it's an inconvenience to you to carry it, one's often glad to have one's card back. The fortune one spends in them!'

Then he saw both that his way of marching with his own prepared tribute had affected her as a deviation in one of those directions he couldn't yet measure, and that she supposed this emblem to be still the one he had received from her. He accordingly handed her the card as if in restitution, but as soon as she

had it she felt the difference and, with her eyes on it, stopped
short for apology. 'I like,' she observed, 'your name.'

'Oh,' he answered, 'you won't have heard of it!' Yet he had
his reasons for not being sure but that she perhaps might.

Ah it was but too visible! She read it over again as one
who had never seen it. '"Mr. Lewis Lambert Strether"' – she
sounded it almost as freely as for any stranger. She repeated
however that she liked it – 'particularly the Lewis Lambert. It's
the name of a novel of Balzac's.'[3]

'Oh I know that!' said Strether.

'But the novel's an awfully bad one.'

'I know that too,' Strether smiled. To which he added with
an irrelevance that was only superficial: 'I come from Woollett
Massachusetts.' It made her for some reason – the irrelevance
or whatever – laugh. Balzac had described many cities, but
hadn't described Woollett Massachusetts. 'You say that,' she
returned, 'as if you wanted one immediately to know the worst.'

'Oh I think it's a thing,' he said, 'that you must already have
made out. I feel it so that I certainly must look it, speak it, and,
as people say there, "act" it. It sticks out of me, and you knew
surely for yourself as soon as you looked at me.'

'The worst, you mean?'

'Well, the fact of where I come from. There at any rate it *is*;
so that you won't be able, if anything happens, to say I've not
been straight with you.'

'I see' – and Miss Gostrey looked really interested in the point
he had made. 'But what do you think of as happening?'

Though he wasn't shy – which was rather anomalous –
Strether gazed about without meeting her eyes; a motion that
was frequent with him in talk, yet of which his words often
seemed not at all the effect. 'Why that you should find me too
hopeless.' With which they walked on again together while
she answered, as they went, that the most 'hopeless' of her
countryfolk were in general precisely those she liked best. All
sorts of other pleasant small things – small things that were yet
large for him – flowered in the air of the occasion; but the
bearing of the occasion itself on matters still remote concerns
us too closely to permit us to multiply our illustrations. Two

or three, however, in truth, we should perhaps regret to lose. The tortuous wall[4] – girdle, long since snapped, of the little swollen city, half held in place by careful civic hands – wanders in narrow file between parapets smoothed by peaceful generations, pausing here and there for a dismantled gate or a bridged gap, with rises and drops, steps up and steps down, queer twists, queer contacts, peeps into homely streets and under the brows of gables, views of cathedral tower and waterside fields, of huddled English town and ordered English country. Too deep almost for words was the delight of these things to Strether; yet as deeply mixed with it were certain images of his inward picture. He had trod this walk in the far-off time, at twenty-five; but that, instead of spoiling it, only enriched it for present feeling and marked his renewal as a thing substantial enough to share. It was with Waymarsh he should have shared it, and he was now accordingly taking from him something that was his due. He looked repeatedly at his watch, and when he had done so for the fifth time Miss Gostrey took him up.

'You're doing something that you think not right.'

It so touched the place that he quite changed colour and his laugh grew almost awkward. 'Am I enjoying it as much as *that*?'

'You're not enjoying it, I think, so much as you ought.'

'I see' – he appeared thoughtfully to agree. 'Great is my privilege.'

'Oh it's not your privilege! It has nothing to do with *me*. It has to do with yourself. Your failure's general.'

'Ah there you are!' he laughed. 'It's the failure of Woollett. *That's* general.'

'The failure to enjoy,' Miss Gostrey explained, 'is what I mean.'

'Precisely. Woollett isn't sure it ought to enjoy. If it were it would. But it hasn't, poor thing,' Strether continued, 'any one to show it how. It's not like me. I have somebody.'

They had stopped, in the afternoon sunshine – constantly pausing, in their stroll, for the sharper sense of what they saw – and Strether rested on one of the high sides of the old stony groove of the little rampart. He leaned back on this support

with his face to the tower of the cathedral, now admirably commanded by their station, the high red-brown mass, square and subordinately spired and crocketed,[5] retouched and restored, but charming to his long-sealed eyes and with the first swallows of the year weaving their flight all round it. Miss Gostrey lingered near him, full of an air, to which she more and more justified her right, of understanding the effect of things. She quite concurred. 'You've indeed somebody.' And she added: 'I wish you *would* let me show you how!'

'Oh I'm afraid of you!' he cheerfully pleaded.

She kept on him a moment, through her glasses and through his own, a certain pleasant pointedness. 'Ah no, you're not! You're not in the least, thank goodness! If you had been we shouldn't so soon have found ourselves here together. I think,' she comfortably concluded, 'you trust me.'

'I think I do! – but that's exactly what I'm afraid of. I shouldn't mind if I didn't. It's falling thus in twenty minutes so utterly into your hands. I dare say,' Strether continued, 'it's a sort of thing you're thoroughly familiar with; but nothing more extraordinary has ever happened to me.'

She watched him with all her kindness. 'That means simply that you've recognized me – which *is* rather beautiful and rare. You see what I am.' As on this, however, he protested, with a good-humoured headshake, a resignation of any such claim, she had a moment of explanation. 'If you'll only come on further as you *have* come you'll at any rate make out. My own fate has been too many for me, and I've succumbed to it. I'm a general guide – to "Europe", don't you know? I wait for people – I put them through. I pick them up – I set them down. I'm a sort of superior "courier-maid". I'm a companion at large. I take people, as I've told you, about. I never sought it – it has come to me. It has been my fate, and one's fate one accepts. It's a dreadful thing to have to say, in so wicked a world, but I verily believe that, such as you see me, there's nothing I don't know. I know all the shops and the prices – but I know worse things still. I bear on my back the huge load of our national consciousness, or, in other words – for it comes to that – of our nation itself. Of what is our nation composed but of the men

and women individually on my shoulders? I don't do it, you
know, for any particular advantage. I don't do it, for instance
– some people do, you know – for money.'

Strether could only listen and wonder and weigh his chance.
'And yet, affected as you are then to so many of your clients,
you can scarcely be said to do it for love.' He waited a moment.
'How do we reward you?'

She had her own hesitation, but 'You don't!' she finally
returned, setting him again in motion. They went on, but in a
few minutes, though while still thinking over what she had said,
he once more took out his watch; mechanically, unconsciously
and as if made nervous by the mere exhilaration of what struck
him as her strange and cynical wit. He looked at the hour
without seeing it, and then, on something again said by his
companion, had another pause. 'You're really in terror of him.'

He smiled a smile that he almost felt to be sickly. 'Now you
can see why I'm afraid of you.'

'Because I've such illuminations? Why they're all for your
help! It's what I told you,' she added, 'just now. You feel as if
this were wrong.'

He fell back once more, settling himself against the parapet
as if to hear more about it. 'Then get me out!'

Her face fairly brightened for the joy of the appeal, but, as if
it were a question of immediate action, she visibly considered.
'Out of waiting for him? – of seeing him at all?'

'Oh no – not that,' said poor Strether, looking grave. 'I've
got to wait for him – and I want very much to see him. But out
of the terror. You did put your finger on it a few minutes ago.
It's general, but it avails itself of particular occasions. That's
what it's doing for me now. I'm always considering something
else; something else, I mean, than the thing of the moment. The
obsession of the other thing is the terror. I'm considering at
present for instance something else than *you*.'

She listened with charming earnestness. 'Oh you oughtn't to
do that!'

'It's what I admit. Make it then impossible.'

She continued to think. 'Is it really an "order" from you? –
that I shall take the job? *Will* you give yourself up?'

Poor Strether heaved his sigh. 'If I only could! But that's the deuce of it – that I never can. No – I can't.'

She wasn't, however, discouraged. 'But you want to at least?'

'Oh unspeakably!'

'Ah then, if you'll try!' – and she took over the job, as she had called it, on the spot. 'Trust me!' she exclaimed; and the action of this, as they retraced their steps, was presently to make him pass his hand into her arm in the manner of a benign dependent paternal old person who wishes to be 'nice' to a younger one. If he drew it out again indeed as they approached the inn this may have been because, after more talk had passed between them, the relation of age, or at least of experience – which, for that matter, had already played to and fro with some freedom – affected him as incurring a readjustment. It was at all events perhaps lucky that they arrived in sufficiently separate fashion within range of the hotel-door. The young lady they had left in the glass cage watched as if she had come to await them on the threshold. At her side stood a person equally interested, by his attitude, in their return, and the effect of the sight of whom was instantly to determine for Strether another of those responsive arrests that we have had so repeatedly to note. He left it to Miss Gostrey to name, with the fine full bravado, as it almost struck him, of her 'Mr. Waymarsh!' what was to have been, what – he more than ever felt as his short stare of suspended welcome took things in – would have been, but for herself, his doom. It was already upon him even at that distance – Mr. Waymarsh was for *his* part joyless.

II

He had none the less to confess to this friend that evening that he knew almost nothing about her, and it was a deficiency that Waymarsh, even with his memory refreshed by contact, by her own prompt and lucid allusions and enquiries, by their having publicly partaken of dinner in her company, and by another stroll, to which she was not a stranger, out into the town to look at the cathedral by moonlight – it was a blank that the resident of Milrose, though admitting acquaintance with the Munsters, professed himself unable to fill. He had no recollection of Miss Gostrey, and two or three questions that she put to him about those members of his circle had, to Strether's observation, the same effect he himself had already more directly felt – the effect of appearing to place all knowledge, for the time, on this original woman's side. It interested him indeed to mark the limits of any such relation for her with his friend as there could possibly be a question of, and it particularly struck him that they were to be marked altogether in Waymarsh's quarter. This added to his own sense of having gone far with her – gave him an early illustration of a much shorter course. There was a certitude he immediately grasped – a conviction that Waymarsh would quite fail, as it were, and on whatever degree of acquaintance, to profit by her.

There had been after the first interchange among the three a talk of some five minutes in the hall, and then the two men had adjourned to the garden, Miss Gostrey for the time disappearing. Strether in due course accompanied his friend to the room he had bespoken and had, before going out, scrupulously visited; where at the end of another half-hour he had no less

discreetly left him. On leaving him he repaired straight to his own room, but with the prompt effect of feeling the compass of that chamber resented by his condition. There he enjoyed at once the first consequence of their reunion. A place was too small for him after it that had seemed large enough before. He had awaited it with something he would have been sorry, have been almost ashamed not to recognize as emotion, yet with a tacit assumption at the same time that emotion would in the event find itself relieved. The actual oddity was that he was only more excited; and his excitement – to which indeed he would have found it difficult instantly to give a name – brought him once more downstairs and caused him for some minutes vaguely to wander. He went once more to the garden; he looked into the public room, found Miss Gostrey writing letters and backed out; he roamed, fidgeted and wasted time; but he was to have his more intimate session with his friend before the evening closed.

It was late – not till Strether had spent an hour upstairs with him – that this subject consented to betake himself to doubtful rest. Dinner and the subsequent stroll by moonlight – a dream, on Strether's part, of romantic effects rather prosaically merged in a mere missing of thicker coats – had measurably intervened, and this midnight conference was the result of Waymarsh's having (when they were free, as he put it, of their fashionable friend) found the smoking-room not quite what he wanted, and yet bed what he wanted less. His most frequent form of words was that he knew himself, and they were applied on this occasion to his certainty of not sleeping. He knew himself well enough to know that he should have a night of prowling unless he should succeed, as a preliminary, in getting prodigiously tired. If the effort directed to this end involved till a late hour the presence of Strether – consisted, that is, in the detention of the latter for full discourse – there was yet an impression of minor discipline involved for our friend in the picture Waymarsh made as he sat in trousers and shirt on the edge of his couch. With his long legs extended and his large back much bent, he nursed alternately, for an almost incredible time, his elbows and his beard. He struck his visitor as extremely, as

almost wilfully uncomfortable; yet what had this been for Strether, from that first glimpse of him disconcerted in the porch of the hotel, but the predominant note? The discomfort was in a manner contagious, as well as also in a manner inconsequent and unfounded; the visitor felt that unless he should get used to it – or unless Waymarsh himself should – it would constitute a menace for his own prepared, his own already confirmed, consciousness of the agreeable. On their first going up together to the room Strether had selected for him Waymarsh had looked it over in silence and with a sigh that represented for his companion, if not the habit of disapprobation, at least the despair of felicity; and this look had recurred to Strether as the key of much he had since observed. 'Europe', he had begun to gather from these things, had up to now rather failed of its message to him; he hadn't got into tune with it and had at the end of three months almost renounced any such expectation.

He really appeared at present to insist on that by just perching there with the gas in his eyes. This of itself somehow conveyed the futility of single rectifications in a multiform failure. He had a large handsome head and a large sallow seamed face – a striking significant physiognomic total, the upper range of which, the great political brow, the thick loose hair, the dark fuliginous eyes, recalled even to a generation whose standard had dreadfully deviated the impressive image, familiar by engravings and busts, of some great national worthy of the earlier part of the mid-century. He was of the personal type – and it was an element in the power and promise that in their early time Strether had found in him – of the American statesman, the statesman trained in 'Congressional halls', of an elder day. The legend had been in later years that as the lower part of his face, which was weak, and slightly crooked, spoiled the likeness, this was the real reason for the growth of his beard, which might have seemed to spoil it for those not in the secret. He shook his mane; he fixed, with his admirable eyes, his auditor or his observer; he wore no glasses and had a way, partly formidable, yet also partly encouraging, as from a representative to a constituent, of looking very hard at those who approached him. He met you as if you had knocked and he had

bidden you enter. Strether, who hadn't seen him for so long an interval, apprehended him now with a freshness of taste, and had perhaps never done him such ideal justice. The head was bigger, the eyes finer, than they need have been for the career; but that only meant, after all, that the career was itself express- ive. What it expressed at midnight in the gas-glaring bedroom at Chester was that the subject of it had, at the end of years, barely escaped, by flight in time, a general nervous collapse. But this very proof of the full life, as the full life was understood at Milrose, would have made to Strether's imagination an element in which Waymarsh could have floated easily had he only consented to float. Alas nothing so little resembled floating as the rigour with which, on the edge of his bed, he hugged his posture of prolonged impermanence. It suggested to his com- rade something that always, when kept up, worried him – a person established in a railway-coach with a forward incli- nation. It represented the angle at which poor Waymarsh was to sit through the ordeal of Europe.

Thanks to the stress of occupation, the strain of professions, the absorption and embarrassment of each, they had not, at home, during years before this sudden brief and almost bewil- dering reign of comparative ease, found so much as a day for a meeting; a fact that was in some degree an explanation of the sharpness with which most of his friend's features stood out to Strether. Those he had lost sight of since the early time came back to him; others that it was never possible to forget struck him now as sitting, clustered and expectant, like a somewhat defiant family-group, on the door-step of their residence. The room was narrow for its length, and the occupant of the bed thrust so far a pair of slippered feet that the visitor had almost to step over them in his recurrent rebounds from his chair to fidget back and forth. There were marks the friends made on things to talk about, and on things not to, and one of the latter in particular fell like the tap of chalk on the blackboard. Married at thirty, Waymarsh had not lived with his wife for fifteen years, and it came up vividly between them in the glare of the gas that Strether wasn't to ask about her. He knew they were still separate and that she lived at hotels, travelled in

Europe, painted her face and wrote her husband abusive letters, of not one of which, to a certainty, that sufferer spared himself the perusal; but he respected without difficulty the cold twilight that had settled on this side of his companion's life. It was a province in which mystery reigned and as to which Waymarsh had never spoken the informing word. Strether, who wanted to do him the highest justice wherever he *could* do it, singularly admired him for the dignity of this reserve, and even counted it as one of the grounds – grounds all handled and numbered – for ranking him, in the range of their acquaintance, as a success. He *was* a success, Waymarsh, in spite of overwork, or prostration, of sensible shrinkage, of his wife's letters and of his not liking Europe. Strether would have reckoned his own career less futile had he been able to put into it anything so handsome as so much fine silence. One might one's self easily have left Mrs. Waymarsh; and one would assuredly have paid one's tribute to the ideal in covering with that attitude the derision of having been left by her. Her husband had held his tongue and had made a large income; and these were in especial the achievements as to which Strether envied him. Our friend had had indeed on his side too a subject for silence, which he fully appreciated; but it was a matter of a different sort, and the figure of the income he had arrived at had never been high enough to look any one in the face.

'I don't know as I quite see what you require it for. You don't appear sick to speak of.' It was of Europe Waymarsh thus finally spoke.

'Well,' said Strether, who fell as much as possible into step, 'I guess I don't *feel* sick now that I've started. But I had pretty well run down before I did start.'

Waymarsh raised his melancholy look. 'Ain't you about up to your usual average?'

It was not quite pointedly sceptical, but it seemed somehow a plea for the purest veracity, and it thereby affected our friend as the very voice of Milrose. He had long since made a mental distinction – though never in truth daring to betray it – between the voice of Milrose and the voice even of Woollett. It was the former, he felt, that was most in the real tradition. There had

been occasions in his past when the sound of it had reduced him to temporary confusion, and the present, for some reason, suddenly became such another. It was nevertheless no light matter that the very effect of his confusion should be to make him again prevaricate. 'That description hardly does justice to a man to whom it has done such a lot of good to see *you*.'

Waymarsh fixed on his washing-stand the silent detached stare with which Milrose in person, as it were, might have marked the unexpectedness of a compliment from Woollett; and Strether, for his part, felt once more like Woollett in person. 'I mean,' his friend presently continued, 'that your appearance isn't as bad as I've seen it: it compares favourably with what it was when I last noticed it.' On this appearance Waymarsh's eyes yet failed to rest; it was almost as if they obeyed an instinct of propriety, and the effect was still stronger when, always considering the basin and jug, he added: 'You've filled out some since then.'

'I'm afraid I have,' Strether laughed: 'one does fill out some with all one takes in, and I've taken in, I dare say, more than I've natural room for. I was dog-tired when I sailed.' It had the oddest sound of cheerfulness.

'*I* was dog-tired,' his companion returned, 'when I arrived, and it's this wild hunt for rest that takes all the life out of me. The fact is, Strether – and it's a comfort to have you here at last to say it to; though I don't know, after all, that I've really waited; I've told it to people I've met in the cars – the fact is, such a country as this ain't my *kind* of country anyway. There ain't a country I've seen over here that *does* seem my kind. Oh I don't say but what there are plenty of pretty places and remarkable old things; but the trouble is that I don't seem to feel anywhere in tune. That's one of the reasons why I suppose I've gained so little. I haven't had the first sign of that lift I was led to expect.' With this he broke out more earnestly. 'Look here – I want to go back.'

His eyes were all attached to Strether's now, for he was one of the men who fully face you when they talk of themselves. This enabled his friend to look at him hard and immediately to appear to the highest advantage in his eyes by doing so. 'That's

a genial thing to say to a fellow who has come out on purpose to meet you!'

Nothing could have been finer, on this, than Waymarsh's sombre glow. '*Have* you come out on purpose?'

'Well – very largely.'

'I thought from the way you wrote there was something back of it.'

Strether hesitated. 'Back of my desire to be with you?'

'Back of your prostration.'

Strether, with a smile made more dim by a certain consciousness, shook his head. 'There are all the causes of it!'

'And no particular cause that seemed most to drive you?'

Our friend could at last conscientiously answer. 'Yes. One. There *is* a matter that has had much to do with my coming out.'

Waymarsh waited a little. 'Too private to mention?'

'No, not too private – for *you*. Only rather complicated.'

'Well,' said Waymarsh, who had waited again, 'I *may* lose my mind over here, but I don't know as I've done so yet.'

'Oh you shall have the whole thing. But not tonight.'

Waymarsh seemed to sit stiffer and to hold his elbows tighter. 'Why not – if I can't sleep?'

'Because, my dear man, I *can*!'

'Then where's your prostration?'

'Just in that – that I can put in eight hours.' And Strether brought it out that if Waymarsh didn't 'gain' it was because he didn't go to bed: the result of which was, in its order, that, to do the latter justice, he permitted his friend to insist on his really getting settled. Strether, with a kind coercive hand for it, assisted him to this consummation, and again found his own part in their relation auspiciously enlarged by the smaller touches of lowering the lamp and seeing to a sufficiency of blanket. It somehow ministered for him to indulgence to feel Waymarsh, who looked unnaturally big and black in bed, as much tucked in as a patient in a hospital and, with his covering up to his chin, as much simplified by it. He hovered in vague pity, to be brief, while his companion challenged him out of the bedclothes. 'Is she really after you? Is that what's behind?'

Strether felt an uneasiness at the direction taken by his companion's insight, but he played a little at uncertainty. 'Behind my coming out?'

'Behind your prostration or whatever. It's generally felt, you know, that she follows you up pretty close.'

Strether's candour was never very far off. 'Oh it has occurred to you that I'm literally running away from Mrs. Newsome?'

'Well, I haven't *known* but what you are. You're a very attractive man, Strether. You've seen for yourself,' said Waymarsh, 'what that lady downstairs makes of it. Unless indeed,' he rambled on with an effect between the ironic and the anxious, 'it's you who are after *her*. Is Mrs. Newsome *over* here?' He spoke as with a droll dread of her.

It made his friend – though rather dimly – smile. 'Dear no; she's safe, thank goodness – as I think I more and more feel – at home. She thought of coming, but she gave it up. I've come in a manner instead of her; and come to that extent – for you're right in your inference – on her business. So you see there *is* plenty of connexion.'

Waymarsh continued to see at least all there was. 'Involving accordingly the particular one I've referred to?'

Strether took another turn about the room, giving a twitch to his companion's blanket and finally gaining the door. His feeling was that of a nurse who had earned personal rest by having made everything straight. 'Involving more things than I can think of breaking ground on now. But don't be afraid – you shall have them from me: you'll probably find yourself having quite as much of them as you can do with. I shall – if we keep together – very much depend on your impression of some of them.'

Waymarsh's acknowledgement of this tribute was characteristically indirect. 'You mean to say you don't believe we *will* keep together?'

'I only glance at the danger,' Strether paternally said, 'because when I hear you wail to go back I seem to see you open up such possibilities of folly.'

Waymarsh took it – silent a little – like a large snubbed child. 'What are you going to do with me?'

It was the very question Strether himself had put to Miss Gostrey, and he wondered if he had sounded like that. But *he* at least could be more definite. 'I'm going to take you right down to London.'

'Oh I've *been* down to London!' Waymarsh more softly moaned. 'I've no use, Strether, for anything down there.'

'Well,' said Strether, good-humouredly, 'I guess you've some use for *me*.'

'So I've got to go?'

'Oh you've got to go further yet.'

'Well,' Waymarsh sighed, 'do your damnedest! Only you *will* tell me before you lead me on all the way –?'

Our friend had again so lost himself, both for amusement and for contrition, in the wonder of whether he had made, in his own challenge that afternoon, such another figure, that he for an instant missed the thread. 'Tell you –?'

'Why what you've got on hand.'

Strether hesitated. 'Why it's such a matter as that even if I positively wanted I shouldn't be able to keep it from you.'

Waymarsh gloomily gazed. 'What does that mean then but that your trip is just *for* her?'

'For Mrs. Newsome? Oh it certainly is, as I say. Very much.'

'Then why do you also say it's for me?'

Strether, in impatience, violently played with his latch. 'It's simple enough. It's for both of you.'

Waymarsh at last turned over with a groan. 'Well, *I* won't marry you!'

'Neither, when it comes to that –!' But the visitor had already laughed and escaped.

III

He had told Miss Gostrey he should probably take, for departure with Waymarsh, some afternoon train, and it thereupon
in the morning appeared that this lady had made her own plan
for an earlier one. She had breakfasted when Strether came into
the coffee-room; but, Waymarsh not having yet emerged, he
was in time to recall her to the terms of their understanding
and to pronounce her discretion overdone. She was surely not
to break away at the very moment she had created a want. He
had met her as she rose from her little table in a window, where,
with the morning papers beside her, she reminded him, as he
let her know, of Major Pendennis breakfasting at his club[1] – a
compliment of which she professed a deep appreciation; and
he detained her as pleadingly as if he had already – and notably
under pressure of the visions of the night – learned to be unable
to do without her. She must teach him at all events, before she
went, to order breakfast as breakfast was ordered in Europe,
and she must especially sustain him in the problem of ordering
for Waymarsh. The latter had laid upon his friend, by desperate
sounds through the door of his room, dreadful divined responsibilities in respect to beefsteak and oranges – responsibilities
which Miss Gostrey took over with an alertness of action that
matched her quick intelligence. She had before this weaned the
expatriated from traditions compared with which the matutinal
beefsteak was but the creature of an hour, and it was not for
her, with some of her memories, to falter in the path; though
she freely enough declared, on reflexion, that there was always
in such cases a choice of opposed policies. 'There are times
when to give them their head, you know –!'

They had gone to wait together in the garden for the dressing of the meal, and Strether found her more suggestive than ever. 'Well, what?'

'Is to bring about for them such a complexity of relations – unless indeed we call it a simplicity! – that the situation *has* to wind itself up. They want to go back.'

'And you want them to go!' Strether gaily concluded.

'I always want them to go, and I send them as fast as I can.'

'Oh I know – you take them to Liverpool.'

'Any port will serve in a storm. I'm – with all my other functions – an agent for repatriation. I want to re-people our stricken country. What will become of it else? I want to discourage others.'

The ordered English garden, in the freshness of the day, was delightful to Strether, who liked the sound, under his feet, of the tight fine gravel, packed with the chronic damp, and who had the idlest eye for the deep smoothness of turf and the clean curves of paths. 'Other people?'

'Other countries. Other people – yes. I want to encourage our own.'

Strether wondered. 'Not to come? Why then do you "meet" them? – since it doesn't appear to be to stop them?'

'Oh that they shouldn't come is as yet too much to ask. What I attend to is that they come quickly and return still more so. I meet them to help it to be over as soon as possible, and though I don't stop them I've my way of putting them through. That's my little system; and, if you want to know,' said Maria Gostrey, 'it's my real secret, my innermost mission and use. I only seem, you see, to beguile and approve; but I've thought it all out and I'm working all the while underground. I can't perhaps quite give you my formula, but I think that practically I succeed. I send you back spent. So you stay back. Passed through my hands –'

'We don't turn up again?' The further she went the further he always saw himself able to follow. 'I don't want your formula – I feel quite enough, as I hinted yesterday, your abysses. Spent!' he echoed. 'If that's how you're arranging so subtly to send me I thank you for the warning.'

For a minute, amid the pleasantness – poetry in tariffed items, but all the more, for guests already convicted, a challenge to consumption – they smiled at each other in confirmed fellowship. 'Do you call it subtly? It's a plain poor tale. Besides, you're a special case.'

'Oh special cases – that's weak!' She was weak enough, further still, to defer her journey and agree to accompany the gentlemen on their own, might a separate carriage mark her independence; though it was in spite of this to befall after luncheon that she went off alone and that, with a tryst taken for a day of her company in London, they lingered another night. She had, during the morning – spent in a way that he was to remember later on as the very climax of his foretaste, as warm with presentiments, with what he would have called collapses – had all sorts of things out with Strether; and among them the fact that though there was never a moment of her life when she wasn't 'due' somewhere, there was yet scarce a perfidy to others of which she wasn't capable for his sake. She explained moreover that wherever she happened to be she found a dropped thread to pick up, a ragged edge to repair, some familiar appetite in ambush, jumping out as she approached, yet appeasable with a temporary biscuit. It became, on her taking the risk of the deviation imposed on him by her insidious arrangement of his morning meal, a point of honour for her not to fail with Waymarsh of the larger success too; and her subsequent boast to Strether was that she had made their friend fare – and quite without his knowing what was the matter – as Major Pendennis would have fared at the Megatherium.[2] She had made him breakfast like a gentleman, and it was nothing, she forcibly asserted, to what she would yet make him do. She made him participate in the slow reiterated ramble with which, for Strether, the new day amply filled itself; and it was by her art that he somehow had the air, on the ramparts and in the Rows,[3] of carrying a point of his own.

The three strolled and stared and gossiped, or at least the two did; the case really yielding for their comrade, if analysed, but the element of stricken silence. This element indeed affected Strether as charged with audible rumblings, but he was conscious

of the care of taking it explicitly as a sign of pleasant peace. He wouldn't appeal too much, for that provoked stiffness; yet he wouldn't be too freely tacit, for that suggested giving up. Waymarsh himself adhered to an ambiguous dumbness that might have represented either the growth of a perception or the despair of one; and at times and in places – where the low-browed galleries were darkest, the opposite gables queerest, the solicitations of every kind densest – the others caught him fixing hard some object of minor interest, fixing even at moments nothing discernible, as if he were indulging it with a truce. When he met Strether's eye on such occasions he looked guilty and furtive, fell the next minute into some attitude of re-tractation. Our friend couldn't show him the right things for fear of provoking some total renouncement, and was tempted even to show him the wrong in order to make him differ with triumph. There were moments when he himself felt shy of professing the full sweetness of the taste of leisure, and there were others when he found himself feeling as if his passages of interchange with the lady at his side might fall upon the third member of their party very much as Mr. Burchell, at Dr. Prim-rose's fireside, was influenced by the high flights of the visitors from London.[4] The smallest things so arrested and amused him that he repeatedly almost apologized – brought up afresh in explanation his plea of a previous grind. He was aware at the same time that his grind had been as nothing to Waymarsh's, and he repeatedly confessed that, to cover his frivolity, he was doing his best for his previous virtue. Do what he might, in any case, his previous virtue was still there, and it seemed fairly to stare at him out of the windows of shops that were not as the shops of Woollett, fairly to make him want things that he shouldn't know what to do with. It was by the oddest, the least admissible of laws demoralizing him now; and the way it boldly took was to make him want more wants. These first walks in Europe were in fact a kind of finely lurid intimation of what one might find at the end of that process. Had he come back after long years, in something already so like the evening of life, only to be exposed to it? It was at all events over the shop-windows that he made, with Waymarsh, most free;

though it would have been easier had not the latter most sensibly yielded to the appeal of the merely useful trades. He pierced with his sombre detachment the plate-glass of ironmongers and saddlers, while Strether flaunted an affinity with the dealers in stamped letter-paper and in smart neckties. Strether was in fact recurrently shameless in the presence of the tailors, though it was just over the heads of the tailors that his countryman most loftily looked. This gave Miss Gostrey a grasped opportunity to back up Waymarsh at his expense. The weary lawyer – it was unmistakeable – had a conception of dress; but that, in view of some of the features of the effect produced, was just what made the danger of insistence on it. Strether wondered if he by this time thought Miss Gostrey less fashionable or Lambert Strether more so; and it appeared probable that most of the remarks exchanged between this latter pair about passers, figures, faces, personal types, exemplified in their degree the disposition to talk as 'society' talked.

Was what was happening to himself then, was what already *had* happened, really that a woman of fashion was floating him into society and that an old friend deserted on the brink was watching the force of the current? When the woman of fashion permitted Strether – as she permitted him at the most – the purchase of a pair of gloves, the terms she made about it, the prohibition of neckties and other items till she should be able to guide him through the Burlington Arcade,[5] were such as to fall upon a sensitive ear as a challenge to just imputations. Miss Gostrey was such a woman of fashion as could make without a symptom of vulgar blinking an appointment for the Burlington Arcade. Mere discriminations about a pair of gloves could thus at any rate represent – always for such sensitive ears as were in question – possibilities of something that Strether could make a mark against only as the peril of apparent wantonness. He had quite the consciousness of his new friend, for their companion, that he might have had of a Jesuit in petticoats, a representative of the recruiting interests of the Catholic Church. The Catholic Church, for Waymarsh – that was to say the enemy, the monster of bulging eyes and far-reaching quivering groping tentacles – was exactly society, exactly the

multiplication of shibboleths, exactly the discrimination of
types and tones, exactly the wicked old Rows of Chester, rank
with feudalism; exactly in short Europe.

There was light for observation, however, in an incident that
occurred just before they turned back to luncheon. Waymarsh
had been for a quarter of an hour exceptionally mute and
distant, and something, or other – Strether was never to make
out exactly what – proved, as it were, too much for him after
his comrades had stood for three minutes taking in, while they
leaned on an old balustrade that guarded the edge of the Row,
a particularly crooked and huddled street-view. 'He thinks us
sophisticated, he thinks us worldly, he thinks us wicked, he
thinks us all sorts of queer things,' Strether reflected; for wondrous were the vague quantities our friend had within a couple
of short days acquired the habit of conveniently and conclus-
ively lumping together. There seemed moreover a direct connexion between some such inference and a sudden grim dash
taken by Waymarsh to the opposite side. This movement was
startlingly sudden, and his companions at first supposed him to
have espied, to be pursuing, the glimpse of an acquaintance.
They next made out, however, that an open door had instantly
received him, and they then recognized him as engulfed in the
establishment of a jeweller, behind whose glittering front he
was lost to view. The act had somehow the note of a demonstration, and it left each of the others to show a face almost of
fear. But Miss Gostrey broke into a laugh. 'What's the matter
with him?'

'Well,' said Strether, 'he can't stand it.'

'But can't stand what?'

'Anything. Europe.'

'Then how will that jeweller help him?'

Strether seemed to make it out, from their position, between
the interstices of arrayed watches, of close-hung dangling gew-
gaws. 'You'll see.'

'Ah that's just what – if he buys anything – I'm afraid of:
that I shall see something rather dreadful.'

Strether studied the finer appearances. 'He may buy everything.'

'Then don't you think we ought to follow him?'

'Not for worlds. Besides we can't. We're paralysed. We exchange a long scared look, we publicly tremble. The thing is, you see, we "realize". He has struck for freedom.'

She wondered but she laughed. 'Ah what a price to pay! And I was preparing some for him so cheap.'

'No, no,' Strether went on, frankly amused now; 'don't call it that: the kind of freedom *you* deal in is dear.' Then as to justify himself: 'Am I not in *my* way trying it? It's this.'

'Being here, you mean, with me?'

'Yes, and talking to you as I do. I've known you a few hours, and I've known *him* all my life; so that if the ease I thus take with you about him isn't magnificent' – and the thought of it held him a moment – 'why it's rather base.'

'It's magnificent!' said Miss Gostrey to make an end of it. 'And you should hear,' she added, 'the ease *I* take – and I above all intend to take – with Mr. Waymarsh.'

Strether thought. 'About *me*? Ah that's no equivalent. The equivalent would be Waymarsh's himself serving me up – his remorseless analysis of me. And he'll never do that' – he was sadly clear. 'He'll never remorselessly analyse me.' He quite held her with the authority of this. 'He'll never say a word to you about me.'

She took it in; she did it justice; yet after an instant her reason, her restless irony, disposed of it. 'Of course he won't. For what do you take people, that they're able to say words about anything, able remorselessly to analyse? There are not many like you and me. It will be only because he's too stupid.'

It stirred in her friend a sceptical echo which was at the same time the protest of the faith of years. 'Waymarsh stupid?'

'Compared with you.'

Strether had still his eyes on the jeweller's front, and he waited a moment to answer. 'He's a success of a kind that I haven't approached.'

'Do you mean he has made money?'

'He makes it – to my belief. And I,' said Strether, 'though with a back quite as bent, have never made anything. I'm a perfectly equipped failure.'

He feared an instant she'd ask him if he meant he was poor; and he was glad she didn't, for he really didn't know to what the truth on this unpleasant point mightn't have prompted her. She only, however, confirmed his assertion. 'Thank goodness you're a failure – it's why I so distinguish you! Anything else to-day is too hideous. Look about you – look at the successes. Would you *be* one, on your honour? Look, moreover,' she continued, 'at me.'

For a little accordingly their eyes met. 'I see,' Strether returned. 'You too are out of it.'

'The superiority you discern in me,' she concurred, 'announces my futility. If you knew,' she sighed, 'the dreams of my youth! But our realities are what has brought us together. We're beaten brothers in arms.'

He smiled at her kindly enough, but he shook his head. 'It doesn't alter the fact that you're expensive. You've cost me already –!'

But he had hung fire. 'Cost you what?'

'Well, my past – in one great lump. But no matter,' he laughed: 'I'll pay with my last penny.'

Her attention had unfortunately now been engaged by their comrade's return, for Waymarsh met their view as he came out of his shop. 'I hope he hasn't paid,' she said, 'with *his* last; though I'm convinced he has been splendid, and has been so for you.'

'Ah no – not that!'

'Then for me?'

'Quite as little.' Waymarsh was by this time near enough to show signs his friend could read, though he seemed to look almost carefully at nothing in particular.

'Then for himself?'

'For nobody. For nothing. For freedom.'

'But what has freedom to do with it?'

Strether's answer was indirect. 'To be as good as you and me. But different.'

She had had time to take in their companion's face; and with it, as such things were easy for her, she took in all. 'Different – yes. But better!'

If Waymarsh was sombre he was also indeed almost sublime. He told them nothing, left his absence unexplained, and though they were convinced he had made some extraordinary purchase they were never to learn its nature. He only glowered grandly at the tops of the old gables. 'It's the sacred rage,' Strether had had further time to say; and this sacred rage was to become between them, for convenient comprehension, the description of one of his periodical necessities. It was Strether who eventually contended that it did make him better than they. But by that time Miss Gostrey was convinced that she didn't want to be better than Strether.

BOOK SECOND

I

Those occasions on which Strether was, in association with the exile from Milrose, to see the sacred rage glimmer through would doubtless have their due periodicity; but our friend had meanwhile to find names for many other matters. On no evening of his life perhaps, as he reflected, had he had to supply so many as on the third of his short stay in London; an evening spent by Miss Gostrey's side at one of the theatres, to which he had found himself transported, without his own hand raised, on the mere expression of a conscientious wonder. She knew her theatre, she knew her play, as she had triumphantly known, three days running, everything else, and the moment filled to the brim, for her companion, that apprehension of the interesting which, whether or no the interesting happened to filter through his guide, strained now to its limits his brief opportunity. Waymarsh hadn't come with them; he had seen plays enough, he signified, before Strether had joined him – an affirmation that had its full force when his friend ascertained by questions that he had seen two and a circus. Questions as to what he had seen had on him indeed an effect only less favourable than questions as to what he hadn't. He liked the former to be discriminated; but how could it be done, Strether asked of their constant counsellor, without discriminating the latter?

Miss Gostrey had dined with him at his hotel, face to face over a small table on which the lighted candles had rose-coloured shades; and the rose-coloured shades and the small table and the soft fragrance of the lady – had anything to his mere sense ever been so soft? – were so many touches in he

scarce knew what positive high picture. He had been to the
theatre, even to the opera, in Boston, with Mrs. Newsome,
more than once acting as her only escort; but there had been
no little confronted dinner, no pink lights, no whiff of vague
sweetness, as a preliminary: one of the results of which was
that at present, mildly rueful, though with a sharpish accent,
he actually asked himself *why* there hadn't. There was much
the same difference in his impression of the noticed state of his
companion, whose dress was 'cut down', as he believed the
term to be, in respect to shoulders and bosom, in a manner
quite other than Mrs. Newsome's, and who wore round her
throat a broad red velvet band with an antique jewel – he was
rather complacently sure it was antique – attached to it in front.
Mrs. Newsome's dress was never in any degree 'cut down', and
she never wore round her throat a broad red velvet band: if she
had, moreover, would it ever have served so to carry on and
complicate, as he now almost felt, his vision?

It would have been absurd of him to trace into ramifications
the effect of the ribbon from which Miss Gostrey's trinket
depended, had he not for the hour, at the best, been so given
over to uncontrolled perceptions. What was it but an uncontrolled perception that his friend's velvet band somehow added,
in her appearance, to the value of every other item – to that of
her smile and of the way she carried her head, to that of her
complexion, of her lips, her teeth, her eyes, her hair? What,
certainly, had a man conscious of a man's work in the world
to do with red velvet bands? He wouldn't for anything have so
exposed himself as to tell Miss Gostrey how much he liked
hers, yet he *had* none the less not only caught himself in the act
– frivolous, no doubt, idiotic, and above all unexpected – of
liking it: he had in addition taken it as a starting-point for fresh
backward, fresh forward, fresh lateral flights. The manner in
which Mrs. Newsome's throat *was* encircled suddenly represented for him, in an alien order, almost as many things as
the manner in which Miss Gostrey's was. Mrs. Newsome wore,
at operatic hours, a black silk dress – very handsome, he knew
it was 'handsome' – and an ornament that his memory was able
further to identify as a ruche. He had his association indeed

with the ruche, but it was rather imperfectly romantic. He had once said to the wearer – and it was as 'free' a remark as he had ever made to her – that she looked, with her ruff and other matters, like Queen Elizabeth;[1] and it had after this in truth been his fancy that, as a consequence of that tenderness and an acceptance of the idea, the form of this special tribute to the 'frill' had grown slightly more marked. The connexion, as he sat there and let his imagination roam, was to strike him as vaguely pathetic; but there it all was, and pathetic was doubtless in the conditions the best thing it could possibly be. It had assuredly existed at any rate; for it seemed now to come over him that no gentleman of his age at Woollett could ever, to a lady of Mrs. Newsome's, which was not much less than his, have embarked on such a smile.

All sorts of things in fact now seemed to come over him, comparatively few of which his chronicler can hope for space to mention. It came over him for instance that Miss Gostrey looked perhaps like Mary Stuart: Lambert Strether had a candour of fancy which could rest for an instant gratified in such an antithesis. It came over him that never before – no, literally never – had a lady dined with him at a public place before going to the play. The publicity of the place was just, in the matter, for Strether, the rare strange thing; it affected him almost as the achievement of privacy might have affected a man of a different experience. He had married, in the far-away years, so young as to have missed the time natural in Boston for taking girls to the Museum;[2] and it was absolutely true of him that – even after the close of the period of conscious detachment occupying the centre of his life, the grey middle desert of the two deaths, that of his wife and that, ten years later, of his boy – he had never taken any one anywhere. It came over him in especial – though the monition had, as happened, already sounded, fitfully gleamed, in other forms – that the business he had come out on hadn't yet been so brought home to him as by the sight of the people about him. She gave him the impression, his friend, at first, more straight than he got it for himself – gave it simply by saying with off-hand illumination: 'Oh yes, they're types!' – but after he had taken it he made to the full

his own use of it; both while he kept silence for the four acts and while he talked in the intervals. It was an evening, it was a world of types, and this was a connexion above all in which the figures and faces in the stalls were interchangeable with those on the stage.

He felt as if the play itself penetrated him with the naked elbow of his neighbour, a great stripped handsome red-haired lady who conversed with a gentleman on her other side in stray dissyllables which had for his ear, in the oddest way in the world, so much sound that he wondered they hadn't more sense; and he recognized by the same law, beyond the footlights, what he was pleased to take for the very flush of English life. He had distracted drops in which he couldn't have said if it were actors or auditors who were most true, and the upshot of which, each time, was the consciousness of new contacts. However he viewed his job it was 'types' he should have to tackle. Those before him and around him were not as the types of Woollett, where, for that matter, it had begun to seem to him that there must only have been the male and the female. These made two exactly, even with the individual varieties. Here, on the other hand, apart from the personal and the sexual range – which might be greater or less – a series of strong stamps had been applied, as it were, from without; stamps that his observation played with as, before a glass case on a table, it might have passed from medal to medal and from copper to gold. It befell that in the drama precisely there was a bad woman in a yellow frock who made a pleasant weak good-looking young man in perpetual evening dress do the most dreadful things. Strether felt himself on the whole not afraid of the yellow frock, but he was vaguely anxious over a certain kindness into which he found himself drifting for its victim. He hadn't come out, he reminded himself, to be too kind, or indeed to be kind at all, to Chadwick Newsome. Would Chad also be in perpetual evening dress? He somehow rather hoped it – it seemed so to add to *this* young man's general amenability; though he wondered too if, to fight him with his own weapons, he himself (a thought almost startling) would have likewise to be. This young man furthermore would have been much more easy to

handle – at least for *him* – than appeared probable in respect
to Chad.

It came up for him with Miss Gostrey that there were things
of which she would really perhaps after all have heard; and
she admitted when a little pressed that she was never quite sure
of what she heard as distinguished from things such as, on
occasions like the present, she only extravagantly guessed. 'I
seem with this freedom, you see, to have guessed Mr. Chad.
He's a young man on whose head high hopes are placed at
Woollett; a young man a wicked woman has got hold of and
whom his family over there have sent you out to rescue. You've
accepted the mission of separating him from the wicked
woman. Are you quite sure she's very bad for him?'

Something in his manner showed it as quite pulling him up.
'Of course we are. Wouldn't *you* be?'

'Oh I don't know. One never does – does one? – beforehand.
One can only judge on the facts. Yours are quite new to me;
I'm really not in the least, as you see, in possession of them: so
it will be awfully interesting to have them from you. If you're
satisfied, that's all that's required. I mean if you're sure you *are*
sure: sure it won't do.'

'That he should lead such a life? Rather!'

'Oh but I don't know, you see, about his life; you've not told
me about his life. She may be charming – his life!'

'Charming?' – Strether stared before him. 'She's base, venal
– out of the streets.'

'I see. And *he* –?'

'Chad, wretched boy?'

'Of what type and temper is he?' she went on as Strether had
lapsed.

'Well – the obstinate.' It was as if for a moment he had been
going to say more and had then controlled himself.

That was scarce what she wished. 'Do you like him?'

This time he was prompt. 'No. How *can* I?'

'Do you mean because of your being so saddled with him?'

'I'm thinking of his mother,' said Strether after a moment.
'He has darkened her admirable life.' He spoke with austerity.
'He has worried her half to death.'

'Oh that's of course odious.' She had a pause as if for renewed emphasis of this truth, but it ended on another note. 'Is her life very admirable?'

'Extraordinarily.'

There was so much in the tone that Miss Gostrey had to devote another pause to the appreciation of it. 'And has he only *her*? I don't mean the bad woman in Paris,' she quickly added – 'for I assure you I shouldn't even at the best be disposed to allow him more than one. But has he only his mother?'

'He has also a sister, older than himself and married; and they're both remarkably fine women.'

'Very handsome, you mean?'

This promptitude – almost, as he might have thought, this precipitation, gave him a brief drop; but he came up again. 'Mrs. Newsome, I think, is handsome, though she's not of course, with a son of twenty-eight and a daughter of thirty, in her very first youth. She married, however, extremely young.'

'And is wonderful,' Miss Gostrey asked, 'for her age?'

Strether seemed to feel with a certain disquiet the pressure of it. 'I don't say she's wonderful. Or rather,' he went on the next moment, 'I do say it. It's exactly what she *is* – wonderful. But I wasn't thinking of her appearance,' he explained – 'striking as that doubtless is. I was thinking – well, of many other things.' He seemed to look at these as if to mention some of them; then took, pulling himself up, another turn. 'About Mrs. Pocock people may differ.'

'Is that the daughter's name – "Pocock"?'

'That's the daughter's name,' Strether sturdily confessed.

'And people may differ, you mean, about *her* beauty?'

'About everything.'

'But *you* admire her?'

He gave his friend a glance as to show how he could bear this. 'I'm perhaps a little afraid of her.'

'Oh,' said Miss Gostrey, 'I see her from here! You may say then I see very fast and very far, but I've already shown you I do. The young man and the two ladies,' she went on, 'are at any rate all the family?'

'Quite all. His father has been dead ten years, and there's

no brother, nor any other sister. They'd do,' said Strether, 'anything in the world for him.'

'And you'd do anything in the world for *them*?'

He shifted again; she had made it perhaps just a shade too affirmative for his nerves. 'Oh I don't know!'

'You'd do at any rate this, and the "anything" they'd do is represented by their *making* you do it.'

'Ah they couldn't have come – either of them. They're very busy people and Mrs. Newsome in particular has a large full life. She's moreover highly nervous – and not at all strong.'

'You mean she's an American invalid?'

He carefully distinguished. 'There's nothing she likes less than to be called one, but she would consent to be one of those things, I think,' he laughed, 'if it were the only way to be the other.'

'Consent to be an American in order to be an invalid?'

'No,' said Strether, 'the other way round. She's at any rate delicate sensitive high-strung. She puts so much of herself into everything –'

Ah Maria knew these things! 'That she has nothing left for anything else? Of course she hasn't. To whom do you say it? High-strung? Don't I spend my life, for them, jamming down the pedal?³ I see moreover how it has told on you.'

Strether took this more lightly. 'Oh I jam down the pedal too!'

'Well,' she lucidly returned, 'we must from this moment bear on it together with all our might.' And she forged ahead. 'Have they money?'

But it was as if, while her energetic image still held him, her enquiry fell short. 'Mrs. Newsome,' he wished further to explain, 'hasn't moreover your courage on the question of contact. If she had come it would have been to see the person herself.'

'The woman? Ah but that's courage.'

'No – it's exaltation, which is a very different thing. Courage,' he, however, accommodatingly threw out, 'is what *you* have.'

She shook her head. 'You say that only to patch me up – to cover the nudity of my want of exaltation. I've neither the one

nor the other. I've mere battered indifference. I see that what
you mean,' Miss Gostrey pursued, 'is that if your friend *had*
come she would take great views, and the great views, to put it
simply, would be too much for her.'

Strether looked amused at her notion of the simple, but he
adopted her formula. 'Everything's too much for her.'

'Ah then such a service as this of yours –'

'Is more for her than anything else? Yes – far more. But so
long as it isn't too much for *me* –!'

'Her condition doesn't matter? Surely not; we leave her condition out; we take it, that is, for granted. I see it, her condition,
as behind and beneath you; yet at the same time I see it as
bearing you up.'

'Oh it does bear me up!' Strether laughed.

'Well then as yours bears *me* nothing more's needed.' With
which she put again her question. 'Has Mrs. Newsome money?'

This time he heeded. 'Oh plenty. That's the root of the evil.
There's money, to very large amounts, in the concern. Chad
has had the free use of a great deal. But if he'll pull himself
together and come home, all the same, he'll find his account
in it.'

She had listened with all her interest. 'And I hope to goodness
you'll find yours!'

'He'll take up his definite material reward,' said Strether
without acknowledgement of this. 'He's at the parting of the
ways. He can come into the business now – he can't come later.'

'Is there a business?'

'Lord, yes – a big brave bouncing business. A roaring trade.'

'A great shop?'

'Yes – a workshop; a great production, a great industry. The
concern's a manufacture – and a manufacture that, if it's only
properly looked after, may well be on the way to become a
monopoly. It's a little thing they make – make better, it appears,
than other people can, or than other people, at any rate, do.
Mr. Newsome, being a man of ideas, at least in that particular
line,' Strether explained, 'put them on it with great effect, and
gave the place altogether, in his time, an immense lift.'

'It's a place in itself?'

'Well, quite a number of buildings; almost a little industrial colony. But above all it's a thing. The article produced.'

'And what *is* the article produced?'

Strether looked about him as in slight reluctance to say; then the curtain, which he saw about to rise, came to his aid. 'I'll tell you next time.' But when the next time came he only said he'd tell her later on – after they should have left the theatre; for she had immediately reverted to their topic, and even for himself the picture of the stage was now overlaid with another image. His postponements, however, made her wonder – wonder if the article referred to were anything bad. And she explained that she meant improper or ridiculous or wrong. But Strether, so far as that went, could satisfy her. 'Unmentionable? Oh no, we constantly talk of it; we are quite familiar and brazen about it. Only, as a small, trivial, rather ridiculous object of the commonest domestic use, it's just wanting in – what shall I say? Well, dignity, or the least approach to distinction. Right here therefore, with everything about us so grand –!' In short he shrank.

'It's a false note?'

'Sadly. It's vulgar.'

'But surely not vulgarer than this.' Then on his wondering as she herself had done: 'Than everything about us.' She seemed a trifle irritated. 'What do you take this for?'

'Why for – comparatively – divine!'

'This dreadful London theatre? It's impossible, if you really want to know.'

'Oh then,' laughed Strether, 'I *don't* really want to know!'

It made between them a pause, which she, however, still fascinated by the mystery of the production at Woollett, presently broke. '"Rather ridiculous"? Clothes-pins? Saleratus?[4] Shoe-polish?'

It brought him round. 'No – you don't even "burn".[5] I don't think, you know, you'll guess it.'

'How then can I judge how vulgar it is?'

'You'll judge when I do tell you' – and he persuaded her to patience. But it may even now frankly be mentioned that he in the sequel never *was* to tell her. He actually never did so, and it moreover oddly occurred that by the law, within her, of the

incalculable, her desire for the information dropped and her attitude to the question converted itself into a positive cultivation of ignorance. In ignorance she could humour her fancy, and that proved a useful freedom. She could treat the little nameless object as indeed unnameable – she could make their abstention enormously definite. There might indeed have been for Strether the portent of this in what she next said.

'Is it perhaps then because it's so bad – because your industry, as you call it, *is* so vulgar – that Mr. Chad won't come back? Does he feel the taint? Is he staying away not to be mixed up in it?'

'Oh,' Strether laughed, 'it wouldn't appear – would it? – that he feels "taints"! He's glad enough of the money from it, and the money's his whole basis. There's appreciation in that – I mean as to the allowance his mother has hitherto made him. She has of course the resource of cutting this allowance off; but even then he has unfortunately, and on no small scale, his independent supply – money left him by his grandfather, her own father.'

'Wouldn't the fact you mention then,' Miss Gostrey asked, 'make it just more easy for him to be particular? Isn't he conceivable as fastidious about the source – the apparent and public source – of his income?'

Strether was able quite good-humouredly to entertain the proposition. 'The source of his grandfather's wealth – and thereby of his own share in it – was not particularly noble.'

'And what source was it?'

Strether cast about. 'Well – practices.'

'In business? Infamies? He was an old swindler?'

'Oh,' he said with more emphasis than spirit, 'I shan't describe *him* nor narrate his exploits.'

'Lord, what abysses! And the late Mr. Newsome then?'

'Well, what about him?'

'Was he like the grandfather?'

'No – he was on the other side of the house. And he was different.'

Miss Gostrey kept it up. 'Better?'

Her friend for a moment hung fire. 'No.'

Her comment on his hesitation was scarce the less marked

for being mute. 'Thank you. *Now* don't you see,' she went on, 'why the boy doesn't come home? He's drowning his shame.'

'His shame? What shame?'

'What shame? Comment donc? *The* shame.'

'But where and when,' Strether asked, 'is "*the* shame" – where is any shame – to-day? The men I speak of – they did as every one does; and (besides being ancient history) it was all a matter of appreciation.'

She showed how she understood. 'Mrs. Newsome has appreciated?'

'Ah I can't speak for *her*!'

'In the midst of such doings – and, as I understand you, profiting by them, she at least has remained exquisite?'

'Oh I can't talk of her!' Strether said.

'I thought she was just what you *could* talk of. You *don't* trust me,' Miss Gostrey after a moment declared.

It had its effect. 'Well, her money is spent, her life conceived and carried on with a large beneficence –'

'That's a kind of expiation of wrongs? Gracious,' she added before he could speak, 'how intensely you make me see her!'

'If you see her,' Strether dropped, 'it's all that's necessary.'

She really seemed to have her. 'I feel that. She *is*, in spite of everything, handsome.'

This at least enlivened him. 'What do you mean by everything?'

'Well, I mean *you*.' With which she had one of her swift changes of ground. 'You say the concern needs looking after; but doesn't Mrs. Newsome look after it?'

'So far as possible. She's wonderfully able, but it's not her affair, and her life's a good deal over-charged. She has many, many things.'

'And you also?'

'Oh yes – I've many too, if you will.'

'I see. But what I mean is,' Miss Gostrey amended, 'do you also look after the business?'

'Oh no, I don't touch the business.'

'Only everything else?'

'Well, yes – some things.'

'As for instance – ?'

Strether obligingly thought. 'Well, the Review.'

'The Review? – you have a Review?'

'Certainly. Woollett has a Review – which Mrs. Newsome, for the most part, magnificently pays for and which I, not at all magnificently, edit. My name's on the cover,' Strether pursued, 'and I'm really rather disappointed and hurt that you seem never to have heard of it.'

She neglected for a moment this grievance. 'And what kind of a Review is it?'

His serenity was now completely restored. 'Well, it's green.'

'Do you mean in political colour as they say here – in thought?'

'No; I mean the cover's green – of the most lovely shade.'

'And with Mrs. Newsome's name on it too?'

He waited a little. 'Oh as for that you must judge if she peeps out. She's behind the whole thing; but she's of a delicacy and a discretion –!'

Miss Gostrey took it all. 'I'm sure. She *would* be. I don't underrate her. She must be rather a swell.'

'Oh yes, she's rather a swell!'

'A Woollett swell – *bon*! I like the idea of a Woollett swell. And you must be rather one too, to be so mixed up with her.'

'Ah no,' said Strether, 'that's not the way it works.'

But she had already taken him up. 'The way it works – you needn't tell me! – is of course that you efface yourself.'

'With my name on the cover?' he lucidly objected.

'Ah but you don't put it on for yourself.'

'I beg your pardon – that's exactly what I do put it on for. It's exactly the thing that I'm reduced to doing for myself. It seems to rescue a little, you see, from the wreck of hopes and ambitions, the refuse-heap of disappointments and failures, my one presentable little scrap of an identity.'

On this she looked at him as to say many things, but what she at last simply said was: 'She likes to see it there. You're the bigger swell of the two,' she immediately continued, 'because you think you're not one. She thinks she *is* one. However,' Miss Gostrey added, 'she thinks you're one too. You're at all events

the biggest she can get hold of.' She embroidered, she abounded.
'I don't say it to interfere between you, but on the day she gets
hold of a bigger one –!' Strether had thrown back his head as
in silent mirth over something that struck him in her audacity or
felicity, and her flight meanwhile was already higher. 'Therefore
close with her –!'

'Close with her?' he asked as she seemed to hang poised.

'Before you lose your chance.'

Their eyes met over it. 'What do you mean by closing?'

'And what do I mean by your chance? I'll tell you when you
tell me all the things *you* don't. Is it her *greatest* fad?' she briskly
pursued.

'The Review?' He seemed to wonder how he could best
describe it. This resulted however but in a sketch. 'It's her
tribute to the ideal.'

'I see. You go in for tremendous things.'

'We go in for the unpopular side – that is so far as we dare.'

'And how far *do* you dare?'

'Well, she very far. I much less. I don't begin to have her
faith. She provides,' said Strether, 'three fourths of that. And
she provides, as I've confided to you, *all* the money.'

It evoked somehow a vision of gold that held for a little Miss
Gostrey's eyes, and she looked as if she heard the bright dollars
shovelled in. 'I hope then you make a good thing –'

'I *never* made a good thing!' he at once returned.

She just waited. 'Don't you call it a good thing to be loved?'

'Oh we're not loved. We're not even hated. We're only just
sweetly ignored.'

She had another pause. 'You don't trust me!' she once more
repeated.

'Don't I when I lift the last veil? – tell you the very secret of
the prison-house?'[6]

Again she met his eyes, but to the result that after an instant
her own turned away with impatience. 'You don't sell? Oh I'm
glad of *that*!' After which however, and before he could protest,
she was off again. 'She's just a *moral* swell.'

He accepted gaily enough the definition. 'Yes – I really think
that describes her.'

But it had for his friend the oddest connexion. 'How does she do her hair?'

He laughed out. 'Beautifully!'

'Ah that doesn't tell me. However, it doesn't matter – I know. It's tremendously neat – a real reproach; quite remarkably thick and without, as yet, a single strand of white. There!'

He blushed for her realism, but gaped at her truth. 'You're the very deuce.'[7]

'What else *should* I be? It was as the very deuce I pounced on you. But don't let it trouble you, for everything but the very deuce – at our age – is a bore and a delusion, and even he himself, after all, but half a joy.' With which, on a single sweep of her wing, she resumed. 'You assist her to expiate – which is rather hard when you've yourself not sinned.'

'It's she who hasn't sinned,' Strether replied. 'I've sinned the most.'

'Ah,' Miss Gostrey cynically laughed, 'what a picture of *her*! Have you robbed the widow and the orphan?'

'I've sinned enough,' said Strether.

'Enough for whom? Enough for what?'

'Well, to be where I am.'

'Thank you!' They were disturbed at this moment by the passage between their knees and the back of the seats before them of a gentleman who had been absent during a part of the performance and who now returned for the close; but the interruption left Miss Gostrey time, before the subsequent hush, to express as a sharp finality her sense of the moral of all their talk. 'I knew you had something up your sleeve!' This finality, however, left them in its turn, at the end of the play, as disposed to hang back as if they had still much to say; so that they easily agreed to let every one go before them – they found an interest in waiting. They made out from the lobby that the night had turned to rain; yet Miss Gostrey let her friend know that he wasn't to see her home. He was simply to put her, by herself, into a four-wheeler;[8] she liked so in London, of wet nights after wild pleasures, thinking things over, on the return, in lonely four-wheelers. This was her great time, she intimated, for pulling herself together. The delays caused by the weather, the

struggle for vehicles at the door, gave them occasion to subside on a divan at the back of the vestibule and just beyond the reach of the fresh damp gusts from the street. Here Strether's comrade resumed that free handling of the subject to which his own imagination of it already owed so much. 'Does your young friend in Paris like you?'

It had almost, after the interval, startled him. 'Oh I hope not! Why *should* he?'

'Why shouldn't he?' Miss Gostrey asked. 'That you're coming down on him need have nothing to do with it.'

'You see more in it,' he presently returned, 'than I.'

'Of course I see *you* in it.'

'Well then you see more in "me"!'

'Than you see in yourself? Very likely. That's always one's right. What I was thinking of,' she explained, 'is the possible particular effect on him of his *milieu*.'

'Oh his *milieu* –!' Strether really felt he could imagine it better now than three hours before.

'Do you mean it can only have been so lowering?'

'Why that's my very starting-point.'

'Yes, but you start so far back. What do his letters say?'

'Nothing. He practically ignores us – or spares us. He doesn't write.'

'I see. But there are all the same,' she went on, 'two quite distinct things that – given the wonderful place he's in – may have happened to him. One is that he may have got brutalized. The other is that he may have got refined.'

Strether stared – this *was* a novelty. 'Refined?'

'Oh,' she said quietly, 'there *are* refinements.'

The way of it made him, after looking at her, break into a laugh. '*You* have them!'

'As one of the signs,' she continued in the same tone, 'they constitute perhaps the worst.'

He thought it over and his gravity returned. 'Is it a refinement not to answer his mother's letters?'

She appeared to have a scruple, but she brought it out. 'Oh I should say the greatest of all.'

'Well,' said Strether, '*I'm* quite content to let it, as one of the

signs, pass for the worst that I know he believes he can do what he likes with me.'

This appeared to strike her. 'How do you know it?'

'Oh I'm sure of it. I feel it in my bones.'

'Feel he *can* do it?'

'Feel that he believes he can. It may come to the same thing!' Strether laughed.

She wouldn't, however, have this. 'Nothing for you will ever come to the same thing as anything else.' And she understood what she meant, it seemed, sufficiently to go straight on. 'You say that if he does break he'll come in for things at home?'

'Quite positively. He'll come in for a particular chance – a chance that any properly constituted young man would jump at. The business has so developed that an opening scarcely apparent three years ago, but which his father's will took account of as in certain conditions possible and which, under that will, attaches to Chad's availing himself of it a large contingent advantage – this opening, the conditions having come about, now simply awaits him. His mother has kept it for him, holding out against strong pressure, till the last possible moment. It requires, naturally, as it carries with it a handsome "part", a large share in profits, his being on the spot and making a big effort for a big result. That's what I mean by his chance. If he misses it he comes in, as you say, for nothing. And to see that he doesn't miss it is, in a word, what I've come out for.'

She let it all sink in. 'What you've come out for then is simply to render him an immense service.'

Well, poor Strether was willing to take it so. 'Ah if you like.'

'He stands, as they say, if you succeed with him, to gain –'

'Oh a lot of advantages.' Strether had them clearly at his fingers' ends.

'By which you mean of course a lot of money.'

'Well, not only. I'm acting with a sense for him of other things too. Consideration and comfort and security – the general safety of being anchored by a strong chain. He wants, as I see him, to be protected. Protected I mean from life.'

'Ah voilà!' – her thought fitted with a click. 'From life. What you *really* want to get him home for is to marry him.'

'Well, that's about the size of it.'

'Of course,' she said, 'it's rudimentary. But to any one in particular?'

He smiled at this, looking a little more conscious. 'You get everything out.'

For a moment again their eyes met. 'You put everything in!'

He acknowledged the tribute by telling her. 'To Mamie Pocock.'

She wondered; then gravely, even exquisitely, as if to make the oddity also fit: 'His own niece?'

'Oh you must yourself find a name for the relation. His brother-in-law's sister. Mrs. Jim's sister-in-law.'

It seemed to have on Miss Gostrey a certain hardening effect. 'And who in the world's Mrs. Jim?'

'Chad's sister – who was Sarah Newsome. She's married – didn't I mention it? – to Jim Pocock.'

'Ah yes,' she tacitly replied; but he had mentioned things –! Then, however, with all the sound it could have, 'Who in the world's Jim Pocock?' she asked.

'Why Sally's husband. That's the only way we distinguish people at Woollett,' he good-humouredly explained.

'And is it a great distinction – being Sally's husband?'

He considered. 'I think there can be scarcely a greater – unless it may become one, in the future, to be Chad's wife.'

'Then how do they distinguish *you*?'

'They *don't* – except, as I've told you, by the green cover.'

Once more their eyes met on it, and she held him an instant. 'The green cover won't – nor will *any* cover – avail you with *me*. You're of a depth of duplicity!' Still, she could in her own large grasp of the real condone it. 'Is Mamie a great *parti*?'

'Oh the greatest we have – our prettiest brightest girl.'

Miss Gostrey seemed to fix the poor child. 'I know what they *can* be. And with money?'

'Not perhaps with a great deal of that – but with so much of everything else that we don't miss it. We *don't* miss money much, you know,' Strether added, 'in general, in America, in pretty girls.'

'No,' she conceded; 'but I know also what you do sometimes miss. And do you,' she asked, 'yourself admire her?'

It was a question, he indicated, that there might be several ways of taking; but he decided after an instant for the humorous. 'Haven't I sufficiently showed you how I admire *any* pretty girl?'

Her interest in his problem was by this time such that it scarce left her freedom, and she kept close to the facts. 'I supposed that at Woollett you wanted them – what shall I call it? – blameless. I mean your young men for your pretty girls.'

'So did I!' Strether confessed. 'But you strike there a curious fact – the fact that Woollett too accommodates itself to the spirit of the age and the increasing mildness of manners. Everything changes, and I hold that our situation precisely marks a date. We *should* prefer them blameless, but we have to make the best of them as we find them. Since the spirit of the age and the increasing mildness send them so much more to Paris –'

'You've to take them back as they come. When they *do* come. *Bon!*' Once more she embraced it all, but she had a moment of thought. 'Poor Chad!'

'Ah,' said Strether cheerfully, 'Mamie will save him!'

She was looking away, still in her vision, and she spoke with impatience and almost as if he hadn't understood her. '*You'll* save him. That's who'll save him.'

'Oh but with Mamie's aid. Unless indeed you mean,' he added, 'that I shall effect so much more with yours!'

It made her at last again look at him. 'You'll do more – as you're so much better – than all of us put together.'

'I think I'm only better since I've known *you*!' Strether bravely returned.

The depletion of the place, the shrinkage of the crowd and now comparatively quiet withdrawal of its last elements had already brought them nearer the door and put them in relation with a messenger of whom he bespoke Miss Gostrey's cab. But this left them a few minutes more, which she was clearly in no mood not to use. 'You've spoken to me of what – by your success – Mr. Chad stands to gain. But you've not spoken to me of what you do.'

'Oh I've nothing more to gain,' said Strether very simply.

She took it as even quite too simple. 'You mean you've got it all "down"? You've been paid in advance?'

'Ah don't talk about payment!' he groaned.

Something in the tone of it pulled her up, but as their messenger still delayed she had another chance and she put it in another way. 'What – by failure – do you stand to lose?'

He still, however, wouldn't have it. 'Nothing!' he exclaimed, and on the messenger's at this instant reappearing he was able to sink the subject in their responsive advance. When, a few steps up the street, under a lamp, he had put her into her four-wheeler and she had asked him if the man had called for him no second conveyance, he replied before the door was closed. 'You won't take me with you?'

'Not for the world.'

'Then I shall walk.'

'In the rain?'

'I like the rain,' said Strether. 'Good-night!'

She kept him a moment, while his hand was on the door, by not answering; after which she answered by repeating her question. 'What do you stand to lose?'

Why the question now affected him as other he couldn't have said; he could only this time meet it otherwise. 'Everything.'

'So I thought. Then you shall succeed. And to that end I'm yours –'

'Ah, dear lady!' he kindly breathed.

'Till death!' said Maria Gostrey. 'Good-night.'

II

Strether called, his second morning in Paris, on the bankers of the Rue Scribe[1] to whom his letter of credit was addressed, and he made this visit attended by Waymarsh, in whose company he had crossed from London two days before. They had hastened to the Rue Scribe on the morrow of their arrival, but Strether had not then found the letters the hope of which prompted this errand. He had had as yet none at all; hadn't expected them in London, but had counted on several in Paris, and, disconcerted now, had presently strolled back to the Boulevard with a sense of injury that he felt himself taking for as good a start as any other. It would serve, this spur to his spirit, he reflected, as, pausing at the top of the street, he looked up and down the great foreign avenue, it would serve to begin business with. His idea was to begin business immediately, and it did much for him the rest of his day that the beginning of business awaited him. He did little else till night but ask himself what he should do if he hadn't fortunately had so much to do; but he put himself the question in many different situations and connexions. What carried him hither and yon was an admirable theory that nothing he could do wouldn't be in some manner related to what he fundamentally had on hand, or *would* be – should he happen to have a scruple – wasted for it. He did happen to have a scruple – a scruple about taking no definite step till he should get letters; but this reasoning carried it off. A single day to feel his feet – he had felt them as yet only at Chester and in London – was, he could consider, none too much; and having, as he had often privately expressed it, Paris to reckon with, he threw these hours of freshness consciously

into the reckoning. They made it continually greater, but that was what it had best be if it was to be anything at all, and he gave himself up till far into the evening, at the theatre and on the return, after the theatre, along the bright congested Boulevard, to feeling it grow. Waymarsh had accompanied him this time to the play, and the two men had walked together, as a first stage, from the Gymnase to the Café Riche,[2] into the crowded 'terrace' of which establishment – the night, or rather the morning, for midnight had struck, being bland and populous – they had wedged themselves for refreshment. Waymarsh, as a result of some discussion with his friend, had made a marked virtue of his having now let himself go; and there had been elements of impression in their half-hour over their watered beer-glasses that gave him his occasion for conveying that he held this compromise with his stiffer self to have become extreme. He conveyed it – for it was still, after all, his stiffer self who gloomed out of the glare of the terrace – in solemn silence; and there was indeed a great deal of critical silence, every way, between the companions, even till they gained the Place de l'Opéra, as to the character of their nocturnal progress.

This morning there *were* letters – letters which had reached London, apparently all together, the day of Strether's journey, and had taken their time to follow him; so that, after a controlled impulse to go into them in the reception-room of the bank, which, reminding him of the post-office at Woollett, affected him as the abutment of some transatlantic bridge, he slipped them into the pocket of his loose grey overcoat with a sense of the felicity of carrying them off. Waymarsh, who had had letters yesterday, had had them again to-day, and Waymarsh suggested in this particular no controlled impulses. The last one he was at all events likely to be observed to struggle with was clearly that of bringing to a premature close any visit to the Rue Scribe. Strether had left him there yesterday; he wanted to see the papers, and he had spent, by what his friend could make out, a succession of hours with the papers. He spoke of the establishment, with emphasis, as a post of superior observation; just as he spoke generally of his actual damnable doom as a device for hiding from him what was going on.

Europe was best described, to his mind, as an elaborate engine
for dissociating the confined American from that indispensable
knowledge, and was accordingly only rendered bearable by
these occasional stations of relief, traps for the arrest of wandering western airs. Strether, on his side, set himself to walk again
– he had his relief in his pocket; and indeed, much as he had
desired his budget,[3] the growth of restlessness might have been
marked in him from the moment he had assured himself of
the superscription of most of the missives it contained. This
restlessness became therefore his temporary law; he knew he
should recognize as soon as see it the best place of all for settling
down with his chief correspondent. He had for the next hour
an accidental air of looking for it in the windows of shops; he
came down the Rue de la Paix[4] in the sun and, passing across
the Tuileries and the river, indulged more than once – as if on
finding himself determined – in a sudden pause before the
book-stalls of the opposite quay. In the garden of the Tuileries
he had lingered, on two or three spots, to look; it was as if the
wonderful Paris spring had stayed him as he roamed. The
prompt Paris morning struck its cheerful notes – in a soft breeze
and a sprinkled smell, in the light flit, over the garden-floor, of
bareheaded girls with the buckled strap of oblong boxes, in the
type of ancient thrifty persons basking betimes where terrace-
walls were warm, in the blue-frocked brass-labelled officialism
of humble rakers and scrapers, in the deep references of a
straight-pacing priest or the sharp ones of a white-gaitered
red-legged soldier. He watched little brisk figures, figures whose
movement was as the tick of the great Paris clock, take their
smooth diagonal from point to point; the air had a taste as of
something mixed with art, something that presented nature as
a white-capped master-chef. The palace was gone,[5] Strether
remembered the palace; and when he gazed into the irremediable void of its site the historic sense in him might have been
freely at play – the play under which in Paris indeed it so often
winces like a touched nerve. He filled out spaces with dim
symbols of scenes; he caught the gleam of white statues at
the base of which, with his letters out, he could tilt back a
straw-bottomed chair. But his drift was, for reasons, to the

other side, and it floated him unspent up the Rue de Seine and as far as the Luxembourg.

In the Luxembourg Gardens[6] he pulled up; here at last he found his nook, and here, on a penny chair from which terraces, alleys, vistas, fountains, little trees in green tubs, little women in white caps and shrill little girls at play all sunnily 'composed' together, he passed an hour in which the cup of his impressions seemed truly to overflow. But a week had elapsed since he quitted the ship, and there were more things in his mind than so few days could account for. More than once, during the time, he had regarded himself as admonished; but the admonition this morning was formidably sharp. It took as it hadn't done yet the form of a question – the question of what he was doing with such an extraordinary sense of escape. This sense was sharpest after he had read his letters, but that was also precisely why the question pressed. Four of the letters were from Mrs. Newsome and none of them short; she had lost no time, had followed on his heels while he moved, so expressing herself that he now could measure the probable frequency with which he should hear. They would arrive, it would seem, her communications, at the rate of several a week; he should be able to count, it might even prove, on more than one by each mail. If he had begun yesterday with a small grievance he had therefore an opportunity to begin to-day with its opposite. He read the letters successively and slowly, putting others back into his pocket but keeping these for a long time afterwards gathered in his lap. He held them there, lost in thought, as if to prolong the presence of what they gave him; or as if at the least to assure them their part in the constitution of some lucidity. His friend wrote admirably, and her tone was even more in her style than in her voice – he might almost, for the hour, have had to come this distance to get its full carrying quality; yet the plentitude of his consciousness of difference consorted perfectly with the deepened intensity of the connexion. It was the difference, the difference of being just where he was and *as* he was, that formed the escape – this difference was so much greater than he had dreamed it would be; and what he finally sat there turning over was the strange logic of his finding himself so free. He felt it in

a manner his duty to think out his state, to approve the process, and when he came in fact to trace the steps and add up the items they sufficiently accounted for the sum. He had never expected – that was the truth of it – again to find himself young, and all the years and other things it had taken to make him so were exactly his present arithmetic. He had to make sure of them to put his scruple to rest.

It all sprang at bottom from the beauty of Mrs. Newsome's desire that he should be worried with nothing that was not of the essence of his task; by insisting that he should thoroughly intermit and break she had so provided for his freedom that she would, as it were, have only herself to thank. Strether could not at this point indeed have completed his thought by the image of what she might have to thank herself *for*: the image, at best, of his own likeness – poor Lambert Strether washed up on the sunny strand by the waves of a single day, poor Lambert Strether thankful for breathing-time and stiffening himself while he gasped. There he was, and with nothing in his aspect or his posture to scandalize: it was only true that if he had seen Mrs. Newsome coming he would instinctively have jumped up to walk away a little. He would have come round and back to her bravely, but he would have had first to pull himself together. She abounded in news of the situation at home, proved to him how perfectly she was arranging for his absence, told him who would take up this and who take up that exactly where he had left it, gave him in fact chapter and verse for the moral that nothing would suffer. It filled for him, this tone of hers, all the air; yet it struck him at the same time as the hum of vain things. This latter effect was what he tried to justify – and with the success that, grave though the appearance, he at last lighted on a form that was happy. He arrived at it by the inevitable recognition of his having been a fortnight before one of the weariest of men. If ever a man had come off tired Lambert Strether was that man; and hadn't it been distinctly on the ground of his fatigue that his wonderful friend at home had so felt for him and so contrived? It seemed to him somehow at these instants that, could he only maintain with sufficient firmness his grasp of that truth, it might become in a manner his

compass and his helm. What he wanted most was some idea that would simplify, and nothing would do this so much as the fact that he was done for and finished. If it had been in such a light that he had just detected in his cup the dregs of youth, that was a mere flaw of the surface of his scheme. He was so distinctly fagged-out that it must serve precisely as his convenience, and if he could but consistently be good for little enough he might do everything he wanted.

Everything he wanted was comprised moreover in a single boon – the common unattainable art of taking things as they came. He appeared to himself to have given his best years to an active appreciation of the way they didn't come; but perhaps – as they would seemingly here be things quite other – this long ache might at last drop to rest. He could easily see that from the moment he should accept the notion of his foredoomed collapse the last thing he would lack would be reasons and memories. Oh if he *should* do the sum no slate would hold the figures! The fact that he had failed, as he considered, in everything, in each relation and in half a dozen trades, as he liked luxuriously to put it, might have made, might still make, for an empty present; but it stood solidly for a crowded past. It had not been, so much achievement missed, a light yoke nor a short road. It was at present as if the backward picture had hung there, the long crooked course, grey in the shadow of his solitude. It had been a dreadful cheerful sociable solitude, a solitude of life or choice, of community; but though there had been people enough all round it there had been but three or four persons *in* it. Waymarsh was one of these, and the fact struck him just now as marking the record. Mrs. Newsome was another, and Miss Gostrey had of a sudden shown signs of becoming a third. Beyond, behind them was the pale figure of his real youth, which held against its breast the two presences paler than itself – the young wife he had early lost and the young son he had stupidly sacrificed. He had again and again made out for himself that he might have kept his little boy, his little dull boy who had died at school of rapid diphtheria, if he had not in those years so insanely given himself to merely missing the mother. It was the soreness of his remorse that the

child had in all likelihood not really been dull – had been dull, as he had been banished and neglected, mainly because the father had been unwittingly selfish. This was doubtless but the secret habit of sorrow, which had slowly given way to time; yet there remained an ache sharp enough to make the spirit, at the sight now and again of some fair young man just growing up, wince with the thought of an opportunity lost. Had ever a man, he had finally fallen into the way of asking himself, lost so much and even done so much for so little? There had been particular reasons why all yesterday, beyond other days, he should have had in one ear this cold enquiry. His name on the green cover, where he had put it for Mrs. Newsome, expressed him doubtless just enough to make the world – the world as distinguished, both for more and for less, from Woollett – ask who he was. He had incurred the ridicule of having to have his explanation explained. He was Lambert Strether because he was on the cover, whereas it should have been, for anything like glory, that he was on the cover because he was Lambert Strether. He would have done anything for Mrs. Newsome, have been still more ridiculous – as he might, for that matter, have occasion to be yet; which came to saying that this acceptance of fate was all he had to show at fifty-five.

He judged the quantity as small because it *was* small, and all the more egregiously since it couldn't, as he saw the case, so much as thinkably have been larger. He hadn't had the gift of making the most of what he tried, and if he had tried and tried again – no one but himself knew how often – it appeared to have been that he might demonstrate what else, in default of that, *could* be made. Old ghosts of experiments came back to him, old drudgeries and delusions, and disgusts, old recoveries with their relapses, old fevers with their chills, broken moments of good faith, others of still better doubt; adventures, for the most part, of the sort qualified as lessons. The special spring that had constantly played for him the day before was the recognition – frequent enough to surprise him – of the promises to himself that he had after his other visit never kept. The reminiscence to-day most quickened for him was that of the vow taken in the course of the pilgrimage that, newly-married,

with the War[7] just over, and helplessly young in spite of it, he
had recklessly made with the creature who was so much
younger still. It had been a bold dash, for which they had taken
money set apart for necessities, but kept sacred at the moment
in a hundred ways, and in none more so than by this private
pledge of his own to treat the occasion as a relation formed
with the higher culture and see that, as they said at Woollett, it
should bear a good harvest. He had believed, sailing home
again, that he had gained something great, and his theory –
with an elaborate innocent plan of reading, digesting, coming
back even, every few years – had then been to preserve, cherish
and extend it. As such plans as these had come to nothing,
however, in respect to acquisitions still more precious, it was
doubtless little enough of a marvel that he should have
lost account of that handful of seed. Buried for long years in
dark corners at any rate these few germs had sprouted again
under forty-eight hours of Paris. The process of yesterday had
really been the process of feeling the general stirred life of connexions long since individually dropped. Strether had become
acquainted even on this ground with short gusts of speculation
– sudden flights of fancy in Louvre galleries, hungry gazes
through clear plates behind which lemon-coloured volumes[8]
were as fresh as fruit on the tree.

There were instants at which he could ask whether, since
there had been fundamentally so little question of his keeping
anything, the fate after all decreed for him hadn't been only to
be kept. Kept for something, in that event, that he didn't pretend, didn't possibly dare as yet to divine; something that made
him hover and wonder and laugh and sigh, made him advance
and retreat, feeling half ashamed of his impulse to plunge and
more than half afraid of his impulse to wait. He remembered
for instance how he had gone back in the sixties with lemon-
coloured volumes in general on the brain as well as with a
dozen – selected for his wife too – in his trunk; and nothing
had at the moment shown more confidence than this invocation
of the finer taste. They were still somewhere at home, the dozen
– stale and soiled and never sent to the binder; but what
had become of the sharp initiation they represented? They

represented now the mere sallow paint on the door of the
temple of taste that he had dreamed of raising up – a structure he
had practically never carried further. Strether's present highest
flights were perhaps those in which this particular lapse figured
to him as a symbol, a symbol of his long grind and his want of
odd moments, his want moreover of money, of opportunity, of
positive dignity. That the memory of the vow of his youth
should, in order to throb again, have had to wait for this last,
as he felt it, of all his accidents – that was surely proof enough
of how his conscience had been encumbered. If any further
proof were needed it would have been to be found in the fact
that, as he perfectly now saw, he had ceased even to measure
his meagreness, a meagreness that sprawled, in this retrospect,
vague and comprehensive, stretching back like some unmapped
Hinterland from a rough coast-settlement. His conscience had
been amusing itself for the forty-eight hours by forbidding him
the purchase of a book; he held off from that, held off from
everything; from the moment he didn't yet call on Chad he
wouldn't for the world have taken any other step. On this
evidence, however, of the way they actually affected him he
glared at the lemon-coloured covers in confession of the subcon-
sciousness that, all the same, in the great desert of the years, he
must have had of them. The green covers at home comprised,
by the law of their purpose, no tribute to letters; it was of a
mere rich kernel of economics, politics, ethics that, glazed and,
as Mrs. Newsome maintained rather against *his* view, pre-
eminently pleasant to touch, they formed the specious shell.
Without therefore any needed instinctive knowledge of what
was coming out, in Paris, on the bright highway, he struck
himself at present as having more than once flushed with a
suspicion: he couldn't otherwise at present be feeling so many
fears confirmed. There were 'movements' he was too late for:
weren't they, with the fun of them, already spent? There were
sequences he had missed and great gaps in the procession: he
might have been watching it all recede in a golden cloud of
dust. If the playhouse wasn't closed his seat had at least fallen
to somebody else. He had had an uneasy feeling the night before
that if he was at the theatre at all – though he indeed justified

the theatre, in the specific sense, and with a grotesqueness to which his imagination did all honour, as something he owed poor Waymarsh – he should have been there with, and as might have been said, *for* Chad.

This suggested the question of whether he could properly have taken him to such a play, and what effect – it was a point that suddenly rose – his peculiar responsibility might be held in general to have on his choice of entertainment. It had literally been present to him at the Gymnase – where one was held moreover comparatively safe – that having his young friend at his side would have been an odd feature of the work of redemption; and this quite in spite of the fact that the picture presented might well, confronted with Chad's own private stage, have seemed the pattern of propriety. He clearly hadn't come out in the name of propriety but to visit unattended equivocal performances; yet still less had he done so to undermine his authority by sharing them with the graceless youth. Was he to renounce all amusement for the sweet sake of that authority? and *would* such renouncement give him for Chad a moral glamour? The little problem bristled the more by reason of poor Strether's fairly open sense of the irony of things. Were there then sides on which his predicament threatened to look rather droll to him? Should he have to pretend to believe – either to himself or the wretched boy – that there was anything that could make the latter worse? Wasn't some such pretence on the other hand involved in the assumption of possible processes that would make him better? His greatest uneasiness seemed to peep at him out of the imminent impression that almost any acceptance of Paris might give one's authority away. It hung before him this morning, the vast bright Babylon, like some huge iridescent object, a jewel brilliant and hard, in which parts were not to be discriminated nor differences comfortably marked. It twinkled and trembled and melted together, and what seemed all surface one moment seemed all depth the next. It was a place of which, unmistakeably, Chad was fond; wherefore if he, Strether, should like it too much, what on earth, with such a bond, would become of either of them? It all depended of course – which was a gleam of light – on how the

'too much' was measured; though indeed our friend fairly felt, while he prolonged the meditation I describe, that for himself even already a certain measure had been reached. It will have been sufficiently seen that he was not a man to neglect any good chance for reflexion. Was it at all possible for instance to like Paris enough without liking it too much? He luckily however hadn't promised Mrs. Newsome not to like it at all. He was ready to recognize at this stage that such an engagement *would* have tied his hands. The Luxembourg Gardens were incontestably just so adorable at this hour by reason – in addition to their intrinsic charm – of his not having taken it. The only engagement he had taken, when he looked the thing in the face, was to do what he reasonably could.

It upset him a little none the less and after a while to find himself at last remembering on what current of association he had been floated so far. Old imaginations of the Latin Quarter had played their part for him, and he had duly recalled its having been with this scene of rather ominous legend that, like so many young men in fiction as well as in fact, Chad had begun. He was now quite out of it, with his 'home', as Strether figured the place, in the Boulevard Malesherbes;[9] which was perhaps why, repairing, not to fail of justice either, to the elder neighbourhood, our friend had felt he could allow for the element of the usual, the immemorial, without courting perturbation. He was not at least in danger of seeing the youth and the particular Person flaunt by together; and yet he was in the very air of which – just to feel what the early natural note must have been – he wished most to take counsel. It became at once vivid to him that he had originally had, for a few days, an almost envious vision of the boy's romantic privilege. Melancholy Mürger, with Francine and Musette and Rodolphe,[10] at home, in the company of the tattered, one – if he not in his single self two or three – of the unbound, the paper-covered dozen on the shelf; and when Chad had written, five years ago, after a sojourn then already prolonged to six months, that he had decided to go in for economy and the real thing, Strether's fancy had quite fondly accompanied him in this migration, which was to convey him, as they somewhat confusedly learned

at Woollett, across the bridges and up the Montagne Sainte-
Geneviève.[11] This was the region – Chad had been quite distinct
about it – in which the best French, and many other things,
were to be learned at least cost, and in which all sorts of clever
fellows, compatriots there for a purpose, formed an awfully
pleasant set. The clever fellows, the friendly countrymen were
mainly young painters, sculptors, architects, medical students;
but they were, Chad sagely opined, a much more profitable lot
to be with – even on the footing of not being quite one of them
– than the 'terrible toughs' (Strether remembered the edifying
discrimination) of the American bars and banks roundabout
the Opéra. Chad had thrown out, in the communications
following this one – for at that time he did once in a while
communicate – that several members of a band of earnest
workers under one of the great artists had taken him right in,
making him dine every night, almost for nothing, at their place,
and even pressing him not to neglect the hypothesis of there
being as much 'in him' as in any of them. There had been
literally a moment at which it appeared there might be something in him; there had been at any rate a moment at which he
had written that he didn't know but what a month or two more
might see him enrolled in some atelier. The season had been
one at which Mrs. Newsome was moved to gratitude for small
mercies; it had broken on them all as a blessing that their
absentee *had* perhaps a conscience – that he was sated in fine
with idleness, was ambitious of variety. The exhibition was
doubtless as yet not brilliant, but Strether himself, even by that
time much enlisted and immersed, had determined, on the part
of the two ladies, a temperate approval and in fact, as he now
recollected, a certain austere enthusiasm.

But the very next thing that happened had been a dark drop
of the curtain. The son and brother had not browsed long on
the Montagne Sainte-Geneviève – his effective little use of the
name of which, like his allusion to the best French, appeared
to have been but one of the notes of his rough cunning. The
light refreshment of these vain appearances had not accordingly
carried any of them very far. On the other hand it had gained
Chad time; it had given him a chance, unchecked, to strike his

roots, had paved the way for initiations more direct and more deep. It was Strether's belief that he had been comparatively innocent before this first migration, and even that the first effects of the migration would not have been, without some particular bad accident, to have been deplored. There had been three months – he had sufficiently figured it out – in which Chad had wanted to try. He *had* tried, though not very hard – he had had his little hour of good faith. The weakness of this principle in him was that almost any accident attestedly bad enough was stronger. Such had at any rate markedly been the case for the precipitation of a special series of impressions. They had proved, successively, these impressions – all of Musette and Francine, but Musette and Francine vulgarized by the larger evolution of the type – irresistibly sharp: he had 'taken up', by what was at the time to be shrinkingly gathered, as it was scantly mentioned, with one ferociously 'interested' little person after another. Strether had read somewhere of a Latin motto, a description of the hours, observed on a clock by a traveller in Spain; and he had been led to apply it in thought to Chad's number one, number two, number three. *Omnes vulnerant, ultima necat* – they had all morally wounded, the last had morally killed.[12] The last had been longest in possession – in possession, that is, of whatever was left of the poor boy's finer mortality. And it hadn't been she, it had been one of her early predecessors, who had determined the second migration, the expensive return and relapse, the exchange again, as was fairly to be presumed, of the vaunted best French for some special variety of the worst.

He pulled himself then at last together for his own progress back; not with the feeling that he had taken his walk in vain. He prolonged it a little, in the immediate neighbourhood, after he had quitted his chair; and the upshot of the whole morning for him was that his campaign had begun. He had wanted to put himself in relation, and he would be hanged if he were *not* in relation. He was that at no moment so much as while, under the old arches of the Odéon,[13] he lingered before the charming open-air array of literature classic and casual. He found the effect of tone and tint, in the long charged tables and shelves,

delicate and appetizing; the impression – substituting one kind
of low-priced *consommation* for another – might have been
that of one of the pleasant cafés that overlapped, under an
awning, to the pavement; but he edged along, grazing the tables,
with his hands firmly behind him. He wasn't there to dip, to
consume – he was there to reconstruct. He wasn't there for his
own profit – not, that is, the direct; he was there on some chance
of feeling the brush of the wing of the stray spirit of youth. He
felt it in fact, he had it beside him; the old arcade indeed, as his
inner sense listened, gave out the faint sound, as from far off,
of the wild waving of wings. They were folded now over the
breasts of buried generations; but a flutter or two lived again in
the turned page of shock-headed slouch-hatted loiterers whose
young intensity of type, in the direction of pale acuteness,
deepened his vision, and even his appreciation, of racial differences, and whose manipulation of the uncut volume was too
often, however, but a listening at closed doors. He recon-
structed a possible groping Chad of three or four years before,
a Chad who had, after all, simply – for that was the only way
to see it – been too vulgar for his privilege. Surely it *was* a
privilege to have been young and happy just there. Well, the
best thing Strether knew of him was that he had had such a
dream.

But his own actual business half an hour later was with a
third floor on the Boulevard Malesherbes – so much as that
was definite; and the fact of the enjoyment by the third-floor
windows of a continuous balcony, to which he was helped by
this knowledge, had perhaps something to do with his lingering
for five minutes on the opposite side of the street. There were
points as to which he had quite made up his mind, and one of
these bore precisely on the wisdom of the abruptness to which
events had finally committed him, a policy that he was pleased
to find not at all shaken as he now looked at his watch and
wondered. He *had* announced himself – six months before; had
written out at least that Chad wasn't to be surprised should he
see him some day turn up. Chad had thereupon, in a few words
of rather carefully colourless answer, offered him a general
welcome; and Strether, ruefully reflecting that he might have

understood the warning as a hint to hospitality, a bid for an invitation, had fallen back upon silence as the corrective most to his own taste. He had asked Mrs. Newsome moreover not to announce him again; he had so distinct an opinion on his attacking his job, should he attack it at all, in his own way. Not the least of this lady's high merits for him was that he could absolutely rest on her word. She was the only woman he had known, even at Woollett, as to whom his conviction was positive that to lie was beyond her art. Sarah Pocock, for instance, her own daughter, though with social ideals, as they said, in some respects different – Sarah who *was*, in her way, aesthetic, had never refused to human commerce that mitigation of rigour; there were occasions when he had distinctly seen her apply it. Since, accordingly, at all events, he had had it from Mrs. Newsome that she had, at whatever cost to her more strenuous view, conformed, in the matter of preparing Chad, wholly to his restrictions, he now looked up at the fine continuous balcony with a safe sense that if the case had been bungled the mistake was at least his property. Was there perhaps just a suspicion of that in his present pause on the edge of the Boulevard and well in the pleasant light?

Many things came over him here, and one of them was that he should doubtless presently know whether he had been shallow or sharp. Another was that the balcony in question didn't somehow show as a convenience easy to surrender. Poor Strether had at this very moment to recognize the truth that wherever one paused in Paris the imagination reacted before one could stop it. This perpetual reaction put a price, if one would, on pauses; but it piled up consequences till there was scarce room to pick one's steps among them. What call had he, at such a juncture, for example, to like Chad's very house? High broad clear – he was expert enough to make out in a moment that it was admirably built – it fairly embarrassed our friend by the quality that, as he would have said, it 'sprang' on him. He had struck off the fancy that it might, as a preliminary, be of service to him to be seen, by a happy accident, from the third-story windows, which took all the March sun, but of what service was it to find himself making out after a moment

that the quality 'sprung', the quality produced by measure and balance, the fine relation of part to part and space to space, was probably – aided by the presence of ornament as positive as it was discreet, and by the complexion of the stone, a cold fair grey, warmed and polished a little by life – neither more nor less than a case of distinction, such a case as he could only feel unexpectedly as a sort of delivered challenge? Meanwhile, however, the chance he had allowed for – the chance of being seen in time from the balcony – had become a fact. Two or three of the windows stood open to the violet air; and, before Strether had cut the knot by crossing, a young man had come out and looked about him, had lighted a cigarette and tossed the match over, and then, resting on the rail, had given himself up to watching the life below while he smoked. His arrival contributed, in its order, to keeping Strether in position; the result of which in turn was that Strether soon felt himself noticed. The young man began to look at him as in acknowledgement of his being himself in observation.

This was interesting so far as it went, but the interest was affected by the young man's not being Chad. Strether wondered at first if he were perhaps Chad altered, and then saw that this was asking too much of alteration. The young man was light bright and alert – with an air too pleasant to have been arrived at by patching. Strether had conceived Chad as patched, but not beyond recognition. He was in presence, he felt, of amendments enough as they stood; it was a sufficient amendment that the gentleman up there should be Chad's friend. He was young too then, the gentleman up there – he was very young; young enough apparently to be amused at an elderly watcher, to be curious even to see what the elderly watcher would do on finding himself watched. There was youth in that, there was youth in the surrender to the balcony, there was youth for Strether at this moment in everything but his own business; and Chad's thus pronounced association with youth had given the next instant an extraordinary quick lift to the issue. The balcony, the distinguished front, testified suddenly, for Strether's fancy, to something that was up and up; they placed the whole case materially, and as by an admirable image, on a level that

he found himself at the end of another moment rejoicing to think he might reach. The young man looked at him still, he looked at the young man; and the issue, by a rapid process, was that this knowledge of a perched privacy appeared to him the last of luxuries. To him too the perched privacy was open, and he saw it now but in one light – that of the only domicile, the only fireside, in the great ironic city, on which he had the shadow of a claim. Miss Gostrey had a fireside; she had told him of it, and it was something that doubtless awaited him; but Miss Gostrey hadn't yet arrived – she mightn't arrive for days; and the sole attenuation of his excluded state was his vision of the small, the admittedly secondary hotel in the bye-street from the Rue de la Paix, in which her solicitude for his purse had placed him, which affected him somehow as all indoor chill, glass-roofed court and slippery staircase, and which, by the same token, expressed the presence of Waymarsh even at times when Waymarsh might have been certain to be round at the bank. It came to pass before he moved that Waymarsh, and Waymarsh alone, Waymarsh not only undiluted but positively strengthened, struck him as the present alternative to the young man in the balcony. When he did move it was fairly to escape that alternative. Taking his way over the street at last and passing through the *porte-cochère* of the house was like consciously leaving Waymarsh out. However, he would tell him all about it.

BOOK THIRD

I

Strether told Waymarsh all about it that very evening, on their dining together at the hotel;[1] which needn't have happened, he was all the while aware, hadn't he chosen to sacrifice to this occasion a rarer opportunity. The mention to his companion of the sacrifice was moreover exactly what introduced his recital – or, as he would have called it with more confidence in his interlocutor, his confession. His confession was that he had been captured and that one of the features of the affair had just failed to be his engaging himself on the spot to dinner. As by such a freedom Waymarsh would have lost him he had obeyed his scruple; and he had likewise obeyed another scruple – which bore on the question of his himself bringing a guest.

Waymarsh looked gravely ardent, over the finished soup, at this array of scruples; Strether hadn't yet got quite used to being so unprepared for the consequences of the impression he produced. It was comparatively easy to explain, however, that he hadn't felt sure his guest would please. The person was a young man whose acquaintance he had made but that afternoon in the course of rather a hindered enquiry for another person – an enquiry his new friend had just prevented in fact from being vain. 'Oh,' said Strether, 'I've all sorts of things to tell you!' – and he put it in a way that was a virtual hint to Waymarsh to help him to enjoy the telling. He waited for his fish, he drank of his wine, he wiped his long moustache, he leaned back in his chair, he took in the two English ladies who had just creaked past them and whom he would even have articulately greeted if they hadn't rather chilled the impulse; so that all he could do was – by way of doing something – to say 'Merci, François!'

out quite loud when his fish was brought. Everything was there that he wanted, everything that could make the moment an occasion, that would do beautifully – everything but what Waymarsh might give. The little waxed salle-à-manger was sallow and sociable; François, dancing over it, all smiles, was a man and a brother; the high-shouldered patronne, with her high-held, much-rubbed hands, seemed always assenting exuberantly to something unsaid; the Paris evening in short was, for Strether, in the very taste of the soup, in the goodness, as he was innocently pleased to think it, of the wine, in the pleasant coarse texture of the napkin and the crunch of the thick-crusted bread. These all were things congruous with his confession, and his confession was that he *had* – it would come out properly just there if Waymarsh would only take it properly – agreed to breakfast out, at twelve literally, the next day. He didn't quite know where; the delicacy of the case came straight up in the remembrance of his new friend's 'We'll see; I'll take you somewhere!' – for it had required little more than that, after all, to let him right in. He was affected after a minute, face to face with his actual comrade, by the impulse to overcolour. There had already been things in respect to which he knew himself tempted by this perversity. If Waymarsh thought them bad he should at least have his reason for his discomfort; so Strether showed them as worse. Still, he was now, in his way, sincerely perplexed.

Chad had been absent from the Boulevard Malesherbes – was absent from Paris altogether; he had learned that from the concierge, but had nevertheless gone up, and gone up – there were no two ways about it – from an uncontrollable, a really, if one would, depraved curiosity. The concierge had mentioned to him that a friend of the tenant of the troisième was for the time in possession; and this had been Strether's pretext for a further enquiry, an experiment carried on, under Chad's roof, without his knowledge. 'I found his friend in fact there keeping the place warm, as he called it, for him; Chad himself being, as appears, in the south. He went a month ago to Cannes[2] and though his return begins to be looked for it can't be for some days. I might, you see, perfectly have waited a week; might have

beaten a retreat as soon as I got this essential knowledge. But I beat no retreat; I did the opposite; I stayed, I dawdled, I trifled; above all I looked round. I saw, in fine; and – I don't know what to call it – I sniffed. It's a detail, but it's as if there were something – something very good – *to* sniff.'

Waymarsh's face had shown his friend an attention apparently so remote that the latter was slightly surprised to find it at this point abreast with him. 'Do you mean a smell? What of?'

'A charming scent. But I don't know.'

Waymarsh gave an inferential grunt. 'Does he live there with a woman?'

'I don't know.'

Waymarsh waited an instant for more, then resumed. 'Has he taken her off with him?'

'And will he bring her back?' – Strether fell into the enquiry. But he wound it up as before. 'I don't know.'

The way he wound it up, accompanied as this was with another drop back, another degustation of the Léoville,[3] another wipe of his moustache and another good word for François, seemed to produce in his companion a slight irritation. 'Then what the devil *do* you know?'

'Well,' said Strether almost gaily, 'I guess I don't know anything!' His gaiety might have been a tribute to the fact that the state he had been reduced to did for him again what had been done by his talk of the matter with Miss Gostrey at the London theatre. It was somehow enlarging; and the air of that amplitude was now doubtless more or less – and all for Waymarsh to feel – in his further response. 'That's what I found out from the young man.'

'But I thought you said you found out nothing.'

'Nothing but that – that I don't know anything.'

'And what good does that do you?'

'It's just,' said Strether, 'what I've come to you to help me to discover. I mean anything about anything over here. I *felt* that, up there. It regularly rose before me in its might. The young man moreover – Chad's friend – as good as told me so.'

'As good as told you you know nothing about anything?'

Waymarsh appeared to look at some one who might have as good as told *him*. 'How old is he?'

'Well, I guess not thirty.'

'Yet you had to take that from him?'

'Oh I took a good deal more – since, as I tell you, I took an invitation to déjeuner.'

'And are you *going* to that unholy meal?'

'If you'll come with me. He wants you too, you know. I told him about you. He gave me his card,' Strether pursued, 'and his name's rather funny. It's John Little Bilham, and he says his two surnames are, on account of his being small, inevitably used together.'

'Well,' Waymarsh asked with due detachment from these details, 'what's he doing up there?'

'His account of himself is that he's "only a little artist-man". That seemed to me perfectly to describe him. But he's yet in the phase of study; this, you know, is the great art-school – to pass a certain number of years in which he came over. And he's a great friend of Chad's, and occupying Chad's rooms just now because they're so pleasant. *He's* very pleasant and curious too,' Strether added – 'though he's not from Boston.'

Waymarsh looked already rather sick of him. 'Where *is* he from?'

Strether thought. 'I don't know that, either. But he's "notoriously", as he put it himself, not from Boston.'

'Well,' Waymarsh moralized from dry depths, 'everyone can't notoriously *be* from Boston. Why,' he continued, 'is he curious?'

'Perhaps just for *that* – for one thing! But really,' Strether added, 'for everything. When you meet him you'll see.'

'Oh I don't want to meet him,' Waymarsh impatiently growled. 'Why don't he go home?'

Strether hesitated. 'Well, because he likes it over here.'

This appeared in particular more than Waymarsh could bear. 'He ought then to be ashamed of himself, and, as you admit that you think so too, why drag him in?'

Strether's reply again took time. 'Perhaps I do think so myself

– though I don't quite yet admit it. I'm not a bit sure – it's again one of the things I want to find out. I liked him, and *can* you like people –? But no matter.' He pulled himself up. 'There's no doubt I want you to come down on me and squash me.'

Waymarsh helped himself to the next course, which, however, proving not the dish he had just noted as supplied to the English ladies, had the effect of causing his imagination temporarily to wander. But it presently broke out at a softer spot. 'Have they got a handsome place up there?'

'Oh a charming place; full of beautiful and valuable things. I never saw such a place' – and Strether's thought went back to it. 'For a little artist-man –!' He could in fact scarce express it.

But his companion, who appeared now to have a view, insisted. 'Well?'

'Well, life can hold nothing better. Besides, they're things of which he's in charge.'

'So that he does doorkeeper for your precious pair? Can life,' Waymarsh enquired, 'hold nothing better than *that*?' Then as Strether, silent, seemed even yet to wonder, 'Doesn't he know what *she* is?' he went on.

'*I* don't know. I didn't ask him. I couldn't. It was impossible. You wouldn't either. Besides I didn't want to. No more would you.' Strether in short explained it at a stroke. 'You can't make out over here what people do know.'

'Then what did you come over for?'

'Well, I suppose exactly to see for myself – without their aid.'

'Then what do you want mine for?'

'Oh,' Strether laughed, 'you're not one of *them*! I do know what *you* know.'

As, however, this last assertion caused Waymarsh again to look at him hard – such being the latter's doubt of its implications – he felt his justification lame. Which was still more the case when Waymarsh presently said: 'Look here, Strether. Quit this.'.

Our friend smiled with a doubt of his own. 'Do you mean my tone?'

'No – damn your tone. I mean your nosing round. Quit the

whole job. Let them stew in their juice. You're being used for a thing you ain't fit for. People don't take a fine-tooth comb to groom a horse.'

'Am I a fine-tooth comb?' Strether laughed. 'It's something I never called myself!'

'It's what you are, all the same. You ain't so young as you were, but you've kept your teeth.'

He acknowledged his friend's humour. 'Take care I don't get them into *you*! You'd like them, my friends at home, Waymarsh,' he declared; 'you'd really particularly like them. And I know' – it was slightly irrelevant, but he gave it sudden and singular force – 'I know they'd like you!'

'Oh don't work them off on *me*!' Waymarsh groaned.

Yet Strether still lingered with his hands in his pockets. 'It's really quite as indispensable as I say that Chad should be got back.'

'Indispensable to whom? To you?'

'Yes,' Strether presently said.

'Because if you get him you also get Mrs. Newsome?'

Strether faced it. 'Yes.'

'And if you don't get him you don't get her?'

It might be merciless, but he continued not to flinch. 'I think it might have some effect on our personal understanding. Chad's of real importance – or can easily become so if he will – to the business.'

'And the business is of real importance to his mother's husband?'

'Well, I naturally want what my future wife wants. And the thing will be much better if we have our own man in it.'

'If you have your own man in it, in other words,' Waymarsh said, 'you'll marry – you personally – more money. She's already rich, as I understand you, but she'll be richer still if the business can be made to boom on certain lines that you've laid down.'

'*I* haven't laid them down,' Strether promptly returned. 'Mr. Newsome – who knew extraordinarily well what he was about – laid them down ten years ago.'

Oh well, Waymarsh seemed to indicate with a shake of his mane, *that* didn't matter! 'You're fierce for the boom anyway.'

His friend weighed a moment in silence the justice of the charge. 'I can scarcely be called fierce, I think, when I so freely take my chance of the possibility, the danger, of being influenced in a sense counter to Mrs. Newsome's own feelings.'

Waymarsh gave this proposition a long hard look. 'I see. You're afraid yourself of being squared. But you're a humbug,' he added, 'all the same.'

'Oh!' Strether quickly protested.

'Yes, you ask me for protection – which makes you very interesting; and then you won't take it. You say you want to be squashed –'

'Ah but not so easily! Don't you see,' Strether demanded, 'where my interest, as already shown you, lies? It lies in my not being squared. If I'm squared where's my marriage? If I miss my errand I miss that; and if I miss that I miss everything – I'm nowhere.'

Waymarsh – but all relentlessly – took this in. 'What do I care where you are if you're spoiled?'

Their eyes met on it an instant. 'Thank you awfully,' Strether at last said. 'But don't you think *her* judgement of that –?'

'Ought to content me? No.'

It kept them again face to face, and the end of this was that Strether again laughed. 'You do her injustice. You really *must* know her. Good-night.'

He breakfasted with Mr. Bilham on the morrow, and, as inconsequently befell, with Waymarsh massively of the party. The latter announced, at the eleventh hour and much to his friend's surprise, that, damn it, he would as soon join him as do anything else; on which they proceeded together, strolling in a state of detachment practically luxurious for them to the Boulevard Malesherbes, a couple engaged that day with the sharp spell of Paris as confessedly, it might have been seen, as any couple among the daily thousands so compromised. They walked, wandered, wondered and, a little, lost themselves; Strether hadn't had for years so rich a consciousness of time – a bag of gold into which he constantly dipped for a handful. It was present to him that when the little business with Mr. Bilham should be over he would still have shining hours[4] to use

absolutely as he liked. There was no great pulse of haste yet in
this process of saving Chad; nor was that effect a bit more
marked as he sat, half an hour later, with his legs under Chad's
mahogany, with Mr. Bilham on one side, with a friend of Mr.
Bilham's on the other, with Waymarsh stupendously opposite,
and with the great hum of Paris coming up in softness, vagueness – for Strether himself indeed already positive sweetness –
through the sunny windows toward which, the day before, his
curiosity had raised its wings from below. The feeling strongest
with him at that moment had borne fruit almost faster than he
could taste it, and Strether literally felt at the present hour that
there was a precipitation in his fate. He had known nothing
and nobody as he stood in the street; but hadn't his view now
taken a bound in the direction of every one and of every thing?

'What's he up to, what's he up to?' – something like that was
at the back of his head all the while in respect to little Bilham;
but meanwhile, till he should make out, every one and every
thing were as good as represented for him by the combination
of his host and the lady on his left. The lady on his left, the lady
thus promptly and ingeniously invited to 'meet' Mr. Strether
and Mr. Waymarsh – it was the way she herself expressed her
case – was a very marked person, a person who had much to
do with our friend's asking himself if the occasion weren't in
its essence the most baited, the most gilded of traps. Baited it
could properly be called when the repast was of so wise a
savour, and gilded surrounding objects seemed inevitably to
need to be when Miss Barrace – which was the lady's name
– looked at them with convex Parisian eyes and through a
glass[5] with a remarkably long tortoise-shell handle. Why
Miss Barrace, mature meagre erect and eminently gay, highly
adorned, perfectly familiar, freely contradictious and reminding
him of some last-century portrait of a clever head without
powder – why Miss Barrace should have been in particular the
note of a 'trap' Strether couldn't on the spot have explained;
he blinked in the light of a conviction that he should know later
on, and know well – as it came over him, for that matter, with
force, that he should need to. He wondered what he was to
think exactly of either of his new friends; since the young man,

Chad's intimate and deputy, had, in thus constituting the scene, practised so much more subtly than he had been prepared for, and since in especial Miss Barrace, surrounded clearly by every consideration, hadn't scrupled to figure as a familiar object. It was interesting to him to feel that he was in the presence of new measures, other standards, a different scale of relations, and that evidently here were a happy pair who didn't think of things at all as he and Waymarsh thought. Nothing was less to have been calculated in the business than that it should now be for him as if he and Waymarsh were comparatively quite at one.

The latter was magnificent – this at least was an assurance privately given him by Miss Barrace. 'Oh your friend's a type, the grand old American – what shall one call it? The Hebrew prophet, Ezekiel, Jeremiah, who used when I was a little girl in the Rue Montaigne[6] to come to see my father and who was usually the American Minister to the Tuileries or some other court. I haven't seen one these ever so many years; the sight of it warms my poor old chilled heart; this specimen is wonderful; in the right quarter, you know, he'll have a *succès fou*.' Strether hadn't failed to ask what the right quarter might be, much as he required his presence of mind to meet such a change in their scheme. 'Oh the artist-quarter and that kind of thing; *here* already, for instance, as you see.' He had been on the point of echoing '"Here"? – is *this* the artist-quarter?' but she had already disposed of the question with a wave of all her tortoise-shell and an easy 'Bring him to *me*!' He knew on the spot how little he should be able to bring him, for the very air was by this time, to his sense, thick and hot with poor Waymarsh's judgement of it. He was in the trap still more than his companion and, unlike his companion, not making the best of it; which was precisely what doubtless gave him his admirable sombre glow. Little did Miss Barrace know that what was behind it was his grave estimate of her own laxity. The general assumption with which our two friends had arrived had been that of finding Mr. Bilham ready to conduct them to one or other of those resorts of the earnest, the aesthetic fraternity which were shown among the sights of Paris. In this character it would have justified them in a proper insistence on discharging

their score. Waymarsh's only proviso at the last had been that
nobody should pay for him; but he found himself, as the
occasion developed, paid for on a scale as to which Strether
privately made out that he already nursed retribution. Strether
was conscious across the table of what worked in him, conscious when they passed back to the small salon to which, the
previous evening, he himself had made so rich a reference;
conscious most of all as they stepped out to the balcony in
which one would have had to be an ogre not to recognize the
perfect place for easy after-tastes. These things were enhanced
for Miss Barrace by a succession of excellent cigarettes –
acknowledged, acclaimed, as a part of the wonderful supply
left behind him by Chad – in an almost equal absorption of
which Strether found himself blindly, almost wildly pushing
forward. He might perish by the sword as well as by famine,
and he knew that his having abetted the lady by an excess
that was rare with him would count for little in the sum – as
Waymarsh might so easily add it up – of her licence. Waymarsh
had smoked of old, smoked hugely; but Waymarsh did nothing
now, and that gave him his advantage over people who took
things up lightly just when others had laid them heavily down.
Strether had never smoked, and he felt as if he flaunted at his
friend that this had been only because of a reason. The reason,
it now began to appear even to himself, was that he had never
had a lady to smoke with.

It was this lady's being there at all, however, that was the
strange free thing; perhaps, since she *was* there, her smoking
was the least of her freedoms. If Strether had been sure at each
juncture of what – with Bilham in especial – she talked about,
he might have traced others and winced at them and felt Waymarsh wince; but he was in fact so often at sea that his sense of
the range of reference was merely general and that he on several
different occasions guessed and interpreted only to doubt. He
wondered what they meant, but there were things he scarce
thought they could be supposed to mean, and 'Oh no – not
that!' was at the end of most of his ventures. This was the very
beginning with him of a condition as to which, later on, it will
be seen, he found cause to pull himself up; and he was to

remember the moment duly as the first step in a process. The central fact of the place was neither more nor less, when analysed – and a pressure superficial sufficed – than the fundamental impropriety of Chad's situation, round about which they thus seemed cynically clustered. Accordingly, since they took it for granted, they took for granted all that was in connexion with it taken for granted at Woollett – matters as to which, verily, he had been reduced with Mrs. Newsome to the last intensity of silence. That was the consequence of their being too bad to be talked about, and was the accompaniment, by the same token, of a deep conception of their badness. It befell therefore that when poor Strether put it to himself that their badness was ultimately, or perhaps even insolently, what such a scene as the one before him was, so to speak, built upon, he could scarce shirk the dilemma of reading a roundabout echo of them into almost anything that came up. This, he was well aware, was a dreadful necessity; but such was the stern logic, he could only gather, of a relation to the irregular life.

It was the way the irregular life sat upon Bilham and Miss Barrace that was the insidious, the delicate marvel. He was eager to concede that their relation to it was all indirect, for anything else in him would have shown the grossness of bad manners; but the indirectness was none the less consonant – *that* was striking – with a grateful enjoyment of everything that was Chad's. They spoke of him repeatedly, invoking his good name and good nature, and the worst confusion of mind for Strether was that all their mention of him was of a kind to do him honour. They commended his munificence and approved his taste, and in doing so sat down, as it seemed to Strether, in the very soil out of which these things flowered. Our friend's final predicament was that he himself was sitting down, for the time, *with* them, and there was a supreme moment at which, compared with his collapse, Waymarsh's erectness affected him as really high. One thing was certain – he saw he must make up his mind. He must approach Chad, must wait for him, deal with him, master him, but he mustn't dispossess himself of the faculty of seeing things as they were. He must bring him to *him* – not go himself, as it were, so much of the way. He must at

any rate be clearer as to what – should he continue to do that
for convenience – he was still condoning. It was on the detail
of this quantity – and what could the fact be but mystifying?
– that Bilham and Miss Barrace threw so little light. So there
they were.

II

When Miss Gostrey arrived, at the end of a week, she made him a sign; he went immediately to see her, and it wasn't till then that he could again close his grasp on the idea of a corrective. This idea however was luckily all before him again from the moment he crossed the threshold of the little entresol of the Quartier Marboeuf[1] into which she had gathered, as she said, picking them up in a thousand flights and funny little passionate pounces, the makings of a final nest. He recognized in an instant that there really, there only, he should find the boon with the vision of which he had first mounted Chad's stairs. He might have been a little scared at the picture of how much more, in this place, he should know himself 'in' hadn't his friend been on the spot to measure the amount to his appetite. Her compact and crowded little chambers, almost dusky, as they at first struck him, with accumulations, represented a supreme general adjustment to opportunities and conditions. Wherever he looked he saw an old ivory or an old brocade, and he scarce knew where to sit for fear of a misappliance. The life of the occupant struck him of a sudden as more charged with possession even than Chad's or than Miss Barrace's; wide as his glimpse had lately become of the empire of 'things', what was before him still enlarged it; the lust of the eyes and the pride of life had indeed thus their temple. It was the innermost nook of the shrine – as brown as a pirate's cave. In the brownness were glints of gold; patches of purple were in the gloom; objects all that caught, through the muslin, with their high rarity, the light of the low windows. Nothing was clear about them but that they were precious, and they brushed his ignorance with their

contempt as a flower, in a liberty taken with him, might have been whisked under his nose. But after a full look at his hostess he knew none the less what most concerned him. The circle in which they stood together was warm with life, and every question between them would live there as nowhere else. A question came up as soon as they had spoken, for his answer, with a laugh, was quickly: 'Well, they've got hold of me!' Much of their talk on this first occasion was his development of that truth. He was extraordinarily glad to see her, expressing to her frankly what she most showed him, that one might live for years without a blessing unsuspected, but that to know it at last for no more than three days was to need it or miss it for ever. She was the blessing that had now become his need, and what could prove it better than that without her he had lost himself?

'What do you mean?' she asked with an absence of alarm that, correcting him as if he had mistaken the 'period' of one of her pieces, gave him afresh a sense of her easy movement through the maze he had but begun to tread. 'What in the name of all the Pococks have you managed to do?'

'Why exactly the wrong thing. I've made a frantic friend of little Bilham.'

'Ah that sort of thing was of the essence of your case and to have been allowed for from the first.' And it was only after this that, quite as a minor matter, she asked who in the world little Bilham might be. When she learned that he was a friend of Chad's and living for the time in Chad's rooms in Chad's absence, quite as if acting in Chad's spirit and serving Chad's cause, she showed, however, more interest. 'Should you mind my seeing him? Only once, you know,' she added.

'Oh the oftener the better: he's amusing – he's original.'

'He doesn't shock you?' Miss Gostrey threw out.

'Never in the world! We escape that with a perfection –! I feel it to be largely, no doubt, because I don't half-understand him; but our *modus vivendi* isn't spoiled even by that. You must dine with me to meet him,' Strether went on. 'Then you'll see.'

'Are you giving dinners?'

'Yes – there I am. That's what I mean.'

All her kindness wondered. 'That you're spending too much money?'

'Dear no – they seem to cost so little. But that I do it to *them*. I ought to hold off.'

She thought again – she laughed. 'The money you must be spending to think it cheap! But I must be out of it – to the naked eye.'

He looked for a moment as if she were really failing him. 'Then you won't meet them?' It was almost as if she had developed an unexpected personal prudence.

She hesitated. 'Who are they – first?'

'Why little Bilham to begin with.' He kept back for the moment Miss Barrace. 'And Chad – when he comes – you must absolutely see.'

'When then does he come?'

'When Bilham has had time to write him, and hear from him, about me. Bilham, however,' he pursued, 'will report favourably – favourably for Chad. That will make him not afraid to come. I want you the more therefore, you see, for my bluff.'

'Oh you'll do yourself for your bluff.' She was perfectly easy. 'At the rate you've gone I'm quiet.'

'Ah but I haven't,' said Strether, 'made one protest.'

She turned it over. 'Haven't you been seeing what there's to protest about?'

He let her, with this, however ruefully, have the whole truth. 'I haven't yet found a single thing.'

'Isn't there anyone *with* him then?'

'Of the sort I came out about?' Strether took a moment. 'How do I know? And what do I care?'

'Oh oh!' – and her laughter spread. He was struck in fact by the effect on her of his joke. He saw now how he meant it as a joke. *She* saw, however, still other things, though in an instant she had hidden them. 'You've got at no facts at all?'

He tried to muster them. 'Well, he has a lovely home.'

'Ah that, in Paris,' she quickly returned, 'proves nothing. That is rather it *dis*proves nothing. They may very well, you see,

the people your mission is concerned with, have done it *for* him.'

'Exactly. And it was on the scene of their doings then that Waymarsh and I sat guzzling.'

'Oh if you forbore to guzzle here on scenes of doings,' she replied, 'you might easily die of starvation.' With which she smiled at him. 'You've worse before you.'

'Ah I've *everything* before me. But on our hypothesis, you know, they must be wonderful.'

'They *are*!' said Miss Gostrey. 'You're not therefore, you see,' she added, 'wholly without facts. They've *been*, in effect, wonderful.'

To have got at something comparatively definite appeared at last a little to help – a wave by which moreover, the next moment, recollection was washed. 'My young man does admit furthermore that they're our friend's great interest.'

'Is that the expression he uses?'

Strether more exactly recalled. 'No – not quite.'

'Something more vivid? Less?'

He had bent, with neared glasses, over a group of articles on a small stand; and at this he came up. 'It was a mere allusion, but, on the lookout as I was, it struck me. "Awful, you know, as Chad is" – those were Bilham's words.'

'"Awful, you know" – ? Oh!' – and Miss Gostrey turned them over. She seemed, however, satisfied. 'Well, what more do you want?'

He glanced once more at a bibelot or two, and everything sent him back. 'But it *is* all the same as if they wished to let me have it between the eyes.'

She wondered. 'Quoi donc?'

'Why what I speak of. The amenity. They can stun you with that as well as with anything else.'

'Oh,' she answered, 'you'll come round! I must see them each,' she went on, 'for myself. I mean Mr. Bilham and Mr. Newsome – Mr. Bilham naturally first. Once only – once for each; that will do. But face to face – for half an hour. What's Mr. Chad,' she immediately pursued, 'doing at Cannes? Decent men don't go to Cannes with the – well, with the kind of ladies you mean.'

'Don't they?' Strether asked with an interest in decent men that amused her.

'No; elsewhere, but not to Cannes. Cannes is different. Cannes is better. Cannes is best. I mean it's all people you know – when you do know them. And if *he* does, why that's different too. He must have gone alone. She can't be with him.'

'I haven't,' Strether confessed in his weakness, 'the least idea.' There seemed much in what she said, but he was able after a little to help her to a nearer impression. The meeting with little Bilham took place, by easy arrangement, in the great gallery of the Louvre; and when, standing with his fellow visitor before one of the splendid Titians – the overwhelming portrait of the young man with the strangely-shaped glove and the blue-grey eyes[2] – he turned to see the third member of their party advance from the end of the waxed and gilded vista, he had a sense of having at last taken hold. He had agreed with Miss Gostrey – it dated even from Chester – for a morning at the Louvre, and he had embraced independently the same idea as thrown out by little Bilham, whom he had already accompanied to the museum of the Luxembourg.[3] The fusion of these schemes presented no difficulty, and it was to strike him again that in little Bilham's company contrarieties in general dropped.

'Oh he's all right – he's one of *us*!' Miss Gostrey, after the first exchange, soon found a chance to murmur to her companion; and Strether, as they proceeded and paused and while a quick unanimity between the two appeared to have phrased itself in half a dozen remarks – Strether knew that he knew almost immediately what she meant, and took it as still another sign that he had got his job in hand. This was the more grateful to him that he could think of the intelligence now serving him as an acquisition positively new. He wouldn't have known even the day before what she meant – that is if she meant, what he assumed, that they were intense Americans together. He had just worked round – and with a sharper turn of the screw than any yet – to the conception of an American intense as little Bilham was intense. The young man was his first specimen; the specimen had profoundly perplexed him; at present however there was light. It was by little Bilham's

amazing serenity that he had at first been affected, but he had
inevitably, in his circumspection, felt it as the trail of the ser-
pent, the corruption, as he might conveniently have said, of
Europe; whereas the promptness with which it came up for
Miss Gostrey but as a special little form of the oldest thing they
knew justified it at once to his own vision as well. He wanted
to be able to like his specimen with a clear good conscience,
and this fully permitted it. What had muddled him was precisely
the small artist-man's way – it was so complete – of being more
American than anybody. But it now for the time put Strether
vastly at his ease to have this view of a new way.

The amiable youth then looked out, as it had first struck
Strether, at a world in respect to which he hadn't a prejudice.
The one our friend most instantly missed was the usual one
in favour of an occupation accepted. Little Bilham had an
occupation, but it was only an occupation declined; and it was
by his general exemption from alarm, anxiety or remorse on
this score that the impression of his serenity was made. He had
come out to Paris to paint – to fathom, that is, at large, that
mystery; but study had been fatal to him so far as anything
could be fatal, and his productive power faltered in proportion
as his knowledge grew. Strether had gathered from him that at
the moment of his finding him in Chad's rooms he hadn't
saved from his shipwreck a scrap of anything but his beautiful
intelligence and his confirmed habit of Paris. He referred to
these things with an equal fond familiarity, and it was sufficiently clear that, as an outfit, they still served him. They were
charming to Strether through the hour spent at the Louvre,
where indeed they figured for him as an unseparated part of
the charged iridescent air, the glamour of the name, the splendour of the space, the colour of the masters. Yet they were
present too wherever the young man led, and the day after the
visit to the Louvre they hung, in a different walk, about the
steps of our party. He had invited his companions to cross
the river with him, offering to show them his own poor place;
and his own poor place, which was very poor, gave to his
idiosyncrasies, for Strether – the small sublime indifferences
and independences that had struck the latter as fresh – an odd

and engaging dignity. He lived at the end of an alley that went out of an old short cobbled street, a street that went in turn out of a new long smooth avenue – street and avenue and alley having, however, in common a sort of social shabbiness; and he introduced them to the rather cold and blank little studio which he had lent to a comrade for the term of his elegant absence. The comrade was another ingenuous compatriot, to whom he had wired that tea was to await them 'regardless', and this reckless repast, and the second ingenuous compatriot, and the faraway makeshift life, with its jokes and its gaps, its delicate daubs and its three or four chairs, its overflow of taste and conviction and its lack of nearly all else – these things wove round the occasion a spell to which our hero unreservedly surrendered.

He liked the ingenuous compatriots – for two or three others soon gathered; he liked the delicate daubs and the free discrimi-nations – involving references indeed, involving enthusiasms and execrations that made him, as they said, sit up; he liked above all the legend of good-humoured poverty, of mutual accommodation fairly raised to the romantic, that he soon read into the scene. The ingenuous compatriots showed a candour, he thought, surpassing even the candour of Woollett; they were red-haired and long-legged, they were quaint and queer and dear and droll; they made the place resound with the vernacular, which he had never known so marked as when figuring for the chosen language, he must suppose, of contemporary art. They twanged with a vengeance the aesthetic lyre – they drew from it wonderful airs. This aspect of their life had an admirable innocence; and he looked on occasion at Maria Gostrey to see to what extent that element reached her. She gave him however for the hour, as she had given him the previous day, no further sign than to show how she dealt with boys; meeting them with the air of old Parisian practice that she had for every one, for everything, in turn. Wonderful about the delicate daubs, masterful about the way to make tea, trustful about the legs of chairs and familiarly reminiscent of those, in the other time, the named, the numbered or the caricatured, who had flourished or failed, disappeared or arrived, she had accepted with the best

grace her second course of little Bilham, and had said to
Strether, the previous afternoon, on his leaving them, that, since
her impression was to be renewed, she would reserve judgement
till after the new evidence.

The new evidence was to come, as it proved, in a day or two.
He soon had from Maria a message to the effect that an excellent box at the Français[4] had been lent her for the following
night; it seeming on such occasions not the least of her merits
that she was subject to such approaches. The sense of how she
was always paying for something in advance was equalled on
Strether's part only by the sense of how she was always being
paid; all of which made for his consciousness, in the larger air,
of a lively bustling traffic, the exchange of such values as were
not for him to handle. She hated, he knew, at the French play,
anything but a box – just as she hated at the English anything
but a stall; and a box was what he was already in this phase
girding himself to press upon her. But she had for that matter
her community with little Bilham: she too always, on the great
issues, showed as having known in time. It made her constantly
beforehand with him and gave him mainly the chance to ask
himself how on the day of their settlement their account would
stand. He endeavoured even now to keep it a little straight by
arranging that if he accepted her invitation she should dine with
him first; but the upshot of this scruple was that at eight o'clock
on the morrow he awaited her with Waymarsh under the pil-
lared portico. She hadn't dined with him, and it was characteristic of their relation that she had made him embrace her refusal
without in the least understanding it. She ever caused her
rearrangements to affect him as her tenderest touches. It was
on that principle for instance that, giving him the opportunity
to be amiable again to little Bilham, she had suggested his
offering the young man a seat in their box. Strether had dispatched for this purpose a small blue missive[5] to the Boulevard
Malesherbes, but up to the moment of their passing into the
theatre he had received no response to his message. He held,
however, even after they had been for some time conveniently
seated, that their friend, who knew his way about, would come
in at his own right moment. His temporary absence moreover

seemed, as never yet, to make the right moment for Miss Gostrey. Strether had been waiting till to-night to get back from her in some mirrored form her impressions and conclusions. She had elected, as they said, to see little Bilham once; but now she had seen him twice and had nevertheless not said more than a word.

Waymarsh meanwhile sat opposite him with their hostess between; and Miss Gostrey spoke of herself as an instructor of youth introducing her little charges to a work that was one of the glories of literature. The glory was happily unobjectionable, and the little charges were candid; for herself she had travelled that road and she merely waited on their innocence. But she referred in due time to their absent friend, whom it was clear they should have to give up. 'He either won't have got your note,' she said, 'or you won't have got his: he has had some kind of hindrance, and, of course, for that matter, you know, a man never writes about coming to a box.' She spoke as if, with her look, it might have been Waymarsh who had written to the youth, and the latter's face showed a mixture of austerity and anguish. She went on however as if to meet this. 'He's far and away, you know, the best of them.'

'The best of whom, ma'am?'

'Why of all the long procession – the boys, the girls, or the old men and old women as they sometimes really are; the hope, as one may say, of our country. They've all passed, year after year; but there has been no one in particular I've ever wanted to stop. I feel – don't *you*? – that I want to stop little Bilham; he's so exactly right as he is.' She continued to talk to Waymarsh. 'He's too delightful. If he'll only not spoil it! But they always *will*; they always do; they always have.'

'I don't think Waymarsh knows,' Strether said after a moment, 'quite what it's open to Bilham to spoil.'

'It can't be a good American,' Waymarsh lucidly enough replied; 'for it didn't strike me the young man had developed much in *that* shape.'

'Ah,' Miss Gostrey sighed, 'the name of the good American is as easily given as taken away! What *is* it, to begin with, to *be* one, and what's the extraordinary hurry? Surely nothing

that's so pressing was ever so little defined. It's such an order, really, that before we cook you the dish we must at least have your receipt. Besides, the poor chicks have time! What I've seen so often spoiled,' she pursued, 'is the happy attitude itself, the state of faith and – what shall I call it? – the sense of beauty. You're right about him' – she now took in Strether; 'little Bilham has them to a charm; we must keep little Bilham along.' Then she was all again for Waymarsh. 'The others have all wanted so dreadfully to do something, and they've gone and done it in too many cases indeed. It leaves them never the same afterwards; the charm's always somehow broken. Now *he*, I think, you know, really won't. He won't do the least dreadful little thing. We shall continue to enjoy him just as he is. No – he's quite beautiful. He sees everything. He isn't a bit ashamed. He has every scrap of the courage of it that one could ask. Only think what he *might* do. One wants really – for fear of some accident – to keep him in view. At this very moment perhaps what mayn't he be up to? I've had my disappointments – the poor things are never really safe; or only at least when you have them under your eye. One can never completely trust them. One's uneasy, and I think that's why I most miss him now.'

She had wound up with a laugh of enjoyment over her embroidery of her idea – an enjoyment that her face communicated to Strether, who almost wished none the less at this moment that she would let poor Waymarsh alone. *He* knew more or less what she meant; but the fact wasn't a reason for her not pretending to Waymarsh that he didn't. It was craven of him perhaps, but he would, for the high amenity of the occasion, have liked Waymarsh not to be so sure of his wit. Her recognition of it gave him away and, before she had done with him or with that article, would give him worse. What was he, all the same, to do? He looked across the box at his friend; their eyes met; something queer and stiff, something that bore on the situation but that it was better not to touch, passed in silence between them. Well, the effect of it for Strether was an abrupt reaction, a final impatience of his own tendency to temporize. Where was that taking him anyway? It was one of

the quiet instants that sometimes settle more matters than the outbreaks dear to the historic muse. The only qualification of the quietness was the synthetic 'Oh hang it!' into which Strether's share of the silence soundlessly flowered. It represented, this mute ejaculation, a final impulse to burn his ships. These ships, to the historic muse, may seem of course mere cockles, but when he presently spoke to Miss Gostrey it was with the sense at least of applying the torch. 'Is it then a conspiracy?'

'Between the two young men? Well, I don't pretend to be a seer or a prophetess,' she presently replied; 'but if I'm simply a woman of sense he's working for you to-night. I don't quite know how – but it's in my bones.' And she looked at him at last as if, little material as she yet gave him, he'd really understand. 'For an opinion *that's* my opinion. He makes you out too well not to.'

'Not to work for me to-night?' Strether wondered. 'Then I hope he isn't doing anything very bad.'

'They've got you,' she portentously answered.

'Do you mean he *is* – ?'

'They've got you,' she merely repeated. Though she disclaimed the prophetic vision she was at this instant the nearest approach he had ever met to the priestess of the oracle. The light was in her eyes. 'You must face it now.'

He faced it on the spot. 'They *had* arranged – ?'

'Every move in the game. And they've been arranging ever since. He has had every day his little telegram from Cannes.'

It made Strether open his eyes. 'Do you *know* that?'

'I do better. I see it. This was, before I met him, what I wondered whether I *was* to see. But as soon as I met him I ceased to wonder, and our second meeting made me sure. I took him all in. He was acting – he is still – on his daily instructions.'

'So that Chad has done the whole thing?'

'Oh no – not the whole. *We've* done some of it. You and I and "Europe".'

'Europe – yes,' Strether mused.

'Dear old Paris,' she seemed to explain. But there was more,

and, with one of her turns, she risked it. 'And dear old Waymarsh. You,' she declared, 'have been a good bit of it.'

He sat massive. 'A good bit of what, ma'am?'

'Why of the wonderful consciousness of our friend here. You've helped too in your way to float him to where he is.'

'And where the devil *is* he?'

She passed it on with a laugh. 'Where the devil, Strether, are you?'

He spoke as if he had just been thinking it out. 'Well, quite already in Chad's hands, it would seem.' And he had had with this another thought. 'Will that be – just all through Bilham – the way he's going to work it? It would be, for him, you know, an idea. And Chad with an idea –!'

'Well?' she asked while the image held him.

'Well, is Chad – what shall I say? – monstrous?'

'Oh as much as you like! But the idea you speak of,' she said, 'won't have been his best. He'll have a better. It won't be all through little Bilham that he'll work it.'

This already sounded almost like a hope destroyed. 'Through whom else then?'

'That's what we shall see!' But quite as she spoke she turned, and Strether turned; for the door of the box had opened, with the click of the *ouvreuse*, from the lobby, and a gentleman, a stranger to them, had come in with a quick step. The door closed behind him, and, though their faces showed him his mistake, his air, which was striking, was all good confidence. The curtain had just again arisen, and, in the hush of the general attention, Strether's challenge was tacit, as was also the greeting, with a quickly-deprecating hand and smile, of the unannounced visitor. He discreetly signed that he would wait, would stand, and these things and his face, one look from which she had caught, had suddenly worked for Miss Gostrey. She fitted to them all an answer for Strether's last question. The solid stranger was simply the answer – as she now, turning to her friend, indicated. She brought it straight out for him – it presented the intruder. 'Why, through this gentleman!' The gentleman indeed, at the same time, though sounding for Strether a very short name, did practically as much to explain.

Strether gasped the name back – then only had he seen. Miss Gostrey had said more than she knew. They were in presence of Chad himself.

Our friend was to go over it afterwards again and again – he was going over it much of the time that they were together, and they were together constantly for three or four days: the note had been so strongly struck during that first half-hour that everything happening since was comparatively a minor development. The fact was that his perception of the young man's identity – so absolutely checked for a minute – had been quite one of the sensations that count in life; he certainly had never known one that had acted, as he might have said, with more of a crowded rush. And the rush, though both vague and multitudinous, had lasted a long time, protected, as it were, yet at the same time aggravated, by the circumstance of its coinciding with a stretch of decorous silence. They couldn't talk without disturbing the spectators in the part of the balcony just below them; and it, for that matter, came to Strether – being a thing of the sort that did come to him – that these were the accidents of a high civilization; the imposed tribute to propriety, the frequent exposure to conditions, usually brilliant, in which relief has to await its time. Relief was never quite near at hand for kings, queens, comedians and other such people, and though you might be yourself not exactly one of those, you could yet, in leading the life of high pressure, guess a little how they sometimes felt. It was truly the life of high pressure that Strether had seemed to feel himself lead while he sat there, close to Chad, during the long tension of the act. He was in presence of a fact that occupied his whole mind, that occupied for the half-hour his senses themselves all together; but he couldn't without inconvenience show anything – which moreover might count really as luck. What he might have shown, had he shown at all, was exactly the kind of emotion – the emotion of bewilderment – that he had proposed to himself from the first, whatever should occur, to show least. The phenomenon that had suddenly sat down there with him was a phenomenon of change so complete that his imagination, which had worked so beforehand, felt itself, in the connexion, without margin or allowance.

It had faced every contingency but that Chad should not *be* Chad, and this was what it now had to face with a mere strained smile and an uncomfortable flush.

He asked himself if, by any chance, before he should have in some way to commit himself, he might feel his mind settled to the new vision, might habituate it, so to speak, to the remarkable truth. But oh it was too remarkable, the truth; for what could be more remarkable than this sharp rupture of an identity? You could deal with a man as himself – you couldn't deal with him as somebody else. It was a small source of peace moreover to be reduced to wondering how little he might know in such an event what a sum he was setting you. He couldn't absolutely not know, for you couldn't absolutely not let him. It was a *case* then simply, a strong case, as people nowadays called such things, a case of transformation unsurpassed, and the hope was but in the general law that strong cases were liable to control from without. Perhaps he, Strether himself, was the only person after all aware of it. Even Miss Gostrey, with all her science, wouldn't be, would she? – and he had never seen anyone less aware of anything than Waymarsh as he glowered at Chad. The social sightlessness of his old friend's survey marked for him afresh, and almost in an humiliating way, the inevitable limits of direct aid from this source. He was not certain, however, of not drawing a shade of compensation from the privilege, as yet untasted, of knowing more about something in particular than Miss Gostrey did. His situation too was a case, for that matter, and he was now so interested, quite so privately agog, about it, that he had already an eye to the fun it would be to open up to her afterwards. He derived during his half-hour no assistance from her, and just this fact of her not meeting his eyes played a little, it must be confessed, into his predicament.

He had introduced Chad, in the first minutes, under his breath, and there was never the primness in her of the person unacquainted; but she had none the less betrayed at first no vision but of the stage, where she occasionally found a pretext for an appreciative moment that she invited Waymarsh to share. The latter's faculty of participation had never had, all round,

such an assault to meet; the pressure on him being the sharper for this chosen attitude in her, as Strether judged it, of isolating, for their natural intercourse, Chad and himself. This intercourse was meanwhile restricted to a frank friendly look from the young man, something markedly like a smile, but falling far short of a grin, and to the vivacity of Strether's private speculation as to whether *he* carried himself like a fool. He didn't quite see how he could so feel as one without somehow showing as one. The worst of that question moreover was that he knew it as a symptom the sense of which annoyed him. 'If I'm going to be odiously conscious of how I may strike the fellow,' he reflected, 'it was so little what I came out for that I may as well stop before I begin.' This sage consideration too, distinctly, seemed to leave untouched the fact that he *was* going to be conscious. He was conscious of everything but of what would have served him.

He was to know afterwards, in the watches of the night, that nothing would have been more open to him than after a minute or two to propose to Chad to seek with him the refuge of the lobby. He hadn't only not proposed it, but had lacked even the presence of mind to see it as possible. He had stuck there like a school-boy wishing not to miss a minute of the show; though for that portion of the show then presented he hadn't had an instant's real attention. He couldn't when the curtain fell have given the slightest account of what had happened. He had therefore, further, not at that moment acknowledged the amenity added by this acceptance of his awkwardness to Chad's general patience. Hadn't he none the less known at the very time – known it stupidly and without reaction – that the boy was accepting something? He was modestly benevolent, the boy – that was at least what he had been capable of the superiority of making out his chance to be; and one had one's self literally not had the gumption to get in ahead of him. If we should go into all that occupied our friend in the watches of the night we should have to mend our pen; but an instance or two may mark for us the vividness with which he could remember. He remembered the two absurdities that, if his presence of mind *had* failed, were the things that had had most to do with it. He

had never in his life seen a young man come into a box at ten
o'clock at night, and would, if challenged on the question in
advance, have scarce been ready to pronounce as to different
ways of doing so. But it was in spite of this definite to him that
Chad had had a way that was wonderful: a fact carrying with
it an implication that, as one might imagine it, he knew, he had
learned, how.

Here already then were abounding results; he had on the spot
and without the least trouble of intention taught Strether that
even in so small a thing as that there were different ways. He
had done in the same line still more than this; had by a mere
shake or two of the head made his old friend observe that the
change in him was perhaps more than anything else, for the
eye, a matter of the marked streaks of grey, extraordinary at
his age, in his thick black hair; as well as that this new feature
was curiously becoming to him, did something for him, as
characterization, also even – of all things in the world – as
refinement, that had been a good deal wanted. Strether felt,
however, he would have had to confess, that it wouldn't have
been easy just now, on this and other counts, in the presence of
what had been supplied, to be quite clear as to what had been
missed. A reflexion a candid critic might have made of old, for
instance, was that it would have been happier for the son to
look more like the mother; but this was a reflexion that at
present would never occur. The ground had quite fallen away
from it, yet no resemblance whatever to the mother had super-
vened. It would have been hard for a young man's face and air
to disconnect themselves more completely than Chad's at this
juncture from any discerned, from any imaginable aspect of a
New England female parent. That of course was no more than
had been on the cards; but it produced in Strether none the less
one of those frequent phenomena of mental reference with
which all judgement in him was actually beset.

Again and again as the days passed he had had a sense of the
pertinence of communicating quickly with Woollett – communicating with a quickness with which telegraphy alone
would rhyme; the fruit really of a fine fancy in him for keeping
things straight, for the happy forestalment of error. No one

could explain better when needful, nor put more conscience into an account or a report; which burden of conscience is perhaps exactly the reason why his heart always sank when the clouds of explanation gathered. His highest ingenuity was in keeping the sky of life clear of them. Whether or no he had a grand idea of the lucid, he held that nothing ever was in fact – for any one else – explained. One went through the vain motions, but it was mostly a waste of life. A personal relation was a relation only so long as people either perfectly understood or, better still, didn't care if they didn't. From the moment they cared if they didn't it was living by the sweat of one's brow; and the sweat of one's brow was just what one might buy one's self off from by keeping the ground free of the wild weed of delusion. It easily grew too fast, and the Atlantic cable now alone could race with it. That agency would each day have testified for him to something that was not what Woollett had argued. He was not at this moment absolutely sure that the effect of the morrow's – or rather of the night's – appreciation of the crisis wouldn't be to determine some brief missive. 'Have at last seen him, but oh dear!' – some temporary relief of that sort seemed to hover before him. It hovered somehow as preparing them all – yet preparing them for what? If he might do so more luminously and cheaply he would tick out in four words: 'Awfully old – grey hair.' To this particular item in Chad's appearance he constantly, during their mute half-hour, reverted; as if so very much more than he could have said had been involved in it. The most he could have said would have been: 'If he's going to make me feel young –!' which indeed, however, carried with it quite enough. If Strether was to feel young, that is, it would be because Chad was to feel old; and an aged and hoary sinner had been no part of the scheme.

The question of Chadwick's true time of life was, doubtless, what came up quickest after the adjournment of the two, when the play was over, to a café in the Avenue de l'Opéra.[6] Miss Gostrey had in due course been perfect for such a step; she had known exactly what they wanted – to go straight somewhere and talk; and Strether had even felt she had known what he wished to say and that he was arranging immediately to begin.

She hadn't pretended this, as she *had* pretended on the other hand, to have divined Waymarsh's wish to extend to her an independent protection homeward; but Strether nevertheless found how, after he had Chad opposite to him at a small table in the brilliant halls that his companion straightway selected, sharply and easily discriminated from others, it was quite, to his mind, as if she heard him speak; as if, sitting up, a mile away, in the little apartment he knew, she would listen hard enough to catch. He found too that he liked that idea, and he wished that, by the same token, Mrs. Newsome might have caught as well. For what had above all been determined in him as a necessity of the first order was not to lose another hour, nor a fraction of one; was to advance, to overwhelm, with a rush. This was how he would anticipate – by a night-attack, as might be – any forced maturity that a crammed consciousness of Paris was likely to take upon itself to assert on behalf of the boy. He knew to the full, on what he had just extracted from Miss Gostrey, Chad's marks of alertness; but they were a reason the more for not dawdling. If he was himself moreover to be treated as young he wouldn't at all events be so treated before he should have struck out at least once. His arms might be pinioned afterwards, but it would have been left on record that he was fifty. The importance of this he had indeed begun to feel before they left the theatre; it had become a wild unrest, urging him to seize his chance. He could scarcely wait for it as they went; he was on the verge of the indecency of bringing up the question in the street; he fairly caught himself going on – so he afterwards invidiously named it – as if there would be for him no second chance should the present be lost. Not till, on the purple divan before the perfunctory *bock*, he had brought out the words themselves, was he sure, for that matter, that the present would be saved.

BOOK FOURTH

I

'I've come, you know, to make you break with everything, neither more nor less, and take you straight home; so you'll be so good as immediately and favourably to consider it!' – Strether, face to face with Chad after the play, had sounded these words almost breathlessly, and with an effect at first positively disconcerting to himself alone. For Chad's receptive attitude was that of a person who had been gracefully quiet while the messenger at last reaching him has run a mile through the dust. During some seconds after he had spoken Strether felt as if *he* had made some such exertion; he was not even certain that the perspiration wasn't on his brow. It was the kind of consciousness for which he had to thank the look that, while the strain lasted, the young man's eyes gave him. They reflected – and the deuce of the thing was that they reflected really with a sort of shyness of kindness – his momentarily disordered state; which fact brought on in its turn for our friend the dawn of a fear that Chad might simply 'take it out' – take everything out – in being sorry for him. Such a fear, any fear, was unpleasant. But everything was unpleasant; it was odd how everything had suddenly turned so. This however was no reason for letting the least thing go. Strether had the next minute proceeded as roundly as if with an advantage to follow up. 'Of course I'm a busybody, if you want to fight the case to the death; but after all mainly in the sense of having known you and having given you such attention as you kindly permitted when you were in jackets and knickerbockers. Yes – it was knickerbockers, I'm busybody enough to remember that; and that you had, for your age – I speak of the first far-away time – tremendously stout

legs. Well, we want you to break. Your mother's heart's passionately set upon it, but she has above and beyond that excellent arguments and reasons. I've not put them into her head – I needn't remind you how little she's a person who needs that. But they exist – you must take it from me as a friend both of hers and yours – for myself as well. I didn't invent them, I didn't originally work them out; but I understand them, I think I can explain them – by which I mean make you actively do them justice; and that's why you see me here. You had better know the worst at once. It's a question of an immediate rupture and an immediate return. I've been conceited enough to dream I can sugar that pill. I take at any rate the greatest interest in the question. I took it already before I left home; and I don't mind telling you that, altered as you are, I take it still more now that I've seen you. You're older and – I don't know what to call it! – more of a handful; but you're by so much the more, I seem to make out, to our purpose.'

'Do I strike you as improved?' Strether was to recall that Chad had at this point enquired.

He was likewise to recall – and it had to count for some time as his greatest comfort – that it had been 'given' him, as they said at Woollett, to reply with some presence of mind: 'I haven't the least idea.' He was really for a while to like thinking he had been positively hard. On the point of conceding that Chad had improved in appearance, but that to the question of appearance the remark must be confined, he checked even that compromise and left his reservation bare. Not only his moral, but also, as it were, his aesthetic sense had a little to pay for this, Chad being unmistakeably – and wasn't it a matter of the confounded grey hair again? – handsomer than he had ever promised. That however fell in perfectly with what Strether had said. They had no desire to keep down his proper expansion, and he wouldn't be less to their purpose for not looking, as he had too often done of old, only bold and wild. There was indeed a signal particular in which he would distinctly be more so. Strether didn't, as he talked, absolutely follow himself; he only knew he was clutching his thread and that he held it from moment to moment a little tighter; his mere uninterruptedness during the

few minutes helped him to do that. He had frequently, for a
month, turned over what he should say on this very occasion,
and he seemed at last to have said nothing he had thought of –
everything was so totally different.

But in spite of all he had put the flag at the window. This
was what he had done, and there was a minute during which
he affected himself as having shaken it hard, flapped it with a
mighty flutter, straight in front of his companion's nose. It gave
him really almost the sense of having already acted his part.
The momentary relief – as if from the knowledge that nothing
of *that* at least could be undone – sprang from a particular
cause, the cause that had flashed into operation, in Miss
Gostrey's box, with direct apprehension, with amazed recognition, and that had been concerned since then in every throb
of his consciousness. What it came to was that with an absolutely *new* quantity to deal with one simply couldn't know. The
new quantity was represented by the fact that Chad had been
made over. That was all; whatever it was it was everything.
Strether had never seen the thing so done before – it was perhaps
a speciality of Paris. If one had been present at the process one
might little by little have mastered the result; but he was face
to face, as matters stood, with the finished business. It had
freely been noted for him that he might be received as a dog
among skittles, but that was on the basis of the old quantity.
He had originally thought of lines and tones as things to be
taken, but these possibilities had now quite melted away. There
was no computing at all what the young man before him would
think or feel or say on any subject whatever. This intelligence
Strether had afterwards, to account for his nervousness, reconstituted as he might, just as he had also reconstituted the
promptness with which Chad had corrected his uncertainty. An
extraordinarily short time had been required for the correction,
and there had ceased to be anything negative in his companion's
face and air as soon as it was made. 'Your engagement to my
mother has become then what they call here a *fait accompli*?' –
it had consisted, the determinant touch, in nothing more
than that.

Well, that was enough, Strether had felt while his answer

hung fire. He had felt at the same time, however, that nothing could less become him than that it should hang fire too long. 'Yes,' he said brightly, 'it was on the happy settlement of the question that I started. You see therefore to what tune I'm in your family. Moreover,' he added, 'I've been supposing you'd suppose it.'

'Oh I've been supposing it for a long time, and what you tell me helps me to understand that you should want to do something. To do something, I mean,' said Chad, 'to commemorate an event so – what do they call it? – so auspicious. I see you make out, and not unnaturally,' he continued, 'that bringing me home in triumph as a sort of wedding-present to Mother would commemorate it better than anything else. You want to make a bonfire in fact,' he laughed, 'and you pitch me on. Thank you, thank you!' he laughed again.

He was altogether easy about it, and this made Strether now see how at bottom, and in spite of the shade of shyness that really cost him nothing, he had from the first moment been easy about everything. The shade of shyness was mere good taste. People with manners formed could apparently have, as one of their best cards, the shade of shyness too. He had leaned a little forward to speak; his elbows were on the table; and the inscrutable new face that he had got somewhere and somehow was brought by the movement nearer to his critic's. There was a fascination for that critic in its not being, this ripe physiognomy, the face that, under observation at least, he had originally carried away from Woollett. Strether found a certain freedom on his own side in defining it as that of a man of the world – a formula that indeed seemed to come now in some degree to his relief; that of a man to whom things had happened and were variously known. In gleams, in glances, the past did perhaps peep out of it; but such lights were faint and instantly merged. Chad was brown and thick and strong, and of old Chad had been rough. Was all the difference therefore that he was actually smooth? Possibly; for that he *was* smooth was as marked as in the taste of a sauce or in the rub of a hand. The effect of it was general – it had retouched his features, drawn them with a cleaner line. It had cleared his eyes and settled his colour and

polished his fine square teeth – the main ornament of his face;
and at the same time that it had given him a form and a surface,
almost a design, it had toned his voice, established his accent,
encouraged his smile to more play and his other motions to
less. He had formerly, with a great deal of action, expressed
very little; and he now expressed whatever was necessary with
almost none at all. It was as if in short he had really, copious
perhaps but shapeless, been put into a firm mould and turned
successfully out. The phenomenon – Strether kept eyeing it as
a phenomenon, an eminent case – was marked enough to be
touched by the finger. He finally put his hand across the table
and laid it on Chad's arm. 'If you'll promise me – here on the
spot and giving me your word of honour – to break straight
off, you'll make the future the real right thing for all of us alike.
You'll ease off the strain of this decent but none the less acute
suspense in which I've for so many days been waiting for you,
and let me turn in to rest. I shall leave you with my blessing
and go to bed in peace.'

Chad again fell back at this and, his hands pocketed, settled
himself a little; in which posture he looked, though he rather
anxiously smiled, only the more earnest. Then Strether seemed
to see that he was really nervous, and he took that as what he
would have called a wholesome sign. The only mark of it
hitherto had been his more than once taking off and putting on
his wide-brimmed crush hat.[1] He had at this moment made the
motion again to remove it, then had only pushed it back, so
that it hung informally on his strong young grizzled crop. It
was a touch that gave the note of the familiar – the intimate
and the belated – to their quiet colloquy; and it was indeed by
some such trivial aid that Strether became aware at the same
moment of something else. The observation was at any rate
determined in him by some light too fine to distinguish from so
many others, but it was none the less sharply determined. Chad
looked unmistakeably during these instants – well, as Strether
put it to himself, all he was worth. Our friend had a sudden
apprehension of what that would on certain sides be. He saw
him in a flash as the young man marked out by women; and for
a concentrated minute the dignity, the comparative austerity, as

he funnily fancied it, of this character affected him almost with awe. There was an experience on his interlocutor's part that looked out at him from under the displaced hat, and that looked out moreover by a force of its own, the deep fact of its quantity and quality, and not through Chad's intending bravado or swagger. That was then the way men marked out by women *were* – and also the men by whom the women were doubtless in turn sufficiently distinguished. It affected Strether for thirty seconds as a relevant truth; a truth which, however, the next minute, had fallen into its relation. 'Can't you imagine there being some questions,' Chad asked, 'that a fellow – however much impressed by your charming way of stating things – would like to put to you first?'

'Oh yes – easily. I'm here to answer everything. I think I can even tell you things, of the greatest interest to you, that you won't know enough to ask me. We'll take as many days to it as you like. But I want,' Strether wound up, 'to go to bed now.'

'Really?'

Chad had spoken in such surprise that he was amused. 'Can't you believe it? – with what you put me through?'

The young man seemed to consider. 'Oh I haven't put you through much – yet.'

'Do you mean there's so much more to come?' Strether laughed. 'All the more reason then that I should gird myself.' And as if to mark what he felt he could by this time count on he was already on his feet.

Chad, still seated, stayed him, with a hand against him, as he passed between their table and the next. 'Oh we shall get on!'

The tone was, as who should say, everything Strether could have desired; and quite as good the expression of face with which the speaker had looked up at him and kindly held him. All these things lacked was their not showing quite so much as the fruit of experience. Yes, experience was what Chad did play on him, if he didn't play any grossness of defiance. Of course experience was in a manner defiance; but it wasn't, at any rate – rather indeed quite the contrary! – grossness; which was so much gained. He fairly grew older, Strether thought, while he himself so reasoned. Then with his mature pat of his visitor's

arm he also got up; and there had been enough of it all by this time to make the visitor feel that something *was* settled. Wasn't it settled that he had at least the testimony of Chad's own belief in a settlement? Strether found himself treating Chad's profession that they would get on as a sufficient basis for going to bed. He hadn't nevertheless after this gone to bed directly; for when they had again passed out together into the mild bright night a check had virtually sprung from nothing more than a small circumstance which might have acted only as confirming quiescence. There were people, expressive sound, projected light, still abroad, and after they had taken in for a moment, through everything, the great clear architectural street, they turned off in tacit union to the quarter of Strether's hotel. 'Of course,' Chad here abruptly began, 'of course Mother's making things out with you about me has been natural – and of course also you've had a good deal to go upon. Still, you must have filled out.'

He had stopped, leaving his friend to wonder a little what point he wished to make; and this it was that enabled Strether meanwhile to make one. 'Oh we've never pretended to go into detail. We weren't in the least bound to *that*. It was "filling out" enough to miss you as we did.'

But Chad rather oddly insisted, though under the high lamp at their corner, where they paused, he had at first looked as if touched by Strether's allusion to the long sense, at home, of his absence. 'What I mean is you must have imagined.'

'Imagined what?'

'Well – horrors.'

It affected Strether: horrors were so little – superficially at least – in this robust and reasoning image. But he was none the less there to be veracious. 'Yes, I dare say we *have* imagined horrors. But where's the harm if we haven't been wrong?'

Chad raised his face to the lamp, and it was one of the moments at which he had, in his extraordinary way, most his air of designedly showing himself. It was as if at these instants he just presented himself, his identity so rounded off, his palpable presence and his massive young manhood, as such a link in the chain as might practically amount to a kind of demonstration.

It was as if – and how but anomalously? – he couldn't after all help thinking sufficiently well of these things to let them go for what they were worth. What could there be in this for Strether but the hint of some self-respect, some sense of power, oddly perverted; something latent and beyond access, ominous and perhaps enviable? The intimation had the next thing, in a flash, taken on a name – a name on which our friend seized as he asked himself if he weren't perhaps really dealing with an irreducible young Pagan. This description – he quite jumped at it – had a sound that gratified his mental ear, so that of a sudden he had already adopted it. Pagan – yes, that was, wasn't it? what Chad *would* logically be. It was what he must be. It was what he was. The idea was a clue and, instead of darkening the prospect, projected a certain clearness. Strether made out in this quick ray that a Pagan was perhaps, at the pass they had come to, the thing most wanted at Woollett. They'd be able to do with one – a good one; he'd find an opening – yes; and Strether's imagination even now prefigured and accompanied the first appearance there of the rousing personage. He had only the slight discomfort of feeling, as the young man turned away from the lamp, that his thought had in the momentary silence possibly been guessed. 'Well, I've no doubt,' said Chad, 'you've come near enough. The details, as you say, don't matter. It *has* been generally the case that I've let myself go. But I'm coming round – I'm not so bad now.' With which they walked on again to Strether's hotel.

'Do you mean,' the latter asked as they approached the door, 'that there isn't any woman with you now?'

'But pray what has that to do with it?'

'Why it's the whole question.'

'Of my going home?' Chad was clearly surprised. 'Oh not much! Do you think that when I want to go any one will have any power –'

'To keep you' – Strether took him straight up – 'from carrying out your wish? Well, our idea has been that somebody has hitherto – or a good many persons perhaps – kept you pretty well from "wanting". That's what – if you're in anybody's hands – may again happen. You don't answer my question' –

he kept it up; 'but if you aren't in anybody's hands so much the better. There's nothing then but what makes for your going.'

Chad turned this over. 'I don't answer your question?' He spoke quite without resenting it. 'Well, such questions have always a rather exaggerated side. One doesn't know quite what you mean by being in women's "hands". It's all so vague. One is when one isn't. One isn't when one is. And then one can't quite give people away.' He seemed kindly to explain. 'I've *never* got stuck – so very hard; and, as against anything at any time really better, I don't think I've ever been afraid.' There was something in it that held Strether to wonder, and this gave him time to go on. He broke out as with a more helpful thought. 'Don't you know how I like Paris itself?'

The upshot was indeed to make our friend marvel. 'Oh if *that's* all that's the matter with you –!' It was *he* who almost showed resentment.

Chad's smile of a truth more than met it. 'But isn't that enough?'

Strether hesitated, but it came out. 'Not enough for your mother!' Spoken, however, it sounded a trifle odd – the effect of which was that Chad broke into a laugh. Strether, at this, succumbed as well, though with extreme brevity. 'Permit us to have still our theory. But if you *are* so free and so strong you're inexcusable. I'll write in the morning,' he added with decision. 'I'll say I've got you.'

This appeared to open for Chad a new interest. 'How often do you write?'

'Oh perpetually.'

'And at great length?'

Strether had become a little impatient. 'I hope it's not found too great.'

'Oh I'm sure not. And you hear as often?'

Again Strether paused. 'As often as I deserve.'

'Mother writes,' said Chad, 'a lovely letter.'

Strether, before the closed porte-cochère, fixed him a moment. 'It's more, my boy, than *you* do! But our suppositions don't matter,' he added, 'if you're actually not entangled.'

Chad's pride seemed none the less a little touched. 'I never

was that – let me insist. I always had my own way.' With which he pursued: 'And I have it at present.'

'Then what are you here for? What has kept you,' Strether asked, 'if you *have* been able to leave?'

It made Chad, after a stare, throw himself back. 'Do you think one's kept only by women?' His surprise and his verbal emphasis rang out so clear in the still street that Strether winced till he remembered the safety of their English speech. 'Is that,' the young man demanded, 'what they think at Woollett?' At the good faith in the question Strether had changed colour, feeling that, as he would have said, he had put his foot in it. He had appeared stupidly to misrepresent what they thought at Woollett; but before he had time to rectify Chad again was upon him. 'I must say then you show a low mind!'

It so fell in, unhappily for Strether, with that reflexion of his own prompted in him by the pleasant air of the Boulevard Malesherbes, that its disconcerting force was rather unfairly great. It was a dig that, administered by himself – and administered even to poor Mrs. Newsome – was no more than salutary; but administered by Chad – and quite logically – it came nearer drawing blood. They *hadn't* a low mind – nor any approach to one; yet incontestably they had worked, and with a certain smugness, on a basis that might be turned against them. Chad had at any rate pulled his visitor up; he had even pulled up his admirable mother; he had absolutely, by a turn of the wrist and a jerk of the far-flung noose, pulled up, in a bunch, Woollett browsing in its pride. There was no doubt Woollett *had* insisted on his coarseness; and what he at present stood there for in the sleeping street was, by his manner of striking the other note, to make of such insistence a preoccupation compromising to the insisters. It was exactly as if they had imputed to him a vulgarity that he had by a mere gesture caused to fall from him. The devil of the case was that Strether felt it, by the same stroke, as falling straight upon himself. He had been wondering a minute ago if the boy weren't a Pagan, and he found himself wondering now if he weren't by chance a gentleman. It didn't in the least, on the spot, spring up helpfully for him that a person couldn't at the same time be both. There was nothing at this moment in

the air to challenge the combination; there was everything to give it on the contrary something of a flourish. It struck Strether into the bargain as doing something to meet the most difficult of the questions; though perhaps indeed only by substituting another. Wouldn't it be precisely by having learned to be a gentleman that he had mastered the consequent trick of looking so well that one could scarce speak to him straight? But what in the world was the clue to such a prime producing cause? There were too many clues then that Strether still lacked, and these clues to clues were among them. What it accordingly amounted to for him was that he had to take full in the face a fresh attribution of ignorance. He had grown used by this time to reminders, especially from his own lips, of what he didn't know; but he had borne them because in the first place they were private and because in the second they practically conveyed a tribute. He didn't know what was bad, and – as others didn't know how little he knew it – he could put up with his state. But if he didn't know, in so important a particular, what was good, Chad at least was now aware he didn't; and that, for some reason, affected our friend as curiously public. It was in fact an exposed condition that the young man left him in long enough for him to feel its chill – till he saw fit, in a word, generously again to cover him. This last was in truth what Chad quite gracefully did. But he did it as with a simple thought that met the whole of the case. 'Oh I'm all right!' It was what Strether had rather bewilderedly to go to bed on.

II

It really looked true moreover from the way Chad was to behave after this. He was full of attentions to his mother's ambassador; in spite of which, all the while, the latter's other relations rather remarkably contrived to assert themselves. Strether's sittings pen in hand with Mrs. Newsome up in his own room were broken, yet they were richer; and they were more than ever interspersed with the hours in which he reported himself, in a different fashion, but with scarce less earnestness and fulness, to Maria Gostrey. Now that, as he would have expressed it, he had really something to talk about he found himself, in respect to any oddity that might reside for him in the double connexion, at once more aware and more indifferent. He had been fine to Mrs. Newsome about his useful friend, but it had begun to haunt his imagination that Chad, taking up again for her benefit a pen too long disused, might possibly be finer. It wouldn't at all do, he saw, that anything should come up for him at Chad's hand but what specifically *was* to have come; the greatest divergence from which would be precisely the element of any lubrication of their intercourse by levity. It was accordingly to forestall such an accident that he frankly put before the young man the several facts, just as they had occurred, of his funny alliance. He spoke of these facts, pleasantly and obligingly, as 'the whole story', and felt that he might qualify the alliance as funny if he remained sufficiently grave about it. He flattered himself that he even exaggerated the wild freedom of his original encounter with the wonderful lady; he was scrupulously definite about the absurd conditions in which they had made acquaintance – their having picked each other up almost in the street; and he had

(finest inspiration of all!) a conception of carrying the war into the enemy's country by showing surprise at the enemy's ignorance.

He had always had a notion that this last was the grand style of fighting; the greater therefore the reason for it, as he couldn't remember that he had ever before fought in the grand style. Every one, according to this, knew Miss Gostrey: how came it Chad didn't know her? The difficulty, the impossibility, was really to escape it; Strether put on him, by what he took for granted, the burden of proof of the contrary. This tone was so far successful as that Chad quite appeared to recognize her as a person whose fame had reached him, but against his acquaintance with whom much mischance had worked. He made the point at the same time that his social relations, such as they could be called, were perhaps not to the extent Strether supposed with the rising flood of their compatriots. He hinted at his having more and more given way to a different principle of selection; the moral of which seemed to be that he went about little in the 'colony'. For the moment certainly he had quite another interest. It was deep, what he understood; and Strether, for himself, could only so observe it. He couldn't see as yet how deep. Might he not all too soon! For there was really too much of their question that Chad had already committed himself to liking. He liked, to begin with, his prospective stepfather; which was distinctly what had not been on the cards. His hating him was the untowardness for which Strether had been best prepared; he hadn't expected the boy's actual form to give him more to do than his imputed. It gave him more through suggesting that he must somehow make up to himself for not being sure he was sufficiently disagreeable. That had really been present to him as his only way to be sure he was sufficiently thorough. The point was that if Chad's tolerance of his thoroughness were insincere, were but the best of devices for gaining time, it none the less did treat everything as tacitly concluded.

That seemed at the end of ten days the upshot of the abundant, the recurrent talk through which Strether poured into him all it concerned him to know, put him in full possession of facts

and figures. Never cutting these colloquies short by a minute, Chad behaved, looked and spoke as if he were rather heavily, perhaps even a trifle gloomily, but none the less fundamentally and comfortably free. He made no crude profession of eagerness to yield, but he asked the most intelligent questions, probed, at moments, abruptly, even deeper than his friend's layer of information, justified by these touches the native estimate of his latent stuff, and had in every way the air of trying to live, reflectively, into the square bright picture. He walked up and down in front of this production, sociably took Strether's arm at the points at which he stopped, surveyed it repeatedly from the right and from the left, inclined a critical head to either quarter, and, while he puffed a still more critical cigarette, animadverted to his companion on this passage and that. Strether sought relief – there were hours when he required it – in repeating himself; it was in truth not to be blinked that Chad had a way. The main question as yet was of what it was a way *to*. It made vulgar questions no more easy; but that was unimportant when all questions save those of his own asking had dropped. That he was free was answer enough, and it wasn't quite ridiculous that this freedom should end by presenting itself as what was difficult to move. His changed state, his lovely home, his beautiful things, his easy talk, his very appetite for Strether, insatiable and, when all was said, flattering – what were such marked matters all but the notes of his freedom? He had the effect of making a sacrifice of it just in these handsome forms to his visitor; which was mainly the reason the visitor was privately, for the time, a little out of countenance. Strether was at this period again and again thrown back on a felt need to remodel somehow his plan. He fairly caught himself shooting rueful glances, shy looks of pursuit, toward the embodied influence, the definite adversary, who had by a stroke of her own failed him and on a fond theory of whose palpable presence he had, under Mrs. Newsome's inspiration, altogether proceeded. He had once or twice, in secret, literally expressed the irritated wish that *she* would come out and find her.

He couldn't quite yet force it upon Woollett that such a career, such a perverted young life, showed after all a certain

plausible side, *did* in the case before them flaunt something like an impunity for the social man; but he could at least treat himself to the statement that would prepare him for the sharpest echo. This echo – as distinct over there in the dry thin air as some shrill 'heading' above a column of print – seemed to reach him even as he wrote. 'He says there's no woman,' he could hear Mrs. Newsome report, in capitals almost of newspaper size, to Mrs. Pocock; and he could focus in Mrs. Pocock the response of the reader of the journal. He could see in the younger lady's face the earnestness of her attention and catch the full scepticism of her but slightly delayed 'What is there then?' Just so he could again as little miss the mother's clear decision: 'There's plenty of disposition, no doubt, to pretend there isn't.' Strether had, after posting his letter, the whole scene out; and it was a scene during which, coming and going, as befell, he kept his eye not least upon the daughter. He had his fine sense of the conviction Mrs. Pocock would take occasion to reaffirm – a conviction bearing, as he had from the first deeply divined it to bear, on Mr. Strether's essential inaptitude. She had looked him in his conscious eyes even before he sailed, and that she didn't believe *he* would find the woman had been written in her look. Hadn't she at the best but a scant faith in his ability to find women? It wasn't even as if he had found her mother – so much more, to her discrimination, had her mother performed the finding. Her mother had, in a case her private judgement of which remained educative of Mrs. Pocock's critical sense, found the man. The man owed his unchallenged state, in general, to the fact that Mrs. Newsome's discoveries were accepted at Woollett; but he knew in his bones, our friend did, how almost irresistibly Mrs. Pocock would now be moved to show what she thought of his own. Give *her* a free hand, would be the moral, and the woman would soon be found.

His impression of Miss Gostrey after her introduction to Chad was meanwhile an impression of a person almost unnaturally on her guard. He struck himself as at first unable to extract from her what he wished; though indeed *of* what he wished at this special juncture he would doubtless have contrived to make but a crude statement. It sifted and settled nothing to put to

her, *tout bêtement*, as she often said, 'Do you like him, eh?' –
thanks to his feeling it actually the least of his needs to heap up
the evidence in the young man's favour. He repeatedly knocked
at her door to let her have it afresh that Chad's case – whatever
else of minor interest it might yield – was first and foremost a
miracle almost monstrous. It was the alteration of the entire
man, and was so signal an instance that nothing else, for the
intelligent observer, could – *could* it? – signify. 'It's a plot,'
he declared – 'there's more in it than meets the eye.' He gave
the rein to his fancy. 'It's a plant!'

His fancy seemed to please her. 'Whose then?'

'Well, the party responsible is, I suppose, the fate that waits
for one, the dark doom that rides. What I mean is that with
such elements one can't count. I've but my poor individual, my
modest human means. It isn't playing the game to turn on the
uncanny. All one's energy goes to facing it, to tracking it. One
wants, confound it, don't you see?' he confessed with a queer
face – 'one wants to enjoy anything so rare. Call it then life' –
he puzzled it out – 'call it poor dear old life simply that springs
the surprise. Nothing alters the fact that the surprise is paralys-
ing, or at any rate engrossing – all, practically, hang it, that one
sees, that one *can* see.'

Her silences were never barren, nor even dull. 'Is that what
you've written home?'

He tossed it off. 'Oh dear, yes!'

She had another pause while, across her carpets, he had
another walk. 'If you don't look out you'll have them straight
over.'

'Oh but I've said he'll go back.'

'And *will* he?' Miss Gostrey asked.

The special tone of it made him, pulling up, look at her
long. 'What's that but just the question I've spent treasures of
patience and ingenuity in giving *you*, by the sight of him – after
everything had led up – every facility to answer? What is it but
just the thing I came here to-day to get out of you? Will he?'

'No – he won't,' she said at last. 'He's not free.'

The air of it held him. 'Then you've all the while known –?'

'I've known nothing but what I've seen; and I wonder,' she

declared with some impatience, 'that you didn't see as much. It was enough to be with him there –'

'In the box? Yes,' he rather blankly urged.

'Well – to feel sure.'

'Sure of what?'

She got up from her chair, at this, with a nearer approach than she had ever yet shown to dismay at his dimness. She even, fairly pausing for it, spoke with a shade of pity. 'Guess!'

It was a shade, fairly, that brought a flush into his face; so that for a moment, as they waited together, their difference was between them. 'You mean that just your hour with him told you so much of his story? Very good; I'm not such a fool, on my side, as that I don't understand you, or as that I didn't in some degree understand *him*. That he has done what he liked most isn't, among any of us, a matter the least in dispute. There's equally little question at this time of day of what it is he does like most. But I'm not talking,' he reasonably explained, 'of any mere wretch he may still pick up. I'm talking of some person who in his present situation may have held her own, may really have counted.'

'That's exactly what *I* am!' said Miss Gostrey. But she as quickly made her point. 'I thought you thought – or that they think at Woollett – that that's what mere wretches necessarily do. Mere wretches necessarily *don't*!' she declared with spirit. 'There must, behind every appearance to the contrary, still be somebody – somebody who's not a mere wretch, since we accept the miracle. What else but such a somebody can such a miracle be?'

He took it in. 'Because the fact itself *is* the woman?'

'*A* woman. Some woman or other. It's one of the things that *have* to be.'

'But you mean then at least a good one.'

'A good woman?' She threw up her arms with a laugh. 'I should call her excellent!'

'Then why does he deny her?'

Miss Gostrey thought a moment. 'Because she's too good to admit! Don't you see,' she went on, 'how she accounts for him?'

Strether clearly, more and more, did see; yet it made him also

see other things. 'But isn't what we want that he shall account
for *her*?'

'Well, he does. What you have before you is his way. You
must forgive him if it isn't quite outspoken. In Paris such debts
are tacit.'

Strether could imagine; but still –! 'Even when the woman's
good?'

Again she laughed out. 'Yes, and even when the man is!
There's always a caution in such cases,' she more seriously
explained – 'for what it may seem to show. There's nothing
that's taken as showing so much here as sudden unnatural
goodness.'

'Ah then you're speaking now,' Strether said, 'of people who
are *not* nice.'

'I delight,' she replied, 'in your classifications. But do you
want me,' she asked, 'to give you in the matter, on this ground,
the wisest advice I'm capable of? Don't consider her, don't
judge her at all in herself. Consider her and judge her only in
Chad.'

He had the courage at least of his companion's logic. 'Because
then I shall like her?' He almost looked, with his quick imagination, as if he already did, though seeing at once also the full
extent of how little it would suit his book. 'But is that what
I came out for?'

She had to confess indeed that it wasn't. But there was something else. 'Don't make up your mind. There are all sorts of
things. You haven't seen him all.'

This on his side Strether recognized; but his acuteness none
the less showed him the danger. 'Yes, but if the more I see the
better he seems?'

Well, she found something. 'That may be – but his disavowal
of her isn't, all the same, pure consideration. There's a hitch.'
She made it out. 'It's the effort to sink her.'

Strether winced at the image. 'To "sink" – ?'

'Well, I mean there's a struggle, and a part of it is just what
he hides. Take time – that's the only way not to make some
mistake that you'll regret. Then you'll see. He does really want
to shake her off.'

Our friend had by this time so got into the vision that he almost gasped. 'After all she has done for him?'

Miss Gostrey gave him a look which broke the next moment into a wonderful smile. 'He's not so good as you think!'

They remained with him, these words, promising him, in their character of warning, considerable help; but the support he tried to draw from them found itself on each renewal of contact with Chad defeated by something else. What could it be, this disconcerting force, he asked himself, but the sense, constantly renewed, that Chad *was* – quite in fact insisted on being – as good as he thought? It seemed somehow as if he couldn't *but* be as good from the moment he wasn't as bad. There was a succession of days at all events when contact with him – and in its immediate effect, as if it could produce no other – elbowed out of Strether's consciousness everything but itself. Little Bilham once more pervaded the scene, but little Bilham became even in a higher degree than he had originally been one of the numerous forms of the inclusive relation; a consequence promoted, to our friend's sense, by two or three incidents with which we have yet to make acquaintance. Waymarsh himself, for the occasion, was drawn into the eddy; it absolutely, though but temporarily, swallowed him down, and there were days when Strether seemed to bump against him as a sinking swimmer might brush a submarine object. The fathomless medium held them – Chad's manner was the fathomless medium; and our friend felt as if they passed each other, in their deep immersion, with the round impersonal eye of silent fish. It was practically produced between them that Waymarsh was giving him then his chance; and the shade of discomfort that Strether drew from the allowance resembled not a little the embarrassment he had known at school, as a boy, when members of his family had been present at exhibitions. He could perform before strangers, but relatives were fatal, and it was now as if, comparatively, Waymarsh were a relative. He seemed to hear him say 'Strike up then!' and to enjoy a foretaste of conscientious domestic criticism. He *had* struck up, so far as he actually could; Chad knew by this time in profusion what he wanted; and what vulgar violence did his fellow pilgrim expect of him

when he had really emptied his mind? It went somehow to and fro that what poor Waymarsh meant was 'I told you so – that you'd lose your immortal soul!' but it was also fairly explicit that Strether had his own challenge and that, since they must go to the bottom of things, he wasted no more virtue in watching Chad than Chad wasted in watching him. His dip for duty's sake – where was it worse than Waymarsh's own? For *he* needn't have stopped resisting and refusing, needn't have parleyed, at that rate, with the foe.

The strolls over Paris to see something or call somewhere were accordingly inevitable and natural, and the late sessions in the wondrous troisième, the lovely home, when men dropped in and the picture composed more suggestively through the haze of tobacco, of music more or less good and of talk more or less polyglot, were on a principle not to be distinguished from that of the mornings and the afternoons. Nothing, Strether had to recognize as he leaned back and smoked, could well less resemble a scene of violence than even the liveliest of these occasions. They were occasions of discussion, none the less, and Strether had never in his life heard so many opinions on so many subjects. There were opinions at Woollett, but only on three or four. The differences were there to match; if they were doubtless deep, though few, they were quiet – they were, as might be said, almost as shy as if people had been ashamed of them. People showed little diffidence about such things, on the other hand, in the Boulevard Malesherbes, and were so far from being ashamed of them – or indeed of anything else – that they often seemed to have invented them to avert those agreements that destroy the taste of talk. No one had ever done that at Woollett, though Strether could remember times when he himself had been tempted to it without quite knowing why. He saw why at present – he had but wanted to promote intercourse.

These, however, were but parenthetic memories; and the turn taken by his affair on the whole was positively that if his nerves were on the stretch it was because he missed violence. When he asked himself if none would then, in connexion with it, ever come at all, he might almost have passed as wondering how to provoke it. It would be too absurd if such a vision as *that*

should have to be invoked for relief; it was already marked enough as absurd that he should actually have begun with flutters and dignities on the score of a single accepted meal. What sort of a brute had he expected Chad to be, anyway? – Strether had occasion to make the enquiry but was careful to make it in private. He could himself, comparatively recent as it was – it was truly but the fact of a few days since – focus his primal crudity; but he would on the approach of an observer, as if handling an illicit possession, have slipped the reminiscence out of sight. There were echoes of it still in Mrs. Newsome's letters, and there were moments when these echoes made him exclaim on her want of tact. He blushed of course, at once, still more for the explanation than for the ground of it: it came to him in time to save his manners that she couldn't at the best become tactful as quickly as he. Her tact had to reckon with the Atlantic Ocean, the General Post-Office and the extravagant curve of the globe.

Chad had one day offered tea at the Boulevard Malesherbes to a chosen few, a group again including the unobscured Miss Barrace; and Strether had on coming out walked away with the acquaintance whom in his letters to Mrs. Newsome he always spoke of as the little artist-man. He had had full occasion to mention him as the other party, so oddly, to the only close personal alliance observation had as yet detected in Chad's existence. Little Bilham's way this afternoon was not Strether's, but he had none the less kindly come with him, and it was somehow a part of his kindness that as it had sadly begun to rain they suddenly found themselves seated for conversation at a café in which they had taken refuge. He had passed no more crowded hour in Chad's society than the one just ended; he had talked with Miss Barrace, who had reproached him with not having come to see her, and he had above all hit on a happy thought for causing Waymarsh's tension to relax. Something might possibly be extracted for the latter from the idea of his success with that lady, whose quick apprehension of what might amuse her had given Strether a free hand. What had she meant if not to ask whether she couldn't help him with his splendid encumbrance, and mightn't the sacred rage at any rate be kept

a little in abeyance by thus creating for his comrade's mind even in a world of irrelevance the possibility of a relation? What was it but a relation to be regarded as so decorative and, in especial, on the strength of it, to be whirled away, amid flounces and feathers, in a coupé lined, by what Strether could make out, with dark blue brocade? He himself had never been whirled away – never at least in a coupé and behind a footman; he had driven with Miss Gostrey in cabs, with Mrs. Pocock, a few times, in an open buggy, with Mrs. Newsome in a four-seated cart and, occasionally up at the mountains, on a buckboard;[1] but his friend's actual adventure transcended his personal experience. He now showed his companion soon enough indeed how inadequate, as a general monitor, this last queer quantity could once more feel itself.

'What game under the sun is he playing?' He signified the next moment that his allusion was not to the fat gentleman immersed in dominoes on whom his eyes had begun by resting, but to their host of the previous hour, as to whom, there on the velvet bench, with a final collapse of all consistency, he treated himself to the comfort of indiscretion. 'Where do you see him come out?'

Little Bilham, in meditation, looked at him with a kindness almost paternal. 'Don't you like it over here?'

Strether laughed out – for the tone was indeed droll; he let himself go. 'What has that to do with it? The only thing I've any business to like is to feel that I'm moving him. That's why I ask you whether you believe I *am*? Is the creature' – and he did his best to show that he simply wished to ascertain – 'honest?'

His companion looked responsible, but looked it through a small dim smile. 'What creature do you mean?'

It was on this that they did have for a little a mute interchange. 'Is it untrue that he's free? How then,' Strether asked wondering, 'does he arrange his life?'

'Is the creature you mean Chad himself?' little Bilham said.

Strether here, with a rising hope, just thought, 'We must take one of them at a time.' But his coherence lapsed. '*Is* there some

woman? Of whom he's really afraid of course I mean – or who does with him what she likes.'

'It's awfully charming of you,' Bilham presently remarked, 'not to have asked me that before.'

'Oh I'm not fit for my job!'

The exclamation had escaped our friend, but it made little Bilham more deliberate. 'Chad's a rare case!' he luminously observed. 'He's awfully changed,' he added.

'Then you see it too?'

'The way he has improved? Oh yes – I think every one must see it. But I'm not sure,' said little Bilham, 'that I didn't like him about as well in his other state.'

'Then this *is* really a new state altogether?'

'Well,' the young man after a moment returned, 'I'm not sure he was really meant by nature to be quite so good. It's like the new edition of an old book that one has been fond of – revised and amended, brought up to date, but not quite the thing one knew and loved. However that may be at all events,' he pursued, 'I don't think, you know, that he's really playing, as you call it, any game. I believe he really wants to go back and take up a career. He's capable of one, you know, that will improve and enlarge him still more. He won't then,' little Bilham continued to remark, 'be my pleasant well-rubbed old-fashioned volume at all. But of course I'm beastly immoral. I'm afraid it would be a funny world altogether – a world with things the way I like them. I ought, I dare say, to go home and go into business myself. Only I'd simply rather die – simply. And I've not the least difficulty in making up my mind not to, and in knowing exactly why, and in defending my ground against all comers. All the same,' he wound up, 'I assure you I don't say a word against it – for himself, I mean – to Chad. I seem to see it as much the best thing for him. You see he's not happy.'

'*Do* I?' – Strether stared. 'I've been supposing I see just the opposite – an extraordinary case of the equilibrium arrived at and assured.'

'Oh there's a lot behind it.'

'Ah there you are!' Strether exclaimed. 'That's just what

I want to get at. You speak of your familiar volume altered out of recognition. Well, who's the editor?'

Little Bilham looked before him a minute in silence. 'He ought to get married. *That* would do it. And he wants to.'

'Wants to marry her?'

Again little Bilham waited, and, with a sense that he had information, Strether scarce knew what was coming. 'He wants to be free. He isn't used, you see,' the young man explained in his lucid way, 'to being so good.'

Strether hesitated. 'Then I may take it from you that he *is* good?'

His companion matched his pause, but making it up with a quiet fulness. '*Do* take it from me.'

'Well then why isn't he free? He swears to me he is, but meanwhile does nothing – except of course that he's so kind to me – to prove it; and couldn't really act much otherwise if he weren't. My question to you just now was exactly on this queer impression of his diplomacy: as if instead of really giving ground his line were to keep me on here and set me a bad example.'

As the half-hour meanwhile had ebbed Strether paid his score, and the waiter was presently in the act of counting out change. Our friend pushed back to him a fraction of it, with which, after an emphatic recognition, the personage in question retreated. 'You give too much,' little Bilham permitted himself benevolently to observe.

'Oh I always give too much!' Strether helplessly sighed. 'But you don't,' he went on as if to get quickly away from the contemplation of that doom, 'answer my question. Why isn't he free?'

Little Bilham had got up as if the transaction with the waiter had been a signal, and had already edged out between the table and the divan. The effect of this was that a minute later they had quitted the place, the gratified waiter alert again at the open door. Strether had found himself deferring to his companion's abruptness as to a hint that he should be answered as soon as they were more isolated. This happened when after a few steps in the outer air they had turned the next corner. There our friend had kept it up. 'Why isn't he free if he's good?'

Little Bilham looked him full in the face. 'Because it's a virtuous attachment.'

This had settled the question so effectually for the time – that is for the next few days – that it had given Strether almost a new lease of life. It must be added however that, thanks to his constant habit of shaking the bottle in which life handed him the wine of experience, he presently found the taste of the lees rising as usual into his draught. His imagination had in other words already dealt with his young friend's assertion; of which it had made something that sufficiently came out on the very next occasion of his seeing Maria Gostrey. This occasion moreover had been determined promptly by a new circumstance – a circumstance he was the last man to leave her for a day in ignorance of. 'When I said to him last night,' he immediately began, 'that without some definite word from him now that will enable me to speak to them over there of our sailing – or at least of mine, giving them some sort of date – my responsibility becomes uncomfortable and my situation awkward; when I said that to him what do you think was his reply?' And then as she this time gave it up: 'Why that he has two particular friends, two ladies, mother and daughter, about to arrive in Paris – coming back from an absence; and that he wants me so furiously to meet them, know them and like them, that I shall oblige him by kindly not bringing our business to a crisis till he has had a chance to see them again himself. Is that,' Strether enquired, 'the way he's going to try to get off? These are the people,' he explained, 'that he must have gone down to see before I arrived. They're the best friends he has in the world, and they take more interest than any one else in what concerns him. As I'm his next best he sees a thousand reasons why we should comfortably meet. He hasn't broached the question sooner because their return was uncertain – seemed in fact for the present impossible. But he more than intimates that – if you can believe it – their desire to make my acquaintance has had to do with their surmounting difficulties.'

'They're dying to see you?' Miss Gostrey asked.

'Dying. Of course,' said Strether, 'they're the virtuous attachment.' He had already told her about that – had seen her the

day after his talk with little Bilham; and they had then threshed out together the bearing of the revelation. She had helped him to put into it the logic in which little Bilham had left it slightly deficient. Strether hadn't pressed him as to the object of the preference so unexpectedly described; feeling in the presence of it, with one of his irrepressible scruples, a delicacy from which he had in the quest of the quite other article worked himself sufficiently free. He had held off, as on a small principle of pride, from permitting his young friend to mention a name; wishing to make with this the great point that Chad's virtuous attachments were none of his business. He had wanted from the first not to think too much of his dignity, but that was no reason for not allowing it any little benefit that might turn up. He had often enough wondered to what degree his interference might pass for interested; so that there was no want of luxury in letting it be seen whenever he could that he didn't interfere. That had of course at the same time not deprived him of the further luxury of much private astonishment; which however he had reduced to some order before communicating his knowledge. When he had done this at last it was with the remark that, surprised as Miss Gostrey might, like himself, at first be, she would probably agree with him on reflexion that such an account of the matter did after all fit the confirmed appearances. Nothing certainly, on all the indications, could have been a greater change for him than a virtuous attachment, and since they had been in search of the 'word' as the French called it, of that change, little Bilham's announcement – though so long and so oddly delayed – would serve as well as another. She had assured Strether in fact after a pause that the more she thought of it the more it did serve; and yet her assurance hadn't so weighed with him as that before they parted he hadn't ventured to challenge her sincerity. Didn't she believe the attachment *was* virtuous? – he had made sure of her again with the aid of that question. The tidings he brought her on this second occasion were moreover such as would help him to make surer still.

She showed at first none the less as only amused. 'You say there are two? An attachment to them both then would, I suppose, almost necessarily be innocent.'

Our friend took the point, but he had his clue. 'Mayn't he be still in the stage of not quite knowing which of them, mother or daughter, he likes best?'

She gave it more thought. 'Oh it must be the daughter – at his age.'

'Possibly. Yet what do we know,' Strether asked, 'about hers? She may be old enough.'

'Old enough for what?'

'Why to marry Chad. That may be, you know, what they want. And if Chad wants it too, and little Bilham wants it, and even *we*, at a pinch, could do with it – that is if she doesn't prevent repatriation – why it may be plain sailing yet.'

It was always the case for him in these counsels that each of his remarks, as it came, seemed to drop into a deeper well. He had at all events to wait a moment to hear the slight splash of this one. 'I don't see why if Mr. Newsome wants to marry the young lady he hasn't already done it or hasn't been prepared with some statement to you about it. And if he both wants to marry her and is on good terms with them why isn't he "free"?'

Strether, responsively, wondered indeed. 'Perhaps the girl herself doesn't like him.'

'Then why does he speak of them to you as he does?'

Strether's mind echoed the question, but also again met it. 'Perhaps it's with the mother he's on good terms.'

'As against the daughter?'

'Well, if she's trying to persuade the daughter to consent to him, what could make him like the mother more? Only,' Strether threw out, 'why shouldn't the daughter consent to him?'

'Oh,' said Miss Gostrey, 'mayn't it be that every one else isn't quite so struck with him as you?'

'Doesn't regard him you mean as such an "eligible" young man? *Is* that what I've come to?' he audibly and rather gravely sought to know. 'However,' he went on, 'his marriage is what his mother most desires – that is if it will help. And oughtn't *any* marriage to help? They must want him' – he had already worked it out – 'to be better off. Almost any girl he may marry

will have a direct interest in his taking up his chances. It won't suit *her* at least that he shall miss them.'

Miss Gostrey cast about. 'No – you reason well! But of course on the other hand there's always dear old Woollett itself.'

'Oh yes,' he mused – 'there's always dear old Woollett itself.'

She waited a moment. 'The young lady mayn't find herself able to swallow *that* quantity. She may think it's paying too much; she may weigh one thing against another.'

Strether, ever restless in such debates, took a vague turn. 'It will all depend on who she is. That of course – the proved ability to deal with dear old Woollett, since I'm sure she does deal with it – is what makes so strongly for Mamie.'

'Mamie?'

He stopped short, at her tone, before her; then, though seeing that it represented not vagueness, but a momentary embarrassed fulness, let his exclamation come. 'You surely haven't forgotten about Mamie!'

'No, I haven't forgotten about Mamie,' she smiled. 'There's no doubt whatever that there's ever so much to be said for her. Mamie's *my* girl!' she roundly declared.

Strether resumed for a minute his walk. 'She's really perfectly lovely, you know. Far prettier than any girl I've seen over here yet.'

'That's precisely on what I perhaps most build.' And she mused a moment in her friend's way. 'I should positively like to take her in hand!'

He humoured the fancy, though indeed finally to deprecate it. 'Oh but don't, in your zeal, go over to her! I need you most and can't, you know, be left.'

But she kept it up. 'I wish they'd send her out to me!'

'If they knew you,' he returned, 'they would.'

'Ah but don't they? – after all that, as I've understood you, you've told them about me?'

He had paused before her again, but he continued his course. 'They *will* – before, as you say, I've done.' Then he came out with the point he had wished after all most to make. 'It seems to give away now his game. This is what he has been doing – keeping me along for. He has been waiting for them.'

Miss Gostrey drew in her lips. 'You see a good deal in it!'

'I doubt if I see as much as you. Do you pretend,' he went on, 'that you don't see – ?'

'Well, what?' – she pressed him as he paused.

'Why that there must be a lot between them – and that it has been going on from the first; even from before I came.'

She took a minute to answer. 'Who are they then – if it's so grave?'

'It mayn't be grave – it may be gay. But at any rate it's marked. Only I don't know,' Strether had to confess, 'anything about them. Their name for instance was a thing that, after little Bilham's information, I found it a kind of refreshment not to feel obliged to follow up.'

'Oh,' she returned, 'if you think you've got off – !'

Her laugh produced in him a momentary gloom. 'I don't think I've got off. I only think I'm breathing for about five minutes. I dare say I *shall* have, at the best, still to get on.' A look, over it all, passed between them, and the next minute he had come back to good humour. 'I don't meanwhile take the smallest interest in their name.'

'Nor in their nationality? – American, French, English, Polish?'[2]

'I don't care the least little "hang",' he smiled, 'for their nationality. It would be nice if they're Polish!' he almost immediately added.

'Very nice indeed.' The transition kept up her spirits. 'So you see you do care.'

He did this contention a modified justice. 'I think I should if they *were* Polish. Yes,' he thought – 'there might be joy in *that*.'

'Let us then hope for it.' But she came after this nearer to the question. 'If the girl's of the right age of course the mother can't be. I mean for the virtuous attachment. If the girl's twenty – and she can't be less – the mother must be at least forty. So it puts the mother out. *She's* too old for him.'

Strether, arrested again, considered and demurred. 'Do you think so? Do you think any one would be too old for him? *I'm* eighty, and I'm too young. But perhaps the girl,' he continued, '*isn't* twenty. Perhaps she's only ten – but such a little dear that

Chad finds himself counting her in as an attraction of the acquaintance. Perhaps she's only five. Perhaps the mother's but five-and-twenty – a charming young widow.'

Miss Gostrey entertained the suggestion. 'She *is* a widow then?'

'I haven't the least idea!' They once more, in spite of this vagueness, exchanged a look – a look that was perhaps the longest yet. It seemed in fact, the next thing, to require to explain itself; which it did as it could. 'I only feel what I've told you – that he has some reason.'

Miss Gostrey's imagination had taken its own flight. 'Perhaps she's *not* a widow.'

Strether seemed to accept the possibility with reserve. Still he accepted it. 'Then that's why the attachment – if it's to her – is virtuous.'

But she looked as if she scarce followed. 'Why is it virtuous if – since she's free – there's nothing to impose on it any condition?'

He laughed at her question. 'Oh I perhaps don't mean as virtuous as *that*! Your idea is that it can be virtuous – in any sense worthy of the name – only if she's *not* free? But what does it become then,' he asked, 'for *her*?'

'Ah that's another matter.' He said nothing for a moment, and she soon went on. 'I dare say you're right, at any rate, about Mr. Newsome's little plan. He *has* been trying you – has been reporting on you to these friends.'

Strether meanwhile had had time to think more. 'Then where's his straightness?'

'Well, as we say, it's struggling up, breaking out, asserting itself as it can. We can be on the side, you see, of his straightness. We can help him. But he has made out,' said Miss Gostrey, 'that you'll do.'

'Do for what?'

'Why, for *them* – for *ces dames*. He has watched you, studied you, liked you – and recognized that *they* must. It's a great compliment to you, my dear man; for I'm sure they're particular. You came out for a success. Well,' she gaily declared, 'you're having it!'

He took it from her with momentary patience and then turned abruptly away. It was always convenient to him that there were so many fine things in her room to look at. But the examination of two or three of them appeared soon to have determined a speech that had little to do with them. 'You don't believe in it!'

'In what?'

'In the character of the attachment. In its innocence.'

But she defended herself. 'I don't pretend to know anything about it. Everything's possible. We must see.'

'See?' he echoed with a groan. 'Haven't we seen enough?'

'*I* haven't,' she smiled.

'But do you suppose then little Bilham has lied?'

'You must find out.'

It made him almost turn pale. 'Find out any *more*?'

He had dropped on a sofa for dismay; but she seemed, as she stood over him, to have the last word. 'Wasn't what you came out for to find out *all*?'

BOOK FIFTH

I

The Sunday of the next week was a wonderful day, and Chad
Newsome had let his friend know in advance that he had
provided for it. There had already been a question of his taking
him to see the great Gloriani,[1] who was at home on Sunday
afternoons and at whose house, for the most part, fewer bores
were to be met than elsewhere; but the project, through some
accident, had not had instant effect, and now revived in happier
conditions. Chad had made the point that the celebrated sculptor had a queer old garden, for which the weather – spring at
last frank and fair – was propitious; and two or three of his
other allusions had confirmed for Strether the expectation of
something special. He had by this time, for all introductions
and adventures, let himself recklessly go, cherishing the sense
that whatever the young man showed him he was showing at
least himself. He could have wished indeed, so far as this went,
that Chad were less of a mere cicerone; for he was not without
the impression – now that the vision of his game, his plan, his
deep diplomacy, did recurrently assert itself – of his taking
refuge from the realities of their intercourse in profusely dispen-
sing, as our friend mentally phrased it, *panem et circenses*.[2] Our
friend continued to feel rather smothered in flowers, though he
made in his other moments the almost angry inference that this
was only because of his odious ascetic suspicion of any form of
beauty. He periodically assured himself – for his reactions were
sharp – that he shouldn't reach the truth of anything till he had
at least got rid of that.

He had known beforehand that Madame de Vionnet and her
daughter would probably be on view, an intimation to that

effect having constituted the only reference again made by Chad
to his good friends from the south. The effect of Strether's talk
about them with Miss Gostrey had been quite to consecrate his
reluctance to pry; something in the very air of Chad's silence –
judged in the light of that talk – offered it to him as a reserve
he could markedly match. It shrouded them about with he
scarce knew what, a consideration, a distinction; he was in
presence at any rate – so far as it placed him there – of ladies;
and the one thing that was definite for him was that they
themselves should be, to the extent of his responsibility, in
presence of a gentleman. Was it because they were very beautiful, very clever, or even very good – was it for one of these
reasons that Chad was, so to speak, nursing his effect? Did he
wish to spring them, in the Woollett phrase, with a fuller force
– to confound his critic, slight though as yet the criticism, with
some form of merit exquisitely incalculable? The most the critic
had at all events asked was whether the persons in question
were French; and that enquiry had been but a proper comment
on the sound of their name. 'Yes. That is no!' had been Chad's
reply; but he had immediately added that their English was the
most charming in the world, so that if Strether were wanting
an excuse for not getting on with them he wouldn't in the least
find one. Never in fact had Strether – in the mood into which
the place had quickly launched him – felt, for himself, less the
need of an excuse. Those he might have found would have
been, at the worst, all for the others, the people before him, in
whose liberty to be as they were he was aware that he positively
rejoiced. His fellow guests were multiplying, and these things,
their liberty, their intensity, their variety, their conditions at
large, were in fusion in the admirable medium of the scene.

The place itself was a great impression – a small pavilion,
clear-faced and sequestered, an effect of polished parquet, of
fine white panel and spare sallow gilt, of decoration delicate
and rare, in the heart of the Faubourg Saint-Germain[3] and on
the edge of a cluster of gardens attached to old noble houses.
Far back from streets and unsuspected by crowds, reached by
a long passage and a quiet court, it was as striking to the
unprepared mind, he immediately saw, as a treasure dug up;

giving him too, more than anything yet, the note of the range of the immeasurable town and sweeping away, as by a last brave brush, his usual landmarks and terms. It was in the garden, a spacious cherished remnant, out of which a dozen persons had already passed, that Chad's host presently met them; while the tall bird-haunted trees, all of a twitter with the spring and the weather, and the high party-walls, on the other side of which grave *hôtels* stood off for privacy, spoke of survival, transmission, association, a strong indifferent persistent order. The day was so soft that the little party had practically adjourned to the open air, but the open air was in such conditions all a chamber of state. Strether had presently the sense of a great convent, a convent of missions, famous for he scarce knew what, a nursery of young priests, of scattered shade, of straight alleys and chapel-bells, that spread its mass in one quarter; he had the sense of names in the air, of ghosts at the windows, of signs and tokens, a whole range of expression, all about him, too thick for prompt discrimination.

This assault of images became for a moment, in the address of the distinguished sculptor, almost formidable: Gloriani showed him, in such perfect confidence, on Chad's introduction of him, a fine worn handsome face, a face that was like an open letter in a foreign tongue. With his genius in his eyes, his manners on his lips, his long career behind him and his honours and rewards all round, the great artist, in the course of a single sustained look and a few words of delight at receiving him, affected our friend as a dazzling prodigy of type. Strether had seen in museums – in the Luxembourg as well as, more reverently, later on, in the New York of the billionaires – the work of his hand; knowing too that after an earlier time in his native Rome he had migrated, in mid-career, to Paris, where, with a personal lustre almost violent, he shone in a constellation: all of which was more than enough to crown him, for his guest, with the light, with the romance, of glory. Strether, in contact with that element as he had never yet so intimately been, had the consciousness of opening to it, for the happy instant, all the windows of his mind, of letting this rather grey interior drink in for once the sun of a clime not marked in his old geography.

He was to remember again repeatedly the medal-like Italian face, in which every line was an artist's own, in which time told only as tone and consecration; and he was to recall in especial, as the penetrating radiance, as the communication of the illustrious spirit itself, the manner in which, while they stood briefly, in welcome and response, face to face, he was held by the sculptor's eyes. He wasn't soon to forget them, was to think of them, all unconscious, unintending, preoccupied though they were, as the source of the deepest intellectual sounding to which he had ever been exposed. He was in fact quite to cherish his vision of it, to play with it in idle hours; only speaking of it to no one and quite aware he couldn't have spoken without appearing to talk nonsense. Was what it had told him or what it had asked him the greater of the mysteries? Was it the most special flare, unequalled, supreme, of the aesthetic torch, lighting that wondrous world for ever, or was it above all the long straight shaft sunk by a personal acuteness that life had seasoned to steel? Nothing on earth could have been stranger and no one doubtless more surprised than the artist himself, but it was for all the world to Strether just then as if in the matter of his accepted duty he had positively been on trial. The deep human expertness in Gloriani's charming smile – oh the terrible life behind it! – was flashed upon him as a test of his stuff.

Chad meanwhile, after having easily named his companion, had still more easily turned away and was already greeting other persons present. He was as easy, clever Chad, with the great artist as with his obscure compatriot, and as easy with every one else as with either: this fell into its place for Strether and made almost a new light, giving him, as a concatenation, something more he could enjoy. He liked Gloriani, but should never see him again; of that he was sufficiently sure. Chad accordingly, who was wonderful with both of them, was a kind of link for hopeless fancy, an implication of possibilities – oh if everything had been different! Strether noted at all events that he was thus on terms with illustrious spirits, and also that – yes, distinctly – he hadn't in the least swaggered about it. Our friend hadn't come there only for this figure of Abel Newsome's

son, but that presence threatened to affect the observant mind as positively central. Gloriani indeed, remembering something and excusing himself, pursued Chad to speak to him, and Strether was left musing on many things. One of them was the question of whether, since he had been tested, he had passed. Did the artist drop him from having made out that he wouldn't do? He really felt just to-day that he might do better than usual. Hadn't he done well enough, so far as that went, in being exactly so dazzled? and in not having too, as he almost believed, wholly hidden from his host that he felt the latter's plummet? Suddenly, across the garden, he saw little Bilham approach, and it was a part of the fit that was on him that as their eyes met he guessed also *his* knowledge. If he had said to him on the instant what was uppermost he would have said: 'Have I passed? – for of course I know one has to pass here.' Little Bilham would have reassured him, have told him that he exaggerated, and have adduced happily enough the argument of little Bilham's own very presence; which, in truth, he could see, was as easy a one as Gloriani's own or as Chad's. He himself would perhaps then after a while cease to be frightened, would get the point of view for some of the faces – types tremendously alien, alien to Woollett – that he had already begun to take in. Who were they all, the dispersed groups and couples, the ladies even more unlike those of Woollett than the gentlemen? – this was the enquiry that, when his young friend had greeted him, he did find himself making.

'Oh they're every one – all sorts and sizes; of course I mean within limits, though limits down perhaps rather more than limits up. There are always artists – he's beautiful and inimitable to the *cher confrère;* and then *gros bonnets* of many kinds – ambassadors, cabinet ministers, bankers, generals, what do I know? even Jews. Above all always some awfully nice women – and not too many; sometimes an actress, an artist, a great performer – but only when they're not monsters; and in particular the right *femmes du monde.* You can fancy his history on that side – I believe it's fabulous: they *never* give him up. Yet he keeps them down: no one knows how he manages; it's too beautiful and bland. Never too many – and a mighty good thing

too; just a perfect choice. But there are not in any way many
bores; it has always been so; he has some secret. It's extraordinary. And you don't find it out. He's the same to every one. He
doesn't ask questions.'

'Ah doesn't he?' Strether laughed.

Bilham met it with all his candour. 'How then should *I* be
here?'

'Oh for what you tell me. You're part of the perfect choice.'

Well, the young man took in the scene. 'It seems rather good
to-day.'

Strether followed the direction of his eyes. 'Are they all, this
time, *femmes du monde?*'

Little Bilham showed his competence. 'Pretty well.'

This was a category our friend had a feeling for; a light,
romantic and mysterious, on the feminine element, in which he
enjoyed for a little watching it. 'Are there any Poles?'

His companion considered. 'I think I make out a "Portu-
guee". But I've seen Turks.'

Strether wondered, desiring justice. 'They seem – all the
women – very harmonious.'

'Oh in closer quarters they come out!' And then, while
Strether was aware of fearing closer quarters, though giving
himself again to the harmonies, 'Well,' little Bilham went on,
'it *is* at the worst rather good, you know. If you like it, you feel
it, this way, that shows you're not in the least out. But you
always know things,' he handsomely added, 'immediately.'

Strether liked it and felt it only too much; so 'I say, don't lay
traps for me!' he rather helplessly murmured.

'Well,' his companion returned, 'he's wonderfully kind to *us*.'

'To us Americans you mean?'

'Oh no – he doesn't know anything about *that*. That's half
the battle here – that you can never hear politics. We don't talk
them. I mean to poor young wretches of all sorts. And yet it's
always as charming as this; it's as if, by something in the air,
our squalor didn't show. It puts us all back – into the last
century.'

'I'm afraid,' Strether said, amused, 'that it puts me rather
forward: oh ever so far!'

'Into the next? But isn't that only,' little Bilham asked, 'because you're really of the century before?'

'The century before the last? Thank you!' Strether laughed. 'If I ask you about some of the ladies it can't be then that I may hope, as such a specimen of the rococo,[4] to please them.'

'On the contrary they adore – we all adore here – the rococo, and where is there a better setting for it than the whole thing, the pavilion and the garden, together? There are lots of people with collections,' little Bilham smiled as he glanced round. 'You'll be secured!'

It made Strether for a moment give himself again to contemplation. There were faces he scarce knew what to make of. Were they charming or were they only strange? He mightn't talk politics, yet he suspected a Pole or two. The upshot was the question at the back of his head from the moment his friend had joined him. 'Have Madame de Vionnet and her daughter arrived?'

'I haven't seen them yet, but Miss Gostrey has come. She's in the pavilion looking at objects. One can see *she's* a collector,' little Bilham added without offence.

'Oh yes, she's a collector, and I knew she was to come. Is Madame de Vionnet a collector?' Strether went on.

'Rather, I believe; almost celebrated.' The young man met, on it, a little, his friend's eyes. 'I happen to know – from Chad, whom I saw last night – that they've come back; but only yesterday. He wasn't sure – up to the last. This, accordingly,' little Bilham went on, 'will be – if they *are* here – their first appearance after their return.'

Strether, very quickly, turned these things over. 'Chad told you last night? To me, on our way here, he said nothing about it.'

'But did you ask him?'

Strether did him the justice. 'I dare say not.'

'Well,' said little Bilham, 'you're not a person to whom it's easy to tell things you don't want to know. Though it *is* easy, I admit – it's quite beautiful,' he benevolently added, 'when you do want to.'

Strether looked at him with an indulgence that matched his

intelligence. 'Is that the deep reasoning on which – about these ladies – you've been yourself so silent?'

Little Bilham considered the depth of his reasoning. 'I haven't been silent. I spoke of them to you the other day, the day we sat together after Chad's tea-party.'

Strether came round to it. 'They then are the virtuous attachment?'

'I can only tell you that it's what they pass for. But isn't that enough? What more than a vain appearance does the wisest of us know? I commend you,' the young man declared with a pleasant emphasis, 'the vain appearance.'

Strether looked more widely round, and what he saw, from face to face, deepened the effect of his young friend's words. 'Is it so good?'

'Magnificent.'

Strether had a pause. 'The husband's dead?'

'Dear no. Alive.'

'Oh!' said Strether. After which, as his companion laughed: 'How then can it be so good?'

'You'll see for yourself. One does see.'

'Chad's in love with the daughter?'

'That's what I mean.'

Strether wondered. 'Then where's the difficulty?'

'Why, aren't you and I – with our grander bolder ideas?'

'Oh mine –!' Strether said rather strangely. But then as if to attenuate: 'You mean they won't hear of Woollett?'

Little Bilham smiled. 'Isn't that just what you must see about?'

It had brought them, as she caught the last words, into relation with Miss Barrace, whom Strether had already observed – as he had never before seen a lady at a party – moving about alone. Coming within sound of them she had already spoken, and she took again, through her long-handled glass, all her amused and amusing possession. 'How much, poor Mr. Strether, you seem to have to see about! But you can't say,' she gaily declared, 'that I don't do what I can to help you. Mr. Waymarsh is placed. I've left him in the house with Miss Gostrey.'

'The way,' little Bilham exclaimed, 'Mr. Strether gets the ladies to work for him! He's just preparing to draw in another; to pounce – don't you see him? – on Madame de Vionnet.'

'Madame de Vionnet? Oh, oh, oh!' Miss Barrace cried in a wonderful crescendo. There was more in it, our friend made out, than met the ear. Was it after all a joke that he should be serious about anything? He envied Miss Barrace at any rate her power of not being. She seemed, with little cries and protests and quick recognitions, movements like the darts of some fine high-feathered free-pecking bird, to stand before life as before some full shop-window. You could fairly hear, as she selected and pointed, the tap of her tortoise-shell against the glass. 'It's certain that we do need seeing about; only I'm glad it's not I who have to do it. One does, no doubt, begin that way; then suddenly one finds that one has given it up. It's too much, it's too difficult. You're wonderful, you people,' she continued to Strether, 'for not feeling those things – by which I mean impossibilities. You never feel them. You face them with a fortitude that makes it a lesson to watch you.'

'Ah but' – little Bilham put it with discouragement – 'what do we achieve after all? We see about you and report – when we even go so far as reporting. But nothing's done.'

'Oh you, Mr. Bilham,' she replied as with an impatient rap on the glass, 'you're not worth sixpence! You come over to convert the savages – for I know you verily did, I remember you – and the savages simply convert *you*.'

'Not even!' the young man woefully confessed: 'they haven't gone through that form. They've simply – the cannibals! – eaten me; converted me if you like, but converted me into food. I'm but the bleached bones of a Christian.'

'Well then there we are! Only' – and Miss Barrace appealed again to Strether – 'don't let it discourage you. You'll break down soon enough, but you'll meanwhile have had your moments. *Il faut en avoir.* I always like to see you while you last. And I'll tell you who *will* last.'

'Waymarsh?' – he had already taken her up.

She laughed out as at the alarm of it. 'He'll resist even Miss Gostrey: so grand is it not to understand. He's wonderful.'

'He is indeed,' Strether conceded. 'He wouldn't tell me of this affair – only said he had an engagement; but with such a gloom, you must let me insist, as if it had been an engagement to be hanged. Then silently and secretly he turns up here with you. Do you call *that* "lasting"?'

'Oh I hope it's lasting!' Miss Barrace said. 'But he only, at the best, bears with me. He doesn't understand – not one little scrap. He's delightful. He's wonderful,' she repeated.

'Michelangelesque!' – little Bilham completed her meaning. 'He *is* a success. Moses, on the ceiling, brought down to the floor;[5] overwhelming, colossal, but somehow portable.'

'Certainly, if you mean by portable,' she returned, 'looking so well in one's carriage. He's too funny beside me in his corner; he looks like somebody, somebody foreign and famous, *en exil*; so that people wonder – it's very amusing – whom I'm taking about. I show him Paris, show him everything, and he never turns a hair. He's like the Indian chief one reads about, who, when he comes up to Washington to see the Great Father, stands wrapt in his blanket and gives no sign. *I* might be the Great Father – from the way he takes everything.' She was delighted at this hit of her identity with that personage – it fitted so her character; she declared it was the title she meant henceforth to adopt. 'And the way he sits, too, in the corner of my room, only looking at my visitors very hard and as if he wanted to start something! They wonder what he does want to start. But he's wonderful,' Miss Barrace once more insisted. 'He has never started anything yet.'

It presented him none the less, in truth, to her actual friends, who looked at each other in intelligence, with frank amusement on Bilham's part and a shade of sadness on Strether's. Strether's sadness sprang – for the image had its grandeur – from his thinking how little he himself was wrapt in his blanket, how little, in marble halls, all too oblivious of the Great Father, he resembled a really majestic aboriginal. But he had also another reflexion. 'You've all of you here so much visual sense that you've somehow all "run" to it. There are moments when it strikes one that you haven't any other.'

'Any moral,' little Bilham explained, watching serenely,

across the garden, the several *femmes du monde*. 'But Miss Barrace has a moral distinction,' he kindly continued; speaking as if for Strether's benefit not less than for her own.

'*Have* you?' Strether, scarce knowing what he was about, asked of her almost eagerly.

'Oh not a distinction' – she was mightily amused at his tone – 'Mr. Bilham's too good. But I think I may say a sufficiency. Yes, a sufficiency. Have you supposed strange things of me?' – and she fixed him again, through all her tortoise-shell, with the droll interest of it. 'You *are* all indeed wonderful. I should awfully disappoint you. I do take my stand on my sufficiency. But I know, I confess,' she went on, 'strange people. I don't know how it happens; I don't do it on purpose; it seems to be my doom – as if I were always one of their habits: it's wonderful! I dare say moreover,' she pursued with an interested gravity, 'that I do, that we all do here, run too much to mere eye. But how can it be helped? We're all looking at each other – and in the light of Paris one sees what things resemble. That's what the light of Paris seems always to show. It's the fault of the light of Paris – dear old light!'

'Dear old Paris!' little Bilham echoed.

'Everything, every one shows,' Miss Barrace went on.

'But for what they really are?' Strether asked.

'Oh I like your Boston "reallys"! But sometimes – yes.'

'Dear old Paris then!' Strether resignedly sighed while for a moment they looked at each other. Then he broke out: 'Does Madame de Vionnet do that? I mean really show for what she is?'

Her answer was prompt. 'She's charming. She's perfect.'

'Then why did you a minute ago say 'Oh, oh, oh!' at her name?'

She easily remembered. 'Why just because –! She's wonderful.'

'Ah she too?' – Strether had almost a groan.

But Miss Barrace had meanwhile perceived relief. 'Why not put your question straight to the person who can answer it best?'

'No,' said little Bilham; 'don't put any question; wait, rather – it will be much more fun – to judge for yourself. He has come to take you to her.'

II

On which Strether saw that Chad was again at hand, and he afterwards scarce knew, absurd as it may seem, what had then quickly occurred. The moment concerned him, he felt, more deeply than he could have explained, and he had a subsequent passage of speculation as to whether, on walking off with Chad, he hadn't looked either pale or red. The only thing he was clear about was that, luckily, nothing indiscreet had in fact been said, and that Chad himself was more than ever, in Miss Barrace's great sense, wonderful. It was one of the connexions – though really why it should be, after all, was none so apparent – in which the whole change in him came out as most striking. Strether recalled as they approached the house that he had impressed him that first night as knowing how to enter a box. Well, he impressed him scarce less now as knowing how to make a presentation. It did something for Strether's own quality – marked it as estimated; so that our poor friend, conscious and passive, really seemed to feel himself quite handed over and delivered; absolutely, as he would have said, made a present of, given away. As they reached the house a young woman, about to come forth, appeared, unaccompanied, on the steps; at the exchange with whom of a word on Chad's part Strether immediately perceived that, obligingly, kindly, she was there to meet them. Chad had left her in the house, but she had afterwards come halfway and then the next moment had joined them in the garden. Her air of youth, for Strether, was at first almost disconcerting, while his second impression was, not less sharply, a degree of relief at there not having just been, with the others, any freedom used about her. It was upon him at a

touch that she was no subject for that, and meanwhile, on Chad's introducing him, she had spoken to him, very simply and gently, in an English clearly of the easiest to her, yet unlike any other he had ever heard. It wasn't as if she tried; nothing, he could see after they had been a few minutes together, was as if she tried; but her speech, charming correct and odd, was like a precaution against her passing for a Pole. There were precautions, he seemed indeed to see, only when there were really dangers.

Later on he was to feel many more of them, but by that time he was to feel other things besides. She was dressed in black, but in black that struck him as light and transparent; she was exceedingly fair, and, though she was as markedly slim, her face had a roundness, with eyes far apart and a little strange. Her smile was natural and dim; her hat not extravagant; he had only perhaps a sense of the clink, beneath her fine black sleeves, of more gold bracelets and bangles than he had ever seen a lady wear. Chad was excellently free and light about their encounter; it was one of the occasions on which Strether most wished he himself might have arrived at such ease and such humour: 'Here you are then, face to face at last; you're made for each other – *vous allez voir*; and I bless your union.' It was indeed, after he had gone off, as if he had been partly serious too. This latter motion had been determined by an enquiry from him about 'Jeanne'; to which her mother had replied that she was probably still in the house with Miss Gostrey, to whom she had lately committed her. 'Ah but you know,' the young man had rejoined, 'he must see her'; with which, while Strether pricked up his ears, he had started as if to bring her, leaving the other objects of his interest together. Strether wondered to find Miss Gostrey already involved, feeling that he missed a link; but feeling also, with small delay, how much he should like to talk with her of Madame de Vionnet on this basis of evidence.

The evidence as yet in truth was meagre; which, for that matter, was perhaps a little why his expectation had had a drop. There was somehow not quite a wealth in her; and a wealth was all that, in his simplicity, he had definitely prefigured. Still, it was too much to be sure already that there was but a poverty.

They moved away from the house, and, with eyes on a bench at some distance, he proposed that they should sit down. 'I've heard a great deal about you,' she said as they went; but he had an answer to it that made her stop short. 'Well, about *you*, Madame de Vionnet, I've heard, I'm bound to say, almost nothing' – those struck him as the only words he himself could utter with any lucidity; conscious as he was, and as with more reason, of the determination to be in respect to the rest of his business perfectly plain and go perfectly straight. It hadn't at any rate been in the least his idea to spy on Chad's proper freedom. It was possibly, however, at this very instant and under the impression of Madame de Vionnet's pause, that going straight began to announce itself as a matter for care. She had only after all to smile at him ever so gently in order to make him ask himself if he weren't already going crooked. It might be going crooked to find it of a sudden just only clear that she intended very definitely to be what he would have called nice to him. This was what passed between them while, for another instant, they stood still; he couldn't at least remember afterwards what else it might have been. The thing indeed really unmistakeable was its rolling over him as a wave that he had been, in conditions incalculable and unimaginable, a subject of discussion. He had been, on some ground that concerned her, answered for; which gave her an advantage he should never be able to match.

'Hasn't Miss Gostrey,' she asked, 'said a good word for me?'

What had struck him first was the way he was bracketed with that lady; and he wondered what account Chad would have given of their acquaintance. Something not as yet traceable, at all events, had obviously happened. 'I didn't even know of her knowing you.'

'Well, now she'll tell you all. I'm so glad you're in relation with her.'

This was one of the things – the 'all' Miss Gostrey would now tell him – that, with every deference to present preoccupation, was uppermost for Strether after they had taken their seat. One of the others was, at the end of five minutes, that she – oh incontestably, yes – *differed* less; differed, that is, scarcely

at all – well, superficially speaking, from Mrs. Newsome or
even from Mrs. Pocock. She was ever so much younger than
the one and not so young as the other; but what *was* there in
her, if anything, that would have made it impossible he should
meet her at Woollett? And wherein was her talk during their
moments on the bench together not the same as would have
been found adequate for a Woollett garden-party? – unless
perhaps truly in not being quite so bright. She observed to
him that Mr. Newsome had, to her knowledge, taken extraordinary pleasure in his visit; but there was no good lady at
Woollett who wouldn't have been at least up to that. Was
there in Chad, by chance, after all, deep down, a principle of
aboriginal loyalty that had made him, for sentimental ends,
attach himself to elements, happily encountered, that would
remind him most of the old air and the old soil? Why accordingly be in a flutter – Strether could even put it that way – about
this unfamiliar phenomenon of the *femme du monde?* On these
terms Mrs. Newsome herself was as much of one. Little Bilham
verily had testified that they came out, the ladies of the type, in
close quarters; but it was just in these quarters – now comparatively close – that he felt Madame de Vionnet's common
humanity. She did come out, and certainly to his relief, but she
came out as the usual thing. There might be motives behind,
but so could there often be even at Woollett. The only thing
was that if she showed him she wished to like him – as the
motives behind might conceivably prompt – it would possibly
have been more thrilling for him that she should have shown
as more vividly alien. Ah she was neither Turk nor Pole! –
which would be indeed flat once more for Mrs. Newsome
and Mrs. Pocock. A lady and two gentlemen had meanwhile,
however, approached their bench, and this accident stayed for
the time further developments.

They presently addressed his companion, the brilliant
strangers; she rose to speak to them, and Strether noted how
the escorted lady, though mature and by no means beautiful,
had more of the bold high look, the range of expensive reference, that he had, as might have been said, made his plans for.
Madame de Vionnet greeted her as 'Duchesse' and was greeted

in turn, while talk started in French, as 'Ma toute-belle'; little facts that had their due, their vivid interest for Strether. Madame de Vionnet didn't, none the less, introduce him – a note he was conscious of as false to the Woollett scale and the Woollett humanity; though it didn't prevent the Duchess, who struck him as confident and free, very much what he had obscurely supposed duchesses, from looking at him as straight and as hard – for it *was* hard – as if she would have liked, all the same, to know him. 'Oh yes, my dear, it's all right, it's *me*; and who are *you*, with your interesting wrinkles and your most effective (is it the handsomest, is it the ugliest?) of noses?' – some such loose handful of bright flowers she seemed, fragrantly enough, to fling at him. Strether almost wondered – at such a pace was he going – if some divination of the influence of either party were what determined Madame de Vionnet's abstention. One of the gentlemen, in any case, succeeded in placing himself in close relation with our friend's companion; a gentleman rather stout and importantly short, in a hat with a wonderful wide curl to its brim and a frock coat buttoned with an effect of superlative decision. His French had quickly turned to equal English, and it occurred to Strether that he might well be one of the ambassadors. His design was evidently to assert a claim to Madame de Vionnet's undivided countenance, and he made it good in the course of a minute – led her away with a trick of three words; a trick played with a social art of which Strether, looking after them as the four, whose backs were now all turned, moved off, felt himself no master.

He sank again upon his bench and, while his eyes followed the party, reflected, as he had done before, on Chad's strange communities. He sat there alone for five minutes, with plenty to think of; above all with his sense of having suddenly been dropped by a charming woman overlaid now by other impressions and in fact quite cleared and indifferent. He hadn't yet had so quiet a surrender; he didn't in the least care if nobody spoke to him more. He might have been, by his attitude, in for something of a march so broad that the want of ceremony with which he had just been used could fall into its place as but a

minor incident of the procession. Besides, there would be incidents enough, as he felt when this term of contemplation was closed by the reappearance of little Bilham, who stood before him a moment with a suggestive 'Well?' in which he saw himself reflected as disorganized, as possibly floored. He replied with a 'Well!' intended to show that he wasn't floored in the least. No indeed; he gave it out, as the young man sat down beside him, that if, at the worst, he had been overturned at all, he had been overturned into the upper air, the sublimer element with which he had an affinity and in which he might be trusted a while to float. It wasn't a descent to earth to say after an instant and in sustained response to the reference: 'You're quite sure her husband's living?'

'Oh dear, yes.'

'Ah then –!'

'Ah then what?'

Strether had after all to think. 'Well, I'm sorry for them.' But it didn't for the moment matter more than that. He assured his young friend he was quite content. They wouldn't stir; were all right as they were. He didn't want to be introduced; had been introduced already about as far as he could go. He had seen moreover an immensity; liked Gloriani, who, as Miss Barrace kept saying, was wonderful; had made out, he was sure, the half-dozen other men who were distinguished, the artists, the critics and oh the great dramatist – *him* it was easy to spot; but wanted – no, thanks, really – to talk with none of them; having nothing at all to say and finding it would do beautifully as it was; do beautifully because what it was – well, was just simply too late. And when after this little Bilham, submissive and responsive, but with an eye to the consolation nearest, easily threw off some 'Better late than never!' all he got in return for it was a sharp 'Better early than late!' This note indeed the next thing overflowed for Strether into a quiet stream of demonstration that as soon as he had let himself go he felt as the real relief. It had consciously gathered to a head, but the reservoir had filled sooner than he knew, and his companion's touch was to make the waters spread. There were some things that had to

come in time if they were to come at all. If they didn't come in time they were lost for ever. It was the general sense of them that had overwhelmed him with its long slow rush.

'It's not too late for *you*, on any side, and you don't strike me as in danger of missing the train; besides which people can be in general pretty well trusted, of course – with the clock of their freedom ticking as loud as it seems to do here – to keep an eye on the fleeting hour. All the same don't forget that you're young – blessedly young; be glad of it on the contrary and live up to it. Live all you can; it's a mistake not to. It doesn't so much matter what you do in particular, so long as you have your life. If you haven't had that what *have* you had? This place and these impressions – mild as you may find them to wind a man up so; all my impressions of Chad and of people I've seen at *his* place – well, have had their abundant message for me, have just dropped *that* into my mind. I see it now. I haven't done so enough before – and now I'm old; too old at any rate for what I see. Oh I *do* see, at least; and more than you'd believe or I can express. It's too late. And it's as if the train had fairly waited at the station for me without my having had the gumption to know it was there. Now I hear its faint receding whistle miles and miles down the line. What one loses one loses; make no mistake about that. The affair – I mean the affair of life – couldn't, no doubt, have been different for me; for it's at the best a tin mould, either fluted and embossed, with ornamental excrescences, or else smooth and dreadfully plain, into which, a helpless jelly, one's consciousness is poured – so that one "takes" the form, as the great cook says, and is more or less compactly held by it: one lives in fine as one can. Still, one has the illusion of freedom; therefore don't be, like me, without the memory of that illusion. I was either, at the right time, too stupid or too intelligent to have it; I don't quite know which. Of course at present I'm a case of reaction against the mistake; and the voice of reaction should, no doubt, always be taken with an allowance. But that doesn't affect the point that the right time is now yours. The right time is *any* time that one is still so lucky as to have. You've plenty; that's the great thing; you're, as I say, damn you, so happily and hatefully young.

Don't at any rate miss things out of stupidity. Of course I don't take you for a fool, or I shouldn't be addressing you thus awfully. Do what you like so long as you don't make *my* mistake. For it was a mistake. Live!' ... Slowly and sociably, with full pauses and straight dashes, Strether had so delivered himself; holding little Bilham from step to step deeply and gravely attentive. The end of all was that the young man had turned quite solemn, and that this was a contradiction of the innocent gaiety the speaker had wished to promote. He watched for a moment the consequence of his words, and then, laying a hand on his listener's knee and as if to end with the proper joke: 'And now for the eye I shall keep on you!'

'Oh but I don't know that I want to be, at your age, too different from you!'

'Ah prepare while you're about it,' said Strether, 'to be more amusing.'

Little Bilham continued to think, but at last had a smile. 'Well, you *are* amusing – to *me*.'

'*Impayable*, as you say, no doubt. But what am I to myself?' Strether had risen with this, giving his attention now to an encounter that, in the middle of the garden, was in the act of taking place between their host and the lady at whose side Madame de Vionnet had quitted him. This lady, who appeared within a few minutes to have left her friends, awaited Gloriani's eager approach with words on her lips that Strether couldn't catch, but of which her interesting witty face seemed to give him the echo. He was sure she was prompt and fine, but also that she had met her match, and he liked – in the light of what he was quite sure was the Duchess's latent insolence – the good humour with which the great artist asserted equal resources. Were they, this pair, of the 'great world'? – and was he himself, for the moment and thus related to them by his observation, *in* it? Then there was something in the great world covertly tiger-ish, which came to him across the lawn and in the charming air as a waft from the jungle. Yet it made him admire most of the two, made him envy, the glossy male tiger, magnificently marked. These absurdities of the stirred sense, fruits of sugges-tion ripening on the instant, were all reflected in his next words

to little Bilham. 'I know – if we talk of that – whom *I* should enjoy being like!'

Little Bilham followed his eyes; but then as with a shade of knowing surprise: 'Gloriani?'

Our friend had in fact already hesitated, though not on the hint of his companion's doubt, in which there were depths of critical reserve. He had just made out, in the now full picture, something and somebody else; another impression had been superimposed. A young girl in a white dress and a softly plumed white hat had suddenly come into view, and what was presently clear was that her course was toward them. What was clearer still was that the handsome young man at her side was Chad Newsome, and what was clearest of all was that she was therefore Mademoiselle de Vionnet, that she was unmistakeably pretty – bright gentle shy happy wonderful – and that Chad now, with a consummate calculation of effect, was about to present her to his old friend's vision. What was clearest of all indeed was something much more than this, something at the single stroke of which – and wasn't it simply juxtaposition? – all vagueness vanished. It was the click of a spring – he saw the truth. He had by this time also met Chad's look; there was more of it in that; and the truth, accordingly, so far as Bilham's enquiry was concerned, had thrust in the answer. 'Oh Chad!' – it was that rare youth he should have enjoyed being 'like'. The virtuous attachment would be all there before him; the virtuous attachment would be in the very act of appeal for his blessing; Jeanne de Vionnet, this charming creature, would be – exquisitely, intensely now – the object of it. Chad brought her straight up to him, and Chad was, oh yes, at this moment – for the glory of Woollett or whatever – better still even than Gloriani. He had plucked this blossom; he had kept it over-night in water; and at last as he held it up to wonder he did enjoy his effect. That was why Strether had felt at first the breath of calculation – and why moreover, as he now knew, his look at the girl would be, for the young man, a sign of the latter's success. What young man had ever paraded about that way, without a reason, a maiden in her flower? And there was nothing in his reason at present obscure. Her type sufficiently told of it – they wouldn't,

they couldn't, want her to go to Woollett. Poor Woollett, and what it might miss! – though brave Chad indeed too, and what it might gain! Brave Chad however had just excellently spoken. 'This is a good little friend of mine who knows all about you and has moreover a message for you. And this, my dear' – he had turned to the child herself – 'is the best man in the world, who has it in his power to do a great deal for us and whom I want you to like and revere as nearly as possible as much as I do.'

She stood there quite pink, a little frightened, prettier and prettier and not a bit like her mother. There was in this last particular no resemblance but that of youth to youth; and here was in fact suddenly Strether's sharpest impression. It went wondering, dazed, embarrassed, back to the woman he had just been talking with; it was a revelation in the light of which he already saw she would become more interesting. So slim and fresh and fair, she had yet put forth this perfection; so that for really believing it of her, for seeing her to any such developed degree as a mother, comparison would be urgent. Well, what was it now but fairly thrust upon him? 'Mamma wishes me to tell you before we go,' the girl said, 'that she hopes very much you'll come to see us very soon. She has something important to say to you.'

'She quite reproaches herself,' Chad helpfully explained: 'you were interesting her so much when she accidentally suffered you to be interrupted.'

'Ah don't mention it!' Strether murmured, looking kindly from one to the other and wondering at many things.

'And I'm to ask you for myself,' Jeanne continued with her hands clasped together as if in some small learnt prayer – 'I'm to ask you for myself if you won't positively come.'

'Leave it to me, dear – I'll take care of it!' Chad genially declared in answer to this, while Strether himself almost held his breath. What was in the girl was indeed too soft, too unknown for direct dealing; so that one could only gaze at it as at a picture, quite staying one's own hand. But with Chad he was now on ground – Chad he could meet; so pleasant a confidence in that and in everything did the young man freely

exhale. There was the whole of a story in his tone to his companion, and he spoke indeed as if already of the family. It made Strether guess the more quickly what it might be about which Madame de Vionnet was so urgent. Having seen him then she had found him easy; she wished to have it out with him that some way for the young people must be discovered, some way that would not impose as a condition the transplantation of her daughter. He already saw himself discussing with this lady the attractions of Woollett as a residence for Chad's companion. Was that youth going now to trust her with the affair – so that it would be after all with one of his 'lady-friends' that his mother's missionary should be condemned to deal? It was quite as if for an instant the two men looked at each other on this question. But there was no mistaking at last Chad's pride in the display of such a connexion. This was what had made him so carry himself while, three minutes before, he was bringing it into view; what had caused his friend, first catching sight of him, to be so struck with his air. It was, in a word, just when he thus finally felt Chad putting things straight off on him that he envied him, as he had mentioned to little Bilham, most. The whole exhibition however was but a matter of three or four minutes, and the author of it had soon explained that, as Madame de Vionnet was immediately going 'on', this could be for Jeanne but a snatch. They would all meet again soon, and Strether was meanwhile to stay and amuse himself – 'I'll pick you up again in plenty of time.' He took the girl off as he had brought her, and Strether, with the faint sweet foreignness of her 'Au revoir, monsieur!' in his ears as a note almost unprecedented, watched them recede side by side and felt how, once more, her companion's relation to her got an accent from it. They disappeared among the others and apparently into the house; whereupon our friend turned round to give out to little Bilham the conviction of which he was full. But there was no little Bilham any more; little Bilham had within the few moments, for reasons of his own, proceeded further: a circumstance by which, in its order, Strether was also sensibly affected.

III

Chad was not in fact on this occasion to keep his promise of
coming back; but Miss Gostrey had soon presented herself with
an explanation of his failure. There had been reasons at the last
for his going off with *ces dames*; and he had asked her with
much instance to come out and take charge of their friend. She
did so, Strether felt as she took her place beside him, in a
manner that left nothing to desire. He had dropped back on his
bench, alone again for a time, and the more conscious for little
Bilham's defection of his unexpressed thought; in respect to
which however this next converser was a still more capacious
vessel. 'It's the child!' he had exclaimed to her almost as soon
as she appeared; and though her direct response was for some
time delayed he could feel in her meanwhile the working of this
truth. It might have been simply, as she waited, that they were
now in presence altogether of truth spreading like a flood and
not for the moment to be offered her in the mere cupful; inasmuch as who should *ces dames* prove to be but persons about
whom – once thus face to face with them – she found she might
from the first have told him almost everything? This would
have freely come had he taken the simple precaution of giving
her their name. There could be no better example – and she
appeared to note it with high amusement – than the way,
making things out already so much for himself, he was at last
throwing precautions to the winds. They were neither more nor
less, she and the child's mother, than old school-friends – friends
who had scarcely met for years but whom this unlooked-for
chance had brought together with a rush. It was a relief, Miss
Gostrey hinted, to feel herself no longer groping; she was

unaccustomed to grope and as a general thing, he might well have seen, made straight enough for her clue. With the one she had now picked up in her hands there need be at least no waste of wonder. 'She's coming to see me – that's for *you*,' Strether's counsellor continued; 'but I don't require it to know where I am.'

The waste of wonder might be proscribed; but Strether, characteristically, was even by this time in the immensity of space. 'By which you mean that you know where *she* is?'

She just hesitated. 'I mean that if she comes to see me I shall – now that I've pulled myself round a bit after the shock – not be at home.'

Strether hung poised. 'You call it – your recognition – a shock?'

She gave one of her rare flickers of impatience. 'It was a surprise, an emotion. Don't be so literal. I wash my hands of her.'

Poor Strether's face lengthened. 'She's impossible – ?'

'She's even more charming than I remembered her.'

'Then what's the matter?'

She had to think how to put it. 'Well, *I'm* impossible. It's impossible. Everything's impossible.'

He looked at her an instant. 'I see where you're coming out. Everything's possible.' Their eyes had on it in fact an exchange of some duration; after which he pursued: 'Isn't it that beautiful child?' Then as she still said nothing: 'Why don't you mean to receive her?'

Her answer in an instant rang clear. 'Because I wish to keep out of the business.'

It provoked in him a weak wail. 'You're going to abandon me *now*?'

'No, I'm only going to abandon *her*. She'll want me to help her with you. And I won't.'

'You'll only help me with her? Well then –!' Most of the persons previously gathered had, in the interest of tea, passed into the house, and they had the gardens mainly to themselves. The shadows were long, the last call of the birds, who had made a home of their own in the noble interspaced quarter, sounded from the high trees in the other gardens as well, those of the old convent and of the old *hôtels*; it was as if our

friends had waited for the full charm to come out. Strether's impressions were still present; it was as if something had happened that 'nailed' them, made them more intense; but he was to ask himself soon afterwards, that evening, what really *had* happened – conscious as he could after all remain that for a gentleman taken, and taken the first time, into the 'great world', the world of ambassadors and duchesses, the items made a meagre total. It was nothing new to him, however, as we know, that a man might have – at all events such a man as he – an amount of experience out of any proportion to his adventures; so that, though it was doubtless no great adventure to sit on there with Miss Gostrey and hear about Madame de Vionnet, the hour, the picture, the immediate, the recent, the possible – as well as the communication itself, not a note of which failed to reverberate – only gave the moments more of the taste of history.

It was history, to begin with, that Jeanne's mother had been three-and-twenty years before, at Geneva, schoolmate and good girl-friend to Maria Gostrey, who had moreover enjoyed since then, though interruptedly and above all with a long recent drop, other glimpses of her. Twenty-three years put them both on, no doubt; and Madame de Vionnet – though she had married straight after school – couldn't be today an hour less than thirty-eight. This made her ten years older than Chad – though ten years, also, if Strether liked, older than she looked; the least, at any rate, that a prospective mother-in-law could be expected to do with. She would be of all mothers-in-law the most charming; unless indeed, through some perversity as yet insupposeable, she should utterly belie herself in that relation. There was none surely in which, as Maria remembered her, she mustn't be charming; and this frankly in spite of the stigma of failure in the tie where failure always most showed. It was no test there – when indeed *was* it a test there? – for Monsieur de Vionnet had been a brute. She had lived for years apart from him – which was of course always a horrid position; but Miss Gostrey's impression of the matter had been that she could scarce have made a better thing of it had she done it on purpose to show she was amiable. She was so amiable that nobody had

had a word to say; which was luckily not the case for her husband. He was so impossible that she had the advantage of all her merits.

It was still history for Strether that the Comte de Vionnet – it being also history that the lady in question was a Countess – should now, under Miss Gostrey's sharp touch, rise before him as a high distinguished polished impertinent reprobate, the product of a mysterious order; it was history, further, that the charming girl so freely sketched by his companion should have been married out of hand by a mother, another figure of striking outline, full of dark personal motive; it was perhaps history most of all that this company was, as a matter of course, governed by such considerations as put divorce out of the question. '*Ces gens-là* don't divorce, you know, any more than they emigrate or abjure – they think it impious and vulgar'; a fact in the light of which they seemed but the more richly special. It was all special; it was all, for Strether's imagination, more or less rich. The girl at the Genevese school, an isolated interesting attaching creature, then both sensitive and violent, audacious but always forgiven, was the daughter of a French father and an English mother who, early left a widow, had married again – tried afresh with a foreigner; in her career with whom she had apparently given her child no example of comfort. All these people – the people of the English mother's side – had been of condition more or less eminent; yet with oddities and disparities that had often since made Maria, thinking them over, wonder what they really quite rhymed to. It was in any case her belief that the mother, interested and prone to adventure, had been without conscience, had only thought of ridding herself most quickly of a possible, an actual encumbrance. The father, by her impression, a Frenchman with a name one knew, had been a different matter, leaving his child, she clearly recalled, a memory all fondness, as well as an assured little fortune which was unluckily to make her more or less of a prey later on. She had been in particular, at school, dazzlingly, though quite booklessly, clever; as polyglot as a little Jewess (which she wasn't, oh no!) and chattering French, English, German, Italian, anything one would, in a way that made a

clean sweep, if not of prizes and parchments, at least of every 'part', whether memorized or improvised, in the curtained costumed school repertory, and in especial of all mysteries of race and vagueness of reference, all swagger about 'home', among their variegated mates.

It would doubtless be difficult to-day, as between French and English, to name her and place her; she would certainly show, on knowledge, Miss Gostrey felt, as one of those convenient types who don't keep you explaining – minds with doors as numerous as the many-tongued cluster of confessionals at Saint Peter's. You might confess to her with confidence in Roumelian,[1] and even Roumelian sins. Therefore –! But Strether's narrator covered her implication with a laugh; a laugh by which his betrayal of a sense of the lurid in the picture was also perhaps sufficiently protected. He had a moment of wondering, while his friend went on, what sins might be especially Roumelian. She went on at all events to the mention of her having met the young thing – again by some Swiss lake – in her first married state, which had appeared for the few intermediate years not at least violently disturbed. She had been lovely at that moment, delightful to *her*, full of responsive emotion, of amused recognitions and amusing reminders; and then, once more, much later, after a long interval, equally but differently charming – touching and rather mystifying for the five minutes of an encounter at a railway-station *en province*, during which it had come out that her life was all changed. Miss Gostrey had understood enough to see, essentially, what had happened, and yet had beautifully dreamed that she was herself faultless. There were doubtless depths in her, but she was all right; Strether would see if she wasn't. She was another person however – that had been promptly marked – from the small child of nature at the Geneva school; a little person quite made over (as foreign women *were*, compared with American) by marriage. Her situation too had evidently cleared itself up; there would have been – all that was possible – a judicial separation. She had settled in Paris, brought up her daughter, steered her boat. It was no very pleasant boat – especially there – to be in; but Marie de Vionnet would have headed straight.

She would have friends, certainly – and very good ones. There she was at all events – and it was very interesting. Her knowing Mr. Chad didn't in the least prove she hadn't friends; what it proved was what good ones *he* had. 'I saw that,' said Miss Gostrey, 'that night at the Français; it came out for me in three minutes. I saw *her* – or somebody like her. And so,' she immediately added, 'did you.'

'Oh no – not anybody like her!' Strether laughed. 'But you mean,' he as promptly went on, 'that she has had such an influence on him?'

Miss Gostrey was on her feet; it was time for them to go. 'She has brought him up for her daughter.'

Their eyes, as so often, in candid conference, through their settled glasses, met over it long; after which Strether's again took in the whole place. They were quite alone there now. 'Mustn't she rather – in the time then – have rushed it?'

'Ah she won't of course have lost an hour. But that's just the good mother – the good French one. You must remember that of her – that as a mother she's French, and that for them there's a special providence. It precisely however – that she mayn't have been able to begin as far back as she'd have liked – makes her grateful for aid.'

Strether took this in as they slowly moved to the house on their way out. 'She counts on me then to put the thing through?'

'Yes – she counts on you. Oh and first of all of course,' Miss Gostrey added, 'on her – well, convincing you.'

'Ah,' her friend returned, 'she caught Chad young!'

'Yes, but there are women who are for all your "time of life". They're the most wonderful sort.'

She had laughed the words out, but they brought her companion, the next thing, to a stand. 'Is what you mean that she'll try to make a fool of me?'

'Well, I'm wondering what she *will* – with an opportunity – make.'

'What do you call,' Strether asked, 'an opportunity? My going to see her?'

'Ah you must go to see her' – Miss Gostrey was a trifle evasive. 'You can't not do that. You'd have gone to see the

other woman. I mean if there had been one – a different sort. It's what you came out for.'

It might be; but Strether distinguished. 'I didn't come out to see *this* sort.'

She had a wonderful look at him now. 'Are you disappointed she isn't worse?'

He for a moment entertained the question, then found for it the frankest of answers. 'Yes. If she were worse she'd be better for our purpose. It would be simpler.'

'Perhaps,' she admitted. 'But won't this be pleasanter?'

'Ah you know,' he promptly replied, 'I didn't come out – wasn't that just what you originally reproached me with? – for the pleasant.'

'Precisely. Therefore I say again what I said at first. You must take things as they come. Besides,' Miss Gostrey added, 'I'm not afraid for myself.'

'For yourself – ?'

'Of your seeing her. I trust her. There's nothing she'll say about me. In fact there's nothing she *can*.'

Strether wondered – little as he had thought of this. Then he broke out. 'Oh you women!'

There was something in it at which she flushed.

'Yes – there we are. We're abysses.' At last she smiled. 'But I risk her!'

He gave himself a shake. 'Well then so do I!' But he added as they passed into the house that he would see Chad the first thing in the morning.

This was the next day the more easily effected that the young man, as it happened, even before he was down, turned up at his hotel. Strether took his coffee, by habit, in the public room; but on his descending for this purpose Chad instantly proposed an adjournment to what he called greater privacy. He had himself as yet had nothing – they would sit down somewhere together; and when after a few steps and a turn into the Boulevard they had, for their greater privacy, sat down among twenty others, our friend saw in his companion's move a fear of the advent of Waymarsh. It was the first time Chad had to that extent given this personage 'away'; and Strether found

himself wondering of what it was symptomatic. He made out in a moment that the youth was in earnest as he hadn't yet seen him; which in its turn threw a ray perhaps a trifle startling on what they had each up to that time been treating as earnestness. It was sufficiently flattering however that the real thing – if this *was* at last the real thing – should have been determined, as appeared, precisely by an accretion of Strether's importance. For this was what it quickly enough came to – that Chad, rising with the lark, had rushed down to let him know while his morning consciousness was yet young that he had literally made the afternoon before a tremendous impression. Madame de Vionnet wouldn't, couldn't rest till she should have some assurance from him that he *would* consent again to see her. The announcement was made, across their marble-topped table, while the foam of the hot milk was in their cups and its plash still in the air, with the smile of Chad's easiest urbanity; and this expression of his face caused our friend's doubts to gather on the spot into a challenge of the lips. 'See here' – that was all; he only for the moment said again 'See here.' Chad met it with all his air of straight intelligence, while Strether remembered again that fancy of the first impression of him, the happy young Pagan, handsome and hard but oddly indulgent, whose mysterious measure he had under the street-lamp tried mentally to take. The young Pagan, while a long look passed between them, sufficiently understood. Strether scarce needed at last to say the rest – 'I want to know where I am.' But he said it, adding before any answer something more. 'Are you engaged to be married – is that your secret? – to the young lady?'

Chad shook his head with the slow amenity that was one of his ways of conveying that there was time for everything. 'I have no secret – though I may have secrets! I haven't at any rate that one. We're not engaged. No.'

'Then where's the hitch?'

'Do you mean why I haven't already started with you?' Chad, beginning his coffee and buttering his roll, was quite ready to explain. 'Nothing would have induced me – nothing will still induce me – not to try to keep you here as long as you can be made to stay. It's too visibly good for you.' Strether had himself

plenty to say about this, but it was amusing also to measure the
march of Chad's tone. He had never been more a man of the
world, and it was always in his company present to our friend
that one was seeing how in successive connexions a man of the
world acquitted himself. Chad kept it up beautifully. 'My idea
– *voyons*! – is simply that you should let Madame de Vionnet
know you, simply that you should consent to know *her*. I don't
in the least mind telling you that, clever and charming as she
is, she's ever so much in my confidence. All I ask of you is to
let her talk to you. You've asked me about what you call my
hitch, and so far as it goes she'll explain it to you. She's herself
my hitch, hang it – if you must really have it all out. But in a
sense,' he hastened in the most wonderful manner to add, 'that
you'll quite make out for yourself. She's too good a friend,
confound her. Too good, I mean, for me to leave without –
without –' It was his first hesitation.

'Without what?'

'Well, without my arranging somehow or other the damnable
terms of my sacrifice.'

'It *will* be a sacrifice then?'

'It will be the greatest loss I ever suffered. I owe her so much.'

It was beautiful, the way Chad said these things, and his
plea was now confessedly – oh quite flagrantly and publicly –
interesting. The moment really took on for Strether an intensity.
Chad owed Madame de Vionnet so much? What *did* that do
then but clear up the whole mystery? He was indebted for
alterations, and she was thereby in a position to have sent in
her bill for expenses incurred in reconstruction. What was this
at bottom but what had been to be arrived at? Strether sat there
arriving at it while he munched toast and stirred his second
cup. To do this with the aid of Chad's pleasant earnest face was
also to do more besides. No, never before had he been so ready
to take him as he was. What was it that had suddenly so cleared
up? It was just everybody's character; that is everybody's but –
in a measure – his own. Strether felt *his* character receive for
the instant a smutch from all the wrong things he had suspected
or believed. The person to whom Chad owed it that he could
positively turn out such a comfort to other persons – such a

person was sufficiently raised above any 'breath' by the nature of her work and the young man's steady light. All of which was vivid enough to come and go quickly; though indeed in the midst of it Strether could utter a question. 'Have I your word of honour that if I surrender myself to Madame de Vionnet you'll surrender yourself to *me*?'

Chad laid his hand firmly on his friend's. 'My dear man, you have it.'

There was finally something in his felicity almost embarrassing and oppressive – Strether had begun to fidget under it for the open air and the erect posture. He had signed to the waiter that he wished to pay, and this transaction took some moments, during which he thoroughly felt, while he put down money and pretended – it was quite hollow – to estimate change, that Chad's higher spirit, his youth, his practice, his paganism, his felicity, his assurance, his impudence, whatever it might be, had consciously scored a success. Well, that was all right so far as it went; his sense of the thing in question covered our friend for a minute like a veil through which – as if he had been muffled – he heard his interlocutor ask him if he mightn't take him over about five. 'Over' was over the river, and over the river was where Madame de Vionnet lived, and five was that very afternoon. They got at last out of the place – got out before he answered. He lighted, in the street, a cigarette, which again gave him more time. But it was already sharp for him that there was no use in time. 'What does she propose to do to me?' he had presently demanded.

Chad had no delays. 'Are you afraid of her?'

'Oh immensely. Don't you see it?'

'Well,' said Chad, 'she won't do anything worse to you than make you like her.'

'It's just of that I'm afraid.'

'Then it's not fair to me.'

Strether cast about. 'It's fair to your mother.'

'Oh,' said Chad, 'are you afraid of *her*?'

'Scarcely less. Or perhaps even more. But is this lady against your interests at home?' Strether went on.

'Not directly, no doubt; but she's greatly in favour of them here.'

'And what – "here" – does she consider them to be?'

'Well, good relations!'

'With herself?'

'With herself.'

'And what is it that makes them so good?'

'What? Well, that's exactly what you'll make out if you'll only go, as I'm supplicating you, to see her.'

Strether stared at him with a little of the wanness, no doubt, that the vision of more to 'make out' could scarce help producing. 'I mean *how* good are they?'

'Oh awfully good.'

Again Strether had faltered, but it was brief. It was all very well, but there was nothing now he wouldn't risk. 'Excuse me, but I must really – as I began by telling you – know where I am. Is she bad?'

' "Bad"?' – Chad echoed it, but without a shock. 'Is that what's implied – ?'

'When relations are good?' Strether felt a little silly, and was even conscious of a foolish laugh, at having it imposed on him to have appeared to speak so. What indeed was he talking about? His stare had relaxed; he looked now all round him. But something in him brought him back, though he still didn't know quite how to turn it. The two or three ways he thought of, and one of them in particular, were, even with scruples dismissed, too ugly. He none the less at last found something. 'Is her life without reproach?'

It struck him, directly he had found it, as pompous and priggish; so much so that he was thankful to Chad for taking it only in the right spirit. The young man spoke so immensely to the point that the effect was practically of positive blandness. 'Absolutely without reproach. A beautiful life. *Allez donc voir*!'

These last words were, in the liberality of their confidence, so imperative that Strether went through no form of assent; but before they separated it had been confirmed that he should be picked up at a quarter to five.

BOOK SIXTH

I

It was quite by half-past five – after the two men had been together in Madame de Vionnet's drawing-room not more than a dozen minutes – that Chad, with a look at his watch and then another at their hostess, said genially, gaily: 'I've an engagement, and I know you won't complain if I leave him with you. He'll interest you immensely; and as for her,' he declared to Strether, 'I assure you, if you're at all nervous, she's perfectly safe.'

He had left them to be embarrassed or not by this guarantee, as they could best manage, and embarrassment was a thing that Strether wasn't at first sure Madame de Vionnet escaped. He escaped it himself, to his surprise; but he had grown used by this time to thinking of himself as brazen. She occupied, his hostess, in the Rue de Bellechasse,[1] the first floor of an old house to which our visitors had had access from an old clean court. The court was large and open, full of revelations, for our friend, of the habit of privacy, the peace of intervals, the dignity of distances and approaches; the house, to his restless sense, was in the high homely style of an elder day, and the ancient Paris that he was always looking for – sometimes intensely felt, sometimes more acutely missed – was in the immemorial polish of the wide waxed staircase and in the fine *boiseries*, the medallions, mouldings, mirrors, great clear spaces, of the greyish-white salon into which he had been shown. He seemed at the very outset to see her in the midst of possessions not vulgarly numerous, but hereditary cherished charming. While his eyes turned after a little from those of his hostess and Chad freely

talked – not in the least about *him*, but about other people, people he didn't know, and quite as if he did know them – he found himself making out, as a background of the occupant, some glory, some prosperity of the First Empire,[2] some Napoleonic glamour, some dim lustre of the great legend; elements clinging still to all the consular chairs and mythological brasses and sphinxes' heads and faded surfaces of satin striped with alternate silk.

The place itself went further back – that he guessed, and how old Paris continued in a manner to echo there; but the post-revolutionary period, the world he vaguely thought of as the world of Châteaubriand, of Madame de Staël, even of the young Lamartine,[3] had left its stamp of harps and urns and torches, a stamp impressed on sundry small objects, ornaments and relics. He had never before, to his knowledge, had present to him relics, of any special dignity, of a private order – little old miniatures, medallions, pictures, books; books in leather bindings, pinkish and greenish, with gilt garlands on the back, ranged, together with other promiscuous properties, under the glass of brass-mounted cabinets. His attention took them all tenderly into account. They were among the matters that marked Madame de Vionnet's apartment as something quite different from Miss Gostrey's little museum of bargains and from Chad's lovely home; he recognized it as founded much more on old accumulations that had possibly from time to time shrunken than on any contemporary method of acquisition or form of curiosity. Chad and Miss Gostrey had rummaged and purchased and picked up and exchanged, sifting, selecting, comparing; whereas the mistress of the scene before him, beautifully passive under the spell of transmission – transmission from her father's line, he quite made up his mind – had only received, accepted and been quiet. When she hadn't been quiet she had been moved at the most to some occult charity for some fallen fortune. There had been objects she or her predecessors might even conceivably have parted with under need, but Strether couldn't suspect them of having sold old pieces to get 'better' ones. They would have felt no difference as to better or worse. He could but imagine their having felt – perhaps in emigration,

in proscription, for his sketch was slight and confused –
the pressure of want or the obligation of sacrifice.

The pressure of want – whatever might be the case with the
other force – was, however, presumably not active now, for the
tokens of a chastened ease still abounded after all, many marks
of a taste whose discriminations might perhaps have been called
eccentric. He guessed at intense little preferences and sharp
little exclusions, a deep suspicion of the vulgar and a personal
view of the right. The general result of this was something for
which he had no name on the spot quite ready, but something
he would have come nearest to naming in speaking of it as the
air of supreme respectability, the consciousness, small, still,
reserved, but none the less distinct and diffused, of private
honour. The air of supreme respectability – that was a strange
blank wall for his adventure to have brought him to break his
nose against. It had in fact, as he was now aware, filled all
the approaches, hovered in the court as he passed, hung on the
staircase as he mounted, sounded in the grave rumble of the
old bell, as little electric as possible, of which Chad, at the door,
had pulled the ancient but neatly-kept tassel; it formed in short
the clearest medium of its particular kind that he had ever
breathed. He would have answered for it at the end of a quarter
of an hour that some of the glass cases contained swords and
epaulettes of ancient colonels and generals; medals and orders
once pinned over hearts that had long since ceased to beat;
snuff-boxes bestowed on ministers and envoys; copies of works
presented, with inscriptions, by authors now classic. At bottom
of it all for him was the sense of her rare unlikeness to the
women he had known. This sense had grown, since the day
before, the more he recalled her, and had been above all singularly fed by his talk with Chad in the morning. Everything in
fine made her immeasurably new, and nothing so new as the
old house and the old objects. There were books, two or three,
on a small table near his chair, but they hadn't the lemon-
coloured covers with which his eye had begun to dally from
the hour of his arrival and to the opportunity of a further
acquaintance with which he had for a fortnight now altogether
succumbed. On another table, across the room, he made out

the great *Revue*;[4] but even that familiar face, conspicuous in
Mrs. Newsome's parlours, scarce counted here as a modern
note. He was sure on the spot – and he afterwards knew he was
right – that this was a touch of Chad's own hand. What would
Mrs. Newsome say to the circumstance that Chad's interested
'influence' kept her paper-knife in the *Revue*? The interested
influence at any rate had, as we say, gone straight to the point
– had in fact soon left it quite behind.

She was seated, near the fire, on a small stuffed and fringed
chair, one of the few modern articles in the room; and she
leaned back in it with her hands clasped in her lap and no
movement, in all her person, but the fine prompt play of her
deep young face. The fire, under the low white marble, un-
draped and academic, had burnt down to the silver ashes of
light wood; one of the windows, at a distance, stood open to
the mildness and stillness, out of which, in the short pauses,
came the faint sound, pleasant and homely, almost rustic, of a
plash and a clatter of *sabots* from some coach-house on the
other side of the court. Madame de Vionnet, while Strether sat
there, wasn't to shift her posture by an inch. 'I don't think you
seriously believe in what you're doing,' she said; 'but all the
same, you know, I'm going to treat you quite as if I did.'

'By which you mean,' Strether directly replied, 'quite as if
you didn't! I assure you it won't make the least difference with
me how you treat me.'

'Well,' she said, taking that menace bravely and philosophi-
cally enough, 'the only thing that really matters is that you shall
get on with me.'

'Ah but I don't!' he immediately returned.

It gave her another pause; which, however, she happily
enough shook off. 'Will you consent to go on with me a little –
provisionally – as if you did?'

Then it was that he saw how she had decidedly come all the
way; and there accompanied it an extraordinary sense of her
raising from somewhere below him her beautiful suppliant eyes.
He might have been perched at his door-step or at his window
and she standing in the road. For a moment he let her stand
and couldn't moreover have spoken. It had been sad, of a

sudden, with a sadness that was like a cold breath in his face. 'What can I do,' he finally asked, 'but listen to you as I promised Chadwick?'

'Ah but what I'm asking you,' she quickly said, 'isn't what Mr. Newsome had in mind.' She spoke at present, he saw, as if to take courageously *all* her risk. 'This is my own idea and a different thing.'

It gave poor Strether in truth – uneasy as it made him too – something of the thrill of a bold perception justified. 'Well,' he answered kindly enough, 'I was sure a moment since that some idea of your own had come to you.'

She seemed still to look up at him, but now more serenely. 'I made out you were sure – and that helped it to come. So you see,' she continued, 'we do get on.'

'Oh but it appears to me I don't at all meet your request. How can I when I don't understand it?'

'It isn't at all necessary you should understand; it will do quite well enough if you simply remember it. Only feel I trust you – and for nothing so tremendous after all. Just,' she said with a wonderful smile, 'for common civility.'

Strether had a long pause while they sat again face to face, as they had sat, scarce less conscious, before the poor lady had crossed the stream. She was the poor lady for Strether now because clearly she had some trouble, and her appeal to him could only mean that her trouble was deep. He couldn't help it; it wasn't his fault; he had done nothing; but by a turn of the hand she had somehow made their encounter a relation. And the relation profited by a mass of things that were not strictly in it or of it; by the very air in which they sat, by the high cold delicate room, by the world outside and the little plash in the court, by the First Empire and the relics in the stiff cabinets, by matters as far off as those and by others as near as the unbroken clasp of her hands in her lap and the look her expression had of being most natural when her eyes were most fixed. 'You count upon me of course for something really much greater than it sounds.'

'Oh it sounds great enough too!' she laughed at this.

He found himself in time on the point of telling her that she

was, as Miss Barrace called it, wonderful; but, catching himself up, he said something else instead. 'What was it Chad's idea then that you should say to me?'

'Ah his idea was simply what a man's idea always is – to put every effort off on the woman.'

'The "woman" – ?' Strether slowly echoed.

'The woman he likes – and just in proportion as he likes her. In proportion too – for shifting the trouble – as she likes *him*.'

Strether followed it; then with an abruptness of his own: 'How much do you like Chad?'

'Just as much as *that* – to take all, with you, on myself.' But she got at once again away from this. 'I've been trembling as if we were to stand or fall by what you may think of me; and I'm even now,' she went on wonderfully, 'drawing a long breath – and, yes, truly taking a great courage – from the hope that I don't in fact strike you as impossible.'

'That's at all events, clearly,' he observed after an instant, 'the way I don't strike *you*.'

'Well,' she so far assented, 'as you haven't yet said you *won't* have the little patience with me I ask for –'

'You draw splendid conclusions? Perfectly. But I don't understand them,' Strether pursued. 'You seem to me to ask for much more than you need. What, at the worst for you, what at the best for myself, can I after all do? I can use no pressure that I haven't used. You come really late with your request. I've already done all that for myself the case admits of. I've said my say, and here I am.'

'Yes, here you are, fortunately!' Madame de Vionnet laughed. 'Mrs. Newsome,' she added in another tone, 'didn't think you can do so little.'

He had an hesitation, but he brought the words out. 'Well, she thinks so now.'

'Do you mean by that – ?' But she also hung fire.

'Do I mean what?'

She still rather faltered. 'Pardon me if I touch on it, but if I'm saying extraordinary things, why, perhaps, mayn't I? Besides, doesn't it properly concern us to know?'

'To know what?' he insisted as after thus beating about the bush she had again dropped.

She made the effort. 'Has she given you up?'

He was amazed afterwards to think how simply and quietly he had met it. 'Not yet.' It was almost as if he were a trifle disappointed – had expected still more of her freedom. But he went straight on. 'Is that what Chad has told you will happen to me?'

She was evidently charmed with the way he took it. 'If you mean if we've talked of it – most certainly. And the question's not what has had least to do with my wishing to see you.'

'To judge if I'm the sort of man a woman *can* – ?'

'Precisely,' she exclaimed – 'you wonderful gentleman! I do judge – I *have* judged. A woman can't. You're safe – with every right to be. You'd be much happier if you'd only believe it.'

Strether was silent a little; then he found himself speaking with a cynicism of confidence of which even at the moment the sources were strange to him. 'I try to believe it. But it's a marvel,' he exclaimed, 'how *you* already get at it!'

Oh she was able to say. 'Remember how much I was on the way to it through Mr. Newsome – before I saw you. He thinks everything of your strength.'

'Well, I can bear almost anything!' our friend briskly interrupted. Deep and beautiful on this her smile came back, and with the effect of making him hear what he had said just as she had heard it. He easily enough felt that it gave him away, but what in truth had everything done but that? It had been all very well to think at moments that he was holding her nose down and that he had coerced her: what had he by this time done but let her practically see that he accepted their relation? What was their relation moreover – though light and brief enough in form as yet – but whatever she might choose to make it? Nothing could prevent her – certainly he couldn't – from making it pleasant. At the back of his head, behind everything, was the sense that she was – there, before him, close to him, in vivid imperative form – one of the rare women he had so often heard of, read of, thought of, but never met, whose very presence,

look, voice, the mere contemporaneous *fact* of whom, from the moment it was at all presented, made a relation of mere recognition. That was not the kind of woman he had ever found Mrs. Newsome, a contemporaneous fact who had been distinctly slow to establish herself; and at present, confronted with Madame de Vionnet, he felt the simplicity of his original impression of Miss Gostrey. She certainly had been a fact of rapid growth; but the world was wide, each day was more and more a new lesson. There were at any rate even among the stranger ones relations and relations. 'Of course I suit Chad's grand way,' he quickly added. 'He hasn't had much difficulty in working me in.'

She seemed to deny a little, on the young man's behalf, by the rise of her eyebrows, an intention of any process at all inconsiderate. 'You must know how grieved he'd be if you were to lose anything. He believes you can keep his mother patient.'

Strether wondered with his eyes on her. 'I see. *That's* then what you really want of me. And how am I to do it? Perhaps you'll tell me that.'

'Simply tell her the truth.'

'And what do you call the truth?'

'Well, *any* truth – about us all – that you see yourself. I leave it to you.'

'Thank you very much. I like,' Strether laughed with a slight harshness, 'the way you leave things!'

But she insisted kindly, gently, as if it wasn't so bad. 'Be perfectly honest. Tell her all.'

'All?' he oddly echoed.

'Tell her the simple truth,' Madame de Vionnet again pleaded.

'But what *is* the simple truth? The simple truth is exactly what I'm trying to discover.'

She looked about a while, but presently she came back to him. 'Tell her, fully and clearly, about *us*.'

Strether meanwhile had been staring. 'You and your daughter?'

'Yes – little Jeanne and me. Tell her,' she just slightly quavered, 'you like us.'

'And what good will that do me? Or rather' – he caught himself up – 'what good will it do *you*?'

She looked graver. 'None, you believe, really?'

Strether debated. 'She didn't send me out to "like" you.'

'Oh,' she charmingly contended, 'she sent you out to face the facts.'

He admitted after an instant that there was something in that. 'But how can I face them till I know what they are? Do you want him,' he then braced himself to ask, 'to marry your daughter?'

She gave a headshake as noble as it was prompt. 'No – not that.'

'And he really doesn't want to himself?'

She repeated the movement, but now with a strange light in her face. 'He likes her too much.'

Strether wondered. 'To be willing to consider, you mean, the question of taking her to America?'

'To be willing to do anything with her but be immensely kind and nice – really tender of her. We watch over her, and you must help us. You must see her again.'

Strether felt awkward. 'Ah with pleasure – she's so remarkably attractive.'

The mother's eagerness with which Madame de Vionnet jumped at this was to come back to him later as beautiful in its grace. 'The dear thing *did* please you?' Then as he met it with the largest 'Oh!' of enthusiasm: 'She's perfect. She's my joy.'

'Well, I'm sure that – if one were near her and saw more of her – she'd be mine.'

'Then,' said Madame de Vionnet, 'tell Mrs. Newsome that!'

He wondered the more. 'What good will that do you?' As she appeared unable at once to say, however, he brought out something else. 'Is your daughter in love with our friend?'

'Ah,' she rather startlingly answered, 'I wish you'd find out!'

He showed his surprise. 'I? A stranger?'

'Oh you won't be a stranger – presently. You shall see her quite, I assure you, as if you weren't.'

It remained for him none the less an extraordinary notion. 'It seems to me surely that if her mother can't –'

'Ah little girls and their mothers to-day!' she rather inconsequently broke in. But she checked herself with something she
seemed to give out as after all more to the point. 'Tell her I've
been good for him. Don't you think I have?'

It had its effect on him – more than at the moment he quite
measured. Yet he was consciously enough touched. 'Oh if it's
all *you* –!'

'Well, it may not be "all",' she interrupted, 'but it's to a great
extent. Really and truly,' she added in a tone that was to take
its place with him among things remembered.

'Then it's very wonderful.' He smiled at her from a face that
he felt as strained, and her own face for a moment kept him so.
At last she also got up. 'Well, don't you think that for that –'

'I ought to save you?' So it was that the way to meet her –
and the way, as well, in a manner, to get off – came over him.
He heard himself use the exorbitant word, the very sound of
which helped to determine his flight. 'I'll save you if I can.'

II

In Chad's lovely home, however, one evening ten days later, he felt himself present at the collapse of the question of Jeanne de Vionnet's shy secret. He had been dining there in the company of that young lady and her mother, as well as of other persons, and he had gone into the *petit salon*, at Chad's request, on purpose to talk with her. The young man had put this to him as a favour – 'I should like so awfully to know what you think of her. It will really be a chance for you,' he had said, 'to see the *jeune fille* – I mean the type – as she actually is, and I don't think that, as an observer of manners, it's a thing you ought to miss. It will be an impression that – whatever else you take – you can carry home with you, where you'll find again so much to compare it with.'

Strether knew well enough with what Chad wished him to compare it, and though he entirely assented he hadn't yet somehow been so deeply reminded that he was being, as he constantly though mutely expressed it, used. He was as far as ever from making out exactly to what end; but he was none the less constantly accompanied by a sense of the service he rendered. He conceived only that this service was highly agreeable to those who profited by it; and he was indeed still waiting for the moment at which he should catch it in the act of proving disagreeable, proving in some degree intolerable, to himself. He failed quite to see how his situation could clear up at all logically except by some turn of events that would give him the pretext of disgust. He was building from day to day on the possibility of disgust, but each day brought forth meanwhile a new and more engaging bend of the road. That possibility was now ever

so much further from sight than on the eve of his arrival, and he perfectly felt that, should it come at all, it would have to be at best inconsequent and violent. He struck himself as a little nearer to it only when he asked himself what service, in such a life of utility, he was after all rendering Mrs. Newsome. When he wished to help himself to believe that he was still all right he reflected – and in fact with wonder – on the unimpaired frequency of their correspondence; in relation to which what was after all more natural than that it should become more frequent just in proportion as their problem became more complicated?

Certain it is at any rate that he now often brought himself balm by the question, with the rich consciousness of yesterday's letter, 'Well, what can I do more than that – what can I do more than tell her everything?' To persuade himself that he did tell her, had told her, everything, he used to try to think of particular things he hadn't told her. When at rare moments and in the watches of the night he pounced on one it generally showed itself to be – to a deeper scrutiny – not quite truly of the essence. When anything new struck him as coming up, or anything already noted as reappearing, he always immediately wrote, as if for fear that if he didn't he would miss something; and also that he might be able to say to himself from time to time 'She knows it *now* – even while I worry.' It was a great comfort to him in general not to have left past things to be dragged to light and explained; not to have to produce at so late a stage anything not produced, or anything even veiled and attenuated, at the moment. She knew it now: that was what he said to himself to-night in relation to the fresh fact of Chad's acquaintance with the two ladies – not to speak of the fresher one of his own. Mrs. Newsome knew in other words that very night at Woollett that he himself knew Madame de Vionnet and that he had conscientiously been to see her; also that he had found her remarkably attractive and that there would probably be a good deal more to tell. But she further knew, or would know very soon, that, again conscientiously, he hadn't repeated his visit; and that when Chad had asked him on the Countess's behalf – Strether made her out vividly, with a thought at the back of his head, a Countess – if he wouldn't name a day for

dining with her, he had replied lucidly: 'Thank you very much
– impossible.' He had begged the young man would present his
excuses and had trusted him to understand that it couldn't
really strike one as quite the straight thing. He hadn't reported
to Mrs. Newsome that he had promised to 'save' Madame de
Vionnet; but, so far as he was concerned with that reminiscence,
he hadn't at any rate promised to haunt her house. What Chad
had understood could only, in truth, be inferred from Chad's
behaviour, which had been in this connexion as easy as in every
other. He was easy, always, when he understood; he was easier
still, if possible, when he didn't; he had replied that he would
make it all right; and he had proceeded to do this by substituting
the present occasion – as he was ready to substitute others – for
any, for every occasion as to which his old friend should have
a funny scruple.

'Oh but I'm not a little foreign girl; I'm just as English as I
can be,' Jeanne de Vionnet had said to him as soon as, in the
petit salon, he sank, shyly enough on his own side, into the
place near her vacated by Madame Gloriani at his approach.
Madame Gloriani, who was in black velvet, with white lace
and powdered hair, and whose somewhat massive majesty
melted, at any contact, into the graciousness of some incom-
prehensible tongue, moved away to make room for the vague
gentleman, after benevolent greetings to him which embodied,
as he believed, in baffling accents, some recognition of his
face from a couple of Sundays before. Then he had remarked
– making the most of the advantage of his years – that it
frightened him quite enough to find himself dedicated to the
entertainment of a little foreign girl. There were girls he wasn't
afraid of – he was quite bold with little Americans. Thus it was
that she had defended herself to the end – 'Oh but I'm almost
American too. That's what mamma has wanted me to be – I
mean *like* that; for she has wanted me to have lots of freedom.
She has known such good results from it.'

She was fairly beautiful to him – a faint pastel in an oval
frame: he thought of her already as of some lurking image in a
long gallery, the portrait of a small old-time princess of whom
nothing was known but that she had died young. Little Jeanne

wasn't, doubtless, to die young, but one couldn't, all the same, bear on her lightly enough. It was bearing hard, it was bearing as *he*, in any case, wouldn't bear, to concern himself, in relation to her, with the question of a young man. Odious really the question of a young man; one didn't treat such a person as a maidservant suspected of a 'follower'. And then young men, young men – well, the thing was their business simply, or was at all events hers. She was fluttered, fairly fevered – to the point of a little glitter that came and went in her eyes and a pair of pink spots that stayed in her cheeks – with the great adventure of dining out and with the greater one still, possibly, of finding a gentleman whom she must think of as very, very old, a gentleman with eye-glasses, wrinkles, a long grizzled moustache. She spoke the prettiest English, our friend thought, that he had ever heard spoken, just as he had believed her a few minutes before to be speaking the prettiest French. He wondered almost wistfully if such a sweep of the lyre didn't react on the spirit itself; and his fancy had in fact, before he knew it, begun so to stray and embroider that he finally found himself, absent and extravagant, sitting with the child in a friendly silence. Only by this time he felt her flutter to have fortunately dropped and that she was more at her ease. She trusted him, liked him, and it was to come back to him afterwards that she had told him things. She had dipped into the waiting medium at last and found neither surge nor chill – nothing but the small splash she could herself make in the pleasant warmth, nothing but the safety of dipping and dipping again. At the end of the ten minutes he was to spend with her his impression – with all it had thrown off and all it had taken in – was complete. She had been free, as she knew freedom, partly to show him that, unlike other little persons she knew, she had imbibed that ideal. She was delightfully quaint about herself, but the vision of what she had imbibed was what most held him. It really consisted, he was soon enough to feel, in just one great little matter, the fact that, whatever her nature, she was thoroughly – he had to cast about for the word, but it came – bred. He couldn't of course on so short an acquaintance speak for her nature, but the idea of breeding was what she had meanwhile dropped into

his mind. He had never yet known it so sharply presented. Her mother gave it, no doubt; but her mother, to make that less sensible, gave so much else besides, and on neither of the two previous occasions, extraordinary woman, Strether felt, anything like what she was giving to-night. Little Jeanne was a case, an exquisite case of education; whereas the Countess, whom it so amused him to think of by that denomination, was a case, also exquisite, of – well, he didn't know what.

'He has wonderful taste, *notre jeune homme*': this was what Gloriani said to him on turning away from the inspection of a small picture suspended near the door of the room. The high celebrity in question had just come in, apparently in search of Mademoiselle de Vionnet, but while Strether had got up from beside her their fellow guest, with his eye sharply caught, had paused for a long look. The thing was a landscape, of no size, but of the French school, as our friend was glad to feel he knew, and also of a quality – which he liked to think he should also have guessed; its frame was large out of proportion to the canvas, and he had never seen a person look at anything, he thought, just as Gloriani, with his nose very near and quick movements of the head from side to side and bottom to top, examined this feature of Chad's collection. The artist used that word the next moment, smiling courteously, wiping his nippers and looking round him further – paying the place in short by the very manner of his presence and by something Strether fancied he could make out in this particular glance, such a tribute as, to the latter's sense, settled many things once for all. Strether was conscious at this instant, for that matter, as he hadn't yet been, of how, round about him, quite without him, they *were* consistently settled. Gloriani's smile, deeply Italian, he considered, and finely inscrutable, had had for him, during dinner, at which they were not neighbours, an indefinite greeting; but the quality in it was gone that had appeared on the other occasion to turn him inside out; it was as if even the momentary link supplied by the doubt between them had snapped. He was conscious now of the final reality, which was that there wasn't so much a doubt as a difference altogether; all the more that over the difference the famous sculptor seemed

to signal almost condolingly, yet oh how vacantly! as across
some great flat sheet of water. He threw out the bridge of a
charming hollow civility on which Strether wouldn't have
trusted his own full weight a moment. That idea, even though
but transient and perhaps belated, had performed the office of
putting Strether more at his ease, and the blurred picture had
already dropped – dropped with the sound of something else
said and with his becoming aware, by another quick turn, that
Gloriani was now on the sofa talking with Jeanne, while he
himself had in his ears again the familiar friendliness and
the elusive meaning of the 'Oh, oh, oh!' that had made him, a
fortnight before, challenge Miss Barrace in vain. She had always
the air, this picturesque and original lady, who struck him, so
oddly, as both antique and modern – she had always the air of
taking up some joke that one had already had out with her.
The point itself, no doubt, was what was antique, and the use
she made of it what was modern. He felt just now that her
good-natured irony did bear on something, and it troubled him
a little that she wouldn't be more explicit, only assuring him,
with the pleasure of observation so visible in her, that she
wouldn't tell him more for the world. He could take refuge but
in asking her what she had done with Waymarsh, though it
must be added that he felt himself a little on the way to a clue
after she had answered that this personage was, in the other
room, engaged in conversation with Madame de Vionnet. He
stared a moment at the image of such a conjunction; then, for
Miss Barrace's benefit, he wondered. 'Is she too then under the
charm – ?'

'No, not a bit' – Miss Barrace was prompt. 'She makes
nothing of him. She's bored. She won't help you with him.'

'Oh,' Strether laughed, 'she can't do everything.'

'Of course not – wonderful as she is. Besides, he makes
nothing of *her*. She won't take him from me – though she
wouldn't, no doubt, having other affairs in hand, even if she
could. I've never,' said Miss Barrace, 'seen her fail with any one
before. And to-night, when she's so magnificent, it would seem
to her strange – if she minded. So at any rate I have him all. *Je
suis tranquille!*'

Strether understood, so far as that went; but he was feeling for his clue. 'She strikes you to-night as particularly magnificent?'

'Surely. Almost as I've never seen her. Doesn't she you? Why it's *for* you.'

He persisted in his candour. ' "For" me – ?'

'Oh, oh, oh!' cried Miss Barrace, who persisted in the opposite of that quality.

'Well,' he acutely admitted, 'she *is* different. She's gay.'

'She's gay!' Miss Barrace laughed. 'And she has beautiful shoulders – though there's nothing different in that.'

'No,' said Strether, 'one was sure of her shoulders. It isn't her shoulders.'

His companion, with renewed mirth and the finest sense, between the puffs of her cigarette, of the drollery of things, appeared to find their conversation highly delightful. 'Yes, it isn't her shoulders.'

'What then is it?' Strether earnestly enquired.

'Why, it's *she* – simply. It's her mood. It's her charm.'

'Of course it's her charm, but we're speaking of the difference.'

'Well,' Miss Barrace explained, 'she's just brilliant, as we used to say. That's all. She's various. She's fifty women.'

'Ah but only one' – Strether kept it clear – 'at a time.'

'Perhaps. But in fifty times – !'

'Oh we shan't come to that,' our friend declared; and the next moment he had moved in another direction. 'Will you answer me a plain question? Will she ever divorce?'

Miss Barrace looked at him through all her tortoise-shell. 'Why should she?'

It wasn't what he had asked for, he signified; but he met it well enough. 'To marry Chad.'

'Why should she marry Chad?'

'Because I'm convinced she's very fond of him. She has done wonders for him.'

'Well then, how could she do more? Marrying a man, or a woman either,' Miss Barrace sagely went on, 'is never the wonder, for any Jack and Jill can bring *that* off. The wonder is their doing such things without marrying.'

Strether considered a moment this proposition. 'You mean it's so beautiful for our friends simply to go on so?'

But whatever he said made her laugh. 'Beautiful.'

He nevertheless insisted. 'And *that* because it's disinterested?'

She was now, however, suddenly tired of the question. 'Yes, then – call it that. Besides, she'll never divorce. Don't, moreover,' she added, 'believe everything you hear about her husband.'

'He's not then,' Strether asked, 'a wretch?'

'Oh yes. But charming.'

'Do you know him?'

'I've met him. He's *bien aimable*.'

'To every one but his wife?'

'Oh for all I know, to her too – to any, to every woman. I hope you at any rate,' she pursued with a quick change, 'appreciate the care I take of Mr. Waymarsh.'

'Oh immensely.' But Strether was not yet in line. 'At all events,' he roundly brought out, 'the attachment's an innocent one.'

'Mine and his? Ah,' she laughed, 'don't rob it of *all* interest!'

'I mean our friend's here – to the lady we've been speaking of.' That was what he had settled to as an indirect but none the less closely involved consequence of his impression of Jeanne. That was where he meant to stay. 'It's innocent,' he repeated – 'I see the whole thing.'

Mystified by his abrupt declaration, she had glanced over at Gloriani as at the unnamed subject of his allusion, but the next moment she had understood; though indeed not before Strether had noticed her momentary mistake and wondered what might possibly be behind that too. He already knew that the sculptor admired Madame de Vionnet; but did this admiration also represent an attachment of which the innocence was discussable? He was moving verily in a strange air and on ground not of the firmest. He looked hard for an instant at Miss Barrace, but she had already gone on. 'All right with Mr. Newsome? Why of course she is!' – and she got gaily back to the question of her own good friend. 'I dare say you're surprised that I'm not worn out with all I see – it being so much! – of

Sitting Bull.[1] But I'm not, you know – I don't mind him; I bear up, and we get on beautifully. I'm very strange; I'm like that; and often I can't explain. There are people who are supposed interesting or remarkable or whatever, and who bore me to death; and then there are others as to whom nobody can understand what anybody sees in them – in whom I see no end of things.' Then after she had smoked a moment, 'He's touching, you know,' she said.

'"Know"?' Strether echoed – 'don't I, indeed? We must move you almost to tears.'

'Oh but I don't mean *you*!' she laughed.

'You ought to then, for the worst sign of all – as I must have it for you – is that you can't help me. That's when a woman pities.'

'Ah but I do help you!' she cheerfully insisted.

Again he looked at her hard, and then after a pause: 'No you don't!'

Her tortoise-shell, on its long chain, rattled down. 'I help you with Sitting Bull. That's a good deal.'

'Oh that, yes.' But Strether hesitated. 'Do you mean he talks of me?'

'So that I have to defend you? No, never.'

'I see,' Strether mused. 'It's too deep.'

'That's his only fault,' she returned – 'that everything, with him, is too deep. He has depths of silence – which he breaks only at the longest intervals by a remark. And when the remark comes it's always something he has seen or felt for himself – never a bit banal. *That* would be what one might have feared and what would kill me. But never.' She smoked again as she thus, with amused complacency, appreciated her acquisition. 'And never about you. We keep clear of you. We're wonderful. But I'll tell you what he does do,' she continued: 'he tries to make me presents.'

'Presents?' poor Strether echoed, conscious with a pang that *he* hadn't yet tried that in any quarter.

'Why you see,' she explained, 'he's as fine as ever in the victoria;[2] so that when I leave him, as I often do almost for hours – he likes it so – at the doors of shops, the sight of him

there helps me, when I come out, to know my carriage away off in the rank. But sometimes, for a change, he goes with me into the shops, and then I've all I can do to prevent his buying me things.'

'He wants to "treat" you?' Strether almost gasped at all he himself hadn't thought of. He had a sense of admiration. 'Oh he's much more in the real tradition than I. Yes,' he mused; 'it's the sacred rage.'

'The sacred rage, exactly!' – and Miss Barrace, who hadn't before heard this term applied, recognized its bearing with a clap of her gemmed hands. 'Now I do know why he's not banal. But I do prevent him all the same – and if you saw what he sometimes selects – from buying. I save him hundreds and hundreds. I only take flowers.'

'Flowers?' Strether echoed again with a rueful reflexion. How many nosegays had her present converser sent?

'Innocent flowers,' she pursued, 'as much as he likes. And he sends me splendours; he knows all the best places – he has found them for himself; he's wonderful.'

'He hasn't told them to *me*,' her friend smiled; 'he has a life of his own.' But Strether had swung back to the consciousness that for himself after all it never would have done. Waymarsh hadn't Mrs. Waymarsh in the least to consider, whereas Lambert Strether had constantly, in the inmost honour of his thoughts, to consider Mrs. Newsome. He liked moreover to feel how much his friend was in the real tradition. Yet he had his conclusion. '*What* a rage it is!' He had worked it out. 'It's an opposition.'

She followed, but at a distance. 'That's what I feel. Yet to what?'

'Well, he thinks, you know, that *I've* a life of my own. And I haven't!'

'You haven't?' She showed doubt, and her laugh confirmed it. 'Oh, oh, oh!'

'No – not for myself. I seem to have a life only for other people.'

'Ah for them and *with* them! Just now for instance with –'

'Well, with whom?' he asked before she had had time to say.

His tone had the effect of making her hesitate and even, as he guessed, speak with a difference. 'Say with Miss Gostrey. What do you do for *her*?'

It really made him wonder. 'Nothing at all!'

III

Madame de Vionnet, having meanwhile come in, was at present
close to them, and Miss Barrace hereupon, instead of risking a
rejoinder, became again with a look that measured her from
top to toe all mere long-handled appreciative tortoise-shell. She
had struck our friend, from the first of her appearing, as dressed
for a great occasion, and she met still more than on either of
the others the conception reawakened in him at their garden-
party, the idea of the *femme du monde* in her habit as she lived.[1]
Her bare shoulders and arms were white and beautiful; the
materials of her dress, a mixture, as he supposed, of silk and
crape, were of a silvery grey so artfully composed as to give an
impression of warm splendour; and round her neck she wore a
collar of large old emeralds, the green note of which was more
dimly repeated, at other points of her apparel, in embroidery,
in enamel, in satin, in substances and textures vaguely rich. Her
head, extremely fair and exquisitely festal, was like a happy
fancy, a notion of the antique, on an old precious medal, some
silver coin of the Renaissance; while her slim lightness and
brightness, her gaiety, her expression, her decision, contributed
to an effect that might have been felt by a poet as half mythological and half conventional. He could have compared her to
a goddess still partly engaged in a morning cloud, or to a
sea-nymph waist-high in the summer surge. Above all she suggested to him the reflexion that the *femme du monde* – in these
finest developments of the type – was, like Cleopatra in the
play,[2] indeed various and multifold. She had aspects, characters,
days, nights – or had them at least, showed them by a mysterious law of her own, when in addition to everything she

happened also to be a woman of genius. She was an obscure person, a muffled person one day, and a showy person, an uncovered person the next. He thought of Madame de Vionnet to-night as showy and uncovered, though he felt the formula rough, because, thanks to one of the short-cuts of genius, she had taken all his categories by surprise. Twice during dinner he had met Chad's eyes in a longish look; but these communications had in truth only stirred up again old ambiguities – so little was it clear from them whether they were an appeal or an admonition. 'You see how I'm fixed', was what they appeared to convey; yet how he was fixed was exactly what Strether didn't see. However, perhaps he should see now.

'Are you capable of the very great kindness of going to relieve Newsome, for a few minutes, of the rather crushing responsibility of Madame Gloriani, while I say a word, if he'll allow me, to Mr. Strether, of whom I've a question to ask? Our host ought to talk a bit to those other ladies, and I'll come back in a minute to your rescue.' She made this proposal to Miss Barrace as if her consciousness of a special duty had just flickered up, but that lady's recognition of Strether's little start at it – as at a betrayal on the speaker's part of a domesticated state – was as mute as his own comment; and after an instant, when their fellow guest had good-naturedly left them, he had been given something else to think of. 'Why has Maria so suddenly gone? Do you know?' That was the question Madame de Vionnet had brought with her.

'I'm afraid I've no reason to give you but the simple reason I've had from her in a note – the sudden obligation to join in the south a sick friend who has got worse.'

'Ah then she has been writing you?'

'Not since she went – I had only a brief explanatory word before she started. I went to see her,' Strether explained – 'it was the day after I called on you – but she was already on her way, and her concierge told me that in case of my coming I was to be informed she had written to me. I found her note when I got home.'

Madame de Vionnet listened with interest and with her eyes on Strether's face; then her delicately decorated head had a

small melancholy motion. 'She didn't write to *me*. I went to see her,' she added, 'almost immediately after I had seen you, and as I assured her I would do when I met her at Gloriani's. She hadn't then told me she was to be absent, and I felt at her door as if I understood. She's absent – with all respect to her sick friend, though I know indeed she has plenty – so that I may not see her. She doesn't want to meet me again. Well,' she continued with a beautiful conscious mildness, 'I liked and admired her beyond every one in the old time, and she knew it – perhaps that's precisely what has made her go – and I dare say I haven't lost her for ever.' Strether still said nothing; he had a horror, as he now thought of himself, of being in question between women – was in fact already quite enough on his way to that; and there was moreover, as it came to him, perceptibly, something behind these allusions and professions that, should he take it in, would square but ill with his present resolve to simplify. It was as if, for him, all the same, her softness and sadness were sincere. He felt that not less when she soon went on: 'I'm extremely glad of her happiness.' But it also left him mute – sharp and fine though the imputation it conveyed. What it conveyed was that *he* was Maria Gostrey's happiness, and for the least little instant he had the impulse to challenge the thought. He could have done so however only by saying 'What then do you suppose to be between us?' and he was wonderfully glad a moment later not to have spoken. He would rather seem stupid any day than fatuous, and he drew back as well, with a smothered inward shudder, from the consideration of what women – of highly-developed type in particular – might think of each other. Whatever he had come out for he hadn't come to go into that; so that he absolutely took up nothing his interlocutress had now let drop. Yet, though he had kept away from her for days, had laid wholly on herself the burden of their meeting again, she hadn't a gleam of irritation to show him. 'Well, about Jeanne now?' she smiled – it had the gaiety with which she had originally come in. He felt it on the instant to represent her motive and real errand. But he had been schooling her of a truth to say much in proportion to his little. '*Do* you make out that she has a sentiment? I mean for Mr. Newsome.'

Almost resentful, Strether could at last be prompt. 'How can I make out such things?'

She remained perfectly good-natured. 'Ah but they're beautiful little things, and you make out – don't pretend! – everything in the world. Haven't you,' she asked, 'been talking with her?'

'Yes, but not about Chad. At least not much.'

'Oh you don't require "much"!' she reassuringly declared. But she immediately changed her ground. 'I hope you remember your promise of the other day.'

'To "save" you, as you called it?'

'I call it so still. You *will*?' she insisted. 'You haven't repented?'

He wondered. 'No – but I've been thinking what I meant.'

She kept it up. 'And not, a little, what *I* did?'

'No – that's not necessary. It will be enough if I know what I meant myself.'

'And don't you know,' she asked, 'by this time?'

Again he had a pause. 'I think you ought to leave it to me. But how long,' he added, 'do you give me?'

'It seems to me much more a question of how long you give *me*. Doesn't our friend here himself, at any rate,' she went on, 'perpetually make me present to you?'

'Not,' Strether replied, 'by ever speaking of you to me.'

'He never does that?'

'Never.'

She considered, and, if the fact was disconcerting to her, effectually concealed it. The next minute indeed she had recovered. 'No, he wouldn't. But do you *need* that?'

Her emphasis was wonderful, and though his eyes had been wandering he looked at her longer now. 'I see what you mean.'

'Of course you see what I mean.'

Her triumph was gentle, and she really had tones to make justice weep. 'I've before me what he owes you.'

'Admit then that that's something,' she said, yet still with the same discretion in her pride.

He took in this note but went straight on. 'You've made of him what I see, but what I don't see is how in the world you've done it.'

'Ah that's another question!' she smiled. 'The point is of what use is your declining to know me when to know Mr. Newsome – as you do me the honour to find him – *is* just to know me.'

'I see,' he mused, still with his eyes on her. 'I shouldn't have met you to-night.'

She raised and dropped her linked hands. 'It doesn't matter. If I trust you why can't you a little trust me too? And why can't you also,' she asked in another tone, 'trust yourself?' But she gave him no time to reply. 'Oh I shall be so easy for you! And I'm glad at any rate you've seen my child.'

'I'm glad too,' he said; 'but she does you no good.'

'No good?' – Madame de Vionnet had a clear stare. 'Why she's an angel of light.'

'That's precisely the reason. Leave her alone. Don't try to find out. I mean,' he explained, 'about what you spoke to me of – the way she feels.'

His companion wondered. 'Because one really won't?'

'Well, because I ask you, as a favour to myself, not to. She's the most charming creature I've ever seen. Therefore don't touch her. Don't know – don't want to know. And moreover – yes – you *won't*.'

It was an appeal, of a sudden, and she took it in. 'As a favour to you?'

'Well – since you ask me.'

'Anything, everything you ask,' she smiled. 'I shan't know then – never. Thank you,' she added with peculiar gentleness as she turned away.

The sound of it lingered with him, making him fairly feel as if he had been tripped up and had a fall. In the very act of arranging with her for his independence he had, under pressure from a particular perception, inconsistently, quite stupidly, committed himself, and, with her subtlety sensitive on the spot to an advantage, she had driven in by a single word a little golden nail, the sharp intention of which he signally felt. He hadn't detached, he had more closely connected himself, and his eyes, as he considered with some intensity this circumstance, met another pair which had just come within their range and

which struck him as reflecting his sense of what he had done. He recognized them at the same moment as those of little Bilham, who had apparently drawn near on purpose to speak to him, and little Bilham wasn't, in the conditions, the person to whom his heart would be most closed. They were seated together a minute later at the angle of the room obliquely opposite the corner in which Gloriani was still engaged with Jeanne de Vionnet, to whom at first and in silence their attention had been benevolently given. 'I can't see for my life,' Strether had then observed, 'how a young fellow of any spirit – such a one as you for instance – can be admitted to the sight of that young lady without being hard hit. Why don't you go in, little Bilham?' He remembered the tone into which he had been betrayed on the garden-bench at the sculptor's reception, and this might make up for that by being much more the right sort of thing to say to a young man worthy of any advice at all. 'There *would* be some reason.'

'Some reason for what?'

'Why for hanging on here.'

'To offer my hand and fortune to Mademoiselle de Vionnet?'

'Well,' Strether asked, 'to what lovelier apparition *could* you offer them? She's the sweetest little thing I've ever seen.'

'She's certainly immense. I mean she's the real thing. I believe the pale pink petals are folded up there for some wondrous efflorescence in time; to open, that is, to some great golden sun. *I'm* unfortunately but a small farthing candle. What chance in such a field for a poor little painter-man?'

'Oh you're good enough,' Strether threw out.

'Certainly I'm good enough. We're good enough, I consider, *nous autres*, for anything. But she's *too* good. There's the difference. They wouldn't look at me.'

Strether, lounging on his divan and still charmed by the young girl, whose eyes had consciously strayed to him, he fancied, with a vague smile – Strether, enjoying the whole occasion as with dormant pulses at last awake and in spite of new material thrust upon him, thought over his companion's words. 'Whom do you mean by "they"? She and her mother?'

'She and her mother. And she has a father too, who, whatever

else he may be, certainly can't be indifferent to the possibilities she represents. Besides, there's Chad.'

Strether was silent a little. 'Ah but he doesn't care for her – not, I mean, it appears, after all, in the sense I'm speaking of. He's *not* in love with her.'

'No – but he's her best friend; after her mother. He's very fond of her. He has his ideas about what can be done for her.'

'Well, it's very strange!' Strether presently remarked with a sighing sense of fulness.

'Very strange indeed. That's just the beauty of it. Isn't it very much the kind of beauty you had in mind,' little Bilham went on, 'when you were so wonderful and so inspiring to me the other day? Didn't you adjure me, in accents I shall never forget, to see, while I've a chance, everything I can? – and *really* to see, for it must have been that only you meant. Well, you did me no end of good, and I'm doing my best. I *do* make it out a situation.'

'So do I!' Strether went on after a moment. But he had the next minute an inconsequent question. 'How comes Chad so mixed up, anyway?'

'Ah, ah, ah!' – and little Bilham fell back on his cushions.

It reminded our friend of Miss Barrace, and he felt again the brush of his sense of moving in a maze of mystic closed allusions. Yet he kept hold of his thread. 'Of course I understand really; only the general transformation makes me occasionally gasp. Chad with such a voice in the settlement of the future of a little countess – no,' he declared, 'it takes more time! You say moreover,' he resumed, 'that we're inevitably, people like you and me, out of the running. The curious fact remains that Chad himself isn't. The situation doesn't make for it, but in a different one he could have her if he would.'

'Yes, but that's only because he's rich and because there's a possibility of his being richer. They won't think of anything but a great name or a great fortune.'

'Well,' said Strether, 'he'll have no great fortune on *these* lines. He must stir his stumps.'

'Is that,' little Bilham enquired, 'what you were saying to Madame de Vionnet?'

'No – I don't say much to her. Of course, however,' Strether continued, 'he can make sacrifices if he likes.'

Little Bilham had a pause. 'Oh he's not keen for sacrifices; or thinks, that is, possibly, that he has made enough.'

'Well, it *is* virtuous,' his companion observed with some decision.

'That's exactly,' the young man dropped after a moment, 'what I mean.'

It kept Strether himself silent a little. 'I've made it out for myself,' he then went on; 'I've really, within the last half-hour, got hold of it. I understand it in short at last; which at first – when you originally spoke to me – I didn't. Nor when Chad originally spoke to me either.'

'Oh,' said little Bilham, 'I don't think that at that time you believed me.'

'Yes – I did; and I believed Chad too. It would have been odious and unmannerly – as well as quite perverse – if I hadn't. What interest have you in deceiving me?'

The young man cast about. 'What interest have *I*?'

'Yes. Chad *might* have. But you?'

'Ah, ah, ah!' little Bilham exclaimed.

It might, on repetition, as a mystification, have irritated our friend a little; but he knew, once more, as we have seen, where he was, and his being proof against everything was only another attestation that he meant to stay there. 'I couldn't, without my own impression, realize. She's a tremendously clever brilliant capable woman, and with an extraordinary charm on top of it all – the charm we surely all of us this evening know what to think of. It isn't every clever brilliant capable woman that has it. In fact it's rare with any woman. So there you are,' Strether proceeded as if not for little Bilham's benefit alone. 'I understand what a relation with such a woman – what such a high fine friendship – may be. It can't be vulgar or coarse, anyway – and that's the point.'

'Yes, that's the point,' said little Bilham. 'It can't be vulgar or coarse. And, bless us and save us, it *isn't*! It's, upon my word, the very finest thing I ever saw in my life, and the most distinguished.'

Strether, from beside him and leaning back with him as he leaned, dropped on him a momentary look which filled a short interval and of which he took no notice. He only gazed before him with intent participation. 'Of course what it has done for him,' Strether at all events presently pursued, 'of course what it has done for him – that is as to *how* it has so wonderfully worked – isn't a thing I pretend to understand. I've to take it as I find it. There he is.'

'There he is!' little Bilham echoed. 'And it's really and truly she. I don't understand either, even with my longer and closer opportunity. But I'm like you,' he added; 'I can admire and rejoice even when I'm a little in the dark. You see I've watched it for some three years, and especially for this last. He wasn't so bad before it as I seem to have made out that you think –'

'Oh I don't think anything now!' Strether impatiently broke in: 'that is but what I *do* think! I mean that originally, for her to have cared for him –'

'There must have been stuff in him? Oh yes, there was stuff indeed, and much more of it than ever showed, I dare say, at home. Still, you know,' the young man in all fairness developed, 'there was room for her, and that's where she came in. She saw her chance and took it. That's what strikes me as having been so fine. But of course,' he wound up, 'he liked her first.'

'Naturally,' said Strether.

'I mean that they first met somehow and somewhere – I believe in some American house – and she, without in the least then intending it, made her impression. Then with time and opportunity he made his; and after *that* she was as bad as he.'

Strether vaguely took it up. 'As "bad"?'

'She began, that is, to care – to care very much. Alone, and in her horrid position, she found it, when once she had started, an interest. It was, it is, an interest; and it did – it continues to do – a lot for herself as well. So she still cares. She cares in fact,' said little Bilham thoughtfully, 'more.'

Strether's theory that it was none of his business was somehow not damaged by the way he took this. 'More, you mean, than he?' On which his companion looked round at him, and now for an instant their eyes met. 'More than he?' he repeated.

Little Bilham, for as long, hung fire. 'Will you never tell any one?'

Strether thought. 'Whom should I tell?'

'Why I supposed you reported regularly –'

'To people at home?' – Strether took him up. 'Well, I won't tell them this.'

The young man at last looked away. 'Then she does now care more than he.'

'Oh!' Strether oddly exclaimed.

But his companion immediately met it. 'Haven't you after all had your impression of it? That's how you've got hold of him.'

'Ah but I haven't got hold of him!'

'Oh I say!' But it was all little Bilham said.

'It's at any rate none of my business. I mean,' Strether explained, 'nothing else than getting hold of him is.' It appeared, however, to strike him as his business to add: 'The fact remains nevertheless that she has saved him.'

Little Bilham just waited. 'I thought that was what *you* were to do.'

But Strether had his answer ready. 'I'm speaking – in connexion with her – of his manners and morals, his character and life. I'm speaking of him as a person to deal with and talk with and live with – speaking of him as a social animal.'

'And isn't it as a social animal that you also want him?'

'Certainly; so that it's as if she had saved him *for* us.'

'It strikes you accordingly then,' the young man threw out, 'as for you all to save *her*?'

'Oh for us "all" – !' Strether could but laugh at that. It brought him back, however, to the point he had really wished to make. 'They've accepted their situation – hard as it is. They're not free – at least she's not; but they take what's left to them. It's a friendship, of a beautiful sort; and that's what makes them so strong. They're straight, they feel; and they keep each other up. It's doubtless she, however, who, as you yourself have hinted, feels it most.'

Little Bilham appeared to wonder what he had hinted. 'Feels most that they're straight?'

'Well, feels that *she* is, and the strength that comes from it. She keeps *him* up – she keeps the whole thing up. When people are able to it's fine. She's wonderful, wonderful, as Miss Barrace says; and he is, in his way, too; however, as a mere man, he may sometimes rebel and not feel that he finds his account in it. She has simply given him an immense moral lift, and what that can explain is prodigious. That's why I speak of it as a situation. It *is* one, if there ever was.' And Strether, with his head back and his eyes on the ceiling, seemed to lose himself in the vision of it.

His companion attended deeply. 'You state it much better than I could.'

'Oh you see it doesn't concern you.'

Little Bilham considered. 'I thought you said just now that it doesn't concern you either.'

'Well, it doesn't a bit as Madame de Vionnet's affair. But as we were again saying just now, what did I come out for but to save him?'

'Yes – to remove him.'

'To save him *by* removal; to win him over to *himself* thinking it best he shall take up business – thinking he must immediately do therefore what's necessary to that end.'

'Well,' said little Bilham after a moment, 'you *have* won him over. He does think it best. He has within a day or two again said to me as much.'

'And that,' Strether asked, 'is why you consider that he cares less than she?'

'Cares less for her than she for him? Yes, that's one of the reasons. But other things too have given me the impression. A man, don't you think?' little Bilham presently pursued, '*can't*, in such conditions, care so much as a woman. It takes different conditions to make him, and then perhaps he cares more. Chad,' he wound up, 'has his possible future before him.'

'Are you speaking of his business future?'

'No – on the contrary; of the other, the future of what you so justly call their situation. M. de Vionnet may live for ever.'

'So that they can't marry?'

The young man waited a moment. 'Not being able to marry

is all they've with any confidence to look forward to. A woman
– a particular woman – may stand that strain. But can a man?'
he propounded.

Strether's answer was as prompt as if he had already, for
himself, worked it out. 'Not without a very high ideal of conduct. But that's just what we're attributing to Chad. And how,
for that matter,' he mused, 'does his going to America diminish
the particular strain? Wouldn't it seem rather to add to it?'

'Out of sight out of mind!' his companion laughed. Then
more bravely: 'Wouldn't distance lessen the torment?' But
before Strether could reply, 'The thing is, you see, Chad ought
to marry!' he wound up.

Strether, for a little, appeared to think of it. 'If you talk of
torments you don't diminish mine!' he then broke out. The
next moment he was on his feet with a question. 'He ought to
marry whom?'

Little Bilham rose more slowly. 'Well, some one he *can* –
some thoroughly nice girl.'

Strether's eyes, as they stood together, turned again to Jeanne.
'Do you mean *her*?'

His friend made a sudden strange face. 'After being in love
with her mother? No.'

'But isn't it exactly your idea that he *isn't* in love with her
mother?'

His friend once more had a pause. 'Well, he isn't at any rate
in love with Jeanne.'

'I dare say not.'

'How *can* he be with any other woman?'

'Oh that I admit. But being in love isn't, you know, here' –
little Bilham spoke in friendly reminder – 'thought necessary,
in strictness, for marriage.'

'And what torment – to call a torment – can there ever
possibly be with a woman like that?' As if from the interest of
his own question Strether had gone on without hearing. 'Is it
for her to have turned a man out so wonderfully, too, only for
somebody else?' He appeared to make a point of this, and little
Bilham looked at him now. 'When it's for each other that people
give things up they don't miss them.' Then he threw off as with

an extravagance of which he was conscious: 'Let them face the future together!'

Little Bilham looked at him indeed. 'You mean that after all he shouldn't go back?'

'I mean that if he gives her up –!'

'Yes?'

'Well, he ought to be ashamed of himself.' But Strether spoke with a sound that might have passed for a laugh.

BOOK SEVENTH

I

It wasn't the first time Strether had sat alone in the great dim church – still less was it the first of his giving himself up, so far as conditions permitted, to its beneficent action on his nerves. He had been to Notre Dame[1] with Waymarsh, he had been there with Miss Gostrey, he had been there with Chad Newsome, and had found the place, even in company, such a refuge from the obsession of his problem that, with renewed pressure from that source, he had not unnaturally recurred to a remedy meeting the case, for the moment, so indirectly, no doubt, but so relievingly. He was conscious enough that it was only for the moment, but good moments – if he could call them good – still had their value for a man who by this time struck himself as living almost disgracefully from hand to mouth. Having so well learnt the way, he had lately made the pilgrimage more than once by himself – had quite stolen off, taking an unnoticed chance and making no point of speaking of the adventure when restored to his friends.

His great friend, for that matter, was still absent, as well as remarkably silent; even at the end of three weeks Miss Gostrey hadn't come back. She wrote to him from Mentone,[2] admitting that he must judge her grossly inconsequent – perhaps in fact for the time odiously faithless; but asking for patience, for a deferred sentence, throwing herself in short on his generosity. For her too, she could assure him, life was complicated – more complicated than he could have guessed; she had moreover made certain of him – certain of not wholly missing him on her return – before her disappearance. If furthermore she didn't burden him with letters it was frankly because of her sense of

the other great commerce he had to carry on. He himself, at the end of a fortnight, had written twice, to show how his generosity could be trusted; but he reminded himself in each case of Mrs. Newsome's epistolary manner at the times when Mrs. Newsome kept off delicate ground. He sank his problem, he talked of Waymarsh and Miss Barrace, of little Bilham and the set over the river, with whom he had again had tea, and he was easy, for convenience, about Chad and Madame de Vionnet and Jeanne. He admitted that he continued to see them, he was decidedly so confirmed a haunter of Chad's premises and that young man's practical intimacy with them was so undeniably great; but he had his reason for not attempting to render for Miss Gostrey's benefit the impression of these last days. That would be to tell her too much about himself – it being at present just from himself he was trying to escape.

This small struggle sprang not a little, in its way, from the same impulse that had now carried him across to Notre Dame; the impulse to let things be, to give them time to justify themselves or at least to pass. He was aware of having no errand in such a place but the desire not to be, for the hour, in certain other places; a sense of safety, of simplification, which each time he yielded to it he amused himself by thinking of as a private concession to cowardice. The great church had no altar for his worship, no direct voice for his soul; but it was none the less soothing even to sanctity; for he could feel while there what he couldn't elsewhere, that he was a plain tired man taking the holiday he had earned. He was tired, but he wasn't plain – that was the pity and the trouble of it; he was able, however, to drop his problem at the door very much as if it had been the copper piece that he deposited, on the threshold, in the receptacle of the inveterate blind beggar. He trod the long dim nave, sat in the splendid choir, paused before the clustered chapels of the east end, and the mighty monument laid upon him its spell. He might have been a student under the charm of a museum – which was exactly what, in a foreign town, in the afternoon of life, he would have liked to be free to be. This form of sacrifice did at any rate for the occasion as well as another; it made him quite sufficiently understand how, within the precinct, for the

real refugee, the things of the world could fall into abeyance.
That was the cowardice, probably – to dodge them, to beg the
question, not to deal with it in the hard outer light; but his own
oblivions were too brief, too vain, to hurt any one but himself,
and he had a vague and fanciful kindness for certain persons
whom he met, figures of mystery and anxiety, and whom, with
observation for his pastime, he ranked as those who were fleeing
from justice. Justice was outside, in the hard light, and injustice
too; but one was as absent as the other from the air of the long
aisles and the brightness of the many altars.

Thus it was at all events that, one morning some dozen
days after the dinner in the Boulevard Malesherbes at which
Madame de Vionnet had been present with her daughter, he
was called upon to play his part in an encounter that deeply
stirred his imagination. He had the habit, in these contem-
plations, of watching a fellow visitant, here and there, from a
respectable distance, remarking some note of behaviour, of
penitence, of prostration, of the absolved, relieved state; this
was the manner in which his vague tenderness took its course,
the degree of demonstration to which it naturally had to confine
itself. It hadn't indeed so felt its responsibility as when on this
occasion he suddenly measured the suggestive effect of a lady
whose supreme stillness, in the shade of one of the chapels, he
had two or three times noticed as he made, and made once
more, his slow circuit. She wasn't prostrate – not in any degree
bowed, but she was strangely fixed, and her prolonged immobility showed her, while he passed and paused, as wholly given
up to the need, whatever it was, that had brought her there.
She only sat and gazed before her, as he himself often sat; but
she had placed herself, as he never did, within the focus of the
shrine, and she had lost herself, he could easily see, as he would
only have liked to do. She was not a wandering alien, keeping
back more than she gave, but one of the familiar, the intimate,
the fortunate, for whom these dealings had a method and a
meaning. She reminded our friend – since it was the way of nine
tenths of his current impressions to act as recalls of things
imagined – of some fine firm concentrated heroine of an old
story, something he had heard, read, something that, had he

had a hand for drama, he might himself have written, renewing her courage, renewing her clearness, in splendidly-protected meditation. Her back, as she sat, was turned to him, but his impression absolutely required that she should be young and interesting, and she carried her head moreover, even in the sacred shade, with a discernible faith in herself, a kind of implied conviction of consistency, security, impunity. But what had such a woman come for if she hadn't come to pray? Strether's reading of such matters was, it must be owned, confused; but he wondered if her attitude were some congruous fruit of absolution, of 'indulgence'. He knew but dimly what indulgence, in such a place, might mean; yet he had, as with a soft sweep, a vision of how it might indeed add to the zest of active rites. All this was a good deal to have been denoted by a mere lurking figure who was nothing to him; but, the last thing before leaving the church, he had the surprise of a still deeper quickening.

He had dropped upon a seat halfway down the nave and, again in the museum mood, was trying with head thrown back and eyes aloft, to reconstitute a past, to reduce it in fact to the convenient terms of Victor Hugo,[3] whom, a few days before, giving the rein for once in a way to the joy of life, he had purchased in seventy bound volumes, a miracle of cheapness, parted with, he was assured by the shopman, at the price of the red-and-gold alone. He looked, doubtless, while he played his eternal nippers over Gothic glooms, sufficiently rapt in reverence; but what his thought had finally bumped against was the question of where, among packed accumulations, so multiform a wedge would be able to enter. Were seventy volumes in red-and-gold to be perhaps what he should most substantially have to show at Woollett as the fruit of his mission? It was a possibility that held him a minute – held him till he happened to feel that some one, unnoticed, had approached him and paused. Turning, he saw that a lady stood there as for a greeting, and he sprang up as he next took her, securely, for Madame de Vionnet, who appeared to have recognized him as she passed near him on her way to the door. She checked, quickly and gaily, a certain confusion in him, came to meet it, turned it

back, by an art of her own; the confusion having threatened him as he knew her for the person he had lately been observing. She was the lurking figure of the dim chapel; she had occupied him more than she guessed; but it came to him in time, luckily, that he needn't tell her and that no harm, after all, had been done. She herself, for that matter, straightway showing she felt their encounter as the happiest of accidents, had for him a 'You come here too?' that despoiled surprise of every awkwardness.

'I come often,' she said. 'I love this place, but I'm terrible, in general, for churches. The old women who live in them all know me; in fact I'm already myself one of the old women. It's like that, at all events, that I foresee I shall end.' Looking about for a chair, so that he instantly pulled one nearer, she sat down with him again to the sound of an 'Oh, I like so much your also being fond –!'

He confessed the extent of his feeling, though she left the object vague; and he was struck with the tact, the taste of her vagueness, which simply took for granted in him a sense of beautiful things. He was conscious of how much it was affected, this sense, by something subdued and discreet in the way she had arranged herself for her special object and her morning walk – he believed her to have come on foot; the way her slightly thicker veil was drawn – a mere touch, but everything; the composed gravity of her dress, in which, here and there, a dull wine-colour seemed to gleam faintly through black; the charming discretion of her small compact head; the quiet note, as she sat, of her folded, grey-gloved hands. It was, to Strether's mind, as if she sat on her own ground, the light honours of which, at an open gate, she thus easily did him, while all the vastness and mystery of the domain stretched off behind. When people were so completely in possession they could be extra-ordinarily civil; and our friend had indeed at this hour a kind of revelation of her heritage. She was romantic for him far beyond what she could have guessed, and again he found his small comfort in the conviction that, subtle though she was, his impression must remain a secret from her. The thing that, once more, made him uneasy for secrets in general was this particular patience she could have with his own want of colour; albeit

that on the other hand his uneasiness pretty well dropped after
he had been for ten minutes as colourless as possible and at the
same time as responsive.

The moments had already, for that matter, drawn their deepest tinge from the special interest excited in him by his vision
of his companion's identity with the person whose attitude
before the glimmering altar had so impressed him. This attitude
fitted admirably into the stand he had privately taken about her
connexion with Chad on the last occasion of his seeing them
together. It helped him to stick fast at the point he had then
reached; it was there he had resolved that he *would* stick, and
at no moment since had it seemed as easy to do so. Unassailably
innocent was a relation that could make one of the parties to it
so carry herself. If it wasn't innocent why did she haunt the
churches? – into which, given the woman he could believe he
made out, she would never have come to flaunt an insolence of
guilt. She haunted them for continued help, for strength, for
peace – sublime support which, if one were able to look at it
so, she found from day to day. They talked, in low easy tones
and with lifted lingering looks, about the great monument and
its history and its beauty – all of which, Madame de Vionnet
professed, came to her most in the other, the outer view. 'We'll
presently, after we go,' she said, 'walk round it again if you
like. I'm not in a particular hurry, and it will be pleasant to
look at it well with you.' He had spoken of the great romancer
and the great romance,[4] and of what, to his imagination, they
had done for the whole, mentioning to her moreover the exorbi-
tance of his purchase, the seventy blazing volumes that were so
out of proportion.

'Out of proportion to what?'

'Well, to any other plunge.' Yet he felt even as he spoke how
at that instant he was plunging. He had made up his mind and
was impatient to get into the air; for his purpose was a purpose
to be uttered outside, and he had a fear that it might with delay
still slip away from him. She however took her time; she drew
out their quiet gossip as if she had wished to profit by their
meeting, and this confirmed precisely an interpretation of her
manner, of her mystery. While she rose, as he would have called

it, to the question of Victor Hugo, her voice itself, the light low
quaver of her deference to the solemnity about them, seemed
to make her words mean something that they didn't mean
openly. Help, strength, peace, a sublime support – she hadn't
found so much of these things as that the amount wouldn't be
sensibly greater for any scrap his appearance of faith in her
might enable her to feel in her hand. Every little, in a long
strain, helped, and if he happened to affect her as a firm object
she could hold on by, he wouldn't jerk himself out of her reach.
People in difficulties held on by what was nearest, and he was
perhaps after all not further off than sources of comfort more
abstract. It was as to this he had made up his mind; he had
made it up, that is, to give her a sign. The sign would be that –
though it was her own affair – he understood; the sign would
be that – though it was her own affair – she was free to clutch.
Since she took him for a firm object – much as he might to his
own sense appear at times to rock – he would do his best to
be one.

The end of it was that half an hour later they were seated
together for an early luncheon at a wonderful, a delightful
house of entertainment on the left bank[5] – a place of pilgrimage
for the knowing, they were both aware, the knowing who came,
for its great renown, the homage of restless days, from the other
end of the town. Strether had already been there three times –
first with Miss Gostrey, then with Chad, then with Chad again
and with Waymarsh and little Bilham, all of whom he had
himself sagaciously entertained; and his pleasure was deep now
on learning that Madame de Vionnet hadn't yet been initiated.
When he had said, as they strolled round the church, by the
river, acting at last on what, within, he had made up his mind
to, 'Will you, if you have time, come to déjeuner with me
somewhere? For instance, if you know it, over there on the
other side, which is so easy a walk' – and then had named the
place; when he had done this she stopped short as for quick
intensity, and yet deep difficulty, of response. She took in the
proposal as if it were almost too charming to be true; and there
had perhaps never yet been for her companion so unexpected
a moment of pride – so fine, so odd a case, at any rate, as his

finding himself thus able to offer to a person in such universal possession a new, a rare amusement. She had heard of the happy spot, but she asked him in reply to a further question how in the world he could suppose her to have been there. He supposed himself to have supposed that Chad might have taken her, and she guessed this the next moment, to his no small discomfort.

'Ah, let me explain,' she smiled, 'that I don't go about with him in public; I never have such chances – not having them otherwise – and it's just the sort of thing that, as a quiet creature living in my hole, I adore.' It was more than kind of him to have thought of it – though, frankly, if he asked whether she had time she hadn't a single minute. That however made no difference – she'd throw everything over. Every duty at home, domestic, maternal, social, awaited her; but it was a case for a high line. Her affairs would go to smash, but hadn't one a right to one's snatch of scandal when one was prepared to pay? It was on this pleasant basis of costly disorder, consequently, that they eventually seated themselves, on either side of a small table, at a window adjusted to the busy quay and the shining barge-burdened Seine; where, for an hour, in the matter of letting himself go, of diving deep, Strether was to feel he had touched bottom. He was to feel many things on this occasion, and one of the first of them was that he had travelled far since that evening in London, before the theatre, when his dinner with Maria Gostrey, between the pink-shaded candles, had struck him as requiring so many explanations. He had at that time gathered them in, the explanations – he had stored them up; but it was at present as if he had either soared above or sunk below them – he couldn't tell which; he could somehow think of none that didn't seem to leave the appearance of collapse and cynicism easier for him than lucidity. How could he wish it to be lucid for others, for any one, that he, for the hour, saw reasons enough in the mere way the bright clean ordered water-side life came in at the open window? – the mere way Madame de Vionnet, opposite him over their intensely white table-linen, their *omelette aux tomates*, their bottle of straw-coloured Chablis, thanked him for everything almost

with the smile of a child, while her grey eyes moved in and out of their talk, back to the quarter of the warm spring air, in which early summer had already begun to throb, and then back again to his face and their human questions.

Their human questions became many before they had done – many more, as one after the other came up, than our friend's free fancy had at all foreseen. The sense he had had before, the sense he had had repeatedly, the sense that the situation was running away with him, had never been so sharp as now; and all the more that he could perfectly put his finger on the moment it had taken the bit in its teeth. That accident had definitely occurred, the other evening, after Chad's dinner; it had occurred, as he fully knew, at the moment when he interposed between this lady and her child, when he suffered himself so to discuss with her a matter closely concerning them that her own subtlety, marked by its significant 'Thank you!' instantly sealed the occasion in her favour. Again he had held off for ten days, but the situation had continued out of hand in spite of that; the fact that it was running so fast being indeed just *why* he had held off. What had come over him as he recognized her in the nave of the church was that holding off could be but a losing game from the instant she was worked for not only by her subtlety, but by the hand of fate itself. If all the accidents were to fight on her side – and by the actual showing they loomed large – he could only give himself up. This was what he had done in privately deciding then and there to propose she should breakfast with him. What did the success of his proposal in fact resemble but the smash in which a regular runaway properly ends? The smash was their walk, their déjeuner, their omelette, the Chablis, the place, the view, their present talk and his present pleasure in it – to say nothing, wonder of wonders, of her own. To this tune and nothing less, accordingly, was his surrender made good. It sufficiently lighted up at least the folly of holding off. Ancient proverbs sounded, for his memory, in the tone of their words and the clink of their glasses, in the hum of the town and the plash of the river. It *was* clearly better to suffer as a sheep than as a lamb.[6] One might as well perish by the sword as by famine.

'Maria's still away?' – that was the first thing she had asked him; and when he had found the frankness to be cheerful about it in spite of the meaning he knew her to attach to Miss Gostrey's absence, she had gone on to enquire if he didn't tremendously miss her. There were reasons that made him by no means sure, yet he nevertheless answered 'Tremendously'; which she took in as if it were all she had wished to prove. Then, 'A man in trouble *must* be possessed somehow of a woman,' she said; 'if she doesn't come in one way she comes in another.'

'Why do you call me a man in trouble?'

'Ah because that's the way you strike me.' She spoke ever so gently and as if with all fear of wounding him while she sat partaking of his bounty. '*Aren't* you in trouble?'

He felt himself colour at the question, and then hated that – hated to pass for anything so idiotic as woundable. Woundable by Chad's lady, in respect to whom he had come out with such a fund of indifference – was he already at that point? Perversely, none the less, his pause gave a strange air of truth to her supposition; and what was he in fact but disconcerted at having struck her just in the way he had most dreamed of not doing? 'I'm not in trouble yet,' he at last smiled. 'I'm not in trouble now.'

'Well, I'm always so. But that you sufficiently know.' She was a woman who, between courses, could be graceful with her elbows on the table. It was a posture unknown to Mrs. Newsome, but it was easy for a *femme du monde*. 'Yes – I am "now"!'

'There was a question you put to me,' he presently returned, 'the night of Chad's dinner. I didn't answer it then, and it has been very handsome of you not to have sought an occasion for pressing me about it since.'

She was instantly all there. 'Of course I know what you allude to. I asked you what you had meant by saying, the day you came to see me, just before you left me, that you'd save me. And you then said – at our friend's – that you'd have really to wait to see, for yourself, what you did mean.'

'Yes, I asked for time,' said Strether. 'And it sounds now, as you put it, like a very ridiculous speech.'

'Oh!' she murmured – she was full of attenuation. But she had another thought. 'If it does sound ridiculous why do you deny that you're in trouble?'

'Ah if I were,' he replied, 'it wouldn't be the trouble of fearing ridicule. I don't fear it.'

'What then do you?'

'Nothing – now.' And he leaned back in his chair.

'I like your "now"!' she laughed across at him.

'Well, it's precisely that it fully comes to me at present that I've kept you long enough. I know by this time, at any rate, what I meant by my speech; and I really knew it the night of Chad's dinner.'

'Then why didn't you tell me?'

'Because it was difficult at the moment. I had already at that moment done something for you, in the sense of what I had said the day I went to see you; but I wasn't then sure of the importance I might represent this as having.'

She was all eagerness. 'And you're sure now?'

'Yes; I see that, practically, I've done for you – had done for you when you put me your question – all that it's as yet possible to me to do. I feel now,' he went on, 'that it may go further than I thought. What I did after my visit to you,' he explained, 'was to write straight off to Mrs. Newsome about you, and I'm at last, from one day to the other, expecting her answer. It's this answer that will represent, as I believe, the consequences.'

Patient and beautiful was her interest. 'I see – the consequences of your speaking for me.' And she waited as if not to hustle him.

He acknowledged it by immediately going on. 'The question, you understand, was *how* I should save you. Well, I'm trying it by thus letting her know that I consider you worth saving.'

'I see – I see.' Her eagerness broke through.

'How can I thank you enough?' He couldn't tell her that, however, and she quickly pursued. 'You do really, for yourself, consider it?'

His only answer at first was to help her to the dish that had been freshly put before them. 'I've written to her again since then – I've left her in no doubt of what I think. I've told her all about you.'

'Thanks – not so much. "All about" me,' she went on – 'yes.'

'All it seems to me you've done for him.'

'Ah and you might have added all it seems to *me*!' She laughed again, while she took up her knife and fork, as in the cheer of these assurances. 'But you're not sure how she'll take it.'

'No, I'll not pretend I'm sure.'

'Voilà.' And she waited a moment. 'I wish you'd tell me about her.'

'Oh,' said Strether with a slightly strained smile, 'all that need concern you about her is that she's really a grand person.'

Madame de Vionnet seemed to demur. 'Is that all that need concern me about her?'

But Strether neglected the question. 'Hasn't Chad talked to you?'

'Of his mother? Yes, a great deal – immensely. But not from your point of view.'

'He can't,' our friend returned, 'have said any ill of her.'

'Not the least bit. He has given me, like you, the assurance that she's really grand. But her being really grand is somehow just what hasn't seemed to simplify our case. Nothing,' she continued, 'is further from me than to wish to say a word against her; but of course I feel how little she can like being told of her owing me anything. No woman ever enjoys such an obligation to another woman.'

This was a proposition Strether couldn't contradict. 'And yet what other way could I have expressed to her what I felt? It's what there was most to say about you.'

'Do you mean then that she *will* be good to me?'

'It's what I'm waiting to see. But I've little doubt she would,' he added, 'if she could comfortably see you.'

It seemed to strike her as a happy, a beneficent thought. 'Oh then couldn't that be managed? Wouldn't she come out? Wouldn't she if you so put it to her? *Did* you by any possibility?' she faintly quavered.

'Oh no' – he was prompt. 'Not that. It would be, much more, to give an account of you that – since there's no question of *your* paying the visit – I should go home first.'

It instantly made her graver. 'And are you thinking of that?'

'Oh all the while, naturally.'

'Stay with us – stay with us!' she exclaimed on this. 'That's your only way to make sure.'

'To make sure of what?'

'Why that he doesn't break up. You didn't come out to do that to him.'

'Doesn't it depend,' Strether returned after a moment, 'on what you mean by breaking up?'

'Oh you know well enough what I mean!'

His silence seemed again for a little to denote an understanding. 'You take for granted remarkable things.'

'Yes, I do – to the extent that I don't take for granted vulgar ones. You're perfectly capable of seeing that what you came out for wasn't really at all to do what you'd now have to do.'

'Ah it's perfectly simple,' Strether good-humouredly pleaded. 'I've had but one thing to do – to put our case before him. To put it as it could only be put here on the spot – by personal pressure. My dear lady,' he lucidly pursued, 'my work, you see, is really done, and my reasons for staying on even another day are none of the best. Chad's in possession of our case and professes to do it full justice. What remains is with himself. I've had my rest, my amusement and refreshment; I've had, as we say at Woollett, a lovely time. Nothing in it has been more lovely than this happy meeting with you – in these fantastic conditions to which you've so delightfully consented. I've a sense of success. It's what I wanted. My getting all this good is what Chad has waited for, and I gather that if I'm ready to go he's the same.'

She shook her head with a finer deeper wisdom. 'You're not ready. If you're ready why did you write to Mrs. Newsome in the sense you've mentioned to me?'

Strether considered. 'I shan't go before I hear from her. You're too much afraid of her,' he added.

It produced between them a long look from which neither

shrank. 'I don't think you believe that – believe I've not really reason to fear her.'

'She's capable of great generosity,' Strether presently stated.

'Well then let her trust me a little. That's all I ask. Let her recognize in spite of everything what I've done.'

'Ah remember,' our friend replied, 'that she can't effectually recognize it without seeing it for herself. Let Chad go over and show her what you've done, and let him plead with her there for it and, as it were, for *you*.'

She measured the depth of this suggestion. 'Do you give me your word of honour that if she once has him there she won't do her best to marry him?'

It made her companion, this enquiry, look again a while out at the view; after which he spoke without sharpness. 'When she sees for herself what he is –'

But she had already broken in. 'It's when she sees for herself what he is that she'll want to marry him most.'

Strether's attitude, that of due deference to what she said, permitted him to attend for a minute to his luncheon. 'I doubt if that will come off. It won't be easy to make it.'

'It will be easy if he remains there – and he'll remain for the money. The money appears to be, as a probability, so hideously much.'

'Well,' Strether presently concluded, 'nothing *could* really hurt you but his marrying.'

She gave a strange light laugh. 'Putting aside what may really hurt *him*.'

But her friend looked at her as if he had thought of that too. 'The question will come up, of course, of the future that you yourself offer him.'

She was leaning back now, but she fully faced him. 'Well, let it come up!'

'The point is that it's for Chad to make of it what he can. His being proof against marriage will show what he does make.'

'If he *is* proof, yes' – she accepted the proposition. 'But for myself,' she added, 'the question is what *you* make.'

'Ah I make nothing. It's not my affair.'

'I beg your pardon. It's just there that, since you've taken it

up and are committed to it, it most intensely becomes yours. You're not saving me, I take it, for your interest in myself, but for your interest in our friend. The one's at any rate wholly dependent on the other. You can't in honour not see me through,' she wound up, 'because you can't in honour not see *him*.'

Strange and beautiful to him was her quiet soft acuteness. The thing that most moved him was really that she was so deeply serious. She had none of the portentous forms of it, but he had never come in contact, it struck him, with a force brought to so fine a head. Mrs. Newsome, goodness knew, was serious; but it was nothing to this. He took it all in, he saw it all together. 'No,' he mused, 'I can't in honour not see him.'

Her face affected him as with an exquisite light. 'You *will* then?'

'I will.'

At this she pushed back her chair and was the next moment on her feet. 'Thank you!' she said with her hand held out to him across the table and with no less a meaning in the words than her lips had so particularly given them after Chad's dinner. The golden nail she had then driven in pierced a good inch deeper. Yet he reflected that he himself had only meanwhile done what he had made up his mind to on the same occasion. So far as the essence of the matter went he had simply stood fast on the spot on which he had then planted his feet.

II

He received three days after this a communication from America, in the form of a scrap of blue paper folded and gummed, not reaching him through his bankers, but delivered at his hotel by a small boy in uniform, who, under instructions from the concierge, approached him as he slowly paced the little court. It was the evening hour, but daylight was long now and Paris more than ever penetrating. The scent of flowers was in the streets, he had the whiff of violets perpetually in his nose; and he had attached himself to sounds and suggestions, vibrations of the air, human and dramatic, he imagined, as they were not in other places, that came out for him more and more as the mild afternoons deepened – a far-off hum, a sharp near click on the asphalt, a voice calling, replying, somewhere and as full of tone as an actor's in a play. He was to dine at home, as usual, with Waymarsh – they had settled to that for thrift and simplicity; and he now hung about before his friend came down.

He read his telegram in the court, standing still a long time where he had opened it and giving five minutes afterwards to the renewed study of it. At last, quickly, he crumpled it up as if to get it out of the way; in spite of which, however, he kept it there – still kept it when, at the end of another turn, he had dropped into a chair placed near a small table. Here, with his scrap of paper compressed in his fist and further concealed by his folding his arms tight, he sat for some time in thought, gazed before him so straight that Waymarsh appeared and approached him without catching his eye. The latter in fact, struck with his appearance, looked at him hard for a single

instant and then, as if determined to that course by some special vividness in it, dropped back into the *salon de lecture* without addressing him. But the pilgrim from Milrose permitted himself still to observe the scene from behind the clear glass plate of that retreat. Strether ended, as he sat, by a fresh scrutiny of his compressed missive, which he smoothed out carefully again as he placed it on his table. There it remained for some minutes, until, at last looking up, he saw Waymarsh watching him from within. It was on this that their eyes met – met for a moment during which neither moved. But Strether then got up, folding his telegram more carefully and putting it into his waistcoat pocket.

A few minutes later the friends were seated together at dinner; but Strether had meanwhile said nothing about it, and they eventually parted, after coffee in the court, with nothing said on either side. Our friend had moreover the consciousness that even less than usual was on this occasion said between them, so that it was almost as if each had been waiting for something from the other. Waymarsh had always more or less the air of sitting at the door of his tent,[1] and silence, after so many weeks, had come to play its part in their concert. This note indeed, to Strether's sense, had lately taken a fuller tone, and it was his fancy to-night that they had never quite so drawn it out. Yet it befell, none the less, that he closed the door to confidence when his companion finally asked him if there were anything particular the matter with him. 'Nothing,' he replied, 'more than usual.'

On the morrow, however, at an early hour, he found occasion to give an answer more in consonance with the facts. What was the matter had continued to be so all the previous evening, the first hours of which, after dinner, in his room, he had devoted to the copious composition of a letter. He had quitted Waymarsh for this purpose, leaving him to his own resources with less ceremony than their wont, but finally coming down again with his letter unconcluded and going forth into the streets without enquiry for his comrade. He had taken a long vague walk, and one o'clock had struck before his return and his re-ascent to his room by the aid of the glimmering candle-end

left for him on the shelf outside the porter's lodge. He had possessed himself, on closing his door, of the numerous loose sheets of his unfinished composition, and then, without reading them over, had torn them into small pieces. He had thereupon slept – as if it had been in some measure thanks to that sacrifice – the sleep of the just, and had prolonged his rest considerably beyond his custom. Thus it was that when, between nine and ten, the tap of the knob of a walking-stick sounded on his door, he had not yet made himself altogether presentable. Chad Newsome's bright deep voice determined quickly enough none the less the admission of the visitor. The little blue paper of the evening before, plainly an object the more precious for its escape from premature destruction, now lay on the sill of the open window, smoothed out afresh and kept from blowing away by the superincumbent weight of his watch. Chad, looking about with careless and competent criticism, as he looked wherever he went, immediately espied it and permitted himself to fix it for a moment rather hard. After which he turned his eyes to his host. 'It has come then at last?'

Strether paused in the act of pinning his necktie. 'Then you know –? You've had one too?'

'No, I've had nothing, and I only know what I see. I see that thing and I guess. Well,' he added, 'it comes as pat as in a play, for I've precisely turned up this morning – as I would have done yesterday, but it was impossible – to take you.'

'To take me?' Strether had turned again to his glass.

'Back, at last, as I promised. I'm ready – I've really been ready this month. I've only been waiting for you – as was perfectly right. But you're better now; you're safe – I see that for myself; you've got all your good. You're looking, this morning, as fit as a flea.'

Strether, at his glass, finished dressing; consulting that witness moreover on this last opinion. *Was* he looking preternaturally fit? There was something in it perhaps for Chad's wonderful eye, but he had felt himself for hours rather in pieces. Such a judgement, however, was after all but a contribution to his resolve; it testified unwittingly to his wisdom. He was still firmer, apparently – since it shone in him as a light – than he

had flattered himself. His firmness indeed was slightly compromised, as he faced about to his friend, by the way this very
personage looked – though the case would of course have been
worse hadn't the secret of personal magnificence been at every
hour Chad's unfailing possession. There he was in all the pleasant morning freshness of it – strong and sleek and gay, easy
and fragrant and fathomless, with happy health in his colour,
and pleasant silver in his thick young hair, and the right word
for everything on the lips that his clear brownness caused to
show as red. He had never struck Strether as personally such a
success; it was as if now, for his definite surrender, he had
gathered himself vividly together. This, sharply and rather
strangely, was the form in which he was to be presented to
Woollett. Our friend took him in again – he was always taking
him in and yet finding that parts of him still remained out;
though even thus his image showed through a mist of other
things. 'I've had a cable,' Strether said, 'from your mother.'

'I dare say, my dear man. I hope she's well.'

Strether hesitated. 'No – she's not well, I'm sorry to have to
tell you.'

'Ah,' said Chad, 'I must have had the instinct of it. All the
more reason then that we should start straight off.'

Strether had now got together hat, gloves and stick, but Chad
had dropped on the sofa as if to show where he wished to make
his point. He kept observing his companion's things; he might
have been judging how quickly they could be packed. He might
even have wished to hint that he'd send his own servant to
assist. 'What do you mean,' Strether enquired, 'by "straight
off"?'

'Oh by one of next week's boats. Everything at this season
goes out so light that berths will be easy anywhere.'

Strether had in his hand his telegram, which he had kept
there after attaching his watch, and he now offered it to Chad,
who, however, with an odd movement, declined to take it.
'Thanks, I'd rather not. Your correspondence with Mother's
your own affair. I'm only *with* you both on it, whatever it is.'
Strether, at this, while their eyes met, slowly folded the missive
and put it in his pocket; after which, before he had spoken

again, Chad broke fresh ground. 'Has Miss Gostrey come back?'

But when Strether presently spoke it wasn't in answer. 'It's not, I gather, that your mother's physically ill; her health, on the whole, this spring, seems to have been better than usual. But she's worried, she's anxious, and it appears to have risen within the last few days to a climax. We've tired out, between us, her patience.'

'Oh it isn't *you*!' Chad generously protested.

'I beg your pardon – it *is* me.' Strether was mild and melancholy, but firm. He saw it far away and over his companion's head. 'It's very particularly me.'

'Well then all the more reason. *Marchons, marchons*!'[2] said the young man gaily. His host, however, at this, but continued to stand agaze; and he had the next thing repeated his question of a moment before. 'Has Miss Gostrey come back?'

'Yes, two days ago.'

'Then you've seen her?'

'No – I'm to see her to-day.' But Strether wouldn't linger now on Miss Gostrey. 'Your mother sends me an ultimatum. If I can't bring you I'm to leave you; I'm to come at any rate myself.'

'Ah but you *can* bring me now,' Chad, from his sofa, reassuringly replied.

Strether had a pause. 'I don't think I understand you. Why was it that, more than a month ago, you put it to me so urgently to let Madame de Vionnet speak for you?'

'"Why"?' Chad considered, but he had it at his fingers' ends. 'Why but because I knew how well she'd do it? It was the way to keep you quiet and, to that extent, do you good. Besides,' he happily and comfortably explained, 'I wanted you really to know her and to get the impression of her – and you see the good that *has* done you.'

'Well,' said Strether, 'the way she has spoken for you, all the same – so far as I've given her a chance – has only made me feel how much she wishes to keep you. If you make nothing of that I don't see why you wanted me to listen to her.'

'Why my dear man,' Chad exclaimed, 'I make everything of it! How can you doubt –?'

'I doubt only because you come to me this morning with your signal to start.'

Chad stared, then gave a laugh. 'And isn't my signal to start just what you've been waiting for?'

Strether debated; he took another turn. 'This last month I've been awaiting, I think, more than anything else, the message I have here.'

'You mean you've been afraid of it?'

'Well, I was doing my business in my own way. And I suppose your present announcement,' Strether went on, 'isn't merely the result of your sense of what I've expected. Otherwise you wouldn't have put me in relation –' But he paused, pulling up.

At this Chad rose. 'Ah *her* wanting me not to go has nothing to do with it! It's only because she's afraid – afraid of the way that, over there, I may get caught. But her fear's groundless.'

He had met again his companion's sufficiently searching look. 'Are you tired of her?'

Chad gave him in reply to this, with a movement of the head, the strangest slow smile he had ever had from him. 'Never.'

It had immediately, on Strether's imagination, so deep and soft an effect that our friend could only for the moment keep it before him. 'Never?'

'Never,' Chad obligingly and serenely repeated.

It made his companion take several more steps. 'Then *you're* not afraid.'

'Afraid to go?'

Strether pulled up again. 'Afraid to stay.'

The young man looked brightly amazed. 'You want me now to "stay"?'

'If I don't immediately sail the Pococks will immediately come out. That's what I mean,' said Strether, 'by your mother's ultimatum.'

Chad showed a still livelier, but not an alarmed interest. 'She has turned on Sarah and Jim?'

Strether joined him for an instant in the vision. 'Oh and you may be sure Mamie. *That's* whom she's turning on.'

This also Chad saw – he laughed out. 'Mamie – to corrupt me?'

'Ah,' said Strether, 'she's very charming.'

'So you've already more than once told me. I should like to see her.'

Something happy and easy, something above all unconscious, in the way he said this, brought home again to his companion the facility of his attitude and the enviability of his state. 'See her then by all means. And consider too,' Strether went on, 'that you really give your sister a lift in letting her come to you. You give her a couple of months of Paris, which she hasn't seen, if I'm not mistaken, since just after she was married, and which I'm sure she wants but the pretext to visit.'

Chad listened, but with all his own knowledge of the world. 'She has had it, the pretext, these several years, yet she has never taken it.'

'Do you mean *you*?' Strether after an instant enquired.

'Certainly – the lone exile. And whom do you mean?' said Chad.

'Oh I mean *me*. I'm her pretext. That is – for it comes to the same thing – I'm your mother's.'

'Then why,' Chad asked, 'doesn't Mother come herself?'

His friend gave him a long look. 'Should you like her to?' And as he for the moment said nothing: 'It's perfectly open to you to cable for her.'

Chad continued to think. 'Will she come if I do?'

'Quite possibly. But try, and you'll see.'

'Why don't *you* try?' Chad after a moment asked.

'Because I don't want to.'

Chad thought. 'Don't desire her presence here?'

Strether faced the question, and his answer was the more emphatic. 'Don't put it off, my dear boy, on *me*!'

'Well – I see what you mean. I'm sure you'd behave beautifully, but you *don't* want to see her. So I won't play you that trick.'

'Ah,' Strether declared, 'I shouldn't call it a trick. You've a perfect right, and it would be perfectly straight of you.' Then he added in a different tone: 'You'd have moreover, in the person of Madame de Vionnet, a very interesting relation prepared for her.'

Their eyes, on this proposition, continued to meet, but

Chad's, pleasant and bold, never flinched for a moment. He got up at last, and he said something with which Strether was struck. 'She wouldn't understand her, but that makes no difference. Madame de Vionnet would like to see her. She'd like to be charming to her. She believes she could work it.'

Strether thought a moment, affected by this, but finally turning away. 'She couldn't!'

'You're quite sure?' Chad asked.

'Well, risk it if you like!'

Strether, who uttered this with serenity, had urged a plea for their now getting into the air; but the young man still waited. 'Have you sent your answer?'

'No, I've done nothing yet.'

'Were you waiting to see me?'

'No, not that.'

'Only waiting' – and Chad, with this, had a smile for him – 'to see Miss Gostrey?'

'No – not even Miss Gostrey. I wasn't waiting to see anyone. I had only waited, till now, to make up my mind – in complete solitude; and, since I of course absolutely owe you the information, was on the point of going out with it quite made up. Have therefore a little more patience with me. Remember,' Strether went on, 'that that's what you originally asked *me* to have. I've had it, you see, and you see what has come of it. Stay on with me.'

Chad looked grave. 'How much longer?'

'Well, till I make you a sign. I can't myself, you know, at the best, or at the worst, stay for ever. Let the Pococks come,' Strether repeated.

'Because it gains you time?'

'Yes – it gains me time.'

Chad, as if it still puzzled him, waited a minute. 'You don't want to get back to Mother?'

'Not just yet. I'm not ready.'

'You feel,' Chad asked in a tone of his own, 'the charm of life over here?'

'Immensely.' Strether faced it. 'You've helped me so to feel it that that surely needn't surprise you.'

'No, it doesn't surprise me, and I'm delighted. But what, my dear man,' Chad went on with conscious queerness, 'does it all lead to for you?'

The change of position and of relation, for each, was so oddly betrayed in the question that Chad laughed out as soon as he had uttered it – which made Strether also laugh. 'Well, to my having a certitude that has been tested – that has passed through the fire. But oh,' he couldn't help breaking out, 'if within my first month here you had been willing to move with me –!'

'Well?' said Chad, while he broke down as for weight of thought.

'Well, we should have been over there by now.'

'Ah but you wouldn't have had your fun!'

'I should have had a month of it; and I'm having now, if you want to know,' Strether continued, 'enough to last me for the rest of my days.'

Chad looked amused and interested, yet still somewhat in the dark; partly perhaps because Strether's estimate of fun had required of him from the first a good deal of elucidation. 'It wouldn't do if I left you –?'

'Left me?' – Strether remained blank.

'Only for a month or two – time to go and come. Madame de Vionnet,' Chad smiled, 'would look after you in the interval.'

'To go back by yourself, I remaining here?' Again for an instant their eyes had the question out; after which Strether said: 'Grotesque!'

'But I want to see Mother,' Chad presently returned. 'Remember how long it is since I've seen Mother.'

'Long indeed; and that's exactly why I was originally so keen for moving you. Hadn't you shown us enough how beautifully you could do without it?'

'Oh but,' said Chad wonderfully, 'I'm better now.'

There was an easy triumph in it that made his friend laugh out again. 'Oh if you were worse I *should* know what to do with you. In that case I believe I'd have you gagged and strapped down, carried on board resisting, kicking. How *much*,' Strether asked, 'do you want to see Mother?'

'How much?' – Chad seemed to find it in fact difficult to say.

'How much.'

'Why as much as you've made me. I'd give anything to see her. And you've left me,' Chad went on, 'in little enough doubt as to how much *she* wants it.'

Strether thought a minute. 'Well then if those things are really your motive catch the French steamer and sail to-morrow. Of course, when it comes to that, you're absolutely free to do as you choose. From the moment you can't hold yourself I can only accept your flight.'

'I'll fly in a minute then,' said Chad, 'if you'll stay here.'

'I'll stay here till the next steamer – then I'll follow you.'

'And do you call that,' Chad asked, 'accepting my flight?'

'Certainly – it's the only thing to call it. The only way to keep me here, accordingly,' Strether explained, 'is by staying yourself.'

Chad took it in. 'All the more that I've really dished[3] you, eh?'

'Dished me?' Strether echoed as inexpressively as possible.

'Why if she sends out the Pococks it will be that she doesn't trust you, and if she doesn't trust you, that bears upon – well, you know what.'

Strether decided after a moment that he did know what, and in consonance with this he spoke. 'You see then all the more what you owe me.'

'Well, if I do see, how can I pay?'

'By not deserting me. By standing by me.'

'Oh I say –!' But Chad, as they went downstairs, clapped a firm hand, in the manner of a pledge, upon his shoulder. They descended slowly together and had, in the court of the hotel, some further talk, of which the upshot was that they presently separated. Chad Newsome departed, and Strether, left alone, looked about, superficially, for Waymarsh. But Waymarsh hadn't yet, it appeared, come down, and our friend finally went forth without sight of him.

III

At four o'clock that afternoon he had still not seen him, but he was then, as to make up for this, engaged in talk about him with Miss Gostrey. Strether had kept away from home all day, given himself up to the town and to his thoughts, wandered and mused, been at once restless and absorbed – and all with the present climax of a rich little welcome in the Quartier Marboeuf. 'Waymarsh has been, "unbeknown" to me, I'm convinced' – for Miss Gostrey had enquired – 'in communication with Woollett: the consequence of which was, last night, the loudest possible call for me.'

'Do you mean a letter to bring you home?'

'No – a cable, which I have at this moment in my pocket: a "Come back by the first ship."'

Strether's hostess, it might have been made out, just escaped changing colour. Reflexion arrived but in time and established a provisional serenity. It was perhaps exactly this that enabled her to say with duplicity: 'And you're going –?'

'You almost deserve it when you abandon me so.'

She shook her head as if this were not worth taking up. 'My absence has helped you – as I've only to look at you to see. It was my calculation, and I'm justified. You're not where you were. And the thing,' she smiled, 'was for me not to be there either. You can go of yourself.'

'Oh but I feel to-day,' he comfortably declared, 'that I shall want you yet.'

She took him all in again. 'Well, I promise you not again to leave you, but it will only be to follow you. You've got your momentum and can toddle alone.'

He intelligently accepted it. 'Yes – I suppose I can toddle. It's the sight of that in fact that has upset Waymarsh. He can bear it – the way I strike him as going – no longer. That's only the climax of his original feeling. He wants me to quit; and he must have written to Woollett that I'm in peril of perdition.'

'Ah good!' she murmured. 'But is it only your supposition?'

'I make it out – it explains.'

'Then he denies? – or you haven't asked him?'

'I've not had time,' Strether said; 'I made it out but last night, putting various things together, and I've not been since then face to face with him.'

She wondered. 'Because you're too disgusted? You can't trust yourself?'

He settled his glasses on his nose. 'Do I look in a great rage?'

'You look divine!'

'There's nothing,' he went on, 'to be angry about. He has done me on the contrary a service.'

She made it out. 'By bringing things to a head?'

'How well you understand!' he almost groaned. 'Waymarsh won't in the least, at any rate, when I have it out with him, deny or extenuate. He has acted from the deepest conviction, with the best conscience and after wakeful nights. He'll recognize that he's fully responsible, and will consider that he has been highly successful; so that any discussion we may have will bring us quite together again – bridge the dark stream that has kept us so thoroughly apart. We shall have at last, in the consequences of his act, something we can definitely talk about.'

She was silent a little. 'How wonderfully you take it! But you're always wonderful.'

He had a pause that matched her own; then he had, with an adequate spirit, a complete admission. 'It's quite true. I'm extremely wonderful just now. I dare say in fact I'm quite fantastic, and I shouldn't be at all surprised if I were mad.'

'Then tell me!' she earnestly pressed. As he, however, for the time answered nothing, only returning the look with which she watched him, she presented herself where it was easier to meet her. 'What will Mr. Waymarsh exactly have done?'

'Simply have written a letter. One will have been quite enough. He has told them I want looking after.'

'And *do* you?' – she was all interest.

'Immensely. And I shall get it.'

'By which you mean you don't budge?'

'I don't budge.'

'You've cabled?'

'No – I've made Chad do it.'

'That you decline to come?'

'That *he* declines. We had it out this morning and I brought him round. He had come in, before I was down, to tell me he was ready – ready, I mean, to return. And he went off, after ten minutes with me, to say he wouldn't.'

Miss Gostrey followed with intensity. 'Then you've *stopped* him?'

Strether settled himself afresh in his chair. 'I've stopped him. That is for the time. That' – he gave it to her more vividly – 'is where I am.'

'I see, I see. But where's Mr. Newsome? He was ready,' she asked, 'to go?'

'All ready.'

'And sincerely – believing *you'd* be?'

'Perfectly, I think; so that he was amazed to find the hand I had laid on him to pull him over suddenly converted into an engine for keeping him still.'

It was an account of the matter Miss Gostrey could weigh. 'Does he think the conversion sudden?'

'Well,' said Strether, 'I'm not altogether sure what he thinks. I'm not sure of anything that concerns him, except that the more I've seen of him the less I've found him what I originally expected. He's obscure, and that's why I'm waiting.'

She wondered. 'But for what in particular?'

'For the answer to his cable.'

'And what was his cable?'

'I don't know,' Strether replied; 'it was to be, when he left me, according to his own taste. I simply said to him: "I want to stay, and the only way for me to do so is for *you* to." That I wanted to stay seemed to interest him, and he acted on that.'

Miss Gostrey turned it over. 'He wants then himself to stay.'

'He half wants it. That is he half wants to go. My original appeal has to that extent worked in him. Nevertheless,' Strether pursued, 'he won't go. Not, at least, so long as I'm here.'

'But you can't,' his companion suggested, 'stay here always. I wish you could.'

'By no means. Still, I want to see him a little further. He's not in the least the case I supposed; he's quite another case. And it's as such that he interests me.' It was almost as if for his own intelligence that, deliberate and lucid, our friend thus expressed the matter. 'I don't want to give him up.'

Miss Gostrey but desired to help his lucidity. She had however to be light and tactful. 'Up, you mean – a – to his mother?'

'Well, I'm not thinking of his mother now. I'm thinking of the plan of which I was the mouthpiece, which, as soon as we met, I put before him as persuasively as I knew how, and which was drawn up, as it were, in complete ignorance of all that, in this last long period, has been happening to him. It took no account whatever of the impression I was here on the spot immediately to begin to receive from him – impressions of which I feel sure I'm far from having had the last.'

Miss Gostrey had a smile of the most genial criticism. 'So your idea is – more or less – to stay out of curiosity?'

'Call it what you like! I don't care what it's called –'

'So long as you do stay? Certainly not then. I call it, all the same, immense fun,' Maria Gostrey declared; 'and to see you work it out will be one of the sensations of my life. It *is* clear you can toddle alone!'

He received this tribute without elation. 'I shan't be alone when the Pococks have come.'

Her eyebrows went up. 'The Pococks are coming?'

'That, I mean, is what will happen – and happen as quickly as possible – in consequence of Chad's cable. They'll simply embark. Sarah will come to speak for her mother – with an effect different from *my* muddle.'

Miss Gostrey more gravely wondered. '*She* then will take him back?'

'Very possibly – and we shall see. She must at any rate have the chance, and she may be trusted to do all she can.'

'And do you *want* that?'

'Of course,' said Strether, 'I want it. I want to play fair.'

But she had lost for a moment the thread. 'If it devolves on the Pococks why do you stay?'

'Just to see that I *do* play fair – and a little also, no doubt, that they do.' Strether was luminous as he had never been. 'I came out to find myself in presence of new facts – facts that have kept striking me as less and less met by our old reasons. The matter's perfectly simple. New reasons – reasons as new as the facts themselves – are wanted; and of this our friends at Woollett – Chad's and mine – were at the earliest moment definitely notified. If any are producible Mrs. Pocock will produce them; she'll bring over the whole collection. They'll be,' he added with a pensive smile, 'a part of the "fun" you speak of.'

She was quite in the current now and floating by his side. 'It's Mamie – so far as I've had it from you – who'll be their great card.' And then as his contemplative silence wasn't a denial she significantly added: 'I think I'm sorry for her.'

'I think *I* am!' – and Strether sprang up, moving about a little as her eyes followed him. 'But it can't be helped.'

'You mean her coming out can't be?'

He explained after another turn what he meant. 'The only way for her not to come is for me to go home – as I believe that on the spot I could prevent it. But the difficulty as to that is that if I do go home –'

'I see, I see' – she had easily understood. 'Mr. Newsome will do the same, and that's not' – she laughed out now – 'to be thought of.'

Strether had no laugh; he had only a quiet comparatively placid look that might have shown him as proof against ridicule. 'Strange, isn't it?'

They had, in the matter that so much interested them, come so far as this without sounding another name – to which however their present momentary silence was full of a conscious reference. Strether's question was a sufficient implication of the weight it had gained with him during the absence of his hostess;

and just for that reason a single gesture from her could pass for him as a vivid answer. Yet he was answered still better when she said in a moment: 'Will Mr. Newsome introduce his sister –?'

'To Madame de Vionnet?' Strether spoke the name at last. 'I shall be greatly surprised if he doesn't.'

She seemed to gaze at the possibility. 'You mean you've thought of it and you're prepared.'

'I've thought of it and I'm prepared.'

It was to her visitor now that she applied her consideration. 'Bon! You *are* magnificent!'

'Well,' he answered after a pause and a little wearily, but still standing there before her – 'well, that's what, just once in all my dull days, I think I shall like to have been!'

Two days later he had news from Chad of a communication from Woollett in response to their determinant telegram, this missive being addressed to Chad himself and announcing the immediate departure for France of Sarah and Jim and Mamie. Strether had meanwhile on his own side cabled; he had but delayed that act till after his visit to Miss Gostrey, an interview by which, as so often before, he felt his sense of things cleared up and settled. His message to Mrs. Newsome, in answer to her own, had consisted of the words: 'Judge best to take another month, but with full appreciation of all re-enforcements.' He had added that he was writing, but he was of course always writing; it was a practice that continued, oddly enough, to relieve him, to make him come nearer than anything else to the consciousness of doing something: so that he often wondered if he hadn't really, under his recent stress, acquired some hollow trick, one of the specious arts of make-believe. Wouldn't the pages he still so freely dispatched by the American post have been worthy of a showy journalist, some master of the great new science of beating the sense out of words? Wasn't he writing against time, and mainly to show he was kind? – since it had become quite his habit not to like to read himself over. On those lines he could still be liberal, yet it was at best a sort of whistling in the dark. It was unmistakeable moreover that the sense of being in the dark now pressed on him more sharply – creating thereby the need for a louder and livelier whistle. He

whistled long and hard after sending his message; he whistled
again and again in celebration of Chad's news; there was an
interval of a fortnight in which this exercise helped him. He
had no great notion of what, on the spot, Sarah Pocock would
have to say, though he had indeed confused premonitions; but
it shouldn't be in her power to say – it shouldn't be in anyone's
anywhere to say – that he was neglecting her mother. He might
have written before more freely, but he had never written more
copiously; and he frankly gave for a reason at Woollett that he
wished to fill the void created there by Sarah's departure.

The increase of his darkness, however, and the quickening,
as I have called it, of his tune, resided in the fact that he was
hearing almost nothing. He had for some time been aware
that he was hearing less than before, and he was now clearly
following a process by which Mrs. Newsome's letters could but
logically stop. He hadn't had a line for many days, and he
needed no proof – though he was, in time, to have plenty – that
she wouldn't have put pen to paper after receiving the hint
that had determined her telegram. She wouldn't write till Sarah
should have seen him and reported on him. It was strange,
though it might well be less so than his own behaviour appeared
at Woollett. It was at any rate significant, and what *was* remarkable was the way his friend's nature and manner put on for him,
through this very drop of demonstration, a greater intensity. It
struck him really that he had never so lived with her as during
this period of her silence; the silence was a sacred hush, a finer
clearer medium, in which her idiosyncrasies showed. He walked
about with her, sat with her, drove with her and dined face-to-
face with her – a rare treat 'in his life', as he could perhaps have
scarce escaped phrasing it; and if he had never seen her so
soundless he had never, on the other hand, felt her so highly,
so almost austerely, herself: pure and by the vulgar estimate
'cold', but deep devoted delicate sensitive noble. Her vividness
in these respects became for him, in the special conditions,
almost an obsession; and though the obsession sharpened his
pulses, adding really to the excitement of life, there were hours
at which, to be less on the stretch, he directly sought forgetful-
ness. He knew it for the queerest of adventures – a circumstance

capable of playing such a part only for Lambert Strether – that in Paris itself, of all places, he should find this ghost of the lady of Woollett more importunate than any other presence.

When he went back to Maria Gostrey it was for the change to something else. And yet after all the change scarcely operated, for he talked to her of Mrs. Newsome in these days as he had never talked before. He had hitherto observed in that particular a discretion and a law; considerations that at present broke down quite as if relations had altered. They hadn't *really* altered, he said to himself, so much as that came to; for if what had occurred was of course that Mrs. Newsome had ceased to trust him, there was nothing on the other hand to prove that he shouldn't win back her confidence. It was quite his present theory that he would leave no stone unturned to do so; and in fact if he now told Maria things about her that he had never told before this was largely because it kept before him the idea of the honour of such a woman's esteem. His relation with Maria as well was, strangely enough, no longer quite the same; this truth – though not too disconcertingly – had come up between them on the renewal of their meetings. It was all contained in what she had then almost immediately said to him; it was represented by the remark she had needed but ten minutes to make and that he hadn't been disposed to gainsay. He could toddle alone, and the difference that showed was extraordinary. The turn taken by their talk had promptly confirmed this difference; his larger confidence on the score of Mrs. Newsome did the rest; and the time seemed already far off when he had held out his small thirsty cup to the spout of her pail. Her pail was scarce touched now, and other fountains had flowed for him; she fell into her place as but one of his tributaries; and there was a strange sweetness – a melancholy mildness that touched him – in her acceptance of the altered order.

It marked for himself the flight of time, or at any rate what he was pleased to think of with irony and pity as the rush of experience; it having been but the day before yesterday that he sat at her feet and held on by her garment and was fed by her hand. It was the proportions that were changed, and the proportions were at all times, he philosophized, the very

conditions of perception, the terms of thought. It was as if, with her effective little *entresol* and her wide acquaintance, her activities, varieties, promiscuities, the duties and devotions that took up nine tenths of her time and of which he got, guardedly, but the side-wind – it was as if she had shrunk to a secondary element and had consented to the shrinkage with the perfection of tact. This perfection had never failed her; it had originally been greater than his prime measure for it; it had kept him quite apart, kept him out of the shop, as she called her huge general acquaintance, made their commerce as quiet, as much a thing of the home alone – the opposite of the shop – as if she had never another customer. She had been wonderful to him at first, with the memory of her little *entresol*, the image to which, on most mornings at that time, his eyes directly opened; but now she mainly figured for him as but part of the bristling total – though of course always as a person to whom he should never cease to be indebted. It would never be given to him certainly to inspire a greater kindness. She had decked him out for others, and he saw at this point at least nothing she would ever ask for. She only wondered and questioned and listened, rendering him the homage of a wistful speculation. She expressed it repeatedly; he was already far beyond her, and she must prepare herself to lose him. There was but one little chance for her.

Often as she had said it he met it – for it was a touch he liked – each time the same way. 'My coming to grief?'

'Yes – then I might patch you up.'

'Oh for my real smash, if it takes place, there will be no patching.'

'But you surely don't mean it will kill you.'

'No – worse. It will make me old.'

'Ah nothing can do that! The wonderful and special thing about you is that you *are*, at this time of day, youth.' Then she always made, further, one of those remarks that she had completely ceased to adorn with hesitations or apologies, and that had, by the same token, in spite of their extreme straightness, ceased to produce in Strether the least embarrassment. She made him believe them, and they became thereby as impersonal as truth itself. 'It's just your particular charm.'

His answer too was always the same. 'Of course I'm youth – youth for the trip to Europe. I began to be young, or at least to get the benefit of it, the moment I met you at Chester, and that's what has been taking place ever since. I never had the benefit at the proper time – which comes to saying that I never had the thing itself. I'm having the benefit at this moment; I had it the other day when I said to Chad "Wait"; I shall have it still again when Sarah Pocock arrives. It's a benefit that would make a poor show for many people; and I don't know who else but you and I, frankly, could begin to see in it what I feel. I don't get drunk; I don't pursue the ladies; I don't spend money; I don't even write sonnets. But nevertheless I'm making up late for what I didn't have early. I cultivate my little benefit in my own little way. It amuses me more than anything that has happened to me in all my life. They may say what they like – it's my surrender, it's my tribute, to youth. One puts that in where one can – it has to come in somewhere, if only out of the lives, the conditions, the feelings of other persons. Chad gives me the sense of it, for all his grey hairs, which merely make it solid in him and safe and serene; and *she* does the same, for all her being older than he, for all her marriageable daughter, her separated husband, her agitated history. Though they're young enough, my pair, I don't say they're, in the freshest way, their *own* absolutely prime adolescence; for that has nothing to do with it. The point is that they're mine. Yes, they're my youth; since somehow at the right time nothing else ever was. What I meant just now therefore is that it would all go – go before doing its work – if they were to fail me.'

On which, just here, Miss Gostrey inveterately questioned. 'What do you, in particular, call its work?'

'Well, to see me through.'

'But through what?' – she liked to get it all out of him.

'Why through this experience.' That was all that would come.

It regularly gave her none the less the last word. 'Don't you remember how in those first days of our meeting it was *I* who was to see you through?'

'Remember? Tenderly, deeply' – he always rose to it. 'You're just doing your part in letting me maunder to you thus.'

'Ah don't speak as if my part were small; since whatever else fails you –'

'*You* won't, ever, ever, ever?' – he thus took her up. 'Oh I beg your pardon; you necessarily, you inevitably *will*. Your conditions – that's what I mean – won't allow me anything to do for you.'

'Let alone – I see what you mean – that I'm drearily dreadfully old. I *am*, but there's a service – possible for you to render – that I know, all the same, I shall think of.'

'And what will it be?'

This, in fine, however, she would never tell him. 'You shall hear only if your smash takes place. As that's really out of the question, I won't expose myself' – a point at which, for reasons of his own, Strether ceased to press.

He came round, for publicity – it was the easiest thing – to the idea that his smash *was* out of the question, and this rendered idle the discussion of what might follow it. He attached an added importance, as the days elapsed, to the arrival of the Pococks; he had even a shameful sense of waiting for it insincerely and incorrectly. He accused himself of making believe to his own mind that Sarah's presence, her impression, her judgement would simplify and harmonize; he accused himself of being so afraid of what they *might* do that he sought refuge, to beg the whole question, in a vain fury. He had abundantly seen at home what they were in the habit of doing, and he had not at present the smallest ground. His clearest vision was when he made out that what he most desired was an account more full and free of Mrs. Newsome's state of mind than any he felt he could now expect from herself; that calculation at least went hand in hand with the sharp consciousness of wishing to prove to himself that he was not afraid to look his behaviour in the face. If he was by an inexorable logic to pay for it he was literally impatient to know the cost, and he held himself ready to pay in instalments. The first instalment would be precisely this entertainment of Sarah; as a consequence of which, moreover, he should know vastly better how he stood.

BOOK EIGHTH

I

Strether rambled alone during these few days, the effect of the incident of the previous week having been to simplify in a marked fashion his mixed relations with Waymarsh. Nothing had passed between them in reference to Mrs. Newsome's summons but that our friend had mentioned to his own the departure of the deputation actually at sea – giving him thus an opportunity to confess to the occult intervention he imputed to him. Waymarsh however in the event confessed to nothing; and though this falsified in some degree Strether's forecast the latter amusedly saw in it the same depth of good conscience out of which the dear man's impertinence had originally sprung. He was patient with the dear man now and delighted to observe how unmistakeably he had put on flesh; he felt his own holiday so successfully large and free that he was full of allowances and charities in respect to those cabined and confined:[1] his instinct toward a spirit so strapped down as Waymarsh's was to walk round it on tiptoe for fear of waking it up to a sense of losses by this time irretrievable. It was all very funny, he knew, and but the difference, as he often said to himself, of tweedledum and tweedledee – an emancipation so purely comparative that it was like the advance of the door-mat on the scraper; yet the present crisis was happily to profit by it and the pilgrim from Milrose to know himself more than ever in the right.

Strether felt that when he heard of the approach of the Pococks the impulse of pity quite sprang up in him beside the impulse of triumph. That was exactly why Waymarsh had looked at him with eyes in which the heat of justice was measured and shaded. He had looked very hard, as if

affectionately sorry for the friend – the friend of fifty-five – whose frivolity had had thus to be recorded; becoming, however, but obscurely sententious and leaving his companion to formulate a charge. It was in this general attitude that he had of late altogether taken refuge; with the drop of discussion they were solemnly sadly superficial; Strether recognized in him the mere portentous rumination to which Miss Barrace had so good-humouredly described herself as assigning a corner of her salon. It was quite as if he knew his surreptitious step had been divined, and it was also as if he missed the chance to explain the purity of his motive; but this privation of relief should be precisely his small penance: it was not amiss for Strether that he should find himself to that degree uneasy. If he had been challenged or accused, rebuked for meddling or otherwise pulled up, he would probably have shown, on his own system, all the height of his consistency, all the depth of his good faith. Explicit resentment of his course would have made him take the floor, and the thump of his fist on the table would have affirmed him as consciously incorruptible. Had what now really prevailed with Strether been but a dread of that thump – a dread of wincing a little painfully at what it might invidiously demonstrate? However this might be, at any rate, one of the marks of the crisis was a visible, a studied lapse, in Waymarsh, of betrayed concern. As if to make up to his comrade for the stroke by which he had played providence he now conspicuously ignored his movements, withdrew himself from the pretension to share them, stiffened up his sensibility to neglect, and, clasping his large empty hands and swinging his large restless foot, clearly looked to another quarter for justice.

This made for independence on Strether's part, and he had in truth at no moment of his stay been so free to go and come. The early summer brushed the picture over and blurred everything but the near; it made a vast warm fragrant medium in which the elements floated together on the best of terms, in which rewards were immediate and reckonings postponed. Chad was out of town again, for the first time since his visitor's first view of him; he had explained this necessity – without

detail, yet also without embarrassment; the circumstance was one of those which, in the young man's life, testified to the variety of his ties. Strether wasn't otherwise concerned with it than for its so testifying – a pleasant multitudinous image in which he took comfort. He took comfort, by the same stroke, in the swing of Chad's pendulum back from that other swing, the sharp jerk towards Woollett, so stayed by his own hand. He had the entertainment of thinking that if he had for that moment stopped the clock it was to promote the next minute this still livelier motion. He himself did what he hadn't done before; he took two or three times whole days off – irrespective of others, of two or three taken with Miss Gostrey, two or three taken with little Bilham: he went to Chartres and cultivated, before the front of the cathedral, a general easy beatitude; he went to Fontainebleau and imagined himself on the way to Italy; he went to Rouen[2] with a little handbag and inordinately spent the night.

One afternoon he did something quite different; finding himself in the neighbourhood of a fine old house across the river, he passed under the great arch of its doorway and asked at the porter's lodge for Madame de Vionnet. He had already hovered more than once about that possibility, been aware of it, in the course of ostensible strolls, as lurking but round the corner. Only it had perversely happened, after his morning at Notre Dame, that his consistency, as he considered and intended it, had come back to him; whereby he had reflected that the encounter in question had been none of his making; clinging again intensely to the strength of his position, which was precisely that there was nothing in it for himself. From the moment he actively pursued the charming associate of his adventure, from that moment his position weakened, for he was then acting in an interested way. It was only within a few days that he had fixed himself a limit: he promised himself his consistency should end with Sarah's arrival. It was arguing correctly to feel the title to a free hand conferred on him by this event. If he wasn't to be let alone he should be merely a dupe to act with delicacy. If he wasn't to be trusted he could at least take his ease. If he was to be placed under control he gained leave to try

what his position *might* agreeably give him. An ideal rigour
would perhaps postpone the trial till after the Pococks had
shown their spirit; and it was to an ideal rigour that he had
quite promised himself to conform.

Suddenly, however, on this particular day, he felt a particular
fear under which everything collapsed. He knew abruptly that
he was afraid of himself – and yet not in relation to the effect
on his sensibilities of another hour of Madame de Vionnet.
What he dreaded was the effect of a single hour of Sarah
Pocock, as to whom he was visited, in troubled nights, with
fantastic waking dreams. She loomed at him larger than life;
she increased in volume as she drew nearer; she so met his eyes
that, his imagination taking, after the first step, all, and more
than all, the strides, he already felt her come down on him,
already burned, under her reprobation, with the blush of guilt,
already consented, by way of penance, to the instant forfeiture
of everything. He saw himself, under her direction, recommitted
to Woollett as juvenile offenders are committed to reforma-
tories. It wasn't of course that Woollett was really a place of
discipline; but he knew in advance that Sarah's salon at the
hotel would be. His danger, at any rate, in such moods of
alarm, was some concession, on this ground, that would involve
a sharp rupture with the actual; therefore if he waited to take
leave of that actual he might wholly miss his chance. It was
represented with supreme vividness by Madame de Vionnet,
and that is why, in a word, he waited no longer. He had
seen in a flash that he must anticipate Mrs. Pocock. He was
accordingly much disappointed on now learning from the port-
ress that the lady of his quest was not in Paris. She had gone
for some days to the country. There was nothing in this accident
but what was natural; yet it produced for poor Strether a drop
of all confidence. It was suddenly as if he should never see her
again, and as if moreover he had brought it on himself by not
having been quite kind to her.

It was the advantage of his having let his fancy lose itself
for a little in the gloom that, as by reaction, the prospect
began really to brighten from the moment the deputation from
Woollett alighted on the platform of the station. They had come

straight from Havre,³ having sailed from New York to that
port, and having also, thanks to a happy voyage, made land
with a promptitude that left Chad Newsome, who had meant
to meet them at the dock, belated. He had received their telegram, with the announcement of their immediate further
advance, just as he was taking the train for Havre, so that
nothing had remained for him but to await them in Paris. He
hastily picked up Strether, at the hotel, for this purpose, and
he even, with easy pleasantry, suggested the attendance of
Waymarsh as well – Waymarsh, at the moment his cab rattled
up, being engaged, under Strether's contemplative range, in a
grave perambulation of the familiar court. Waymarsh had
learned from his companion, who had already had a note,
delivered by hand, from Chad, that the Pococks were due, and
had ambiguously, though, as always, impressively, glowered at
him over the circumstance; carrying himself in a manner in
which Strether was now expert enough to recognize his uncertainty, in the premises, as to the best tone. The only tone he
aimed at with confidence was a full tone – which was necessarily
difficult in the absence of a full knowledge. The Pococks were
a quantity as yet unmeasured, and, as he had practically brought
them over, so this witness had to that extent exposed himself.
He wanted to feel right about it, but could only, at the best, for
the time, feel vague. 'I shall look to you, you know, immensely,'
our friend had said, 'to help me with them', and he had been
quite conscious of the effect of the remark, and of others of the
same sort, on his comrade's sombre sensibility. He had insisted
on the fact that Waymarsh would quite like Mrs. Pocock –
one could be certain he would: he would be with her about
everything, and she would also be with *him*, and Miss Barrace's
nose, in short, would find itself out of joint.

Strether had woven this web of cheerfulness while they waited
in the court for Chad; he had sat smoking cigarettes to keep
himself quiet while, caged and leonine, his fellow traveller paced
and turned before him. Chad Newsome was doubtless to be
struck, when he arrived, with the sharpness of their opposition
at this particular hour; he was to remember, as a part of it, how
Waymarsh came with him and with Strether to the street and

stood there with a face half-wistful and half-rueful. They talked
of him, the two others, as they drove, and Strether put Chad in
possession of much of his own strained sense of things. He had
already, a few days before, named to him the wire he was
convinced their friend had pulled – a confidence that had made
on the young man's part quite hugely for curiosity and diversion. The action of the matter, moreover, Strether could see,
was to penetrate; he saw, that is, how Chad judged a system of
influence in which Waymarsh had served as a determinant – an
impression just now quickened again; with the whole bearing
of such a fact on the youth's view of his relatives. As it came
up between them that they might now take their friend for a
feature of the control of these latter now sought to be exerted
from Woollett, Strether felt indeed how it would be stamped
all over him, half an hour later, for Sarah Pocock's eyes, that
he was as much on Chad's 'side' as Waymarsh had probably
described him. He was letting himself, at present, go; there was
no denying it; it might be desperation, it might be confidence;
he should offer himself to the arriving travellers bristling with
all the lucidity he had cultivated.

He repeated to Chad what he had been saying in the court
to Waymarsh; how there was no doubt whatever that his sister
would find the latter a kindred spirit, no doubt of the alliance,
based on an exchange of views, that the pair would successfully
strike up. They would become as thick as thieves – which
moreover was but a development of what Strether remembered
to have said in one of his first discussions with his mate, struck
as he had then already been with the elements of affinity
between that personage and Mrs. Newsome herself. 'I told him,
one day, when he had questioned me on your mother, that she
was a person who, when he should know her, would rouse in
him, I was sure, a special enthusiasm; and that hangs together
with the conviction we now feel – this certitude that Mrs.
Pocock will take him into her boat. For it's your mother's own
boat that she's pulling.'

'Ah,' said Chad, 'Mother's worth fifty of Sally!'

'A thousand; but when you presently meet her, all the same,
you'll be meeting your mother's representative – just as I shall.

I feel like the outgoing ambassador,' said Strether, 'doing honour to his appointed successor.' A moment after speaking as he had just done he felt he had inadvertently rather cheapened Mrs. Newsome to her son; an impression audibly reflected, as at first seen, in Chad's prompt protest. He had recently rather failed of apprehension of the young man's attitude and temper – remaining principally conscious of how little worry, at the worst, he wasted; and he studied him at this critical hour with renewed interest. Chad had done exactly what he had promised him a fortnight previous – had accepted without another question his plea for delay. He was waiting cheerfully and handsomely, but also inscrutably and with a slight increase perhaps of the hardness originally involved in his acquired high polish. He was neither excited nor depressed; was easy and acute and deliberate – unhurried unflurried unworried, only at most a little less amused than usual. Strether felt him more than ever a justification of the extraordinary process of which his own absurd spirit had been the arena; he knew as their cab rolled along, knew as he hadn't even yet known, that nothing else than what Chad had done and had been would have led to his present showing. They had made him, these things, what he was, and the business hadn't been easy; it had taken time and trouble, it had cost, above all, a price. The result at any rate was now to be offered to Sally; which Strether, so far as that was concerned, was glad to be there to witness. Would she in the least make it out or take it in, the result, or would she in the least care for it if she did? He scratched his chin as he asked himself by what name, when challenged – as he was sure he should be – he could call it for her. Oh those were determinations she must herself arrive at; since she wanted so much to see, let her see then and welcome. She had come out in the pride of her competence, yet it hummed in Strether's inner sense that she practically wouldn't see.

That this was moreover what Chad shrewdly suspected was clear from a word that next dropped from him. 'They're children; they play at life!' – and the exclamation was significant and reassuring. It implied that he hadn't then, for his companion's sensibility, appeared to give Mrs. Newsome away; and

it facilitated our friend's presently asking him if it were his idea that Mrs. Pocock and Madame de Vionnet should become acquainted. Strether was still more sharply struck, hereupon, with Chad's lucidity. 'Why, isn't that exactly – to get a sight of the company I keep – what she has come out for?'

'Yes – I'm afraid it is,' Strether unguardedly replied.

Chad's quick rejoinder lighted his precipitation. 'Why do you say you're afraid?'

'Well, because I feel a certain responsibility. It's my testimony, I imagine, that will have been at the bottom of Mrs. Pocock's curiosity. My letters, as I've supposed you to understand from the beginning, have spoken freely. I've certainly said my little say about Madame de Vionnet.'

All that, for Chad, was beautifully obvious. 'Yes, but you've only spoken handsomely.'

'Never more handsomely of any woman. But it's just that tone –!'

'That tone,' said Chad, 'that has fetched her? I dare say; but I've no quarrel with you about it. And no more has Madame de Vionnet. Don't you know by this time how she likes you?'

'Oh!' – and Strether had, with his groan, a real pang of melancholy. 'For all I've done for her!'

'Ah you've done a great deal.'

Chad's urbanity fairly shamed him, and he was at this moment absolutely impatient to see the face Sarah Pocock would present to a sort of thing, as he synthetically phrased it to himself, with no adequate forecast of which, despite his admonitions, she would certainly arrive. 'I've done *this*!'

'Well, this is all right. She likes,' Chad comfortably remarked, 'to be liked.'

It gave his companion a moment's thought. 'And she's sure Mrs. Pocock *will* –?'

'No, I say that for you. She likes your liking her; it's so much, as it were,' Chad laughed, 'to the good. However, she doesn't despair of Sarah either, and is prepared, on her own side, to go all lengths.'

'In the way of appreciation?'

'Yes, and of everything else. In the way of general amiability,

hospitality and welcome. She's under arms,' Chad laughed again; 'she's prepared.'

Strether took it in; then as if an echo of Miss Barrace were in the air: 'She's wonderful.'

'You don't begin to know *how* wonderful!'

There was a depth in it, to Strether's ear, of confirmed luxury – almost a kind of unconscious insolence of proprietorship; but the effect of the glimpse was not at this moment to foster speculation: there was something so conclusive in so much graceful and generous assurance. It was in fact a fresh evocation; and the evocation had before many minutes another consequence. 'Well, I shall see her oftener now. I shall see her as much as I like – by your leave; which is what I hitherto haven't done.'

'It has been,' said Chad, but without reproach, 'only your own fault. I tried to bring you together, and *she*, my dear fellow – I never saw her more charming to any man. But you've got your extraordinary ideas.'

'Well, I *did* have,' Strether murmured; while he felt both how they had possessed him and how they had now lost their authority. He couldn't have traced the sequence to the end, but it was all because of Mrs. Pocock. Mrs. Pocock might be because of Mrs. Newsome, but that was still to be proved. What came over him was the sense of having stupidly failed to profit where profit would have been precious. It had been open to him to see so much more of her, and he had but let the good days pass. Fierce in him almost was the resolve to lose no more of them, and he whimsically reflected, while at Chad's side he drew nearer to his destination, that it was after all Sarah who would have quickened his chance. What her visit of inquisition might achieve in other directions was as yet all obscure – only not obscure that it would do supremely much to bring two earnest persons together. He had but to listen to Chad at this moment to feel it; for Chad was in the act of remarking to him that they of course both counted on him – he himself and the other earnest person – for cheer and support. It was brave to Strether to hear him talk as if the line of wisdom they had struck out was to make things ravishing to the Pococks. No, if

Madame de Vionnet compassed *that*, compassed the ravishment of the Pococks, Madame de Vionnet would be prodigious. It would be a beautiful plan if it succeeded, and it all came to the question of Sarah's being really bribeable. The precedent of his own case helped Strether perhaps but little to consider she might prove so; it being distinct that her character would rather make for every possible difference. This idea of his own bribeability set him apart for himself; with the further mark in fact that his case was absolutely proved. He liked always, where Lambert Strether was concerned, to know the worst, and what he now seemed to know was not only that he was bribeable, but that he had been effectually bribed. The only difficulty was that he couldn't quite have said with what. It was as if he had sold himself, but hadn't somehow got the cash. That, however, was what, characteristically, *would* happen to him. It would naturally be his kind of traffic. While he thought of these things he reminded Chad of the truth they mustn't lose sight of – the truth that, with all deference to her susceptibility to new interests, Sarah would have come out with a high firm definite purpose. 'She hasn't come out, you know, to be bamboozled. We may all be ravishing – nothing perhaps can be more easy for us; but she hasn't come out to be ravished. She has come out just simply to take you home.'

'Oh well, with *her* I'll go,' said Chad good-humouredly. 'I suppose you'll allow *that*.' And then as for a minute Strether said nothing: 'Or is your idea that when I've seen her I shan't want to go?' As this question, however, again left his friend silent he presently went on: 'My own idea at any rate is that they shall have while they're here the best sort of time.'

It was at this that Strether spoke. 'Ah there you are! I think if you really wanted to go – !'

'Well?' said Chad to bring it out.

'Well, you wouldn't trouble about our good time. You wouldn't care what sort of a time we have.'

Chad could always take in the easiest way in the world any ingenious suggestion. 'I see. But can I help it? I'm too decent.'

'Yes, you're too decent!' Strether heavily sighed. And he felt for the moment as if it were the preposterous end of his mission.

It ministered for the time to this temporary effect that Chad made no rejoinder. But he spoke again as they came in sight of the station. 'Do you mean to introduce her to Miss Gostrey?'

As to this Strether was ready. 'No.'

'But haven't you told me they know about her?'

'I think I've told you your mother knows.'

'And won't she have told Sally?'

'That's one of the things I want to see.'

'And if you find she *has* –?'

'Will I then, you mean, bring them together?'

'Yes,' said Chad with his pleasant promptness: 'to show her there's nothing in it.'

Strether hesitated. 'I don't know that I care very much what she may think there's in it.'

'Not if it represents what Mother thinks?'

'Ah what *does* your mother think?' There was in this some sound of bewilderment.

But they were just driving up, and help, of a sort, might after all be quite at hand. 'Isn't that, my dear man, what we're both just going to make out?'

II

Strether quitted the station half an hour later in different company. Chad had taken charge, for the journey to the hotel, of Sarah, Mamie, the maid and the luggage, all spaciously installed and conveyed; and it was only after the four had rolled away that his companion got into a cab with Jim. A strange new feeling had come over Strether, in consequence of which his spirits had risen; it was as if what had occurred on the alighting of his critics had been something other than his fear, though his fear had yet not been of an instant scene of violence. His impression had been nothing but what was inevitable – he said that to himself; yet relief and reassurance had softly dropped upon him. Nothing could be so odd as to be indebted for these things to the look of faces and the sound of voices that had been with him to satiety, as he might have said, for years; but he now knew, all the same, how uneasy he had felt; that was brought home to him by his present sense of a respite. It had come moreover in the flash of an eye; it had come in the smile with which Sarah, whom, at the window of her compartment, they had effusively greeted from the platform, rustled down to them a moment later, fresh and handsome from her cool June progress through the charming land. It was only a sign, but enough: she was going to be gracious and unallusive, she was going to play the larger game – which was still more apparent, after she had emerged from Chad's arms, in her direct greeting to the valued friend of her family.

Strether *was* then as much as ever the valued friend of her family; it was something he could at all events go on with; and the manner of his response to it expressed even for himself how

little he had enjoyed the prospect of ceasing to figure in that likeness. He had always seen Sarah gracious – had in fact rarely seen her shy or dry; her marked thin-lipped smile, intense without brightness and as prompt to act as the scrape of a safety-match; the protrusion of her rather remarkably long chin, which in her case represented invitation and urbanity, and not, as in most others, pugnacity and defiance; the penetration of her voice to a distance, the general encouragement and approval of her manner, were all elements with which intercourse had made him familiar, but which he noted to-day almost as if she had been a new acquaintance. This first glimpse of her had given a brief but vivid accent to her resemblance to her mother; he could have taken her for Mrs. Newsome while she met his eyes as the train rolled into the station. It was an impression that quickly dropped; Mrs. Newsome was much handsomer, and while Sarah inclined to the massive her mother had, at an age, still the girdle of a maid; also the latter's chin was rather short, than long, and her smile, by good fortune, much more, oh ever so much more, mercifully vague. Strether had seen Mrs. Newsome reserved; he had literally heard her silent, though he had never known her unpleasant. It was the case with Mrs. Pocock that he had known *her* unpleasant, even though he had never known her not affable. She had forms of affability that were in a high degree assertive; nothing for instance had ever been more striking than that she was affable to Jim.

What had told in any case at the window of the train was her high clear forehead, that forehead which her friends, for some reason, always thought of as a 'brow'; the long reach of her eyes – it came out at this juncture in such a manner as to remind him, oddly enough, also of that of Waymarsh's; and the unusual gloss of her dark hair, dressed and hatted, after her mother's refined example, with such an avoidance of extremes that it was always spoken of at Woollett as 'their own'. Though this analogy dropped as soon as she was on the platform it had lasted long enough to make him feel all the advantage, as it were, of his relief. The woman at home, the woman to whom he was attached, was before him just long enough to give him

again the measure of the wretchedness, in fact really of the shame, of their having to recognize the formation, between them, of a 'split'. He had taken this measure in solitude and meditation; but the catastrophe, as Sarah steamed up, looked for its seconds unprecedentedly dreadful – or proved, more exactly, altogether unthinkable; so that his finding something free and familiar to respond to brought with it an instant renewal of his loyalty. He had suddenly sounded the whole depth, had gasped at what he might have lost.

Well, he could now, for the quarter of an hour of their detention, hover about the travellers as soothingly as if their direct message to him was that he had lost nothing. He wasn't going to have Sarah write to her mother that night that he was in any way altered or strange. There had been times enough for a month when it had seemed to him that he was strange, that he was altered, in every way; but that was a matter for himself; he knew at least whose business it was *not*; it was not at all events such a circumstance as Sarah's own unaided lights would help her to. Even if she had come out to flash those lights more than yet appeared she wouldn't make much headway against mere pleasantness. He counted on being able to be merely pleasant to the end, and if only from incapacity moreover to formulate anything different. He couldn't even formulate to himself his being changed and queer; it had taken place, the process, somewhere deep down; Maria Gostrey had caught glimpses of it; but how was he to fish it up, even if he desired, for Mrs. Pocock? This was then the spirit in which he hovered, and with the easier throb in it much indebted furthermore to the impression of high and established adequacy as a pretty girl promptly produced in him by Mamie. He had wondered vaguely – turning over many things in the fidget of his thoughts – if Mamie *were* as pretty as Woollett published her; as to which issue seeing her now again was to be so swept away by Woollett's opinion that this consequence really let loose for the imagination an avalanche of others. There were positively five minutes in which the last word seemed of necessity to abide with a Woollett represented by a Mamie. This was the sort of truth the place itself would feel; it would send her forth in

confidence; it would point to her with triumph; it would take its stand on her with assurance; it would be conscious of no requirements she didn't meet, of no question she couldn't answer.

Well, it was right, Strether slipped smoothly enough into the cheerfulness of saying: granted that a community *might* be best represented by a young lady of twenty-two, Mamie perfectly played the part, played it as if she were used to it, and looked and spoke and dressed the character. He wondered if she mightn't, in the high light of Paris, a cool full studio-light, becoming yet treacherous, show as too conscious of these matters; but the next moment he felt satisfied that her consciousness was after all empty for its size, rather too simple than too mixed, and that the kind way with her would be not to take many things out of it, but to put as many as possible in. She was robust and conveniently tall; just a trifle too bloodlessly fair perhaps, but with a pleasant public familiar radiance that affirmed her vitality. She might have been 'receiving' for Woollett, wherever she found herself, and there was something in her manner, her tone, her motion, her pretty blue eyes, her pretty perfect teeth and her very small, too small, nose, that immediately placed her, to the fancy, between the windows of a hot bright room in which voices were high – up at that end to which people were brought to be 'presented'. They were there to congratulate, these images, and Strether's renewed vision, on this hint, completed the idea. What Mamie was like was the happy bride, the bride after the church and just before going away. She wasn't the mere maiden, and yet was only as much married as that quantity came to. She was in the brilliant acclaimed festal stage. Well, might it last her long!

Strether rejoiced in these things for Chad, who was all genial attention to the needs of his friends, besides having arranged that his servant should re-enforce him; the ladies were certainly pleasant to see, and Mamie would be at any time and anywhere pleasant to exhibit. She would look extraordinarily like his young wife – the wife of a honeymoon, should he go about with her; but that was his own affair – or perhaps it was hers; it was at any rate something she couldn't help. Strether

remembered how he had seen him come up with Jeanne de Vionnet in Gloriani's garden, and the fancy he had had about that – the fancy obscured now, thickly overlaid with others; the recollection was during these minutes his only note of trouble. He had often, in spite of himself, wondered if Chad but too probably were not with Jeanne the object of a still and shaded flame. It was on the cards that the child *might* be tremulously in love, and this conviction now flickered up not a bit the less for his disliking to think of it, for its being, in a complicated situation, a complication the more, and for something indescribable in Mamie, something at all events straightway lent her by his own mind, something that gave her value, gave her intensity and purpose, as the symbol of an opposition. Little Jeanne wasn't really at all in question – how *could* she be? – yet from the moment Miss Pocock had shaken her skirts on the platform, touched up the immense bows of her hat and settled properly over her shoulder the strap of her morocco-and-gilt travelling-satchel, from that moment little Jeanne was opposed.

It was in the cab with Jim that impressions really crowded on Strether, giving him the strangest sense of length of absence from people among whom he had lived for years. Having them thus come out to him was as if he had returned to find them; and the droll promptitude of Jim's mental reaction threw his own initiation far back into the past. Whoever might or mightn't be suited by what was going on among them, Jim, for one, would certainly be: his instant recognition – frank and whimsical – of what the affair was for *him* gave Strether a glow of pleasure. 'I say, you know, this *is* about my shape, and if it hadn't been for *you* – !' so he broke out as the charming streets met his healthy appetite; and he wound up, after an expressive nudge, with a clap of his companion's knee and an 'Oh you, you – you *are* doing it!' that was charged with rich meaning. Strether felt in it the intention of homage, but, with a curiosity otherwise occupied, postponed taking it up. What he was asking himself for the time was how Sarah Pocock, in the opportunity already given her, had judged her brother – from whom he himself, as they finally, at the station, separated for their different conveyances, had had a look into which he could read more

than one message. However Sarah was judging her brother, Chad's conclusion about his sister, and about her husband and her husband's sister, was at the least on the way not to fail of confidence. Strether felt the confidence, and that, as the look between them was an exchange, what he himself gave back was relatively vague. This comparison of notes however could wait; everything struck him as depending on the effect produced by Chad. Neither Sarah nor Mamie had in any way, at the station – where they had had after all ample time – broken out about it; which, to make up for this, was what our friend had expected of Jim as soon as they should find themselves together.

It was queer to him that he had that noiseless brush with Chad; an ironic intelligence with this youth on the subject of his relatives, an intelligence carried on under their nose and, as might be said, at their expense – such a matter marked again for him strongly the number of stages he had come; albeit that if the number seemed great the time taken for the final one was but the turn of a hand. He had before this had many moments of wondering if he himself weren't perhaps changed even as Chad was changed. Only what in Chad was conspicuous improvement – well, he had no name ready for the working, in his own organism, of his own more timid dose. He should have to see first what this action would amount to. And for his occult passage with the young man, after all, the directness of it had no greater oddity than the fact that the young man's way with the three travellers should have been so happy a manifestation. Strether liked him for it, on the spot, as he hadn't yet liked him; it affected him while it lasted as he might have been affected by some light pleasant perfect work of art: to that degree that he wondered if they were really worthy of it, took it in and did it justice; to that degree that it would have been scarce a miracle if, there in the luggage-room, while they waited for their things, Sarah had pulled his sleeve and drawn him aside. 'You're right; we haven't quite known what you mean, Mother and I, but now we see. Chad's magnificent; what can one want more? If *this* is the kind of thing –!' On which they might, as it were, have embraced and begun to work together.

Ah how much, as it was, for all her bridling brightness –

which was merely general and noticed nothing – *would* they work together? Strether knew he was unreasonable; he set it down to his being nervous: people couldn't notice everything and speak of everything in a quarter of an hour. Possibly, no doubt, also, he made too much of Chad's display. Yet, none the less, when, at the end of five minutes, in the cab, Jim Pocock had said nothing either – hadn't said, that is, what Strether wanted, though he had said much else – it all suddenly bounced back to their being either stupid or wilful. It was more probably on the whole the former; so that that would be the drawback of the bridling brightness. Yes, they would bridle and be bright; they would make the best of what was before them, but their observation would fail; it would be beyond them; they simply wouldn't understand. Of what use would it be then that they had come? – if they weren't to be intelligent up to *that* point: unless indeed he himself were utterly deluded and extravagant? Was he, on this question of Chad's improvement, fantastic and away from the truth? Did he live in a false world, a world that had grown simply to suit him, and was his present slight irritation – in the face now of Jim's silence in particular – but the alarm of the vain thing menaced by the touch of the real? Was this contribution of the real possibly the mission of the Pococks? – had they come to make the work of observation, as *he* had practised observation, crack and crumble, and to reduce Chad to the plain terms in which honest minds could deal with him? Had they come in short to be sane where Strether was destined to feel that he himself had only been silly?

He glanced at such a contingency, but it failed to hold him long when once he had reflected that he would have been silly, in this case, with Maria Gostrey and little Bilham, with Madame de Vionnet and little Jeanne, with Lambert Strether, in fine, and above all with Chad Newsome himself. Wouldn't it be found to have made more for reality to be silly with these persons than sane with Sarah and Jim? Jim in fact, he presently made up his mind, was individually out of it; Jim didn't care; Jim hadn't come out either for Chad or for him; Jim in short left the moral side to Sally and indeed simply availed himself now, for the sense of recreation, of the fact that he left almost every-

thing to Sally. He was nothing compared to Sally, and not so much by reason of Sally's temper and will as by that of her more developed type and greater acquaintance with the world. He quite frankly and serenely confessed, as he sat there with Strether, that he felt his type hang far in the rear of his wife's and still further, if possible, in the rear of his sister's. Their types, he well knew, were recognized and acclaimed; whereas the most a leading Woollett business-man could hope to achieve socially, and for that matter industrially, was a certain freedom to play into this general glamour.

The impression he made on our friend was another of the things that marked our friend's road. It was a strange impression, especially as so soon produced; Strether had received it, he judged, all in the twenty minutes; it struck him at least as but in a minor degree the work of the long Woollett years. Pocock was normally and consentingly though not quite wittingly out of the question. It was despite his being normal; it was despite his being cheerful; it was despite his being a leading Woollett business-man; and the determination of his fate left him thus perfectly usual – as everything else about it was clearly, to his sense, not less so. He seemed to say that there was a whole side of life on which the perfectly usual *was* for leading Woollett business-men to be out of the question. He made no more of it than that, and Strether, so far as Jim was concerned, desired to make no more. Only Strether's imagination, as always, worked, and he asked himself if this side of life were not somehow connected, for those who figured on it, with the fact of marriage. Would *his* relation to it, had he married ten years before, have become now the same as Pocock's? Might it even become the same should he marry in a few months? Should he ever know himself as much out of the question for Mrs. Newsome as Jim knew himself – in a dim way – for Mrs. Jim?

To turn his eyes in that direction was to be personally reassured; he was different from Pocock; he had affirmed himself differently and was held after all in higher esteem. What none the less came home to him, however, at this hour, was that the society over there, that of which Sarah and Mamie – and, in a more eminent way, Mrs. Newsome herself – were

specimens, was essentially a society of women, and that poor
Jim wasn't in it. He himself, Lambert Strether, *was* as yet in
some degree – which was an odd situation for a man; but it
kept coming back to him in a whimsical way that he should
perhaps find his marriage had cost him his place. This occasion
indeed, whatever that fancy represented, was not a time of
sensible exclusion for Jim, who was in a state of manifest
response to the charm of his adventure. Small and fat and
constantly facetious, straw-coloured and destitute of marks,
he would have been practically indistinguishable hadn't his
constant preference for light-grey clothes, for white hats, for
very big cigars and very little stories, done what it could for his
identity. There were signs in him, though none of them plain-
tive, of always paying for others; and the principal one perhaps
was just this failure of type. It was with this that he paid, rather
than with fatigue or waste; and also doubtless a little with the
effort of humour – never irrelevant to the conditions, to the
relations, with which he was acquainted.

He gurgled his joy as they rolled through the happy streets;
he declared that his trip was a regular windfall, and that he
wasn't there, he was eager to remark, to hang back from anything: he didn't know quite what Sally had come for, but *he*
had come for a good time. Strether indulged him even while
wondering if what Sally wanted her brother to go back for was
to become like her husband. He trusted that a good time was
to be, out and out, the programme for all of them; and he
assented liberally to Jim's proposal that, disencumbered and
irresponsible – his things were in the omnibus with those of the
others – they should take a further turn round before going to
the hotel. It wasn't for *him* to tackle Chad – it was Sally's job;
and as it would be like her, he felt, to open fire on the spot, it
wouldn't be amiss of them to hold off and give her time.
Strether, on his side, only asked to give her time; so he jogged
with his companion along boulevards and avenues, trying to
extract from meagre material some forecast of his catastrophe.
He was quick enough to see that Jim Pocock declined judgement, had hovered quite round the outer edge of discussion
and anxiety, leaving all analysis of their question to the ladies

alone and now only feeling his way toward some small droll cynicism. It broke out afresh, the cynicism – it had already shown a flicker – in a but slightly deferred: 'Well, hanged if I would if *I* were he!'

'You mean you wouldn't in Chad's place – ?'

'Give up this to go back and boss the advertising!' Poor Jim, with his arms folded and his little legs out in the open fiacre,[1] drank in the sparkling Paris noon and carried his eyes from one side of their vista to the other. 'Why I want to come right out and live here myself. And I want to live while I *am* here too. I feel with *you* – oh you've been grand, old man, and I've twigged – that it ain't right to worry Chad. *I* don't mean to persecute him; I couldn't in conscience. It's thanks to you at any rate that I'm here, and I'm sure I'm much obliged. You're a lovely pair.'

There were things in this speech that Strether let pass for the time. 'Don't you then think it important the advertising should be thoroughly taken in hand? Chad *will* be, so far as capacity is concerned,' he went on, 'the man to do it.'

'Where did he get his capacity,' Jim asked, 'over here?'

'He didn't get it over here, and the wonderful thing is that over here he hasn't inevitably lost it. He has a natural turn for business, an extraordinary head. He comes by that,' Strether explained, 'honestly enough. He's in that respect his father's son, and also – for she's wonderful in her way too – his mother's. He has other tastes and other tendencies; but Mrs. Newsome and your wife are quite right about his having that. He's very remarkable.'

'Well, I guess he is!' Jim Pocock comfortably sighed. 'But if you've believed so in his making us hum, why have you so prolonged the discussion? Don't you know we've been quite anxious about you?'

These questions were not informed with earnestness, but Strether saw he must none the less make a choice and take a line. 'Because, you see, I've greatly liked it. I've liked my Paris. I dare say I've liked it too much.'

'Oh you old wretch!' Jim gaily exclaimed.

'But nothing's concluded,' Strether went on. 'The case is more complex than it looks from Woollett.'

'Oh well, it looks bad enough from Woollett!' Jim declared.

'Even after all I've written?'

Jim bethought himself. 'Isn't it what you've written that has made Mrs. Newsome pack us off? That at least and Chad's not turning up?'

Strether made a reflexion of his own. 'I see. That she should do something was, no doubt, inevitable, and your wife has therefore of course come out to act.'

'Oh yes,' Jim concurred – 'to act. But Sally comes out to act, you know,' he lucidly added, 'every time she leaves the house. She never comes out but she *does* act. She's acting moreover now for her mother, and that fixes the scale.' Then he wound up, opening all his senses to it, with a renewed embrace of pleasant Paris. 'We haven't all the same at Woollett got anything like this.'

Strether continued to consider. 'I'm bound to say for you all that you strike me as having arrived in a very mild and reasonable frame of mind. You don't show your claws. I felt just now in Mrs. Pocock no symptom of that. She isn't fierce,' he went on. 'I'm such a nervous idiot that I thought she might be.'

'Oh don't you know her well enough,' Pocock asked, 'to have noticed that she never gives herself away, any more than her mother ever does? They ain't fierce, either of 'em; they let you come quite close. They wear their fur the smooth side out – the warm side in. Do you know what they are?' Jim pursued as he looked about him, giving the question, as Strether felt, but half his care – 'do you know what they are? They're about as intense as they can live.'

'Yes' – and Strether's concurrence had a positive precipitation; 'they're about as intense as they can live.'

'They don't lash about and shake the cage,' said Jim, who seemed pleased with his analogy; 'and it's at feeding-time that they're quietest. But they always get there.'

'They do indeed – they always get there!' Strether replied with a laugh that justified his confession of nervousness. He disliked to be talking sincerely of Mrs. Newsome with Pocock; he could have talked insincerely. But there was something he wanted to know, a need created in him by her recent inter-

mission, by his having given from the first so much, as now more than ever appeared to him, and got so little. It was as if a queer truth in his companion's metaphor had rolled over him with a rush. She *had* been quiet at feeding-time; she had fed, and Sarah had fed with her, out of the big bowl of all his recent free communication, his vividness and pleasantness, his ingenuity and even his eloquence, while the current of her response had steadily run thin. Jim meanwhile however, it was true, slipped characteristically into shallowness from the moment he ceased to speak out of the experience of a husband.

'But of course Chad has now the advantage of being there before her. If he doesn't work that for all it's worth –!' He sighed with contingent pity at his brother-in-law's possible want of resource. 'He has worked it on *you*, pretty well, eh?' and he asked the next moment if there were anything new at the Varieties[2] which he pronounced in the American manner. They talked about the Varieties – Strether confessing to a knowledge which produced again on Pocock's part a play of innuendo as vague as a nursery-rhyme, yet as aggressive as an elbow in his side; and they finished their drive under the protection of easy themes. Strether waited to the end, but still in vain, for any show that Jim had seen Chad as different; and he could scarce have explained the discouragement he drew from the absence of this testimony. It was what he had taken his own stand on, so far as he had taken a stand; and if they were all only going to see nothing he had only wasted his time. He gave his friend till the very last moment, till they had come into sight of the hotel; and when poor Pocock only continued cheerful and envious and funny he fairly grew to dislike him, to feel him extravagantly common. If they were *all* going to see nothing! – Strether knew, as this came back to him, that he was also letting Pocock represent for him what Mrs. Newsome wouldn't see. He went on disliking, in the light of Jim's commonness, to talk to him about that lady; yet just before the cab pulled up he knew the extent of his desire for the real word from Woollett.

'Has Mrs. Newsome at all given way –?'

'"Given way"?' – Jim echoed it with the practical derision of his sense of a long past.

'Under the strain, I mean, of hope deferred, of disappointment repeated and thereby intensified.'

'Oh is she prostrate, you mean?' – he had his categories in
hand. 'Why yes, she's prostrate – just as Sally is. But they're
never so lively, you know, as when they're prostrate.'

'Ah Sarah's prostrate?' Strether vaguely murmured.

'It's when they're prostrate that they most sit up.'

'And Mrs. Newsome's sitting up?'

'All night, my boy – for *you*!' And Jim fetched him, with a
vulgar little guffaw, a thrust that gave relief to the picture. But
he had got what he wanted. He felt on the spot that this *was*
the real word from Woollett. 'So don't you go home!' Jim added
while he alighted and while his friend, letting him profusely pay
the cabman, sat on in a momentary muse. Strether wondered if
that were the real word too.

III

As the door of Mrs. Pocock's salon was pushed open for him, the next day, well before noon, he was reached by a voice with a charming sound that made him just falter before crossing the threshold. Madame de Vionnet was already on the field, and this gave the drama a quicker pace than he felt it as yet – though his suspense had increased – in the power of any act of his own to do. He had spent the previous evening with all his old friends together; yet he would still have described himself as quite in the dark in respect to a forecast of their influence on his situation. It was strange now, none the less, that in the light of this unexpected note of her presence he felt Madame de Vionnet a part of that situation as she hadn't even yet been. She was alone, he found himself assuming, with Sarah, and there was a bearing in that – somehow beyond his control – on his personal fate. Yet she was only saying something quite easy and independent – the thing she had come, as a good friend of Chad's, on purpose to say. 'There isn't anything at all –? I should be so delighted.'

It was clear enough, when they were there before him, how she had been received. He saw this, as Sarah got up to greet him, from something fairly hectic in Sarah's face. He saw furthermore that they weren't, as had first come to him, alone together; he was at no loss as to the identity of the broad high back presented to him in the embrasure of the window furthest from the door. Waymarsh, whom he had to-day not yet seen, whom he only knew to have left the hotel before him, and who had taken part, the night previous, on Mrs. Pocock's kind invitation, conveyed by Chad, in the entertainment, informal but cordial, promptly offered by that lady – Waymarsh had

anticipated him even as Madame de Vionnet had done, and,
with his hands in his pockets and his attitude unaffected by
Strether's entrance, was looking out, in marked detachment, at
the Rue de Rivoli.[1] The latter felt it in the air – it was immense
how Waymarsh could mark things – that he had remained
deeply dissociated from the overture to their hostess that we
have recorded on Madame de Vionnet's side. He had, conspicuously, tact, besides a stiff general view; and this was why he
had left Mrs. Pocock to struggle alone. He would outstay the
visitor; he would unmistakeably wait; to what had he been
doomed for months past but waiting? Therefore she was to feel
that she had him in reserve. What support she drew from this
was still to be seen, for, although Sarah was vividly bright, she
had given herself up for the moment to an ambiguous flushed
formalism. She had had to reckon more quickly than she
expected; but it concerned her first of all to signify that she was
not to be taken unawares. Strether arrived precisely in time for
her showing it. 'Oh you're too good; but I don't think I feel
quite helpless. I have my brother – and these American friends.
And then you know I've been to Paris. I *know* Paris,' said Sally
Pocock in a tone that breathed a certain chill on Strether's
heart.

'Ah but a woman, in this tiresome place where everything's
always changing, a woman of good will,' Madame de Vionnet
threw off, 'can always help a woman. I'm sure you "know" –
but we know perhaps different things.' She too, visibly, wished
to make no mistake; but it was a fear of a different order and
more kept out of sight. She smiled in welcome at Strether; she
greeted him more familiarly than Mrs. Pocock; she put out her
hand to him without moving from her place; and it came to
him in the course of a minute and in the oddest way that – yes,
positively – she was giving him over to ruin. She was all kindness
and ease, but she couldn't help so giving him; she was exquisite,
and her being just as she was poured for Sarah a sudden rush
of meaning into his own equivocations. How could she know
how she was hurting him? She wanted to show as simple and
humble – in the degree compatible with operative charm; but
it was just this that seemed to put him on her side. She struck

him as dressed, as arranged, as prepared infinitely to conciliate
– with the very poetry of good taste in her view of the conditions
of her early call. She was ready to advise about dressmakers
and shops; she held herself wholly at the disposition of Chad's
family. Strether noticed her card on the table – her coronet and
her 'Comtesse' – and the imagination was sharp in him of
certain private adjustments in Sarah's mind. She had never, he
was sure, sat with a 'Comtesse' before, and such was the specimen of that class he had been keeping to play on her. She had
crossed the sea very particularly for a look at her; but he read
in Madame de Vionnet's own eyes that this curiosity hadn't
been so successfully met as that she herself wouldn't now have
more than ever need of him. She looked much as she had looked
to him that morning at Notre Dame; he noted in fact the
suggestive sameness of her discreet and delicate dress. It seemed
to speak – perhaps a little prematurely or too finely – of the
sense in which she would help Mrs. Pocock with the shops.
The way that lady took her in, moreover, added depth to his
impression of what Miss Gostrey, by their common wisdom,
had escaped. He winced as he saw himself but for that timely
prudence ushering in Maria as a guide and an example. There
was however a touch of relief for him in his glimpse, so far as
he had got it, of Sarah's line. She 'knew Paris'. Madame de
Vionnet had, for that matter, lightly taken this up. 'Ah then
you've a turn for that, an affinity that belongs to your family.
Your brother, though his long experience makes a difference, I
admit, has become one of us in a marvellous way.' And she
appealed to Strether in the manner of a woman who could
always glide off with smoothness into another subject. Wasn't
he struck with the way Mr. Newsome had made the place his
own, and hadn't he been in a position to profit by his friend's
wondrous expertness?

Strether felt the bravery, at the least, of her presenting herself
so promptly to sound that note, and yet asked himself what
other note, after all, she *could* strike from the moment she
presented herself at all. She could meet Mrs. Pocock only on
the ground of the obvious, and what feature of Chad's situation
was more eminent than the fact that he had created for himself

a new set of circumstances? Unless she hid herself altogether
she could show but as one of these, an illustration of his domi-
ciled and indeed of his confirmed condition. And the consciousness of all this in her charming eyes was so clear and fine that
as she thus publicly drew him into her boat she produced in
him such a silent agitation as he was not to fail afterwards to
denounce as pusillanimous. 'Ah don't be so charming to me! –
for it makes us intimate, and after all what *is* between us when
I've been so tremendously on my guard and have seen you but
half a dozen times?' He recognized once more the perverse law
that so inveterately governed his poor personal aspects: it would
be exactly *like* the way things always turned out for him that
he should affect Mrs. Pocock and Waymarsh as launched in a
relation in which he had really never been launched at all. They
were at this very moment – they could only be – attributing to
him the full licence of it, and all by the operation of her own
tone with him; whereas his sole licence had been to cling with
intensity to the brink, not to dip so much as a toe into the flood.
But the flicker of his fear on this occasion was not, as may be
added, to repeat itself; it sprang up, for its moment, only to die
down and then go out for ever. To meet his fellow visitor's
invocation and, with Sarah's brilliant eyes on him, answer, *was*
quite sufficiently to step into her boat. During the rest of the
time her visit lasted he felt himself proceed to each of the proper
offices, successively, for helping to keep the adventurous skiff
afloat. It rocked beneath him, but he settled himself in his place.
He took up an oar and, since he was to have the credit of
pulling, pulled.

   'That will make it all the pleasanter if it so happens that we
do meet,' Madame de Vionnet had further observed in reference
to Mrs. Pocock's mention of her initiated state; and she had
immediately added that, after all, her hostess couldn't be in
need with the good offices of Mr. Strether so close at hand. 'It's
he, I gather, who has learnt to know his Paris, and to love it,
better than any one ever before in so short a time; so that
between him and your brother, when it comes to the point,
how can you possibly want for good guidance? The great thing,

Mr. Strether will show you,' she smiled, 'is just to let one's self go.'

'Oh I've not let myself go very far,' Strether answered, feeling quite as if he had been called upon to hint to Mrs. Pocock how Parisians could talk. 'I'm only afraid of showing I haven't let myself go far enough. I've taken a good deal of time, but I must quite have had the air of not budging from one spot.' He looked at Sarah in a manner that he thought she might take as engaging, and he made, under Madame de Vionnet's protection, as it were, his first personal point. 'What has really happened has been that, all the while, I've done what I came out for.'

Yet it only at first gave Madame de Vionnet a chance immediately to take him up. 'You've renewed acquaintance with your friend – you've learnt to know him again.' She spoke with such cheerful helpfulness that they might, in a common cause, have been calling together and pledged to mutual aid.

Waymarsh, at this, as if he had been in question, straightway turned from the window. 'Oh yes, Countess – he has renewed acquaintance with *me*, and he *has*, I guess, learnt something about me, though I don't know how much he has liked it. It's for Strether himself to say whether he has felt it justifies his course.'

'Oh but *you*,' said the Countess gaily, 'are not in the least what he came out for – is he really, Strether? and I hadn't you at all in my mind. I was thinking of Mr. Newsome, of whom we think so much and with whom, precisely, Mrs. Pocock has given herself the opportunity to take up threads. What a pleasure for you both!' Madame de Vionnet, with her eyes on Sarah, bravely continued.

Mrs. Pocock met her handsomely, but Strether quickly saw she meant to accept no version of her movements or plans from any other lips. She required no patronage and no support, which were but other names for a false position; she would show in her own way what she chose to show, and this she expressed with a dry glitter that recalled to him a fine Woollett winter morning. 'I've never wanted for opportunities to see my brother. We've many things to think of at home, and great

responsibilities and occupations, and our home's not an impossible place. We've plenty of reasons,' Sarah continued a little piercingly, 'for everything we do' – and in short she wouldn't give herself the least little scrap away. But she added as one who was always bland and who could afford a concession; 'I've come because – well, because we do come.'

'Ah then fortunately!' – Madame de Vionnet breathed it to the air. Five minutes later they were on their feet for her to take leave, standing together in an affability that had succeeded in surviving a further exchange of remarks; only with the emphasized appearance on Waymarsh's part of a tendency to revert, in a ruminating manner and as with an instinctive or a precautionary lightening of his tread, to an open window and his point of vantage. The glazed and gilded room, all red damask, ormolu, mirrors, clocks, looked south, and the shutters were bowed upon the summer morning; but the Tuileries garden and what was beyond it, over which the whole place hung, were things visible through gaps; so that the far-spreading presence of Paris came up in coolness, dimness and invitation, in the twinkle of gilt-tipped palings, the crunch of gravel, the click of hoofs, the crack of whips, things that suggested some parade of the circus. 'I think it probable,' said Mrs. Pocock, 'that I shall have the opportunity of going to my brother's. I've no doubt it's very pleasant indeed.' She spoke as to Strether, but her face was turned with an intensity of brightness to Madame de Vionnet, and there was a moment during which, while she thus fronted her, our friend expected to hear her add: 'I'm much obliged to you, I'm sure, for inviting me there.' He guessed that for five seconds these words were on the point of coming; he heard them as clearly as if they had been spoken; but he presently knew they had just failed – knew it by a glance, quick and fine, from Madame de Vionnet, which told him that she too had felt them in the air, but that the point had luckily not been made in any manner requiring notice. This left her free to reply only to what had been said.

'That the Boulevard Malesherbes may be common ground for us offers me the best prospect I see for the pleasure of meeting you again.'

'Oh I shall come to see you, since you've been so good': and Mrs. Pocock looked her invader well in the eyes. The flush in Sarah's cheeks had by this time settled to a small definite crimson spot that was not without its own bravery; she held her head a good deal up, and it came to Strether that of the two, at this moment, she was the one who most carried out the idea of a Countess. He quite took in, however, that she would really return her visitor's civility: she wouldn't report again at Woollett without at least so much producible history as that in her pocket.

'I want extremely to be able to show you my little daughter.' Madame de Vionnet went on; 'and I should have brought her with me if I hadn't wished first to ask your leave. I was in hopes I should perhaps find Miss Pocock, of whose being with you I've heard from Mr. Newsome and whose acquaintance I should so much like my child to make. If I have the pleasure of seeing her and you do permit it I shall venture to ask her to be kind to Jeanne. Mr. Strether will tell you' – she beautifully kept it up – 'that my poor girl is gentle and good and rather lonely. They've made friends, he and she, ever so happily, and he doesn't, I believe, think ill of her. As for Jeanne herself he has had the same success with her that I know he has had here wherever he has turned.' She seemed to ask him for permission to say these things, or seemed rather to take it, softly and happily, with the ease of intimacy, for granted, and he had quite the consciousness now that not to meet her at any point more than halfway would be odiously, basely to abandon her. Yes, he was *with* her, and, opposed even in this covert, this semi-safe fashion to those who were not, he felt, strangely and confusedly, but excitedly, inspiringly, how much and how far. It was as if he had positively waited in suspense for something from her that would let him in deeper, so that he might show her how he could take it. And what did in fact come as she drew out a little her farewell served sufficiently the purpose. 'As his success is a matter that I'm sure he'll never mention for himself, I feel, you see, the less scruple; which it's very good of me to say, you know, by the way,' she added as she addressed herself to him; 'considering how little direct advantage I've

gained from your triumphs with *me*. When does one ever see you? I wait at home and I languish. You'll have rendered me the service, Mrs. Pocock, at least,' she wound up, 'of giving me one of my much-too-rare glimpses of this gentleman.'

'I certainly should be sorry to deprive you of anything that seems so much, as you describe it, your natural due. Mr. Strether and I are very old friends,' Sarah allowed, 'but the privilege of his society isn't a thing I shall quarrel about with any one.'

'And yet, dear Sarah,' he freely broke in, 'I feel, when I hear you say that, that you don't quite do justice to the important truth of the extent to which – as you're also mine – I'm *your* natural due. I should like much better,' he laughed, 'to see you fight for me.'

She met him, Mrs. Pocock, on this, with an arrest of speech – with a certain breathlessness, as he immediately fancied, on the score of a freedom for which she wasn't quite prepared. It had flared up – for all the harm he had intended by it – because, confoundedly, he didn't want any more to be afraid about her than he wanted to be afraid about Madame de Vionnet. He had never, naturally, called her anything but Sarah at home, and though he had perhaps never quite so markedly invoked her as his 'dear', that was somehow partly because no occasion had hitherto laid so effective a trap for it. But something admonished him now that it was too late – unless indeed it were possibly too early; and that he at any rate shouldn't have pleased Mrs. Pocock the more by it. 'Well, Mr. Strether –!' she murmured with vagueness, yet with sharpness, while her crimson spots burned a trifle brighter and he was aware that this must be for the present the limit of her response. Madame de Vionnet had already, however, come to his aid, and Waymarsh, as if for further participation, moved again back to them. It was true that the aid rendered by Madame de Vionnet was questionable; it was a sign that, for all one might confess to with her, and for all she might complain of not enjoying, she could still insidiously show how much of the material of conversation had accumulated between them.

'The real truth is, you know, that you sacrifice one without

mercy to dear old Maria. She leaves no room in your life for anybody else. Do you know,' she enquired of Mrs. Pocock, 'about dear old Maria? The worst is that Miss Gostrey is really a wonderful woman.'

'Oh yes indeed,' Strether answered for her, 'Mrs. Pocock knows about Miss Gostrey. Your mother, Sarah, must have told you about her; your mother knows everything,' he sturdily pursued. 'And I cordially admit,' he added with his conscious gaiety of courage, 'that she's as wonderful a woman as you like.'

'Ah it isn't *I* who "like", dear Mr. Strether, anything to do with the matter!' Sarah Pocock promptly protested; 'and I'm by no means sure I have – from my mother or from any one else – a notion of whom you're talking about.'

'Well, he won't let you see her, you know,' Madame de Vionnet sympathetically threw in. 'He never lets *me* – old friends as we are: I mean as I am with Maria. He reserves her for his best hours; keeps her consummately to himself; only gives us others the crumbs of the feast.'

'Well, Countess, *I've* had some of the crumbs,' Waymarsh observed with weight and covering her with his large look; which led her to break in before he could go on.

'*Comment donc*, he shares her with *you*?' she exclaimed in droll stupefaction. 'Take care you don't have, before you go much further, rather more of all *ces dames* than you may know what to do with!'

But he only continued in his massive way. 'I can post you about the lady, Mrs. Pocock, so far as you may care to hear. I've seen her quite a number of times, and I was practically present when they made acquaintance. I've kept my eye on her right along, but I don't know as there's any real harm in her.'

'"Harm"?' Madame de Vionnet quickly echoed. 'Why she's the dearest and cleverest of all the clever and dear.'

'Well, you run her pretty close, Countess,' Waymarsh returned with spirit; 'though there's no doubt she's pretty well up in things. She knows her way round Europe. Above all there's no doubt she does love Strether.'

'Ah but we all do that – we all love Strether: it isn't a merit!'

their fellow visitor laughed, keeping to her idea with a good conscience at which our friend was aware that he marvelled, though he trusted also for it, as he met her exquisitely expressive eyes, to some later light.

The prime effect of her tone, however – and it was a truth which his own eyes gave back to her in sad ironic play – could only be to make him feel that, to say such things to a man in public, a woman must practically think of him as ninety years old. He had turned awkwardly, responsively red, he knew, at her mention of Maria Gostrey; Sarah Pocock's presence – the particular quality of it – had made this inevitable; and then he had grown still redder in proportion as he hated to have shown anything at all. He felt indeed that he was showing much, as, uncomfortably and almost in pain, he offered up his redness to Waymarsh, who, strangely enough, seemed now to be looking at him with a certain explanatory yearning. Something deep – something built on their old old relation – passed, in this complexity, between them; he got the side-wind of a loyalty that stood behind all actual queer questions. Waymarsh's dry bare humour – as it gave itself to be taken – gloomed out to demand justice. 'Well, if you talk of Miss Barrace I've *my* chance too,' it appeared stiffly to nod, and it granted that it was giving him away, but struggled to add that it did so only to save him. The sombre glow stared it at him till it fairly sounded out – 'to save you, poor old man, to save you; to save you in spite of yourself.' Yet it was somehow just this communication that showed him to himself as more than ever lost. Still another result of it was to put before him as never yet that between his comrade and the interest represented by Sarah there was already a basis. Beyond all question now, yes: Waymarsh had been in occult relation with Mrs. Newsome – out, out it all came in the very effort of his face. 'Yes, you're feeling my hand' – he as good as proclaimed it; 'but only because this at least I *shall* have got out of the damned Old World: that I shall have picked up the pieces into which it has caused you to crumble.' It was as if in short, after an instant, Strether had not only had it from him, but had recognized that so far as this went the instant had cleared the air. Our friend understood and approved; he had

the sense that they wouldn't otherwise speak of it. This would be all, and it would mark in himself a kind of intelligent generosity. It was with grim Sarah then – Sarah grim for all her grace – that Waymarsh had begun at ten o'clock in the morning to save him. Well – if he *could*, poor dear man, with his big bleak kindness! The upshot of which crowded perception was that Strether, on his own side, still showed no more than he absolutely had to. He showed the least possible by saying to Mrs. Pocock after an interval much briefer than our glance at the picture reflected in him: 'Oh it's as true as they please! – There's no Miss Gostrey for any one but me – not the least little peep. I keep her to myself.'

'Well, it's very good of you to notify me,' Sarah replied without looking at him and thrown for a moment by this discrimination, as the direction of her eyes showed, upon a dimly desperate little community with Madame de Vionnet. 'But I hope I shan't miss her too much.'

Madame de Vionnet instantly rallied. 'And you know – though it might occur to one – it isn't in the least that he's ashamed of her. She's really – in a way – extremely good-looking.'

'Ah but extremely!' Strether laughed while he wondered at the odd part he found thus imposed on him.

It continued to be so by every touch from Madame de Vionnet. 'Well, as I say, you know, I wish you would keep *me* a little more to yourself. Couldn't you name some day for me, some hour – and better soon than late? I'll be at home whenever it best suits you. There – I can't say fairer.'

Strether thought a moment while Waymarsh and Mrs. Pocock affected him as standing attentive. 'I did lately call on you. Last week – while Chad was out of town.'

'Yes – and I was away, as it happened, too. You choose your moments well. But don't wait for my next absence, for I shan't make another,' Madame de Vionnet declared, 'while Mrs. Pocock's here.'

'That vow needn't keep you long, fortunately,' Sarah observed with reasserted suavity. 'I shall be at present but a short time in Paris. I have my plans for other countries. I meet

a number of charming friends' – and her voice seemed to caress
that description of these persons.

'Ah then,' her visitor cheerfully replied, 'all the more reason!
To-morrow, for instance, or next day?' she continued to
Strether. 'Tuesday would do for me beautifully.'

'Tuesday then with pleasure.'

'And at half-past five? – or at six?'

It was ridiculous, but Mrs. Pocock and Waymarsh struck him
as fairly waiting for his answer. It was indeed as if they were
arranged, gathered for a performance, the performance of
'Europe' by his confederate and himself. Well, the performance
could only go on. 'Say five forty-five.'

'Five forty-five – good.' And now at last Madame de Vionnet
must leave them, though it carried, for herself, the performance
a little further. 'I *did* hope so much also to see Miss Pocock.
Mayn't I still?'

Sarah hesitated, but she rose equal. 'She'll return your visit
with me. She's at present out with Mr. Pocock and my brother.'

'I see – of course Mr. Newsome has everything to show them.
He has told me so much about her. My great desire's to give
my daughter the opportunity of making her acquaintance. I'm
always on the lookout for such chances for her. If I didn't bring
her to-day it was only to make sure first that you'd let me.'
After which the charming woman risked a more intense appeal.
'It wouldn't suit *you* also to mention some near time, so that
we shall be sure not to lose you?' Strether on his side waited,
for Sarah likewise had, after all, to perform; and it occupied
him to have been thus reminded that she had stayed at home –
and on her first morning of Paris – while Chad led the others
forth. Oh she was up to her eyes; if she had stayed at home she
had stayed by an understanding, arrived at the evening before,
that Waymarsh would come and find her alone. This was beginning well – for a first day in Paris; and the thing might be
amusing yet. But Madame de Vionnet's earnestness was meanwhile beautiful. 'You may think me indiscreet, but I've *such* a
desire my Jeanne shall know an American girl of the really
delightful kind. You see I throw myself for it on your charity.'

The manner of this speech gave Strether such a sense of

depths below it and behind it as he hadn't yet had – ministered in a way that almost frightened him to his dim divinations of reasons; but if Sarah still, in spite of it, faltered, this was why he had time for a sign of sympathy with her petitioner. 'Let me say then, dear lady, to back your plea, that Miss Mamie is of the most delightful kind of all – is charming among the charming.'

Even Waymarsh, though with more to produce on the subject, could get into motion in time. 'Yes, Countess, the American girl's a thing that your country must at least allow ours the privilege to say we *can* show you. But her full beauty is only for those who know how to make use of her.'

'Ah then,' smiled Madame de Vionnet, 'that's exactly what I want to do. I'm sure she has much to teach us.'

It was wonderful, but what was scarce less so was that Strether found himself, by the quick effect of it, moved another way. 'Oh that may be! But don't speak of your own exquisite daughter, you know, as if she weren't pure perfection. *I* at least won't take that from you. Mademoiselle de Vionnet,' he explained, in considerable form, to Mrs. Pocock, '*is* pure perfection. Mademoiselle de Vionnet *is* exquisite.'

It had been perhaps a little portentous, but 'Ah?' Sarah simply glittered.

Waymarsh himself, for that matter, apparently recognized, in respect to the facts, the need of a larger justice, and he had with it an inclination to Sarah. 'Miss Jane's strikingly handsome – in the regular French style.'

It somehow made both Strether and Madame de Vionnet laugh out, though at the very moment he caught in Sarah's eyes, as glancing at the speaker, a vague but unmistakeable 'You too?' It made Waymarsh in fact look consciously over her head. Madame de Vionnet meanwhile, however, made her point in her own way. 'I wish indeed I could offer you my poor child as a dazzling attraction: it would make one's position simple enough! She's as good as she can be, but of course she's different, and the question is now – in the light of the way things seem to go – if she isn't after all *too* different: too different I mean from the splendid type every one is so agreed

that your wonderful country produces. On the other hand of course Mr. Newsome, who knows it so well, has, as a good friend, dear kind man that he is, done everything he can – to keep us from fatal benightedness – for my small shy creature. Well,' she wound up after Mrs. Pocock had signified, in a murmur still a little stiff, that she would speak to her own young charge on the question – 'well, we shall sit, my child and I, and wait and wait and wait for you.' But her last fine turn was for Strether. 'Do speak of us in such a way –!'

'As that something can't but come of it? Oh something *shall* come of it! I take a great interest!' he further declared; and in proof of it, the next moment, he had gone with her down to her carriage.

BOOK NINTH

I

'The difficulty is,' Strether said to Madame de Vionnet a couple of days later, 'that I can't surprise them into the smallest sign of his not being the same old Chad they've been for the last three years glowering at across the sea. They simply won't give any, and as a policy, you know – what you call a *parti pris*,[1] a deep game – that's positively remarkable.'

It was so remarkable that our friend had pulled up before his hostess with the vision of it; he had risen from his chair at the end of ten minutes and begun, as a help not to worry, to move about before her quite as he moved before Maria. He had kept his appointment with her to the minute and had been intensely impatient, though divided in truth between the sense of having everything to tell her and the sense of having nothing at all. The short interval had, in the face of their complication, multiplied his impressions – it being meanwhile to be noted, moreover, that he already frankly, already almost publicly, viewed the complication as common to them. If Madame de Vionnet, under Sarah's eyes, had pulled him into her boat, there was by this time no doubt whatever that he had remained in it and that what he had really most been conscious of for many hours together was the movement of the vessel itself. They were in it together this moment as they hadn't yet been, and he hadn't at present uttered the least of the words of alarm or remonstrance that had died on his lips at the hotel. He had other things to say to her than that she had put him in a position; so quickly had his position grown to affect him as quite excitingly, altogether richly, inevitable. That the outlook, however – given the point of exposure – hadn't cleared up half so much as he had reckoned

was the first warning she received from him on his arrival. She had replied with indulgence that he was in too great a hurry, and had remarked soothingly that if she knew how to be patient surely *he* might be. He felt her presence, on the spot, he felt her tone and everything about her, as an aid to that effort; and it was perhaps one of the proofs of her success with him that he seemed so much to take his ease while they talked. By the time he had explained to her why his impressions, though multiplied, still baffled him, it was as if he had been familiarly talking for hours. They baffled him because Sarah – well, Sarah was deep; deeper than she had ever yet had a chance to show herself. He didn't say that this was partly the effect of her opening so straight down, as it were, into her mother, and that, given Mrs. Newsome's profundity, the shaft thus sunk might well have a reach; but he wasn't without a resigned apprehension that, at such a rate of confidence between the two women, he was likely soon to be moved to show how already, at moments, it had been for him as if he were dealing directly with Mrs. Newsome. Sarah, to a certainty, would have begun herself to feel it in him – and this naturally put it in her power to torment him the more. From the moment she knew he *could* be tormented –!

'But *why* can you be?' – his companion was surprised at his use of the word.

'Because I'm made so – I think of everything.'

'Ah one must never do that,' she smiled. 'One must think of as few things as possible.'

'Then,' he answered, 'one must pick them out right. But all I mean is – for I express myself with violence – that she's in a position to watch me. There's an element of suspense for me, and she can see me wriggle. But my wriggling doesn't matter,' he pursued. 'I can bear it. Besides, I shall wriggle out.'

The picture at any rate stirred in her an appreciation that he felt to be sincere. 'I don't see how a man can be kinder to a woman than you are to me.'

Well, kind was what he wanted to be; yet even while her charming eyes rested on him with the truth of this he none the less had his humour of honesty. 'When I say suspense I mean, you know,' he laughed, 'suspense about my own case too!'

'Oh yes – about your own case too!' It diminished his magnanimity, but she only looked at him the more tenderly.

'Not, however,' he went on, 'that I want to talk to you about that. It's my own little affair, and I mentioned it simply as part of Mrs. Pocock's advantage.' No, no; though there was a queer present temptation in it, and his suspense was so real that to fidget was a relief, he wouldn't talk to her about Mrs. Newsome, wouldn't work off on her the anxiety produced in him by Sarah's calculated omissions of reference. The effect she produced of representing her mother had been produced – and that was just the immense, the uncanny part of it – without her having so much as mentioned that lady. She had brought no message, had alluded to no question, had only answered his enquiries with hopeless limited propriety. She had invented a way of meeting them – as if he had been a polite perfunctory poor relation, of distant degree – that made them almost ridiculous in him. He couldn't moreover on his own side ask much without appearing to publish how he had lately lacked news; a circumstance of which it was Sarah's profound policy not to betray a suspicion. These things, all the same, he wouldn't breathe to Madame de Vionnet – much as they might make him walk up and down. And what he didn't say – as well as what *she* didn't, for she had also her high decencies – enhanced the effect of his being there with her at the end of ten minutes more intimately on the basis of saving her than he had yet had occasion to be. It ended in fact by being quite beautiful between them, the number of things they had a manifest consciousness of not saying. He would have liked to turn her, critically, to the subject of Mrs. Pocock, but he so stuck to the line he felt to be the point of honour and of delicacy that he scarce even asked her what her personal impression had been. He knew it, for that matter, without putting her to trouble: that she wondered how, with such elements, Sarah could still have no charm, was one of the principal things she held her tongue about. Strether would have been interested in her estimate of the elements – indubitably there, some of them, and to be appraised according to taste – but he denied himself even the luxury of this diversion. The way Madame de Vionnet affected him to-day was in itself

a kind of demonstration of the happy employment of gifts. How could a woman think Sarah had charm who struck one as having arrived at it herself by such different roads? On the other hand of course Sarah wasn't obliged to have it. He felt as if somehow Madame de Vionnet *was*. The great question meanwhile was what Chad thought of his sister; which was naturally ushered in by that of Sarah's apprehension of Chad. *That* they could talk of, and with a freedom purchased by their discretion in other senses. The difficulty however was that they were reduced as yet to conjecture. He had given them in the day or two as little of a lead as Sarah, and Madame de Vionnet mentioned that she hadn't seen him since his sister's arrival.

'And does that strike you as such an age?'

She met it in all honesty. 'Oh I won't pretend I don't miss him. Sometimes I see him every day. Our friendship's like that. Make what you will of it!' she whimsically smiled; a little flicker of the kind, occasional in her, that had more than once moved him to wonder what he might best make of *her*. 'But he's perfectly right,' she hastened to add, 'and I wouldn't have him fail in any way at present for the world. I'd sooner not see him for three months. I begged him to be beautiful to them, and he fully feels it for himself.'

Strether turned away under his quick perception; she was so odd a mixture of lucidity and mystery. She fell in at moments with the theory about her he most cherished, and she seemed at others to blow it into air. She spoke now as if her art were all an innocence, and then again as if her innocence were all an art. 'Oh he's giving himself up, and he'll do so to the end. How can he but want, now that it's within reach, his full impression? – which is much more important, you know, than either yours or mine. But he's just soaking,' Strether said as he came back; 'he's going in conscientiously for a saturation. I'm bound to say he *is* very good.'

'Ah,' she quietly replied, 'to whom do you say it?' And then more quietly still: 'He's capable of anything.'

Strether more than reaffirmed – 'Oh he's excellent. I more and more like,' he insisted, 'to see him with them'; though the oddity of this tone between them grew sharper for him even

while they spoke. It placed the young man so before them as the result of her interest and the product of her genius, acknowledged so her part in the phenomenon and made the phenomenon so rare, that more than ever yet he might have been on the very point of asking her for some more detailed account of the whole business than he had yet received from her. The occasion almost forced upon him some question as to how she had managed and as to the appearance such miracles presented from her own singularly close place of survey. The moment in fact however passed, giving way to more present history, and he continued simply to mark his appreciation of the happy truth. 'It's a tremendous comfort to feel how one can trust him.' And then again while for a little she said nothing – as if after all to *her* trust there might be a special limit: 'I mean for making a good show to them.'

'Yes,' she thoughtfully returned – 'but if they shut their eyes to it!'

Strether for an instant had his own thought. 'Well perhaps that won't matter!'

'You mean because he probably – do what they will – won't like them?'

'Oh "do what they will" –! They won't do much; especially if Sarah hasn't more – well, more than one has yet made out – to give.'

Madame de Vionnet weighed it. 'Ah she has all her grace!' It was a statement over which, for a little, they could look at each other sufficiently straight, and though it produced no protest from Strether the effect was somehow as if he had treated it as a joke. 'She may be persuasive and caressing with him; she may be eloquent beyond words. She may get hold of him,' she wound up – 'well, as neither you nor I have.'

'Yes, she *may*' – and now Strether smiled. 'But he has spent all his time each day with Jim. He's still showing Jim round.'

She visibly wondered. 'Then how about Jim?'

Strether took a turn before he answered. 'Hasn't he given you Jim? Hasn't he before this "done" him for you?' He was a little at a loss. 'Doesn't he tell you things?'

She hesitated. 'No' – and their eyes once more gave and took.

'Not as you do. You somehow make me see them – or at least feel them. And I haven't asked too much,' she added; 'I've of late wanted so not to worry him.'

'Ah for that, so have I,' he said with encouraging assent; so that – as if she had answered everything – they were briefly sociable on it. It threw him back on his other thought, with which he took another turn; stopping again, however, presently with something of a glow. 'You see Jim's really immense. I think it will be Jim who'll do it.'

She wondered. 'Get hold of him?'

'No – just the other thing. Counteract Sarah's spell.' And he showed now, our friend, how far he had worked it out. 'Jim's intensely cynical.'

'Oh dear Jim!' Madame de Vionnet vaguely smiled.

'Yes, literally – dear Jim! He's awful. What *he* wants, heaven forgive him, is to help us.'

'You mean' – she was eager – 'help *me*?'

'Well, Chad and me in the first place. But he throws you in too, though without as yet seeing you much. Only, so far as he does see you – if you don't mind – he sees you as awful.'

' "Awful"?' – she wanted it all.

'A regular bad one – though of course of a tremendously superior kind. Dreadful, delightful, irresistible.'

'Ah dear Jim! I should like to know him. I *must*.'

'Yes, naturally. But will it do? You may, you know,' Strether suggested, 'disappoint him.'

She was droll and humble about it. 'I can but try. But my wickedness then,' she went on, 'is my recommendation for him?'

'Your wickedness and the charms with which, in such a degree as yours, he associates it. He understands, you see, that Chad and I have above all wanted to have a good time, and his view is simple and sharp. Nothing will persuade him – in the light, that is, of my behaviour – that I really didn't, quite as much as Chad, come over to have one before it was too late. He wouldn't have expected it of me; but men of my age, at Woollett – and especially the least likely ones – have been noted as liable to strange outbreaks, belated uncanny clutches at the

unusual, the ideal. It's an effect that a lifetime of Woollett has quite been observed as having; and I thus give it to you, in Jim's view, for what it's worth. Now his wife and his mother-in-law,' Strether continued to explain, 'have, as in honour bound, no patience with such phenomena, late or early – which puts Jim, as against his relatives, on the other side. Besides,' he added, 'I don't think he really wants Chad back. If Chad doesn't come –'

'He'll have' – Madame de Vionnet quite apprehended – 'more of the free hand?'

'Well, Chad's the bigger man.'

'So he'll work now, *en dessous*, to keep him quiet?'

'No – he won't "work" at all, and he won't do anything *en dessous*. He's very decent and won't be a traitor in the camp. But he'll be amused with his own little view of our duplicity, he'll sniff up what he supposes to be Paris from morning till night, and he'll be, as to the rest, for Chad – well, just what he is.'

She thought it over. 'A warning?'

He met it almost with glee. 'You *are* as wonderful as everybody says!' And then to explain all he meant: 'I drove him about for his first hour, and do you know what – all beautifully unconscious – he most put before me? Why that something like *that* is at bottom, as an improvement to his present state, as in fact the real redemption of it, what they think it may not be too late to make of our friend.' With which, as, taking it in, she seemed, in her recurrent alarm, bravely to gaze at the possibility, he completed his statement. 'But it *is* too late. Thanks to you!'

It drew from her again one of her indefinite reflexions. 'Oh "me" – after all!'

He stood before her so exhilarated by his demonstration that he could fairly be jocular. 'Everything's comparative. You're better than *that*.'

'You' – she could but answer him – 'are better than anything.' But she had another thought. '*Will* Mrs. Pocock come to me?'

'Oh yes – she'll do that. As soon, that is, as my friend Waymarsh – *her* friend now – leaves her leisure.'

She showed an interest. 'Is he so much her friend as that?'

'Why, didn't you see it all at the hotel?'

'Oh' – she was amused – ' "all" is a good deal to say. I don't know – I forget. I lost myself in *her*.'

'You were splendid,' Strether returned – 'but "all" isn't a good deal to say: it's only a little. Yet it's charming so far as it goes. She wants a man to herself.'

'And hasn't she got *you*?'

'Do you think she looked at me – or even at you – as if she had?' Strether easily dismissed that irony. 'Every one, you see, must strike her as having somebody. You've got Chad – and Chad has got you.'

'I see' – she made of it what she could. 'And you've got Maria.'

Well, he on his side accepted that. 'I've got Maria. And Maria has got me. So it goes.'

'But Mr. Jim – whom has he got?'

'Oh he has got – or it's as *if* he had – the whole place.'

'But for Mr. Waymarsh' – she recalled – 'isn't Miss Barrace before any one else?'

He shook his head. 'Miss Barrace is a *raffinée*, and her amusement won't lose by Mrs. Pocock. It will gain rather – especially if Sarah triumphs and she comes in for a view of it.'

'How well you know us!' Madame de Vionnet, at this, frankly sighed.

'No – it seems to me it's we that I know. I know Sarah – it's perhaps on that ground only that my feet are firm. Waymarsh will take her round while Chad takes Jim – and I shall be, I assure you, delighted for both of them. Sarah will have had what she requires – she will have paid her tribute to the ideal; and he will have done about the same. In Paris it's in the air – so what can one do less? If there's a point that, beyond any other, Sarah wants to make, it's that she didn't come out to be narrow. We shall feel at least that.'

'Oh,' she sighed, 'the quantity we seem likely to "feel"! But what becomes, in these conditions, of the girl?'

'Of Mamie – if we're all provided? Ah for that,' said Strether, 'you can trust Chad.'

'To be, you mean, all right to her?'

'To pay her every attention as soon as he has polished off Jim. He wants what Jim can give him – and what Jim really won't – though he has had it all, and more than all, from me. He wants in short his own personal impression, and he'll get it – strong. But as soon as he has got it Mamie won't suffer.'

'Oh Mamie mustn't *suffer*!' Madame de Vionnet soothingly emphasized.

But Strether could reassure her. 'Don't fear. As soon as he has done with Jim, Jim will fall to me. And then you'll see.'

It was as if in a moment she saw already; yet she still waited. Then 'Is she really quite charming?' she asked.

He had got up with his last words and gathered in his hat and gloves. 'I don't know; I'm watching. I'm studying the case, as it were – and I dare say I shall be able to tell you.'

She wondered. 'Is it a case?'

'Yes – I think so. At any rate I shall see.'

'But haven't you known her before?'

'Yes,' he smiled – 'but somehow at home she wasn't a case. She has become one since.' It was as if he made it out for himself. 'She has become one here.'

'So very very soon?'

He measured it, laughing. 'Not sooner than I did.'

'And you became one –?'

'Very very soon. The day I arrived.'

Her intelligent eyes showed her thought of it. 'Ah but the day you arrived you met Maria. Whom has Miss Pocock met?'

He paused again, but he brought it out. 'Hasn't she met Chad?'

'Certainly – but not for the first time. He's an old friend.' At which Strether had a slow amused significant headshake that made her go on: 'You mean that for *her* at least he's a new person – that she sees him as different?'

'She sees him as different.'

'And how does she see him?'

Strether gave it up. 'How can one tell how a deep little girl sees a deep young man?'

'Is every one so deep? Is she too?'

'So it strikes me – deeper than I thought. But wait a little – between us we'll make it out. You'll judge for that matter yourself.'

Madame de Vionnet looked for the moment fairly bent on the chance. 'Then she *will* come with her? – I mean Mamie with Mrs. Pocock?'

'Certainly. Her curiosity, if nothing else, will in any case work that. But leave it all to Chad.'

'Ah,' wailed Madame de Vionnet, turning away a little wearily, 'the things I leave to Chad!'

The tone of it made him look at her with a kindness that showed his vision of her suspense. But he fell back on his confidence. 'Oh well – trust him. Trust him all the way.' He had indeed no sooner so spoken than the queer displacement of his point of view appeared again to come up for him in the very sound, which drew from him a short laugh, immediately checked. He became still more advisory. 'When they do come give them plenty of Miss Jeanne. Let Mamie see her well.'

She looked for a moment as if she placed them face to face. 'For Mamie to hate her?'

He had another of his corrective headshakes. 'Mamie won't. Trust *them*.'

She looked at him hard, and then as if it were what she must always come back to: 'It's *you* I trust. But I was sincere,' she said, 'at the hotel. I did, I do, want my child –'

'Well?' – Strether waited with deference while she appeared to hesitate as to how to put it.

'Well, to do what she can for me.'

Strether for a little met her eyes on it; after which something that might have been unexpected to her came from him. 'Poor little duck!'

Not more expected for himself indeed might well have been her echo of it. 'Poor little duck! But she immensely wants herself,' she said, 'to see our friend's cousin.'

'Is that what she thinks her?'

'It's what we call the young lady.'

He thought again; then with a laugh: 'Well, your daughter will help you.'

And now at last he took leave of her, as he had been intending for five minutes. But she went part of the way with him, accompanying him out of the room and into the next and the next. Her noble old apartment offered a succession of three, the first two of which indeed, on entering, smaller than the last, but each with its faded and formal air, enlarged the office of the antechamber and enriched the sense of approach. Strether fancied them, liked them, and, passing through them with her more slowly now, met a sharp renewal of his original impression. He stopped, he looked back; the whole thing made a vista, which he found high melancholy and sweet – full, once more, of dim historic shades, of the faint far-away cannon-roar of the great Empire. It was doubtless half the projection of his mind, but his mind was a thing that, among old waxed parquets, pale shades of pink and green, pseudo-classic candelabra, he had always needfully to reckon with. They could easily make him irrelevant. The oddity, the originality, the poetry – he didn't know what to call it – of Chad's connexion reaffirmed for him its romantic side. 'They ought to see this, you know. They *must*.'

'The Pococks?' – she looked about in deprecation; she seemed to see gaps he didn't.

'Mamie and Sarah – Mamie in particular.'

'My shabby old place? But *their* things – !'

'Oh their things! You were talking of what will do something for you –'

'So that it strikes you,' she broke in, 'that my poor place may? Oh,' she ruefully mused, 'that *would* be desperate!'

'Do you know what I wish?' he went on. 'I wish Mrs. Newsome herself could have a look.'

She stared, missing a little his logic. 'It would make a difference?'

Her tone was so earnest that as he continued to look about he laughed. 'It might!'

'But you've told her, you tell me –'

'All about you? Yes, a wonderful story. But there's all the indescribable – what one gets only on the spot.'

'Thank you!' she charmingly and sadly smiled.

'It's all about me here,' he freely continued. 'Mrs. Newsome feels things.'

But she seemed doomed always to come back to doubt. 'No one feels so much as *you*. No – not any one.'

'So much the worse then for every one. It's very easy.'

They were by this time in the antechamber, still alone together, as she hadn't rung for a servant. The antechamber was high and square, grave and suggestive too, a little cold and slippery even in summer, and with a few old prints that were precious, Strether divined, on the walls. He stood in the middle, slightly lingering, vaguely directing his glasses, while, leaning against the door-post of the room, she gently pressed her cheek to the side of the recess. '*You* would have been a friend.'

'I?' – it startled him a little.

'For the reason you say. You're not stupid.' And then abruptly, as if bringing it out were somehow founded on that fact: 'We're marrying Jeanne.'

It affected him on the spot as a move in a game, and he was even then not without the sense that that wasn't the way Jeanne should be married. But he quickly showed his interest, though – as quickly afterwards struck him – with an absurd confusion of mind. '"You"? You and – a – not Chad?' Of course it was the child's father who made the 'we', but to the child's father it would have cost him an effort to allude. Yet didn't it seem the next minute that Monsieur de Vionnet was after all not in question? – since she had gone on to say that it was indeed to Chad she referred and that he had been in the whole matter kindness itself.

'If I must tell you all, it is he himself who has put us in the way. I mean in the way of an opportunity that, so far as I can yet see, is all I could possibly have dreamed of. For all the trouble Monsieur de Vionnet will ever take!' It was the first time she had spoken to him of her husband, and he couldn't have expressed how much more intimate with her it suddenly made him feel. It wasn't much, in truth – there were other things in what she was saying that were far more; but it was as if, while they stood there together so easily in these cold chambers of the past, the single touch had shown the reach of her

confidence. 'But our friend,' she asked, 'hasn't then told you?'

'He has told me nothing.'

'Well, it has come with rather a rush – all in a very few days; and hasn't moreover yet taken a form that permits an announcement. It's only for you – absolutely you alone – that I speak; I so want you to know.' The sense he had so often had, since the first hour of his disembarkment, of being further and further 'in', treated him again at this moment to another twinge; but in this wonderful way of her putting him in there continued to be something exquisitely remorseless. 'Monsieur de Vionnet will accept what he *must* accept. He has proposed half a dozen things – each one more impossible than the other; and he wouldn't have found this if he lives to a hundred. Chad found it,' she continued with her lighted, faintly flushed, her conscious confidential face, 'in the quietest way in the world. Or rather it found *him* – for everything finds him; I mean finds him right. You'll think we do such things strangely – but at my age,' she smiled, 'one has to accept one's conditions. Our young man's people had seen her; one of his sisters, a charming woman – we know all about them – had observed her somewhere with me. She had spoken to her brother – turned him on; and we were again observed, poor Jeanne and I, without our in the least knowing it. It was at the beginning of the winter; it went on for some time; it outlasted our absence; it began again on our return; and it luckily seems all right. The young man had met Chad, and he got a friend to approach him – as having a decent interest in us. Mr. Newsome looked well before he leaped; he kept beautifully quiet and satisfied himself fully; then only he spoke. It's what has for some time past occupied us. It seems as if it were what would do; really, really all one could wish. There are only two or three points to be settled – they depend on her father. But this time I think we're safe.'

Strether, consciously gaping a little, had fairly hung upon her lips. 'I hope so with all my heart.' And then he permitted himself: 'Does nothing depend on *her*?'

'Ah naturally; everything did. But she's pleased *comme tout*. She has been perfectly free; and he – our young friend – is really a combination. I quite adore him.'

Strether just made sure. 'You mean your future son-in-law?'

'Future if we all bring it off.'

'Ah well,' said Strether decorously, 'I heartily hope you may.' There seemed little else for him to say, though her communication had the oddest effect on him. Vaguely and confusedly he was troubled by it; feeling as if he had even himself been concerned in something deep and dim. He had allowed for depths, but these were greater: and it was as if, oppressively – indeed absurdly – he was responsible for what they had now thrown up to the surface. It was – through something ancient and cold in it – what he would have called the real thing. In short his hostess's news, though he couldn't have explained why, was a sensible shock, and his oppression a weight he felt he must somehow or other immediately get rid of. There were too many connexions missing to make it tolerable he should do anything else. He was prepared to suffer – before his own inner tribunal – for Chad; he was prepared to suffer even for Madame de Vionnet. But he wasn't prepared to suffer for the little girl. So now having said the proper thing, he wanted to get away. She held him an instant, however, with another appeal.

'Do I seem to you very awful?'

'Awful? Why so?' But he called it to himself, even as he spoke, his biggest insincerity yet.

'Our arrangements are so different from yours.'

'Mine?' Oh he could dismiss that too! 'I haven't any arrangements.'

'Then you must accept mine; all the more that they're excellent. They're founded on a *vieille sagesse*. There will be much more, if all goes well, for you to hear and to know, and everything, believe me, for you to like. Don't be afraid; you'll be satisfied.' Thus she could talk to him of what, of her innermost life – for that was what it came to – he must 'accept'; thus she could extraordinarily speak as if in such an affair his being satisfied had an importance. It was all a wonder and made the whole case larger. He had struck himself at the hotel, before Sarah and Waymarsh, as being in her boat; but where on earth was he now? This question was in the air till her own lips

quenched it with another. 'And do you suppose *he* – who loves her so – would do anything reckless or cruel?'

He wondered what he supposed. 'Do you mean your young man – ?'

'I mean yours. I mean Mr. Newsome.' It flashed for Strether the next moment a finer light, and the light deepened as she went on. 'He takes, thank God, the truest tenderest interest in her.'

It deepened indeed. 'Oh I'm sure of that!'

'You were talking,' she said, 'about one's trusting him. You see then how I do.'

He waited a moment – it all came. 'I see – I see.' He felt he really did see.

'He wouldn't hurt her for the world, nor – assuming she marries at all – risk anything that might make against her happiness. And – willingly, at least – he would never hurt *me*.'

Her face, with what he had by this time grasped, told him more than her words; whether something had come into it, or whether he only read clearer, her whole story – what at least he then took for such – reached out to him from it. With the initiative she now attributed to Chad it all made a sense, and this sense – a light, a lead, was what had abruptly risen before him. He wanted, once more, to get off with these things; which was at last made easy, a servant having, for his assistance, on hearing voices in the hall, just come forward. All that Strether had made out was, while the man opened the door and imper-sonally waited, summed up in his last word. 'I don't think, you know, Chad will tell me anything.'

'No – perhaps not yet.'

'And I won't as yet speak to him.'

'Ah that's as you'll think best. You must judge.'

She had finally given him her hand, which he held a moment. 'How *much* I have to judge!'

'Everything,' said Madame de Vionnet: a remark that was indeed – with the refined disguised suppressed passion of her face – what he most carried away.

II

So far as a direct approach was concerned Sarah had neglected him, for the week now about to end, with a civil consistency of chill that, giving him a higher idea of her social resource, threw him back on the general reflexion that a woman could always be amazing. It indeed helped a little to console him that he felt sure she had for the same period also left Chad's curiosity hanging; though on the other hand, for his personal relief, Chad could at least go through the various motions – and he made them extraordinarily numerous – of seeing she had a good time. There wasn't a motion on which, in her presence, poor Strether could so much as venture, and all he could do when he was out of it was to walk over for a talk with Maria. He walked over of course much less than usual, but he found a special compensation in a certain half-hour during which, toward the close of a crowded empty expensive day, his several companions seemed to him so disposed of as to give his forms and usages a rest. He had been with them in the morning and had nevertheless called on the Pococks in the afternoon; but their whole group, he then found, had dispersed after a fashion of which it would amuse Miss Gostrey to hear. He was sorry again, gratefully sorry she was so out of it – she who had really put him in; but she had fortunately always her appetite for news. The pure flame of the disinterested burned in her cave of treasures as a lamp in a Byzantine vault. It was just now, as happened, that for so fine a sense as hers a near view would have begun to pay. Within three days, precisely, the situation on which he was to report had shown signs of an equilibrium; the effect of his look in at the hotel was to confirm this appearance. If the equilibrium

might only prevail! Sarah was out with Waymarsh, Mamie was out with Chad, and Jim was out alone. Later on indeed he himself was booked to Jim, was to take him that evening to the Varieties – which Strether was careful to pronounce as Jim pronounced them.

Miss Gostrey drank it in. 'What then to-night do the others do?'

'Well, it has been arranged. Waymarsh takes Sarah to dine at Bignon's.'[1]

She wondered. 'And what do they do after? They can't come straight home.'

'No, they can't come straight home – at least Sarah can't. It's their secret, but I think I've guessed it.' Then as she waited: 'The circus.'

It made her stare a moment longer, then laugh almost to extravagance. 'There's no one like you!'

'Like *me*?' – he only wanted to understand.

'Like all of you together – like all of us: Woollett, Milrose and their products. We're abysmal – but may we never be less so! Mr. Newsome,' she continued, 'meanwhile takes Miss Pocock – ?'

'Precisely – to the Français: to see what *you* took Waymarsh and me to, a family-bill.'

'Ah then may Mr. Chad enjoy it as *I* did!' But she saw so much in things. 'Do they spend their evening, your young people, like that, alone together?'

'Well, they're young people – but they're old friends.'

'I see, I see. And do *they* dine – for a difference – at Brébant's?'[2]

'Oh where they dine is their secret too. But I've my idea that it will be, very quietly, at Chad's own place.'

'She'll come to him there alone?'

They looked at each other a moment. 'He has known her from a child. Besides,' said Strether with emphasis, 'Mamie's remarkable. She's splendid.'

She wondered. 'Do you mean she expects to bring it off?'

'Getting hold of him? No – I think not.'

'She doesn't want him enough? – or doesn't believe in her

power?' On which as he said nothing she continued: 'She finds she doesn't care for him?'

'No – I think she finds she does. But that's what I mean by so describing her. It's *if* she does that she's splendid. But we'll see,' he wound up, 'where she comes out.'

'You seem to show me sufficiently,' Miss Gostrey laughed, 'where she goes in! But is her childhood's friend,' she asked, 'permitting himself recklessly to flirt with her?'

'No – not that. Chad's also splendid. They're *all* splendid!' he declared with a sudden strange sound of wistfulness and envy. 'They're at least *happy*.'

'Happy?' – it appeared, with their various difficulties, to surprise her.

'Well – I seem to myself among them the only one who isn't.'

She demurred. 'With your constant tribute to the ideal?'

He had a laugh at his tribute to the ideal, but he explained after a moment his impression. 'I mean they're living. They're rushing about. I've already had my rushing. I'm waiting.'

'But aren't you,' she asked by way of cheer, 'waiting with *me*?'

He looked at her in all kindness. 'Yes – if it weren't for that!'

'And you help me to wait,' she said. 'However,' she went on, 'I've really something for you that will help you to wait and which you shall have in a minute. Only there's something more I want from you first. I revel in Sarah.'

'So do I. If it weren't,' he again amusedly sighed, 'for *that* –!'

'Well, you owe more to women than any man I ever saw. We do seem to keep you going. Yet Sarah, as I see her, must be great.'

'She *is*' – Strether fully assented: 'great! Whatever happens, she won't, with these unforgettable days, have lived in vain.'

Miss Gostrey had a pause. 'You mean she has fallen in love?'

'I mean she wonders if she hasn't – and it serves all her purpose.'

'It has indeed,' Maria laughed, 'served women's purposes before!'

'Yes – for giving in. But I doubt if the idea – as an idea – has ever up to now answered so well for holding out. That's *her*

tribute to the ideal – we each have our own. It's her romance – and it seems to me better on the whole than mine. To have it in Paris too,' he explained – 'on this classic ground, in this charged infectious air, with so sudden an intensity: well, it's more than she expected. She has had in short to recognize the breaking out for her of a real affinity – and with everything to enhance the drama.'

Miss Gostrey followed. 'Jim for instance?'

'Jim. Jim hugely enhances. Jim was made to enhance. And then Mrs. Waymarsh. It's the crowning touch – it supplies the colour. He's positively separated.'

'And she herself unfortunately isn't – that supplies the colour too.' Miss Gostrey was all there. But somehow –! 'Is *he* in love?'

Strether looked at her a long time; then looked all about the room; then came a little nearer. 'Will you never tell any one in the world as long as ever you live?'

'Never.' It was charming.

'He thinks Sarah really is. But he has no fear,' Strether hastened to add.

'Of her being affected by it?'

'Of *his* being. He likes it, but he knows she can hold out. He's helping her, he's floating her over, by kindness.'

Maria rather funnily considered it. 'Floating her over in champagne? The kindness of dining her, nose to nose, at the hour when all Paris is crowding to profane delights, and in the – well, in the great temple, as one hears of it, of pleasure?'

'That's just *it*, for both of them,' Strether insisted – 'and all of a supreme innocence. The Parisian place, the feverish hour, the putting before her of a hundred francs' worth of food and drink, which they'll scarcely touch – all that's the dear man's own romance; the expensive kind, expensive in francs and centimes, in which he abounds. And the circus afterwards – which is cheaper, but which he'll find some means of making as dear as possible – that's also *his* tribute to the ideal. It does for him. He'll see her through. They won't talk of anything worse than you and me.'

'Well, we're bad enough perhaps, thank heaven,' she laughed,

'to upset them! Mr. Waymarsh at any rate is a hideous old coquette.' And the next moment she had dropped everything for a different pursuit. 'What you don't appear to know is that Jeanne de Vionnet has become engaged. She's to marry – it has been definitely arranged – young Monsieur de Montbron.'

He fairly blushed. 'Then – if you know it – it's "out"?'

'Don't I often know things that are *not* out? However,' she said, 'this will be out to-morrow. But I see I've counted too much on your possible ignorance. You've been before me, and I don't make you jump as I hoped.'

He gave a gasp at her insight. 'You never fail! I've *had* my jump. I had it when I first heard.'

'Then if you knew why didn't you tell me as soon as you came in?'

'Because I had it from her as a thing not yet to be spoken of.'

Miss Gostrey wondered. 'From Madame de Vionnet herself?'

'As a probability – not quite a certainty: a good cause in which Chad has been working. So I've waited.'

'You need wait no longer,' she returned. 'It reached me yester-day – roundabout and accidental, but by a person who had had it from one of the young man's own people – as a thing quite settled. I was only keeping it for you.'

'You thought Chad wouldn't have told me?'

She hesitated. 'Well, if he hasn't –'

'He hasn't. And yet the thing appears to have been practically his doing. So there we are.'

'There we are!' Maria candidly echoed.

'That's why I jumped. I jumped,' he continued to explain, 'because it means, this disposition of the daughter, that there's now nothing else: nothing else but him and the mother.'

'Still – it simplifies.'

'It simplifies' – he fully concurred. 'But that's precisely where we are. It marks a stage in his relation. The act is his answer to Mrs. Newsome's demonstration.'

'It tells,' Maria asked, 'the worst?'

'The worst.'

'But is the worst what he wants Sarah to know?'

'He doesn't care for Sarah.'

At which Miss Gostrey's eyebrows went up. 'You mean she has already dished herself?'

Strether took a turn about; he had thought it out again and again before this, to the end; but the vista seemed each time longer. 'He wants his good friend to know the best. I mean the measure of his attachment. She asked for a sign, and he thought of that one. There it is.'

'A concession to her jealousy?'

Strether pulled up. 'Yes – call it that. Make it lurid – for that makes my problem richer.'

'Certainly, let us have it lurid – for I quite agree with you that we want none of our problems poor. But let us also have it clear. Can he, in the midst of such a preoccupation, or on the heels of it, have seriously cared for Jeanne? – cared, I mean, as a young man at liberty would have cared?'

Well, Strether had mastered it. 'I think he can have thought it would be charming if he *could* care. It would be nicer.'

'Nicer than being tied up to Marie?'

'Yes – than the discomfort of an attachment to a person he can never hope, short of a catastrophe, to marry. And he was quite right,' said Strether. 'It would certainly have been nicer. Even when a thing's already nice there mostly *is* some other thing that would have been nicer – or as to which we wonder if it wouldn't. But his question was all the same a dream. He *couldn't* care in that way. He *is* tied up to Marie. The relation is too special and has gone too far. It's the very basis, and his recent lively contribution toward establishing Jeanne in life has been his definite and final acknowledgement to Madame de Vionnet that he has ceased squirming. I doubt meanwhile,' he went on, 'if Sarah has at all directly attacked him.'

His companion brooded. 'But won't he wish for his own satisfaction to make his ground good to her?'

'No – he'll leave it to me, he'll leave everything to me. I "sort of" feel' – he worked it out – 'that the whole thing will come upon me. Yes, I shall have every inch and every ounce of it. I shall be *used* for it –!' And Strether lost himself in the prospect. Then he fancifully expressed the issue. 'To the last drop of my blood.'

Maria, however, roundly protested. 'Ah you'll please keep a drop for *me*. *I* shall have a use for it!' – which she didn't however follow up. She had come back the next moment to another matter. 'Mrs. Pocock, with her brother, is trusting only to her general charm?'

'So it would seem.'

'And the charm's not working?'

Well, Strether put it otherwise, 'She's sounding the note of home – which is the very best thing she can do.'

'The best for Madame de Vionnet?'

'The best for home itself. The natural one; the right one.'

'Right,' Maria asked, 'when it fails?'

Strether had a pause. 'The difficulty's Jim. Jim's the note of home.'

She debated. 'Ah surely not the note of Mrs. Newsome.'

But he had it all. 'The note of the home for which Mrs. Newsome wants him – the home of the business. Jim stands, with his little legs apart, at the door of *that* tent; and Jim *is*, frankly speaking, extremely awful.'

Maria stared. 'And you in, you poor thing, for your evening with him?'

'Oh he's all right for *me*!' Strether laughed. 'Any one's good enough for *me*. But Sarah shouldn't, all the same, have brought him. She doesn't appreciate him.'

His friend was amused with this statement of it. 'Doesn't know, you mean, how bad he is?'

Strether shook his head with decision. 'Not really.'

She wondered. 'Then doesn't Mrs. Newsome?'

It made him frankly do the same. 'Well, no – since you ask me.'

Maria rubbed it in. 'Not really either?'

'Not at all. She rates him rather high.' With which indeed, immediately, he took himself up. 'Well, he *is* good too, in his way. It depends on what you want him for.'

Miss Gostrey, however, wouldn't let it depend on anything – wouldn't have it, and wouldn't want him, at any price. 'It suits my book,' she said, 'that he should be impossible; and it suits it still better,' she more imaginatively added, 'that Mrs. Newsome doesn't know he is.'

Strether, in consequence, had to take it from her, but he fell back on something else. 'I'll tell you who does really know.'

'Mr. Waymarsh? Never!'

'Never indeed. I'm not *always* thinking of Mr. Waymarsh; in fact I find now I never am.' Then he mentioned the person as if there were a good deal in it. 'Mamie.'

'His own sister?' Oddly enough it but let her down. 'What good will that do?'

'None perhaps. But there – as usual – we are!'

III

There they were yet again, accordingly, for two days more; when Strether, on being, at Mrs. Pocock's hotel, ushered into that lady's salon, found himself at first assuming a mistake on the part of the servant who had introduced him and retired. The occupants hadn't come in, for the room looked empty as only a room can look in Paris, of a fine afternoon, when the faint murmur of the huge collective life, carried on out of doors, strays among scattered objects even as a summer air idles in a lonely garden. Our friend looked about and hesitated; observed, on the evidence of a table charged with purchases and other matters, that Sarah had become possessed – by no aid from *him* – of the last number of the salmon-coloured Revue; noted further that Mamie appeared to have received a present of Fromentin's 'Maîtres d'Autrefois'[1] from Chad, who had written her name on the cover; and pulled up at the sight of a heavy letter addressed in a hand he knew. This letter, forwarded by a banker and arriving in Mrs. Pocock's absence, had been placed in evidence, and it drew from the fact of its being unopened a sudden queer power to intensify the reach of its author. It brought home to him the scale on which Mrs. Newsome – for she had been copious indeed this time – was writing to her daughter while she kept *him* in durance; and it had altogether such an effect upon him as made him for a few minutes stand still and breathe low. In his own room, at his own hotel, he had dozens of well-filled envelopes superscribed in that character; and there was actually something in the renewal of his interrupted vision of the character that played straight into the so frequent question of whether he weren't already disinherited

beyond appeal. It was such an assurance as the sharp downstrokes of her pen hadn't yet had occasion to give him; but they somehow at the present crisis stood for a probable absoluteness in any decree of the writer. He looked at Sarah's name and address, in short, as if he had been looking hard into her mother's face, and then turned from it as if the face had declined to relax. But since it was in a manner as if Mrs. Newsome were thereby all the more, instead of the less, in the room, and were conscious, sharply and sorely conscious, of himself, so he felt both held and hushed, summoned to stay at least and take his punishment. By staying, accordingly, he took it – creeping softly and vaguely about and waiting for Sarah to come in. She *would* come in if he stayed long enough, and he had now more than ever the sense of her success in leaving him a prey to anxiety. It wasn't to be denied that she had had a happy instinct, from the point of view of Woollett, in placing him thus at the mercy of her own initiative. It was very well to try to say he didn't care – that she might break ground when she would, might never break it at all if she wouldn't, and that he had no confession whatever to wait upon her with: he breathed from day to day an air that damnably required clearing, and there were moments when he quite ached to precipitate that process. He couldn't doubt that, should she only oblige him by surprising him just as he then was, a clarifying scene of some sort would result from the concussion.

He humbly circulated in this spirit till he suddenly had a fresh arrest. Both the windows of the room stood open to the balcony, but it was only now that, in the glass of the leaf of one of them, folded back, he caught a reflexion quickly recognized as the colour of a lady's dress. Somebody had been then all the while on the balcony, and the person, whoever it might be, was so placed between the windows as to be hidden from him; while on the other hand the many sounds of the street had covered his own entrance and movements. If the person were Sarah he might on the spot therefore be served to his taste. He might lead her by a move or two up to the remedy for his vain tension; as to which, should he get nothing else from it, he would at least have the relief of pulling down the roof on their heads.

There was fortunately no one at hand to observe – in respect
to his valour – that even on this completed reasoning he still
hung fire. He had been waiting for Mrs. Pocock and the sound
of the oracle; but he had to gird himself afresh – which he
did in the embrasure of the window, neither advancing, nor
retreating – before provoking the revelation. It was apparently
for Sarah to come more into view; he was in that case there at
her service. She did however, as meanwhile happened, come
more into view; only she luckily came at the last minute as a
contradiction of Sarah. The occupant of the balcony was after
all quite another person, a person presented, on a second look,
by a charming back and a slight shift of her position, as beautiful brilliant unconscious Mamie – Mamie alone at home,
Mamie passing her time in her own innocent way, Mamie in
short rather shabbily used, but Mamie absorbed interested and
interesting. With her arms on the balustrade and her attention
dropped to the street she allowed Strether to watch her, to
consider several things, without her turning round.

But the oddity was that when he *had* so watched and considered he simply stepped back into the room without following
up his advantage. He revolved there again for several minutes,
quite as with something new to think of and as if the bearings
of the possibility of Sarah had been superseded. For frankly,
yes, it *had* bearings thus to find the girl in solitary possession.
There was something in it that touched him to a point not to
have been reckoned beforehand, something that softly but quite
pressingly spoke to him, and that spoke the more each time
he paused again at the edge of the balcony and saw her still
unaware. Her companions were plainly scattered; Sarah would
be off somewhere with Waymarsh and Chad off somewhere
with Jim. Strether didn't at all mentally impute to Chad that he
was with his 'good friend'; he gave him the benefit of supposing
him involved in appearances that, had he had to describe them
– for instance to Maria – he would have conveniently qualified
as more subtle. It came to him indeed the next thing that
there was perhaps almost an excess of refinement in having left
Mamie in such weather up there alone; however she might in
fact have extemporized, under the charm of the Rue de Rivoli,

a little makeshift Paris of wonder and fancy. Our friend in
any case now recognized – and it was as if at the recognition
Mrs. Newsome's fixed intensity had suddenly, with a deep
audible gasp, grown thin and vague – that day after day he had
been conscious in respect to his young lady of something odd
and ambiguous, yet something into which he could at last read
a meaning. It had been at the most, this mystery, an obsession
– oh an obsession agreeable; and it had just now fallen into
its place as at the touch of a spring. It had represented the
possibility between them of some communication baffled by
accident and delay – the possibility even of some relation as yet
unacknowledged.

There was always their old relation, the fruit of the Woollett
years; but that – and it was what was strangest – had nothing
whatever in common with what was now in the air. As a child,
as a 'bud', and then again as a flower of expansion, Mamie
had bloomed for him, freely, in the almost incessantly open
doorways of home; where he remembered her as first very
forward, as then very backward – for he had carried on at
one period, in Mrs. Newsome's parlours (oh Mrs. Newsome's
phases and his own!) a course of English Literature re-enforced
by exams and teas – and once more, finally, as very much in
advance. But he had kept no great sense of points of contact; it
not being in the nature of things at Woollett that the freshest
of the buds should find herself in the same basket with the most
withered of the winter apples. The child had given sharpness,
above all, to his sense of the flight of time; it was but the day
before yesterday that he had tripped up on her hoop, yet his
experience of remarkable women – destined, it would seem,
remarkably to grow – felt itself ready this afternoon, quite
braced itself, to include her. She had in fine more to say to him
than he had ever dreamed the pretty girl of the moment *could*
have; and the proof of the circumstance was that, visibly, unmistakeably, she had been able to say it to no one else. It was
something she could mention neither to her brother, to her
sister-in-law nor to Chad; though he could just imagine that
had she still been at home she might have brought it out, as
a supreme tribute to age, authority and attitude, for Mrs.

Newsome. It was moreover something in which they all took
an interest; the strength of their interest was in truth just the
reason of her prudence. All this then, for five minutes, was vivid
to Strether, and it put before him that, poor child, she had now
but her prudence to amuse her. That, for a pretty girl in Paris,
struck him, with a rush, as a sorry state; so that under the
impression he went out to her with a step as hypocritically
alert, he was well aware, as if he had just come into the room.
She turned with a start at his voice; preoccupied with him
though she might be, she was just a scrap disappointed. 'Oh I
thought you were Mr. Bilham!'

The remark had been at first surprising and our friend's
private thought, under the influence of it, temporarily blighted;
yet we are able to add that he presently recovered his inward
tone and that many a fresh flower of fancy was to bloom in the
same air. Little Bilham – since little Bilham was, somewhat
incongruously, expected – appeared behindhand; a circumstance by which Strether was to profit. They came back into
the room together after a little, the couple on the balcony, and
amid its crimson-and-gold elegance, with the others still absent,
Strether passed forty minutes that he appraised even at the time
as far, in the whole queer connexion, from his idlest. Yes indeed,
since he had the other day so agreed with Maria about the
inspiration of the lurid, here was something for his problem
that surely didn't make it shrink and that was floated in upon
him as part of a sudden flood. He was doubtless not to know
till afterwards, on turning them over in thought, of how many
elements his impression was composed; but he none the less
felt, as he sat with the charming girl, the signal growth of a
confidence. For she *was* charming, when all was said – and
none the less so for the visible habit and practice of freedom
and fluency. She was charming, he was aware, in spite of the
fact that if he hadn't found her so he would have found her
something he should have been in peril of expressing as 'funny'.
Yes, she was funny, wonderful Mamie, and without dreaming
it; she was bland, she was bridal – with never, that he could
make out as yet, a bridegroom to support it; she was handsome
and portly and easy and chatty, soft and sweet and almost

disconcertingly reassuring. She was dressed, if we might so far discriminate, less as a young lady than as an old one – had an old one been supposable to Strether as so committed to vanity; the complexities of her hair missed moreover also the looseness of youth; and she had a mature manner of bending a little, as to encourage and reward, while she held neatly together in front of her a pair of strikingly polished hands: the combination of all of which kept up about her the glamour of her 'receiving', placed her again perpetually between the windows and within sound of the ice-cream plates, suggested the enumeration of all the names, all the Mr. Brookses and Mr. Snookses, gregarious specimens of a single type, she was happy to 'meet'.

But if all this was where she was funny, and if what was funnier than the rest was the contrast between her beautiful benevolent patronage – such a hint of the polysyllabic as might make her something of a bore toward middle age – and her rather flat little voice, the voice, naturally, unaffectedly yet, of a girl of fifteen; so Strether, none the less, at the end of ten minutes, felt in her a quiet dignity that pulled things bravely together. If quiet dignity, almost more than matronly, with voluminous, too voluminous clothes, was the effect she proposed to produce, that was an ideal one could like in her when once one had got into relation. The great thing now for her visitor was that this was exactly what he had done; it made so extraordinary a mixture of the brief and crowded hour. It was the mark of a relation that he had begun so quickly to find himself sure she was, of all people, as might have been said, on the side and of the party of Mrs. Newsome's original ambassador. She was in *his* interest and not in Sarah's; and some sign of that was precisely what he had been feeling in her, these last days, as imminent. Finally placed, in Paris, in immediate presence of the situation and of the hero of it – by whom Strether was incapable of meaning any one but Chad – she had accomplished, and really in a manner all unexpected to herself, a change of base; deep still things had come to pass within her, and by the time she had grown sure of them Strether had become aware of the little drama. When she knew where she was, in short, he had made it out; and he made it out at present

still better; though with never a direct word passing between them all the while on the subject of his own predicament. There had been at first, as he sat there with her, a moment during which he wondered if she meant to break ground in respect to his prime undertaking. That door stood so strangely ajar that he was half-prepared to be conscious, at any juncture, of her having, of any one's having, quite bounced in. But, friendly, familiar, light of touch and happy of tact, she exquisitely stayed out; so that it was for all the world as if to show she could deal with him without being reduced to – well, scarcely anything.

It fully came up for them then, by means of their talking of everything *but* Chad, that Mamie, unlike Sarah, unlike Jim, knew perfectly what had become of him. It fully came up that she had taken to the last fraction of an inch the measure of the change in him, and that she wanted Strether to know what a secret she proposed to make of it. They talked most conveniently – as if they had had no chance yet – about Woollett; and that had virtually the effect of their keeping the secret more close. The hour took on for Strether, little by little, a queer sad sweetness of quality; he had such a revulsion in Mamie's favour and on behalf of her social value as might have come from remorse at some early injustice. She made him, as under the breath of some vague western whiff, homesick and freshly restless; he could really for the time have fancied himself stranded with her on a far shore, during an ominous calm, in a quaint community of shipwreck. Their little interview was like a picnic on a coral strand; they passed each other, with melancholy smiles and looks sufficiently allusive, such cupfuls of water as they had saved. Especially sharp in Strether meanwhile was the conviction that his companion really knew, as we have hinted, where she had come out. It was at a very particular place – only *that* she would never tell him; it would be above all what he should have to puzzle for himself. This was what he hoped for, because his interest in the girl wouldn't be complete without it. No more would the appreciation to which she was entitled – so assured was he that the more he saw of her process the more he should see of her pride. She saw, herself, everything; but she knew what she didn't want, and that it was that had

helped her. What didn't she want? – there was a pleasure lost for her old friend in not yet knowing, as there would doubtless be a thrill in getting a glimpse. Gently and sociably she kept that dark to him, and it was as if she soothed and beguiled him in other ways to make up for it. She came out with her impression of Madame de Vionnet – of whom she had 'heard so much'; she came out with her impression of Jeanne, whom she had been 'dying to see': she brought it out with a blandness by which her auditor was really stirred that she had been with Sarah early that very afternoon, and after dreadful delays caused by all sorts of things, mainly, eternally, by the purchase of clothes – clothes that unfortunately wouldn't be themselves eternal – to call in the Rue de Bellechasse.

At the sound of these names Strether almost blushed to feel that he couldn't have sounded them first – and yet couldn't either have justified his squeamishness. Mamie made them easy as he couldn't have begun to do, and yet it could only have cost her more than he should ever have had to spend. It was as friends of Chad's, friends special, distinguished, desirable, enviable, that she spoke of them, and she beautifully carried it off that much as she had heard of them – though she didn't say how or where, which was a touch of her own – she had found them beyond her supposition. She abounded in praise of them, and after the manner of Woollett – which made the manner of Woollett a loveable thing again to Strether. He had never so felt the true inwardness of it as when his blooming companion pronounced the elder of the ladies of the Rue de Bellechasse too fascinating for words and declared of the younger that she was perfectly ideal, a real little monster of charm. 'Nothing,' she said of Jeanne, 'ought ever to happen to her – she's so awfully right as she is. Another touch will spoil her – so she oughtn't to *be* touched.'

'Ah but things, here in Paris,' Strether observed, 'do happen to little girls.' And then for the joke's and the occasion's sake: 'Haven't you found that yourself?'

'That things happen –? Oh I'm not a little girl. I'm a big battered blowsy one. *I* don't care,' Mamie laughed, '*what* happens.'

Strether had a pause while he wondered if it mightn't happen that he should give her the pleasure of learning that he found her nicer than he had really dreamed – a pause that ended when he had said to himself that, so far as it at all mattered for her, she had in fact perhaps already made this out. He risked accordingly a different question – though conscious, as soon as he had spoken, that he seemed to place it in relation to her last speech. 'But that Mademoiselle de Vionnet is to be married – I suppose you've heard of *that*.'

For all, he then found, he need fear! 'Dear, yes; the gentleman was there: Monsieur de Montbron, whom Madame de Vionnet presented to us.'

'And was he nice?'

Mamie bloomed and bridled with her best reception manner. 'Any man's nice when he's in love.'

It made Strether laugh. 'But is Monsieur de Montbron in love – already – with *you*?'

'Oh that's not necessary – it's so much better he should be so with *her*: which, thank goodness, I lost no time in discovering for myself. He's perfectly gone – and I couldn't have borne it for her if he hadn't been. She's just too sweet.'

Strether hesitated. 'And through being in love too?'

On which with a smile that struck him as wonderful Mamie had a wonderful answer. 'She doesn't know if she is or not.'

It made him again laugh out. 'Oh but *you* do!'

She was willing to take it that way. 'Oh yes, I know everything.' And as she sat there rubbing her polished hands and making the best of it – only holding her elbows perhaps a little too much out – the momentary effect for Strether was that every one else, in all their affair, seemed stupid.

'Know that poor little Jeanne doesn't know what's the matter with her?'

It was as near as they came to saying that she was probably in love with Chad; but it was quite near enough for what Strether wanted; which was to be confirmed in his certitude that, whether in love or not, she appealed to something large and easy in the girl before him. Mamie would be fat, too fat, at thirty; but she would always be the person who, at the present

sharp hour, had been disinterestedly tender. 'If I see a little more of her, as I hope I shall, I think she'll like me enough – for she seemed to like me to-day – to want me to tell her.'

'And *shall* you?'

'Perfectly. I shall tell her the matter with her is that she wants only too much to do right. To do right for her, naturally,' said Mamie, 'is to please.'

'Her mother, do you mean?'

'Her mother first.'

Strether waited. 'And then?'

'Well, "then" – Mr. Newsome.'

There was something really grand for him in the serenity of this reference. 'And last only Monsieur de Montbron?'

'Last only' – she good-humouredly kept it up.

Strether considered. 'So that every one after all then will be suited?'

She had one of her few hesitations, but it was a question only of a moment; and it was her nearest approach to being explicit with him about what was between them. 'I think I can speak for myself. *I* shall be.'

It said indeed so much, told such a story of her being ready to help him, so committed to him that truth, in short, for such use as he might make of it toward those ends of his own with which, patiently and trustfully, she had nothing to do – it so fully achieved all this that he appeared to himself simply to meet it in its own spirit by the last frankness of admiration. Admiration was of itself almost accusatory, but nothing less would serve to show her how nearly he understood. He put out his hand for good-bye with a 'Splendid, splendid, splendid!' And he left her, in her splendour, still waiting for little Bilham.

BOOK TENTH

I

Strether occupied beside little Bilham, three evenings after his interview with Mamie Pocock, the same deep divan they had enjoyed together on the first occasion of our friend's meeting Madame de Vionnet and her daughter in the apartment of the Boulevard Malesherbes, where his position affirmed itself again as ministering to an easy exchange of impressions. The present evening had a different stamp; if the company was much more numerous, so, inevitably, were the ideas set in motion. It was on the other hand, however, now strongly marked that the talkers moved, in respect to such matters, round an inner, a protected circle. They knew at any rate what really concerned them to-night, and Strether had begun by keeping his companion close to it. Only a few of Chad's guests had dined – that is fifteen or twenty, a few compared with the large concourse offered to sight by eleven o'clock; but number and mass, quantity and quality, light, fragrance, sound, the overflow of hospitality meeting the high tide of response, had all from the first pressed upon Strether's consciousness, and he felt himself somehow part and parcel of the most festive scene, as the term was, in which he had ever in his life been engaged. He had perhaps seen, on Fourths of July and on dear old domestic Commencements, more people assembled, but he had never seen so many in proportion to the space, or had at all events never known so great a promiscuity to show so markedly as picked. Numerous as was the company, it had still been made so by selection, and what was above all rare for Strether was that, by no fault of his own, he was in the secret of the principle that had worked. He hadn't enquired, he had averted his head, but Chad had put

him a pair of questions that themselves smoothed the ground. He hadn't answered the questions, he had replied that they were the young man's own affair; and he had then seen perfectly that the latter's direction was already settled.

Chad had applied for counsel only by way of intimating that he knew what to do; and he had clearly never known it better than in now presenting to his sister the whole circle of his society. This was all in the sense and the spirit of the note struck by him on that lady's arrival; he had taken at the station itself a line that led him without a break, and that enabled him to lead the Pococks – though dazed a little, no doubt, breathless, no doubt, and bewildered – to the uttermost end of the passage accepted by them perforce as pleasant. He had made it for them violently pleasant and mercilessly full; the upshot of which was, to Strether's vision, that they had come all the way without discovering it to be really no passage at all. It was a brave blind alley, where to pass was impossible and where, unless they stuck fast, they would have – which was always awkward – publicly to back out. They were touching bottom assuredly tonight; the whole scene represented the terminus of the *cul-de-sac*. So could things go when there was a hand to keep them consistent – a hand that pulled the wire with a skill at which the elder man more and more marvelled. The elder man felt responsible, but he also felt successful, since what had taken place was simply the issue of his own contention, six weeks before, that they properly should wait to see what their friends would have really to say. He had determined Chad to wait, he had determined him to see; he was therefore not to quarrel with the time given up to the business. As much as ever, accordingly, now that a fortnight had elapsed, the situation created for Sarah, and against which she had raised no protest, was that of her having accommodated herself to her adventure as to a pleasure-party surrendered perhaps even somewhat in excess to bustle and to 'pace'. If her brother had been at any point the least bit open to criticism it might have been on the ground of his spicing the draught too highly and pouring the cup too full. Frankly treating the whole occasion of the presence of his relatives as an opportunity for amusement, he left it, no doubt,

but scant margin as an opportunity for anything else. He suggested, invented, abounded – yet all the while with the loosest
easiest rein. Strether, during his own weeks, had gained a sense
of knowing Paris; but he saw it afresh, and with fresh emotion,
in the form of the knowledge offered to his colleague.

A thousand unuttered thoughts hummed for him in the air
of these observations; not the least frequent of which was that
Sarah might well of a truth not quite know whither she was
drifting. She was in no position not to appear to expect that
Chad should treat her handsomely; yet she struck our friend as
privately stiffening a little each time she missed the chance of
marking the great *nuance*. The great *nuance* was in brief that
of course her brother must treat her handsomely – she should
like to see him not; but that treating her handsomely, none the
less, wasn't all in all – treating her handsomely buttered no
parsnips;[1] and that in fine there were moments when she felt
the fixed eyes of their admirable absent mother fairly screw into
the flat of her back. Strether, watching, after his habit, and
overscoring with thought, positively had moments of his own
in which he found himself sorry for her – occasions on which
she affected him as a person seated in a runaway vehicle and
turning over the question of a possible jump. *Would* she jump,
could she, would *that* be a safe place? – this question, at such
instants, sat for him in her lapse into pallor, her tight lips, her
conscious eyes. It came back to the main point at issue: would
she be, after all, to be squared? He believed on the whole she
would jump; yet his alternations on this subject were the more
especial stuff of his suspense. One thing remained well before
him – a conviction that was in fact to gain sharpness from the
impressions of this evening: that if she *should* gather in her
skirts, close her eyes and quit the carriage while in motion, he
would promptly enough become aware. She would alight from
her headlong course more or less directly upon him; it would be
appointed to him, unquestionably, to receive her entire weight.
Signs and portents of the experience thus in reserve for him
had, as it happened, multiplied even through the dazzle of
Chad's party. It was partly under the nervous consciousness of
such a prospect that, leaving almost every one in the two other

rooms, leaving those of the guests already known to him as well as a mass of brilliant strangers of both sexes and of several varieties of speech, he had desired five quiet minutes with little Bilham, whom he always found soothing and even a little inspiring, and to whom he had actually moreover something distinct and important to say.

He had felt of old – for it already seemed long ago – rather humiliated at discovering he could learn in talk with a personage so much his junior the lesson of a certain moral ease; but he had now got used to that – whether or no the mixture of the fact with other humiliations had made it indistinct, whether or no directly from little Bilham's example, the example of his being contentedly just the obscure and acute little Bilham he was. It worked so for him, Strether seemed to see; and our friend had at private hours a wan smile over the fact that he himself, after so many more years, was still in search of something that would work. However, as we have said, it worked just now for them equally to have found a corner a little apart. What particularly kept it apart was the circumstance that the music in the salon was admirable, with two or three such singers as it was a privilege to hear in private. Their presence gave a distinction to Chad's entertainment, and the interest of calculating their effect on Sarah was actually so sharp as to be almost painful. Unmistakeably, in her single person, the motive of the composition and dressed in a splendour of crimson which affected Strether as the sound of a fall through a skylight, she would now be in the forefront of the listening circle and committed by it up to her eyes. Those eyes during the wonderful dinner itself he hadn't once met; having confessedly – perhaps a little pusillanimously – arranged with Chad that he should be on the same side of the table. But there was no use in having arrived now with little Bilham at an unprecedented point of intimacy unless he could pitch everything into the pot. 'You who sat where you could see her, what does she make of it all? By which I mean on what terms does she take it?'

'Oh she takes it, I judge, as proving that the claim of his family is more than ever justified.'

'She isn't then pleased with what he has to show?'

'On the contrary; she's pleased with it as with his capacity to do this kind of thing – more than she has been pleased with anything for a long time. But she wants him to show it *there*. He has no right to waste it on the likes of us.'

Strether wondered. 'She wants him to move the whole thing over?'

'The whole thing – with an important exception. Everything he has "picked up" – and the way he knows how. She sees no difficulty in that. She'd run the show herself, and she'll make the handsome concession that Woollett would be on the whole in some ways the better for it. Not that it wouldn't be also in some ways the better for Woollett. The people there are just as good.'

'Just as good as you and these others? Ah that may be. But such an occasion as this, whether or no,' Strether said, 'isn't the people. It's what has made the people possible.'

'Well then,' his friend replied, 'there you are; I give you my impression for what it's worth. Mrs. Pocock has *seen*, and that's to-night how she sits there. If you were to have a glimpse of her face you'd understand me. She has made up her mind – to the sound of expensive music.'

Strether took it freely in. 'Ah then I shall have news of her.'

'I don't want to frighten you, but I think that likely. However,' little Bilham continued, 'if I'm of the least use to you to hold on by –!'

'You're not of the least!' – and Strether laid an appreciative hand on him to say it. 'No one's of the least.' With which, to mark how gaily he could take it, he patted his companion's knee. 'I must meet my fate alone, and I *shall* – oh you'll see! And yet,' he pursued the next moment, 'you *can* help me too. You once said to me' – he followed this further – 'that you held Chad should marry. I didn't see then so well as I know now that you meant he should marry Miss Pocock. Do you still consider that he should? Because if you do' – he kept it up – 'I want you immediately to change your mind. You can help me that way.'

'Help you by thinking he should *not* marry?'

'Not marry at all events Mamie.'

'And who then?'

'Ah,' Strether returned, 'that I'm not obliged to say. But Madame de Vionnet – I suggest – when he can.'

'Oh!' said little Bilham with some sharpness.

'Oh precisely! But he needn't marry at all – I'm at any rate not obliged to provide for it. Whereas in your case I rather feel that I *am*.'

Little Bilham was amused. 'Obliged to provide for my marrying?'

'Yes – after all I've done to you!'

The young man weighed it. 'Have you done as much as that?'

'Well,' said Strether, thus challenged, 'of course I must remember what you've also done to *me*. We may perhaps call it square. But all the same,' he went on, 'I wish awfully you'd marry Mamie Pocock yourself.'

Little Bilham laughed out. 'Why it was only the other night, in this very place, that you were proposing to me a different union altogether.'

'Mademoiselle de Vionnet?' Well, Strether easily confessed it. 'That, I admit, was a vain image. *This* is practical politics. I want to do something good for both of you – I wish you each so well; and you can see in a moment the trouble it will save me to polish you off by the same stroke. She likes you, you know. You console her. And she's splendid.'

Little Bilham stared as a delicate appetite stares at an overheaped plate. 'What do I console her for?'

It just made his friend impatient. 'Oh come, you know!'

'And what proves for you that she likes me?'

'Why the fact that I found her three days ago stopping at home alone all the golden afternoon on the mere chance that you'd come to her, and hanging over her balcony on that of seeing your cab drive up. I don't know what you want more.'

Little Bilham after a moment found it. 'Only just to know what proves to you that I like *her*.'

'Oh if what I've just mentioned isn't enough to make you do it, you're a stony-hearted little fiend. Besides' – Strether encouraged his fancy's flight – 'you showed your inclination in

the way you kept her waiting, kept her on purpose to see if she cared enough for you.'

His companion paid his ingenuity the deference of a pause. 'I didn't keep her waiting. I came at the hour. I wouldn't have kept her waiting for the world,' the young man honourably declared.

'Better still – then there you are!' And Strether, charmed, held him the faster. 'Even if you didn't do her justice, moreover,' he continued, 'I should insist on your immediately coming round to it. I want awfully to have worked it. I want' – and our friend spoke now with a yearning that was really earnest – 'at least to have done *that*.'

'To have married me off – without a penny?'

'Well, I shan't live long; and I give you my word, now and here, that I'll leave you every penny of my own. I haven't many, unfortunately, but you shall have them all. And Miss Pocock, I think, has a few. I want,' Strether went on, 'to have been at least to that extent constructive – even expiatory. I've been sacrificing so to strange gods that I feel I want to put on record, somehow, my fidelity – fundamentally unchanged after all – to our own. I feel as if my hands were embrued with the blood of monstrous alien altars – of another faith altogether. There it is – it's done.' And then he further explained. 'It took hold of me because the idea of getting her quite out of the way for Chad helps to clear my ground.'

The young man, at this, bounced about, and it brought them face to face in admitted amusement. 'You want me to marry as a convenience to Chad?'

'No,' Strether debated – '*he* doesn't care whether you marry or not. It's as a convenience simply to my own plan *for* him.'

' "Simply"!' – and little Bilham's concurrence was in itself a lively comment. 'Thank you. But I thought,' he continued, 'you had exactly *no* plan "for" him.'

'Well then call it my plan for myself – which may be well, as you say, to have none. His situation, don't you see? is reduced now to the bare facts one has to recognize. Mamie doesn't want him, and he doesn't want Mamie: so much as that these days

have made clear. It's a thread we can wind up and tuck in.'

But little Bilham still questioned. '*You* can – since you seem so much to want to. But why should I?'

Poor Strether thought it over, but was obliged of course to admit that his demonstration did superficially fail. 'Seriously, there *is* no reason. It's my affair – I must do it alone. I've only my fantastic need of making my dose stiff.'

Little Bilham wondered. 'What do you call your dose?'

'Why what I have to swallow. I want my conditions unmitigated.'

He had spoken in the tone of talk for talk's sake, and yet with an obscure truth lurking in the loose folds; a circumstance presently not without its effect on his young friend. Little Bilham's eyes rested on him a moment with some intensity; then suddenly, as if everything had cleared up, he gave a happy laugh. It seemed to say that if pretending, or even trying, or still even hoping, to be able to care for Mamie would be of use, he was all there for the job. 'I'll do anything in the world for you!'

'Well,' Strether smiled, 'anything in the world is all I want. I don't know anything that pleased me in her more,' he went on, 'than the way that, on my finding her up there all alone, coming on her unawares and feeling greatly for her being so out of it, she knocked down my tall house of cards with her instant and cheerful allusion to the next young man. It was somehow so the note I needed – her staying at home to receive him.'

'It was Chad of course,' said little Bilham, 'who asked the next young man – I like your name for me! – to call.'

'So I supposed – all of which, thank God, is in our innocent and natural manners. But do you know,' Strether asked, 'if Chad knows – ?' And then as this interlocutor seemed at a loss: 'Why where she has come out.'

Little Bilham, at this, met his face with a conscious look; it was as if, more than anything yet, the allusion had penetrated. 'Do you know yourself?'

Strether lightly shook his head. 'There I stop. Oh, odd as it may appear to you, there *are* things I don't know. I only got the sense from her of something very sharp, and yet very deep

down, that she was keeping all to herself. That is I had begun with the belief that she *had* kept it to herself; but face to face with her there I soon made out that there was a person with whom she would have shared it. I had thought she possibly might with *me* – but I saw then that I was only half in her confidence. When, turning to me to greet me – for she was on the balcony and I had come in without her knowing it – she showed me she had been expecting *you* and was proportionately disappointed, I got hold of the tail of my conviction. Half an hour later I was in possession of all the rest of it. You know what has happened.' He looked at his young friend hard – then he felt sure. 'For all you say, you're up to your eyes. So there you are.'

Little Bilham after an instant pulled half round. 'I assure you she hasn't told me anything.'

'Of course she hasn't. For what do you suggest that I suppose her to take you? But you've been with her every day, you've seen her freely, you've liked her greatly – I stick to that – and you've made your profit of it. You know what she has been through as well as you know that she has dined here to-night – which must have put her, by the way, through a good deal more.'

The young man faced this blast; after which he pulled round the rest of the way. 'I haven't in the least said she hasn't been nice to me. But she's proud.'

'And quite properly. But not too proud for that.'

'It's just her pride that has made her. Chad,' little Bilham loyally went on, 'has really been as kind to her as possible. It's awkward for a man when a girl's in love with him.'

'Ah but she isn't – now.'

Little Bilham sat staring before him; then he sprang up as if his friend's penetration, recurrent and insistent, made him really after all too nervous. 'No – she isn't now. It isn't in the least,' he went on, 'Chad's fault. He's really all right. I mean he would have been willing. But she came over with ideas. Those she had got at home. They had been her motive and support in joining her brother and his wife. She was to *save* our friend.'

'Ah like me, poor thing?' Strether also got to his feet.

'Exactly – she had a bad moment. It was very soon distinct to her, to pull her up, to let her down, that, alas, he was, he *is*, saved. There's nothing left for her to do.'

'Not even to love him?'

'She would have loved him better as she originally believed him.'

Strether wondered. 'Of course one asks one's self what notion a little girl forms, where a young man's in question, of such a history and such a state.'

'Well, this little girl saw them, no doubt, as obscure, but she saw them practically as wrong. The wrong for her *was* the obscure. Chad turns out at any rate right and good and disconcerting, while what she was all prepared for, primed and girded and wound up for, was to deal with him as the general opposite.'

'Yet wasn't her whole point' – Strether weighed it – 'that he was to be, that he *could* be, made better, redeemed?'

Little Bilham fixed it all a moment, and then with a small headshake that diffused a tenderness: 'She's too late. Too late for the miracle.'

'Yes' – his companion saw enough. 'Still, if the worst fault of his condition is that it may be all there for her to profit by –?'

'Oh she doesn't want to "profit", in that flat way. She doesn't want to profit by another woman's work – she wants the miracle to have been her own miracle. *That's* what she's too late for.'

Strether quite felt how it all fitted, yet there seemed one loose piece. 'I'm bound to say, you know, that she strikes one, on these lines, as fastidious – what you call here *difficile*.'

Little Bilham tossed up his chin. 'Of course she's *difficile* – on any lines! What else in the world *are* our Mamies – the real, the right ones?'

'I see, I see,' our friend repeated, charmed by the responsive wisdom he had ended by so richly extracting. 'Mamie is one of the real and the right.'

'The very thing itself.'

'And what it comes to then,' Strether went on, 'is that poor awful Chad is simply too good for her.'

'Ah too good was what he was after all to be; but it was she herself, and she herself only, who was to have made him so.'

It hung beautifully together, but with still a loose end. 'Wouldn't he do for her even if he should after all break –'

'With his actual influence?' Oh little Bilham had for this enquiry the sharpest of all his controls. 'How can he "do" – on any terms whatever – when he's flagrantly spoiled?'

Strether could only meet the question with his passive, his receptive pleasure. 'Well, thank goodness, *you're* not! *You* remain for her to save, and I come back, on so beautiful and full a demonstration, to my contention of just now – that of your showing distinct signs of her having already begun.'

The most he could further say to himself – as his young friend turned away – was that the charge encountered for the moment no renewed denial. Little Bilham, taking his course back to the music, only shook his good-natured ears an instant, in the manner of a terrier who has got wet; while Strether relapsed into the sense – which had for him in these days most of comfort – that he was free to believe in anything that from hour to hour kept him going. He had positively motions and flutters of this conscious hour-to-hour kind, temporary surrenders to irony, to fancy, frequent instinctive snatches at the growing rose of observation, constantly stronger for him, as he felt, in scent and colour, and in which he could bury his nose even to wantonness. This last resource was offered him, for that matter, in the very form of his next clear perception – the vision of a prompt meeting, in the doorway of the room, between little Bilham and brilliant Miss Barrace, who was entering as Bilham withdrew. She had apparently put him a question, to which he had replied by turning to indicate his late interlocutor; toward whom, after an interrogation further aided by a resort to that optical machinery which seemed, like her other ornaments, curious and archaic, the genial lady, suggesting more than ever for her fellow guest the old French print, the historic portrait, directed herself with an intention that Strether instantly met. He knew in advance the first note she would sound, and took in as she approached all her need of sounding it. Nothing yet had been so 'wonderful' between them as the present occasion; and it was her special sense of this quality in occasions that she was there, as she was in most places, to feed. That sense

had already been so well fed by the situation about them that she had quitted the other room, forsaken the music, dropped out of the play, abandoned, in a word, the stage itself, that she might stand a minute behind the scenes with Strether and so perhaps figure as one of the famous augurs replying, behind the oracle, to the wink of the other. Seated near him presently where little Bilham had sat, she replied in truth to many things; beginning as soon as he had said to her – what he hoped he said without fatuity – 'All you ladies are extraordinarily kind to me.'

She played her long handle, which shifted her observation; she saw in an instant all the absences that left them free. 'How can we be anything else? But isn't that exactly your plight? "We ladies" – oh we're nice, and you must be having enough of us! As one of us, you know, I don't pretend I'm crazy about us. But Miss Gostrey at least to-night has left you alone, hasn't she?' With which she again looked about as if Maria might still lurk.

'Oh yes,' said Strether; 'she's only sitting up for me at home.' And then as this elicited from his companion her gay 'Oh, oh, oh!' he explained that he meant sitting up in suspense and prayer. 'We thought it on the whole better she shouldn't be present; and either way of course it's a terrible worry for her.' He abounded in the sense of his appeal to the ladies, and they might take their choice of his doing so from humility or from pride. 'Yet she inclines to believe I shall come out.'

'Oh I incline to believe too you'll come out!' – Miss Barrace, with her laugh, was not to be behind. 'Only the question's about *where*, isn't it? However,' she happily continued, 'if it's anywhere at all it must be very far on, mustn't it? To do us justice, I think, you know,' she laughed, 'we do, among us all, want you rather far on. Yes, yes,' she repeated in her quick droll way; 'we want you very, *very* far on!' After which she wished to know why he had thought it better Maria shouldn't be present.

'Oh,' he replied, 'it was really her own idea. I should have wished it. But she dreads responsibility.'

'And isn't that a new thing for her?'

'To dread it? No doubt – no doubt. But her nerve has given way.'

Miss Barrace looked at him a moment. 'She has too much at stake.' Then less gravely: 'Mine, luckily for me, holds out.'

'Luckily for me too' – Strether came back to that. 'My own isn't so firm, *my* appetite for responsibility isn't so sharp, as that I haven't felt the very principle of this occasion to be "the more the merrier". If we *are* so merry it's because Chad has understood so well.'

'He has understood amazingly,' said Miss Barrace.

'It's wonderful!' – Strether anticipated for her.

'It's wonderful!' she, to meet it, intensified; so that, face to face over it, they largely and recklessly laughed. But she presently added: 'Oh I see the principle. If one didn't one would be lost. But when once one has got hold of it –'

'It's as simple as twice two! From the moment he had to do something –'

'A crowd' – she took him straight up – 'was the only thing? Rather, rather: a rumpus of sound,' she laughed, 'or nothing. Mrs. Pocock's built in, or built out – whichever you call it; she's packed so tight she can't move. She's in splendid isolation' – Miss Barrace embroidered the theme.

Strether followed, but scrupulous of justice. 'Yet with everyone in the place successively introduced to her.'

'Wonderfully – but just so that it does build her out. She's bricked up, she's buried alive!'

Strether seemed for a moment to look at it; but it brought him to a sigh. 'Oh but she's not dead! It will take more than this to kill her.'

His companion had a pause that might have been for pity. 'No, I can't pretend I think she's finished – or that it's for more than to-night.' She remained pensive as if with the same compunction. 'It's only up to her chin.' Then again for the fun of it: 'She can breathe.'

'She can breathe!' – he echoed it in the same spirit. 'And do you know,' he went on, 'what's really all this time happening to me? – through the beauty of music, the gaiety of voices, the uproar in short of our revel and the felicity of your wit? The

sound of Mrs. Pocock's respiration drowns for me, I assure you, every other. It's literally all I hear.'

She focussed him with her clink of chains. 'Well –!' she breathed ever so kindly.

'Well, what?'

'She *is* free from her chin up,' she mused; 'and that *will* be enough for her.'

'It will be enough for me!' Strether ruefully laughed. 'Waymarsh has really,' he then asked, 'brought her to see you?'

'Yes – but that's the worst of it. I could do you no good. And yet I tried hard.'

Strether wondered. 'And how did you try?'

'Why I didn't speak of you.'

'I see. That was better.'

'Then what would have been worse? For speaking or silent,' she lightly wailed, 'I somehow "compromise". And it has never been any one but you.'

'That shows' – he was magnanimous – 'that it's something not in you, but in one's self. It's *my* fault.'

She was silent a little. 'No, it's Mr. Waymarsh's. It's the fault of his having brought her.'

'Ah then,' said Strether good-naturedly, 'why *did* he bring her?'

'He couldn't afford not to.'

'Oh you were a trophy – one of the spoils of conquest? But why in that case, since you do "compromise" –'

'Don't I compromise *him* as well? I do compromise him as well,' Miss Barrace smiled. 'I compromise him as hard as I can. But for Mr. Waymarsh it isn't fatal. It's – so far as his wonderful relation with Mrs. Pocock is concerned – favourable.' And then, as he still seemed slightly at sea: 'The man who had succeeded with *me*, don't you see? For her to get him from me was such an added incentive.'

Strether saw, but as if his path was still strewn with surprises. 'It's "from" you then that she has got him?'

She was amused at his momentary muddle. 'You can fancy my fight! She believes in her triumph. I think it has been part of her joy.'

'Oh her joy!' Strether sceptically murmured.

'Well, she thinks she has had her own way. And what's to-night for her but a kind of apotheosis? Her frock's really good.'

'Good enough to go to heaven in? For after a real apotheosis,' Strether went on, 'there's nothing *but* heaven. For Sarah there's only to-morrow.'

'And you mean that she won't find to-morrow heavenly?'

'Well, I mean that I somehow feel to-night – on her behalf – too good to be true. She has had her cake; that is she's in the act now of having it, of swallowing the largest and sweetest piece. There won't be another left for her. Certainly *I* haven't one. It can only, at the best, be Chad.' He continued to make it out as for their common entertainment. 'He may have one, as it were, up his sleeve; yet it's borne in upon me that if he had –'

'He wouldn't' – she quite understood – 'have taken all *this* trouble? I dare say not, and, if I may be quite free and dreadful, I very much hope he won't take any more. Of course I won't pretend now,' she added, 'not to know what it's a question of.'

'Oh everyone must know now,' poor Strether thoughtfully admitted; 'and it's strange enough and funny enough that one should feel everybody here at this very moment to be knowing and watching and waiting.'

'Yes – isn't it indeed funny?' Miss Barrace quite rose to it. 'That's the way we *are* in Paris.' She was always pleased with a new contribution to that queerness. 'It's wonderful! But, you know,' she declared, 'it all depends on you. I don't want to turn the knife in your vitals, but that's naturally what you just now meant by our all being on top of you. We know you as the hero of the drama, and we're gathered to see what you'll do.'

Strether looked at her a moment with a light perhaps slightly obscured. 'I think that must be why the hero has taken refuge in this corner. He's scared at his heroism – he shrinks from his part.'

'Ah but we nevertheless believe he'll play it. That's why,' Miss Barrace kindly went on, 'we take such an interest in you. We feel you'll come up to the scratch.' And then as he seemed perhaps not quite to take fire: 'Don't let him do it.'

'Don't let Chad go?'

'Yes, keep hold of him. With all this' – and she indicated the general tribute – 'he has done enough. We love him here – he's charming.'

'It's beautiful,' said Strether, 'the way you all can simplify when you will.'

But she gave it to him back. 'It's nothing to the way *you* will when you must.'

He winced at it as at the very voice of prophecy, and it kept him a moment quiet. He detained her, however, on her appearing about to leave him alone in the rather cold clearance their talk had made. 'There positively isn't a sign of a hero to-night; the hero's dodging and shirking, the hero's ashamed. Therefore, you know, I think, what you must all *really* be occupied with is the heroine.'

Miss Barrace took a minute. 'The heroine?'

'The heroine. I've treated her,' said Strether, 'not a bit like a hero. Oh,' he sighed, 'I don't do it well!'

She eased him off. 'You do it as you can.' And then after another hesitation: 'I think she's satisfied.'

But he remained compunctious. 'I haven't been near her. I haven't looked at her.'

'Ah then you've lost a good deal!'

He showed he knew it. 'She's more wonderful than ever?'

'Than ever. With Mr. Pocock.'

Strether wondered. 'Madame de Vionnet – with Jim?'

'Madame de Vionnet – with "Jim".' Miss Barrace was historic.

'And what's she doing with him?'

'Ah you must ask *him*!'

Strether's face lighted again at the prospect. 'It *will* be amusing to do so.' Yet he continued to wonder. 'But she must have some idea.'

'Of course she has – she has twenty ideas. She has in the first place,' said Miss Barrace, swinging a little her tortoise-shell, 'that of doing her part. Her part is to help *you*.'

It came out as nothing had come yet; links were missing and connexions unnamed, but it was suddenly as if they were at the heart of their subject. 'Yes; how much more she does it,' Strether

gravely reflected, 'than I help *her*!' It all came over him as with the near presence of the beauty, the grace, the intense, dissimulated spirit with which he had, as he said, been putting off contact. '*She* has courage.'

'Ah she has courage!' Miss Barrace quite agreed; and it was as if for a moment they saw the quantity in each other's face.

But indeed the whole thing was present. 'How much she must care!'

'Ah there it is. She does care. But it isn't, is it,' Miss Barrace considerately added, 'as if you had ever had any doubt of that?'

Strether seemed suddenly to like to feel that he really never had. 'Why of course it's the whole point.'

'Voilà!' Miss Barrace smiled.

'It's why one came out,' Strether went on. 'And it's why one has stayed so long. And it's also' – he abounded – 'why one's going home. It's why, it's why –'

'It's why everything!' she concurred. 'It's why she might be to-night – for all she looks and shows, and for all your friend "Jim" does – about twenty years old. That's another of her ideas; to be for him, and to be quite easily and charmingly, as young as a little girl.'

Strether assisted at his distance. ' "For him"? For Chad – ?'

'For Chad, in a manner, naturally, always. But in particular to-night for Mr. Pocock.' And then as her friend still stared: 'Yes, it *is* of a bravery! But that's what she has: her high sense of duty.' It was more than sufficiently before them. 'When Mr. Newsome has his hands so embarrassed with his sister –'

'It's quite the least' – Strether filled it out – 'that she should take his sister's husband? Certainly – quite the least. So she has taken him.'

'She has taken him.' It was all Miss Barrace had meant.

Still it remained enough. 'It must be funny.'

'Oh it *is* funny.' That of course essentially went with it.

But it brought them back. 'How indeed then she must care!' In answer to which Strether's entertainer dropped a comprehensive 'Ah!' expressive perhaps of some impatience for the time he took to get used to it. She herself had got used to it long before.

II

When one morning within the week he perceived the whole thing to be really at last upon him Strether's immediate feeling was all relief. He had known this morning that something was about to happen – known it, in a moment, by Waymarsh's manner when Waymarsh appeared before him during his brief consumption of coffee and a roll in the small slippery *salle-à-manger* so associated with rich rumination. Strether had taken there of late various lonely and absent-minded meals; he communed there, even at the end of June, with a suspected chill, the air of old shivers mixed with old savours, the air in which so many of his impressions had perversely matured; the place meanwhile renewing its message to him by the very circumstance of his single state. He now sat there, for the most part, to sigh softly, while he vaguely tilted his carafe, over the vision of how much better Waymarsh was occupied. That was really his success by the common measure – to have led this companion so on and on. He remembered how at first there had been scarce a squatting-place he could beguile him into passing; the actual outcome of which at last was that there was scarce one that could arrest him in his rush. His rush – as Strether vividly and amusedly figured it – continued to be all with Sarah, and contained perhaps moreover the word of the whole enigma, whipping up in its fine full-flavoured froth the very principle, for good or for ill, of his own, of Strether's destiny. It might after all, to the end, only be that they had united to save him, and indeed, so far as Waymarsh was concerned, that *had* to be the spring of action. Strether was glad at all events, in connexion with the case, that the saving he required was not more scant;

so constituted a luxury was it in certain lights just to lurk there out of the full glare. He had moments of quite seriously wondering whether Waymarsh wouldn't in fact, thanks to old friendship and a conceivable indulgence, make about as good terms for him as he might make for himself. They wouldn't be the same terms of course; but they might have the advantage that he himself probably should be able to make none at all.

He was never in the morning very late, but Waymarsh had already been out, and, after a peep into the dim refectory, he presented himself with much less than usual of his large looseness. He had made sure, through the expense of glass exposed to the court, that they would be alone; and there was now in fact that about him that pretty well took up the room. He was dressed in the garments of summer; and save that his white waistcoat was redundant and bulging these things favoured, they determined, his expression. He wore a straw hat such as his friend hadn't yet seen in Paris, and he showed a buttonhole freshly adorned with a magnificent rose. Strether read on the instant his story – how, astir for the previous hour, the sprinkled newness of the day, so pleasant at that season in Paris, he was fairly panting with the pulse of adventure and had been with Mrs. Pocock, unmistakeably, to the Marché aux Fleurs.[1] Strether really knew in this vision of him a joy that was akin to envy; so reversed as he stood there did their old positions seem; so comparatively doleful now showed, by the sharp turn of the wheel, the posture of the pilgrim from Woollett. He wondered, this pilgrim, if he had originally looked to Waymarsh so brave and well, so remarkably launched, as it was at present the latter's privilege to appear. He recalled that his friend had remarked to him even at Chester that his aspect belied his plea of prostration; but there certainly couldn't have been, for an issue, an aspect less concerned than Waymarsh's with the menace of decay. Strether had at any rate never resembled a Southern planter of the great days – which was the image picturesquely suggested by the happy relation between the fuliginous face and the wide panama of his visitor. This type, it further amused him to guess, had been, on Waymarsh's part, the object of Sarah's care; he was convinced that her taste had

not been a stranger to the conception and purchase of the hat, any more than her fine fingers had been guiltless of the bestowal of the rose. It came to him in the current of thought, as things so oddly did come, that *he* had never risen with the lark to attend a brilliant woman to the Marché aux Fleurs; this could be fastened on him in connexion neither with Miss Gostrey nor with Madame de Vionnet; the practice of getting up early for adventures could indeed in no manner be fastened on him. It came to him in fact that just here was his usual case: he was for ever missing things through his general genius for missing them, while others were for ever picking them up through a contrary bent. And it was others who looked abstemious and he who looked greedy; it was he somehow who finally paid, and it was others who mainly partook. Yes, he should go to the scaffold yet for he wouldn't know quite whom. He almost, for that matter, felt on the scaffold now and really quite enjoying it. It worked out as *because* he was anxious there – it worked out as for this reason that Waymarsh was so blooming. It was *his* trip for health, for a change, that proved the success – which was just what Strether, planning and exerting himself, had desired it should be. That truth already sat full-blown on his companion's lips; benevolence breathed from them as with the warmth of active exercise, and also a little as with the bustle of haste.

'Mrs. Pocock, whom I left a quarter of an hour ago at her hotel, has asked me to mention to you that she would like to find you at home here in about another hour. She wants to see you; she has something to say – or considers, I believe, that you may have: so that I asked her myself why she shouldn't come right round. She hasn't *been* round yet – to see our place; and I took upon myself to say that I was sure you'd be glad to have her. The thing's therefore, you see, to keep right here till she comes.'

The announcement was sociably, even though, after Waymarsh's wont, somewhat solemnly made; but Strether quickly felt other things in it than these light features. It was the first approach, from that quarter, to admitted consciousness; it quickened his pulse; it simply meant at last that he should have

but himself to thank if he didn't know where he was. He had finished his breakfast; he pushed it away and was on his feet. There were plenty of elements of surprise, but only one of doubt. 'The thing's for *you* to keep here too?' Waymarsh had been slightly ambiguous.

He wasn't ambiguous, however, after this enquiry; and Strether's understanding had probably never before opened so wide and effective a mouth as it was to open during the next five minutes. It was no part of his friend's wish, as appeared, to help to receive Mrs. Pocock; he quite understood the spirit in which she was to present herself, but his connexion with her visit was limited to his having – well, as he might say – perhaps a little promoted it. He had thought, and had let her know it, that Strether possibly would think she might have been round before. At any rate, as turned out, she had been wanting herself, quite a while, to come. 'I told her,' said Waymarsh, 'that it would have been a bright idea if she had only carried it out before.'

Strether pronounced it so bright as to be almost dazzling. 'But why *hasn't* she carried it out before? She has seen me every day – she had only to name her hour. I've been waiting and waiting.'

'Well, I told her you had. And she has been waiting too.' It was, in the oddest way in the world, on the showing of this tone, a genial new pressing coaxing Waymarsh; a Waymarsh conscious with a different consciousness from any he had yet betrayed, and actually rendered by it almost insinuating. He lacked only time for full persuasion, and Strether was to see in a moment why. Meantime, however, our friend perceived, he was announcing a step of some magnanimity on Mrs. Pocock's part, so that he could deprecate a sharp question. It was his own high purpose in fact to have smoothed sharp questions to rest. He looked his old comrade very straight in the eyes, and he had never conveyed to him in so mute a manner so much kind confidence and so much good advice. Everything that was between them was again in his face, but matured and shelved and finally disposed of. 'At any rate,' he added, 'she's coming now.'

Considering how many pieces had to fit themselves, it all fell,

in Strether's brain, into a close rapid order. He saw on the spot what had happened, and what probably would yet; and it was all funny enough. It was perhaps just this freedom of appreciation that wound him up to his flare of high spirits. 'What is she coming *for*? – to kill me?'

'She's coming to be very *very* kind to you, and you must let me say that I greatly hope you'll not be less so to herself.'

This was spoken by Waymarsh with much gravity of admonition, and as Strether stood there he knew he had but to make a movement to take the attitude of a man gracefully receiving a present. The present was that of the opportunity dear old Waymarsh had flattered himself he had divined in him the slight soreness of not having yet thoroughly enjoyed; so he had brought it to him thus, as on a little silver breakfast-tray, familiarly though delicately – without oppressive pomp; and he was to bend and smile and acknowledge, was to take and use and be grateful. He was not – that was the beauty of it – to be asked to deflect too much from his dignity. No wonder the old boy bloomed in this bland air of his own distillation. Strether felt for a moment as if Sarah were actually walking up and down outside. Wasn't she hanging about the porte-cochère while her friend thus summarily opened a way? Strether would meet her but to take it, and everything would be for the best in the best of possible worlds. He had never so much known what any one meant as, in the light of this demonstration, he knew what Mrs. Newsome did. It had reached Waymarsh from Sarah, but it had reached Sarah from her mother, and there was no break in the chain by which it reached *him*. 'Has anything particular happened,' he asked after a minute – 'so suddenly to determine her? Has she heard anything unexpected from home?'

Waymarsh, on this, it seemed to him, looked at him harder than ever. '"Unexpected"?' He had a brief hesitation; then, however, he was firm. 'We're leaving Paris.'

'Leaving? That *is* sudden.'

Waymarsh showed a different opinion. 'Less so than it may seem. The purpose of Mrs. Pocock's visit is to explain to you in fact that it's *not*.'

Strether didn't at all know if he had really an advantage –
anything that would practically count as one; but he enjoyed
for the moment – as for the first time in his life – the sense of
so carrying it off. He wondered – it was amusing – if he felt as
the impudent feel. 'I shall take great pleasure, I assure you, in
any explanation. I shall be delighted to receive Sarah.'

The sombre glow just darkened in his comrade's eyes; but he
was struck with the way it died out again. It was too mixed
with another consciousness – it was too smothered, as might
be said, in flowers. He really for the time regretted it – poor
dear old sombre glow! Something straight and simple, something heavy and empty, had been eclipsed in its company;
something by which he had best known his friend. Waymarsh
wouldn't *be* his friend, somehow, without the occasional ornament of the sacred rage, and the right to the sacred rage –
inestimably precious for Strether's charity – he also seemed in a
manner, and at Mrs. Pocock's elbow, to have forfeited. Strether
remembered the occasion early in their stay when on that very
spot he had come out with his earnest, his ominous 'Quit it!' –
and, so remembering, felt it hang by a hair that he didn't himself
now utter the same note. Waymarsh was having a good time –
this was the truth that was embarrassing for him, and he was
having it then and there, he was having it in Europe, he was
having it under the very protection of circumstances of which
he didn't in the least approve; all of which placed him in a false
position, with no issue possible – none at least by the grand
manner. It was practically in the manner of any one – it was all
but in poor Strether's own – that instead of taking anything up
he merely made the most of having to be himself explanatory.
'I'm not leaving for the United States direct. Mr. and Mrs.
Pocock and Miss Mamie are thinking of a little trip before their
own return, and we've been talking for some days past of our
joining forces. We've settled it that we do join and that we sail
together the end of next month. But we start to-morrow for
Switzerland. Mrs. Pocock wants some scenery. She hasn't had
much yet.'

He was brave in his way too, keeping nothing back, confessing all there was, and only leaving Strether to make certain

connexions. 'Is what Mrs. Newsome had cabled her daughter an injunction to break off short?'

The grand manner indeed at this just raised its head a little. 'I know nothing about Mrs. Newsome's cables.'

Their eyes met on it with some intensity – during the few seconds of which something happened quite out of proportion to the time. It happened that Strether, looking thus at his friend, didn't take his answer for truth – and that something more again occurred in consequence of *that*. Yes – Waymarsh just *did* know about Mrs. Newsome's cables: to what other end than that had they dined together at Bignon's? Strether almost felt for the instant that it was to Mrs. Newsome herself the dinner had been given; and, for that matter, quite felt how she must have known about it and, as he might think, protected and consecrated it. He had a quick blurred view of daily cables, questions, answers, signals: clear enough was his vision of the expense that, when so wound up, the lady at home was prepared to incur. Vivid not less was his memory of what, during his long observation of her, some of her attainments of that high pitch had cost her. Distinctly she was at the highest now, and Waymarsh, who imagined himself an independent performer, was really, forcing his fine old natural voice, an overstrained accompanist. The whole reference of his errand seemed to mark her for Strether as by this time consentingly familiar to him, and nothing yet had so despoiled her of a special shade of consideration. 'You don't know,' he asked, 'whether Sarah has been directed from home to try me on the matter of my also going to Switzerland?'

'I know,' said Waymarsh as manfully as possible, 'nothing whatever about her private affairs; though I believe her to be acting in conformity with things that have my highest respect.' It was as manful as possible, but it was still the false note – as it had to be to convey so sorry a statement. He knew everything, Strether more and more felt, that he thus disclaimed, and his little punishment was just in this doom to a second fib. What falser position – given the man – could the most vindictive mind impose? He ended by squeezing through a passage in which three months before he would certainly have stuck fast. 'Mrs.

Pocock will probably be ready herself to answer any enquiry you may put to her. But,' he continued, '*but* –!' He faltered on it.

'But what? Don't put her too many?'

Waymarsh looked large, but the harm was done; he couldn't, do what he would, help looking rosy. 'Don't do anything you'll be sorry for.'

It was an attenuation, Strether guessed, of something else that had been on his lips; it was a sudden drop to directness, and was thereby the voice of sincerity. He had fallen to the supplicating note, and that immediately, for our friend, made a difference and reinstated him. They were in communication as they had been, that first morning, in Sarah's salon and in her presence and Madame de Vionnet's; and the same recognition of a great good will was again, after all, possible. Only the amount of response Waymarsh had then taken for granted was doubled, decupled now. This came out when he presently said: 'Of course I needn't assure you *I* hope you'll come with us.' Then it was that his implications and expectations loomed up for Strether as almost pathetically gross.

The latter patted his shoulder while he thanked him, giving the go-by to the question of joining the Pococks; he expressed the joy he felt at seeing him go forth again so brave and free, and he in fact almost took leave of him on the spot. 'I shall see you again of course before you go; but I'm meanwhile much obliged to you for arranging so conveniently for what you've told me. I shall walk up and down in the court there – dear little old court which we've each bepaced so, this last couple of months, to the tune of our flights and our drops, our hesitations and our plunges: I shall hang about there, all impatience and excitement, please let Sarah know, till she graciously presents herself. Leave me with her without fear,' he laughed; 'I assure you I shan't hurt her. I don't think either she'll hurt *me*: I'm in a situation in which damage was some time ago discounted. Besides, *that* isn't what worries you – but don't, don't explain! We're all right as we are: which was the degree of success our adventure was pledged to for each of us. We weren't, it seemed, all right as we were before; and we've got over the ground, all

things considered, quickly. I hope you'll have a lovely time in the Alps.'

Waymarsh fairly looked up at him as from the foot of them. 'I don't know as I *ought* really to go.'

It was the conscience of Milrose in the very voice of Milrose, but, oh it was feeble and flat! Strether suddenly felt quite ashamed for him; he breathed a greater boldness. '*Let* yourself, on the contrary, go – in all agreeable directions. These are precious hours – at our age they mayn't recur. Don't have it to say to yourself at Milrose, next winter, that you hadn't courage for them.' And then as his comrade queerly stared: 'Live up to Mrs. Pocock.'

'Live up to her?'

'You're a great help to her.'

Waymarsh looked at it as at one of the uncomfortable things that were certainly true and that it was yet ironical to say. 'It's more then than you are.'

'That's exactly your own chance and advantage. Besides,' said Strether, 'I do in my way contribute. I know what I'm about.'

Waymarsh had kept on his great panama, and, as he now stood nearer the door, his last look beneath the shade of it had turned again to darkness and warning. 'So do I! See here, Strether.'

'I know what you're going to say. "Quit this"?'

'Quit this!' But it lacked its old intensity; nothing of it remained; it went out of the room with him.

III

Almost the first thing, strangely enough, that, about an hour later, Strether found himself doing in Sarah's presence was to remark articulately on this failure, in their friend, of what had been superficially his great distinction. It was as if – he alluded of course to the grand manner – the dear man had sacrificed it to some other advantage; which would be of course only for himself to measure. It might be simply that he was physically so much more sound than on his first coming out; this was all prosaic, comparatively cheerful and vulgar. And fortunately, if one came to that, his improvement in health was really itself grander than any manner it could be conceived as having cost him. 'You yourself alone, dear Sarah' – Strether took the plunge – 'have done him, it strikes me, in these three weeks, as much good as all the rest of his time together.'

It was a plunge because somehow the range of reference was, in the conditions, 'funny', and made funnier still by Sarah's attitude, by the turn the occasion had, with her appearance, so sensibly taken. Her appearance was really indeed funnier than anything else – the spirit in which he felt her to be there as soon as she *was* there, the shade of obscurity that cleared up for him as soon as he was seated with her in the small *salon de lecture* that had, for the most part, in all the weeks, witnessed the wane of his early vivacity of discussion with Waymarsh. It was an immense thing, quite a tremendous thing, for her to have come: this truth opened out to him in spite of his having already arrived for himself at a fairly vivid view of it. He had done exactly what he had given Waymarsh his word for – had walked and re-walked the court while he awaited her advent; acquiring

in this exercise an amount of light that affected him at the time
as flooding the scene. She had decided upon the step in order
to give him the benefit of a doubt, in order to be able to say to
her mother that she had, even to abjectness, smoothed the way
for him. The doubt had been as to whether he mightn't take
her as not having smoothed it – and the admonition had possibly come from Waymarsh's more detached spirit. Waymarsh
had at any rate, certainly, thrown his weight into the scale – he
had pointed to the importance of depriving their friend of a
grievance. She had done justice to the plea, and it was to set
herself right with a high ideal that she actually sat there in her
state. Her calculation was sharp in the immobility with which
she held her tall parasol-stick upright and at arm's length, quite
as if she had struck the place to plant her flag; in the separate
precautions she took not to show as nervous; in the aggressive
repose in which she did quite nothing but wait for him. Doubt
ceased to be possible from the moment he had taken in that she
had arrived with no proposal whatever; that her concern was
simply to show what she had come to receive. She had come to
receive his submission, and Waymarsh was to have made it
plain to him that she would expect nothing less. He saw fifty
things, her host, at this convenient stage; but one of those he
most saw was that their anxious friend hadn't quite had
the hand required of him. Waymarsh *had*, however, uttered the
request that she might find him mild, and while hanging about
the court before her arrival he had turned over with zeal the
different ways in which he could be so. The difficulty was that
if he was mild he wasn't, for her purpose, conscious. If she
wished him conscious – as everything about her cried aloud
that she did – she must accordingly be at costs to make him so.
Conscious he *was*, for himself – but only of too many things;
so she must choose the one she required.

Practically, however, it at last got itself named, and when
once that had happened they were quite at the centre of their
situation. One thing had really done as well as another; when
Strether had spoken of Waymarsh's leaving him, and that had
necessarily brought on a reference to Mrs. Pocock's similar
intention, the jump was but short to supreme lucidity. Light

became indeed after that so intense that Strether would doubtless have but half made out, in the prodigious glare, by which
of the two the issue had been in fact precipitated. It was, in
their contracted quarters, as much there between them as if it
had been something suddenly spilled with a crash and a splash
on the floor. The form of his submission was to be an engagement to acquit himself within the twenty-four hours. 'He'll go
in a moment if you give him the word – he assures me on his
honour he'll do that': this came in its order, out of its order, in
respect to Chad, after the crash had occurred. It came repeatedly
during the time taken by Strether to feel that he was even more
fixed in his rigour than he had supposed – the time he was not
above adding to a little by telling her that such a way of putting
it on her brother's part left him sufficiently surprised. She wasn't
at all funny at last – she was really fine; and he felt easily where
she was strong – strong for herself. It hadn't yet so come home
to him that she was nobly and appointedly officious. She was
acting in interests grander and clearer than that of her poor
little personal, poor little Parisian equilibrium, and all his consciousness of her mother's moral pressure profited by this proof
of its sustaining force. She would be held up; she would be
strengthened; he needn't in the least be anxious for her. What
would once more have been distinct to him had he tried to
make it so was that, as Mrs. Newsome was essentially all moral
pressure, the presence of this element was almost identical with
her own presence. It wasn't perhaps that he felt he was dealing
with her straight, but it was certainly as if she had been dealing
straight with *him*. She was reaching him somehow by the
lengthened arm of the spirit, and he was having to that extent
to take her into account; but he wasn't reaching her in turn,
not making her take *him*; he was only reaching Sarah, who
appeared to take so little of him. 'Something has clearly passed
between you and Chad,' he presently said, 'that I think I ought
to know something more about. Does he put it all,' he smiled,
'on me?'

'Did you come out,' she asked, 'to put it all on *him*?'

But he replied to this no further than, after an instant, by
saying: 'Oh it's all right. Chad I mean's all right in having said

to you – well anything he may have said. I'll *take* it all – what he does put on me. Only I must see him before I see you again.'

She hesitated, but she brought it out. 'Is it absolutely necessary you should see me again?'

'Certainly, if I'm to give you any definite word about anything.'

'Is it your idea then,' she returned, 'that I shall keep on meeting you only to be exposed to fresh humiliation?'

He fixed her a longer time. 'Are your instructions from Mrs. Newsome that you shall, even at the worst, absolutely and irretrievably break with me?'

'My instructions from Mrs. Newsome are, if you please, my affair. You know perfectly what your own were, and you can judge for yourself of what it can do for you to have made what you have of them. You can perfectly see, at any rate, I'll go so far as to say, that if I wish not to expose myself I must wish still less to expose *her*.' She had already said more than she had quite expected; but, though she had also pulled up, the colour in her face showed him he should from one moment to the other have it all. He now indeed felt the high importance of his having it. 'What is your conduct,' she broke out as if to explain – 'what is your conduct but an outrage to women like *us*? I mean your acting as if there can be a doubt – as between us and such another – of his duty?'

He thought a moment. It was rather much to deal with at once; not only the question itself, but the sore abysses it revealed. 'Of course they're totally different kinds of duty.'

'And do you pretend that he has any at all – to such another?'

'Do you mean to Madame de Vionnet?' He uttered the name not to affront her, but yet again to gain time – time that he needed for taking in something still other and larger than her demand of a moment before. It wasn't at once that he could see all that was in her actual challenge; but when he did he found himself just checking a low vague sound, a sound which was perhaps the nearest approach his vocal chords had ever known to a growl. Everything Mrs. Pocock had failed to give a sign of recognizing in Chad as a particular part of a transformation – everything that had lent intention to this particular failure –

affected him as gathered into a large loose bundle and thrown, in her words, into his face. The missile made him to that extent catch his breath; which however he presently recovered. 'Why when a woman's at once so charming and so beneficent –'

'You can sacrifice mothers and sisters to her without a blush, and can make them cross the ocean on purpose to feel the more, and take from you the straighter, *how* you do it?'

Yes, she had taken him up as short and as sharply as that; but he tried not to flounder in her grasp. 'I don't think there's anything I've done in any such calculated way as you describe. Everything has come as a sort of indistinguishable part of every-thing else. Your coming out belonged closely to my having come before you, and my having come was a result of our general state of mind. Our general state of mind had proceeded, on its side, from our queer ignorance, our queer misconceptions and confusions – from which, since then, an inexorable tide of light seems to have floated us into our perhaps still queerer knowledge. Don't you *like* your brother as he is,' he went on, 'and haven't you given your mother an intelligible account of all that that comes to?'

It put to her also, doubtless, his own tone, too many things; this at least would have been the case hadn't his final chal-lenge directly helped her. Everything, at the stage they had reached, directly helped her, because everything betrayed in him such a basis of intention. He saw – the odd way things came out! – that he would have been held less monstrous had he only been a little wilder. What exposed him was just his poor old trick of quiet inwardness, what exposed him was his *thinking* such offence. He hadn't in the least however the desire to irritate that Sarah imputed to him, and he could only at last temporize, for the moment, with her indignant view. She was altogether more inflamed than he had expected, and he would probably understand this better when he should learn what had occurred for her with Chad. Till then her view of his particular blackness, her clear surprise at his not clutching the pole she held out, must pass as extravagant. 'I leave you to flatter your-self,' she returned, 'that what you speak of is what *you've* beautifully done. When a thing has been already described in

such a lovely way – !' But she caught herself up, and her comment on his description rang out sufficiently loud. 'Do you consider her even an apology for a decent woman?'

Ah there it was at last! She put the matter more crudely than, for his own mixed purposes, he had yet had to do; but essentially it was all one matter. It was so much – so much; and she treated it, poor lady, as so little. He grew conscious, as he was now apt to do, of a strange smile, and the next moment he found himself talking like Miss Barrace. 'She has struck me from the first as wonderful. I've been thinking too moreover that, after all, she would probably have represented even for yourself something rather new and rather good.'

He was to have given Mrs. Pocock with this, however, but her best opportunity for a sound of derision. 'Rather new? I hope so with all my heart!'

'I mean,' he explained, 'that she might have affected you by her exquisite amiability – a real revelation, it has seemed to myself; her high rarity, her distinction of every sort.'

He had been, with these words, consciously a little 'precious'; but he had had to be – he couldn't give her the truth of the case without them; and it seemed to him moreover now that he didn't care. He had at all events not served his cause, for she sprang at its exposed side. 'A "revelation" – to *me*: I've come to such a woman for a revelation? You talk to me about "distinction" – *you*, you who've had your privilege? – when the most distinguished woman we shall either of us have seen in this world sits there insulted, in her loneliness, by your incredible comparison!'

Strether forbore, with an effort, from straying; but he looked all about him. 'Does your mother herself make the point that she sits insulted?'

Sarah's answer came so straight, so 'pat', as might have been said, that he felt on the instant its origin. 'She has confided to my judgement and my tenderness the expression of her personal sense of everything, and the assertion of her personal dignity.'

They were the very words of the lady of Woollett – he would have known them in a thousand; her parting charge to her child. Mrs. Pocock accordingly spoke to this extent by book,

and the fact immensely moved him. 'If she does really feel as you say it's of course very very dreadful. I've given sufficient proof, one would have thought,' he added, 'of my deep admiration for Mrs. Newsome.'

'And pray what proof would one have thought you'd *call* sufficient? That of thinking this person here so far superior to her?'

He wondered again; he waited. 'Ah dear Sarah, you must *leave* me this person here!'

In his desire to avoid all vulgar retorts, to show how, even perversely, he clung to his rag of reason, he had softly almost wailed this plea. Yet he knew it to be perhaps the most positive declaration he had ever made in his life, and his visitor's reception of it virtually gave it that importance. 'That's exactly what I'm delighted to do. God knows *we* don't want her! You take good care not to meet,' she observed in a still higher key, 'my question about their life. If you do consider it a thing one can even *speak* of, I congratulate you on your taste!'

The life she alluded to was of course Chad's and Madame de Vionnet's, which she thus bracketed together in a way that made him wince a little; there being nothing for him but to take home her full intention. It was none the less his inconsequence that while he had himself been enjoying for weeks the view of the brilliant woman's specific action, he just suffered from any characterization of it by other lips. 'I think tremendously well of her, at the same time that I seem to feel her "life" to be really none of my business. It's my business, that is, only so far as Chad's own life is affected by it; and what has happened, don't you see? is that Chad's has been affected so beautifully. The proof of the pudding's in the eating' – he tried, with no great success, to help it out with a touch of pleasantry, while she let him go on as if to sink and sink. He went on however well enough, as well as he could do without fresh counsel; he indeed shouldn't stand quite firm, he felt, till he should have re-established his communications with Chad. Still, he could always speak for the woman he had so definitely promised to 'save'. This wasn't quite for her the air of salvation; but as that chill fairly deepened what did it become but a reminder that

one might at the worst perish *with* her? And it was simple enough – it was rudimentary: not, not to give her away. 'I find in her more merits than you would probably have patience with my counting over. And do you know,' he enquired, 'the effect you produce on me by alluding to her in such terms? It's as if you had some motive in not recognizing all she has done for your brother, and so shut your eyes to each side of the matter, in order, whichever side comes up, to get rid of the other. I don't, you must allow me to say, see how you can with any pretence to candour get rid of the side nearest you.'

'Near me – *that* sort of thing?' And Sarah gave a jerk back of her head that well might have nullified any active proximity.

It kept her friend himself at his distance, and he respected for a moment the interval. Then with a last persuasive effort he bridged it. 'You don't, on your honour, appreciate Chad's fortunate development?'

'Fortunate?' she echoed again. And indeed she was prepared. 'I call it hideous.'

Her departure had been for some minutes marked as imminent, and she was already at the door that stood open to the court, from the threshold of which she delivered herself of this judgement. It rang out so loud as to produce for the time the hush of everything else. Strether quite, as an effect of it, breathed less bravely; he could acknowledge it, but simply enough. 'Oh if you think *that* – !'

'Then all's at an end? So much the better. I do think that!' She passed out as she spoke and took her way straight across the court, beyond which, separated from them by the deep arch of the porte-cochère, the low victoria that had conveyed her from her own hotel was drawn up. She made for it with decision, and the manner of her break, the sharp shaft of her rejoinder, had an intensity by which Strether was at first kept in arrest. She had let fly at him as from a stretched cord, and it took him a minute to recover from the sense of being pierced. It was not the penetration of surprise; it was that, much more, of certainty; his case being put for him as he had as yet only put it to himself. She was away at any rate; she had distanced him – with rather a grand spring, an effect of pride and ease,

after all; she had got into her carriage before he could overtake her, and the vehicle was already in motion. He stopped halfway; he stood there in the court only seeing her go and noting that she gave him no other look. The way he had put it to himself was that all quite *might* be at an end. Each of her movements, in this resolute rupture, re-affirmed, re-enforced that idea. Sarah passed out of sight in the sunny street while, planted there in the centre of the comparatively grey court, he continued merely to look before him. It probably *was* all at an end.

BOOK ELEVENTH

I

He went late that evening to the Boulevard Malesherbes, having his impression that it would be vain to go early, and having also, more than once in the course of the day, made enquiries of the concierge. Chad hadn't come in and had left no intimation; he had affairs, apparently, at this juncture – as it occurred to Strether he so well might have – that kept him long abroad. Our friend asked once for him at the hotel in the Rue de Rivoli, but the only contribution offered there was the fact that every one was out. It was with the idea that he would have to come home to sleep that Strether went up to his rooms, from which however he was still absent, though, from the balcony, a few moments later, his visitor heard eleven o'clock strike. Chad's servant had by this time answered for his reappearance; he *had*, the visitor learned, come quickly in to dress for dinner and vanish again. Strether spent an hour in waiting for him – an hour full of strange suggestions, persuasions, recognitions; one of those that he was to recall, at the end of his adventure, as the particular handful that most had counted. The mellowest lamplight and the easiest chair had been placed at his disposal by Baptiste, subtlest of servants; the novel half-uncut, the novel lemon-coloured and tender, with the ivory knife athwart it like the dagger in a contadina's[1] hair, had been pushed within the soft circle – a circle which, for some reason, affected Strether as softer still after the same Baptiste had remarked that in the absence of a further need of anything by Monsieur he would betake himself to bed. The night was hot and heavy and the single lamp sufficient; the great flare of the lighted city, rising high, spending itself afar, played up from the Boulevard and,

through the vague vista of the successive rooms, brought objects into view and added to their dignity. Strether found himself in possession as he never yet had been; he had been there alone, had turned over books and prints, had invoked, in Chad's absence, the spirit of the place, but never at the witching hour and never with a relish quite so like a pang.

He spent a long time on the balcony; he hung over it as he had seen little Bilham hang the day of his first approach, as he had seen Mamie hang over her own the day little Bilham himself might have seen her from below; he passed back into the rooms, the three that occupied the front and that communicated by wide doors; and, while he circulated and rested, tried to recover the impression that they had made on him three months before, to catch again the voice in which they had seemed then to speak to him. That voice, he had to note, failed audibly to sound; which he took as the proof of all the change in himself. He had heard, of old, only what he *could* then hear; what he could do now was to think of three months ago as a point in the far past. All voices had grown thicker and meant more things; they crowded on him as he moved about – it was the way they sounded together that wouldn't let him be still. He felt, strangely, as sad as if he had come for some wrong, and yet as excited as if he had come for some freedom. But the freedom was what was most in the place and the hour; it was the freedom that most brought him round again to the youth of his own that he had long ago missed. He could have explained little enough to-day either why he had missed it or why, after years and years, he should care that he had; the main truth of the actual appeal of everything was none the less that everything represented the substance of his loss, put it within reach, within touch, made it, to a degree it had never been, an affair of the senses. That was what it became for him at this singular time, the youth he had long ago missed – a queer concrete presence, full of mystery, yet full of reality, which he could handle, taste, smell, the deep breathing of which he could positively hear. It was in the outside air as well as within; it was in the long watch, from the balcony, in the summer night, of the wide late life of Paris, the unceasing soft quick rumble, below, of the little

lighted carriages that, in the press, always suggested the gamblers he had seen of old at Monte Carlo pushing up to the tables. This image was before him when he at last became aware that Chad was behind.

'She tells me you put it all on *me*' – he had arrived after this promptly enough at that information; which expressed the case however quite as the young man appeared willing for the moment to leave it. Other things, with this advantage of their virtually having the night before them, came up for them, and had, as well, the odd effect of making the occasion, instead of hurried and feverish, one of the largest, loosest and easiest to which Strether's whole adventure was to have treated him. He had been pursuing Chad from an early hour and had overtaken him only now; but now the delay was repaired by their being so exceptionally confronted. They had foregathered enough of course in all the various times; they had again and again, since that first night at the theatre, been face to face over their question; but they had never been so alone together as they were actually alone – their talk hadn't yet been so supremely for themselves. And if many things moreover passed before them, none passed more distinctly for Strether than that striking truth about Chad of which he had been so often moved to take note: the truth that everything came happily back with him to his knowing how to live. It had been seated in his pleased smile – a smile that pleased exactly in the right degree – as his visitor turned round, on the balcony, to greet his advent; his visitor in fact felt on the spot that there was nothing their meeting would so much do as bear witness to that facility. He surrendered himself accordingly to so approved a gift; for what was the meaning of the facility but that others *did* surrender themselves? He didn't want, luckily, to prevent Chad from living; but he was quite aware that even if he had he would himself have thoroughly gone to pieces. It was in truth essentially by bringing down his personal life to a function all subsidiary to the young man's own that he held together. And the great point, above all, the sign of how completely Chad possessed the knowledge in question, was that one thus became, not only with a proper cheerfulness, but with wild native impulses, the feeder of his

stream. Their talk had accordingly not lasted three minutes without Strether's feeling basis enough for the excitement in which he had waited. This overflow fairly deepened, wastefully abounded, as he observed the smallness of anything corresponding to it on the part of his friend. That was exactly this friend's happy case; he 'put out' his excitement, or whatever other emotion the matter involved, as he put out his washing; than which no arrangement could make more for domestic order. It was quite for Strether himself in short to feel a personal analogy with the laundress bringing home the triumphs of the mangle.

When he had reported on Sarah's visit, which he did very fully, Chad answered his question with perfect candour. 'I positively referred her to you – told her she must absolutely see you. This was last night, and it all took place in ten minutes. It was our first free talk – really the first time she had tackled me. She knew I also knew what her line had been with yourself; knew moreover how little you had been doing to make anything difficult for her. So I spoke for you frankly – assured her you were all at her service. I assured her *I* was too,' the young man continued; 'and I pointed out how she could perfectly, at any time, have got at me. Her difficulty has been simply her not finding the moment she fancied.'

'Her difficulty,' Strether returned, 'has been simply that she finds she's afraid of you. She's not afraid of *me*, Sarah, one little scrap; and it was just because she has seen how I can fidget when I give my mind to it that she has felt her best chance, rightly enough, to be in making me as uneasy as possible. I think she's at bottom as pleased to *have* you put it on me as you yourself can possibly be to put it.'

'But what in the world, my dear man,' Chad enquired in objection to this luminosity, 'have I done to make Sally afraid?'

'You've been "wonderful, wonderful", as we say – we poor people who watch the play from the pit; and that's what has, admirably, made her. Made her all the more effectually that she could see you didn't set about it on purpose – I mean set about affecting her as with fear.'

Chad cast a pleasant backward glance over his possibilities

of motive. 'I've only wanted to be kind and friendly, to be decent and attentive – and I still only want to be.'

Strether smiled at his comfortable clearness. 'Well, there can certainly be no way for it better than by my taking the onus. It reduces your personal friction and your personal offence to almost nothing.'

Ah but Chad, with his completer conception of the friendly, wouldn't quite have this! They had remained on the balcony, where, after their day of great and premature heat, the midnight air was delicious; and they leaned back in turn against the balustrade, all in harmony with the chairs and the flower-pots, the cigarettes and the starlight. 'The onus isn't *really* yours – after our agreeing so to wait together and judge together. That was all my answer to Sally,' Chad pursued – 'that we have been, that we are, just judging together.'

'I'm not afraid of the burden,' Strether explained; 'I haven't come in the least that you should take it off me. I've come very much, it seems to me, to double up my forelegs in the manner of the camel when he gets down on his knees to make his back convenient. But I've supposed you all this while to have been doing a lot of special and private judging – about which I haven't troubled you; and I've only wished to have your con-clusion first from you. I don't ask more than that; I'm quite ready to take it as it has come.'

Chad turned up his face to the sky with a slow puff of his smoke. 'Well, I've seen.'

Strether waited a little. 'I've left you wholly alone; haven't, I think I may say, since the first hour or two – when I merely preached patience – so much as breathed on you.'

'Oh you've been awfully good!'

'We've both been good then – we've played the game. We've given them the most liberal conditions.'

'Ah,' said Chad, 'splendid conditions! It was open to them, open to them' – he seemed to make it out, as he smoked, with his eyes still on the stars. He might in quiet sport have been reading their horoscope. Strether wondered meanwhile what had been open to them, and he finally let him have it. 'It was open to them simply to let me alone; to have made up their

minds, on really seeing me for themselves, that I could go on well enough as I was.'

Strether assented to this proposition with full lucidity, his companion's plural pronoun, which stood all for Mrs. Newsome and her daughter, having no ambiguity for him. There was nothing, apparently, to stand for Mamie and Jim; and this added to our friend's sense of Chad's knowing what he thought. 'But they've made up their minds to the opposite – that you *can't* go on as you are.'

'No,' Chad continued in the same way; 'they won't have it for a minute.'

Strether on his side also reflectively smoked. It was as if their high place really represented some moral elevation from which they could look down on their recent past. 'There never was the smallest chance, do you know, that they *would* have it for a moment.'

'Of course not – no real chance. But if they were willing to think there was –!'

'They weren't willing.' Strether had worked it all out. 'It wasn't for you they came out, but for me. It wasn't to see for themselves what you're doing, but what I'm doing. The first branch of their curiosity was inevitably destined, under my culpable delay, to give way to the second; and it's on the second that, if I may use the expression and you don't mind my marking the invidious fact, they've been of late exclusively perched. When Sarah sailed it was me, in other words, they were after.'

Chad took it in both with intelligence and with indulgence. 'It *is* rather a business then – what I've let you in for!'

Strether had again a brief pause; which ended in a reply that seemed to dispose once for all of this element of compunction. Chad was to treat it, at any rate, so far as they were again together, as having done so. 'I was "in" when you found me.'

'Ah but it was you,' the young man laughed, 'who found *me*.'

'I only found you out. It was you who found me in. It was all in the day's work for them, at all events, that they should come. And they've greatly enjoyed it,' Strether declared.

'Well, I've tried to make them,' said Chad.

His companion did himself presently the same justice. 'So

have I. I tried even this very morning – while Mrs. Pocock was with me. She enjoys for instance, almost as much as anything else, not being, as I've said, afraid of me; and I think I gave her help in that.'

Chad took a deeper interest. 'Was she very very nasty?'

Strether debated. 'Well, she was the most important thing – she was definite. She was – at last – crystalline. And I felt no remorse. I saw that they must have come.'

'Oh I wanted to see them for myself; so that if it were only for *that* –!' Chad's own remorse was as small.

This appeared almost all Strether wanted. 'Isn't your having seen them for yourself then *the* thing, beyond all others, that has come of their visit?'

Chad looked as if he thought it nice of his old friend to put it so. 'Don't you count it as anything that you're dished – if you *are* dished? Are you, my dear man, dished?'

It sounded as if he were asking if he had caught cold or hurt his foot, and Strether for a minute but smoked and smoked. 'I want to see her again. I must see her.'

'Of course you must.' Then Chad hesitated. 'Do you mean – a – Mother herself?'

'Oh your mother – that will depend.'

It was as if Mrs. Newsome had somehow been placed by the words very far off. Chad however endeavoured in spite of this to reach the place. 'What do you mean it will depend on?'

Strether, for all answer, gave him a longish look. 'I was speaking of Sarah. I must positively – though she quite cast me off – see *her* again. I can't part with her that way.'

'Then she was awfully unpleasant?'

Again Strether exhaled. 'She was what she had to be. I mean that from the moment they're not delighted they can only be – well what I admit she was. We gave them,' he went on, 'their chance to be delighted, and they've walked up to it, and looked all round it, and not taken it.'

'You can bring a horse to water –!' Chad suggested.

'Precisely. And the tune to which this morning Sarah wasn't delighted – the tune to which, to adopt your metaphor, she refused to drink – leaves us on that side nothing more to hope.'

Chad had a pause, and then as if consolingly: 'It was never of course really the least on the cards that they would be "delighted".'

'Well, I don't know, after all,' Strether mused. 'I've had to come as far round. However' – he shook it off – 'it's doubtless *my* performance that's absurd.'

'There are certainly moments,' said Chad, 'when you seem to me too good to be true. Yet if you are true,' he added, 'that seems to be all that need concern me.'

'I'm true, but I'm incredible. I'm fantastic and ridiculous – I don't explain myself even *to* myself. How can they then,' Strether asked, 'understand me? So I don't quarrel with them.'

'I see. They quarrel,' said Chad rather comfortably, 'with *us*.' Strether noted once more the comfort, but his young friend had already gone on. 'I should feel greatly ashamed, all the same, if I didn't put it before you again that you ought to think, after all, tremendously well. I mean before giving up beyond recall –' With which insistence, as from a certain delicacy, dropped.

Ah but Strether wanted it. 'Say it all, say it all.'

'Well, at your age, and with what – when all's said and done – Mother might do for you and be for you.'

Chad had said it all, from his natural scruple, only to that extent; so that Strether after an instant himself took a hand. 'My absence of an assured future. The little I have to show toward the power to take care of myself. The way, the wonderful way, she would certainly take care of me. Her fortune, her kindness, and the constant miracle of her having been disposed to go even so far. Of course, of course' – he summed it up. 'There are those sharp facts.'

Chad had meanwhile thought of another still. 'And don't you really care –?'

His friend slowly turned round to him. 'Will you go?'

'I'll go if you'll say you now consider I should. You know,' he went on, 'I was ready six weeks ago.'

'Ah,' said Strether, 'that was when you didn't know *I* wasn't! You're ready at present because you do know it.'

'That may be,' Chad returned; 'but all the same I'm sincere. You talk about taking the whole thing on your shoulders, but

in what light do you regard me that you think me capable of letting you pay?' Strether patted his arm, as they stood together against the parapet, reassuringly – seeming to wish to contend that he *had* the wherewithal; but it was again round this question of purchase and price that the young man's sense of fairness continued to hover. 'What it literally comes to for you, if you'll pardon my putting it so, is that you give up money. Possibly a good deal of money.'

'Oh,' Strether laughed, 'if it were only just enough you'd still be justified in putting it so! But I've on my side to remind you too that *you* give up money; and more than "possibly" – quite certainly, as I should suppose – a good deal.'

'True enough; but I've got a certain quantity,' Chad returned after a moment. 'Whereas you, my dear man, you –'

'I can't be at all said' – Strether took him up – 'to have a "quantity" certain or uncertain? Very true. Still, I shan't starve.'

'Oh you mustn't *starve*!' Chad pacifically emphasized; and so, in the pleasant conditions, they continued to talk; though there was, for that matter, a pause in which the younger companion might have been taken as weighing again the delicacy of his then and there promising the elder some provision against the possibility just mentioned. This, however, he presumably thought best not to do, for at the end of another minute they had moved in quite a different direction. Strether had broken in by returning to the subject of Chad's passage with Sarah and enquiring if they had arrived, in the event, at anything in the nature of a 'scene'. To this Chad replied that they had on the contrary kept tremendously polite; adding moreover that Sally was after all not the woman to have made the mistake of not being. 'Her hands are a good deal tied, you see. I got so, from the first,' he sagaciously observed, 'the start of her.'

'You mean she has taken so much from you?'

'Well, I couldn't of course in common decency give less: only she hadn't expected, I think, that I'd give her nearly so much. And she began to take it before she knew it.'

'And she began to like it,' said Strether, 'as soon as she began to take it!'

'Yes, she has liked it – also more than she expected.' After

which Chad observed: 'But she doesn't like *me*. In fact she hates me.'

Strether's interest grew. 'Then why does she want you at home?'

'Because when you hate you want to triumph, and if she should get me neatly stuck there she *would* triumph.'

Strether followed afresh, but looking as he went. 'Certainly – in a manner. But it would scarce be a triumph worth having if, once entangled, feeling her dislike and possibly conscious in time of a certain quantity of your own, you should on the spot make yourself unpleasant to her.'

'Ah,' said Chad, 'she can bear *me* – could bear me at least at home. It's my being there that would be her triumph. She hates me in Paris.'

'She hates in other words –'

'Yes, *that's* it!' – Chad had quickly understood this understanding; which formed on the part of each as near an approach as they had yet made to naming Madame de Vionnet. The limitations of their distinctness didn't, however, prevent its fairly lingering in the air that it was this lady Mrs. Pocock hated. It added one more touch moreover to their established recognition of the rare intimacy of Chad's association with her. He had never yet more twitched away the last light veil from this phenomenon than in presenting himself as confounded and submerged in the feeling she had created at Woollett. 'And I'll tell you who hates me too,' he immediately went on.

Strether knew as immediately whom he meant, but with as prompt a protest. 'Ah no! Mamie doesn't hate – well,' he caught himself in time – 'anybody at all. Mamie's beautiful.'

Chad shook his head. 'That's just why I mind it. She certainly doesn't like me.'

'How much do you mind it? What would you do for her?'

'Well, I'd like her if she'd like me. Really, really,' Chad declared.

It gave his companion a moment's pause. 'You asked me just now if I don't, as you said, "care" about a certain person. You rather tempt me therefore to put the question in my turn. Don't *you* care about a certain other person?'

Chad looked at him hard in the lamplight of the window. 'The difference is that I don't want to.'

Strether wondered. ' "Don't want" to?'

'I try not to – that is I *have* tried. I've done my best. You can't be surprised,' the young man easily went on, 'when you yourself set me on it. I was indeed,' he added, 'already on it a little; but you set me harder. It was six weeks ago that I thought I had come out.'

Strether took it well in. 'But you haven't come out!'

'I don't know – it's what I *want* to know,' said Chad. 'And if I could have sufficiently wanted – by myself – to go back, I think I might have found out.'

'Possibly' – Strether considered. 'But all you were able to achieve was to want to want to! And even then,' he pursued, 'only till our friends there came. Do you want to want to still?' As with a sound half-dolorous, half-droll and all vague and equivocal, Chad buried his face for a little in his hands, rubbing it in a whimsical way that amounted to an evasion, he brought it out more sharply: '*Do* you?'

Chad kept for a time his attitude, but at last he looked up, and then abruptly, 'Jim *is* a damned dose!'[2] he declared.

'Oh I don't ask you to abuse or describe or in any way pronounce on your relatives; I simply put it to you once more whether you're *now* ready. You say you've "seen". Is what you've seen that you can't resist?'

Chad gave him a strange smile – the nearest approach he had ever shown to a troubled one. 'Can't you make me *not* resist?'

'What it comes to,' Strether went on very gravely now and as if he hadn't heard him, 'what it comes to is that more has been done for you, I think, than I've ever seen done – attempted perhaps, but never so successfully done – by one human being for another.'

'Oh an immense deal certainly' – Chad did it full justice. 'And you yourself are adding to it.'

It was without heeding this either that his visitor continued. 'And our friends there won't have it.'

'No, they simply won't.'

'They demand you on the basis, as it were, of repudiation

and ingratitude; and what has been the matter with me,'
Strether went on, 'is that I haven't seen my way to working
with you for repudiation.'

Chad appreciated this. 'Then as you haven't seen yours you
naturally haven't seen mine. There it is.' After which he proceeded, with a certain abruptness, to a sharp interrogation.
'*Now* do you say she doesn't hate me?'

Strether hesitated. '"She" – ?'

'Yes – Mother. We called it Sarah, but it comes to the same
thing.'

'Ah,' Strether objected, 'not to the same thing as her hating
you.'

On which – though as if for an instant it had hung fire –
Chad remarkably replied: 'Well, if they hate my good friend,
that comes to the same thing.' It had a note of inevitable truth
that made Strether take it as enough, feel he wanted nothing
more. The young man spoke in it for his 'good friend' more
than he had ever yet directly spoken, confessed to such deep
identities between them as he might play with the idea of working free from, but which at a given moment could still draw
him down like a whirlpool. And meanwhile he had gone on.
'Their hating you too moreover – that also comes to a good
deal.'

'Ah,' said Strether, 'your mother doesn't.'

Chad, however, loyally stuck to it – loyally, that is, to
Strether. 'She will if you don't look out.'

'Well, I do look out. I am, after all, looking out. That's just
why,' our friend explained, 'I want to see her again.'

It drew from Chad again the same question. 'To see Mother?'

'To see – for the present – Sarah.'

'Ah then there you are! And what I don't for the life of me
make out,' Chad pursued with resigned perplexity, 'is what you
gain by it.'

Oh it would have taken his companion too long to say!
'That's because you have, I verily believe, no imagination.
You've other qualities. But no imagination, don't you see? at all.'

'I dare say. I do see.' It was an idea in which Chad showed
interest. 'But haven't you yourself rather too much?'

'Oh *rather* –!' So that after an instant, under this reproach and as if it were at last a fact really to escape from, Strether made his move for departure.

II

One of the features of the restless afternoon passed by him after Mrs. Pocock's visit was an hour spent, shortly before dinner, with Maria Gostrey, whom of late, in spite of so sustained a call on his attention from other quarters, he had by no means neglected. And that he was still not neglecting her will appear from the fact that he was with her again at the same hour on the very morrow – with no less fine a consciousness moreover of being able to hold her ear. It continued inveterately to occur, for that matter, that whenever he had taken one of his greater turns he came back to where she so faithfully awaited him. None of these excursions had on the whole been livelier than the pair of incidents – the fruit of the short interval since his previous visit – on which he had now to report to her. He had seen Chad Newsome late the night before, and he had had that morning, as a sequel to this conversation, a second interview with Sarah. 'But they're all off,' he said, 'at last.'

It puzzled her a moment. 'All? – Mr. Newsome with them?'

'Ah not yet! Sarah and Jim and Mamie. But Waymarsh with them – for Sarah. It's too beautiful,' Strether continued; 'I find I don't get over that – it's always a fresh joy. But it's a fresh joy too,' he added, 'that – well, what do you think? Little Bilham also goes. But he of course goes for Mamie.'

Miss Gostrey wondered. '"For" her? Do you mean they're already engaged?'

'Well,' said Strether, 'say then for *me*. He'll do anything for me; just as I will, for that matter – anything I can – for him. Or for Mamie either. *She'll* do anything for me.'

Miss Gostrey gave a comprehensive sigh. 'The way you reduce people to subjection!'

'It's certainly, on one side, wonderful. But it's quite equalled, on another, by the way I don't. I haven't reduced Sarah, since yesterday; though I've succeeded in seeing her again, as I'll presently tell you. The others however are really all right. Mamie, by that blessed law of ours, absolutely must have a young man.'

'But what must poor Mr. Bilham have? Do you mean they'll *marry* for you?'

'I mean that, by the same blessed law, it won't matter a grain if they don't – I shan't have in the least to worry.'

She saw as usual what he meant. 'And Mr. Jim? – who goes for him?'

'Oh,' Strether had to admit, 'I couldn't manage *that*. He's thrown, as usual, on the world; the world which, after all, by his account – for he has prodigious adventures – seems very good to him. He fortunately – "over here", as he says – finds the world everywhere; and his most prodigious adventure of all,' he went on, 'has been of course of the last few days.'

Miss Gostrey, already knowing, instantly made the connexion. 'He has seen Marie de Vionnet again?'

'He went, all by himself, the day after Chad's party – didn't I tell you? – to tea with her. By her invitation – all alone.'

'Quite like yourself!' Maria smiled.

'Oh but he's more wonderful about her than I am!' And then as his friend showed how she could believe it, filling it out, fitting it on to old memories of the wonderful woman: 'What I should have liked to manage would have been *her* going.'

'To Switzerland with the party?'

'For Jim – and for symmetry. If it had been workable moreover for a fortnight she'd have gone. She's ready' – he followed up his renewed vision of her – 'for anything.'

Miss Gostrey went with him a minute. 'She's too perfect!'

'She *will*, I think,' he pursued, 'go to-night to the station.'

'To see him off?'

'With Chad – marvellously – as part of their general attention.

And she does it' – it kept before him – 'with a light, light grace, a free, free gaiety, that may well softly bewilder Mr. Pocock.'

It kept her so before him that his companion had after an instant a friendly comment. 'As in short it has softly bewildered a saner man. Are you really in love with her?' Maria threw off.

'It's of no importance I should know,' he replied. 'It matters so little – has nothing to do, practically, with either of us.'

'All the same' – Maria continued to smile – 'they go, the five, as I understand you, and you and Madame de Vionnet stay.'

'Oh and Chad.' To which Strether added: 'And you.'

'Ah "me"!' – she gave a small impatient wail again, in which something of the unreconciled seemed suddenly to break out. '*I* don't stay, it somehow seems to me, much to my advantage. In the presence of all you cause to pass before me I've a tremendous sense of privation.'

Strether hesitated. 'But your privation, your keeping out of everything, has been – hasn't it? – by your own choice.'

'Oh yes; it has been necessary – that is it has been better for you. What I mean is only that I seem to have ceased to serve you.'

'How can you tell that?' he asked. 'You don't know how you serve me. When you cease –'

'Well?' she said as he dropped.

'Well, I'll *let* you know. Be quiet till then.'

She thought a moment. 'Then you positively like me to stay?'

'Don't I treat you as if I did?'

'You're certainly very kind to me. But that,' said Maria, 'is for myself. It's getting late, as you see, and Paris turning rather hot and dusty. People are scattering, and some of them, in other places, want me. But if you want me here –!'

She had spoken as resigned to his word, but he had of a sudden a still sharper sense than he would have expected of desiring not to lose her. 'I want you here.'

She took it as if the words were all she had wished; as if they brought her, gave her something that was the compensation of her case. 'Thank you,' she simply answered. And then as he looked at her a little harder, 'Thank you very much,' she repeated.

It had broken as with a slight arrest into the current of their

talk, and it held him a moment longer. 'Why, two months, or whatever the time was, ago, did you so suddenly dash off? The reason you afterwards gave me for having kept away three weeks wasn't the real one.'

She recalled. 'I never supposed you believed it was. Yet,' she continued, 'if you didn't guess it that was just what helped you.'

He looked away from her on this; he indulged, so far as space permitted, in one of his slow absences. 'I've often thought of it, but never to feel that I could guess it. And you see the consideration with which I've treated you in never asking till now.'

'Now then why *do* you ask?'

'To show you how I miss you when you're not here, and what it does for me.'

'It doesn't seem to have done,' she laughed, 'all it might! However,' she added, 'if you've really never guessed the truth I'll tell it you.'

'I've never guessed it,' Strether declared.

'Never?'

'Never.'

'Well then I dashed off, as you say, so as not to have the confusion of being there if Marie de Vionnet should tell you anything to my detriment.'

He looked as if he considerably doubted. 'You even then would have had to face it on your return.'

'Oh if I had found reason to believe it something very bad I'd have left you altogether.'

'So then,' he continued, 'it was only on guessing she had been on the whole merciful that you ventured back?'

Maria kept it together. 'I owe her thanks. Whatever her temptation she didn't separate us. That's one of my reasons,' she went on, 'for admiring her so.'

'Let it pass then,' said Strether, 'for one of mine as well. But what would have been her temptation?'

'What are ever the temptations of women?'

He thought – but hadn't, naturally, to think too long. 'Men?'

'She would have had you, with it, more for herself. But she saw she could have you without it.'

'Oh "have" me!' Strether a trifle ambiguously sighed. '*You*,' he

handsomely declared, 'would have had me at any rate *with* it.'

'Oh "have" you!' – she echoed it as he had done. 'I do have you, however,' she less ironically said, 'from the moment you express a wish.'

He stopped before her, full of the disposition. 'I'll express fifty.'

Which indeed begot in her, with a certain inconsequence, a return of her small wail. 'Ah there you are!'

There, if it were so, he continued for the rest of the time to be, and it was as if to show her how she could still serve him that, coming back to the departure of the Pococks, he gave her the view, vivid with a hundred more touches than we can reproduce, of what had happened for him that morning. He had had ten minutes with Sarah at her hotel, ten minutes recon-quered, by irresistible pressure, from the time over which he had already described her to Miss Gostrey as having, at the end of their interview on his own premises, passed the great sponge of the future. He had caught her by not announcing himself, had found her in her sitting-room with a dressmaker and a *lingère* whose accounts she appeared to have been more or less ingenuously settling and who soon withdrew. Then he had explained to her how he had succeeded, late the night before, in keeping his promise of seeing Chad. 'I told her I'd take it all.'

'You'd "take" it?'

'Why if he doesn't go.'

Maria waited. 'And who takes it if he does?' she enquired with a certain grimness of gaiety.

'Well,' said Strether, 'I think I take, in any event, everything.'

'By which I suppose you mean,' his companion brought out after a moment, 'that you definitely understand you now lose everything.'

He stood before her again. 'It does come perhaps to the same thing. But Chad, now that he has seen, doesn't really want it.'

She could believe that, but she made, as always, for clearness. 'Still, what, after all, *has* he seen?'

'What they want of him. And it's enough.'

'It contrasts so unfavourably with what Madame de Vionnet wants?'

'It contrasts – just so; all round, and tremendously.'

'Therefore, perhaps, most of all with what *you* want?'

'Oh,' said Strether, 'what I want is a thing I've ceased to measure or even to understand.'

But his friend none the less went on. 'Do you want Mrs. Newsome – after such a way of treating you?'

It was a straighter mode of dealing with this lady than they had as yet – such was their high form – permitted themselves; but it seemed not wholly for this that he delayed a moment. 'I dare say it has been, after all, the only way she could have imagined.'

'And does that make you want her any more?'

'I've tremendously disappointed her,' Strether thought it worth while to mention.

'Of course you have. That's rudimentary; that was plain to us long ago. But isn't it almost as plain,' Maria went on, 'that you've even yet your straight remedy? Really drag him away, as I believe you still can, and you'd cease to have to count with her disappointment.'

'Ah then,' he laughed, 'I should have to count with yours!'

But this barely struck her now. 'What, in that case, should you call counting? You haven't come out where you are, I think, to please *me*.'

'Oh,' he insisted, 'that too, you know, has been part of it. I can't separate – it's all one; and that's perhaps why, as I say, I don't understand.' But he was ready to declare again that this didn't in the least matter; all the more that, as he affirmed, he *hadn't* really as yet 'come out'. 'She gives me after all, on its coming to the pinch, a last mercy, another chance. They don't sail, you see, for five or six weeks more, and they haven't – she admits that – expected Chad would take part in their tour. It's still open to him to join them, at the last, at Liverpool.'

Miss Gostrey considered. 'How in the world is it "open" unless you open it? How can he join them at Liverpool if he but sinks deeper into his situation here?'

'He has given her – as I explained to you that she let me know yesterday – his word of honour to do as I say.'

Maria stared. 'But if you say nothing!'

Well, he as usual walked about on it. 'I did say something this morning. I gave her my answer – the word I had promised her after hearing from himself what *he* had promised. What she demanded of me yesterday, you'll remember, was the engagement then and there to make him take up this vow.'

'Well then,' Miss Gostrey enquired, 'was the purpose of your visit to her only to decline?'

'No; it was to ask, odd as that may seem to you, for another delay.'

'Ah that's weak!'

'Precisely!' She had spoken with impatience, but, so far as that at least, he knew where he was. 'If I *am* weak I want to find it out. If I don't find it out I shall have the comfort, the little glory, of thinking I'm strong.'

'It's all the comfort, I judge,' she returned, 'that you *will* have!'

'At any rate,' he said, 'it will have been a month more. Paris may grow, from day to day, hot and dusty, as you say; but there are other things that are hotter and dustier. I'm not afraid to stay on; the summer here must be amusing in a wild – if it isn't a tame – way of its own; the place at no time more picturesque. I think I shall like it. And then,' he benevolently smiled for her, 'there will be always you.'

'Oh,' she objected, 'it won't be as a part of the picturesqueness that I shall stay, for I shall be the plainest thing about you. You may, you see, at any rate,' she pursued, 'have nobody else. Madame de Vionnet may very well be going off, mayn't she? – and Mr. Newsome by the same stroke: unless indeed you've had an assurance from them to the contrary. So that if your idea's to stay for them' – it was her duty to suggest it – 'you may be left in the lurch. Of course if they do stay' – she kept it up – 'they would be part of the picturesqueness. Or else indeed you might join them somewhere.'

Strether seemed to face it as if it were a happy thought; but the next moment he spoke more critically. 'Do you mean that they'll probably go off together?'

She just considered. 'I think it will be treating you quite without ceremony if they do; though after all,' she added, 'it

would be difficult to see now quite what degree of ceremony properly meets your case.'

'Of course,' Strether conceded, 'my attitude toward them is extraordinary.'

'Just so; so that one may ask one's self what style of proceeding on their own part can altogether match it. The attitude of their own that won't pale in its light they've doubtless still to work out. The really handsome thing perhaps,' she presently threw off, '*would* be for them to withdraw into more secluded conditions, offering at the same time to share them with you.' He looked at her, on this, as if some generous irritation – all in his interest – had suddenly again flickered in her; and what she next said indeed half-explained it. 'Don't really be afraid to tell me if what now holds you *is* the pleasant prospect of the empty town, with plenty of seats in the shade, cool drinks, deserted museums, drives to the Bois[1] in the evening, and our wonderful woman all to yourself.' And she kept it up still more. 'The handsomest thing of *all*, when one makes it out, would, I dare say, be that Mr. Chad should for a while go off by himself. It's a pity, from that point of view,' she wound up, 'that he doesn't pay his mother a visit. It would at least occupy your interval.' The thought in fact held her a moment. 'Why doesn't he pay his mother a visit? Even a week, at this good moment, would do.'

'My dear lady,' Strether replied – and he had it even to himself surprisingly ready – 'my dear lady, his mother has paid *him* a visit. Mrs. Newsome has been with him, this month, with an intensity that I'm sure he has thoroughly felt; he has lavishly entertained her, and she has let him have her thanks. Do you suggest he shall go back for more of them?'

Well, she succeeded after a little in shaking it off. 'I see. It's what you don't suggest – what you haven't suggested. And you know.'

'So would you, my dear,' he kindly said, 'if you had so much as seen her.'

'As seen Mrs. Newsome?'

'No, Sarah – which, both for Chad and for myself, has served all the purpose.'

'And served it in a manner,' she responsively mused, 'so extraordinary!'

'Well, you see,' he partly explained, 'what it comes to is that she's all cold thought – which Sarah could serve to us cold without its really losing anything. So it is that we know what she thinks of us.'

Maria had followed, but she had an arrest. 'What I've never made out, if you come to that, is what you think – I mean you personally – of *her*. Don't you so much, when all's said, as care a little?'

'That,' he answered with no loss of promptness, 'is what even Chad himself asked me last night. He asked me if I don't mind the loss – well, the loss of an opulent future. Which moreover,' he hastened to add, 'was a perfectly natural question.'

'I call your attention, all the same,' said Miss Gostrey, 'to the fact that I don't ask it. What I venture to ask is whether it's to Mrs. Newsome herself that you're indifferent.'

'I haven't been so' – he spoke with all assurance. 'I've been the very opposite. I've been, from the first moment, preoccupied with the impression everything might be making on her – quite oppressed, haunted, tormented by it. I've been interested *only* in her seeing what I've seen. And I've been as disappointed in her refusal to see it as she has been in what has appeared to her the perversity of my insistence.'

'Do you mean that she has shocked you as you've shocked her?'

Strether weighed it. 'I'm probably not so shockable. But on the other hand I've gone much further to meet her. She, on her side, hasn't budged an inch.'

'So that you're now at last' – Maria pointed the moral – 'in the sad stage of recriminations.'

'No – it's only to you I speak. I've been like a lamb to Sarah. I've only put my back to the wall. It's to *that* one naturally staggers when one has been violently pushed there.'

She watched him a moment. 'Thrown over?'

'Well, as I feel I've landed somewhere I think I must have been thrown.'

She turned it over, but as hoping to clarify much rather

than to harmonize. 'The thing is that I suppose you've been disappointing –'

'Quite from the very first of my arrival? I dare say. I admit I was surprising even to myself.'

'And then of course,' Maria went on, 'I had much to do with it.'

'With my being surprising –?'

'That will do,' she laughed, 'if you're too delicate to call it *my* being! Naturally,' she added, 'you came over more or less for surprises.'

'Naturally!' – he valued the reminder.

'But they were to have been all for you' – she continued to piece it out – 'and none of them for *her*.'

Once more he stopped before her as if she had touched the point. 'That's just her difficulty – that she doesn't admit surprises. It's a fact that, I think, describes and represents her; and it falls in with what I tell you – that she's all, as I've called it, fine cold thought. She had, to her own mind, worked the whole thing out in advance, and worked it out for me as well as for herself. Whenever she has done that, you see, there's no room left; no margin, as it were, for any alteration. She's filled as full, packed as tight, as she'll hold, and if you wish to get anything more or different either out or in –'

'You've got to make over altogether the woman herself?'

'What it comes to,' said Strether, 'is that you've got morally and intellectually to get rid of her.'

'Which would appear,' Maria returned, 'to be practically what you've done.'

But her friend threw back his head. 'I haven't touched her. She won't *be* touched. I see it now as I've never done; and she hangs together with a perfection of her own,' he went on, 'that does suggest a kind of wrong in *any* change of her composition. It was at any rate,' he wound up, 'the woman herself, as you call her, the whole moral and intellectual being or block, that Sarah brought me over to take or to leave.'

It turned Miss Gostrey to deeper thought. 'Fancy having to take at the point of the bayonet a whole moral and intellectual being or block!'

'It was in fact,' said Strether, 'what, at home, I *had* done. But somehow over there I didn't quite know it.'

'One never does, I suppose,' Miss Gostrey concurred, 'realize in advance, in such a case, the size, as you may say, of the block. Little by little it looms up. It has been looming for you more and more till at last you see it all.'

'I see it all,' he absently echoed, while his eyes might have been fixing some particularly large iceberg in a cool blue northern sea. 'It's magnificent!' he then rather oddly exclaimed.

But his friend, who was used to this kind of inconsequence in him, kept the thread. 'There's nothing so magnificent – for making others feel you – as to have no imagination.'

It brought him straight round. 'Ah there you are! It's what I said last night to Chad. That he himself, I mean, has none.'

'Then it would appear,' Maria suggested, 'that he has, after all, something in common with his mother.'

'He has in common that he makes one, as you say, "feel" him. And yet,' he added, as if the question were interesting, 'one feels others too, even when they have plenty.'

Miss Gostrey continued suggestive. 'Madame de Vionnet?'

'*She* has plenty.'

'Certainly – she had quantities of old. But there are different ways of making one's self felt.'

'Yes, it comes, no doubt, to that. You now –'

He was benevolently going on, but she wouldn't have it. 'Oh I *don't* make myself felt; so my quantity needn't be settled. Yours, you know,' she said, 'is monstrous. No one has ever had so much.'

It struck him for a moment. 'That's what Chad also thinks.'

'There *you* are then – though it isn't for him to complain of it!'

'Oh he doesn't complain of it,' said Strether.

'That's all that would be wanting! But apropos of what,' Maria went on, 'did the question come up?'

'Well, of his asking me what it is I gain.'

She had a pause. 'Then as I've asked you too it settles *my* case. Oh you *have*,' she repeated, 'treasures of imagination.'

But he had been for an instant thinking away from this, and

he came up in another place. 'And yet Mrs. Newsome – it's a thing to remember – *has* imagined, did, that is, imagine, and apparently still does, horrors about what I should have found. I was booked, by her vision – extraordinarily intense, after all – to find them; and that I didn't, that I couldn't, that, as she evidently felt, I wouldn't – this evidently didn't at all, as they say, "suit" her book. It was more than she could bear. That was her disappointment.'

'You mean you were to have found Chad himself horrible?'

'I was to have found the woman.'

'Horrible?'

'Found her as she imagined her.' And Strether paused as if for his own expression of it he could add no touch to that picture.

His companion had meanwhile thought. 'She imagined stupidly – so it comes to the same thing.'

'Stupidly? Oh!' said Strether.

But she insisted. 'She imagined meanly.'

He had it, however, better. 'It couldn't but be ignorantly.'

'Well, intensity with ignorance – what do you want worse?'

This question might have held him, but he let it pass. 'Sarah isn't ignorant – now; she keeps up the theory of the horrible.'

'Ah but she's intense – and that by itself will do sometimes as well. If it doesn't do, in this case, at any rate, to deny that Marie's charming, it will do at least to deny that she's good.'

'What I claim is that she's good for Chad.'

'You don't claim' – she seemed to like it clear – 'that she's good for *you*.'

But he continued without heeding. 'That's what I wanted them to come out for – to see for themselves if she's bad for him.'

'And now that they've done so they won't admit that she's good even, for anything?'

'They do think,' Strether presently admitted, 'that she's on the whole about as bad for me. But they're consistent of course, inasmuch as they've their clear view of what's good for both of us.'

'For you, to begin with' – Maria, all responsive, confined the

question for the moment – 'to eliminate from your existence and if possible even from your memory the dreadful creature that *I* must gruesomely shadow forth for them, even more than to eliminate the distincter evil – thereby a little less portentous – of the person whose confederate you've suffered yourself to become. However, that's comparatively simple. You can easily, at the worst, after all, give me up.'

'I can easily at the worst, after all, give you up.' The irony was so obvious that it needed no care. 'I can easily at the worst, after all, even forget you.'

'Call that then workable. But Mr. Newsome has much more to forget. How can *he* do it?'

'Ah there again we are! That's just what I was to have made him do; just where I was to have worked with him and helped.'

She took it in silence and without attenuation – as if perhaps from very familiarity with the facts; and her thought made a connexion without showing the links. 'Do you remember how we used to talk at Chester and in London about my seeing you through?' She spoke as of far-off things and as if they had spent weeks at the places she named.

'It's just what you *are* doing.'

'Ah but the worst – since you've left such a margin – may be still to come. You may yet break down.'

'Yes, I may yet break down. But will you take me – ?'

He had hesitated, and she waited. 'Take you – ?'

'For as long as I can bear it.'

She also debated. 'Mr. Newsome and Madame de Vionnet may, as we were saying, leave town. How long do you think you can bear it without them?'

Strether's reply to this was at first another question. 'Do you mean in order to get away from me?'

Her answer had an abruptness. 'Don't find me rude if I say I should think they'd want to!'

He looked at her hard again – seemed even for an instant to have an intensity of thought under which his colour changed. But he smiled. 'You mean after what they've done to me?'

'After what *she* has.'

At this, however, with a laugh, he was all right again. 'Ah but she hasn't done it yet!'

III

He had taken the train a few days after this from a station – as well as *to* a station – selected almost at random; such days, whatever should happen, were numbered, and he had gone forth under the impulse – artless enough, no doubt – to give the whole of one of them to that French ruralism, with its cool special green, into which he had hitherto looked only through the little oblong window of the picture-frame. It had been as yet for the most part but a land of fancy for him – the background of fiction, the medium of art, the nursery of letters; practically as distant as Greece, but practically also well-nigh as consecrated. Romance could weave itself, for Strether's sense, out of elements mild enough; and even after what he had, as he felt, lately 'been through', he could thrill a little at the chance of seeing something somewhere that would remind him of a certain small Lambinet[1] that had charmed him, long years before, at a Boston dealer's and that he had quite absurdly never forgotten. It had been offered, he remembered, at a price he had been instructed to believe the lowest ever named for a Lambinet, a price he had never felt so poor as on having to recognize, all the same, as beyond a dream of possibility. He had dreamed – had turned and twisted possibilities for an hour: it had been the only adventure of his life in connexion with the purchase of a work of art. The adventure, it will be perceived, was modest; but the memory, beyond all reason and by some accident of association, was sweet. The little Lambinet abode with him as the picture he *would* have bought – the particular production that had made him for the moment overstep the modesty of nature. He was quite aware that if he were to see it

again he should perhaps have a drop or a shock, and he never found himself wishing that the wheel of time would turn it up again, just as he had seen it in the maroon-coloured, sky-lighted inner shrine of Tremont Street.[2] It would be a different thing, however, to see the remembered mixture resolved back into its elements – to assist at the restoration to nature of the whole far-away hour: the dusty day in Boston, the background of the Fitchburg Depot, of the maroon-coloured sanctum, the special-green vision, the ridiculous price, the poplars, the willows, the rushes, the river, the sunny silvery sky, the shady woody horizon.

He observed in respect to his train almost no condition save that it should stop a few times after getting out of the *banlieue*; he threw himself on the general amiability of the day for the hint of where to alight. His theory of his excursion was that he could alight anywhere – not nearer Paris than an hour's run – on catching a suggestion of the particular note required. It made its sign, the suggestion – weather, air, light, colour and his mood all favouring – at the end of some eighty minutes; the train pulled up just at the right spot, and he found himself getting out as securely as if to keep an appointment. It will be felt of him that he could amuse himself, at his age, with very small things if it be again noted that his appointment was only with a superseded Boston fashion. He hadn't gone far without the quick confidence that it would be quite sufficiently kept. The oblong gilt frame disposed its enclosing lines; the poplars and willows, the reeds and river – a river of which he didn't know, and didn't want to know, the name – fell into a composition, full of felicity, within them; the sky was silver and turquoise and varnish; the village on the left was white and the church on the right was grey; it was all there, in short – it was what he wanted: it was Tremont Street, it was France, it was Lambinet. Moreover he was freely walking about in it. He did this last, for an hour, to his heart's content, making for the shady woody horizon and boring so deep into his impression and his idleness that he might fairly have got through them again and reached the maroon-coloured wall. It was a wonder, no doubt, that the taste of idleness for him shouldn't need more

time to sweeten; but it had in fact taken the few previous days; it had been sweetening in truth ever since the retreat of the Pococks. He walked and walked as if to show himself how little he had now to do; he had nothing to do but turn off to some hillside where he might stretch himself and hear the poplars rustle, and whence – in the course of an afternoon so spent, an afternoon richly suffused too with the sense of a book in his pocket – he should sufficiently command the scene to be able to pick out just the right little rustic inn for an experiment in respect to dinner. There was a train back to Paris at 9.20, and he saw himself partaking, at the close of the day, with the enhancements of a coarse white cloth and a sanded floor, of something fried and felicitous, washed down with authentic wine; after which he might, as he liked, either stroll back to his station in the gloaming or propose for the local *carriole* and converse with his driver, a driver who naturally wouldn't fail of a stiff clean blouse, of a knitted nightcap and of the genius of response – who, in fine, would sit on the shafts, tell him what the French people were thinking, and remind him, as indeed the whole episode would incidentally do, of Maupassant.[3] Strether heard his lips, for the first time in French air, as this vision assumed consistency, emit sounds of expressive intention without fear of his company. He had been afraid of Chad and of Maria and of Madame de Vionnet; he had been most of all afraid of Waymarsh, in whose presence, so far as they had mixed together in the light of the town, he had never without somehow paying for it aired either his vocabulary or his accent. He usually paid for it by meeting immediately afterwards Waymarsh's eye.

Such were the liberties with which his fancy played after he had turned off to the hillside that did really and truly, as well as most amiably, await him beneath the poplars, the hillside that made him feel, for a murmurous couple of hours, how happy had been his thought. He had the sense of success, of a finer harmony in things; nothing but what had turned out as yet according to his plan. It most of all came home to him, as he lay on his back on the grass, that Sarah had really gone, that his tension was really relaxed; the peace diffused in these ideas

might be delusive, but it hung about him none the less for the
time. It fairly, for half an hour, sent him to sleep; he pulled his
straw hat over his eyes – he had bought it the day before
with a reminiscence of Waymarsh's – and lost himself anew in
Lambinet. It was as if he had found out he was tired – tired not
from his walk, but from that inward exercise which had known,
on the whole, for three months, so little intermission. That was
it – when once they were off he had dropped; this moreover
was what he had dropped to, and now he was touching bottom.
He was kept luxuriously quiet, soothed and amused by the
consciousness of what he had found at the end of his descent.
It was very much what he had told Maria Gostrey he should
like to stay on for, the hugely-distributed Paris of summer,
alternately dazzling and dusky, with a weight lifted for him off
its columns and cornices and with shade and air in the flutter
of awnings as wide as avenues. It was present to him without
attenuation that, reaching out, the day after making the remark,
for some proof of his freedom, he had gone that very afternoon
to see Madame de Vionnet. He had gone again the next day
but one, and the effect of the two visits, the after-sense of the
couple of hours spent with her, was almost that of fulness and
frequency. The brave intention of frequency, so great with him
from the moment of his finding himself unjustly suspected at
Woollett, had remained rather theoretic, and one of the things
he could muse about under his poplars was the source of the
special shyness that had still made him careful. He had surely
got rid of it now, this special shyness; what had become of it if
it hadn't precisely, within the week, rubbed off?

It struck him now in fact as sufficiently plain that if he had
still been careful he had been so for a reason. He had really
feared, in his behaviour, a lapse from good faith; if there was a
danger of one's liking such a woman too much one's best safety
was in waiting at least till one had the right to do so. In the
light of the last few days the danger was fairly vivid; so that
it was proportionately fortunate that the right was likewise
established. It seemed to our friend that he had on each occasion
profited to the utmost by the latter: how could he have done so
more, he at all events asked himself, than in having immediately

let her know that, if it was all the same to her, he preferred not
to talk about anything tiresome? He had never in his life so
sacrificed an armful of high interests as in that remark; he had
never so prepared the way for the comparatively frivolous as in
addressing it to Madame de Vionnet's intelligence. It hadn't
been till later that he quite recalled how in conjuring away
everything but the pleasant he had conjured away almost all
they had hitherto talked about; it was not till later even that he
remembered how, with their new tone, they hadn't so much as
mentioned the name of Chad himself. One of the things that
most lingered with him on his hillside was this delightful facility,
with such a woman, of arriving at a new tone; he thought, as
he lay on his back, of all the tones she might make possible if
one were to try her, and at any rate of the probability that one
could trust her to fit them to occasions. He had wanted her to
feel that, as he was disinterested now, so she herself should be,
and she had showed she felt it, and he had showed he was
grateful, and it had been for all the world as if he were calling
for the first time. They had had other, but irrelevant, meetings;
it was quite as if, had they sooner known how much they *really*
had in common, there were quantities of comparatively dull
matters they might have skipped. Well, they were skipping
them now, even to graceful gratitude, even to handsome 'Don't
mention it!' – and it was amazing what could still come up
without reference to what had been going on between them. It
might have been, on analysis, nothing more than Shakespeare
and the musical glasses;[4] but it had served all the purpose of his
appearing to have said to her: 'Don't like me, if it's a question
of liking me, for anything obvious and clumsy that I've, as they
call it, "done" for you: like me – well, like me, hang it, for
anything else you choose. So, by the same propriety, don't be for
me simply the person I've come to know through my awkward
connexion with Chad – was ever anything, by the way, *more*
awkward? Be for me, please, with all your admirable tact and
trust, just whatever I may show you it's a present pleasure to
me to think you.' It had been a large indication to meet; but if
she hadn't met it what *had* she done, and how had their time
together slipped along so smoothly, mild but not slow, and

melting, liquefying, into his happy illusion of idleness? He could recognize on the other hand that he had probably not been without reason, in his prior, his restricted state, for keeping an eye on his liability to lapse from good faith.

He really continued in the picture – that being for himself his situation – all the rest of this rambling day; so that the charm was still, was indeed more than ever upon him when, toward six o'clock, he found himself amicably engaged with a stout white-capped deep-voiced woman at the door of the *auberge* of the biggest village, a village that affected him as a thing of whiteness, blueness and crookedness, set in coppery green, and that had the river flowing behind or before it – one couldn't say which; at the bottom, in particular, of the inn-garden. He had had other adventures before this; had kept along the height, after shaking off slumber; had admired, had almost coveted, another small old church, all steep roof and dim slate-colour without and all whitewash and paper flowers within; had lost his way and had found it again; had conversed with rustics who struck him perhaps a little more as men of the world than he had expected; had acquired at a bound a fearless facility in French; had had, as the afternoon waned, a watery *bock*, all pale and Parisian, in the café of the furthest village, which was not the biggest; and had meanwhile not once overstepped the oblong gilt frame. The frame had drawn itself out for him, as much as you please; but that was just his luck. He had finally come down again to the valley, to keep within touch of stations and trains, turning his face to the quarter from which he had started; and thus it was that he had at last pulled up before the hostess of the Cheval Blanc, who met him, with a rough readiness that was like the clatter of sabots over stones, on their common ground of a *côtelette de veau à l'oseille* and a subsequent lift. He had walked many miles and didn't know he was tired; but he still knew he was amused, and even that, though he had been alone all day, he had never yet so struck himself as engaged with others and in midstream of his drama. It might have passed for finished, his drama, with its catastrophe all but reached: it had, however, none the less been vivid again for him as he thus gave it its fuller chance. He had only had to

be at last well out of it to feel it, oddly enough, still going on.

For this had been all day at bottom the spell of the picture – that it was essentially more than anything else a scene and a stage, that the very air of the play was in the rustle of the willows and the tone of the sky. The play and the characters had, without his knowing it till now, peopled all his space for him, and it seemed somehow quite happy that they should offer themselves, in the conditions so supplied, with a kind of inevitability. It was as if the conditions made them not only inevitable, but so much more nearly natural and right as that they were at least easier, pleasanter, to put up with. The conditions had nowhere so asserted their difference from those of Woollett as they appeared to him to assert it in the little court of the Cheval Blanc while he arranged with his hostess for a comfortable climax. They were few and simple, scant and humble, but they were *the thing*, as he would have called it, even to a greater degree than Madame de Vionnet's old high salon where the ghost of the Empire walked. 'The' thing was the thing that implied the greatest number of other things of the sort he had had to tackle; and it was queer of course, but so it was – the implication here was complete. Not a single one of his observations but somehow fell into a place in it; not a breath of the cooler evening that wasn't somehow a syllable of the text. The text was simply, when condensed, that in *these* places such things were, and that if it was in them one elected to move about one had to make one's account with what one lighted on. Meanwhile at all events it was enough that they did affect one – so far as the village aspect was concerned – as whiteness, crookedness and blueness set in coppery green; there being positively, for that matter, an outer wall of the White Horse that was painted the most improbable shade. That was part of the amusement – as if to show that the fun was harmless; just as it was enough, further, that the picture and the play seemed supremely to melt together in the good woman's broad sketch of what she could do for her visitor's appetite. He felt in short a confidence, and it was general, and it was all he wanted to feel. It suffered no shock even on her mentioning that she had in fact just laid the cloth for two persons who,

unlike Monsieur, had arrived by the river – in a boat of their own; who had asked her, half an hour before, what she could do for them, and had then paddled away to look at something a little further up – from which promenade they would presently return. Monsieur might meanwhile, if he liked, pass into the garden, such as it was, where she would serve him, should he wish it – for there were tables and benches in plenty – a 'bitter'[5] before his repast. Here she would also report to him on the possibility of a conveyance to his station, and here at any rate he would have the *agrément* of the river.

It may be mentioned without delay that Monsieur had the *agrément* of everything, and in particular, for the next twenty minutes, of a small and primitive pavilion that, at the garden's edge, almost overhung the water, testifying, in its somewhat battered state, to much fond frequentation. It consisted of little more than a platform, slightly raised, with a couple of benches and a table, a protecting rail and a projecting roof; but it raked the full grey-blue stream, which, taking a turn a short distance above, passed out of sight to reappear much higher up; and it was clearly in esteemed requisition for Sundays and other feasts. Strether sat there and, though hungry, felt at peace; the confidence that had so gathered for him deepened with the lap of the water, the ripple of the surface, the rustle of the reeds on the opposite bank, the faint diffused coolness and the slight rock of a couple of small boats attached to a rough landing-place hard by. The valley on the further side was all copper-green level and glazed pearly sky, a sky hatched across with screens of trimmed trees, which looked flat, like espaliers; and though the rest of the village straggled away in the near quarter the view had an emptiness that made one of the boats suggestive. Such a river set one afloat almost before one could take up the oars – the idle play of which would be moreover the aid to the full impression. This perception went so far as to bring him to his feet; but that movement, in turn, made him feel afresh that he was tired, and while he leaned against a post and continued to look out he saw something that gave him a sharper arrest.

IV

What he saw was exactly the right thing – a boat advancing round the bend and containing a man who held the paddles and a lady, at the stern, with a pink parasol. It was suddenly as if these figures, or something like them, had been wanted in the picture, had been wanted more or less all day, and had now drifted into sight, with the slow current, on purpose to fill up the measure. They came slowly, floating down, evidently directed to the landing-place near their spectator and presenting themselves to him not less clearly as the two persons for whom his hostess was already preparing a meal. For two very happy persons he found himself straightway taking them – a young man in shirt-sleeves, a young woman easy and fair, who had pulled pleasantly up from some other place and, being acquainted with the neighbourhood, had known what this particular retreat could offer them. The air quite thickened, at their approach, with further intimations; the intimation that they were expert, familiar, frequent – that this wouldn't at all events be the first time. They knew how to do it, he vaguely felt – and it made them but the more idyllic, though at the very moment of the impression, as happened, their boat seemed to have begun to drift wide, the oarsman letting it go. It had by this time none the less come much nearer – near enough for Strether to dream the lady in the stern had for some reason taken account of his being there to watch them. She had remarked on it sharply, yet her companion hadn't turned round; it was in fact almost as if our friend had felt her bid him keep still. She had taken in something as a result of which their course had wavered, and it continued to waver while they just stood off. This little effect

was sudden and rapid, so rapid that Strether's sense of it was separate only for an instant from a sharp start of his own. He too had within the minute taken in something, taken in that he knew the lady whose parasol, shifting as if to hide her face, made so fine a pink point in the shining scene. It was too prodigious, a chance in a million, but, if he knew the lady, the gentleman, who still presented his back and kept off, the gentleman, the coatless hero of the idyll, who had responded to her start, was, to match the marvel, none other than Chad.

Chad and Madame de Vionnet were then like himself taking a day in the country – though it was as queer as fiction, as farce, that their country could happen to be exactly his; and she had been the first at recognition, the first to feel, across the water, the shock – for it appeared to come to that – of their wonderful accident. Strether became aware, with this, of what was taking place – that her recognition had been even stranger for the pair in the boat, that her immediate impulse had been to control it, and that she was quickly and intensely debating with Chad the risk of betrayal. He saw they would show nothing if they could feel sure he hadn't made them out; so that he had before him for a few seconds his own hesitation. It was a sharp fantastic crisis that had popped up as if in a dream, and it had had only to last the few seconds to make him feel it as quite horrible. They were thus, on either side, *trying* the other side, and all for some reason that broke the stillness like some unprovoked harsh note. It seemed to him again, within the limit, that he had but one thing to do – to settle their common question by some sign of surprise and joy. He hereupon gave large play to these things, agitating his hat and his stick and loudly calling out – a demonstration that brought him relief as soon as he had seen it answered. The boat, in mid-stream, still went a little wild – which seemed natural, however, while Chad turned round, half springing up; and his good friend, after blankness and wonder, began gaily to wave her parasol. Chad dropped afresh to his paddles and the boat headed round, amazement and pleasantry filling the air meanwhile, and relief, as Strether continued to fancy, superseding mere violence. Our friend went down to the water under this odd impression as of violence

averted – the violence of their having 'cut' him, out there in the eye of nature, on the assumption that he wouldn't know it. He awaited them with a face from which he was conscious of not being able quite to banish this idea that they would have gone on, not seeing and not knowing, missing their dinner and disappointing their hostess, had he himself taken a line to match. That at least was what darkened his vision for the moment. Afterwards, after they had bumped at the landing-place and he had assisted their getting ashore, everything found itself sponged over by the mere miracle of the encounter.

They could so much better at last, on either side, treat it as a wild extravagance of hazard, that the situation was made elastic by the amount of explanation called into play. Why indeed – apart from oddity – the situation should have been really stiff was a question naturally not practical at the moment, and in fact, so far as we are concerned, a question tackled, later on and in private, only by Strether himself. He was to reflect later on and in private that it was mainly *he* who had explained – as he had had moreover comparatively little difficulty in doing. He was to have at all events meanwhile the worrying thought of their perhaps secretly suspecting him of having plotted this coincidence, taking such pains as might be to give it the semblance of an accident. That possibility – as their imputation – didn't of course bear looking into for an instant; yet the whole incident was so manifestly, arrange it as they would, an awkward one, that he could scarce keep disclaimers in respect to his own presence from rising to his lips. Disclaimers of intention would have been as tactless as his presence was practically gross; and the narrowest escape they either of them had was his lucky escape, in the event, from making any. Nothing of the sort, so far as surface and sound were involved, was even in question; surface and sound all made for their common ridiculous good fortune, for the general *invraisemblance* of the occasion, for the charming chance that they had, the others, in passing, ordered some food to be ready, the charming chance that he had himself not eaten, the charming chance, even more, that their little plans, their hours, their train, in short, from *là-bas*, would all match for their return together to Paris. The

chance that was most charming of all, the chance that drew from Madame de Vionnet her clearest, gayest 'Comme cela se trouve!' was the announcement made to Strether after they were seated at table, the word given him by their hostess in respect to his carriage for the station, on which he might now count. It settled the matter for his friends as well; the conveyance – it *was* all too lucky! – would serve for them; and nothing was more delightful than his being in a position to make the train so definite. It might have been, for themselves – to hear Madame de Vionnet – almost unnaturally vague, a detail left to be fixed; though Strether indeed was afterwards to remember that Chad had promptly enough intervened to forestall this appearance, laughing at his companion's flightiness and making the point that he had, after all, in spite of the bedazzlement of a day out with her, known what he was about.

Strether was to remember afterwards further that this had had for him the effect of forming Chad's almost sole intervention; and indeed he was to remember further still, in subsequent meditation, many things that, as it were, fitted together. Another of them was for instance that the wonderful woman's overflow of surprise and amusement was wholly into French, which she struck him as speaking with an unprecedented command of idiomatic turns, but in which she got, as he might have said, somewhat away from him, taking all at once little brilliant jumps that he could but lamely match. The question of his own French had never come up for them; it was the one thing she wouldn't have permitted – it belonged, for a person who had been through much, to mere boredom; but the present result was odd, fairly veiling her identity, shifting her back into a mere voluble class or race to the intense audibility of which he was by this time inured. When she spoke the charming slightly strange English he best knew her by he seemed to feel her as a creature, among all the millions, with a language quite to herself, the real monopoly of a special shade of speech, beautifully easy for her, yet of a colour and a cadence that were both inimitable and matters of accident. She came back to these things after they had shaken down in the inn-parlour and knew, as it were, what was to become of them; it was inevitable that

loud ejaculation over the prodigy of their convergence should at last wear itself out. Then it was that his impression took fuller form – the impression, destined only to deepen, to complete itself, that they had something to put a face upon, to carry off and make the best of, and that it was she who, admirably on the whole, was doing this. It was familiar to him of course that they had something to put a face upon; their friendship, their connexion, took any amount of explaining – that would have been made familiar by his twenty minutes with Mrs. Pocock if it hadn't already been so. Yet his theory, as we know, had bountifully been that the facts were specifically none of his business, and were, over and above, so far as one had to do with them, intrinsically beautiful; and this might have prepared him for anything, as well as rendered him proof against mystification. When he reached home that night, however, he knew he had been, at bottom, neither prepared nor proof; and since we have spoken of what he was, after his return, to recall and interpret, it may as well immediately be said that his real experience of these few hours put on, in that belated vision – for he scarce went to bed till morning – the aspect that is most to our purpose.

He then knew more or less how he had been affected – he but half knew at the time. There had been plenty to affect him even after, as has been said, they had shaken down; for his consciousness, though muffled, had its sharpest moments during this passage, a marked drop into innocent friendly Bohemia. They then had put their elbows on the table, deploring the premature end of their two or three dishes; which they had tried to make up with another bottle while Chad joked a little spasmodically, perhaps even a little irrelevantly, with the hostess. What it all came to had been that fiction and fable *were*, inevitably, in the air, and not as a simple term of comparison, but as a result of things said; also that they were blinking it, all round, and that they yet needn't, so much as that, have blinked it – though indeed if they hadn't Strether didn't quite see what else they could have done. Strether didn't quite see *that* even at an hour or two past midnight, even when he had, at his hotel, for a long time, without a light and without undressing, sat

back on his bedroom sofa and stared straight before him. He was, at that point of vantage, in full possession, to make of it all what he could. He kept making of it that there had been simply a *lie* in the charming affair – a lie on which one could now, detached and deliberate, perfectly put one's finger. It was with the lie that they had eaten and drunk and talked and laughed, that they had waited for their *carriole* rather impatiently, and had then got into the vehicle and, sensibly subsiding, driven their three or four miles through the darkening summer night. The eating and drinking, which had been a resource, had had the effect of having served its turn; the talk and laughter had done as much; and it was during their somewhat tedious progress to the station, during the waits there, the further delays, their submission to fatigue, their silences in the dim compartment of the much-stopping train, that he prepared himself for reflexions to come. It had been a performance, Madame de Vionnet's manner, and though it had to that degree faltered toward the end, as through her ceasing to believe in it, as if she had asked herself, or Chad had found a moment surreptitiously to ask her, what after all was the use, a performance it had none the less quite handsomely remained, with the final fact about it that it was on the whole easier to keep up than to abandon.

From the point of view of presence of mind it had been very wonderful indeed, wonderful for readiness, for beautiful assurance, for the way her decision was taken on the spot, without time to confer with Chad, without time for anything. Their only conference could have been the brief instants in the boat before they confessed to recognizing the spectator on the bank, for they hadn't been alone together a moment since and must have communicated all in silence. It was a part of the deep impression for Strether, and not the least of the deep interest, that they *could* so communicate – that Chad in particular could let her know he left it to her. He habitually left things to others, as Strether was so well aware, and it in fact came over our friend in these meditations that there had been as yet no such vivid illustration of his famous knowing how to live. It was as if he had humoured her to the extent of letting her lie without

correction – almost as if, really, he would be coming round in the morning to set the matter, as between Strether and himself, right. Of course he couldn't quite come; it was a case in which a man was obliged to accept the woman's version, even when fantastic; if she had, with more flurry than she cared to show, elected, as the phrase was, to represent that they had left Paris that morning, and with no design but of getting back within the day – if she had so sized-up, in the Woollett phrase, their necessity, she knew best her own measure. There were things, all the same, it was impossible to blink and which made this measure an odd one – the too evident fact for instance that she hadn't started out for the day dressed and hatted and shod, and even, for that matter, pink parasol'd, as she had been in the boat. From what did the drop in her assurance proceed as the tension increased – from what did this slightly baffled ingenuity spring but from her consciousness of not presenting, as night closed in, with not so much as a shawl to wrap her round, an appearance that matched her story? She admitted that she was cold, but only to blame her imprudence, which Chad suffered her to give such account of as she might. Her shawl and Chad's overcoat and her other garments, and his, those they had each worn the day before, were at the place, best known to themselves – a quiet retreat enough, no doubt – at which they had been spending the twenty-four hours, to which they had fully meant to return that evening, from which they had so remarkably swum into Strether's ken,[1] and the tacit repudiation of which had been thus the essence of her comedy. Strether saw how she had perceived in a flash that they couldn't quite look to going back there under his nose; though, honestly, as he gouged deeper into the matter, he was somewhat surprised, as Chad likewise had perhaps been, at the uprising of this scruple. He seemed even to divine that she had entertained it rather for Chad than for herself, and that, as the young man had lacked the chance to enlighten her, she had had to go on with it, he meanwhile mistaking her motive.

He was rather glad, none the less, that they had in point of fact not parted at the Cheval Blanc, that he hadn't been reduced to giving them his blessing for an idyllic retreat down the river.

He had had in the actual case to make-believe more than he
liked, but this was nothing, it struck him, to what the other
event would have required. Could he, literally, quite have faced
the other event? Would he have been capable of making the
best of it with them? This was what he was trying to do now;
but with the advantage of his being able to give more time to it
a good deal counteracted by his sense of what, over and above
the central fact itself, he had to swallow. It was the quantity of
make-believe involved and so vividly exemplified that most
disagreed with his spiritual stomach. He moved, however, from
the consideration of that quantity – to say nothing of the consciousness of that organ – back to the other feature of the show,
the deep, deep truth of the intimacy revealed. That was what,
in his vain vigil, he oftenest reverted to: intimacy, at such a
point, was *like* that – and what in the world else would one
have wished it to be like? It was all very well for him to feel the
pity of its being so much like lying; he almost blushed, in the
dark, for the way he had dressed the possibility in vagueness,
as a little girl might have dressed her doll. He had made them
– and by no fault of their own – momentarily pull it for him,
the possibility, out of this vagueness; and must he not therefore
take it now as they had had simply, with whatever thin attenu-
ations, to give it to him? The very question, it may be added,
made him feel lonely and cold. There was the element of the
awkward all round, but Chad and Madame de Vionnet had at
least the comfort that they could talk it over together. With
whom could *he* talk of such things? – unless indeed always, at
almost any stage, with Maria? He foresaw that Miss Gostrey
would come again into requisition on the morrow; though it
wasn't to be denied that he was already a little afraid of her
'What on earth – that's what I want to know now – had you
then supposed?' He recognized at last that he had really been
trying all along to suppose nothing. Verily, verily, his labour
had been lost. He found himself supposing innumerable and
wonderful things.

BOOK TWELFTH

BOOK TWELFTH

I

Strether couldn't have said he had during the previous hours definitely expected it; yet when, later on, that morning – though no later indeed than for his coming forth at ten o'clock – he saw the concierge produce, on his approach, a *petit bleu* delivered since his letters had been sent up, he recognized the appearance as the first symptom of a sequel. He then knew he had been thinking of some early sign from Chad as more likely, after all, than not; and this would be precisely the early sign. He took it so for granted that he opened the *petit bleu* just where he had stopped, in the pleasant cool draught of the porte-cochère – only curious to see where the young man would, at such a juncture, break out. His curiosity, however, was more than gratified; the small missive, whose gummed edge he had detached without attention to the address, not being from the young man at all, but from the person whom the case gave him on the spot as still more worth while. Worth while or not, he went round to the nearest telegraph-office, the big one on the Boulevard, with a directness that almost confessed to a fear of the danger of delay. He might have been thinking that if he didn't go before he could think he wouldn't perhaps go at all. He at any rate kept, in the lower side-pocket of his morning coat, a very deliberate hand on his blue missive, crumpling it up rather tenderly than harshly. He wrote a reply, on the Boulevard, also in the form of a *petit bleu* – which was quickly done, under pressure of the place, inasmuch as, like Madame de Vionnet's own communication, it consisted of the fewest words. She had asked him if he could do her the very great kindness of coming to see her that evening at half-past nine,

and he answered, as if nothing were easier, that he would present himself at the hour she named. She had added a line of postscript, to the effect that she would come to him elsewhere and at his own hour if he preferred; but he took no notice of this, feeling that if he saw her at all half the value of it would be in seeing her where he had already seen her best. He mightn't see her at all; that was one of the reflexions he made after writing and before he dropped his closed card into the box; he mightn't see any one at all any more at all; he might make an end as well now as ever, leaving things as they were, since he was doubtless not to leave them better, and taking his way home so far as should appear that a home remained to him. This alternative was for a few minutes so sharp that if he at last did deposit his missive it was perhaps because the pressure of the place had an effect.

There was none other, however, than the common and constant pressure, familiar to our friend under the rubric of *Postes et Télégraphes*[1] – the something in the air of these establishments; the vibration of the vast strange life of the town, the influence of the types, the performers concocting their messages; the little prompt Paris women, arranging, pretexting goodness knew what, driving the dreadful needle-pointed public pen at the dreadful sand-strewn public table: implements that symbolized for Strether's too interpretative innocence something more acute in manners, more sinister in morals, more fierce in the national life. After he had put in his paper he had ranged himself, he was really amused to think, on the side of the fierce, the sinister, the acute. He was carrying on a correspondence, across the great city, quite in the key of the *Postes et Télégraphes* in general; and it was fairly as if the acceptance of that fact had come from something in his state that sorted with the occupation of his neighbours. He was mixed up with the typical tale of Paris, and so were they, poor things – how could they all together help being? They were no worse than he, in short, and he no worse than they – if, queerly enough, no better; and at all events he had settled his hash, so that he went out to begin, from that moment, his day of waiting. The great settlement was, as he felt, in his preference for seeing his correspondent in her

own best conditions. *That* was part of the typical tale, the part most significant in respect to himself. He liked the place she lived in, the picture that each time squared itself, large and high and clear, around her: every occasion of seeing it was a pleasure of a different shade. Yet what precisely was he doing with shades of pleasure now, and why hadn't he properly and logically compelled her to commit herself to whatever of disadvantage and penalty the situation might throw up? He might have proposed, as for Sarah Pocock, the cold hospitality of his own *salon de lecture*, in which the chill of Sarah's visit seemed still to abide and shades of pleasure were dim; he might have suggested a stone bench in the dusty Tuileries or a penny chair at the back part of the Champs Elysées. These things would have been a trifle stern, and sternness alone now wouldn't be sinister. An instinct in him cast about for some form of discipline in which they might meet – some awkwardness they would suffer from, some danger, or at least some grave inconvenience, they would incur. This would give a sense – which the spirit required, rather ached and sighed in the absence of – that somebody was paying something somewhere and somehow, that they were at least not all floating together on the silver stream of impunity. Just instead of that to go and see her late in the evening, as if, for all the world – well, as if he were as much in the swim as anybody else: this had as little as possible in common with the penal form.

Even when he had felt that objection melt away, however, the practical difference was small; the long stretch of his interval took the colour it would, and if he lived on thus with the sinister from hour to hour it proved an easier thing than one might have supposed in advance. He reverted in thought to his old tradition, the one he had been brought up on and which even so many years of life had but little worn away; the notion that the state of the wrongdoer, or at least this person's happiness, presented some special difficulty. What struck him now rather was the ease of it – for nothing in truth appeared easier. It was an ease he himself fairly tasted of for the rest of the day; giving himself quite up; not so much as trying to dress it out, in any particular whatever, as a difficulty; not after all going to see

Maria – which would have been in a manner a result of such dressing; only idling, lounging, smoking, sitting in the shade, drinking lemonade and consuming ices. The day had turned to heat and eventual thunder, and he now and again went back to his hotel to find that Chad hadn't been there. He hadn't yet struck himself, since leaving Woollett, so much as a loafer, though there had been times when he believed himself touching bottom. This was a deeper depth than any, and with no foresight, scarcely with a care, as to what he should bring up. He almost wondered if he didn't *look* demoralized and disreputable; he had the fanciful vision, as he sat and smoked, of some accidental, some motived, return of the Pococks, who would be passing along the Boulevard and would catch this view of him. They would have distinctly, on his appearance, every ground for scandal. But fate failed to administer even that sternness; the Pococks never passed and Chad made no sign. Strether meanwhile continued to hold off from Miss Gostrey, keeping her till to-morrow; so that by evening his irresponsibility, his impunity, his luxury, had become – there was no other word for them – immense.

Between nine and ten, at last, in the high clear picture – he was moving in these days, as in a gallery, from clever canvas to clever canvas – he drew a long breath: it was so presented to him from the first that the spell of his luxury wouldn't be broken. He wouldn't have, that is, to become responsible – this was admirably in the air: she had sent for him precisely to let him feel it, so that he might go on with the comfort (comfort already established, hadn't it been?) of regarding his ordeal, the ordeal of the weeks of Sarah's stay and of their climax, as safely traversed and left behind him. Didn't she just wish to assure him that *she* now took it all and so kept it; that he was absolutely not to worry any more, was only to rest on his laurels and continue generously to help her? The light in her beautiful formal room was dim, though it would do, as everything would always do; the hot night had kept out lamps, but there was a pair of clusters of candles that glimmered over the chimney-piece like the tall tapers of an altar. The windows were all open, their redundant hangings swaying a little, and he heard once more, from the

empty court, the small plash of the fountain. From beyond this, and as from a great distance – beyond the court, beyond the *corps de logis* forming the front – came, as if excited and exciting, the vague voice of Paris. Strether had all along been subject to sudden gusts of fancy in connexion with such matters as these – odd starts of the historic sense, suppositions and divinations with no warrant but their intensity. Thus and so, on the eve of the great recorded dates, the days and nights of revolution, the sounds had come in, the omens, the beginnings broken out. They were the smell of revolution, the smell of the public temper – or perhaps simply the smell of blood.

It was at present queer beyond words, 'subtle', he would have risked saying, that such suggestions should keep crossing the scene; but it was doubtless the effect of the thunder in the air, which had hung about all day without release. His hostess was dressed as for thunderous times, and it fell in with the kind of imagination we have just attributed to him that she should be in simplest coolest white, of a character so old-fashioned, if he were not mistaken, that Madame Roland[2] must on the scaffold have worn something like it. This effect was enhanced by a small black fichu or scarf, of crape or gauze, disposed quaintly round her bosom and now completing as by a mystic touch the pathetic, the noble analogy. Poor Strether in fact scarce knew what analogy was evoked for him as the charming woman, receiving him and making him, as she could do such things, at once familiarly and gravely welcome, moved over her great room with her image almost repeated in its polished floor, which had been fully bared for summer. The associations of the place, all felt again; the gleam here and there, in the subdued light, of glass and gilt and parquet, with the quietness of her own note as the centre – these things were at first as delicate as if they had been ghostly, and he was sure in a moment that, whatever he should find he had come for, it wouldn't be for an impression that had previously failed him. That conviction held him from the outset, and, seeming singularly to simplify, certified to him that the objects about would help him, would really help them both. No, he might never see them again – this was only too probably the last time; and he should certainly see

nothing in the least degree like them. He should soon be going
to where such things were not, and it would be a small mercy
for memory, for fancy, to have, in that stress, a loaf on the
shelf. He knew in advance he should look back on the perception actually sharpest with him as on the view of something
old, old, old, the oldest thing he had ever personally touched;
and he also knew, even while he took his companion in as the
feature among features, that memory and fancy couldn't help
being enlisted for her. She might intend what she would, but
this was beyond anything she could intend, with things from
far back – tyrannies of history, facts of type, values, as the
painters said, of expression – all working for her and giving
her the supreme chance, the chance of the happy, the really
luxurious few, the chance, on a great occasion, to be natural
and simple. She had never, with him, been more so; or if it was
the perfection of art it would never – and that came to the same
thing – be proved against her.

What was truly wonderful was her way of differing so from
time to time without detriment to her simplicity. Caprices, he
was sure she felt, were before anything else bad manners, and
that judgement in her was by itself a thing making more for
safety of intercourse than anything that in his various own past
intercourses he had had to reckon on. If therefore her presence
was now quite other than the one she had shown him the night
before, there was nothing of violence in the change – it was all
harmony and reason. It gave him a mild deep person, whereas
he had had on the occasion to which their interview was a
direct reference a person committed to movement and surface
and abounding in them; but she was in either character more
remarkable for nothing than for her bridging of intervals, and
this now fell in with what he understood he was to leave to her.
The only thing was that, if he was to leave it *all* to her, why
exactly had she sent for him? He had had, vaguely, in advance,
his explanation, his view of the probability of her wishing to
set something right, to deal in some way with the fraud so lately
practised on his presumed credulity. Would she attempt to carry
it further or would she blot it out? Would she throw over it
some more or less happy colour; or would she do nothing about

it at all? He perceived soon enough at least that, however reasonable she might be, she wasn't vulgarly confused, and it herewith pressed upon him that their eminent 'lie', Chad's and hers, was simply after all such an inevitable tribute to good taste as he couldn't have wished them not to render. Away from them, during his vigil, he had seemed to wince at the amount of comedy involved; whereas in his present posture he could only ask himself how he should enjoy any attempt from her to take the comedy back. He shouldn't enjoy it at all; but, once more and yet once more, he could trust her. That is he could trust her to make deception right. As she presented things the ugliness – goodness knew why – went out of them; none the less too that she could present them, with an art of her own, by not so much as touching them. She let the matter, at all events, lie where it was – where the previous twenty-four hours had placed it; appearing merely to circle about it respectfully, tenderly, almost piously, while she took up another question.

She knew she hadn't really thrown dust in his eyes; this, the previous night, before they separated, had practically passed between them; and, as she had sent for him to see what the difference thus made for him might amount to, so he was conscious at the end of five minutes that he had been tried and tested. She had settled with Chad after he left them that she would, for her satisfaction, assure herself of this quantity, and Chad had, as usual, let her have her way. Chad was always letting people have their way when he felt that it would some-how turn his wheel for him; it somehow always did turn his wheel. Strether felt, oddly enough, before these facts, freshly and consentingly passive; they again so rubbed it into him that the couple thus fixing his attention were intimate, that his intervention had absolutely aided and intensified their intimacy, and that in fine he must accept the consequence of that. He had absolutely become, himself, with his perceptions and his mistakes, his concessions and his reserves, the droll mixture, as it must seem to them, of his braveries and his fears, the general spectacle of his art and his innocence, almost an added link and certainly a common priceless ground for them to meet upon. It was as if he had been hearing their very tone when she brought

out a reference that was comparatively straight. 'The last twice
that you've been here, you know, I never asked you,' she said
with an abrupt transition – they had been pretending before
this to talk simply of the charm of yesterday and of the interest
of the country they had seen. The effort was confessedly vain;
not for such talk had she invited him; and her impatient
reminder was of their having done for it all the needful on his
coming to her after Sarah's flight. What she hadn't asked him
then was to state to her where and how he stood for her;
she had been resting on Chad's report of their midnight hour
together in the Boulevard Malesherbes. The thing therefore she
at present desired was ushered in by this recall of the two
occasions on which, disinterested and merciful, she hadn't
worried him. To-night truly she *would* worry him, and this was
her appeal to him to let her risk it. He wasn't to mind if she
bored him a little: she had behaved, after all – hadn't she? – so
awfully, awfully well.

II

'Oh, you're all right, you're all right,' he almost impatiently declared; his impatience being moreover not for her pressure, but for her scruple. More and more distinct to him was the tune to which she would have had the matter out with Chad; more and more vivid for him the idea that she had been nervous as to what he might be able to 'stand'. Yes, it had been a question if he had 'stood' what the scene on the river had given him, and, though the young man had doubtless opined in favour of his recuperation, her own last word must have been that she should feel easier in seeing for herself. That was it, unmistakeably; she *was* seeing for herself. What he could stand was thus, in these moments, in the balance for Strether, who reflected, as he became fully aware of it, that he must properly brace himself. He wanted fully to appear to stand all he might; and there was a certain command of the situation for him in this very wish not to look too much at sea. She was ready with everything, but so, sufficiently, was he; that is he was at one point the more prepared of the two, inasmuch as, for all her cleverness, she couldn't produce on the spot – and it was surprising – an account of the motive of her note. He had the advantage that his pronouncing her 'all right' gave him for an enquiry. 'May I ask, delighted as I've been to come, if you've wished to say something special?' He spoke as if she might have seen he had been waiting for it – not indeed with discomfort, but with natural interest. Then he saw that she was a little taken aback, was even surprised herself at the detail she had neglected – the only one ever yet; having somehow assumed he would know, would recognize, would leave some things not to be said. She

looked at him, however, an instant as if to convey that if he wanted them *all* –!

'Selfish and vulgar – that's what I must seem to you. You've done everything for me, and here I am as if I were asking for more. But it isn't,' she went on, 'because I'm afraid – though I *am* of course afraid, as a woman in my position always is. I mean it isn't because one lives in terror – it isn't because of that one is selfish, for I'm ready to give you my word to-night that I don't care; don't care what still may happen and what I may lose. I don't ask you to raise your little finger for me again, nor do I wish so much as to mention to you what we've talked of before, either my danger or my safety, or his mother, or his sister, or the girl he may marry, or the fortune he may make or miss, or the right or the wrong, of any kind, he may do. If after the help one has had from you one can't either take care of one's self or simply hold one's tongue, one must renounce all claim to be an object of interest. It's in the name of what I *do* care about that I've tried still to keep hold of you. How can I be indifferent,' she asked, 'to how I appear to you?' And as he found himself unable immediately to say: 'Why, if you're going, *need* you, after all? Is it impossible you should stay on – so that one mayn't lose you?'

'Impossible I should live with you here instead of going home?'

'Not "with" us, if you object to that, but near enough to us, somewhere, for us to see you – well,' she beautifully brought out, 'when we feel we *must*. How shall we not sometimes feel it? I've wanted to see you often when I couldn't,' she pursued, 'all these last weeks. How shan't I then miss you now, with the sense of your being gone forever?' Then as if the straightness of this appeal, taking him unprepared, had visibly left him wondering: 'Where *is* your "home" moreover now – what has become of it? I've made a change in your life, I know I have; I've upset everything in your mind as well; in your sense of – what shall I call it? – all the decencies and possibilities. It gives me a kind of detestation –' She pulled up short.

Oh but he wanted to hear. 'Detestation of what?'

'Of everything – of life.'

'Ah that's too much,' he laughed – 'or too little!'

'Too little, precisely' – she was eager. 'What I hate is myself – when I think that one has to take so much, to be happy, out of the lives of others, and that one isn't happy even then. One does it to cheat one's self and to stop one's mouth – but that's only at the best for a little. The wretched self is always there, always making one somehow a fresh anxiety. What it comes to is that it's not, that it's never, a happiness, any happiness at all, to *take*. The only safe thing is to give. It's what plays you least false.' Interesting, touching, strikingly sincere as she let these things come from her, she yet puzzled and troubled him – so fine was the quaver of her quietness. He felt what he had felt before with her, that there was always more behind what she showed, and more and more again behind that. 'You know so, at least,' she added, 'where you are!'

'*You* ought to know it indeed then; for isn't what you've been giving exactly what has brought us together this way? You've been making, as I've so fully let you know I've felt,' Strether said, 'the most precious present I've ever seen made, and if you can't sit down peacefully on that performance you *are*, no doubt, born to torment yourself. But you ought,' he wound up, 'to be easy.'

'And not trouble you any more, no doubt – not thrust on you even the wonder and the beauty of what I've done; only let you regard our business as over, and well over, and see you depart in a peace that matches my own? No doubt, no doubt, no doubt,' she nervously repeated – 'all the more that I don't really pretend I believe you couldn't, for yourself, *not* have done what you have. I don't pretend you feel yourself victimized, for this evidently is the way you live, and it's what – we're agreed – is the best way. Yes, as you say,' she continued after a moment, 'I ought to be easy and rest on my work. Well then here am I doing so. I *am* easy. You'll have it for your last impression. When is it you say you go?' she asked with a quick change.

He took some time to reply – his last impression was more and more so mixed a one. It produced in him a vague disappointment, a drop that was deeper even than the fall of his elation the previous night. The good of what he had done, if he

had done so much, wasn't there to enliven him quite to the point that would have been ideal for a grand gay finale. Women were thus endlessly absorbent, and to deal with them was to walk on water.[1] What was at bottom the matter with her, embroider as she might and disclaim as she might – what was at bottom the matter with her was simply Chad himself. It was of Chad she was after all renewedly afraid; the strange strength of her passion was the very strength of her fear; she clung to *him*, Lambert Strether, as to a source of safety she had tested, and, generous graceful truthful as she might try to be, exquisite as she was, she dreaded the term of his being within reach. With this sharpest perception yet, it was like a chill in the air to him, it was almost appalling, that a creature so fine could be, by mysterious forces, a creature so exploited. For at the end of all things they *were* mysterious: she had but made Chad what he was – so why could she think she had made him infinite? She had made him better, she had made him best, she had made him anything one would; but it came to our friend with supreme queerness that he was none the less only Chad. Strether had the sense that *he*, a little, had made him too; his high appreciation had, as it were, consecrated her work. The work, however admirable, was nevertheless of the strict human order, and in short it was marvellous that the companion of mere earthly joys, of comforts, aberrations (however one classed them) within the common experience, should be so transcendently prized. It might have made Strether hot or shy, as such secrets of others brought home sometimes do make us; but he was held there by something so hard that it was fairly grim. This was not the discomposure of last night; that had quite passed – such discomposures were a detail; the real coercion was to see a man ineffably adored. There it was again – it took women, it took women; if to deal with them was to walk on water what wonder that the water rose? And it had never surely risen higher than round this woman. He presently found himself taking a long look from her, and the next thing he knew he had uttered all his thought. 'You're afraid for your life!'

It drew out her long look, and he soon enough saw why. A spasm came into her face, the tears she had already been unable

to hide overflowed at first in silence, and then, as the sound suddenly comes from a child, quickened to gasps, to sobs. She sat and covered her face with her hands, giving up all attempt at a manner. 'It's how you see me, it's how you see me' – she caught her breath with it – 'and it's as I *am*, and as I must take myself, and of course it's no matter.' Her emotion was at first so incoherent that he could only stand there at a loss, stand with his sense of having upset her, though of having done it by the truth. He had to listen to her in a silence that he made no immediate effort to attenuate, feeling her doubly woeful amid all her dim diffused elegance; consenting to it as he had consented to the rest, and even conscious of some vague inward irony in the presence of such a fine free range of bliss and bale. He couldn't say it was *not* no matter; for he was serving her to the end, he now knew, anyway – quite as if what he thought of her had nothing to do with it. It was actually moreover as if he didn't think of her at all, as if he could think of nothing but the passion, mature, abysmal, pitiful, she represented, and the possibilities she betrayed. She was older for him to-night, visibly less exempt from the touch of time; but she was as much as ever the finest and subtlest creature, the happiest apparition, it had been given him, in all his years, to meet; and yet he could see her there as vulgarly troubled, in very truth, as a maid-servant crying for her young man. The only thing was that she judged herself as the maidservant wouldn't; the weakness of which wisdom too, the dishonour of which judgement, seemed but to sink her lower. Her collapse, however, no doubt, was briefer and she had in a manner recovered herself before he intervened. 'Of course I'm afraid for my life. But that's nothing. It isn't that.'

He was silent a little longer, as if thinking what it might be. 'There's something I have in mind that I can still do.'

But she threw off at last, with a sharp sad headshake, drying her eyes, what he could still do. 'I don't care for that. Of course, as I've said, you're acting, in your wonderful way, for yourself; and what's for yourself is no more my business – though I may reach out unholy hands so clumsily to touch it – than if it were something in Timbuctoo. It's only that you don't snub me, as

you've had fifty chances to do – it's only your beautiful patience that makes one forget one's manners. In spite of your patience, all the same,' she went on, 'you'd do anything rather than be with us here, even if that were possible. You'd do everything for us but be mixed up with us – which is a statement you can easily answer to the advantage of your own manners. You can say "What's the use of talking of things that at the best are impossible?" What *is* of course the use? It's only my little madness. You'd talk if you were tormented. And I don't mean now about *him*. Oh for him –!' Positively, strangely, bitterly, as it seemed to Strether, she gave 'him', for the moment, away. 'You don't care what I think of you; but I happen to care what you think of me. And what you *might*,' she added. 'What you perhaps even did.'

He gained time. 'What I did –?'

'Did think before. Before this. *Didn't* you think –?'

But he had already stopped her. 'I didn't think anything. I never think a step further than I'm obliged to.'

'That's perfectly false, I believe,' she returned – 'except that you may, no doubt, often pull up when things become *too* ugly; or even, I'll say, to save you a protest, too beautiful. At any rate, even so far as it's true, we've thrust on you appearances that you've had to take in and that have therefore made your obligation. Ugly or beautiful – it doesn't matter what we call them – you were getting on without them, and that's where we're detestable. We bore you – that's where we are. And we may well – for what we've cost you. All you can do *now* is not to think at all. And I who should have liked to seem to you – well, sublime!'

He could only after a moment re-echo Miss Barrace. 'You're wonderful!'

'I'm old and abject and hideous' – she went on as without hearing him. 'Abject above all. Or old above all. It's when one's old that it's worst. I don't care what becomes of it – let what *will*; there it is. It's a doom – I know it; you can't see it more than I do myself. Things have to happen as they will.' With which she came back again to what, face to face with him, had so quite broken down. 'Of course you wouldn't, even if poss-

ible, and no matter what may happen to you, be near us. But think of me, think of me –!' She exhaled it into air.

He took refuge in repeating something he had already said and that she had made nothing of. 'There's something I believe I can still do.' And he put his hand out for good-bye.

She again made nothing of it; she went on with her insistence. 'That won't help you. There's nothing to help you.'

'Well, it may help *you*,' he said.

She shook her head. 'There's not a grain of certainty in my future – for the only certainty is that I shall be the loser in the end.'

She hadn't taken his hand, but she moved with him to the door. 'That's cheerful,' he laughed, 'for your benefactor!'

'What's cheerful for *me*,' she replied, 'is that we might, you and I, have been friends. That's it – that's it. You see how, as I say, I want everything. I've wanted you too.'

'Ah but you've *had* me!' he declared, at the door, with an emphasis that made an end.

III

His purpose had been to see Chad the next day, and he had prefigured seeing him by an early call; having in general never stood on ceremony in respect to visits at the Boulevard Malesherbes. It had been more often natural for him to go there than for Chad to come to the small hotel, the attractions of which were scant; yet it nevertheless, just now, at the eleventh hour, did suggest itself to Strether to begin by giving the young man a chance. It struck him that, in the inevitable course, Chad would be 'round', as Waymarsh used to say – Waymarsh who already, somehow, seemed long ago. He hadn't come the day before, because it had been arranged between them that Madame de Vionnet should see their friend first; but now that this passage had taken place he would present himself, and their friend wouldn't have long to wait. Strether assumed, he became aware, on this reasoning, that the interesting parties to the arrangement would have met betimes, and that the more interesting of the two – as she was after all – would have communicated to the other the issue of her appeal. Chad would know without delay that his mother's messenger had been with her, and, though it was perhaps not quite easy to see how she could qualify what had occurred, he would at least have been sufficiently advised to feel he could go on. The day, however, brought, early or late, no word from him, and Strether felt, as a result of this, that a change had practically come over their intercourse. It was perhaps a premature judgement; or it only meant perhaps – how could he tell? – that the wonderful pair he protected had taken up again together the excursion he had accidentally checked. They might have gone back to the

country, and gone back but with a long breath drawn; that indeed would best mark Chad's sense that reprobation hadn't rewarded Madame de Vionnet's request for an interview. At the end of the twenty-four hours, at the end of the forty-eight, there was still no overture; so that Strether filled up the time, as he had so often filled it before, by going to see Miss Gostrey.

He proposed amusements to her; he felt expert now in proposing amusements; and he had thus, for several days, an odd sense of leading her about Paris, of driving her in the Bois, of showing her the penny steamboats[1] – those from which the breeze of the Seine was to be best enjoyed – that might have belonged to a kindly uncle doing the honours of the capital to an intelligent niece from the country. He found means even to take her to shops she didn't know, or that she pretended she didn't; while she, on her side, was, like the country maiden, all passive modest and grateful – going in fact so far as to emulate rusticity in occasional fatigues and bewilderments. Strether described these vague proceedings to himself, described them even to her, as a happy interlude; the sign of which was that the companions said for the time no further word about the matter they had talked of to satiety. He proclaimed satiety at the outset, and she quickly took the hint; as docile both in this and in everything else as the intelligent obedient niece. He told her as yet nothing of his late adventure – for as an adventure it now ranked with him; he pushed the whole business temporarily aside and found his interest in the fact of her beautiful assent. She left questions unasked – she who for so long had been all questions; she gave herself up to him with an understanding of which mere mute gentleness might have seemed the sufficient expression. She knew his sense of his situation had taken still another step – of that he was quite aware; but she conveyed that, whatever had thus happened for him, it was thrown into the shade by what was happening for herself. This – though it mightn't to a detached spirit have seemed much – was the major interest, and she met it with a new directness of response, measuring it from hour to hour with her grave hush of acceptance. Touched as he had so often been by her before, he was, for his part too, touched afresh; all the more that though

he could be duly aware of the principle of his own mood he couldn't be equally so of the principle of hers. He knew, that is, in a manner – knew roughly and resignedly – what he himself was hatching; whereas he had to take the chance of what he called to himself Maria's calculations. It was all he needed that she liked him enough for what they were doing, and even should they do a good deal more would still like him enough for that; the essential freshness of a relation so simple was a cool bath to the soreness produced by other relations. These others appeared to him now horribly complex; they bristled with fine points, points all unimaginable beforehand, points that pricked and drew blood; a fact that gave to an hour with his present friend on a *bateau-mouche*, or in the afternoon shade of the Champs Elysées, something of the innocent pleasure of handling rounded ivory. His relation with Chad personally – from the moment he had got his point of view – had been of the simplest; yet this also struck him as bristling, after a third and a fourth blank day had passed. It was as if at last however his care for such indications had dropped; there came a fifth blank day and he ceased to enquire or to heed.

They now took on to his fancy, Miss Gostrey and he, the image of the Babes in the Wood;[2] they could trust the merciful elements to let them continue at peace. He had been great already, as he knew, at postponements; but he had only to get afresh into the rhythm of one to feel its fine attraction. It amused him to say to himself that he might for all the world have been going to die – die resignedly; the scene was filled for him with so deep a death-bed hush, so melancholy a charm. That meant the postponement of everything else – which made so for the quiet lapse of life; and the postponement in especial of the reckoning to come – unless indeed the reckoning to come were to be one and the same thing with extinction. It faced him, the reckoning, over the shoulder of much interposing experience – which also faced him; and one would float to it doubtless duly through these caverns of Kubla Khan.[3] It was really behind everything; it hadn't merged in what he had done; his final appreciation of what he had done – his appreciation on the spot – would provide it with its main sharpness. The spot so

focussed was of course Woollett, and he was to see, at the best, what Woollett would be with everything there changed for him. Wouldn't *that* revelation practically amount to the wind-up of his career? Well, the summer's end would show; his suspense had meanwhile exactly the sweetness of vain delay; and he had with it, we should mention, other pastimes than Maria's company – plenty of separate musings in which his luxury failed him but at one point. He was well in port, the outer sea behind him, and it was only a matter of getting ashore. There was a question that came and went for him, however, as he rested against the side of his ship, and it was a little to get rid of the obsession that he prolonged his hours with Miss Gostrey. It was a question about himself, but it could only be settled by seeing Chad again; it was indeed his principal reason for wanting to see Chad. After that it wouldn't signify – it was a ghost that certain words would easily lay to rest. Only the young man must be there to take the words. Once they were taken he wouldn't have a question left; none, that is, in connexion with this particular affair. It wouldn't then matter even to himself that he might now have been guilty of speaking *because* of what he had forfeited. That was the refinement of his supreme scruple – he wished so to leave what he had forfeited out of account. He wished not to do anything because he had missed something else, because he was sore or sorry or impoverished, because he was maltreated or desperate; he wished to do everything because he was lucid and quiet, just the same for himself on all essential points as he had ever been. Thus it was that while he virtually hung about for Chad he kept mutely putting it: 'You've been chucked, old boy; but what has that to do with it?' It would have sickened him to feel vindictive.

These tints of feeling indeed were doubtless but the iridescence of his idleness, and they were presently lost in a new light from Maria. She had a fresh fact for him before the week was out, and she practically met him with it on his appearing one night. He hadn't on this day seen her, but had planned presenting himself in due course to ask her to dine with him somewhere out of doors, on one of the terraces, in one of the gardens, of which the Paris of summer was profuse. It had then

come on to rain, so that, disconcerted, he changed his mind; dining alone at home, a little stuffily and stupidly, and waiting on her afterwards to make up his loss. He was sure within a minute that something had happened; it was so in the air of the rich little room that he had scarcely to name his thought. Softly lighted, the whole colour of the place, with its vague values, was in cool fusion – an effect that made the visitor stand for a little agaze. It was as if in doing so now he had felt a recent presence – his recognition of the passage of which his hostess in turn divined. She had scarcely to say it – 'Yes, she has been here, and this time I received her.' It wasn't till a minute later that she added: 'There being, as I understand you, no reason *now* – !'

'None for your refusing?'

'No – if you've done what you've had to do.'

'I've certainly so far done it,' Strether said, 'as that you needn't fear the effect, or the appearance of coming between us. There's nothing between us now but what we ourselves have put there, and not an inch of room for anything else whatever. Therefore you're only beautifully *with* us as always – though doubtless now, if she has talked to you, rather more with us than less. Of course if she came,' he added, 'it was to talk to you.'

'It was to talk to me,' Maria returned; on which he was further sure that she was practically in possession of what he himself hadn't yet told her. He was even sure she was in possession of things he himself couldn't have told; for the consciousness of them was now all in her face and accompanied there with a shade of sadness that marked in her the close of all uncertainties. It came out for him more than ever yet that she had had from the first a knowledge she believed him not to have had, a knowledge the sharp acquisition of which might be destined to make a difference for him. The difference for him might not inconceivably be an arrest of his independence and a change in his attitude – in other words a revulsion in favour of the principles of Woollett. She had really prefigured the possibility of a shock that would send him swinging back to Mrs. Newsome. He hadn't, it was true, week after week, shown

signs of receiving it, but the possibility had been none the less
in the air. What Maria accordingly had had now to take in was
that the shock had descended and that he hadn't, all the same,
swung back. He had grown clear, in a flash, on a point long
since settled for herself; but no reapproximation to Mrs. Newsome had occurred in consequence. Madame de Vionnet had
by her visit held up the torch to these truths, and what now
lingered in poor Maria's face was the somewhat smoky light of
the scene between them. If the light however wasn't, as we have
hinted, the glow of joy, the reasons for this also were perhaps
discernible to Strether even through the blur cast over them by
his natural modesty. She had held herself for months with a
firm hand; she hadn't interfered on any chance – and chances
were specious enough – that she might interfere to her profit.
She had turned her back on the dream that Mrs. Newsome's
rupture, their friend's forfeiture – the engagement, the relation
itself, broken beyond all mending – might furnish forth her
advantage; and, to stay her hand from promoting these things,
she had, on private, difficult, but rigid, lines, played strictly fair.
She couldn't therefore but feel that, though, as the end of all,
the facts in question had been stoutly confirmed, her ground
for personal, for what might have been called interested, elation
remained rather vague. Strether might easily have made out
that she had been asking herself, in the hours she had just sat
through, if there were still for her, or were only not, a fair shade
of uncertainty. Let us hasten to add, however, that what he at
first made out on this occasion he also at first kept to himself.
He only asked what in particular Madame de Vionnet had
come for; and as to this his companion was ready.

'She wants tidings of Mr. Newsome, whom she appears not
to have seen for some days.'

'Then she hasn't been away with him again?'

'She seemed to think,' Maria answered, 'that he might have
gone away with *you*.'

'And did you tell her I know nothing of him?'

She had her indulgent headshake. 'I've known nothing of
what you know. I could only tell her I'd ask you.'

'Then I've not seen him for a week – and of course I've

wondered.' His wonderment showed at this moment as sharper, but he presently went on. 'Still, I dare say I can put my hand on him. Did she strike you,' he asked, 'as anxious?'

'She's always anxious.'

'After all I've done for her?' And he had one of the last flickers of his occasional mild mirth. 'To think that was just what I came out to prevent!'

She took it up but to reply. 'You don't regard him then as safe?'

'I was just going to ask you how in that respect you regard Madame de Vionnet.'

She looked at him a little. 'What woman was *ever* safe? She told me,' she added – and it was as if at the touch of the connexion – 'of your extraordinary meeting in the country. After that *à quoi se fier?*'

'It was, as an accident, in all the possible or impossible chapter,' Strether conceded, 'amazing enough. But still, but still –!'

'But still she didn't mind?'

'She doesn't mind anything.'

'Well, then, as you don't either, we may all sink to rest!'

He appeared to agree with her, but he had his reservation. 'I do mind Chad's disappearance.'

'Oh you'll get him back. But now you know,' she said, 'why I went to Mentone.' He had sufficiently let her see that he had by this time gathered things together, but there was nature in her wish to make them clearer still. 'I didn't want you to put it to me.'

'To put it to you –?'

'The question of what you were at last – a week ago – to see for yourself. I didn't want to have to lie for her. I felt that to be too much for me. A man of course is always expected to do it – to do it, I mean, for a woman; but not a woman for another woman; unless perhaps on the tit-for-tat principle, as an indirect way of protecting herself. I don't need protection, so that I was free to "funk" you[4] – simply to dodge your test. The responsibility was too much for me. I gained time, and when I came back the need of a test had blown over.'

Strether thought of it serenely. 'Yes; when you came back little Bilham had shown me what's expected of a gentleman. Little Bilham had lied like one.'

'And like what you believed him?'

'Well,' said Strether, 'it was but a technical lie – he classed the attachment as virtuous. That was a view for which there was much to be said – and the virtue came out for me hugely. There was of course a great deal of it. I got it full in the face, and I haven't, you see, done with it yet.'

'What I see, what I saw,' Maria returned, 'is that you dressed up even the virtue. You were wonderful – you were beautiful, as I've had the honour of telling you before; but, if you wish really to know,' she sadly confessed, 'I never quite knew *where* you were. There were moments,' she explained, 'when you struck me as grandly cynical; there were others when you struck me as grandly vague.'

Her friend considered. 'I had phases. I had flights.'

'Yes, but things must have a basis.'

'A basis seemed to me just what her beauty supplied.'

'Her beauty of person?'

'Well, her beauty of everything. The impression she makes. She has such variety and yet such harmony.'

She considered him with one of her deep returns of indulgence – returns out of all proportion to the irritations they flooded over. 'You're complete.'

'You're always too personal,' he good-humouredly said; 'but that's precisely how I wondered and wandered.'

'If you mean,' she went on, 'that she was from the first for you the most charming woman in the world, nothing's more simple. Only that was an odd foundation.'

'For what I reared on it?'

'For what you didn't!'

'Well, it was all not a fixed quantity. And it had for me – it has still – such elements of strangeness. Her greater age than his, her different world, traditions, association; her other opportunities, liabilities, standards.'

His friend listened with respect to his enumeration of these disparities; then she disposed of them at a stroke. 'Those things

are nothing when a woman's hit. It's very awful. She was hit.'

Strether, on his side, did justice to that plea. 'Oh of course I saw she was hit. That she was hit was what we were busy with; that she was hit was our great affair. But somehow I couldn't think of her as down in the dust. And as put there by *our* little Chad!'

'Yet wasn't "your" little Chad just your miracle?'

Strether admitted it. 'Of course I moved among miracles. It was all phantasmagoric. But the great fact was that so much of it was none of my business – as I saw my business. It isn't even now.'

His companion turned away on this, and it might well have been yet again with the sharpness of a fear of how little his philosophy could bring her personally. 'I wish *she* could hear you!'

'Mrs. Newsome?'

'No – not Mrs. Newsome; since I understand you that it doesn't matter now what Mrs. Newsome hears. Hasn't she heard everything?'

'Practically – yes.' He had thought a moment, but he went on. 'You wish Madame de Vionnet could hear me?'

'Madame de Vionnet.' She had come back to him. 'She thinks just the contrary of what you say. That you distinctly judge her.'

He turned over the scene as the two women thus placed together for him seemed to give it. 'She might have known –!'

'Might have known you don't?' Miss Gostrey asked as he let it drop. 'She was sure of it at first,' she pursued as he said nothing; 'she took it for granted, at least, as any woman in her position would. But after that she changed her mind; she believed you believed –'

'Well?' – he was curious.

'Why in her sublimity. And that belief had remained with her, I make out, till the accident of the other day opened your eyes. For that it did,' said Maria, 'open them –'

'She can't help' – he had taken it up – 'being aware? No,' he mused; 'I suppose she thinks of that even yet.'

'Then they *were* closed? There you are! However, if you see

her as the most charming woman in the world it comes to the same thing. And if you'd like me to tell her that you do still so see her –!' Miss Gostrey, in short, offered herself for service to the end.

It was an offer he could temporarily entertain; but he decided. 'She knows perfectly how I see her.'

'Not favourably enough, she mentioned to me, to wish ever to see her again. She told me you had taken a final leave of her. She says you've done with her.'

'So I have.'

Maria had a pause; then she spoke as if for conscience. 'She wouldn't have done with *you*. She feels she has lost you – yet that she might have been better for you.'

'Oh she has been quite good enough!' Strether laughed.

'She thinks you and she might at any rate have been friends.'

'We might certainly. That's just' – he continued to laugh – 'why I'm going.'

It was as if Maria could feel with this then at last that she had done her best for each. But she had still an idea. 'Shall I tell her that?'

'No. Tell her nothing.'

'Very well then.' To which in the next breath Miss Gostrey added: 'Poor dear thing!'

Her friend wondered; then with raised eyebrows: 'Me?'

'Oh no. Marie de Vionnet.'

He accepted the correction, but he wondered still. 'Are you so sorry for her as that?'

It made her think a moment – made her even speak with a smile. But she didn't really retract. 'I'm sorry for us all!'

IV

He was to delay no longer to re-establish communication with Chad, and we have just seen that he had spoken to Miss Gostrey of this intention on hearing from her of the young man's absence. It was not moreover only the assurance so given that prompted him; it was the need of causing his conduct to square with another profession still – the motive he had described to her as his sharpest for now getting away. If he was to get away because of some of the relations involved in staying, the cold attitude toward them might look pedantic in the light of lingering on. He must do both things; he must see Chad, but he must go. The more he thought of the former of these duties the more he felt himself make a subject of insistence of the latter. They were alike intensely present to him as he sat in front of a quiet little café into which he had dropped on quitting Maria's entresol. The rain that had spoiled his evening with her was over; for it was still to him as if his evening *had* been spoiled – though it mightn't have been wholly the rain. It was late when he left the café, yet not too late; he couldn't in any case go straight to bed, and he would walk round by the Boulevard Malesherbes – rather far round – on his way home. Present enough always was the small circumstance that had originally pressed for him the spring of so big a difference – the accident of little Bilham's appearance on the balcony of the mystic troisième at the moment of his first visit, and the effect of it on his sense of what was then before him. He recalled his watch, his wait, and the recognition that had proceeded from the young stranger, that had played frankly into the air and had presently brought him up – things smoothing the way for his first straight

step. He had since had occasion, a few times, to pass the house without going in; but he had never passed it without again feeling how it had then spoken to him. He stopped short tonight on coming to sight of it: it was as if his last day were oddly copying his first. The windows of Chad's apartment were open to the balcony – a pair of them lighted; and a figure that had come out and taken up little Bilham's attitude, a figure whose cigarette-spark he could see leaned on the rail and looked down at him. It denoted however no reappearance of his younger friend; it quickly defined itself in the tempered darkness as Chad's more solid shape; so that Chad's was the attention that, after he had stepped forward into the street and signalled, he easily engaged; Chad's was the voice that, sounding into the night with promptness and seemingly with joy, greeted him and called him up.

That the young man had been visible there just in this position expressed somehow for Strether that, as Maria Gostrey had reported, he had been absent and silent; and our friend drew breath on each landing – the lift, at that hour, having ceased to work – before the implications of the fact. He had been for a week intensely away, away to a distance and alone; but he was more back than ever, and the attitude in which Strether had surprised him was something more than a return – it was clearly a conscious surrender. He had arrived but an hour before, from London, from Lucerne, from Homburg, from no matter where – though the visitor's fancy, on the staircase, liked to fill it out; and after a bath, a talk with Baptiste and a supper of light cold clever French things, which one could see the remains of there in the circle of the lamp, pretty and ultra-Parisian, he had come into the air again for a smoke, was occupied at the moment of Strether's approach in what might have been called taking up his life afresh. His life, his life! – Strether paused anew, on the last flight, at this final rather breathless sense of what Chad's life was doing with Chad's mother's emissary. It was dragging him, at strange hours, up the staircases of the rich; it was keeping him out of bed at the end of long hot days; it was trans-forming beyond recognition the simple, subtle, conveniently uni-form thing that had anciently passed with him for a life of his

own. Why should it concern him that Chad was to be fortified
in the pleasant practice of smoking on balconies, of supping
on salads, of feeling his special conditions agreeably reaffirm
themselves, of finding reassurance in comparisons and contrasts? There was no answer to such a question but that he was
still practically committed – he had perhaps never yet so much
known it. It made him feel old, and he would buy his railway-
ticket – feeling, no doubt, older – the next day; but he had
meanwhile come up four flights, counting the entresol, at midnight and without a lift, for Chad's life. The young man, hearing
him by this time, and with Baptiste sent to rest, was already at
the door; so that Strether had before him in full visibility the
cause in which he was labouring and even, with the troisième
fairly gained, panting a little.

Chad offered him, as always, a welcome in which the cordial
and the formal – so far as the formal was the respectful –
handsomely met; and after he had expressed a hope that he
would let him put him up for the night Strether was in full
possession of the key, as it might have been called, to what had
lately happened. If he had just thought of himself as old Chad
was at sight of him thinking of him as older: he wanted to put
him up for the night just because he was ancient and weary. It
could never be said the tenant of these quarters wasn't nice to
him; a tenant who, if he might indeed now keep him, was
probably prepared to work it all still more thoroughly. Our
friend had in fact the impression that with the minimum of
encouragement Chad would propose to keep him indefinitely;
an impression in the lap of which one of his own possibilities
seemed to sit. Madame de Vionnet had wished him to stay – so
why didn't that happily fit? He could enshrine himself for the
rest of his days in his young host's *chambre d'ami* and draw
out these days at his young host's expense: there could scarce
be greater logical expression of the countenance he had been
moved to give. There was literally a minute – it was strange
enough – during which he grasped the idea that as he *was*
acting, as he could only act, he was inconsistent. The sign that
the inward forces he had obeyed really hung together would be
that – in default always of another career – he should promote

the good cause by mounting guard on it. These things, during his first minutes, came and went; but they were after all practically disposed of as soon as he had mentioned his errand. He had come to say good-bye – yet that was only a part; so that from the moment Chad accepted his farewell the question of a more ideal affirmation gave way to something else. He proceeded with the rest of his business. 'You'll be a brute, you know – you'll be guilty of the last infamy – if you ever forsake her.'

That, uttered there at the solemn hour, uttered in the place that was full of her influence, was the rest of his business; and when once he had heard himself say it he felt that his message had never before been spoken. It placed his present call immediately on solid ground, and the effect of it was to enable him quite to play with what we have called the key. Chad showed no shade of embarrassment, but had none the less been troubled for him after their meeting in the country; had had fears and doubts on the subject of his comfort. He was disturbed, as it were, only *for* him, and had positively gone away to ease him off, to let him down – if it wasn't indeed rather to screw him up – the more gently. Seeing him now fairly jaded he had come with characteristic good humour, all the way to meet him, and what Strether thereupon supremely made out was that he would abound for him to the end in conscientious assurances. This was what was between them while the visitor remained; so far from having to go over old ground he found his entertainer keen to agree to everything. It couldn't be put too strongly for him that he'd be a brute. 'Oh rather! – if I should do anything of *that* sort. I hope you believe I really feel it.'

'I want it,' said Strether, 'to be my last word of all to you. I can't say more, you know; and I don't see how I can do more, in every way, than I've done.'

Chad took this, almost artlessly, as a direct allusion. 'You've seen her?'

'Oh yes – to say good-bye. And if I had doubted the truth of what I tell you –'

'She'd have cleared up your doubt?' Chad understood – 'rather' – again! It even kept him briefly silent. But he made that up. 'She must have been wonderful.'

'She *was*,' Strether candidly admitted – all of which practically told as a reference to the conditions created by the accident of the previous week.

They appeared for a little to be looking back at it; and that came out still more in what Chad next said. 'I don't know what you've really thought, all along; I never did know – for anything, with you, seemed to be possible. But of course – of course –' Without confusion, quite with nothing but indulgence, he broke down, he pulled up. 'After all, you understand. I spoke to you originally only as I *had* to speak. There's only one way – isn't there? – about such things. However,' he smiled with a final philosophy, 'I see it's all right.'

Strether met his eyes with a sense of multiplying thoughts. What was it that made him at present, late at night and after journeys, so renewedly, so substantially young? Strether saw in a moment what it was – it was that he was younger again than Madame de Vionnet. He himself said immediately none of the things that he was thinking; he said something quite different. 'You *have* really been to a distance?'

'I've been to England.' Chad spoke cheerfully and promptly, but gave no further account of it than to say: 'One must sometimes get off.'

Strether wanted no more facts – he only wanted to justify, as it were, his question. 'Of course you do as you're free to do. But I hope, this time, that you didn't go for *me*.'

'For very shame at bothering you really too much? My dear man,' Chad laughed, 'what *wouldn't* I do for you?'

Strether's easy answer for this was that it was a disposition he had exactly come to profit by. 'Even at the risk of being in your way I've waited on, you know, for a definite reason.'

Chad took it in. 'Oh yes – for us to make if possible a still better impression.' And he stood there happily exhaling his full general consciousness. 'I'm delighted to gather that you feel we've made it.'

There was a pleasant irony in the words, which his guest, preoccupied and keeping to the point, didn't take up. 'If I had my sense of wanting the rest of the time – the time of their being

still on this side,' he continued to explain – 'I know now why I wanted it.'

He was as grave, as distinct, as a demonstrator before a blackboard, and Chad continued to face him like an intelligent pupil. 'You wanted to have been put through the whole thing.'

Strether again, for a moment, said nothing; he turned his eyes away, and they lost themselves, through the open window, in the dusky outer air. 'I shall learn from the Bank here where they're now having their letters, and my last word, which I shall write in the morning and which they're expecting as my ultimatum, will so immediately reach them.' The light of his plural pronoun was sufficiently reflected in his companion's face as he again met it; and he completed his demonstration. He pursued indeed as if for himself. 'Of course I've first to justify what I shall do.'

'You're justifying it beautifully!' Chad declared.

'It's not a question of advising you not to go,' Strether said, 'but of absolutely preventing you, if possible, from so much as thinking of it. Let me accordingly appeal to you by all you hold sacred.'

Chad showed a surprise. 'What makes you think me capable – ?'

'You'd not only be, as I say, a brute; you'd be,' his companion went on in the same way, 'a criminal of the deepest dye.'

Chad gave a sharper look, as if to gauge a possible suspicion. 'I don't know what should make you think I'm tired of her.'

Strether didn't quite know either, and such impressions, for the imaginative mind, were always too fine, too floating, to produce on the spot their warrant. There was none the less for him, in the very manner of his host's allusion to satiety as a thinkable motive, a slight breath of the ominous. 'I feel how much more she can do for you. She hasn't done it all yet. Stay with her at least till she has.'

'And leave her *then*?'

Chad had kept smiling, but its effect in Strether was a shade of dryness. 'Don't leave her *before*. When you've got all that can be got – I don't say,' he added a trifle grimly. 'That will be

the proper time. But as, for you, from such a woman, there will always be something to be got, my remark's not a wrong to her.' Chad let him go on, showing every decent deference, showing perhaps also a candid curiosity for this sharper accent. 'I remember you, you know, as you were.'

'An awful ass, wasn't I?'

The response was as prompt as if he had pressed a spring; it had a ready abundance at which he even winced; so that he took a moment to meet it. 'You certainly then wouldn't have seemed worth all you've let me in for. You've defined yourself better. Your value has quintupled.'

'Well then, wouldn't that be enough –?'

Chad had risked it jocosely, but Strether remained blank. 'Enough?'

'If one *should* wish to live on one's accumulations?' After which, however, as his friend appeared cold to the joke, the young man as easily dropped it. 'Of course I really never forget, night or day, what I owe her. I owe her everything. I give you my word of honour,' he frankly rang out, 'that I'm not a bit tired of her.' Strether at this only gave him a stare: the way youth could express itself was again and again a wonder. He meant no harm, though he might after all be capable of much; yet he spoke of being 'tired' of her almost as he might have spoken of being tired of roast mutton for dinner. 'She has never for a moment yet bored me – never been wanting, as the cleverest women sometimes are, in tact. She has never talked about her tact – as even they too sometimes talk; but she has always had it. She has never had it more' – he handsomely made the point – 'than just lately.' And he scrupulously went further. 'She has never been anything I could call a burden.'

Strether for a moment said nothing; then he spoke gravely, with his shade of dryness deepened. 'Oh if you didn't do her justice –!'

'I *should* be a beast, eh?'

Strether devoted no time to saying what he would be; *that*, visibly, would take them far. If there was nothing for it but to repeat, however, repetition was no mistake. 'You owe her everything – very much more than she can ever owe you. You've

in other words duties to her, of the most positive sort; and I don't see what other duties – as the others are presented to you – can be held to go before them.'

Chad looked at him with a smile. 'And you know of course about the others, eh? – since it's you yourself who have done the presenting.'

'Much of it – yes – and to the best of my ability. But not all – from the moment your sister took my place.'

'She didn't,' Chad returned. 'Sally took a place, certainly; but it was never, I saw from the first moment, to be yours. No one – with us – will ever take yours. It wouldn't be possible.'

'Ah of course,' sighed Strether, 'I knew it. I believe you're right. No one in the world, I imagine, was ever so portentously solemn. There I am,' he added with another sigh, as if weary enough, on occasion, of this truth. 'I was made so.'

Chad appeared for a little to consider the way he was made; he might for this purpose have measured him up and down. His conclusion favoured the fact. '*You* have never needed any one to make you better. There has never been any one good enough. They couldn't,' the young man declared.

His friend hesitated. 'I beg your pardon. They *have*.'

Chad showed, not without amusement, his doubt. 'Who then?'

Strether – though a little dimly – smiled at him. 'Women – too.'

' "Two"?' – Chad stared and laughed. 'Oh I don't believe, for such work, in any more than one! So you're proving too much. And what *is* beastly, at all events,' he added, 'is losing you.'

Strether had set himself in motion for departure, but at this he paused. 'Are you afraid?'

'Afraid –?'

'Of doing wrong. I mean away from my eye.' Before Chad could speak, however, he had taken himself up. 'I *am*, certainly,' he laughed, 'prodigious.'

'Yes, you spoil us for all the stupid –!' This might have been, on Chad's part, in its extreme emphasis, almost too freely extravagant; but it was full, plainly enough, of the intention of comfort, it carried with it a protest against doubt and a promise,

positively, of performance. Picking up a hat in the vestibule
he came out with his friend, came downstairs, took his arm,
affectionately, as to help and guide him, treating him if not
exactly as aged and infirm, yet as a noble eccentric who appealed
to tenderness, and keeping on with him, while they walked, to
the next corner and the next. 'You needn't tell me, you needn't
tell me!' – this again as they proceeded, he wished to make
Strether feel. What he needn't tell him was now at last, in the
geniality of separation, anything at all it concerned him to
know. He knew, up to the hilt – that really came over Chad;
he understood, felt, recorded his vow; and they lingered on it
as they had lingered in their walk to Strether's hotel the night
of their first meeting. The latter took, at this hour, all he could
get; he had given all he had had to give; he was as depleted as
if he had spent his last sou. But there was just one thing for
which, before they broke off, Chad seemed disposed slightly to
bargain. His companion needn't, as he said, tell him, but he
might himself mention that he had been getting some news of
the art of advertisement. He came out quite suddenly with this
announcement, while Strether wondered if his revived interest
were what had taken him, with strange inconsequence, over to
London. He appeared at all events to have been looking into
the question and had encountered a revelation. Advertising
scientifically worked presented itself thus as the great new force.
'It really does the thing, you know.'

They were face to face under the street-lamp as they had been
the first night, and Strether, no doubt, looked blank. 'Affects,
you mean, the sale of the object advertised?'

'Yes – but affects it extraordinarily; really beyond what one
had supposed. I mean of course when it's done as one makes
out that, in our roaring age, it *can* be done. I've been finding
out a little; though it doubtless doesn't amount to much more
than what you originally, so awfully vividly – and all, very
nearly, that first night – put before me. It's an art like another,
and infinite like all the arts.' He went on as if for the joke of it
– almost as if his friend's face amused him. 'In the hands,
naturally, of a master. The right man must take hold. With the
right man to work it *c'est un monde*.'

Strether had watched him quite as if, there on the pavement, without a pretext, he had begun to dance a fancy step. 'Is what you're thinking of that you yourself, in the case you have in mind, would be the right man?'

Chad had thrown back his light coat and thrust each of his thumbs into an armhole of his waistcoat; in which position his fingers played up and down. 'Why, what is he but what you yourself, as I say, took me for when you first came out?'

Strether felt a little faint, but he coerced his attention. 'Oh yes, and there's no doubt that, with your natural parts, you'd have much in common with him. Advertising is clearly at this time of day the secret of trade. It's quite possible it will be open to you – giving the whole of your mind to it – to make the whole place hum with you. Your mother's appeal is to the whole of your mind, and that's exactly the strength of her case.'

Chad's fingers continued to twiddle, but he had something of a drop. 'Ah we've been through my mother's case!'

'So I thought. Why then do you speak of the matter?'

'Only because it was part of our original discussion. To wind up where we began, my interest's purely platonic. There at any rate the fact is – the fact of the possible. I mean the money in it.'

'Oh damn the money in it!' said Strether. And then as the young man's fixed smile seemed to shine out more strange: 'Shall you give your friend up for the money in it?'

Chad preserved his handsome grimace as well as the rest of his attitude. 'You're not altogether – in your so great "solemnity" – kind. Haven't I been drinking you in – showing you all I feel you're worth to me? What have I done, what am I doing, but cleave to her to the death? The only thing is,' he good-humouredly explained, 'that one can't but have it before one, in the cleaving – the point where the death comes in. Don't be afraid for *that*. It's pleasant to a fellow's feelings,' he developed, 'to "size-up" the bribe he applies his foot to.'

'Oh then if all you want's a kickable surface the bribe's enormous.'

'Good. Then there it goes!' Chad administered his kick with fantastic force and sent an imaginary object flying. It was accordingly as if they were once more rid of the question and could

come back to what really concerned him. 'Of course I shall see you tomorrow.'

But Strether scarce heeded the plan proposed for this; he had still the impression – not the slighter for the simulated kick – of an irrelevant hornpipe or jig. 'You're restless.'

'Ah,' returned Chad as they parted, 'you're exciting.'

V

He had, however, within two days, another separation to face. He had sent Maria Gostrey a word early, by hand, to ask if he might come to breakfast; in consequence of which, at noon, she awaited him in the cool shade of her little Dutch-looking dining-room. This retreat was at the back of the house, with a view of a scrap of old garden that had been saved from modern ravage; and though he had on more than one other occasion had his legs under its small and peculiarly polished table of hospitality, the place had never before struck him as so sacred to pleasant knowledge, to intimate charm, to antique order, to a neatness that was almost august. To sit there was, as he had told his hostess before, to see life reflected for the time in ideally kept pewter; which was somehow becoming, improving to life, so that one's eyes were held and comforted. Strether's were comforted at all events now – and the more that it was the last time – with the charming effect, on the board bare of a cloth and proud of its perfect surface, of the small old crockery and old silver, matched by the more substantial pieces happily disposed about the room. The specimens of vivid Delf,[1] in particular, had the dignity of family portraits; and it was in the midst of them that our friend resignedly expressed himself. He spoke even with a certain philosophic humour. 'There's nothing more to wait for; I seem to have done a good day's work. I've let them have it all round. I've seen Chad, who has been to London and come back. He tells me I'm "exciting", and I seem indeed pretty well to have upset every one. I've at any rate excited *him*. He's distinctly restless.'

'You've excited *me*,' Miss Gostrey smiled. '*I'm* distinctly restless.'

'Oh you were that when I found you. It seems to me I've rather got you out of it. What's this,' he asked as he looked about him, 'but a haunt of ancient peace?'

'I wish with all my heart,' she presently replied, 'I could make you treat it as a haven of rest.' On which they fronted each other, across the table, as if things unuttered were in the air.

Strether seemed, in his way, when he next spoke, to take some of them up. 'It wouldn't give me – that would be the trouble – what it will, no doubt, still give you. I'm not,' he explained, leaning back in his chair, but with his eyes on a small ripe round melon – 'in real harmony with what surrounds me. You *are*. I take it too hard. You *don't*. It makes – that's what it comes to in the end – a fool of me.' Then at a tangent, 'What has he been doing in London?' he demanded.

'Ah one may go to London,' Maria laughed. 'You know *I* did.'

Yes – he took the reminder. 'And you brought *me* back.' He brooded there opposite to her, but without gloom. 'Whom has Chad brought? He's full of ideas. And I wrote to Sarah,' he added, 'the first thing this morning. So I'm square. I'm ready for them.'

She neglected certain parts of this speech in the interest of others. 'Marie said to me the other day that she felt him to have the makings of an immense man of business.'

'There it is. He's the son of his father!'

'But *such* a father!'

'Ah just the right one from that point of view! But it isn't his father in him,' Strether added, 'that troubles me.'

'What is it then?' He came back to his breakfast; he partook presently of the charming melon, which she liberally cut for him; and it was only after this that he met her question. Then moreover it was but to remark that he'd answer her presently. She waited, she watched, she served him and amused him, and it was perhaps with this last idea that she soon reminded him of his having never even yet named to her the article produced at Woollett. 'Do you remember our talking of it in London –

that night at the play?' Before he could say yes, however, she
had put it to him for other matters. Did he remember, did he
remember – this and that of their first days? He remembered
everything, bringing up with humour even things of which she
professed no recollection, things she vehemently denied; and
falling back above all on the great interest of their early time,
the curiosity felt by both of them as to where he would 'come
out'. They had so assumed it was to be in some wonderful place
– they had thought of it as so very *much* out. Well, that was
doubtless what it had been – since he had come out just there.
He was out, in truth, as far as it was possible to be, and must
now rather bethink himself of getting in again. He found on
the spot the image of his recent history; he was like one of the
figures of the old clock at Berne.[2] *They* came out, on one side,
at their hour, jigged along their little course in the public eye,
and went in on the other side. He too had jigged his little course
– him too a modest retreat awaited. He offered now, should
she really like to know, to name the great product of Woollett.
It would be a great commentary on everything. At this she
stopped him off; she not only had no wish to know, but she
wouldn't know for the world. She had done with the products
of Woollett – for all the good she had got from them. She desired
no further news of them, and she mentioned that Madame de
Vionnet herself had, to her knowledge, lived exempt from the
information he was ready to supply. She had never consented
to receive it, though she would have taken it, under stress, from
Mrs. Pocock. But it was a matter about which Mrs. Pocock
appeared to have had little to say – never sounding the word –
and it didn't signify now. There was nothing clearly for Maria
Gostrey that signified now – save one sharp point, that is, to
which she came in time. 'I don't know whether it's before you
as a possibility that, left to himself, Mr. Chad may after all go
back. I judge that it *is* more or less so before you, from what
you just now said of him.'

Her guest had his eyes on her, kindly but attentively, as if
foreseeing what was to follow this. 'I don't think it will be for
the money.' And then as she seemed uncertain: 'I mean I don't
believe it will be for that he'll give her up.'

'Then he *will* give her up?'

Strether waited a moment, rather slow and deliberate now, drawing out a little this last soft stage, pleading with her in various suggestive and unspoken ways for patience and understanding. 'What were you just about to ask me?'

'Is there anything he can do that would make you patch it up?'

'With Mrs. Newsome?'

Her assent, as if she had had a delicacy about sounding the name, was only in her face; but she added with it: 'Or is there anything he can do that would make *her* try it?'

'To patch it up with me?' His answer came at last in a conclusive headshake. 'There's nothing anyone can do. It's over. Over for both of us.'

Maria wondered, seemed a little to doubt. 'Are you so sure for her?'

'Oh yes – sure now. Too much has happened. I'm different for her.'

She took it in then, drawing a deeper breath. 'I see. So that as she's different for *you* –'

'Ah but,' he interrupted, 'she's not.' And as Miss Gostrey wondered again: 'She's the same.[3] She's more than ever the same. But I do what I didn't before – I *see* her.'

He spoke gravely and as if responsibly – since he had to pronounce; and the effect of it was slightly solemn, so that she simply exclaimed 'Oh!' Satisfied and grateful, however, she showed in her own next words an acceptance of his statement. 'What then do you go home to?'

He had pushed his plate a little away, occupied with another side of the matter; taking refuge verily in that side and feeling so moved that he soon found himself on his feet. He was affected in advance by what he believed might come from her, and he would have liked to forestall it and deal with it tenderly; yet in the presence of it he wished still more to be – though as smoothly as possible – deterrent and conclusive. He put her question by for the moment; he told her more about Chad. 'It would have been impossible to meet me more than he did last night on the question of the infamy of not sticking to her.'

'Is that what you called it for him – "infamy"?'

'Oh rather! I described to him in detail the base creature he'd be, and he quite agrees with me about it.'

'So that it's really as if you had nailed him?'

'Quite really as if –! I told him I should curse him.'

'Oh,' she smiled, 'you *have* done it.' And then having thought again: 'You *can't* after that propose –!' Yet she scanned his face.

'Propose again to Mrs. Newsome?'

She hesitated afresh, but she brought it out. 'I've never believed, you know, that you did propose. I always believed it was really she – and, so far as that goes, I can understand it. What I mean is,' she explained, 'that with such a spirit – the spirit of curses! – your breach is past mending. She has only to know what you've done to him never again to raise a finger.'

'I've done,' said Strether, 'what I could – one can't do more. He protests his devotion and his horror. But I'm not sure I've saved him. He protests too much. He asks how one can dream of his being tired. But he has all life before him.'

Maria saw what he meant. 'He's formed to please.'

'And it's our friend who has formed him.' Strether felt in it the strange irony.

'So it's scarcely his fault!'

'It's at any rate his danger. I mean,' said Strether, 'it's hers. But she knows it.'

'Yes, she knows it. And is your idea,' Miss Gostrey asked, 'that there was some other woman in London?'

'Yes. No. That is I *have* no ideas. I'm afraid of them. I've done with them.' And he put out his hand to her. 'Good-bye.'

It brought her back to her unanswered question. 'To what do you go home?'

'I don't know. There will always be something.'

'To a great difference,' she said as she kept his hand.

'A great difference – no doubt. Yet I shall see what I can make of it.'

'Shall you make anything so good –?' But, as if remembering what Mrs. Newsome had done, it was as far as she went.

He had sufficiently understood. 'So good as this place at this

moment? So good as what *you* make of everything you touch?'
He took a moment to say, for, really and truly, what stood
about him there in her offer – which was as the offer of exquisite
service, of lightened care, for the rest of his days – might well
have tempted. It built him softly round, it roofed him warmly
over, it rested, all so firm, on selection. And what ruled selection
was beauty and knowledge. It was awkward, it was almost
stupid, not to seem to prize such things; yet, none the less, so
far as they made his opportunity they made it only for a
moment. She'd moreover understand – she always understood.

That indeed might be, but meanwhile she was going on.
'There's nothing, you know, I wouldn't do for you.'

'Oh yes – I know.'

'There's nothing,' she repeated, 'in all the world.'

'I know. I know. But all the same I must go.' He had got it
at last. 'To be right.'

'To be right?'

She had echoed it in vague deprecation, but he felt it already
clear for her. 'That, you see, is my only logic. Not, out of the
whole affair, to have got anything for myself.'

She thought. 'But with your wonderful impressions you'll
have got a great deal.'

'A great deal' – he agreed. 'But nothing like *you*. It's you who
would make me wrong!'

Honest and fine, she couldn't greatly pretend she didn't see
it. Still she could pretend just a little. 'But why should you be
so dreadfully right?'

'That's the way that – if I must go – you yourself would be
the first to want me. And I can't do anything else.'

So then she had to take it, though still with her defeated
protest. 'It isn't so much your *being* "right" – it's your horrible
sharp eye for what makes you so.'

'Oh but you're just as bad yourself. You can't resist me when
I point that out.'

She sighed it at last all comically, all tragically, away. 'I can't
indeed resist you.'

'Then there we are!' said Strether.

Selected Variant Readings

Entries on the left are from this edition, based on the text of the New York Edition (NYE); on the right are variants from the serial version in the *North American Review* (S), from the first American edition by Harper (A) and the first English edition by Methuen (E). See A Note on the Text, pp. xl–xli).

Page/line

22: 38	but on happy terms with each other	but expressive and agreeable S A E
23: 34–5	She appeared to have no reserves	She was frank S A E
24: 15	under this unsought protection	with his new friend S A E
26: 3	intenser	more subtle S A E
37: 21	during years	for some five years S A E
50: 6	hideous	ignoble E
61: 11	American	bad S A E
61: 13–17	but she would consent . . . She's at any rate delicate	But she's delicate S A E
61: 27	she forged ahead	she reappeared further on S A she took the subject up further on E
71: 30	grasp of the real	grasp of the truth S E
73: 4	groaned	murmured S A E
77: 32	plentitude	enormity S A E
83: 5	This suggested the question of whether	With his letters in his lap then, in his Luxembourg nook – letters held with nervous, unconscious intensity – he thought of things in a strange, vast order,

swinging at moments off into
space, into past and future,
and then dropping fast, with
some loss of breath, but with
a soft, reassuring thud, down
to yesterday and today. Thus
it was that he came back to
his puzzle of the evening, the
question of whether E

86: 14	irresistibly sharp: he	overwhelmingly intense; the wretched youth E
86: 17	somewhere of a	somewhere in Théophile Gautier of a E
86: 20	three	three – through numbers indeed as to which it might be a question whether those of mere modest clock-faces wouldn't be exceeded E
86, 25–6	migration, the expensive	migration, the journey retraced, that is, in the sense of demoralisation, the expensive E
86, 27–8	French for some special variety of the worst	French for something that might in a manner be a part of that ambiguous ideal, but was certainly not the part permitting publicity, either of appreciation or of discussion, in respect to varieties of quality. All Mrs. Newsome had now for a long time known of her son was that he had renewed his career in the expensive district – it was so, she felt, that she sufficiently designated it – and that he had not so established himself without intimate countenance. He had travelled, in the dreadful direction, almost like a Pasha – save that his palanquins had

		been by no means curtained and their occupants far from veiled; he had, in short, had company – scandalous, notorious company – across the bridges, company making with him, in the cynical journey, from stage to stage and from period to period, bolder pushes and taking larger freedoms: traces, echoes. almost legends, all these things, left in the wake of the pair E
130: 26	feet	feet. He knew he showed he was glad to bring his effort to an end E
139: 24	her discrimination	*her* fearless sense S E
140: 16	uncanny	abnormal S E
145: 27	sadly	awkwardly S A deplorably E
159: 19–20	in profusely dispensing	in the offered bribe S E in the offer A
159: 21	flowers	sensations S E
159: 23	ascetic	inbred S E
174: 18	importantly short	not very tall S A E
182: 8–9	in the immensity of space	quite in the air S E
209: 9	*notre jeune homme*	our young friend S E
212: 20	interest	romance S A E
217: 23	their fellow guest	the spinster S their friend E
218: 35–6	to represent her motive and real errand	to have been, for her, her real errand S A E
235: 30	domain	property S A E
245: 10–11	with a force brought to so fine a head	with a spirit brought to so fine a point S A with a spirit whose lightest throbs were so full E
254: 19	elucidation	interpretation S E
257: 15	divine	exquisite E
276: 26–7	present to a sort of thing, as he synthetically phrased it to himself	present to a force A E

278: 20	bamboozled	beguiled E
278: 36–7	decent . . . decent!	nice . . . nice! E
281: 17	girdle of a maid	waist of a girl E
281: 19	mercifully vague	restfully dim E
281: 21–2	unpleasant . . . unpleasant	disagreeable . . . disagreeable S A E
283: 16	robust	erect E
285: 3–4	the way not to fail of confidence . . . confidence	the way to be sharp . . . sharpness S A E
302: 34	the damned	your stale E
303: 5	bleak	narrow S A E
305: 18–19	*I* at least won't take that from you.	[only in NYE]
311: 18	lacked news	lacked the direct and intimate news to which he would have been so conspicuously entitled E
314: 20–1	awful . . . "Awful"	very advanced . . . 'Advanced' E
314: 27	droll	funny S A
320: 15	stupid	not, like almost everyone, stupid E
321: 36	she's pleased *comme tout*	she's as pleased as Punch S A E
324: 16	forms and usages	manners S AE
325: 19–20	but may we never be less so!	but long may we wave! S but may we never fill up! A but long may we play our parts! E
325: 37	Getting hold of him?	Winning him over and making him her own? E
327: 21	affected	demoralised E
327: 24	Maria rather funnily considered it	Maria considered it in the light of comedy E
330: 19	awful	fearsome E
337: 11	all the Mr. Brookses and Mr. Snookses	all the Mr. Coxes and Mr. Coleses E
339: 5–8	She came out with . . . she came out with . . . she brought it out	She aired for him . . . she threw off . . . she produced it E
339: 29	monster	miracle E

347: 5	the knowledge offered to his colleague	the knowledge, the *panem et circenses* again, offered to his fellow-emissary E
362: 24	destiny	outlook S A E
364: 36–7	approach, from that quarter, to admitted consciousness	approach to a meaning S A E
365: 25	genial	bright S E
368: 20–3	Distinctly she was at the highest . . . , an overstrained accompanist	Distinctly, she was exalted now, and Waymarsh, who imagined himself standing there on his own feet, was truly but suspended in an air of her making S A E
368: 32	the false note	the small manner S A the same manner E
375: 15–17	queer . . . queer . . . queerer	funny . . . funny . . . funnier S E
378: 12	have nullified any active proximity	have paralyzed any active approach S have placed a penalty on any active approach E
404: 16–17	it's to Mrs. Newsome	it's to the forfeiture of possession of Mrs. Newsome E
404: 22–3	I've been as disappointed in her	I've been as disconcerted, as disappointed, as disillusioned by her E
404: 34	violently	indignantly E
408: 2	the dreadful creature	the dreadful insidious parasite E
410: 26	as the picture he *would* have bought	as the material acquisiton that, in all his time, he had most sharply failed of E
411: 24	superseded Boston fashion	faded Boston enthusiasm E
414: 26–7	nothing more than Shakespeare and the musical glasses; but it	nothing more than such questions as the difference between Victor Hugo and the English poets; Victor Hugo, for whom one could have but a plural comparison, and the English poets, whom his

		friend quite surprisingly, rather quaintly and archaically, knew. Yet it E
420: 12	wild extravagance of hazard	wild fable than as anything else E
420: 30–1	from making any. Nothing of the sort	from so blundering. Nothing either like a challenge or like an apology E
431: 25	penal	disciplinary S A E
434: 19	Caprices	Inequalities E
435: 34	droll	funny S A ridiculous E
445: 2–3	that reprobation hadn't rewarded Madame de Vionnet's request for an interview	that violence had not awaited the presentation of Mme. de Vionnet's plea S E
445: 5	overture	demonstration S E
447: 31	These tints of feeling	These shades S E
449: 4	He had grown clear, in a flash, on	He had shut to, with a click, on E
449: 19	difficult, but, rigid lines	passionate lines S E
451: 25	complete	magnificent S E
451: 26	You're always too personal	You're too much struck with everything E
451: 26–7	but that's precisely how I wondered and wandered	but that is then where I was S E
452: 37	I suppose she thinks of that even yet	I can see that she must have liked better the other idea E
452: 38	Then they *were* closed?	Then you *had* the other idea. E
456: 30	enshrine	instal E
456: 37	the inward forces	the inspiration E
459: 28	the imaginative mind	the sensitive spirit E
461: 37– 462: 1	but it was full, plainly enough, of the intention of comfort, it carried with it a protest against doubt and a promise, positively, of performance. Picking	The intention of kindness was, at any rate all there; Chad continued to show it as a protest and a promise, and, picking E
465: 1	separation to face	report to make E
466: 252	Marie	She S A certain person E

| 469: 1 | 'Is that | Well, he could hold poor Maria with this too. 'Is that E |
| 470: 28 | 'That's the | He considered, but he kept it straight. 'That's the E |

Glossary of French Words and Expressions

à quoi se fier?	what can be trusted?
agrément	pleasure
allez donc voir	go and see then
auberge	inn
banlieue	suburb
bateau-mouche	pleasure boat (on the Seine)
bêtise	stupidity
bien aimable	very likeable
bock	glass of beer
boiseries	wood panelling
bon	good
c'est un monde	it's a whole world
carriole	light cart
ces dames	those ladies
ces gens-là	those people
chambre d'ami	spare room
cher confrère	dear colleague
comme cela se trouve	look how it's worked out
comme tout	like anything, awfully
comment donc?	what's that?
Comtesse	Countess
concierge	door-keeper
consommation	drink (at a bar or café)
corps de logis	main part of a building
côtelette de veau à l'oseille	veal cutlet in sorrel sauce
déjeuner	breakfast or lunch
difficile	difficult (to please)
en dessous	underneath
en exil	in exile
en province	in the country
entresol	mezzanine

fait accompli	accomplished fact
femmes du monde	fashionable society women
ficelles	tricks or devices (literally 'strings')
galère	galley
gros bonnets	bigwigs, important people
hôtels	grand townhouses
il faut en avoir	you must have some
impayable	priceless
invraisemblance	unlikelihood
je suis tranquille	I am not worried
jeune fille	young girl
là-bas	over there
lingère	sewing woman
ma toute-belle	my great beauty
merci	thank you
milieu	surroundings
notre jeune homme	our young man
nous autres	we others
omelette aux tomates	tomato omelette
ouvreuse	usherette
parti	match (as in *c'est un bon parti*; she's a good match)
parti pris	preconceived view
patronne	(female) owner
petit bleu	an express letter
petit salon	small drawing room
porte-cochère	carriage entrance
quoi donc?	what then?
raffinée	refined (female)
sabots	clogs
salle-à-manger	dining room
salon de lecture	reading room
succès fou	wild success
tout bêtement	very stupidly
troisième (étage)	third (floor)
vieille sagesse	ancient wisdom
voilà	there you are
vous allez voir	you will see
voyons	let's see

Notes

For details of other writings by Henry James and of critical works referred to in the Notes, see List of Abbreviations (p. vi) and Further Reading (pp. xxxvi–xxxix). References to Shakespeare are to *The Arden Shakespeare: Complete Works*, ed. Richard Proudfoot, Ann Thompson and David Scott Kastan (Walton-on-Thames: Thomson, 1998). I am indebted to previous editions of *The Ambassadors*, especially to the revised and expanded Norton Critical Edition, ed. S. P. Rosenbaum (New York: W. W. Norton, 1994), and to the Unwin Critical Library edition, ed. Alan W. Bellringer (London: Allen & Unwin, 1984) for the identification of places mentioned in the novel. Readers should consult the Glossary for the meaning of French words and expressions.

PREFACE

1. *its germ*: See Introduction, p. xxiv.
2. *what is he doing ... in that galère?*: What has he let himself in for?
3. *more things than had been dreamt of in the philosophy of Woollett*: Refers to *Hamlet* by William Shakespeare: 'There are more things in heaven and earth, Horatio, / Than are dreamt of in your philosophy' (*Hamlet*, I.v.174–5).
4. *'Gil Blas' ... 'David Copperfield'*: In the novels *Gil Blas* (1715–35) by René Lesage (1668–1747) and *David Copperfield* (1849–50) by Charles Dickens (1812–70), the title-characters narrate their own life-stories.

BOOK FIRST

I

1. *Chester rather than at Liverpool*: Chester is about fifteen miles south of Liverpool, the main port for transatlantic travellers in northwest England. In 1872 James wrote that 'the American traveller arriving at this venerable town finds himself transported, without a sensible gradation, from the edge of the New World to the very heart of the Old' (*EH*, p. 35). Bellringer (p. 97) notes that Strether's hotel is probably the Queen Hotel, near the railway station, where James had himself stayed in 1872.

2. *nippers*: Pince-nez, eye-glasses clipped to the nose.

3. *a novel of Balzac's*: The title-character of *Louis Lambert* (1832–3) by Honoré de Balzac (1799–1850) is a would-be philosopher troubled by the disjunction of spirit and flesh. Inspired by the Swedish philosopher Emanuel Swedenborg (1688–1772), he tries to write a treatise on the will, but falls in love with an heiress. On the eve of the wedding he suffers a cataleptic fit and goes mad. James agreed with his characters that 'the novel's an awfully bad one'. In 1877 he declared that 'as a whole, [it] is now quite unreadable; it contains some admirable descriptions, but the "scientific" portion is mere fantastic verbiage' (*LC*, p. 76). Hazel Hutchison proposes a further perspective on the connotations of Strether's name ('The Other Lambert Strether'). She points to the Alsatian philosopher Johann Heinrich Lambert (1728–77), now little known but eminent in his time, who was a significant figure in the development of phenomenology, a philosophical movement with which James's writings have been thought actively to converse (see Paul B. Armstrong, Collin Meissner, Julie Rivkin and Merle A. Williams). Hutchison concludes: 'These two Lamberts, one idealist [Balzac's] and one phenomenologist, spark a dialectical tension between the two theories of reality that they represent. And this tension mirrors the dilemma facing Strether within the novel: whether to escape into the mind or to embrace the world of experience' (p. 234).

4. *The tortuous wall*: James much admired Chester's ancient city wall. A wonderful vantage-point, it enabled its citizens to 'know their city more intimately than their unbuckled neighbours', so he fantasized. 'The civic consciousness, sunning itself thus on the city's rim and glancing at the little swarming towered and gabled

town within, and then at the blue undulations of the near Welsh border, may easily deepen to delicious complacency' (*EH*, p. 36).

5. *crocketed*: Decorated with crockets, small carved ornaments (buds, leaves, animals) on the sides of Gothic pinnacles or gables.

III

1. *Major Pendennis breakfasting at his club*: *Pendennis* (1848–50) by William Makepeace Thackeray (1811–63) begins with the title-character's uncle Major Pendennis at his usual breakfast. There is a parallel with Strether's situation: the Major opens a letter from his sister-in-law asking him to come and 'save' his nephew from marrying an actress some twelve years his senior.

2. *at the Megatherium*: It is in Thackeray's *The Newcomes* (1853–5), which is related by Pendennis, that we are told of the Major's club, the Megatherium.

3. *the Rows*: The famous streets of Chester with shops on two levels. James wrote: 'Next after its wall – possibly even before it – Chester values its Rows, an architectural idiosyncrasy which must be seen to be appreciated. They are a sort of Gothic edition of the blessed arcades and porticoes of Italy, and consist, roughly speaking, of a running public passage tunnelled through the second story of the houses' (*EH*, p. 38).

4. *the visitors from London*: Refers to an incident in *The Vicar of Wakefield* (1766) by Oliver Goldsmith (1730–74). Two London prostitutes pretending to be ladies of fashion hoodwink the family of the Vicar, Dr Primrose, but fail to deceive Mr Burchell who is also in disguise. Shortly before starting *The Ambassadors* James had written an introduction to an edition of Goldsmith's novel for Century Classics (New York, 1900), in the course of which he admires this episode. Dr Primrose's pursuit of his prodigal daughter Olivia and attempt to save her from debauchery provides a rough analogue with Strether's situation (see Walker, *Reading Henry James*, p. 58). See also Book Eleventh, III and note 4.

5. *the Burlington Arcade*: A fashionable London shopping arcade.

BOOK SECOND

I

1. *Queen Elizabeth*: Queen Elizabeth I of England (1533–1603). In the next paragraph, Strether compares Miss Gostrey to Elizabeth's cousin and rival, Mary Stuart, Queen of Scots (1542–87), Catholic claimant to the throne of England and the focus of consequent conspiracy, who was executed on the orders of Elizabeth in 1587.

2. *the Museum*: The Boston Museum of Fine Arts, founded in 1870.

3. *jamming down the pedal*: Presumably the soft pedal on the piano, picking up the 'high-strung'.

4. *Saleratus*: Compound used as an ingredient in baking powders; its name is derived from the Latin *sal aeratus*, 'aerated salt'.

5. *you don't even "burn"*: You're not even getting warm.

6. *the very secret of the prison-house*: The Ghost tells Hamlet: 'But that I am forbid / To tell the secrets of my prison-house, / I could a tale unfold whose lightest word / Would harrow up thy soul' (*Hamlet*, I.v.13–16).

7. *the very deuce*: A colloquial expression possibly derived from a gambler's unlucky throw of a two (deuce) at dice, in which 'the deuce' is used as a synonym for and interchangeably with 'the devil'.

8. *four-wheeler*: Hired carriage.

II

1. *the bankers of the Rue Scribe*: Probably Munroe & Co., rue Scribe 7 (Fussell, *French Side*, p. 186). Rue Scribe marks the northern boundary of what James described in 1875 as 'the classic region' for American tourists, on the right bank of the Seine just off the Place de l'Opéra (*PS*, p. 6).

2. *the Gymnase to the Café Riche*: The Théâtre du Gymnase, Boulevard Bonne-Nouvelle 38, best known for comedies. The Café Riche was an expensive restaurant nearby at Boulevard des Italiens 16. It was also known as Bignon's, and Waymarsh and Sarah Pocock will dine there later (Book Ninth, II).

3. *budget*: Bundle of letters, news (literally, the contents of a wallet, or budget).

4. *the Rue de la Paix*: Runs from the Place de l'Opéra towards the garden of the Tuileries next to the Louvre.

5. *The palace was gone*: The palace of the Tuileries was burned down in the suppression of the Paris Commune, 22–23 May 1871, amid scenes described in *La Débâcle* (1892), the penultimate volume of the Rougon-Macquart novels of Émile Zola (1840–1902), which James admired in an essay published the same year as *The Ambassadors* (*LC*, II, pp. 871–99).

6. *the Rue de Seine . . . Luxembourg Gardens*: The rue de la Seine runs south from the Left Bank of the river to the Luxembourg Gardens surrounding the seventeenth-century Palais du Luxembourg. James recalls that as a youngster walking in Paris with his brother William they 'hugged' this particular walk 'as if it somehow held the secret of our future'. Of the Luxembourg Gardens he says that they 'formed the right, the sober social antithesis to the "elegant" Tuileries' (*Autobiography*, pp. 190–92).

7. *the War*: The American Civil War, 1861–5. This means that if Strether was twenty-five when he married in 1865 or shortly thereafter, and he is now fifty-five, the novel must be set shortly after 1895. James's characters are unaware of the Métro, work on which began in 1898 and which was operating by 1900.

8. *lemon-coloured volumes*: The usual colour of French paperback novels.

9. *the Latin Quarter . . . Malesherbes*: A colourful district on the Left Bank, the Latin Quarter was particularly frequented by artists and students, hence vaguely disreputable by Victorian standards. The Boulevard Malesherbes was a fashionable modern boulevard on the Right Bank.

10. *Melancholy Mürger . . . Rodolphe*: Born in Paris of a German father, Henry Murger (1822–61) is best remembered for his *Scènes de la vie de Bohème* (*Scenes of Bohemian Life*, 1848), set in the Latin Quarter. Francine, Musette and Rodolphe are characters in these stories, which popularized the idea of 'Bohemia' as the domain of starving but sexually liberated artists and students. Puccini's opera *La Bohème* is based on a play derived from Murger's work. First performed in 1896, it belongs exactly to the time in which *The Ambassadors* is set.

11. *Montagne Sainte-Geneviève*: On this little hill in the Latin Quarter can be found the remains of the abbey where St Geneviève, the patron saint of Paris, is buried.

12. *Strether had read somewhere . . . killed*: The first English edition identifies the source as Théophile Gautier (1811–72), Parisian

poet and novelist. The Latin motto appears in Gautier's *Voyage en Espagne* (*Travels in Spain*, 1845), which James in 1873 thought 'a masterpiece and model' (*LC*, II, p. 364). The Latin means 'All wound, the last kills'; the English edition multiplies the number of Bohemian liaisons Chad is supposed to have enjoyed well beyond the 'three' specified in the American versions (see Selected Variant Readings).

13. *the Odéon*: Theatre ranked next to the Théâtre Français (see Book Third, II, note 4), chiefly devoted to French classical drama.

BOOK THIRD

I

1. *hotel*: Bellringer (p. 97) suggests that Strether's modest hotel might have been the Hôtel Chatham in rue Daunou or Hôtel de Calais in rue des Capucines.

2. *Cannes*: Then as now a fashionable resort on the Mediterranean.

3. *Léoville*: Red Bordeaux wine.

4. *shining hours*: Rosenbaum notes the echo with the lines from 'Against Idleness and Mischief' by Isaac Watts (1674–1748): 'How doth the little busy Bee / Improve each shining Hour'.

5. glass: Eye-glass or lorgnette.

6. *the Rue Montaigne*: Now named the rue Jean-Mermoz, this runs from the Champs Elysées to the Right Bank of the Seine. Louis-Philippe (1830–48) and Napoleon III (1852–70) had their courts at the Tuileries Palace in the nineteenth century.

II

1. *Quartier Marboeuf*: A modern district, in the 1890s, on the Right Bank south of the Champs Elysées. Miss Barrace also seems to live in this area, possibly on the north side of the Champs Elysées, at Avenue Gabriel 42, the address of her original, James's old friend Henrietta Reubell.

2. *Portrait ... blue-grey eyes*: *The Portrait of a Man with Gloves* (1523–4), one of the paintings in the Louvre by the Italian artist Titian (*c*. 1488–1576), depicts a handsome and prosperous young man who would certainly appeal to Strether.

3. *museum of the Luxembourg*: In the Luxembourg Gardens; here

you could see the work of contemporary artists, unlike the Louvre.

4.   *the Français*: The theatre in the rue de Richelieu that was home to the Comédie Française, France's oldest theatre company. It was one of James's favourite haunts and the subject of several reviews by him, including 'The Parisian Stage' and 'The Théâtre Français' (1876, reprinted in *SA*), and a significant presence in *The Tragic Muse* (1890).

5.   *small blue missive*: Literal translation of *un petit bleu*, the affectionate name for a letter-card propelled pneumatically through a network of tubes across Paris, so-called because between 1897 and 1902 it was on blue paper.

6.   *a café in the Avenue de l'Opéra*: The Avenue leads from the Théâtre Français to the Place de l'Opéra. Bellringer suggests the café is either the Café St-Roch at no. 31 or the Café de Paris at no. 41.

BOOK FOURTH

I

1.   *his wide-brimmed crush hat*: A soft hat that can be crushed flat or (as is likely in this case) an opera-hat, that is, a top hat that can be collapsed by means of a spring.

II

1.   *a buckboard*: Four-wheeled country wagon. A coupé was a closed carriage for two, with an outside driver; a buggy, a light one-horse carriage.

2.   *Polish*: Political turmoil in nineteenth-century Poland had attracted large numbers of often upper-class émigrés to Paris. One wonders what James's younger colleague and near neighbour, Polish-born Joseph Conrad (1857–1924) made of this passage. Conrad left Poland in his teens after his father became a political exile, and by 1903 had established himself as a major English novelist.

BOOK FIFTH

I

1. *Gloriani*: James had already introduced Gloriani, an artist, in *Roderick Hudson* (1875). In the revised version of that novel (New York Edition, 1907), he is described as 'an American sculptor of French extraction, or remotely perhaps of Italian' (Chapter 6).

2. *panem et circenses*: Bread and circuses (Latin). The satirist Juvenal (*c.* 55–140) thought this was all the populace wanted to keep them from rebelling (*Satire* 10, 1. 81).

3. *Faubourg Saint-Germain*: Stylish wealthy district on the Left Bank. The garden that provided the setting for the anecdote that inspired the whole novel (see Introduction, p. xxiv) belonged to James's friend, the American artist James McNeill Whistler (1834–1903), who lived at the time in the rue du Bac (and died the same year the novel was published). In his Project James recalled another 'charming old garden' from the year he spent in Paris in 1875–6 when he used to visit an old lady called Madame Mohl (1793–1883) at rue du Bac 120. Her house certainly ministered to his 'historic sense'. He remembers, not quite accurately, its associations with two leading figures of the French Romantic movement, the literary hostess Madame Récamier (1777–1849) and the writer and statesman François René de Chateaubriand (1768–1848), the star of her salon. Madame Mohl, who had known and waited on Madame Récamier in an apartment on the ground floor, gave the novelist 'a strange and touching image of her as she lay there dying, blind, and bereft of Chateaubriand, who was already dead' (*CN*, p. 542). In fact it was Chateaubriand himself who spent the last years of his life in this building. One wonders if James was determined to imagine in this case, as in that of his fictional Madame de Vionnet, the transmissive power of women.

4. *rococo*: An ornate style of art and decoration predominantly associated with the first half of the eighteenth century in France.

5. *Moses, on the ceiling ... to the floor*: Refers to two famous portrayals of Moses by Michelangelo (1475–1564): the painting on the ceiling of the Sistine Chapel and the statue in S. Pietro in Vincoli, both in Rome.

III

1.   *Saint Peter's . . . Roumelian*: The cathedral in the Vatican City, centre of the Roman Catholic faith; a form of Greek spoken in part of the Balkan peninsula.

BOOK SIXTH

I

1.   *Rue de Bellechasse*: In the 7th *arrondissement* (district) of Paris in the Faubourg St-Germain on the Left Bank: the name means 'a fine chase'. James must have had in mind the handsome building at no. 31 where, as a plaque now tells us, his friend and fellow-novelist Alphonse Daudet (1850–97) lived from 1885 until his death. James certainly visited him there in 1893, and Daudet's son Lucien seemed to remember in later life that James and a young Marcel Proust (1875–1922) had dined there together at this time (Leon Edel, *Henry James: The Middle Years, 1884–1894* (1963), p. 275). More officially, the plaque records that Daudet's widow conducted a salon there, and that Proust, who was a member, was moved to write the following testimonial, to which the author of *The Ambassadors* would surely have warmed: *Je n'en sais pas d'aussi pleine de passé, de pensée, d'aussi pieusement consacrée par le souvenir que le 31 Rue de Bellechasse* ('I know nowhere so full of the past, of thought, so devoutly sanctified by memory as 31 Rue de Bellechasse').

2.   *the First Empire*: That of Napoleon (Bonaparte) I (1804–15).

3.   *the world of Châteaubriand, of Madame de Staël, even of the young Lamartine*: Like Chateaubriand (see Book Fifth, I, note 2) the novelist and essayist Madame de Staël (1776–1817) and the poet and statesman Alphonse Marie de Lamartine (1790–1869) were leading figures in French Romanticism during the early decades of the nineteenth century.

4.   *the great Revue*: James had been from his youth an avid reader of the bi-monthly *Revue des deux mondes*, founded in 1829 and from the 1860s until 1914 the most widely read of all French literary journals.

II

1. *Sitting Bull*: I.e., Waymarsh (referring back to the 'Indian chief' on p. 168). See also Book Seventh, II, note 1.
2. *victoria*: Low, four-wheeled carriage.

III

1. *in her habit as she lived*: James was fond of echoing Hamlet's words as the Ghost leaves his mother's chamber: 'Why, look you there! look how it steals away! My father, in his habit as he liv'd!' (*Hamlet*, III.iv.136–7).
2. *like Cleopatra in the play*: Another Shakespearean echo: 'Age cannot wither her, nor custom stale / Her infinite variety' (*Antony and Cleopatra*, II.ii.245–6).

BOOK SEVENTH

I

1. *Notre Dame*: The great cathedral of Paris dedicated to 'Our Lady' is situated on the Ile de la Cité, a small island in the Seine.
2. *Mentone*: Resort on the Mediterranean coast, on the Franco-Italian border. James uses the Italian spelling of its name (Menton in French).
3. *Victor Hugo*: The leading figure of French Romanticism between 1830 and 1850, Hugo (1802–85) won and sustained wide popular acclaim for his poetry, novels and dramas through his years of exile (1851–70) up to his death. His state funeral was attended by two million people and delegates from every country in Europe. 'The joy of Life' was a phrase much current at the time, popularized by William Archer's 1891 translation of Ibsen's gloomy play *Ghosts* (1881).
4. *the great romance*: Hugo's *Notre-Dame de Paris – 1482* (1831), known in English as *The Hunchback of Notre Dame*, was the romantic historical novel that established his reputation; Lamartine called him 'the Shakespeare of prose fiction'. If the sight of Madame de Vionnet seated in Notre Dame reminds Strether of 'some fine firm concentrated heroine of an old story' (p. 233), he may be thinking of Hugo's heroine, at once saviour and victim, the beautiful and innocent gypsy girl Esméralda.

5. *a delightful house of entertainment on the left bank*: Probably the Hostellerie de la Tour d'Argent at Quai de la Tournelle 15.
6. *better to suffer as a sheep than as a lamb*: Curiously inverts the saying that 'one might as well be hanged for a sheep as a lamb'.

II

1. *sitting at the door of his tent*: Though this has been seen as a reference to Homer's Achilles in *Iliad*, Book I, it more obviously recalls Miss Barrace's image of Waymarsh as an 'Indian chief', p. 168.
2. *Marchons, marchons!*: Let's march, let's march! Words from 'La Marseillaise', the French national anthem.
3. *dished*: James loved slang words like this, meaning 'ruined' (from the idea of meat being cooked and served).

BOOK EIGHTH

I

1. *cabined and confined*: 'But now, I am cabin'd, cribb'd, confin'd, bound in / To saucy doubts and fears' (*Macbeth*, III.iv.23–4).
2. *he went to Chartres . . . Rouen*: Chartres, famous for its magnificent Gothic cathedral, is some fifty miles southwest of Paris. The Renaissance palace of Fontainebleau, in Italianate style, is some thirty-five miles southeast of Paris. Rouen, some eighty miles northwest of Paris, also boasts a fine Gothic cathedral.
3. *Havre*: On the north coast at the mouth of Seine, the principal French port for transatlantic passengers.

II

1. *fiacre*: Small hackney cab available for hire.
2. *the Varieties*: At the Boulevard Montmartre 7, the Variétés specialized in vaudevilles, farces and operettas. Reviewing 'The Parisian Stage' in the winter of 1876 James remarked disparagingly that the Variétés was pre-eminent for the *revue*, 'that dreary, flimsy burlesque of the events of the year, which is the pretext for so many bad jokes and undressed *figurantes*' (*SA*, p. 50).

III

1. *at the Rue de Rivoli*: There are many hotels in the rue de Rivoli but Bellringer believes the Pococks stay at the Hôtel Meurice, nos. 228–30.

BOOK NINTH

I

1. *a parti pris*: A preconceived opinion or view, deliberately arrived at. James was always interested in the formation of what we dismissively call 'prejudice'. In 1863 he shared with his friend T. S. Perry some searching reflections on the difficulty and un-desirability of remaining wholly 'clean of prejudice' (*Letters*, I, pp. 45–7). Four years later he told the same correspondent: 'We are Americans born – *il faut en prendre son parti* [one must make up one's mind]. I look upon it as a great blessing; and I think that to be an American is an excellent preparation for culture' (*Letters*, I, p. 77). To Strether's eyes little Bilham looks out at 'a world in respect to which he hadn't a prejudice' (110).

II

1. *Bignon's*: The Café Riche at Boulevard des Italiens 16 (see Book Second, II, note 2). The circus to which Waymarsh and Sarah Pocock go on was probably the New Circus at rue St Honoré 251 (Bellringer, p. 98).

2. *Brébant's*: Well-known tavern, at Boulevard Poissonnière 32 on the Right Bank.

III

1. *Fromentin's 'Maîtres d'Autrefois'*: Eugène Fromentin (1820–76), painter and writer, best known for his only novel, *Dominique* (1862), based on his youthful passion for an older married woman. James described it as 'a singularly exquisite and perfect work', but it would clearly have been a less suitable present for Mamie than Fromentin's *Maîtres d'Autrefois* (*Old Masters*), a

volume of essays on Dutch and Flemish painters published in 1876. James wrote an admiring review (*PE*, pp. 116–21).

BOOK TENTH

I

1. *treating her handsomely buttered no parsnips*: A reference to the tough-minded proverb that 'fair (fine, soft) words butter no parsnips'.

II

1. *Marché aux Fleurs*: Flower market on the Ile de la Cité.

BOOK ELEVENTH

I

1. *contadina's*: Italian peasant woman.
2. *dose*: Slang, conveying the sense of 'hard to swallow'.

II

1. *the Bois*: The Bois de Boulogne, a large wooded park to the west of central Paris.

III

1. *a certain small Lambinet*: Émile Lambinet (1815–77), French Romantic landscape painter, whom James in his younger days had known as one of a group of 'so finely interesting landscapists ... which summed up for the American collector and in the New York and Boston markets the idea of the modern in the masterly' (*Autobiography*, p. 193). Hutchison describes Lambinet as a minor pre-impressionist well suited to Strether's taste for the 'marginal' (like Balzac's *Louis Lambert*).
2. *Tremont Street*: Messrs Doll and Richards had a gallery at 145 Tremont Street, Boston, 1871–80. In 1872 James reviewed an

exhibition there that included 'the first names of the French school' – but Lambinet was not one of them (*PE*, pp. 43–9).

3. *Maupassant*: Guy de Maupassant (1850–93), French short story writer admired by James with reservations: 'at once so licentious and so impeccable' (*LC*, II, pp. 521–49).

4. *Shakespeare and the musical glasses*: Another reference to the scene in Goldsmith's *The Vicar of Wakefield* (see Book First, III, note 4), in which the London visitors 'talk of nothing but high life, and high lived company; with other fashionable topics, such as pictures, taste, Shakespeare, and the musical glasses'. Benjamin Franklin invented the musical glasses, an instrument also known as the glass harmonica, in 1761, five years before the publication of *The Vicar of Wakefield*.

5. *a 'bitter'*: An apéritif flavoured with bitter-tasting herbs.

IV

1. *swum into Strether's ken*: An echo, much favoured by James, of a line from Keats's 'On First Looking into Chapman's Homer' (1816), ll. 9–10: 'Then felt I like some watcher of the skies / When a new planet swims into his ken'.

BOOK TWELFTH

I

1. *Postes et Télégraphes*: Post and telegraph office, perhaps the one at Boulevard Malesherbes 6 or Avenue de l'Opéra 2.

2. *Madame Roland*: (1754–93), wife of Jean-Marie Roland de la Platière (1734–93), minister of the interior, 1792–3. Leading figures of the moderate Girondin party, after the execution of Louis XVI in September 1793 the Rolands fell victim to the violence of the Terror. Just before her execution on the guillotine Madame Roland uttered the famous declaration: *O Liberté, que de crimes on commet en ton nom* ('O Liberty, what crimes are committed in your name'). James divides her first name, Marie-Jeanne, between Madame de Vionnet and her daughter.

II

1. *to walk on water*: Refers to the miracle when Jesus walked on water (Matthew 14: 22–33).

III

1. *penny steamboats*: *Bateaux-mouches* that offered visitors pleasure trips on the Seine.
2. *the Babes in the Wood*: Ballad and folk-tale supply this popular image of two orphaned children, brother and sister, who find refuge in a wood.
3. *these caverns of Kubla Khan*: Refers to the opening lines of Samuel Taylor Coleridge's well-known poem 'Kubla Khan' (1798): 'In Xanadu did Kubla Khan / A stately pleasure-dome decree: / Where Alph, the sacred river, ran / Through caverns measureless to man / Down to a sunless sea.'
4. *to "funk" you*: To shirk, fight shy of.

V

1. *Delf*: Glazed earthenware made at Delf (now Delft) in Holland.
2. *the old clock at Berne*: The clock on the Zeitglockenturm in the centre of Berne, Switzerland, famous for the mechanical bears that parade across its front every hour on the hour.
3. *She's the same*: The motto of Queen Elizabeth I, to whom Mrs Newsome was compared (see Book Second, I, note 1), was *semper eadem*, 'always the same'.

PENGUIN CLASSICS

THE EUROPEANS
HENRY JAMES

'They are sober; they are even severe ... But we shall cheer them up'

Eugenia, an American expatriate brought up in Europe, arrives in rural New England with her charming brother Felix, hoping to find a wealthy second husband after the collapse of her marriage to a German prince. Their exotic, sophisticated airs cause quite a stir with their affluent, God-fearing American cousins, the Wentworths – and provoke the disapproval of their father, suspicious of foreign influences. To Gertrude Wentworth, struggling against her sombre puritan upbringing, the arrival of the handsome Felix is especially enchanting. One of Henry James's most optimistic novels, *The Europeans* is a subtle and gently ironic examination of manners and morals, deftly portraying the impact of experience upon innocence.

Part of a series of new Penguin Classics editions of Henry James's works, this edition contains a chronology, further reading, notes and an introduction by Andrew Taylor exploring the novel's shifting patterns of opposites and James's portrayal of personal and national identity.

'This small book, written so early in James's career, is a masterpiece of major quality' F. R. Leavis

Edited with an introduction and notes by Andrew Taylor
Series editor Philip Horne

PENGUIN CLASSICS

WASHINGTON SQUARE
HENRY JAMES

'Why, you must take me or leave me … You can't please your father and me both; you must choose between us'

When timid and plain Catherine Sloper acquires a dashing and determined suitor, her father, convinced that the young man is nothing more than a fortune-hunter, decides to put a stop to their romance. Torn between a desire to win her father's approval and passion for the first man who has ever declared his love for her, Catherine faces an agonizing choice, and eventually becomes all too aware of the restrictions that others seek to place on her freedom. James's masterly novel deftly interweaves the public and private faces of nineteenth-century New York society, and is also a moving study of innocence destroyed.

Part of a series of new Penguin Classics editions of Henry James's works, this edition contains a chronology, suggested reading, notes and an introduction discussing the novel's lasting influence and James's depiction of the quiet strength of his heroine.

'Perhaps the only novel in which a man has successfully invaded the feminine field and produced a work comparable to Jane Austen's' Graham Greene

Edited with an introduction and notes by Martha Banta
Series editor Philip Horne

PENGUIN CLASSICS

TRAVELS WITH A DONKEY AND THE AMATEUR EMIGRANT
ROBERT LOUIS STEVENSON

'I was not only travelling out of my country in latitude and longitude, but out of myself in diet, associates, and consideration'

In 1878, Robert Louis Stevenson escaped from his numerous troubles – poor health, tormented love, inadequate funds – by embarking on a journey through the Cévennes in France, accompanied by Modestine, a rather single-minded donkey. The notebook Stevenson kept during this time became *Travels with a Donkey*, a highly entertaining account of the French people and their country. *The Amateur Emigrant* is a vivid journal of his travels to and in America – describing the crowded weeks in steerage with the poor and sick, as well as stowaways – and the train journey he took across the country. Filled with sharp-eyed observations, this work brilliantly conveys Stevenson's perceptions of America and the Americans. Together, these two pieces are fascinating examples of nineteenth-century travel writing, revealing as much about the traveller as the places he travels to.

Christopher MacLachlan's introduction places the works in their biographical and literary context. This edition also includes pieces from Stevenson's original notebooks, a chronology, further reading, notes and maps of the journeys.

Edited with an introduction by Christopher MacLachlan

PENGUIN CLASSICS

THE FOX/THE CAPTAIN'S DOLL/THE LADYBIRD
D. H. LAWRENCE

These three novellas show D. H. Lawrence's brilliant and insightful evocation of human relationships – both tender and cruel – and the devastating results of war. In 'The Fox', two young women living on a small farm during the First World War find their solitary life interrupted. As a fox preys on their poultry, a human predator has the women in his sights. 'The Captain's Doll' explores the complex relationship between a German countess and a married Scottish soldier in occupied Germany, while in 'The Ladybird', a wounded prisoner of war has a disturbing influence on the Englishwoman who visits him in hospital.

In her introduction, Helen Dunmore discusses the profound effect the First World War had on Lawrence's writing. Using the restored texts of the Cambridge edition, this volume includes a new chronology and further reading by Paul Poplawski.

'As wonderful to read as they are disturbing … Lawrence's prose is breath-taking' Helen Dunmore

'A marvellous writer … bold and witty' Claire Tomalin

Edited by Dieter Mehl
With an introduction by Helen Dunmore

THE STORY OF PENGUIN CLASSICS

Before 1946 ... 'Classics' are mainly the domain of academics and students; readable editions for everyone else are almost unheard of. This all changes when a little-known classicist, E. V. Rieu, presents Penguin founder Allen Lane with the translation of Homer's *Odyssey* that he has been working on in his spare time.

1946 Penguin Classics debuts with *The Odyssey*, which promptly sells three million copies. Suddenly, classics are no longer for the privileged few.

1950s Rieu, now series editor, turns to professional writers for the best modern, readable translations, including Dorothy L. Sayers's *Inferno* and Robert Graves's unexpurgated *Twelve Caesars*.

1960s The Classics are given the distinctive black covers that have remained a constant throughout the life of the series. Rieu retires in 1964, hailing the Penguin Classics list as 'the greatest educative force of the twentieth century.'

1970s A new generation of translators swells the Penguin Classics ranks, introducing readers of English to classics of world literature from more than twenty languages. The list grows to encompass more history, philosophy, science, religion and politics.

1980s The Penguin American Library launches with titles such as *Uncle Tom's Cabin*, and joins forces with Penguin Classics to provide the most comprehensive library of world literature available from any paperback publisher.

1990s The launch of Penguin Audiobooks brings the classics to a listening audience for the first time, and in 1999 the worldwide launch of the Penguin Classics website extends their reach to the global online community.

The 21st Century Penguin Classics are completely redesigned for the first time in nearly twenty years. This world-famous series now consists of more than 1300 titles, making the widest range of the best books ever written available to millions – and constantly redefining what makes a 'classic'.

The Odyssey continues ...

The best books ever written

PENGUIN CLASSICS

SINCE 1946

Find out more at www.penguinclassics.com

Maule). For Penguin, he has edited Robert Louis Stevenson, *The Master of Ballantrae* (1996) and Charles Dickens, *Our Mutual Friend* (1997), and has provided introductions to Shakespeare, *Romeo and Juliet* and *Henry IV, Part II* (2005).

PHILIP HORNE is a Professor of English at University College London. He is the author of *Henry James and Revision: The New York Edition* (1990); editor of *Henry James: A Life in Letters* (1999); and co-editor of *Thorold Dickinson; A World of Film* (2008). He has also edited Henry James, *A London Life & The Reverberator*; and for Penguin, Henry James, *The Tragic Muse*, and Charles Dickens, *Oliver Twist*. He has written articles on Henry James, and on a wide range of other subjects, including telephones and literature, zombies and consumer culture, the films of Powell and Pressburger and Martin Scorsese, the texts of Emily Dickinson, and the criticism of F. R. Leavis.

THE AMBASSADORS

SERIES ADVISOR: PHILIP HORNE

HENRY JAMES was born in 1843 in Washington Place, New York, of Scottish and Irish ancestry. His father was a prominent theologian and philosopher and his elder brother, William, also became famous as a philosopher. James attended schools in New York and later in London, Paris and Geneva, before briefly entering the Law School at Harvard in 1862. In 1865 he began to contribute reviews and short stories to American journals. He visited Europe twice as an adult before moving to Paris in 1875, where he met Flaubert, Turgenev and other literary figures. However, after a year he moved to London, where he met with such success in society that he confessed to accepting 107 invitations in the winter of 1878–9 alone. In 1898 he left London and went to live at Lamb House, Rye, Sussex. Henry James became a naturalized British citizen in 1915, and was awarded the Order of Merit in 1916, shortly before his death in February of that year.

In addition to many short stories, plays, books of criticism, biography and autobiography, and much travel writing, he wrote some twenty novels, the first of which, *Watch and Ward*, appeared serially in the *Atlantic Monthly* in 1871. His novella 'Daisy Miller' (1878) established him as a literary figure on both sides of the Atlantic. Other novels include *Roderick Hudson* (1875), *The American* (1877), *The Europeans* (1878), *Washington Square* (1880), *The Portrait of a Lady* (1881), *The Bostonians* (1886), *The Princess Casamassima* (1886), *The Tragic Muse* (1890), *The Spoils of Poynton* (1897), *What Maisie Knew* (1897), *The Awkward Age* (1899), *The Wings of the Dove* (1902), *The Ambassadors* (1903) and *The Golden Bowl* (1904).

ADRIAN POOLE is Professor of English Literature at the University of Cambridge and Fellow of Trinity College, Cambridge. His publications include *Shakespeare and the Victorians* (2003), *A Very Short Introduction to Tragedy* (2005) and *The Oxford Book of Classical Verse in Translation* (1995, co-edited with Jeremy